Stand Before
The Children

Book 6

Of The Warrior Series

By

Sandra J Yearman

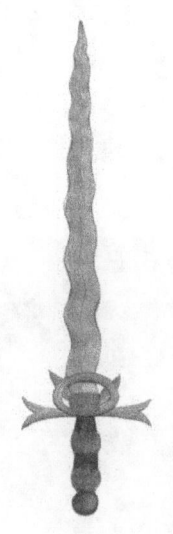

Seraphim Publishing LLC

We Will Bring Light To All The Dark Places

Registered trademark-Sandra J Yearman

Seraphim Publishing
438 Water St
Cambridge, WI 53523
sandrajyearman@gmail.com

Produced in the United States of America

Stand Before The Children is a work of fiction. Names, characters, places and incidents are the product of the author's imagination or used fictitiously. Any resemblance to actual persons, living or dead, events or locale is entirely coincidental.

Library of Congress Catalog Number: 2014913978

ISBN: 978-0-9890263-4-5

First Edition

About The Author

Sandra J Yearman is a native of Wisconsin, where she currently resides. She graduated from the University of Wisconsin with a Bachelor of Arts degree in Journalism. Sandra was a member of the United States Army Reserves for over twenty years. She retired from the Dane County Sheriff's Office in Madison Wisconsin as a sergeant.

Sandra is a cancer survivor. And it is on this journey that she says she found her voice and began to write. She established Seraphim Publishing LLC in 2008. Sandra has spent decades supporting and working with rescued domestic animals.

Books written by Sandra:

Novels

Brother Kings
The Scroll And The Sword
Song Of The Second Son
The Faces Of The Damned
A Single Lion Roars
Stand Before The Children
Tyrants, Dictators And Kings

Politicians And Kings
Armada Of The Dead

Poetry

A Gathering Of Angels
I AM Who You Seek
A Celebration Of Angels
The Time Of Angels Is At Hand
The Warrior On Bended Knees
Celebration of God
On His Wings
The Voice Of An Angel
If I Had Wings
Souls On Fire
As Angels Hover Over
From The Mist The Angels Came
You Are The Song
Be Still
Walking With Angels
When Angels Smile
Angel Dreams
An Angel's Touch
Dancing With Angels

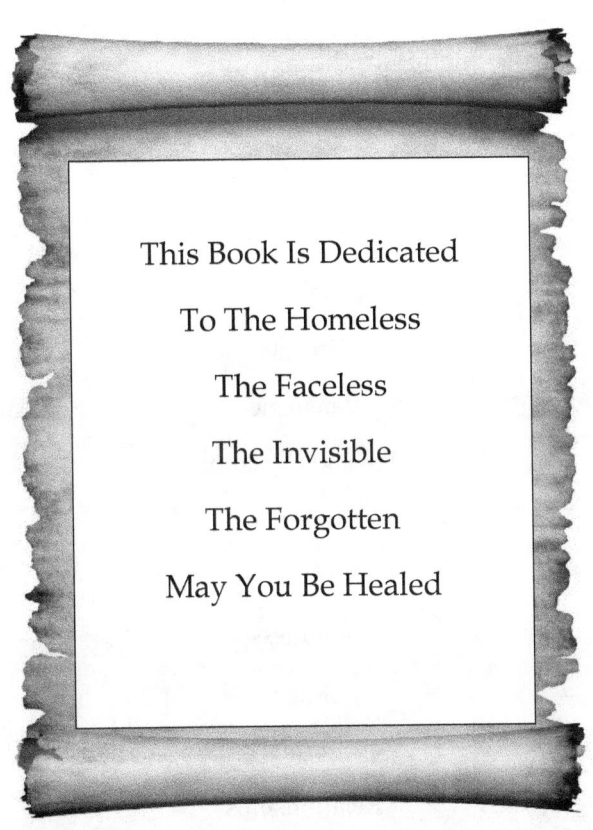

This Book Is Dedicated

To The Homeless

The Faceless

The Invisible

The Forgotten

May You Be Healed

Contents

Contents

Contents

Poem

Glossary of Characters

Glossary of Terms

Maps

Introduction to the Astrum

Solar System

The Astrum Solar System is unique because it has three suns that form a triangle. Seven planets orbit the suns.

Abrax: orbits the closest to the suns. It is a small dry planet that is not inhabited.

Traxsor: is the second planet in the Astrum Solar System. It is larger than Abrax and has one moon.

Nunc: is the third planet orbiting around the three suns. It is the world where the Continent of Opots exists. It has seven continents and one moon.

Planteen: is the fourth planet in the Astrum Solar System. It is inhabited and has two moons.

Sidus: is the fifth planet in this solar system and is unique because of the red fog that always surrounds it. This planet is inhabited but centuries earlier the demons conquered the humans and established the hell dimensions above ground. Sidus has one moon.

Filsum: is the sixth planet from the three suns. This planet has two moons.

Orantho: is the largest planet in the Astrum Solar System and has four moons. This planet is inhabited and it also has more hell dimensions than the other planets.

Chapter I
Fall from Grace

"Close the gates!" the sergeant screamed as dozens upon dozens of prisoners and demons were battling their way across the grounds of Fort Salar. During the night when most of the soldiers were sleeping, the powerful demon Petorus, one of the Old Ones, unlocked the cells to the dungeons. Timothy, son of Fahron of Lentz, sold his soul to the demon. The bargain: Petorus would help Timothy to escape his prison cell and Timothy would murder his family and give half of their riches to the demon.

Until Timothy made his pact with the demon he was not a murderer, he was a rapist, a serial rapist and an arrogant, spoiled son of a wealthy and powerful family. During Timothy's confinement in the dungeons of Fort Salar his antagonistic behavior caused many conflicts among the prisoners so the guards repeatedly moved him to different cells for his own safety. After one such move, he met another prisoner; or so Timothy thought. The prisoner said his name was Agosto and he told Timothy about demons; both their power and their accessibility.

Blinded by hatred and revenge, Timothy immediately called to demons and never realized that Agosto had disappeared from his prison cell. Petorus answered Timothy's call immediately since he was waiting in the darkness. Petorus had watched Timothy for some time because of the blackness of Timothy's soul.

His incarceration for attacking the daughter of King Sudfad only exaggerated Timothy's madness. But his arrogance knew no bounds and he expected the ruling families of Lentz to arrange for his release. Claudius, Stephan and Matthew refused to aid Timothy and threatened to have him killed if he returned to the Kingdom of Lentz.

Timothy's actions broke the hearts and souls of his parents but after many months they traveled to Wetpr and visited their eldest child. It was during this visit that Timothy boasted to his parents that Annabelle was not the only woman he had attacked. This admission and the manner in which it was delivered severed any connection that Fahron and Isadore had to their son.

When Timothy realized his parents were not going to have him released from prison he cursed their souls and swore to kill them. On this morning, before the sun illuminated the sky; Timothy's plans were taking fruition.

When Gabriel's team heard the Horn of Cass blowing in the morning air they realized there was an attack against the kingdom. Grabbing their weapons they stormed out of the house but did not know if the attack was against the castle of King Sudfad or Fort Salar. Gabriel made the decision that they should go to the castle first and protect the Royal Family. As the team ran up the steps to the front doors of the castle they saw a trail of blood, their pulses quickened as they realized there were no guards at the doors.

Natasha stayed in the dining room with the children as Cassandra, Hannah, Lila and Emeral moved quickly up the stairs towards Diana's fearful cries. Bekka followed the others but she was moving much slower because of her wounds.

"I don't know what happened," Diana cried as she was using her hands to put pressure on one of Thor's bleeding wounds. I only stepped out of the room for a moment; he didn't try to get out of bed.

When Hannah saw the amount of blood that Thor was losing again she knew he needed more than her medical skills. "Cassandra fly to the castle and get the Sanuri and please hurry."

"What is happening?" Raphael asked as Gabriel's team ran into the castle and found Archetenus, Raul, Sudfad and Simon coming out of the King's study with weapons.

"We don't know yet," Simon said. "We can't find the guards and someone stabbed Erebus; Gala and the Sanuri are with him now."

"We didn't see any soldiers as we flew over your grounds," Calen said. "But we didn't see any intruders either."

The Sanuri quickly walked down the hallway towards the men. "I just looked into Erebus' mind. Something woke him but he wasn't sure what it was. He felt the presence of demons and started to walk to the castle when he saw a soldier lying on the ground. Erebus bent down to look at the soldier, who suddenly pulled Erebus closer to him and stabbed Erebus in the chest. Very little was clear after that."

Cassandra burst into the foyer, "Sanuri, Hannah wants you; Thor is bleeding badly."

"Go," Sudfad said. "We will find out what deviltry is going on here." Cassandra flew the Sanuri to Gabriel's house while Luca, Calen, Misha, Koby, Elan and Dagon flew around the castle grounds. Gabriel, Raphael and Archetenus stayed inside of the castle to guard the Royal Family. Within moments of exiting the castle the Ruala warriors saw smoke rising in the air.

"The barracks," Luca yelled and the warriors flew as fast as they could towards the buildings. While the vast majority of soldiers either lived at Fort Salar or outside of the fort in their homes; the soldiers assigned to guard the castle lived in barracks on the royal grounds. The five large barracks sat at the rear of the castle close to the back wall that surrounded the royal grounds. Smoke was rising from all five buildings.

"Where are the soldiers?" Elan yelled as they descended towards the building. It wasn't until they landed that the Ruala's could hear the soldiers screaming for help. The doors to the barracks were closed and large timbers were propped against them to prevent the men from escaping fiery deaths. The Ruala's moved quickly pushing away the timbers. The coughing soldiers that escaped from the first two buildings helped to remove the timbers blocking the doors of the remaining barracks. As the sergeants took count of their men, the Rualas resumed their search of the castle grounds.

Timothy laughed hysterically as he hacked a guard to pieces with the guards own sword. "Come we have to get out of here," yelled one of the other prisoners. Timothy had been so caught up in his murderous frenzy that for a few moments he lost tract of reality.

Now Timothy looked around him and saw the battles between the soldiers and the escapees, all of whom were running towards the front gates of the fort. Timothy ran from building to building, trying to hide as he worked his way to the back wall of the fort.

"Sanuri please save him," Diana screamed as Cassandra and the Sanuri ran into the bedroom. Thor was unconscious and bleeding profusely from his stab wounds. Hannah, Lila, Emeral and Diana wore Thor's blood as they tried to stop the bleeding. This was the second such episode for Thor and no one believed he would live through it.

"Give me room," the Sanuri said as he made his way to Thor. "You may remain in the room if you want." The Sanuri placed his large hands over Thor's wounds and silently prayed. The Sanuri closed his eyes and started emitting a high pitched humming sound. Soon the air in the room seemed lighter as holy energy healed the fears and the bodies of all who were present.

"The bleeding stopped," Emeral gasped after just a few moments.

The Sanuri did not remove his hands from Thor but continued to hum with closed eyes for several more minutes before the women realized that the image of the Sanuri was becoming lighter and less dense.

Delilah and Zoya ran into the bedroom to help Gala care for Erebus; while Vitomas and Annabelle grabbed weapons to protect the children. Both Queen Renya and Kyra were still confined to their beds, healing from the wounds they received during the last battle at the castle. Laurel and Alexander helped the nurses with the children, who were hidden in a chambers on the second floor of the castle.

The door to Renya's and Sudfad's bedroom chambers swung open as Petra entered, followed by Jared who was carrying Kyra. "I am sorry My Lady," Jared said. "But Sudfad wants me to guard both of you."

"I heard the horn what is happening?" Renya asked as she picked up the papers she had been reading, to make room for Kyra on the bed. "Lay her down here."

"We aren't sure yet," Jared said. "All I know is that Marie found Erebus unconscious at the front door and bleeding from a knife wound. While Sudfad and your boys were dragging Erebus into the castle the horn sounded. Archetenus ran outside and didn't see any guards around the castle."

Petra was carrying a sword and walked around the windows of his parent's bedroom chambers peering outside. "I don't see anything or anyone; I don't see any soldiers." Whimpering was heard from outside of the bedroom door. "Mama the pups are outside can I let them in?"

"Yes," Renya said and smiled. "But they can't jump on the bed." Petra ran to the door and let his three German shepherds into the room.

As the freed soldiers put out the fires in their barracks a small flock of Enrops flew into the castle through an opened dining room window. Raul, Simon, Archetenus, Raphael and Gabriel were searching the castle for intruders. The Enrops flew through the castle until they found Marie, who let them into Sudfad's study where the King was grabbing weapons from his arsenal.

"The prisoners have escaped," Nica, the leader of the flock, yelled as he landed on Sudfad's desk.

Sudfad quickly came out of his weapon's room, "What did you say?"

"The prisoners have escaped from the dungeons, there were demons among them and they are fighting with the soldiers," Nica explained.

"How many demons?" Sudfad asked.

"Maybe twenty, they were dressed like the prisoners."

"The soldiers greatly outnumber the prisoners," Sudfad said.

"Unless those demons can't be killed by humans. Nica the Sanuri is at Gabriel's house. Will you tell him this information? I am going to the fort."

Sudfad walked into the hallway and called for Marie, who quickly came from the kitchen. "Marie would you find Raul, Simon and the others and tell them I need to see them at once?"

"Yes, My Lord," Marie said and quickly walked up the stairs to the second floor of the castle.

By the time that Raul, Simon, Archetenus, Gabriel and Raphael had gathered at Sudfad's study the Ruala warriors were walking in the front door of the castle. Sudfad was wearing his riding boots and weapons when he met with all of the men. "Nica said all of the prisoners at the fort have escaped and are fighting with the soldiers. He said there were about twenty demons among them dressed like prisoners. We only had about fifty prisoners in the dungeons but I sent Nica to tell the Sanuri in case humans can't kill the demons."

"That doesn't explain what happened to the castle guards," Simon said.

"All of your soldiers were locked inside of the barracks and the buildings were set on fire," Calen said. "We got them out and the sergeants are taking count of their men and putting out the fires."

"So your guards may have either been dragged into the barracks or they were part of this escape plan," Luca added.

"The Sanuri warned us about this," Sudfad reminded them all. "But we thought this was all going to take place with the blood moon ceremonies, I should have had more guards on the prisoners."

Simon, Gabriel, Luca and Jared remained at the castle in case there were problems, while the others went to Fort Salar. Although Simon did not verbalize it, he was concerned that Timothy might come after Annabelle.

By the time Sudfad, Raul, Archetenus, Raphael, Misha, Calen, Dagon and Elan arrived at the fort, Cassandra and the Sanuri were already there. The grounds of the fort were littered with dead bodies, most belonging to the prisoners.

Lieutenant Peters ran up to Sudfad and the others as soon as he realized they had entered the fort. "My Lord, we are still sorting things out," Peters explained. "But about four this morning somehow the prisoners were able to get the cell doors open in the dungeons. They killed the six guards, perhaps killed isn't a good word. The prisoners disemboweled and hacked the guards to death then escaped onto the grounds."

Peters continued, "Most of the soldiers were sleeping so there were few guarding the grounds. One soldier sounded the horn as the others fought with the prisoners. The first three soldiers who encountered the prisoners were killed. Right now we are tending to the wounded and I have groups searching the fort. We think all of the prisoners are dead except for four."

"Any idea who those four are?" asked Sudfad.

"Timothy, who attacked your daughter, Aaron who killed a man in a knife fight in Salar, Josie is a horse thief and Jackson robbed and murdered a family, they might still be hiding inside of the compound."

Sudfad motioned to several Enrops that were flying overhead, "Go to the homes of Fahron, Mathas and Claudius in the Kingdom of Lentz, tell them there has been a major prison break here and that Timothy is still unaccounted for. Tell them that if Timothy has truly escaped he is in the company of some dangerous men."

"Father we should have put him to death," Raul said.

"I know," Sudfad replied with disgust. "But Mathas never asks for anything and he wanted us to spare Timothy's life because of his parents."

The Sanuri and Cassandra had joined the group of men while Lieutenant Peters was giving the briefing. "All the guards are still wearing their sets of keys," the Sanuri said. "I believe a demon opened those cells. In the visions I told you of before, Timothy was bargaining with Petorus; he is one of the Old Ones."

"Do you know why Petorus would help Timothy?" Raphael asked.

"No, but with a heart as black as Timothy's who knows what he offered that demon," the Sanuri replied.

"We will take to the air with the Enrops," Calen said. "Perhaps we can see something from that view."

"How is he?" Gabriel asked as he walked into the chambers that Erebus had been put into.

"He will live," Gala replied. "But he lost a great deal of blood, he won't be going anywhere for a while. Did the Sanuri tell you what he saw when he looked into Erebus' mind?"

"Yes," Gabriel said as he walked closer to the bed. "It sounds like he was coming to the castle to warn them."

"After the Sanuri left I found this in his hand," Gala said as she took an item out of the pocket of her apron and handed it to Gabriel. "Do you know what it is?"

"Yes," Gabriel said solemnly. "It's an aboultis; it's rather like a calling card for demons. It means a bounty has been put on someone and the demon carrying this has killed the person and will be collecting the bounty."

"Was the bounty put on Erebus?" Gala asked. "But why, he is a sorcerer?"

"Yes he is but he has also been helping us so others will view him as a traitor," Gabriel replied. "Or Erebus encountered the assassin as he was looking for someone else."

The majority of Gabriel's team did not return to the house until well after dark that evening. "We've been keeping dinner warm for you," Natasha said as the woman quickly brought food to the table.

"Mother," Calen said when Emeral walked into the dining room. "Father, Misha and Raphael are still at the fort, they won't be home until later."

"Why?" Vivian asked as she entered the dining room from the kitchen.

"There are still four prisoners unaccounted for," Calen explained. "And they are dangerous men. Raphael and Archetenus have assigned shifts of search parties. Father and Misha are both still out with search parties and as soon as they return to the fort they have to attend a meeting."

"Cassandra told us about the escape and what the prisoners did to their guards," Hannah said as she brought a tray of platters to the table.

"It was pretty gruesome," Gabriel said. "We shouldn't talk about it in front of the children." As Gabriel spoke everyone could hear the voices of Christopher, Nicholas and Cerey as they ran towards the dining room. Nicholas and Cerey both ran up to Gabriel and handed him pieces of paper, while Christopher ran up to Luca and also handed him a piece of paper. "What is this?" Gabriel asked, then as he realized what he was looking at he asked, "Did you two draw these?"

"Diana is teaching us to draw maps," Christopher said enthusiastically before Nicholas or Cerey could answer the questions. "She said that when she is better she will take us outside and teach us other ways to draw maps."

"Diana said we could help you if we knew how to draw maps," Nicholas said with a proud smile.

"Well, these are very good," Gabriel said and hugged both of his children.

"I am very proud of you," Luca said and hugged Christopher. "Being able to draw maps is very important."

"How is Thor?" Gabriel asked as he handed the maps to Hannah.

"Thank The Great Ruler the Sanuri was here," Hannah said. "Or he never would have lived. It was beyond what I could do."

"So he will live?" asked Luca.

"Yes, but he will be in bed for weeks," Hannah said. "His wounds were very serious and he lost so much blood. The wounds were close to Thor's spine but the Sanuri said that Thor will walk again and after some time will be his old self."

"Christopher is Diana still in Thor's room?" Natasha asked.

"Yes, she said she wasn't hungry."

"I'll take her up a tray," Emeral said. "She hasn't left his room since this morning."

"She was crying," Nicholas said.

"Who? Diana?" asked Vivian.

"Yes," Christopher said. "That's why we sat with her."

Late that night Maxwell and Misha found Emeral and Diana sitting in Thor's bedroom. Diana jumped out of her chair and kissed Misha on the lips then put her arms around Maxwell and kissed him on the cheek. "We were at the castle and heard about Thor," Misha said as Maxwell kissed Emeral. "How is he now?"

"He's been sleeping peacefully since the Sanuri left," said Emeral.

"What is all this," Maxwell asked and smiled as he saw both Emeral and Diana knitting.

"Emeral's teaching me how to knit," Diana said enthusiastically. "We're going to make things for the babies."

"Diana you haven't left this room all day, why don't you and Misha take a walk," Emeral said. "Maxwell and I have some things to discuss."

Diana kissed Thor on the forehead then took Misha's hand as they walked out of the room. "We have some things to talk about also," Misha said.

"Ok, but first are you hungry, I could fix you something?" Diana asked. "You probably won't believe this but I am a good cook, Iris taught me."

"I believe you are a good cook," Misha said as he smiled. "But we just ate. Our meeting was at the castle. Do you want to help me pack?"

"Pack? Where are you going?"

"That's what I wanted to talk to you about." Misha said as he opened the door to his chambers. Diana stood still until Misha started lighting candles.

"Misha this is where you stay? It's so big. How many rooms do you have?"

"Five, but as you can see I am not much for decorating." Diana looked around the empty rooms. There was little furniture but the floors were covered with dirty laundry and dishes of partially eaten food.

"Misha would you get mad at me if I cleaned your rooms?"

"If it will make you happy go right ahead," Misha said with a chuckle. Diana followed Misha into his bedroom and sat down on his bed.

"This morning I heard Hannah and the Sanuri talking about Thor," Diana said. "Hannah said that some of Thor's wounds are close to his spine and she was afraid he would never be able to walk again, but the Sanuri said he will be fine, eventually. I didn't know about that, did you?"

"No but I think Maxwell and Emeral did."

"Is that why they adopted us?"

"They adopted you for several reasons; you know they really do care about you and Thor."

"I just love Emeral and Maxwell, I wish there was something I could do for them."

Misha looked at Diana for a few moments before he spoke again, "Diana if I tell you some family business do you promise not to repeat it to anyone because I will be very angry if you do."

"I promise Misha."

"Well, you know that Emeral and Maxwell took all us boys in and that Calen is their blood son, well, they also have three daughters who are older than Calen." Misha paused. "Maybe I should go back to the beginning before I tell you about the girls. Do you know that we are members of the Royal Family of Rualas?"

"No, you are?"

"My uncle is King, Maxwell and my blood father are both brothers to the King which makes them princes. Emeral is a princess by marriage and all their children are princes and princesses."

"I don't mean any disrespect but you all act like normal people, not royalty."

"That's where I am going with this story. Now, Gabriel's and Natasha's parents weren't royalty but they were incredibly wealthy. They took Raphael in and those three inherited a great deal of money. Hannah's father was also incredibly wealthy but she didn't find out until recently that he got his money through illegal means. As wealthy as all these people are, you don't see any servants here. Gabriel hires some men to tend to the horses and grounds but that is about it. All the women share in the cooking, cleaning and taking care of the children and every one of them is a warrior."

Misha continued, "I don't know if you have heard some of the stories about Natasha but she is a fierce warrior, I would say she is almost as well trained as you and Vivian. Well, she almost died twice on a mission and now Calen is terrified to let her work on missions because he is afraid he will lose her. Natasha loves Calen and wants to please him but she really misses being a warrior too."

"Now back to my adopted sisters," Misha said. "In your clan women can choose to go through the training to become a Venator but in my race all children are trained to be warriors then when they are adults they can decide if they want to live the life of a warrior. My adopted sisters and their husbands are not warriors they prefer to live the lives of royalty; they are arrogant and selfish people as far as I am concerned."

21

"And although they all have children they make no time for Emeral and Maxwell. Calen and Natasha invited his parents here for a visit and everyone in the household fell in love with them and didn't want them to leave. Most of the people here don't have parents of their own so they look at Emeral and Maxwell as their parents."

"Emeral and Maxwell hadn't spent much time out of the Ice Caves and they were very surprised to see how close we all are. Now this is the part you can't repeat. I think Maxwell and Emeral feel closer to the women here than they do their own daughters; because the women here are just like Emeral. And I don't know if you realize it yet Diana but you fit right in here. Emeral in particular took to you right away. So as I said there are many reasons they adopted the two of you," Misha continued.

"I can't believe those girls don't want to spend time with their parents, I love being with Emeral and Maxwell." Diana frowned. "You know, Misha I think that if I ever meet those girls I am not going to like them."

"Well, be prepared because they might come to Elan's and Cassandra's wedding. Which brings up something else we should talk about."

"Misha before you tell me anything else about the family, why are you packing?"

"Tomorrow Maxwell and I are going to lead search parties for the escaped prisoners, we might be gone a couple of days."

"I wish I could go with you."

"Well, I am glad you aren't."

Diana was both surprised and insulted by Misha's comment. "Why? You know I can fight."

"Diana I will be leading a company of men, if you were along not one of those soldiers would be able to concentrate on his mission." Diana blushed but didn't say anything. Misha put the last of his weapons into a bag and sat down on the bed next to her. "There is a lot we have to talk about but I also need to get a couple of hours of sleep before I leave in the morning."

"Yesterday morning when we were talking about dating, well, we didn't finish that conversation. Our cultures are different and here there are different ways of dating did you know that?"

"No," Diana said suspiciously. She suddenly didn't want to hear what Misha was going to say.

"Two people can date each other but they can also date other people."

"Misha I don't understand what you mean."

"Well, for example you and I are dating but you might also want to date Dagon or Dack or Joao."

"Misha I only want to date you," Diana said then her eyes widened and started to fill with tears. "You're saying this because you want to date other women don't you?"

"Honey don't cry, let me finish talking. The other type of dating is when a couple makes a commitment to each other that they only want to date each other. Diana I have dated a lot of women and I know what I want now but you have never dated anyone before. Do you really know what you want?"

"Misha, I may not go to fancy parties and things but I have been around a lot of men. I have never confronted Thor about my dating privileges because I never met anyone I was that interested in dating. That is until I met you. And Thor is probably not going to be happy about it but it is my decision to make."

"So do you want to be my girl?"

"I'm not sure what that means."

"It means that I don't date other women and you don't date other men, we just date each other."

Diana got a big smile on her face. "Yes I want to be your girl," she said and kissed Misha on the lips.

"Good," he said and paused for a moment. "You could move your things into my chambers; I know it might be too soon but think about it."

"You mean we would be like Koby and Bekka?"

"Yes."

"I want to Misha but I will have to think if I should do that before or after I tell Thor about us."

"Do you want me to talk to him with you?"

"Probably not at first."

"Now that you promised to be my girl I am going to tell you something that will probably make you really mad at me," Misha said as he put his arm around Diana. "Remember what I said about my adopted sisters? Well, a few months ago when Luca and Lila were married, Luca wanted all of his brothers in the wedding but there weren't enough women to walk down the aisle with us, so Emeral asked a couple girls from the Ice Caves to be in the wedding."

"These girls were supposed to walk with me and Dagon, we didn't know them but we knew of them and they are friends with our adopted sisters. And I might say they act just like our adopted sisters. The girls were pretty but neither Dagon or I liked them," Misha paused for a moment. "But that didn't stop us from having sex with them. The girls have been writing to us and I have never answered a letter but Dagon did once. The girl I slept with is Mia and Dagon slept with Melanie. I am telling you this because I just found out they might be at the wedding too and I don't want you to be blindsided if one of them makes a scene."

"I am glad that you told me but what do you want me to do if something happens?"

"You are my girl and my date at the wedding, just be yourself."

Diana looked thoughtfully at Misha for a few moments then she bent over and unfastened her lamsman from her ankle. "In our clan when someone makes a commitment to another person we give them our lamsman to wear. It is the most precious thing a Venator owns and it is a symbol of many things, including commitment. Vivian gave her lamsman to Raphael when she decided to take him for her husband. I am offering you mine as a sign that you are the only man I want to date and you can stop worrying about the others. Will you wear it?"

Misha took the lamsman from Diana's hand and looked at it. "Yes I will wear it but sometime you will have to explain to me what all these stones symbolize."

"I will but it will take a while. I have to put it on you," Diana said and took the lamsman from Misha. She knelt on the floor and fastened it around Misha's ankle. When she stood up, Misha pulled her to him and kissed her on the lips.

"But I have nothing for you."

"That doesn't matter," Diana said and kissed Misha again. "Will you stay with me tonight? We don't have to make love, so you can get some sleep. I just feel better when I am with you."

"You talked me into it," Misha said with a grin.

Chapter II
The Hunt

Both Maxwell and Misha had to leave the house before the rest of the household usually got up for the day. Diana walked into the kitchen to fix breakfast for Misha and found Emeral already cooking for Maxwell. "Did you come down to fix breakfast for Misha?" Emeral asked.

"Yes, I was going to fix a couple of dishes of our clan but what have you started?"

"Just the coffee and the bread. I thought we would fix breakfast and some food for them to take along."

"This is fun," Diana said as she started peeling potatoes. "I love to cook and now that I am healing I can help more around the house." Emeral smiled at this comment.

"So did Misha stay in your room last night?"

"Yes Emeral," Misha said with a grin as he walked into the kitchen. "And nothing happened." Misha walked up to Emeral and kissed her on the cheek.

"Misha that's not really true," Diana said teasingly. "Or don't you want to tell anyone?"

Emeral now looked at Misha suspiciously which made Misha laugh out loud. "Last night Diana and I had a long talk and we made commitments to only date each other. See she gave me her lamsman as a symbol that she doesn't want to date other men."

Before Emeral could say anything Diana started talking. "Misha thinks I am too young and naïve to know what I want. He's afraid I am going to want to date other men too. I keep trying to tell him, he's the only fella for me," Diana said with a big grin.

"I am very happy about all of this," Emeral said. "We have to tell Maxwell."

"We need to get more weapons," Jackson snarled.

"Well, you should have grabbed some off the guards," Timothy said as they crept through the underbrush.

"What we need are some damn horses and dry clothes," Aaron said angrily.

"We are almost to the Village of Phifer," Josie said. "We should be able to get what we need there."

"The problem is, it's gonna be daylight soon and there ain't much between the river and Phifer but farm fields," Jackson said. "I think we need to find a place to hold up; you know those damn Rualas can see us from the air."

"Does anyone know if there are any caves around here?" asked Timothy.

"I know this area," Josie said. "There is a farm house not far from here."

"Any news Father?" Raul asked as the Royal Family of Wetpr started to gather around the breakfast table.

"The search parties didn't find anything last night," Sudfad replied. "Not that I really expected them to. Maxwell and Misha have already left the fort with their men. Since we believe Timothy is headed towards Lentz, these two search parties are concentrating on the areas between here and Lentz. Maxwell is leading his men northeast towards Lentz and Misha is leading his southeast."

"Archetenus is commanding fresh search parties to search the city and close areas and the Patronus at the Cicero headquarters are searching northwest of the fort. Raphael and Edward will remain in command at the fort and I want you boys to command security of the castle. As crazy as Timothy is he might try to get his revenge here before he goes after his family."

"That means all of you are staying inside of the castle until we tell you otherwise," Simon said as he looked at Annabelle, Vitomas and the other women sitting at the table.

Zoya walked into the dining room. "I just looked in on Erebus and he hasn't regained consciousness yet."

"Zoya," Jared said. "All the women are to stay inside of the castle until we find out what has happened to those prisoners."

"That's fine. I'm glad you hired some men to watch our place for us, or those poor animals would starve," Zoya said as she kissed Jared on the cheek and took her seat at the table.

"Zoya you haven't talked about any visions lately," Simon said. "Are you not having any or don't you want to talk about them?"

"It's so strange," Zoya said with emphasis. "Ever since I got pregnant, I'm not hearing as many voices or seeing things. Now why pregnancy would stop the spirits from talking to me I don't understand. It is the most peculiar thing."

As soon as Gabriel and Hannah took their seats at the breakfast table, Diana walked up to them and handed Gabriel a leather pouch. "What is this?" he asked without opening it.

"Misha gave it to me. He said that since I am his girl now he wants to take care of me but I have no idea what I would do with all that money. I think you should have it for feeding me and Thor and all the medical care."

Both Hannah and Gabriel looked at each other and smiled. "Diana, Hannah and I have plenty of money; Misha gave that to you so you should keep it," Gabriel said warmly.

"I feel like I should do something to pay you back," Diana said sincerely.

"This morning Diana told me she wants to help around the house now that she is healing," Emeral said. "And she fixed a wonderful breakfast for Maxwell and Misha. Vivian, Diana said the recipes were your mother's. I was thinking that you girls should fix us some meals using the recipes of your tribe."

Both Vivian and Diana looked at each other and smiled. "We would love to do that," said Vivian.

"That's how you can pay us back," Gabriel said with a grin. "We all love to eat."

"So you are Misha's girl now?" Luca asked as Diana was taking her seat at the table.

"Yes," she replied with a shy smile.

"Does that mean you have seen his chambers?" Luca asked with a grin.

Diana's eyes grew wide, "I asked him if I could clean his rooms," she said seriously and Calen, Dagon, Koby, Luca and Elan roared with laughter.

"Diana you are going to earn every gold coin in that pouch," Dagon said as he laughed.

"Certainly it can't be that bad," said Emeral.

"Mother have you been in his chambers?" Calen asked.

"I don't think any of us have," said Natasha.

"He never bought any furniture except for a bed," Calen said as he continued to laugh. "Misha is a slob; the floors are covered with dirty clothes and dishes of food."

Emeral looked at Diana who nodded with embarrassment. "Emeral I will clean it up, don't worry."

"I have to see this for myself," Emeral said and stood up at the table.

"I want to see it too," Natasha said with a chuckle. "Come on girls."

"I've seen it," Bekka said. "I don't want to go in there again."

"I haven't," Cassandra said as she followed Emeral, Diana, Hannah, Vivian, Natasha and Lila out of the dining room.

"We're getting our brother in trouble," Luca said with a big grin as they watched the women leave the room.

"What is it?" Misha asked as he landed on the ground near three of his scouts. The main body of Misha's men were on the western bank of the River Toba preparing to cross. Misha and his scouts were on the eastern bank of the river.

"Foot prints," one of the soldiers said. "And look at the ground, it looks like they tried to sweep the area as soon as they got out of the water but they missed these two prints."

"Colonel," a second soldier said. "There ain't much between here and the Village of Phifer but fields and that ain't no cover. They might try to hold up some place during the day and move at night."

"I didn't see any caves on the map," Misha said. "But the map doesn't show homes. They are probably heading towards Langa Woods and then into Lentz. Do any of you know the closest farms near here?"

"There's the Stapleton place a few miles east of here," the first soldier replied.

"This is simply disgusting," Emeral said as she looked around Misha's chambers. "He wasn't raised like this. I don't know what's got into that boy."

"Good thing we've got plenty of dishes," Natasha said as she was picking up dishes from the floor.

"Diana I will help you clean then we are going into Salar and buy some furniture," Emeral said with authority.

"We can all help her clean," Natasha said. "This is a big job."

"Emeral I need to tell you something," Diana said and blushed. "Misha asked me to move in here with him. But I want to know how you and Maxwell feel about it." Now every woman in the chambers stopped talking and listened to Diana's and Emeral's conversation.

"Do you want to?" asked Emeral.

"Yes but I don't want to upset you and Maxwell."

"If you moved in would it be right away?"

"I don't know if I should move in before or after I tell Thor about me and Misha."

Emeral smiled, "I am pleased at how you and Misha have been talking things out and taking care of each other; if you want to move in with him that is fine with us. But child you can't live like this."

"I could use the money that Misha gave me for furniture and things," Diana said happily and hugged Emeral. "Thank you."

"You have a great deal to tell Thor when he wakes and I think we should decide how much information to give him at a time depending on his health," Hannah said. "You're afraid that he is going to get really angry, aren't you?"

"Yes," said Diana.

"Thor could try to get out of bed and fight with Misha," Vivian warned.

"You could move in with Misha and we will just keep some of your things in the bedroom you have now," Natasha suggested. "Not that you want to lie to Thor but you could lead him to believe you are living in that room until you are ready to tell him the truth."

"Appreciate the warning," Fred Stapleton said to Misha as soldiers searched the buildings on Stapleton's farm.

"These men are murderers and rapists," Misha warned. "I could have some of my men take your family to the fort for safety."

"Thanks but we can't leave the farm, too damn much work to do," Stapleton replied. "Me and my boys have weapons and we know how to use them."

"Don't take any chances, remember there are four of them," Misha said. "Can you point out the next closest farmhouse?"

"The Jarvis place is just on the other side of that hill yonder," Stapleton pointed out. "He might take you up on the offer for protection. Jarvis only has one son and three daughters."

"Emeral he is too big to spank," Luca joked as the women returned to the dining room.

"I may still try," Emeral said with a grin. "Are there any other secrets I should know about?" Calen, Luca, Koby and Dagon all looked at each other and grinned.

"Is this what they were like when they were boys?" Natasha asked with a laugh and a shake of her head.

"Girls someday I will tell you what these boys were like," Emeral teased. "I only hope their children act the same way."

"We don't," Calen said. "We were monsters."

"Vivian do you feel alright?" Hannah asked. "You've been so quiet."

"I just miss Raphael; he didn't come home last night. Do you think it would be alright if I went to the fort and visited him?"

"You shouldn't be travelling alone with those prisoners on the loose, I will fly you," Cassandra said.

"We're all going to the fort after breakfast," Dagon said. "You could go with us and return with Raphael."

"I want to take him some food and clean clothes," Vivian said as she stood up. "I will only be a few minutes."

"Shut up!" Timothy yelled.

"I didn't sign on for this," Josie yelled. "I ain't no rapist or murderer."

"Well, if you don't have the stomach boy go outside and watch for soldiers," Jackson yelled as he dragged one of the young Jarvis daughters across the kitchen floor by her long red hair.

"Pa help me, Pa," the thirteen year old girl screamed hysterically.

"Your pa ain't gonna be helpin no one," Jackson yelled at the girl.

"Get off from me you pig," Marsha yelled at Timothy. The sixteen year old girl repeatedly hit Timothy with her fists.

"I like em feisty," Timothy said as he grabbed a knife from the kitchen table and cut the front of the girl's dress. "Now you start being nice to me or this here knife is gonna slice through you like it did your dress."

"Shut up, I told you to shut the hell up," Aaron yelled at the eight year old girl who was lying naked on the floor. "I can't stand that damn crying, hell Timothy throw me that knife."

"Private Paterson," Edward said with frustration. "Raphael and I are just trying to figure out what happened we aren't looking to put the blame on anyone. So will you stop being so defensive and just tell us about Timothy."

"Like I was saying I usually work the morning shift," Paterson said. "And you know how prisoners are, they sit up all night talking like they think they are in the taverns then they sleep during the day."

"But that didn't answer my question," Raphael said.

"Have either of you ever worked around prisoners?" Paterson asked the two Generals who were interviewing him in their office.

"No," Raphael said. "That is why we need you to explain things to us."

"Well it's like this," Paterson explained. "You take bad guys and you throw them into small cages with other bad guys and the worse ones become kings of the cells. What is common is that we see the weaker guys puffin out their chests and boasting a lot, not because they are that tough but because they are scared and want the other prisoners and guards to think they are tough."

"The guys that are really tough don't have to put on a show, the presence they give off just tells ya. Timothy was one of those puffin his chest out and talking big. He would start fights and get his ass whipped every damn time; that's why we had to keep moving him, to keep him from being killed by the others."

Paterson cleared his throat then continued, "None of us believed Timothy was a threat of any kind; that bastard was as crazy as a jay bird what with dancing around his cell and talking to imaginary people."

"What about the imaginary people?" Raphael said. "Did he ever call them by names?" Private Paterson looked at Raphael like he was crazy for asking such a question. "We believe Timothy was talking with demons; that is why I am asking you these questions. Now do you remember anything about his conversations with imaginary people?"

"Well, that pretty much started the day he got put into his first cell and now that I think about it he seemed to get crazier the longer he was here. He looked normal when we first locked him up. Did you see what he looks like now?" Paterson asked but did not wait for a response. "His beard and hair are grown out and scraggy and he braids them and decorates them with bones from his food. And his eyes, he has that wild crazy look like a rabid dog."

"Did you ever hear what he was saying to the imaginary people?" asked Edward.

"He would yell at them and argue with them a lot. You know I always heard his voice but his conversations just seemed crazy so I didn't pay them no mind."

"Paterson this is important," Edward said with frustration. "Can you remember anything that Timothy said or something another guard said he heard?"

"Ok, I remember him saying things like a man of his position shouldn't be locked up and if the girl would have been anyone else, no one would have cared what he did. He would scream things like 'stop looking at me' and 'get me out of here.' Did you read any of the stuff he wrote?"

"We searched all of the cells and didn't find any drawings or writings that seemed demonic," Raphael said.

"No he was writing on paper."

"How did he get paper and a pen?" Edward asked.

"From us," Paterson said. "We let the prisoners write to their families and such but with Timothy he didn't send out any letters he just wrote a lot. We kept giving him paper because it was the only way we could shut him up."

"We searched the cells and didn't find any papers," Raphael said, "Other than some letters to different men."

"Did you check the walls? Sometimes the men hide stuff behind loose rocks in the walls."

"They can't be far, these bodies are still warm," Sergeant Tatterd said to Misha.

"I'm covering these bodies," Private Benson said emotionally. "I've got daughters of my own. These aren't men they're animals."

"We found the rest of the family," Lieutenant Haas said as he entered the house and now saw the naked and mutilated bodies of the three girls. "The Great Ruler be with us," Haas said in almost a whisper then he returned his attention to Misha. "The father and the boy are in the barn; they're dead and cut up but not as bad as these girls. And we found the mother's body in the garden, looks like she was raped too."

Misha was so angry at the scene before him that he could barely speak. "Lieutenant, take ten men and bury these bodies, then join us." Misha walked out of the blood soaked farm house and motioned to Enrops flying overhead. He gave the birds verbal messages for Kings Sudfad and Mathas, Raphael and Maxwell. Then he turned to his men "Mount up! Where are the scouts?"

"They're trying to hide their trail but we got blood," Riker, one of the scouts, yelled loudly. Then proceeded to follow the trail.

Patterson led Raphael and Edward through several cells in the dungeons at Fort Salar. "Raphael are you in here?" Calen called out.

"Yes, we're searching cells," Raphael yelled back.

"Vivian's here," Calen said. "She came to visit, I'm here to help."

"Is everything alright?" Raphael asked as he walked out of a cell and up to his wife.

"I just missed you so," Vivian said and kissed Raphael. "Last night was the first night we have been apart."

"Honey I would have come home if I could," Raphael replied and hugged Vivian tightly.

"I know, I just missed you. Is Edward here too?"

"Yes, why?" Raphael asked.

"I have clean clothes for you and we stopped at the castle and got some clean clothes for Edward," Vivian said. "And we brought you food."

"I heard that," Edward said as he walked out of the cell. "Much appreciated."

"Hope you didn't mind us going into your chambers," Calen said to Edward.

"Not at all, I really want to change after spending so much time in these dungeons.

"We put the food and clothes in your office," Vivian said. "Do you need help with anything?"

"If you want to help us search the cells," Raphael said. "Private Paterson said Timothy was always writing on paper and we are trying to find anything he might have left behind."

"We're looking for loose stones in the walls and floor," Edward added.

"Which cells have you already searched?" Calen asked as he and Vivian followed Raphael and Edward deeper into the dungeons.

"It really stinks in here," Vivian said as she wrinkled her nose.

"If it starts to make you sick, you should leave," said Raphael.

"Those herbs that Hannah has been giving me work pretty well," Vivian said as she grabbed a torch from the wall and entered a cell.

"You were supposed to be watching," Jackson yelled and punched Josie in the face. "You could have got us caught, what the hell is wrong with you?" Jackson was more than twice the weight of Josie; he kicked Josie in the side, breaking two of Josie's ribs and throwing his body a small distance.

"I couldn't stand to hear those little girls scream," Josie yelled back. "I can't stop hearing those screams; they were just little girls!"

"Boy you don't have the balls to be with us men," Jackson yelled as he pulled a knife from his belt.

"Jackson what the hell are you doing?" Josie yelled as he tried to stand up. "Aaron, Timothy help me. Help me," Josie choked out as Jackson jumped behind him and grabbed a fist full of Josie's hair. Jackson yanked Josie's head back and slit his throat.

"Come on," growled Aaron. "We're losing time."

"Why the hell do you think they killed one of their own?" Riker asked with disgust as Misha and his men came upon Josie's body.

"That's the horse thief," Tatterd said. "Maybe he didn't fit in with the rapists and murders."

"Well, this one wasn't injured until they killed him," Misha said as he examined Josie's body. "Which means it's someone else's blood trail we have been following."

37

"What I don't understand is why the Enrops can't see them. That demon that helped them escape must be protecting them somehow." Misha motioned to the Enrops flying above and gave them verbal messages to deliver to Sudfad, Mathas, Raphael and Maxwell. "Tatterd have some men bury him," Misha said. "Then catch up with us."

Gabriel's team all came home for a late lunch. As the women were putting food on the table, Raphael asked Vivian to take the children out of the dining room.

"What's wrong?" Hannah asked

"We heard from Misha and the children can't hear what I am going to tell you," Raphael replied.

"Is Misha alright?" Diana asked fearfully.

"Yes," Raphael said then he turned to Hannah. "Would you ask Emeral and Lila to come in here?"

Hannah walked into the kitchen and within a few moments everyone was gathered in the dining room. "Misha's group has found the trail of the prisoners, it led them to a farm house where the escapees raped and hacked to death three little girls; their parents and brother," Raphael explained. "Then just a few moments ago I got a second message from Misha. The prisoners apparently killed one of their own men, the only one among them who was not a rapist or murder."

"Misha thinks the same demon that set up the escape is protecting the prisoners because the Enrops can't see them even though they are hiding in farm fields. Misha thinks something is very wrong but he can't put his finger on it. We..."

Diana interrupted Raphael, "Oh my god this is a trap, I'm going after him."

"Diana what are you talking about?" asked Gabriel.

"I know you all think I am naïve because I don't understand your ways but I have devoted my life to hunting and this demon is using the same strategy that Thor and I do."

"Remember when Misha and I were fighting those demons at the castle? They weren't interested in me just Misha. And one of you said there was a bounty on your team. When you are all together you are too powerful to defeat. Thor and I often hunt packs of demons. We don't attack the group but find ways to separate individuals and kill them. Don't you see? Gabriel can I borrow a horse and can someone show me Misha's location on a map?"

"I'm going with you," Vivian said as she returned to the dining room.

"Vivian if Thor wakes up you are probably the only one who can handle him and besides you are pregnant," Diana said.

"Well you can't go alone," said Vivian.

"She's not going alone," Dagon said. "We will have to divide into two groups because Maxwell is part of the team too."

"I'll start packing food," Natasha said and quickly left the room.

"I'm changing," Diana yelled and ran out of the dining room.

Both of the burial parties joined Misha and his men by late afternoon. "Colonel, when we were burying that poor family I had the men check the farm again. I think we just missed the prisoners because it didn't look like they took anything because there were horses, food and weapons at the farm. I think we scared them off," Haas said.

"I was thinking the same thing," Misha replied. "So why can't we find them in these fields? One of them is bleeding so that should slow them up. I am beginning to wonder if they are close at hand and that demon is protecting them."

"Look to the sky," a soldier yelled. Misha was standing on the ground talking with several of his men, they all looked up and saw a small group of Rualas approaching them from the west. When Misha saw that the Rualas were carrying humans he knew something was wrong.

"Stay here," Misha ordered and he walked away from the soldiers and towards the Rualas who were descending towards the ground.

Dagon, Luca and Koby landed; Dagon was carrying Diana and Koby carried Gabriel. Misha walked up to the group and angrily yelled at Diana. "Diana I told you not to come, what are you doing here?" Before Diana could answer his questions Misha yelled at Dagon, "Why did you bring her?" Everyone in the group was surprised at Misha's behavior.

"Don't yell at me," Dagon said. "Diana was coming here to warn you and the rest of us just tagged a long."

"Warn me about what?"

"Well, if you stopped yelling at her, she might be able to tell you," Luca said with annoyance.

"Luca, you tell him," Diana said with a quivering voice.

Luca was irritated with Misha's behavior and did not try to hide his feelings as he spoke. "We got your messages and we have been trying to figure out why one of the Old Ones would help Timothy and it was your wife here who saw the threat. There is a bounty on our team, as a group the demons haven't been able to defeat us."

"Diana said that she and Thor often hunt packs of demons and they don't attack the pack but find ways to draw individuals away from the group so they can kill them. She thinks that is what this demon is trying to do. And honestly her idea was better than anything we came up with. So Emeral, Calen Raphael and Elan are with Maxwell and we came here."

"Diana your idea has merit but I want you to go home," Misha said.

Diana marched up to Misha; she was both angry and hurt by his behavior which caused her to shake. Diana drew a knife from a sheath on her belt and thrust it into the ground as a challenge to fight. "Misha," she tried to say calmly. "I don't know what I did to make you so mad at me but I am not going home and that is final." Misha glared at Diana who paused then said, "Misha you can just be an ass sometimes." Diana turned and walked back to Dagon. Diana's words made Misha's brothers smile.

Gabriel now stepped forward, "We don't have time for fighting between us. Misha tell us what you have so far."

Misha repeated the same information that was in the messages he had sent. "I know you have seen some horrible things today and have been focused on the prisoners but has there been anything at all that did not seem right to you? Something that might indicate the presence of a demon besides what you have already told us?" asked Gabriel.

"Nothing concrete, just this nagging feeling like something is very wrong here." Misha seemed less tense as he said. "We have been riding hard all day without meals; I was just going to tell my men to make camp, unless you have some concerns?"

"If you mean, do I sense anything, I don't," Gabriel replied. "We brought a lot of food with us so you are welcomed to join us."

"I will, I just have to talk to the men first. I am doubling the guards tonight."

Diana did not speak as she and Koby prepared dinner and set up the campsite. "Are you mad at me too?" Koby asked teasingly.

"No, I'm not even mad I am just so shocked and I'm afraid I am going to cry; which would probably make him madder at me. Koby does it matter where I put my blankets? I mean do any of you like certain spots near the fire?"

"You're not sleeping with Misha?"

"It certainly doesn't sound like it."

"You can lay out the blankets any place but I am pretty sure Misha is going to want you to sleep with him, if for no other reason so he can protect you."

"Protect me from what, demons?"

"Well, everything. I wouldn't be surprised if part of the reason he doesn't want you out here is all these soldiers, besides the escaped prisoners."

"Soldiers?"

"Honey you are a really beautiful woman and we don't know these men. And although you are a great fighter, you can only fight off so many attackers." Diana turned and stared at Koby with disbelief. "Diana I don't want to scare you but I will bet you that is what Misha is thinking. You know you are safe with us, we will protect you."

"I'm not used to being in situations where I need others to protect me," Diana said then paused. "Koby if I ask you a question will you give me an honest answer?"

"I'll try."

"Does Misha get like that often; I mean I have not seen that side of him before."

"Honesty I have never seen him act like that before."

Diana finished laying out everyone's blankets and now sat next to Koby by the fire. "Then do you know what I did that made him so mad?"

"Diana I don't think you did anything wrong. I think Misha senses this is a dangerous situation and he wants you safe at home."

"But I am a Venator."

Koby was cooking the meal and now turned from the pans on the fire and looked into Diana's eyes. "All of us on the team have been very dedicated to our work. It has only been recently that any of us got married or have steady girlfriends, but that doesn't mean we didn't date or have sex, we just maintained distances from relationships. In my opinion I think he is crazy about you but he doesn't know how to handle the emotions. Give him some time."

Gabriel, Luca and Dagon were walking around the outskirts of the campsites studying the land. "Misha is right, there is a sense of foreboding but I can't read anything else," Gabriel said. Misha heard Gabriel's words as he joined them.

"Ever since we left the fort I have been feeling like we are being watched," Misha said.

"I haven't mentioned anything to my men. And that farmhouse, those murders, well, they looked more like the work of demons than men. I looked but I didn't see any drawings or black magic things at either the farmhouse or the place where we found the body of the prisoner."

"Come on, let's get some dinner and talk about this," Gabriel said and turned towards their campsite.

Luca pulled Misha aside as the others walked away. "I don't know what is going on with you; but Diana has been cleaning your chambers and washing your clothes and I think she even went to Salar and bought you some furniture. She's a nice girl, you could treat her better."

"I just don't want her here," Misha said. "What if these soldiers are taken over by demons like we saw at the fort? It is too dangerous."

"Then at least tell her you are yelling because you are worried about her, because none of the rest of us understood that."

"Aren't you eating?" Dagon asked Diana as he sat down near the fire.

"I'm not hungry," Diana said then paused and added. "I had a big breakfast." She did not want to admit that she was too upset to eat.

"What are you working on?" Dagon asked when he saw Diana weaving beads into leather strips.

"I'm making," then she laughed. "I need your opinion. I want to do something for Emeral and Maxwell but well, your whole family just has everything. In my tribe the most valuable thing a Venator has is their lamsman. Thor and I took the same tests so our lamsmans are alike. I am making similar lamsmans for Emeral and Maxwell. Do you think they will like them or do you think they will think them silly?"

"I think they will love them," Misha said as he and Luca walked into the campsite. Diana glanced up at Misha but then quickly looked back at her work.

Luca squatted down by the fire and filled a plate with food. "Diana where is your lamsman?" Diana was wearing the short leather dress of a Venator and Luca could see her lamsman was not on her ankle.

"I'm wearing it," Misha said as he stared at Diana.

"Oh so she really is your wife now," Luca said somewhat jokingly.

Diana never looked up from her work. "No I'm not," she said softly.

"Diana can we talk?" Misha asked.

Diana continued to look at her work. "Misha I'm not leaving."

"Diana will you just come and talk with me?"

Diana put the lamsmans she was working on into a pouch then stood up and faced Misha; she didn't want to look at him because she was afraid she would cry. Misha took her hand and led her away from the campsite. Neither of them spoke until Misha stopped in a small clearing about fifteen feet from the campsite. He turned and faced Diana, who would not look at him. "I am sorry I yelled at you. I don't want you here because I think it is too dangerous; for all we know the soldiers could be demons like they were at the fort. Diana why won't you look at me are you that mad?"

"I don't want to look at you because I am trying not to cry. Misha you really hurt my feelings. And I know it is dangerous here that is why I came." Misha put his arms around Diana and hugged her tightly.

"You sure aren't very obedient," he teased.

"And I probably never will be Misha." Tears were running down Diana's cheeks. "Maybe I shouldn't be your girl anymore."

Misha moved so he could look into Diana's face. "You aren't getting your lamsman back," he said sternly. "I will admit I don't know much about relationships but I do know that people have to work on them and can't quit every time there is a problem."

"I should not have yelled at you but that is not enough for us to break up. Is there something else that I don't know about?"

"No," Diana said in a whisper. "You are right."

Misha kissed Diana then said, "Let's go back."

"No, wait." Diana untied a pouch from her belt. "Here."

"What is this?" he asked as he took the pouch.

"So many of the men at the house wear beautiful necklaces and Natasha told me they all got them from their girls."

"You mean wives," Misha said and smiled warmly as he looked at a necklace with a large dark blue sapphire stone. The chain was braided silver and gold. "It's beautiful, thank you." He bent down and kissed Diana on the lips.

"Emeral told me that was your favorite stone. Do you really like it because if you don't I can get you something else."

"I love it," Misha said as he clasped the necklace around his neck. "But tell me did you buy yourself anything with that money?"

"Not yet." Diana said then paused. "There is something I should tell you."

"What?"

"Emeral saw your rooms and you are probably going to get yelled at when we get home." Misha laughed loudly and hugged Diana. The two young lovers embraced for a moment then they both became very still.

Chapter III
Attacked

"Vivian, Vivian," Cassandra yelled down the staircase. "Thor is awake and he wants to talk to you." Cassandra returned to Thor's bedroom. "Thor please do not get out of bed, the last time you did that you tore all of your stitches open."

Thor had been trying to sit up, now his head collapsed onto the pillow, "I don't remember that. Where am I?"

"You are in the home of my new family," Vivian said as she ran into the room and hugged Thor. "Thor you almost died several times, please do as we tell you so you can get well."

"Where's Diana?"

"She's on a mission but don't worry she is with many of the members of Gabriel's team, she will be fine. Now before I tell you about everything that has happened since you were hurt, how do you feel?"

"Really weak and hungry."

"I'll get him some food," Cassandra said.

"Wait. Thor this is Cassandra, she and her fiancé Elan have been spending many days and nights watching over you. They are members of Gabriel's team and wonderful people."

Thor put his right hand out and Cassandra held it in both of her hands, "Thank you." Thor said weakly.

Cassandra smiled and squeezed his hand. "Elan and I were hoping that you would be in our wedding, I need someone to walk down the aisle with my sister, so you need to concentrate on getting better."

"What?"

"Oh don't worry my sister is beautiful, but she can't walk down the aisle by herself. Now Vivian has much to tell you and I am going to get you some food. Do you think you can eat meat or do you want soup?"

"I would like some meat," Thor said and tried to smile. After Cassandra left the room, he turned to Vivian. "Was she serious about me being in the wedding, I don't' even know them?"

"You're family here," Vivian said as she pulled a chair closer to Thor's bed. "I have so much to tell you but first tell me what you remember."

"Is something wrong? Why are you all here?" Maxwell asked as Emeral, Calen, Raphael and Elan landed on the road in front of Maxwell and his troops.

Without answering his father's question, Calen asked. "You are heading south?"

"Yes, Sudfad sent me a message to join Misha and his men, since they found the trail. The scouts said there is a fine campsite about a mile away, we are heading there for the night."

"Perhaps we should wait and talk after you make camp and we can be alone," Emeral said. "It's already getting dark."

Misha and Diana stood perfectly still, their bodies stiffening as they listened to the sounds of the evening. The sound of movement had interrupted their embrace. As they stood with their arms around each other, they both slowly grabbed knife hilts from the other's belt. Then as one they sprang away from each other and faced the soldier who was walking towards them.

"Kinda jumpy ain't ya," the soldier said with a grin.

"He's not a soldier," Misha said to Diana. "Go warn the others." But as Diana turned other soldiers walked out of the brush towards the couple.

"There's more," Diana said calmly and she now walked over to Misha and stood with her back against his.

Misha yelled the Ruala war cry and the eight soldiers attacked. As soon as the first notes of the war cry were heard by Luca and the others, they were on their feet and running towards the area where they had last seen Misha and Diana.

Both Misha and Diana were trained to fight multiple attackers, so they kept their focus as the soldiers ran towards them. Diana threw a knife which landed in the throat of one of the men running towards her. Misha lunged forward and plunged his knife into the chest of the soldier closest to him then he turned the soldier around and used him as a shield.

Diana kicked an attacker in the groin then quickly turned and plunged her knife into the stomach of another attacker. Misha threw the now dead soldier who he had been using as a shield onto two other soldiers, then quickly Misha moved from left to right stabbing the two men at his sides. Diana turned quickly to throw a knife but stopped herself as it was Dagon that she heard near her. "I almost stabbed you," Diana yelled. Luca and Koby killed two of the three remaining soldiers.

"I want one alive," yelled Gabriel.

Dagon was now on the ground fighting with a soldier, the others ran to them. Gabriel kicked the soldier's arm that held a knife, causing him to drop it. Luca and Gabriel pulled the soldier off from Dagon.

"Are you alright?" Misha asked fearfully as he turned and grabbed Diana.

"Just a scratch, how about you?"

"I am fine," Misha said and hugged her tightly. "I need to check on the rest of the soldiers," he said. "Diana you stay with Gabriel." Misha ascended into the air and Koby flew with him.

"Tie him to a tree," Gabriel said as he grabbed a small vial of blessed water from his pocket. Gabriel sprinkled a few drops of the water onto the soldier's bare arm; nothing happened. "He's not a demon," Gabriel said and took another vial from his pocket. Luca grabbed the soldier's forehead and jaw, opening his mouth as Gabriel poured the truth potion down the soldier's throat.

"What do you want me to do?" asked Diana.

"Watch and listen," Gabriel said. "That was a truth potion we poured down him."

Koby and Misha flew over the campsites of the troops, who were going about their normal duties. None of the soldiers seemed to be paying any attention to the two Ruala warriors, nor were any of the soldiers acting suspicious. Misha and Koby landed in a tree line where they could hide and watch the soldiers.

"If any of them were in on the attack, they know you are still alive," Koby said.

"I know I am hoping it will draw them out."

"Well, I think our new daughter is pretty smart," Maxwell said after Emeral explained Diana's theory of the demon trying to trap members of the team. "Although I have not encountered the same things as Misha I too have had an overwhelming feeling that something is not right."

"We didn't want to say anything to you in front of the soldiers in case any of them are demons or working for a demon," Raphael said.

"I think we should just go about business as normal but be on the lookout," Calen suggested.

"Raphael I am going to fix some dinner," Emeral said. "Then you get some sleep, you haven't slept in two days."

"And I really feel it; I will sleep now and take a late watch."

"Why don't you just sleep and we will stand watch tonight," said Calen.

The Rualas and Raphael prepared a campsite away from the soldiers. Calen gathered wood, while Emeral prepared their evening meal and spread out the blankets. Elan escorted Maxwell as he checked on the troops. Raphael was asleep as soon as he lay down on his blanket. But within moments his sleep was plagued with strange images that flooded his mind.

Almost ten minutes after Koby and Misha hid in the tree line they saw two soldiers leaving their campsite and walking towards them. Within moments three more soldiers started to follow the two. Several times members of this group of five would look back at the main body of soldiers to see if they were being watched. The soldiers were unaware that Koby and Misha were hiding in the tree tops as they met as a group.

"I think we should go look for them," one of the soldiers said. "They should be back by now."

"And what if they are dead?" another replied. "What the hell are we going to say about nosing around the Colonel's campsite?"

"What if they are just captured, we could free them and then all attack the Rualas." As soon as this soldier completed his sentence one of Koby's arrows entered the back of his body with such force that the tip of the arrow was exposed from his chest. The attack caught the soldiers by surprise and their reaction time was slow. Misha killed another soldier and Koby a third before the two remaining soldiers realized where the arrows were coming from, but this knowledge did them little good because Misha and Koby killed them within seconds.

Koby flew down and searched the bodies while Misha watched for more soldiers. They waited another twenty minutes then flew back to their own campsite. This time they did not fly over the campsites of the soldiers. When they returned to their campsite, Gabriel, Diana, Luca and Dagon were eating. "What took you so long?" Luca asked.

"We got five more," Koby said then he walked up to Diana and handed her five pouches. "Here you can buy your husband more furniture."

"Koby that was supposed to be a surprise," Diana said and glanced at Misha who was grinning at her. "What is this?"

"Probably the money they were paid to kill us," Misha said as he squatted near the fire and filled a plate with food.

"How did you know five more were involved?" Gabriel asked.

"We flew over the campsites so they could see us then we hid in some trees, sure enough five men sneak away from the others and hide in the tree line to talk," Misha explained. "They were wondering what happened to their friends. One of them says 'kill Rualas' and Koby has an arrow in him before the guy could finish his sentence."

"We kept one alive long enough to give him that truth potion," Gabriel said. "I tested him and he wasn't a demon. He said there were thirteen here and more with Maxwell. He claimed he never heard of Petorus. He said he was hired by a man named Shanksaw. He said Shanksaw isn't in the army and we can find him any night at the Racing Horse Tavern in Salar, apparently the guy likes to play cards. He described Shanksaw as a large man with red hair and a ruddy colored face. Says the guy's got scars all over his face and the back of his neck and wears three gold earrings in each ear."

"He shouldn't be hard to find with that description," said Luca.

"Actually I want to send someone in that tavern to play cards with him; maybe we can get more information that way. Edward is kind of a new face around here, maybe him," Gabriel said.

"Did he say what Shanksaw wanted with us?" Misha asked.

"No, he just gave them each a bag of gold to kill you and Maxwell then said they would get another bag when the job was done," Gabriel continued. "Shanksaw told them that if he was pleased with their work there would be other jobs for them."

"He called you and Maxwell by name," Diana said. "And he knew who Gabriel was. I wish Thor was better because no one knows us, we could get information for you."

Gabriel now looked at Diana and asked seriously, "Diana how would you get information?"

"She's not going in that tavern," Misha said abruptly.

"I know, but I want to hear what she has to say," Gabriel said. "I can't use any of the Rualas and apparently most of my team is known to whoever wants to kill us."

Diana felt proud that Gabriel was asking her this question. "Two ways that I can think of right now. Thor and I have spent almost our entire lives chasing demons. I can follow someone or sneak up on them without being noticed. And after Natasha asked me to help you with the mission in Ryed she has been teaching me a lot of things. She told me how she talks to people and gets information." Diana now hesitated and looked at Misha. "And she showed me how to flirt." Luca, Dagon and Koby roared with laughter and looked at Misha, who did not look pleased.

Diana turned red and looked at Gabriel. "Hannah told me how good Natasha is at blending in with crowds and getting information. I like to talk to people and I think I could do it but the only problem I have is I am not used to walking in the kinds of shoes the women here wear. I would have to learn or I will be noticed." Diana glanced at Misha again then turned back to Gabriel.

"Gabriel I know some times all of you look at me like I am stupid and I am sure you will look at Thor that way too. We aren't stupid but you have to understand we would be gone from the village for five and six months at a time hunting. Vivian's parents taught us to read and write and well, many other things but Thor and I are more at home in the forest than we are in a house."

"Diana, first of all none of us think you are stupid," Gabriel said. "And I am sorry if we have made you feel that way. On the contrary you are very smart and you think like a warrior. We can teach you the mannerisms to fit in with people in Salar; if you are willing to work with the team."

"I would really like to Gabriel," Diana said enthusiastically. "And I know Thor will too, when he is better. We are both fast learners. And besides Natasha said it would be good for me to help because all of the other women are pregnant."

"I vote her on the team," Luca said.

"So do I," said Koby.

"Me too," said Dagon.

Gabriel turned to Misha. "We can talk in private if you would like."

"No, the family can hear," Misha said. "Diana is an excellent fighter and I think she would be good."

"Misha it is obvious to everyone that you and Diana care a great deal for each other," Gabriel said. "And you know how difficult it has been for all of us to have our wives and girlfriends put into danger. I have never seen you as emotional as you were today when we landed. And while I understand your concerns we have all worked together long enough to know that uncontrolled emotions can get others hurt. So I would feel better if you and Diana talked this matter over and then talked to me."

Gabriel now turned to Diana. "I know Venatores are trained to work alone but this team is strong because we learn how to work together. Today when you realized that Misha was in danger, you were ready to run out of the house and find him. Diana, honestly do you think you can work as part of a team? And I mean no disrespect with this question, it has been a difficult transition for Vivian but she is doing well."

"Gabriel I would really like to work on the team, but I will admit that it will be difficult to change how I react to things but I will work on it. And you are right; I was emotional when I thought Misha was riding into a trap."

"I want you two to really think if you can work together," Gabriel said. "And Misha if you don't want her on the team; now is the time to say something."

"This is a little awkward because there is a lot that Diana and I haven't talked about yet but I would want the same conditions that all of the rest of you have with your wives." Diana spun around and stared at Misha as he spoke. "We work on the same missions and she doesn't work when she is pregnant."

"I think your girl just stopped breathing," Dagon said with a chuckle.

"Misha are we getting married?" Diana gasped as the others all smiled.

"I didn't want to ask you until I had a ring. Vivian was going to help me pick one out but now that it's not a surprise you can pick out your own ring or Luca designed his and Lila's rings; he could help us design ours."

"I don't understand your customs," Diana said with embarrassment. "I don't know the significance of the rings."

"When a man asks a girl to marry him," Misha explained as he walked closer to Diana. "He gives her an engagement ring as a sign of commitment then when they marry they each give the other another ring. Look at Gabriel's and Luca's."

"Is that why everyone has been calling me your wife?"

"No, it's because you two already act like you are married," Luca said with a grin. "Now ask her proper."

Misha took both of Diana's hands and gently pulled her to a standing position. "Diana will you be my wife?"

"Are you serious?" she asked in disbelief which made the others laugh.

"Yes I am serious and this might get embarrassing if you say no," Misha said as he smiled at her.

"You are really serious?"

"Why don't you believe me?"

"I don't know, I guess I am just so shocked."

"Just say yes," Luca said as he was laughing.

Diana now laughed, "Yes Misha I will marry you." Misha picked Diana up and spun her around then kissed her as the others applauded.

"Oh, do we have to ask Emeral and Maxwell if we can get married?"

"No," Misha said. "Why?"

"I asked Emeral if we could live together."

"Why did you do that?" Misha asked with a big grin.

"Because they have been so good to me and I didn't want them upset with us."

54

Misha laughed loudly, "So what did Emeral say?" Diana hesitated and looked at the others who were all watching her and Misha. "You can say it in front of them."

"Emeral said she liked the way that we have been talking things out and she liked the way we have been taking care of each other and she approved of us living together but not in your chambers the way they were." Now everyone started to laugh loudly except for Diana.

"Is that why you were buying furniture with the money I told you to spend on yourself?" Before Diana could answer Misha turned and showed the others his necklace. "She gave me this tonight."

"Very nice," Gabriel said.

"Yes, but Emeral bought a lot of things too and so did all of the other girls," Diana said defensively then she hesitated. "And I bought a necklace for Thor too, but his is different from yours."

"Honey you act like I am going to be mad about this, I just wanted you to buy yourself some things," Misha said warmly. "I will give you more money when we get home."

"Emeral did say she would fix us up homes when we got married," Luca said.

"Misha don't get mad but I don't want to get married until Thor is better, he has to be in the wedding."

"I was thinking the same thing," Misha said and kissed her again.

Vivian walked down the stairs to the dining room carrying Thor's tray. "How is he?" Natasha asked as she was setting plates on the table.

"I will have to say he is handling all of this much better than I expected," Vivian said.

"What do you mean?" Hannah asked as she entered the dining room with a pot of coffee.

"Thor does not trust easily and he has never been wounded this seriously before. He is helpless and in the home of strangers but I think Cassandra set the tone when she asked him to be in their wedding. She was very sweet to him."

"What did he say?" Bekka asked.

"He was shocked that she and Elan wanted him in the wedding because they don't know him but I told him he is family here."

"Just how much did you tell him?" asked Natasha.

"I told him everything that has happened since he was attacked, except for his being adopted and Diana falling in love with Misha; I wasn't going to touch those subjects. He is sleeping now but he wants to thank all of you for taking care of him, so if you could stop up to his room, that would be nice."

"He might be too weak to be in the wedding," Hannah warned. "What did he eat?"

"He said he wanted meat so Cassandra fixed him a steak, potatoes and bread and he ate most of it."

"Well, that is a good sign," Hannah said. "If he keeps eating like that it will help him get his strength back."

"He sure is handsome," Natasha said with a grin. All of the other women looked at her and smiled. "I am just stating the obvious. I wish I knew a girl to set him up with."

"Cassandra's sister is really pretty and very nice," Bekka said. "That might be something."

"Speaking of fixing people up," Natasha said and laughed. "Vivian you did a great job with Diana and Misha, do you have any friends for Dagon?" All of the women laughed loudly.

"I don't know if I should wake him to eat," Emeral said of Raphael when all the Rualas had returned to their campsite.

"Let the poor guy sleep," Calen said to Emeral. "He was able to eat the last couple of days." Calen turned to Maxwell. "So did you see anything suspicious when you checked on your men?"

"No but Elan and I were in the open, they knew we could see them," Maxwell said as he took the plate of food that Emeral was handing him. "That feeling I have been having is getting stronger. I wish we could get Raphael up into the trees. I would rather be hiding when our attackers come."

"He might be waking up," Elan said. "Look at him." Raphael was violently tossing and turning on his blanket.

"Something is wrong," Emeral said. "I am waking him."

"Vivian, Vivian," Thor called out from his room.

"You finish eating, I will go up there," Natasha said and left the dining room. "Thor are you alright?" Natasha asked as she walked into his bedroom.

"I was talking to Vivian and I must have fallen asleep. Did she leave? And who are you?"

"I am Natasha; my brother Gabriel owns this house. My husband Calen and I work on Gabriel's team. Would it hurt you if I sat on the side of the bed?"

"No," Thor said and stared at Natasha intensely. "I think I dreamt about you."

"You probably recognize me from taking care of you," Natasha said sweetly. "You scared us a couple of times."

"I don't really remember."

"The first time you got out of bed and fell and broke your wounds open and the second time, well we don't know what happened but the Sanuri healed you."

"Vivian told me that; sorry I have been so much trouble."

"Thor you came here to help us and you got hurt fighting with us; taking care of you is the very least we can do."

"Well thank you, I'll try to get out of your hair as soon as I can."

"Oh no you aren't," Natasha said with a laugh. "You have a wedding to be in and Diana volunteered you both to help us with our next mission. You will be here for a long time. Does that bother you?"

"Not as long as I can be useful."

"Thor you have been unconscious for most of your stay here but, well, did Vivian tell you what a close family our team is?"

"Yes, I have never heard her speak so highly of people, she really loves all of you so much."

"Well, we have all become very attached to Diana, she just fits in with us and I am sure you will feel the same way when you are feeling better. Did Vivian show you all of the things that Emeral bought for you?"

"No, why would she buy me things?"

"That requires a long answer are you up for it?"

"Yes," Thor said and grinned.

"Did Vivian tell you that Gabriel raised me, like you raised Diana?"

"Yes."

"I am married to Calen, who has been working with Gabriel for many years. Calen comes from a large family and most of the children were adopted. Misha, Koby, Luca and Dagon are Calen's adopted brothers and they all work on the team. Emeral and Maxwell are Calen's parents and they are the most wonderful people you will ever meet. When I got pregnant Calen wanted him and me to move to the Ice Caves where his tribe lives."

"A really important mission came up and we stayed here. We invited his parents to visit us and I know this sounds crazy but I was so nervous because I really didn't know them. Well, once they got here everyone in the house fell in love with them and wanted them to stay. You see most of us don't have parents and we all look at Emeral and Maxwell as our parents. You will just have to meet them to understand what I mean."

58

"I still don't understand why Emeral would buy me things." Natasha stared at Thor as she tried to decide if she should tell him the truth.

"Thor you are a grown man and I want to tell you something that Vivian was afraid to tell you. You look me in the eye and tell me whether you want to hear the truth."

"Did something happen to Diana?" Thor asked fearfully.

"No she is fine now; you know she was wounded too."

Thor stared at Natasha seriously then said, "Tell me."

"If I do, I expect you to act like a grown man and a warrior Thor."

"What is it you have to say?" Thor was getting worried.

"Two of the four knife wounds you have in your back are very close to your spinal cord. We were afraid you would be crippled but don't get scared; the Sanuri just told us you will be fine. When I said you scared us twice, you almost died and Diana was here and saw the blood gushing from you. You know how much she loves you, she was just hysterical."

"Emeral and Maxwell didn't know if you would live and if you did; if you would be crippled and they couldn't bear to see Diana left alone," Natasha continued. "So they asked her if they could adopt both of you and Diana said yes. Diana loves Emeral and Maxwell very much. Now you are a grown man and when you heal you will have many choices to make. But I am asking you to please give Emeral and Maxwell a chance; they are incredible warriors and wonderful people."

Thor stared at Natasha in disbelief. "Thor if you are going to lose your temper then get mad at me," Natasha said confrontationally. "You have a family and a home here with us, it is up to you whether you accept it."

"Why did you think I would get mad? It was a very kind thing they did looking out for my sister. Vivian said they were on a mission, I want to meet them when they come back."

"You really aren't mad?"

"When I would wake up I remember being afraid of what could be happening to Diana without me there to protect her. It sounds like your family took very good care of her and I owe them thanks."

"Thor, it is your family too, now. Diana wanted you to wake up so she could tell you that you finally had a family, please give everyone a chance."

Just as Emeral reached down to touch Raphael's shoulder he shot up to a sitting position. "Miranda, Miranda," Raphael repeated as he tried to wake up.

"What about Miranda?" Maxwell asked.

Suddenly Raphael was awake, "Petorus' men are going to be coming for us soon, we have to prepare.

"Where are your blankets?" Diana asked Misha. "I will put ours together."

"I'll get them, why don't you look at Luca's and Gabriel's wedding rings," Misha said and left the campsite.

"Welcome to the family little sister," Luca said and walked up to Diana and kissed her on the cheek. "I have to tell you Misha is the most difficult of all of us," he said kiddingly. Suddenly they heard a thud in the darkness outside of the ring of the campfire. Everyone grabbed their weapons and ran in the direction that Misha had taken.

"Careful," Misha said. "This thing isn't over with yet." Misha dragged a body into the light of the fire and dropped it onto the ground. He turned the body over to expose the face and said, "Well this is interesting." The body was wearing the uniform of the Wetprian military but the face was not that of a human.

A dozen Wetprian soldiers crept up to the campsite of Maxwell, Emeral, Raphael, Elan and Calen. As one the soldiers ran forward and started to hack what they thought were bodies under the blankets around the fire.

Elan threw a knife from his vantage point in a tree and struck one of the soldiers in the throat. Simultaneously Raphael, Emeral, Calen and Maxwell shot arrows at their attackers.

Five soldiers were dead before the others realized they were hacking only blankets. One soldier screamed with rage as he looked up into the trees. Between the foliage and the darkness of night Maxwell and the others were well concealed from the soldiers.

"Get down here and fight like men," the soldier screamed then collapsed to the ground with one of Calen's arrows in his throat. Maxwell and the others had taken positions in the trees surrounding their campsite and they now fired arrows into the six remaining soldiers who were trying to run away.

"If you each give me a few arrows I can set traps around our campsite. But then you will have to fly over them," Diana said as she ran to her pouch and took out a ball of thin fiber cord and her quiver of arrows.

"Vivian showed me how to set those traps," Luca said. "I will help you. Gabriel you remember that is how Vivian killed those Valdees warriors we brought to the house."

"Why don't you show all of us," said Gabriel.

"First let me fly around and make sure no one is watching us," said Koby and ascended into the air.

Chapter IV
Admissions

"Is that boy still sleeping?" Nicholas asked.

"Can we see him?" asked Christopher.

"As soon as you finish your pie, we will take some desert to Thor and if he is awake you can talk to him," Hannah said. "But he is still very sick so if he is sleeping we won't wake him."

"Can I go get him a toy?" Christopher asked enthusiastically.

"Me too?" asked Nicholas.

"Alright, but don't run," Hannah said then laughed as both boys ran out of the dining room. "I don't know why I even bother saying that."

"You should know I told Thor that Emeral and Maxwell adopted them," Natasha said.

"You did what!" Vivian said. "How did he take it, I didn't hear any yelling."

"Well, first I told him how bad his medical situation was then I told him about Emeral and Maxwell and that they wanted to take care of him and Diana. The way he was staring at me at first I thought he might get mad," Natasha explained. "But he said that he remembered waking up and he was always worried about what was happening to Diana. He said he was grateful that our family was taking care of her. I told him it was his family now and he should give us a chance."

"Boy that really doesn't sound like the Thor I know," Vivian said.

"We're ready," Christopher said loudly. Hannah walked into the kitchen and returned moments later with a tray containing a piece of pie and a glass of milk. "Now remember don't jump on the bed," she said as they walked up the stairs.

"Thor are you awake?"

"Yes, you can come in."

"We brought you some pie and milk." Hannah set the tray on a table and helped Thor sit up. "I am Hannah, I am a physician and this is Christopher, Nicholas and Cerey; they have been wanting to meet you."

"We brought you some toys to help you feel better," Christopher said as he and Nicholas handed Thor two stuffed animals.

"Thank you," Thor said with a weak smile. "And Hannah thank you, I owe you a great deal."

"No you don't, I am just so relieved you are getting better."

"When Diana was hurt we would go in her room and all of us would draw," Christopher said. "Do you like to draw?"

"Sometimes," Thor answered as he smiled at the children.

"Diana is teaching us how to draw maps so we can help our papas," Nicholas said.

"I taught Diana how to draw maps so if I feel better tomorrow why don't you bring your maps and paper and we will work on them."

"Ok," Christopher said enthusiastically then he became somber. "Diana said that your parents were killed when you were kids. My parents and their parents were killed by Hutas." Christopher nodded towards Nicholas and Cerey. "But Luca is my new daddy and Hannah and Gabriel are their new parents." Thor looked at the children but didn't know what to say. "When your parents were killed did you have bad dreams?"

"When I was little; why are you having bad dreams?"

"Yeah, but Luca lets me sleep with him and Lila when I get scared and that helps."

Thor looked at Hannah then back at the children, "The dreams do go away," he said.

"Thor would you like another piece of pie?" Hannah asked as she was trying to change the subject.

"Yes, it was very good."

"I'll get it," Christopher said and ran out of the room.

"I don't know if Vivian said anything to you but we were hoping that you and Diana would help Gabriel on the next mission. You see Natasha just had a baby and Vivian, me and Lila are all pregnant so our husbands won't let us go with them; so they will be very short handed."

"Vivian didn't tell me she was pregnant," Thor said with a big smile. "She has really changed."

"She and Raphael are very much in love."

"Actually Natasha said that Diana had already volunteered us for that mission, which is fine because it is the least I can do to pay you back."

"He ran and dropped the first piece," Bekka said with a chuckle as she and Christopher walked into the bedroom. "Thor I don't know if you remember me from that night at the castle, I am Bekka."

"I remember you, you were with Koby," Thor said then turned to Christopher who was handing him a plate containing a piece of pie. "Thank you Christopher."

"Bekka got hurt that night when you did," Christopher said. "She is my good friend. We had another friend, Fala but the Hutas killed her too."

Thor looked at Christopher then at Hannah. "The children have been through a lot lately and they are still trying to understand it all," Hannah explained. "Thor you are looking really tired again, we should let you get some rest."

"I am feeling tired; sorry I do enjoy talking to you."

Cerey had not said a word since she entered the room, now she walked up to Thor's bed and put her arms up and said, "Hug."

"Oh Honey you might hurt him," Hannah said.

"That's alright but you will have to put her on the bed."

64

"Now be careful," Hannah said as she placed Cerey on top of the bed. Cerey put both of her arms around Thor's neck and hugged him tightly. He hugged her back; then without saying a word Cerey put her arms out for Hannah to take her."

"We'll let you get some sleep now," Hannah said as she held Cerey and took Nicholas' hand. As they were walking out of the bedroom Nicholas asked.

"What is that boy's name again?"

"Thor," Hannah replied with a smile.

"Oh that is right," Nicolas said.

Several hours later, King Mathas called a late night meeting at his castle. The families of Fahron and Claudius were escorted to the castle by details of soldiers. "I apologize for getting you out at this time of night, especially with the children but I did not want to wait until morning to tell you the news," Mathas said as the two families took seats at the dining room table. "I have received several messages from Wetpr and they are all very disturbing. You can read them for yourselves but..." Mathas hesitated because he knew what he was to say would break the hearts of Fahron and Isadore.

"There is no easy way to say this," Mathas continued. "Yesterday morning there was a prison escape in Wetpr. Sudfad believes a demon named Petorus opened all of the cell doors. All of the prisoners were killed in the battle that followed except for four. Timothy." Isadore gasped loudly and grabbed Fahron's hand.

"A man named Aaron who killed a man, a man named Josie who is a horse thief and a man named Jackson who robbed and murdered a family. These four men got away. Sudfad has sent search parties out. One of the parties is led by the Ruala Misha. He has sent me messages also."

"Misha and his men believe the prisoners are heading here." Mathas explained. "They have been following a trail that brought them to a farm house where an entire family was hacked to death and the three little girls and the mother were also raped." Now Isadore started to sob. Fahron put his arm around his wife.

"Misha said a short time later they found the body of the prisoner Josie, he had been beaten and his throat cut. They are following the prisoners through that farm land that is west of Langa Woods. While the prisoners should be exposed because the crops are not high, no one, even the Enrops can see them. Misha believes that demon is somehow protecting Timothy and the others."

"Fahron I would like you to move your family inside of this castle. Claudius I will extend the same offer to you, but your children are grown and warriors so the choice is yours. I have already dispatched troops along our western border and they have orders to kill the prisoners if they find them."

Rosa and Bella both got out of their seats and went to comfort their dear friend Isadore. "Mathas is such an order necessary?" Queen Rosa asked.

"Timothy has threatened to kill both my family and Claudius' family," Fahron said with great sadness. "I no longer consider him my blood, if he raped and killed those children he should be put to death."

"Misha is a great warrior," Matthew said. "He will find Timothy and those others."

"Unless a powerful demon is hiding them," Claudius said. "Does Sudfad have any idea what Timothy promised that demon to help him?"

"No," Mathas replied.

"We are families of great wealth, one can only guess," Fahron said. "Honestly knowing the darkness of my son I would hope that money was all he promised."

"Did Misha say how old those little girls were?" Isadore asked as she sobbed.

"I don't think you really want to know," Mathas said.

"Yes I do, I need to understand the monster my son has turned into; Mathas you had to do the same with Juleta."

"He said the bodies had been stabbed repeatedly but from their sizes he thought the ages might be seven, maybe twelve and the last one was maybe sixteen. The girls were all naked when they found them."

"I am getting everyone some whiskey," Bella said. "I think we could all use some."

Misha and Diana were hiding in the same tree; the others of their team were in trees at other points of the campsite. During the night they kept hearing the release of arrows as assailants set off the booby traps around their camp. "I must say I had planned a more romantic evening for the night that I proposed," Misha said.

Diana laughed, "I still can't believe we are getting married. Do you think Emeral will be surprised?"

"I have a feeling she expected it that is why she is fixing up my chambers, Emeral did that for Luca when he got married and said she would do it for each of us when we took a wife." Misha touched Diana's arm and she looked in the same direction that he was looking. Three demons walked into the campsite but they were not wearing military uniforms. One of the demons kicked a bedroll, thinking it was a sleeping person, when he realized it was just blankets he yelled to the others; all three were impaled with arrows before they could hide in the darkness.

"Stay where you are," Miranda's voice rang in Raphael's ear. Raphael, Calen, Elan, Maxwell and Emeral were still hiding in the tree tops. "Miranda said to stay where we are," Raphael called out. Horrifying screams rang out one after another around the campsite, in the darkness beyond the ring of light made by the fire. There were loud sounds that Raphael and the others did not recognize, loud, groaning sounds filled the air and with these sounds were agonizing screams.

"Daniel," Gabriel said loudly as he saw the Angel appear on the ground near their fire. Daniel called each of them by name and said, "You can come down now."

"What is he?" Diana asked Misha.

"An Angel and a friend of ours."

"An Angel are you serious, is he really an Angel?"

"Ask him yourself," Misha said as he grabbed Diana and flew to the ground.

"I like it when people call us friends," Daniel said warmly. "We don't hear if often enough. Yes Diana I am an Angel." Diana was overwhelmed and never understood why she started to cry. "You have done well," Daniel said when they were all gathered around him. "Too well, Petorus is angry and is sending reinforcements."

"Do all my soldiers work for the demon?" Misha asked.

"No and they are not aware of what is happening here, it is not their fight. Diana was right about the demons trying to separate you and kill you individually; you would be wise to remember that in the future."

"Are they out there now?" Dagon asked.

"They will be shortly but they will not make it to your campsite. Your fight is over this night. Misha you have some very good men who are out here with you. In the morning bring your leaders to this camp and show them the mercenaries of Petorus. Your army will need to have faith that the heavens are watching." Daniel suddenly turned and faced Gabriel. "Yes she is and yes I would like that very much," Daniel said and his smile brought a warmth that touched them all.

"So it is a boy?" Gabriel asked excitedly.

"Yes, you and Raul naming your babies after Angels, your world may not be ready for the miracles that can bring."

"Then we will expect you at his birth," Gabriel said with pride.

"The heavens watch the birth of every new life but I promise I will pay you a visit."

With the assurance that the threats were over, Misha built a separate campfire for him and Diana a short distance from the others. The two cuddled together underneath the blankets, kissing. "You have no idea how badly I want to make love to you," Misha said breathlessly. "I can't wait for us to go home."

Diana was overwhelmed with emotion and started to cry, "Misha I love you so much, I really do."

"I love you too," he whispered into her ear.

The next morning Diana and Misha awoke before the others. Misha added wood to the main fire while Diana started breakfast. "Something really smells good," Luca said as he squatted by the fire and poured himself a cup of coffee. "Where is Misha?"

"He's counting bodies and making sure the booby traps are disarmed."

Gabriel and Dagon joined them at the fire. "Here this batch is done," Diana said as she piled a panful of biscuits onto a plate.

"These are great," Gabriel said. "I know what they taste like." He thought for a moment. "They are Iris's biscuits aren't they?"

"Yes, she taught me how to cook," Diana said as she was smiling and humming.

"That's it," Gabriel said. "You are the official cook on these missions."

"That's fine," Diana said. "I really like to cook. I packed herbs and other things so I could fix you the food of my people." Luca looked at Gabriel and winked as they watched Diana who now started to sing softly while she was cooking.

"You are going to have to see this for yourselves," Misha said as he walked up to the fire. "Afraid I can't do it justice by trying to explain the scene out there."

"We just made your wife the official cook," Dagon said as he grabbed his third biscuit.

Diana filled plates with food and handed one to each man, it was then that she noticed they were all looking at her and smiling. "Is something wrong? Do I have flour on my face?" Diana asked as she brushed her cheeks with her hands. "Tell me why are you all looking at me like that?"

"They can tell we made love last night," Misha said with a smile.

"What!" Diana yelled and turned dark red. "How? Did I change?"

All the men started laughing. Misha bent over and kissed Diana on the forehead. "No you just have that glow," Luca said.

"I am glowing?" Diana asked frantically. "Are you serious?" Her responses made everyone laugh louder.

"You're not literally glowing," Gabriel said. "It's a presence about you. It happens to everyone, don't worry."

"Misha, do you think Thor will see me glowing?" Diana asked fearfully.

"Honey it doesn't matter, we will be married soon. If Thor is awake when we get home, you and I will talk to him right away."

"I don't think that is a very good idea. He can get awfully mad. I should talk to him first."

"No, I am your husband and I am sure he will have questions of me. We will talk to him together."

As Emeral was cooking breakfast, Elan flew up to her. "Emeral follow me, you have got to see this, you will never believe it."

"Elan, I have food on the fire."

"Can't you take them off for just a few minutes?"

"Alright but give me a moment," Emeral said as she took the pot of coffee and the pans off from the fire. Emeral followed Elan into the wooded area that surrounded their campsite.

"We wanted you to see this," Maxwell said as he, Raphael and Calen all stood near some large trees.

"Oh by The Great Ruler," gasped Emeral. "What happened to them?"

"It looks like the forest came alive and attacked the demons," Raphael said. "Look at how those tree branches and roots are wrapped around them and over there that vine is wrapped around a demon's throat."

"This is utterly incredible, I have never heard of such a thing," Emeral gasped.

"Keep walking," Calen said. "Wait until you see how many demons are dead."

"I checked on my men," Maxwell said. "And they were unaware of an attack on us. I will let them see this later."

Later that morning, after Misha had shown his military leaders the bodies of the men and demons that attacked them the previous night; the company headed out. The scouts were in the lead and they were still tracking the trail of the prisoners eastward. Koby was carrying Diana and now flew next to Misha who was leading the soldiers.

"Misha all Venatores are really good trackers," Diana called out. "Can I go up with the scouts?"

"Only if Koby stays with you."

Koby shot out ahead of the troops and within minutes landed near the three scouts who were shocked to see a beautiful woman joining them. "She is a Venator warrior from Ryed," Koby explained. "They are excellent trackers, she would like to help."

The three men stared at Diana for a moment then Riker said, "Excuse our manners but we have never seen a woman tracker before. If you can help us pick up this trail, why I will buy you a drink." Then Riker looked sheepishly at Koby. "Well, I will buy you something." Diana laughed.

"She's the Colonel's wife," Koby said. This comment made Diana smile as she was still getting use to the idea that she had taken Misha for her husband.

"Oh no disrespect meant," Riker said apologetically. "If one of us does good; well, the others buy him a drink."

Diana smiled sweetly, "I'm not offended; please just tell me where you have been searching. Is there still a blood trail?"

It was mid-morning when Misha received a message from Maxwell, telling of the attacks the night before. Misha read the note then handed it to Gabriel who was being carried by Luca. The Enrops that Maxwell and Misha had sent to Kings Sudfad and Mathas had not yet delivered their messages.

Misha and his troops were leaving the second farmhouse that they had come upon that morning. All the soldiers and warriors were relieved to find both families unharmed. Neither family claimed to have seen the escaped prisoners. At the second farm house Diana asked the woman for some dried lynswood; the woman gave Diana a large pouch full.

"Let's go back to the trail before we turned off to check on this family," Diana said. "Then I want to show all of you something."

Once they reached the original trail, Misha stopped the troops and flew forward to land among the scouts. Luca, Dagon and Gabriel joined them also. "My people are trained to hunt demons," Diana was explaining to the scouts. "If a demon is using its powers to prevent us from seeing its prints this dried herb will often make the trail clear to us."

"I don't understand," Riker said with a confused look on his face.

"Let's say the demons put a sort of veil over their prints so we can't see them. But the prints are really on the ground. We sprinkle a little of this herb around and it eats through the veil and shows us the prints. Watch, but everyone stay behind me so you don't step on any prints." Diana carefully walked around the area until she had covered a distance of almost ten feet.

While Diana walked she lightly sprinkled the dried lynswood on the ground. Then she started to retrace her steps. "We got it," she called out. "It takes a few minutes for the lynswood to work."

"They are turning south," Riker said. "They know we think they are headed for Lentz. Bet they plan to cover their trail in the River Toba and enter Lentz from a more southerly location. Damn girl write down the name of that stuff for me will ya?"

"Here," Diana said and opened the pouch so each scout could grab some of the herb. "You don't have to sprinkle much for it to work."

"We can learn a lot from the Venatores," Luca said. "Good thing we got two on our team now."

"Hopefully three, when Thor recovers," said Gabriel.

Misha quickly wrote three notes and gave them to Enrops to deliver to Mathas, Sudfad and Maxwell.

"Is it alright if the children visit you after breakfast?" Vivian asked Thor as she helped him to sit up so he could eat.

"Of course; I was surprised when they talked to me about their parents being killed," he said. "I actually didn't know what to say to them."

Vivian placed a tray of food in front of Thor then sat down in a chair next to his bed. "The children here are so good but they have seen such tragedy that Emeral is afraid it won't hit them until later. I think Christopher, in particular was happy, well maybe happy isn't the right word; but when Diana told him your parents had been killed Christopher suddenly had someone to talk to about it. I expect he will talk to you more."

"What should I tell him?"

"The truth, those children are very bright I think they are just trying to understand their own feelings. I don't know if anyone told you but Cerey stopped talking after her parents were murdered. Hannah said she thought Cerey couldn't talk, then one day Cerey walks up to Calen and asks to sit on his lap and she just starts talking."

"So why were you afraid to tell me about Emeral and Maxwell?" Thor suddenly asked.

Vivian looked Thor in the eyes, "Do you want the truth or do you want me to tell you what you want to hear?"

"The truth," Thor responded sullenly.

"Thor you always get so mad at me when I tell you but you are so filled with anger and hatred that you overreact to things. I didn't want you to get mad because you have to be careful with your health right now. And while we are on that subject, the children might really need to talk to you but don't fill their heads with hatred, that is not the way of this family." Thor did not respond but glared at Vivian.

"Natasha said you handled the information very well," Vivian said. "I will admit I was surprised until she told me you had been worried about Diana and was happy we were watching over her. Thor you will love it here if you just give everyone a chance. You always push people away because you are afraid they will hurt you."

"I am afraid of no one," Thor said hostilely.

"You know exactly what I mean. Your heart was broken when your parents died and you are afraid to feel that pain again. You wouldn't let my parents adopt you now you have a second chance for you and Diana to be happy; don't throw it away because of your ego. Other than my parents you won't find better parents than Emeral and Maxwell, I just love them as does everyone in this household." Thor continued to stare at Vivian. "So tell me Thor have you met anyone in this family that was not good to you?"

"No."

"These people have taken turns sitting at your bedside night and day to help keep you alive and I am talking about the men as well as the women. A total stranger and the entire family has bent over backwards to help you. Think about that before you make any judgments."

"Now Emeral and Maxwell are on a mission and when they return I expect you to be nice to them. If you later decide you don't want to live with this family that is your choice but so help me Thor if you are mean to them. I will call you to battle when you are better."

Thor laughed. "I don't fight with pregnant women, so why didn't you tell me that?"

"I was going to," Vivian said as she too laughed. "Actually there is still so much I have to tell you but you fell asleep on me."

"Well I am awake now; so tell me how did you meet these people?"

"This don't make no sense," Riker said as they followed the trail of the escaped prisoners. "Take a look at this," Riker called to Koby who was flying overhead. "They done met up with someone. Must have been someone they knew because there is no blood or sign of a fight. And that fourth set of prints just showed up out of nowhere."

"Stay right here," Koby said then he picked up Diana and flew back to the main body of soldiers. Within minutes, Misha, Luca, Dagon and Gabriel returned to the scouts along with Koby and Diana. After Riker pointed out the mysterious prints, Gabriel took a vial from his pocket and poured a few drops of blessed water on the prints which instantly began to smoke.

"What the hell?" Riker uttered.

"These prints belong to a demon," Gabriel explained. "But why would the demon reveal himself like this to those men? Misha I think we will need to use more caution going forward. I want to stay up front with the scouts."

Although Raphael was a general in the military he had not donned his uniform when the group headed out to help Maxwell. Maxwell was in charge of these soldiers and Raphael felt he represented the team instead of the military on this mission.

The soldiers that Maxwell led were shown the bodies of the demons that had tried to attack Maxwell's camp. They were shown the bodies for two reasons, one to show the good men among them that the heavens were watching over them and the other to show the men who were aligned with the demons that the heavens were watching and would intervene.

Maxwell was leading his troops southward to assist Misha and his men. Since they were not bogged down with trying to find trails, the contingent was moving quickly and closing up the distance between the two groups. A small flock of Enrops were leading Maxwell to Misha's location. The Enrops that were acting as messengers had less distance to travel between these two groups and were delivering their letters faster than the birds that were sent to either King Sudfad or King Mathas.

"For me?" Emeral asked with surprise when three Enrops flew to her and one of them handed her a note. As Emeral read it her entire face smiled. She flew forward to Maxwell. "I just got a letter from Misha; he said to start planning another wedding; that Diana said yes."

Chapter V
Escaped

Later that afternoon, Raul, Simon, Alexander and Laurel arrived at Gabriel's house. Raul and Simon dismounted and went to the front door of the house first. "We have the fort for the children," Raul told Lila when she answered the door. "Where do you want it?"

"Oh let me see," Lila said excitedly as she closed the door behind her and ran to the back of the boca. "We were going to put it outside but with all that has been going on Hannah wondered if we could set it up in one of the rooms. Alexander it is absolutely wonderful the children will love it."

"It comes in sections," Alexander said as he climbed down from the front seat of the boca. "We should be able to get those pieces through the doorway."

"Just let us know where you want it," Simon said. "Then we wanted to meet with all of you, we have received several letters from your team."

"Wait here a moment," Lila said. "We want it to be a surprise for the children."

Lila ran into the house and within moments, Hannah, Vivian, Natasha, Bekka, Cassandra and Lila all came outside. "Oh this is wonderful," Hannah gasped. "How can we ever thank you?"

"We just want to see the children when they see it," Alexander said.

"They are in Thor's room drawing maps," said Vivian.

"We would like to meet him, if he is awake," Raul said.

"Of course," Hannah replied to Raul then she turned to the other women. "Would one of you show them to the room we prepared and I will make some refreshments?"

Almost twenty minutes later, Vivian walked into Thor's bedroom. "Grandpa Alexander is here with a surprise for you," Vivian said as she looked at Christopher, Nicholas and Cerey.

"He is down stairs by the dining room, don't run." All the children ran out of the bedroom, screaming with delight. Vivian turned to Thor. "The King's sons are here, they helped to assemble the fort that Alexander built for the children. They want to come up and meet you."

"Why?"

"Probably because you were injured defending their family. Raul and Simon are both mighty warriors and they often work on missions with our team. They are good men."

"Certainly I will meet them, are they the husbands of Vitomas and Annabelle?"

"Yes, Raul is married to Vitomas and Simon to Annabelle; I will bring them up in just a moment." Suddenly Vivian and Thor heard the children screaming loudly.

"I guess they like their surprise," Thor said with a grin.

"We will take a break to eat," Misha announced to his officers and to the members of Gabriel's team. "Those Enrops said that Maxwell and his men are very close, we will give them time to catch up to us."

"I'll tell the scouts," Dagon said and flew ahead of the group.

Luca, Gabriel, Koby and Diana were working with the scouts when they received Dagon's message. "We could use some food," Riker said. "We will just make a fire here; you all can go back to the others."

Diana fixed lunch as the members of the team talked among themselves. "I have real concerns about that demon meeting with the prisoners," Gabriel said. "We are either being led into a trap or those prisoners made some important promises to get the demon's help."

"Probably both," Luca said. "Why do you think he met with them? To give them information?"

"I don't know but I will feel better when Maxwell and his forces join up with us," Gabriel said. "I feel stronger when we are all together."

"Thor this is Prince Raul and Prince Simon," Vivian introduced. "And this is my dear friend Thor, his sister Diana also fought at the castle." Both Princes shook hands with Thor as Vivian brought another chair into the bedroom.

"We have heard a great deal about you and your sister," Raul said. "Everyone said you are incredible warriors."

"And we owe you a great deal for risking your lives to protect our families," Simon added.

"May I speak honestly?" Thor asked.

"Of course," said Raul.

"Your family was certainly not what I expected. They were and I don't mean to be disrespectful, they were so normal and fun then when the fighting started everyone, your wives, your parents grabbed swords and fought. It was not as I imagined royalty to be." Both Simon and Raul laughed.

"We took shelter in the castle for some time," Vivian said. "And the Royal Family treated us all like we were members of the family. And I just love Queen Renya she is so glamorous and such a strong warrior at the same time."

"Our wives both want big families," Simon said. "Yet they complain that they can't help us more on missions. But that is what we love about them."

"When Diana and I first arrived at the castle, Raphael and Vivian wanted us to blend in with the others so they dressed us up. Neither Diana or I were used to the kinds of shoes you wear here. Simon your wife was trying to teach me to dance and I am afraid I stepped on her feet more than once."

"Our wives liked you and Father said that Diana killed two demons with her shoes; that I would have liked to have seen," Raul said. "Thor tell me, can you get out of bed yet?"

"No he can't," Vivian said. "The last time he tried be broke open his wounds."

"We were going to tell you about the messages we got from your team; maybe you would like to gather in here and Thor can listen too, since they also talk about Diana," Raul suggested.

"Fahron I really would feel better if you would move your family into the castle," Mathas said. "While I understand your reasoning, I..." Mathas did not finish his sentence.

"You what?" Fahron asked as he and Claudius sat in the King's study.

"Both of you lived through my personal hell with me; with my daughter Juleta," Mathas said emotionally. "You two know better than anyone else how I wanted to believe she would change and how I underestimated the depths she would go to injure our families. Fahron you have been a trusted friend to me for most of my life; I don't want to see you make the same mistakes that I did."

"I just don't want to empower Timothy by allowing him to think we are afraid of him," Fahron said with exasperation."

"It is not Timothy you should fear," Claudius said. "Mathas just showed us all the messages he has been receiving from Maxwell and Misha. Not only is Timothy in the company of murders and rapists but he is consorting with a demon."

"You have not moved your family to the castle," said Fahron.

"That is because, except for Ryan, all my sons and daughters are warriors who are experienced in battle. Fahron your children are just that, they are yet children who cannot defend themselves from Timothy and the others."

"Fahron, I do not mean to add to your distress now," Mathas said. "I just want you to know that you have a home here whenever you like."

Diana got a big smile on her face when she heard Dagon call out, "They're here."

"I'm glad I made extra food," she said to Misha who had just walked up to the fire to get his lunch. Misha walked out to meet Maxwell and the soldiers while Emeral, Raphael, Calen and Elan landed at the campsite. Diana walked up to Emeral and hugged her.

"I made extra food for all of you," Diana said.

"Good, I am starving," Calen replied and walked towards the pans near the fire.

"Misha sent me a message," Emeral said warmly. "He said I should start planning another wedding."

"I know I can hardly believe it," Diana said happily.

"And she means that," Luca said and laughed. "She kept asking him over and over if he was serious."

"He proposed in front of you?" Emeral asked with surprise.

"It's kind of a long story," Luca said. "We can tell you later." Luca walked up to Emeral and kissed her on the cheek.

The members of the team gathered in the campsite and ate lunch while they told of their experiences since leaving Fort Salar.

"I have to see how that lynswood works," Elan said enthusiastically.

Before Diana could say anything Gabriel said, "Diana when we get home I want you and Vivian to make up enough pouches of that herb so every member can carry one on their belt and I would like you to explain the use."

"I would be happy to."

"We officially voted Diana onto the team," Koby said. "She has done well and she is willing to do many of the tasks that Natasha used to do; although I can't say that made Misha particularly happy."

"I think it was when she said that Natasha taught her how to flirt that Misha got grumpy," Luca joked.

81

"Misha you told me I was over reacting in Nora; you just wait until the first time Diana is batting her eyes at some dark lord scum and see how you feel."

"What are you talking about?" asked Diana.

"We were on a very important mission," Gabriel said. "Three priests had sold their souls to demons and were trying to raise a powerful demon from its prison in The Abyss. The demon they were trying to raise would have destroyed the world. We traveled greatly trying to locate these priests and the site they had prepared for the ascension. It was on that mission that Natasha and Calen met and married and Hannah and I met and got married."

"Both our wives worked on the mission with us and did so much but at times they would have to get information or distract men while we were searching rooms. You know how beautiful Hannah and Natasha are, all they had to do was smile and flirt a little and any man was ready to tell them whatever they wanted to know. And it was difficult for Calen and me to watch but it had to be done; it was necessary for the mission and we all knew that."

"When we found the location of the ascension there were thousands of Hutas helping the demons, we were greatly outnumbered," Misha explained. "We all thought we would die on that mission then Hannah comes up with the idea to make crocks of explosives for us. Hannah, Natasha and another woman who was with us made a virtual arsenal of explosives for us."

"How did she know how to make explosives?" Diana asked.

"Hannah grew up in a mining city, where they make explosives to break through the rocks and her science classes at the university," Gabriel said.

"You asked me about all the scars on my back," Misha said to Diana. "Calen and I were on top of a hill dropping crocks of explosives down a hole into a cave that was set up for the ascension. We couldn't get away from the hill fast enough and both of us got hit with flying debris."

"Perhaps I should learn how to make those explosives," Diana said. Calen saw the look on Misha's face and roared with laughter.

"Well this is a treat," Simon said as he grabbed his third piece of pie. Hannah had brought refreshments up to Thor's bedroom while the Princes shared all of the information they had received from Maxwell and Misha to that point.

"You have real Angels helping you?" Thor asked skeptically.

"Yes," Raul said. "But many of us have sworn covenants to The Great Ruler to do His will. The Angels appeared at your village didn't you hear about them?"

"Once we returned from northern Ryed we went straight to Joshua's and Iris' house. We told them about our hunting trip and Joshua told us about you. It seemed like as soon as we got some sleep and cleaned our things, Ruala warriors were at the village to bring us here. We did hear that Vivian had married and we heard about Sampson. It doesn't surprise me that he wants to become a demon; I think he already had a good start. I hate him. He tried to rape Diana right after our parents were killed."

"We can fill you in," Simon said. "Most of us were at your village for a long time."

"You should be proud that Diana was voted onto Gabriel's team, because they are the best," Raul said. "Do you think you would be interested in being on the team when you are better?"

"It's hard for me to say now," Thor said. "I will be working with them on their next mission. The girls told me that Emeral and Maxwell adopted Diana and me; I haven't even met them yet. But life here is very different, I will have to see."

"Diana seems to have settled in nicely," Simon said. "Everyone has been saying that she just fit in with the family right from the beginning. Give it a chance I'll bet you like it here."

"Now that Diana and Misha are courting, I can't imagine she is going to want to leave," Raul said. As the words came out of his mouth Raul saw Vivian's eyes widen and she was shaking her head from side to side.

"What!" Thor yelled angrily. "My sister is not allowed to date."

Natasha moved so that she could look Thor in the eyes. "Thor," Natasha said calmly. "Your sister is a grown woman now she can make her own decisions and Misha is a wonderful man and a great warrior. Instead of being angry you should be happy that she found such a good man."

"Don't tell me how I should be feeling," Thor growled. "She is my sister and my responsibility. Why am I just hearing about this now?"

"Because of the way you are acting Thor," Vivian said. "Misha is my best friend and I wanted him and Diana to meet. So if you are going to get mad at anyone get mad at me. And every word that Natasha said is true."

"You went behind my back and matched her with this man," Thor yelled angrily. Hannah stood up and closed the bedroom door so the children would not hear Thor yelling. "Was he the man she was dancing with at the castle?"

"Yes," Vivian replied. "You will like Misha if you ever stop being angry and get to know him."

"We won't be here long enough to get to know anyone," Thor yelled. "As soon as Diana returns we are leaving."

"Thor I am not on any side in this argument," Hannah said. "I am your physician and if you try to travel now you will die, there is no question in my mind. If you are determined to leave at least wait until you are healed, I don't want to have to explain to the children that another friend has died."

Thor glared at Hannah but did not speak to her. After a few moments he asked. "Would you all please leave now?"

After a short lunch, Misha, Maxwell and their troops resumed their search for the prisoners. An hour later Riker rode back to the main body of troops. "This ain't looking good," he said. "Like we thought they are trying to hide their trail in the river but every once in a while we find a print."

"The problem is they are heading for Stordt, we can't follow them into that Kingdom or there will be a war. Lentz is our friend we could follow the convicts into that kingdom."

"How long before they cross the border?" asked Misha.

"They are real close, I'm thinking within the hour," Riker replied.

"Then let's get moving," Misha said. All of the Rualas now flew forward quickly and the soldiers galloped towards the border between Wetpr and Stordt.

"I am sorry," Raul said as he and Simon were leaving Gabriel's house. "I had no idea he would act like that."

"That is pretty much how Thor reacts to everything," Vivian said. "I should have warned you."

"Wait," Christopher yelled and he, Cerey and Nicolas all ran to Raul and Simon and hugged their legs. "Thanks for the fort." Alexander and Laurel were walking behind the children and smiling.

"Now I can't wait for your children to be big enough for one," Alexander said.

Both Raul and Simon squatted and hugged the three children. "All we did was bring it over," Simon said.

"We love it," Nicholas said happily.

"One day we will take you to a real fort and show you around," said Raul.

"Really," Christopher said in awe.

"Really, I promise."

Misha, Maxwell and their troops were stopped at the border between Stordt and Wetpr. "Misha crossing that border is an act of war," Gabriel warned.

"This is just so damn frustrating," Misha said. "To be this close and just let them get away."

"I'm starting a letter to Mathas," Maxwell said. "We need to send one to Sudfad too, before we head back. Then I think we should prepare for an attack tonight; I can just feel it in my bones."

Dejectedly the army from Wetpr turned around and started the journey back to Fort Salar. "It just makes me sick to think about how many other people those animals are going to rape and kill before they are stopped," Misha said with frustration.

"We did what we could do," Maxwell said. "The rest is up to Mathas and his troops."

Emeral carried Diana so they could talk. "How do you think Thor is going to react when he hears the news?" Emeral asked.

"I think he will be really, really angry. I am not afraid of him I am just afraid he will do something stupid and hurt himself because of his wounds."

"I was thinking that when we get home, perhaps Maxwell and I should meet Thor first," Emeral said. "Maybe we can get him interested in other things so he is not as angry about your engagement."

"What do you mean?"

"Well, as tough as Thor is I am sure part of his anger is actually fear of being alone. It has been just the two of you since you were children. I would like to make him feel like a member of the family. Did I tell you that Natasha told him that we adopted both of you?"

"No," Diana said apprehensively. "What did he do?"

"She said he handled it well because while he was so injured he was worried about you. He was grateful to know we were looking after you."

"I stand up to Thor all of the time," Diana said. "Sometimes our relationship is pretty confrontational."

"But he has always made all of the big decisions concerning us. This is the first time I have just made the decisions."

"My dear you did nothing wrong," Emeral said. "You sound so guilty. You and Thor now have a loving family and you are going to marry a wonderful man who loves you very much." Emeral now laughed. "Of course I might be a little prejudice on the matter."

"Emeral are you happy that we are getting married?"

"Honey I couldn't be happier. I think you and Misha are perfect for each other and I think you will both keep each other on your toes."

As soon as Raul and Simon left the house, Vivian wrote a note and gave it to an Enrop to deliver to Diana. Vivian wanted to warn Diana that Thor knew about her relationship with Misha and was very angry. Then Vivian walked back into the house and went up to Thor's bedroom.

"I don't want any visitors," Thor snapped when he heard the door open.

"I don't care," Vivian said as she closed the door behind her. "You don't have to talk to me; I came here to tell you a story." Thor glared at Vivian as she sat down in one of the chairs next to his bed."

"Thor you are like a brother to me, you know I care about you. Now let me tell you more about my new family. Gabriel and my husband Raphael became close friends when they were boys studying at the monastery. Raphael came from a very poor family and after only a year his father could no longer afford to pay for his education."

"Gabriel went to his parents who were very wealthy and asked for an advance on his inheritance so he could pay for Raphael's education. Gabriel's parents took Raphael into their home and raised him as another son. After Gabriel's parents were killed, Raphael helped Gabriel raise Natasha. You don't really know Natasha but she is a fine warrior, trained as well as us." Thor did not speak but continued to glare at Vivian.

"Natasha and Gabriel devoted their lives to each other like you and Diana have. I have been told that when Calen and Natasha met, it was love at first sight. They married three days later and are very happy. Natasha told me that although she was so in love with Calen that she was filled with guilt because she didn't want to leave Gabriel alone."

"Now mind you, they were still all going to live in the same castle and work on the same missions. It wasn't three weeks later that Gabriel met Hannah and they fell in love. Gabriel has never been happier, especially now that they have Nicholas and Cerey and a baby on the way. Natasha said that she believes Gabriel would never have allowed himself such happiness as long as he was taking care of her."

Vivian paused and stood up. "Thor you are a good man and you too deserve happiness. Think about what I have said. I always said I would never take a husband but since I met Raphael my life is so happy and I feel so complete. Because I love you and Diana I would like the two of you to feel the same way." Vivian turned and walked out of the room, closing the door behind her. Thor picked up a cup of water from the side table near his bed and threw it at the back of the door.

It wasn't until late that night that Kings Mathas and Sudfad received the messages that the prisoners had escaped into the Kingdom of Stordt. Immediately upon reading his message, King Mathas sent troops to escort the families of Claudius and Fahron to the royal castle. Prince Matthew pulled out maps of Lentz and Stordt and tried to determine the prisoner's next moves.

King Sudfad called his family together and told them the news. Misha's letter to the King made it very apparent that Misha was frustrated that he could not have crossed the border into Stordt. Misha apologized to Sudfad for failing at his mission. After his family meeting, Sudfad sent a letter to Misha and Maxwell.

Gabriel's team as well as the soldiers were prepared for a night attack. Emeral and Diana worked over the campfire preparing dough and potatoes for the breakfast meal. "When is Maxwell coming back?" Diana asked.

88

"I think he is just out talking to the boys," Emeral said. "Why; do you want to talk to him?"

Diana suddenly felt embarrassed. "I have gifts for both of you, I was waiting for Misha and Maxwell to come back so I could give them to you. But I know how bad they both feel about the prisoners getting away so maybe I should wait."

"And perhaps it is just what Maxwell needs to cheer him up," Emeral said then cupped her hands around her mouth and made the sound of a night bird. She turned back to Diana, "That's our little signal when we are out in the field; you and Misha should devise one." Within moments Maxwell, Misha, Calen and Luca flew back to the campsite.

"Is everything all right?" Maxwell asked. Moments later the rest of the team ran into camp.

"Now see how well that works dear," Emeral said to Diana who was turning red from embarrassment.

"Are you alright?" Maxwell asked again.

"Yes dear," Emeral said. "Diana has gifts she wants to give us."

Maxwell and several of the others laughed especially when they saw the look on Diana's face. "I feel really embarrassed that you all came running back here," Diana said as she walked over to her things and grabbed a leather pouch. Diana kept turning darker shades of red so Misha walked up to her and put his arm around her shoulders.

"Honey don't be embarrassed, they will like them."

Diana and Misha walked up to Emeral and Maxwell who were both standing. "In my tribe the most important item a Venator can own is their lamsman. I am sure Vivian probably already told you that. The training to become a Venator is very difficult and some people spend most of their lives trying to complete it."

"A Venator must complete a series of very difficult tests on their own; with no assistance to earn each stone of that lamsman. Some of the tests everyone must take but Venatores have choices to take more difficult tasks also."

"Vivian, Thor, Vivian's brothers and I all choose to take these additional tests so our lamsmans are different from others. I gave my lamsman to Misha as a sign of my commitment to him."

Diana now hesitated and looked embarrassed again. "Both of you have been so good to us and I wanted to do something for you but you have so much; so I made you lamsmans that are identical to Thor's and mine. And I am giving them to you as a sign of commitment also." Both Emeral and Maxwell smiled warmly as Diana handed them each a lamsman. "I must put them on you if you chose to wear them."

"Of course we are going to wear them," Emeral said and hugged Diana. "This is a most wonderful gift."

Maxwell waited for Emeral and Diana to finish hugging then he put his arms around Diana and hugged her tightly. "These gifts make us proud," Maxwell said. "But before you put mine on I would really like to hear what the individual stones represent."

"So would I," Raphael said. "Vivian still hasn't explained them to me and she didn't tell me about those additional tests."

"She may not have wanted to worry you," said Diana.

"Now I have to hear too," Misha said.

"I think we would all like to hear," Luca said. "And maybe we should have a drink. I have a bottle of whiskey in my pouch."

For the next two hours the members of Gabriel's team sat captivated by Diana's stories of the training of Venatores. Raphael sat close to Emeral and Maxwell so he could compare lamsmans as Diana spoke. "How old were you when you started this training?" Raphael asked. "Because I know Vivian had been hunting by herself for three years before we met."

"Our parents started to train Thor and me when we were really little, I was about four and I think Thor was the same age but we didn't start the testing until we were older."

"Vivian and I would compete with each other so we tested for certain stones around the same time, we were about ten. It takes several years to complete the testing even if you are really good."

"So this stone, the one you said you got for tracking and killing a group of demons, how old were you two when you got those?" Raphael asked.

"I think we were twelve, but the groups we tracked were small, maybe three or four demons."

"Twelve," Raphael repeated. "I am actually surprised that Joshua and Iris allowed their children to take those tests when they were so young."

"Joshua and Iris were fierce Venatores. They were close friends with my parents and I think the real reason Joshua and Iris stopped hunting is when they saw what the deaths of our parents did to me and Thor. But Raphael that is the way of my people."

Raphael was quiet for a moment. "Diana I hold your clan in the highest respect but Vivian and I haven't talked about the training our children will receive and I am not sure I would want them to start that young." Diana didn't say anything to Raphael but turned and glanced at Misha to see the look on his face.

Misha grinned, "I think we are going to have to have that talk too."

"But isn't it true that all the children of your tribe are trained to be warriors at a young age?" asked Diana.

"They are," Emeral replied. "But they are trained in groups when they are young and not sent off by themselves. Of course this is not my place," Emeral said with a grin. "Diana, King Sudfad is building a learning center for all of our children and grandchildren."

"We can decide what training we want them to have. Gabriel and Raphael have different backgrounds as do my sons. And Raul, Simon and Matthew; you haven't met him yet, have been trained in different fighting forms too. I think all of you should sit down together and decide what types of training you want to do at what ages. Our family is growing quickly and children grow fast."

"It is difficult for me to think of training Nicholas and Christopher at their ages," Gabriel said. "Yet you, Vivian and Thor were training when you were that young."

"When I found Lila and Christopher," Luca explained. "Hutas had skinned their father alive and one Huta was raping their mother while the second Huta was trying to rape Lila. Both Lila and Christopher fought bravely. Christopher stabbed the Huta that was attacking his mother in the back with a pitchfork. Now months later he is having terrible nightmares. I guess I am not sure what age is right to start this type of training."

"After what Christopher, Nicholas and Cerey have gone through, I would ask the Sanuri for advice on this matter," Maxwell said.

"We should probably think about turning in pretty soon," Gabriel suggested.

Diana knelt down and fastened Emeral's lamsman to her ankle and was fastening Maxwell's when a small flock of Enrops flew into camp. "This is for Misha and Diana," one of the birds announced. Misha took the note and read it as Diana finished fastening Maxwell's lamsman.

"What is the matter?" Diana asked when she saw the look on Misha's face. "Is Thor alright?"

Misha handed Diana the note. "It's from Vivian," he explained to everyone. "Raul and Simon visited Thor and mentioned that Diana and I are courting. Thor is very angry and said that when we return home he is taking Diana and returning to Ryed."

"I was afraid of that," Diana moaned and tears filled her eyes. "Misha what are we going to do?"

"What do you mean?" he asked fearfully. "You are still going to marry me aren't you?"

"Yes, I don't know what I mean. I love Thor but you don't know what he can get like when he is mad."

"We will talk to him as soon as we get home," said Misha.

"I think the easiest thing for you to do is just get married right now," Calen said. "Like Natasha and I did. Gabriel and Raphael are here, you can buy rings in Salar."

"Thor won't like it but once you are Misha's wife Thor has no hold over you anymore. You can have a regular ceremony and celebration later."

"That's what Hannah and I did too," Gabriel said. "Calen is right, that might solve your problems."

"I think they are right," Koby said. "Thor is a big guy and might try to force Diana to leave with him."

Misha looked at Diana, "I think they are right too. I wasn't able to give you the proposal I had planned and now not the wedding I imagined but at least we will be married."

Diana smiled, "All right." Then she started to laugh. Diana turned to Emeral and Maxwell. "What do you think?"

"I think it is a lovely night for a wedding," Maxwell said with a huge smile.

"Here you can wear this ring until you buy one," Emeral said. "At least you will feel married that way." Emeral tool off one of her rings and handed it to Diana.

"Diana wants Vivian to be her maid-of-honor," Misha said. "Raphael would you perform the ceremony tonight, then Gabriel can perform our next wedding ceremony and you will be in that wedding?"

The mood around the campsite became very festive as everyone quickly prepared for the ceremony. "Since Maxwell is here, we need a little aisle for you to walk down," Luca said.

"Elan I hope you aren't offended that we are getting married before you," Misha said. "The regular ceremony will be well after your wedding."

"Not at all. I personally think it is the wisest thing to do."

Chapter VI
Vengeance

"It's not often you see a holy man and a sorcerer eating breakfast together," Erebus said with a smirk.

"You are rather isolated in these chambers," the Sanuri responded. "I just thought I would join you and Marie was kind enough to serve our food in here."

"I'm not sure if isolated is the correct word," Erebus said. "I'm just not well enough to venture out yet. But I can't complain I am being treated very well."

"And that surprises you?"

"While I don't know all of the details I am well aware of the role Sophie played in the torture of Vitomas and Annabelle. And although Sophie was not directly involved with Delilah's capture, she was a member of the Insidiae. So yes, it surprised me that Gabriel and his team would risk their lives to try and save Sophie and it surprises me that Sudfad's family is so gracious and forgiving."

"I find your choice of words interesting," the Sanuri said as he sipped his coffee. "For a man whose sole purpose in life is vengeance you applaud these people for being forgiving."

"My situation is different."

"Is it? As you said you don't know the details of the atrocities that were committed against Vitomas and Annabelle. Yet look at those two young women now, as well as Delilah, one would never guess they survived the tortures of hell. They are happy, delightful and grateful women who are a joy to be around and do you know why they are like that now?"

"No, but I am sure you are going to tell me."

"Forgiveness."

"Is this why you joined me for breakfast so you could preach to me?"

"Partly," the Sanuri said and smiled. "I feel that I should tell you that when we first found you wounded I looked inside of your mind to find out what had happened to you. While this is a powerful gift I have I cannot control the scope of what is revealed to me. I saw your life Erebus and I saw what a life dedicated to vengeance will do to you."

"I have no life anymore," Erebus replied. "I died when Sophie did."

"There you are wrong; you are willing yourself to die. Erebus you are a man of great potential; potential that can be used for good or evil. You have many choices to make; do not act in haste. Now that I am done preaching to you," the Sanuri said then laughed. "I have another reason for wanting to talk to you. You have repeatedly said you are grateful to Gabriel and Sudfad, I know a way you can help them."

"I am listening."

"There is a great threat against Sudfad's family originating from members of the Insidiae who live in Ryed. I believe these members are working closely with some of the Grand Masters. Gabriel has been preparing for this mission but his team will be short members. That young girl you met the night of the ball will be replacing four others on the team. But they have no idea of what they are up against. Ryed is your home and I would imagine you are well connected in certain areas. While they may not realize yet that they will need your help, I do. It is just something for you to consider."

"Why did you mention that girl?"

"I told you I read your thoughts."

"And?"

"You liked her and she made you think of the children you should have had. Erebus everything is a matter of choices."

"So do you feel different now that you are married?" Dagon asked as he reached for a freshly baked biscuit.

"I really don't know," Diana said with a big smile. "I am still in shock and I think I do feel different but I can't explain it." Diana was filling cups with coffee and handing them to members of the team who were coming to the fire for breakfast.

"Now might be the time to tell you that Ruala babies fly before they learn to walk," Gabriel said with a grin as he took a cup of coffee.'

"Are you serious?"

"Yes."

Diana turned and looked at Misha who was eating his breakfast. Misha smiled and nodded. Diana was thinking about Gabriel's words then suddenly her eyes widened and she asked Misha in a scolding tone, "How am I supposed to catch flying babies?" Everyone broke into laughter.

"I can get a Ruala nurse," Misha replied.

"Or you could have enough family around to help," Emeral said with a coy smile. "I have three human daughter-in-laws that is one reason I didn't want to take that position in the military.

Both Luca and Calen stared at Emeral. "Mother we didn't know," Calen said. "If you want that position that Sudfad offered you, we can certainly hire nurses. That is a very honorable position."

"And being a grandmother isn't?"

"You know that's not what I meant. I just don't want you to deny yourself to help us," Calen said.

"Diana has anyone told you that Lily is the first baby born that is half Ruala and half human?" Emeral asked

"No," Diana said seriously.

"A former member of Gabriel's team named Rabi married Hannah's friend and they will have a baby soon. Luca and Lila will have the third child that is of both races. I think it is exciting and simply a wonder to behold. I could not be prouder of my family," Emeral said then turned to Calen.

96

"Your father feels alive when he is leading troops and planning missions. When I walk into the house and Christopher, Nicholas and Cerey jump into my arms and yell 'Grandma', I feel alive."

"Thor, its Natasha and I have your breakfast tray," Natasha called through the closed bedroom door. "I am coming in and if you throw anything I will hit you over the head with this tray." Natasha could hear Thor laughing. "You sat up by yourself." Natasha said with surprise when she entered the room.

"I am getting better."

"Since you want to kill all of us you will need your strength so I brought you a big breakfast," Natasha teased as she set the tray on Thor's lap.

"I don't want to kill you."

"Well you could have fooled me yesterday," Natasha said with a grin and sat down on the side of Thor's bed. "Now I have some questions for you; Thor don't you scowl at me like that, Natasha said in a scolding manner which made Thor laugh. "So tell me what kind of girls do you like?'

Thor was obviously surprised by Natasha's question. "I don't understand what you are asking?"

"Short, tall, blonde, brunette, red head, funny or serious, those kind of things."

"I guess I don't really know."

"You don't know! Thor are you saying you have never had a girlfriend?"

"I've always been too busy hunting."

"Thor I grew up a hunter too and you have to make time in life for other things."

"So why are you asking me these questions?"

"Because there will be a lot of single women at Elan's and Cassandra's wedding and I would like to introduce you to some."

"Now let me finish. You don't have to talk to them but if you want to, you should let me teach you how to dance."

"What makes you think they will want to meet me?"

"Are you kidding me, you are such a handsome man. Thor did you see all the women who were admiring you at the ball? I'll tell you if I wasn't married I would be flirting with you." Natasha was surprised to see Thor blush. "So that's it, it's a date. Work on getting better and I will teach you how to dance." Thor laughed as Natasha stood up and started to walk away from the bed. She changed her mind and walked back to Thor.

"You know I understand; every time you kill a demon you are getting vengeance for what they did to your parents. But if you let the demons fill you with hatred, you are just letting them win and it doesn't matter how many of them you kill." Natasha turned and left the room.

"It's just like he said," Timothy said with a laugh as he warmed himself by the fire Aaron had just made. "The troops won't follow us into Stordt." Timothy laughed again loudly.

"Now we don't have to freeze our asses off," Jackson said as he dropped an armload of wood near the fire. "And we can have a fire at night."

"So Timothy," Aaron said. "You always seem like such a little sissy. How is it that you have demons coming to you? Did you call to them because you can't protect yourself?"

"Those demons are what got us out of prison," Timothy retorted. "So you scoff all you want."

"I don't know a lot about demons," Aaron continued. "But I do know they don't do anything for free. So what did you have to give them?"

"Haven't given them anything yet," Timothy said haughtily.

Jackson and Aaron looked at each other and grinned. "So what did you promise them?" Jackson asked.

"Half of my father's fortune after I kill him," Timothy said as if he was showing a badge of honor.

"What else?" Jackson asked.

"What else! That's more than enough."

"Is that what the demon told you?"

"No, that's what I told him," Timothy said as he felt a rising sense of power.

Both Aaron and Jackson roared with laughter, "You really are a fool," Aaron said which greatly irritated Timothy.

"So if you are so damn smart, why didn't you get us out of prison?" Timothy shouted.

"Because I'm not gonna be a slave to no damn demon," Jackson said. "Once they get their hooks into you they don't let go."

"Jackson ask him," Aaron said as he continued to laugh at Timothy.

"Ask me what?"

"Did you barter your soul away you moron?"

Timothy was quiet for a moment as he tried to remember his conversations with the demons, "I don't think so," Timothy said. Aaron and Jackson again roared with laughter.

Dack and Joao walked into Gabriel's house and didn't see anyone so they walked into the kitchen where they found Lila, Natasha and Bekka.

"Well welcome back," Bekka said as she hugged both of her friends. "How was your trip?"

"It was good to go home and see everyone," Dack said. "But Joao has to talk to Cassandra."

"Where is she?" Joao asked.

"Shopping in Salar with Vivian," Lila replied.

"What's wrong?" asked Natasha.

"I don't know if Cassandra told you that she and Elan didn't want Mother to help with the wedding preparations," Joao said. "Well Mother is mad then somehow she found out that Emeral is going to be the maid-of-honor now she's just fuming."

"First why didn't Cassandra want your mother to help with the wedding?" Natasha asked.

"When you meet her you will know," Joao said.

"That doesn't tell us anything," Natasha replied.

Joao thought for a moment then said, "Let's say King Sudfad and Queen Renya invite my parents for coffee. Even though mother has never met them she would start telling the King how to run his kingdom and the Queen how to decorate the castle. If there is a subject, Mother believes she is an expert on it and don't ever tell her I said this but she can't do anything." Everyone laughed at this comment.

"Now I understand about your mother but why is she mad that Emeral is going to be Cassandra's maid-of-honor?" Natasha asked.

"They grew up together and are complete opposites," Bekka said. "Joao don't get mad at me for saying this but Tina would never consider getting her hands dirty let alone fight in battle. And she only had the three children and always had nurses and housekeepers taking care of them. Personally I think Tina is jealous of Emeral because Emeral is well respected among our people."

"I'm not going to argue with anything you said," Joao replied. "Mother is very impressed by wealth and she knows all of you are wealthy. She is just going to have a fit when she finds out you do your own cooking and cleaning and you are warriors."

"And that they adopted children that weren't their own blood," Dack said condescendingly.

"Alright I hate her now," Natasha said. "We will have to warn the others. Where are they going to stay?"

"The King and Queen offered the castle," Joao said.

"We might want to change that," Natasha said. "We shouldn't be punishing Sudfad and Renya for their generosity. There are plenty of hotels in Salar. Tomorrow when Hannah goes to the castle to check on Erebus I am going with her and talk to the Royal Family."

Hecate stepped out of her lair and stood in the cool night air. She and Sampson had been arguing most of the day and night. Finally frustration overtook her and Hecate slipped a sedative into Sampson's glass of whiskey; when he fell asleep Hecate walked out of the lair.

Sampson was not happy with Hecate's decision to postpone the trials he needed to complete his transformation into a demon. Hecate the manipulative, seductress demon was actually honest with her human husband. She was planning on joining the fierce battles in the hell dominions for territory and he was more useful to her cause as a human.

Honesty was not something that came to Hecate easily and she failed to tell Sampson that she had a powerful partner in her plans to take over a hell dimension; her longtime lover Orbus. While Orbus was aware of Sampson, Sampson knew nothing of Orbus. But Sampson was not a fool; he sensed that something had changed in his relationship with Hecate since his return from the monastery at Rubar; where he was sent to steal holy items.

Sampson was demanding the completion of his trials so that he would obtain more power. Power that he desired to be on a more equal basis with his demon wife, power he desired so he could destroy his village; the Clan of Gesmal who had banished him and power so he could feed his dark appetites.

While Misha, Maxwell and the troops they led found their return travel to Salar increasingly faster since they were no longer tracking the escaped prisoners. The prisoners were consumed with paranoia. They found a small cave on the border between the Kingdoms of Stordt and Lentz where they had been hiding for two days.

The cave was small for three men; especially three men who could not get along.

"Timothy so help me if you don't stop your damn whining I am going to beat the hell out of you," Jackson growled. "No wonder your family disowned you, they probably couldn't stand your whining either."

Timothy picked up a small log from the campfire and rushed towards Jackson, whose back was to him. Just as Timothy was about to hit Jackson on the head with the log, Jackson quickly rolled onto his side and kicked Timothy's legs off from under him. Timothy landed hard on his face.

Jackson jumped on top of Timothy and rolled him over so he was lying on his back. Jackson was a powerful man with large fists that he used to beat Timothy until he was almost unconscious. Jackson pulled a large knife out of the sheath on his belt and pressed it against Timothy's throat. "The next time I have to tell you to stop whining I am cutting your damn tongue out; understand me?"

Timothy nodded and Jackson got off from him. Aaron laughed loudly. "Jackson you have more patience than me. I would have killed the bastard."

"Well I've been thinking," Jackson said. "If Timothy's daddy is so wealthy that a demon would bust us out of prison, maybe we should get a little of that wealth for ourselves."

Misha, Maxwell and the soldiers returned to Fort Salar, while the other members of Gabriel's team, other than Emeral and Diana went to the castle to meet with King Sudfad. As soon as Misha completed his necessary duties he picked up Diana and flew along with Emeral into the City of Salar.

During their return trip, Diana and Misha had received several messages form Vivian and Natasha about Thor's angry demeanor. Diana kept begging Emeral and Maxwell not to introduce themselves to Thor until she had a chance to speak with Thor first. Finally Emeral and Maxwell agreed although they both felt they could probably calm Thor down more than Diana, since she appeared to be the subject of his anger.

The members of Gabriel's team who had remained in the house were all women, with the exception of Dack and Joao who returned from the Ice Caves two days prior to the return of Gabriel and the others. As the household was receiving messages from Gabriel and the other members of the team, they decided to keep all the information from Thor so he could not plan some sort of reprisal against Diana and Misha.

On this afternoon an Enrop entered Gabriel's house with the verbal message that the members of the team had returned to Salar but were at the castle of Sudfad. The Enrop continued to say that Misha, Diana and Emeral might be at the house before the others could return. Joao and Dack decided to stay inside of the house in case they had to physically restrain Thor.

"Honey don't be shy just tell me which stones you like," Misha said as he, Diana and Emeral were in Andrew's Jewelry Store in Salar.

"I am not sure," Diana said. "They are all so beautiful and I have never seen things like this before."

"Let her look around," Emeral said to Misha as she took him by the arm. "Now if I were you, I would strongly consider buying these items for your new bride. You two will be attending functions at the castle and you know Diana would never pick out things like this." Misha motioned for Andrew to wrap up two necklaces with matching earrings and bracelets. Then Misha returned to Diana's side.

"Misha all these stones are equally beautiful to me; since you like the dark blue sapphires why don't we have those stones?" Once Diana decided on the stone, it only took a matter of minutes for the young couple to pick out an engagement ring and wedding rings. All were dark blue sapphires and diamonds in yellow gold."

The meeting at the castle was short and Gabriel and his team returned home before Misha, Diana and Emeral. Christopher, Nicholas and Cerey pulled everyone into their playroom to show them the fort that Alexander had built for them.

While the family members were still showering each other with affection, Misha, Diana and Emeral walked into the house.

"I want to get this over with," Diana said as she took a deep breath; then she and Misha walked directly up the stairs hand in hand. "Thor," Diana said as they entered his room. Thor was sitting up in bed and Diana ran up to her brother and hugged him. "You look wonderful," she gushed.

Thor did not return Diana's hug nor did he speak to her. Thor's anger was exploding within him. Diana could feel how tense he was becoming and she moved away from his bed and stood next to Misha.

"Is this the man you are courting? The man you went behind my back to date?"

"No, Thor this is the man I married," Diana said calmly.

Thor was stunned by Diana's admission. The veins protruded from his neck as he stared at the two. "Married!" Thor yelled. "Married!" Thor's voice grew louder. "Diana of all people I never believed you would betray me like this. We have devoted our lives to each other then while I am dying you take a husband. What kind of a person are you. I don't know you anymore. I don't want to know you anymore. I disown you as my blood." Thor's voice carried throughout the house and the rest of the team now became silent and listened to the confrontation between Thor, Diana and Misha.

Misha had promised Diana that he would not get involved with her conversation with Thor. Diana was of the belief that she could calm her brother down. As soon as Misha heard Diana crying he moved so he was now standing between her and Thor.

"Don't you talk to your sister like that," Misha said loudly. "She was stabbed and beaten too and when she was too weak to walk she asked me to carry her in here so she could watch over you." "Diana has been through hell, she saw those demons attack you and she watched you come close to dying twice. Until the last few days she has remained by your side and speaks of little besides you. And you finally wake up and this is how you treat her. Thor you don't deserve a sister like Diana."

Thor stared at Misha as a variety of thoughts and emotions flooded his mind. Without looking at Diana Thor said, "Diana he is right, I am sorry that I yelled at you but I am still angry."

"Then you will take it out on me," Misha said. "If you want to do battle when you are healed, that is fine but you will not talk to Diana in that manner again." Both men became quiet but continued to glare at each other angrily. Diana quickly ran out of the room and returned with a pouch.

"Thor, Misha gave me the money so I could buy you a gift," Diana said as she handed the pouch to her brother. He emptied the pouch into his left hand and stared at the finely crafted golden chain that held a large ruby pendant.

"How can you afford this?" Thor growled. "Are you a criminal?"

Now Misha was visibly angry as he walked closer to Thor's bed. "Hasn't anyone told you about the family that has adopted you; you are royalty now as am I and Diana?"

"What are you talking about?" Thor asked with suspicion.

"Maxwell's brother is King of the Ruala people; Maxwell is a prince and Emeral a princess, which makes all of their children by blood or adoption princes and princesses. Thor whether you choose to live with this family or not is not my concern. But if you are going to accept this family you will act like an honorable warrior and you will assume your responsibilities like a man. Neither of which I am seeing right now."

"What responsibilities?" Thor asked in a normal tone of voice.

"Diana, why don't you leave Thor and me alone to talk?" Misha said while continuing to stare at Thor. As Diana turned to leave the room Misha added. "Wait, why don't you bring us a bottle of whiskey and some glasses."

By the time Diana walked into the dining room, Natasha was walking out of the kitchen with a small tray that held a bottle of whiskey and two glasses. "You heard?" Diana asked with embarrassment.

"Everyone heard," Natasha replied. "I don't know what Misha is doing but it seems to be working. Give them this then come back down and show us your rings."

Misha and Thor were talking but stopped when Diana entered the room. She set the tray on a small table and poured whiskey into two glasses. She handed Misha his glass first then walked over to Thor's bed and handed him a glass. "Let me see your hand," Thor ordered as he saw her new rings.

"In this tribe, people give each other rings when they marry," Diana said. "This is my engagement ring and this is my wedding band, Misha is wearing one just like it." Thor did not respond and Diana turned and started to walk out of the room. Both men watched her as she stopped, stood still for a moment then turned around and walked up to Thor's bed with a determined step.

"Thor you know how much I love you," Diana said angrily then she turned and looked at Misha and her voice softened. "Misha I don't know if you realize yet how much I love you. I don't want the two men I love to hate each other."

Diana turned back to her brother. "For years my life has focused on you. But now I love Emeral and Maxwell and I am falling in love with this entire family. Thor they are the nicest people, they are honorable and fierce warriors. And when you and I were dying they took us in and treated us like their own."

"Look at this," Diana now walked briskly across the room and pulled open several dresser drawers. These are filled with clothing and weapons that Emeral and Maxwell have bought you." Then she walked up to Thor again. "This is my family now and Thor I will not have you showing them disrespect, do you hear me?" Diana glared at Thor.

"Yes," he said.

"Thor do you really hear me?"

Thor started to laugh, "Yes I do. I always love it when the baby lioness in you wakes up." Diana smiled and kissed Thor on the forehead, then kissed Misha on the cheek and walked out of the room.

Misha turned to Thor and said. "It must be unsettling to wake up from an injury and find that your entire life has changed."

"They've been up there for almost two hours," Diana said with concern as she worked in the kitchen. "Do you think they are fighting?"

"They are both big men," Natasha said. "I think we would hear them if they were fighting."

"Do you want me to go up there with you?" Vivian asked Diana.

"Girls," Emeral said. "The cakes are done. Maxwell and I are going to take one to Thor. Diana I would like you to go up with us and introduce us then please leave us with your brother. Would you please get Maxwell while I finish this tray?"

A few minutes later Diana knocked on the open door to Thor's bedroom. "Are you two still alive or drunk?"

"Both," Misha said. "Come in."

"Thor I want you to meet Emeral and Maxwell," Diana said lovingly. Before Thor could speak, Emeral placed a tray on his lap."

"What is this?" Thor asked with a laugh.

"I promised Diana that I would make you one of my special cakes as soon as you woke up," Emeral said.

"Thor you have never tasted anything like that before it is wonderful," Diana said. "I am going to leave you alone to get acquainted."

"Misha the girls have something they have been waiting to show you," Emeral said. "Why don't you go down stairs too?"

"Yes Mother," Misha said with a grin and walked out of the bedroom, closing the door behind him. Misha walked down the stairs and walked up behind Diana and kissed her on the neck.

"You have time for that later," Lila said with a giggle. "We have been waiting for you."

"Where is everyone?" Misha asked.

"In bed already," Vivian said. "We didn't think you would ever leave Thor's room."

"Now come with us," Lila said excitedly. Lila and Vivian led Misha and Diana up the stairs and past his chambers."

"Where are we going?" he asked as he suspected the surprise was that the girls had fixed up his chambers.

A door opened in the hallway and Luca said, "It's about time; we've been drinking all of your whiskey." As Diana and Misha walked into a large room they could see the family was gathered inside and there were tables set up with food and beverages.

"Welcome to your new chambers," Calen announced. Diana squeezed Misha's hand and smiled as she looked around the beautifully decorated parlor.

"Are you serious?" Diana asked Calen.

"Let us show you around," Lila said and she and Vivian led the couple through the rooms of their new home. When they returned to the parlor Misha thanked everyone.

"This is unbelievable," Diana said and started to cry. "Thank you so much."

"There's just one thing Misha," Bekka said with a grin. "We aren't helping Diana clean up this place too."

"Oh I will keep it really clean," Diana said seriously and Misha bent down and kissed her on the head.

"Let's have a toast," Misha said as he poured a glass of wine for Diana and a glass of whiskey for himself. Misha raised his glass and the others followed his example. "To family," Misha said with pride.

Chapter VII
Elan and Cassandra

The next morning Vivian led Elan and Cassandra into the dining room for breakfast. Elan and Cassandra both stopped suddenly and stared at the room and table. There were bouquets of flowers everywhere, lit candles on the table as well as wine glasses. And the entire family was standing in the room smiling at them.

"You are right on time Vivian," Natasha said and smiled.

Vivian turned and looked at Elan and Cassandra, "I was supposed to distract you so they could prepare the room."

"What is all of this?" asked Elan.

"It's a pre-wedding party," Hannah said.

"And you will never believe this," Luca said sarcastically. "It was Misha's idea because he felt like he and Diana stole some of the attention from your wedding. It's amazing how much Diana has changed him already."

"Sit down," Lila said as she handed Cassandra a bouquet of flowers.

"Since we had more advanced notice about your wedding we have had plans in the works for a while," Maxwell said. "You never got back to Emeral with how you wanted your chambers built and decorated and we did not pursue the matter with you because we have been working on a special surprise. The family commissioned Alexander to build all of the furniture for your new home." Both Cassandra and Elan smiled broadly as they listened to Maxwell. "Since it is such a big order he has put his apprentice to work helping him. Do you know who his apprentice is?"

"No," Elan said while Cassandra shook her head from side to side.

"Sudfad, who is trying to talk me into learning the craft because he says' it heals the soul. So my children you will be using furniture built for you by the most powerful king in Opots."

Calen now walked up to Elan and Cassandra and handed them several drawings. "I was going to give these too you as part of a wedding gift. I have made several designs for new chambers for you that will be large enough for your families to stay with you. Just decide on a drawing and we will start construction." Elan and Cassandra looked at the drawings in amazement then looked at each other and smiled.

"Thank you so much," Cassandra said with tears in her eyes.

"I don't know what to say," Elan said. "We are so touched by all of this."

"Oh there is more," Koby said. "Christopher, Nicholas, Cerey it's your turn." The three children ran up to Elan and Cassandra and handed them envelopes and three pouches of gold coins." Elan and Cassandra hugged the children then Elan opened one of the envelopes and after reading the note he showed it to Cassandra.

"I don't understand what this is." Elan said.

"We are sending you on a trip after your wedding," Gabriel said. "Those envelopes contain invitations from the ruling families of Lentz. They all want you to stay at their castles for a few days each as they show you around their kingdom, then Matthew and Angelina, Stephan and Ingr and Thaos and Nikki are taking you to the coast of Lentz, where there are fancy cities and hotels. And the pouches contain money for your trip."

Both Elan and Cassandra looked overwhelmed, "We just don't know how to thank you."

"We will furnish your chambers as we have our other sons," Emeral said. "And since we have more time, Cassandra we can start taking you shopping for the carpets, drapes and other things."

"Can you please excuse us for a moment?" Elan asked and he and Cassandra walked out of the room and into the hallway.

"Where are they going?" Nicholas asked loudly. "We haven't had cake yet."

"They will be back," Hannah assured her son.

110

Elan and Cassandra returned to the room and stood near their chairs. "We both are so appreciative of what you are doing for us and there are things that we wanted to talk to you about but both Cassandra and I have felt like you may think badly of us. While Cassandra and I both have families, we have become closer to all of you than to our own parents and brothers and sisters. We don't want chambers big enough for our families to stay with us because we don't really feel like they are our families any longer. If it would be alright with you we would like to move into Misha's old chambers."

"That's fine," Calen said. "But are you sure?"

"Some of you don't know our families very well," Cassandra said. "And honestly I am embarrassed for you to meet mine. My mother worships money, she is overbearing and I don't think she has ever done a day's work in her life. And she believes in," Cassandra now looked at her brother Joao. "Help me you know what I am trying to say."

"Our mother is a fanatic about what she calls pure blood. She will just throw a fit when she learns you have adopted three children, even though it is none of her business. And for what it is worth I agree with Cassandra and Elan. Our parents are like poison you don't want them here."

"They aren't exaggerating," Dack said.

"We love the life we have here with all of you and wanted to talk to you about something but we don't want Cassandra's parents to know yet," Elan said. "Hannah every week when you go to the orphanage to take care of the children, many of the girls go with you. Cassandra has been going with you so much lately because we have been thinking about adopting a child, if that is alright with all of you."

"Oh course it is alright," Gabriel said. "Children are blessings; you don't need to ask permission to bring one into this home."

Hannah got a big smile on her face and gasped, "Joey isn't it?"

Cassandra smiled, "Yes, I just fell in love with him and yesterday after Elan returned we went to the orphanage so they could meet. And Elan fell in love with him too."

"We thought you were giving him a lot of attention," Natasha said happily.

"Cassandra's mother will make it rain fire if she finds out about this," Dack said. "And Elan and Cassandra are sharing the one bedroom. So Joao and I thought we could share a room so it would open up a room for the boy; then they could bring him home from the orphanage."

"There are plenty of rooms in this house," Gabriel said. "Bring the boy home today."

"Thank you so much," Cassandra said. "Joey is such a good boy he shouldn't be any trouble."

"Nicholas do you remember Joey from the orphanage?" Hannah asked. "He was the quiet little boy with the blonde hair."

"I remember him," Nicholas said. "We played sometimes."

"Cassandra and Elan are going to be his new mommy and daddy so he is coming here to live?"

Nicholas turned to Christopher and said, "You will like Joey; he is really nice."

"Grandma can we go with them to bring Joey home?" Christopher asked and it was at this point that everyone realized that Emeral was crying. "What's wrong Grandma?" Christopher cried and all three children ran up to her.

"I am sorry," Emeral said as she hugged her grandchildren. "Elan and Cassandra I think that it is absolutely wonderful that you are adopting a child. But when I think about how much happiness these children have brought into our lives I can't imagine how cold Tina's heart must be. I hope none of you ever feel like you have to hide something like that from Maxwell and me; it just seems so sad." Maxwell put his arm around Emeral's shoulders.

"The priests at the orphanage don't know Joey's age. But he seems about the same age as Nicholas and Christopher. His entire family was killed in a fire, he was sick and his mother had left him with one of the physicians in Salar."

"Personally I think it sounds suspicious that the entire family burned alive in that house in the middle of the day; I think something more happened to them," Elan explained.

Emeral composed herself, "Elan and Cassandra why don't you get Joey after breakfast. Boys, I will need some of you to move Elan's and Cassandra's things into Misha's old chambers for the time being. Then some of us will need to go shopping for a child's bed and other things for his room."

"I'll go to the orphanage with them," Hannah said. "That way I can take the children."

"I think all of us girls should go shopping," Natasha said then she walked around the table and kissed both Elan and Cassandra on their cheeks. "This is a good thing you are doing."

"There is one more thing," Elan said. "We would like Emeral and Maxwell to come on our trip with us." Now everyone at the table started smiling.

"Us," Emeral gasped. "Why would you want old folks like us to go with you?"

"First of all you aren't old," Cassandra said then laughed. "You two are a lot of fun."

"And you are our maid-of-honor and our best man," Elan said with a big smile.

"You will have a wonderful time," Raphael said. "And you will fit right in with the families of Lentz. I'll bet you all become good friends."

"Go," Calen said. "It can be like a second honeymoon for you."

"We'll take care of Joey," Hannah said to Elan and Cassandra.

Emeral and Maxwell looked at each other and smiled. "What do you think?" Emeral asked.

"I think I am going to need to ask Sudfad for some time off," Maxwell said and hugged his wife.

113

"Here's some money," Misha said to Diana as he handed her a pouch. "Go shopping with the girls. Buy a gift from us for Elan's and Cassandra's new home. Also, it's traditional here for people to give gifts when babies are born, so feel free to start buying things for Vivian, Lila and Hannah." Diana looked up at Misha with pride in her eyes.

"You are such a good man," she said and kissed him.

"That means you should buy something for Joey also," Misha said. "I have to be honest with you I don't like to go shopping."

"But you've taken me shopping."

"That's different," Misha said. "It's fun to buy things for you."

"What are you going to do?" she asked.

"Visit your brother and move furniture." Misha said. "Now that all of us men are home, I am wondering if we can start getting Thor out of bed and walking a little."

"Are you two becoming friends?" Diana asked happily.

"I wouldn't go that far," Misha said. "Your brother can certainly be an ass but I kind of feel sorry for him. This must be like waking up from a dream and finding that your world is completely different. And maybe it will put him in a better mood if he can start feeling a little more independent again."

"Misha I love you so much," Diana said and stretched up to kiss him again.

"I'm glad we don't live here anymore," Nicholas said as he and Cerey took Hannah's hands to walk inside of the orphanage. As usual Christopher held Nicholas' other hand.

"I remember when we came here to get you and Cerey," Christopher said. "You both were so sad."

"I think Joey is kind of sad too," Cassandra said as she and Elan landed near them. Then Cassandra turned to Elan and squeezed his hand. "I am so excited."

114

Once they entered the huge stone building, Hannah said, "Children why don't you go with Elan and Cassandra to find Joey. I am going to find the priests." Elan and Cassandra held the children's hands as they walked down a long dimly lit corridor.

"I don't like it here," Christopher said. They opened a door at the end of the corridor and walked out into a large play yard that was filled with children. "Elan don't any of these kids have parents?" Christopher asked anxiously.

"No and that is sad," Elan said.

"There he is," Cassandra said when she saw Joey sitting by himself and drawing in the dirt. They walked over to Joey and Cassandra squatted down. "Joey, Elan and I would like to have you as our son; we want to take you home today." Joey kept looking back and forth between Elan and Cassandra as if he did not understand what was happening.

"We will be living in the same house with Hannah," Elan said. "And this is Christopher and you know Nicholas and Cerey."

Joey started to cry. Nicholas walked up to Joey and held out his hand. Joey took Nicholas' hand and stood up, then Christopher took a hold of Joey's other hand and the three little boys walked off the play yard in silence. Tears ran down Cassandra's face as she picked Cerey up and followed the boys. As soon as they entered the corridor they met Hannah and Padre Octavos.

"Hannah I don't know if Joey understands," Cassandra said. "When we told him we wanted to bring him home he started crying."

"He understands," Nicholas said.

All of the children rode in the back of the small boca and Elan and Cassandra sat in the front seat with Hannah. "I think the other children will help Joey heal," Hannah whispered to her friends. "Perhaps they should have a little party tonight and all sleep together. We can let them pick the bedroom."

"I thought he would be happy," Cassandra whispered.

"He is," Hannah said. "But you have to understand, you and Elan probably just answered all of his prayers and Joey doesn't know how to handle it emotionally. Just be patient with him."

"I think Cassandra and I are going to be asking you a lot of questions," Elan said. "Also Hannah, I don't feel right about you paying all of the fees. I will pay you back."

"Don't let Padre Octavos hear you calling them fees," Hannah said with a laugh. "We call them contributions. You know my father left me with more money than I will ever know what to do with. And he obtained it in the worse ways; I like to spend it for good things and it just makes me so happy that you are giving a child a home."

"I was thinking about taking Joey shopping for clothes and toys," Cassandra said. "But he seems so emotional I think I should wait."

"I think that is the right decision for today," Hannah said. "Emeral and they girls will buy him things today and if he needs anything else he can borrow the children's." Hannah paused. "Cassandra I think we all were really surprised to hear about your mother because you are such a sweet girl and although I don't know Joao well, he seems like a nice young man."

"We can't stand our mother, don't get me wrong we love her but we have tried to become very different from her. My sister Melinda is like me and Joao I will let her visit but I don't want our parents in your house. Hannah trust me; Mother will be awful to the children and well, everyone else."

"We feel sorry for Melinda because she still lives with Tina and Charles," Elan said. "We thought we would ask her to stay with us, while she is here for the wedding."

"I hope you two realize that although Gabriel owns the house, we consider it a home to all of you. You make it sound like we think of you as guests."

"Thank you so much," Cassandra said. "We meant what we said this morning. Elan and I don't feel like we belong to the families we were born into, we feel like we are members of your family and we have chosen yours over ours."

116

"How are you going to keep the news of Joey from your parents?" Hannah asked. "Are you not going to have him at the wedding?"

"We haven't figured that out yet," Elan said. "You see we didn't expect to find a child this quickly. We don't care if Tina yells at us we just don't want her to upset the children."

"After dinner tonight, when the children are playing let's talk about this as a family; we will come up with something," Hannah said.

"What is going on here?" Hannah asked loudly when they all walked into the dining room and she saw Thor sitting at the table eating cake with Misha, Dagon and Luca.

"We thought Thor wouldn't be so grouchy if we got him out of bed," Luca kidded.

"And it is working," Thor said with a grin.

"How do you feel?" Hannah asked as she felt his forehead.

"Well I am not happy about how weak I am but after hearing about my bleeding episodes I suppose I am lucky to be walking at all."

"That you are," Hannah said. "Did you save any cake for the children?"

"Yes, there's another one in the kitchen," Dagon replied.

"Nicholas, Christopher why don't you introduce Joey to everyone while I get some cake and milk for you," Hannah suggested.

Joey was shy as Christopher and Nicholas took him by the hand and introduced him to Dagon, Misha and Luca all of the men greeted Joey and shook hands with him. Christopher announced with his usual pride, "Luca is my new daddy." When the boys walked up to Thor, Nicholas said, "He was the new boy in the house but now you are Joey." All the men laughed.

"Hi Joey I am Thor." Thor said and shook hands with the boy.

"He's shy like Nicholas was when he first came here," Christopher explained. "Joey this is where we all sit," Christopher said and ran to his chair. Joey ran to the chairs with the other children as Hannah put plates of cake and glasses of milk on the table.

"The girls aren't back from shopping yet," Luca said to Cassandra and Elan. "But we have all of your things moved. We just guessed where you might want the furniture so why don't you go upstairs now and let us know if you want anything moved."

It was almost lunch time before anyone else returned to the house. "Are they here?" Emeral asked as she entered the house with an armload of packages.

"All the children and Elan are playing in the new fort," Cassandra said as she and Hannah worked in the kitchen. "Emeral all Joey did was cry when I told him we wanted him as our son," Cassandra said as the event still upset her.

"Dear I would imagine that is pretty normal," Emeral said. "Now, new mama, why don't you take me in and introduce me to my new grandson?"

"Wait just a moment," Hannah said as she took a pan out of the oven. "I want to see this."

Christopher yelled, "Grandma." As the three women entered the playroom. All the children but Joey ran up to Emeral and hugged her.

"Joey come here she is your grandma too," Nicholas said.

"Well so much for introductions," Cassandra said as Joey slowly walked towards Emeral and the other children. Emeral squatted down.

"Hello Joey I am Emeral," she said and held out her arms. Joey ran to Emeral and she hugged him tightly.

"Are we doing something wrong?" Elan whispered to Cassandra since Joey had not hugged either of them.

"Joey," Emeral said softy after she overheard Elan's question. "Elan and Cassandra don't want you to forget your real mommy and daddy because you should always remember them. But Elan and Cassandra love you and they are going to be your new mommy and daddy and they will be very good to you and you will like living here."

"Now why don't you be a good boy and give them each a hug." Joey turned around and looked at Elan and Cassandra who were both standing, then he held his arms up. Elan picked Joey up and hugged him tightly then handed Joey to Cassandra who hugged and kissed her new son.

Cassandra was crying when Hannah said. "Cassandra why don't you tell the children about their surprise for tonight."

"Grandma Emeral and all the women in the house bought all kinds of things for you Joey and we will put together a bedroom for you today. But to celebrate you becoming part of the family all the children will have a little party tonight. We have treats for you and you can stay up later and play." Christopher and Nicholas started to yell and Cerey added to the noise. "And all of you can sleep in the same room tonight and all of you can decide which room that will be."

"Really," Christopher said with a big grin. "We will have to see Joey's room before we decide."

"Emeral you always know the right thing to say," Natasha said as she, Lila, Vivian, Bekka and Diana stood in the doorway of the playroom.

"Joey, let me introduce you to more family," Cassandra said and walked towards the women.

Chapter VIII
Bounties

"My dear are you sure you should be out of bed?" Sudfad asked as Renya, Laurel, Vitomas, Annabelle and Kyra were walking past his office towards the front foyer of the castle. The women stopped and Renya turned and walked through the open door of Sudfad's study.

"I am losing my mind staying in bed. Hannah said that both Kyra and I can walk about as long as we don't overdo it, so all of us girls are going shopping."

"That sounds like you will be overdoing it to me." Sudfad said and smiled.

"We will come home if Kyra or I get too exhausted. I had wanted to have a celebration for the birth of Thedes' and Ibula's son but from Ibula's letters they aren't planning any trips soon. So the celebration is on hold but with all of the Ruala's coming for Elan's and Cassandra's wedding I thought we could at least send back gifts. And with Vitomas, Hannah, Vivian, Lila, Angelina, Nikki, Delilah and Zoya all pregnant I was thinking of having a huge baby celebration."

"Are you going to open it up to the public?"

"No, I believe we all need a break from worrying about terrorists. But I would like to have the celebration while Vivian's family is here."

"Speaking of families I am going to share something with you from this morning's meeting. Remember how Natasha warned us about Cassandra's parents?" Sudfad did not wait for Renya to respond. "We may regret that we invited them here. This morning Gabriel and Raphael said that Elan and Cassandra want to adopt a little boy from the orphanage but they don't want her parents to know about him because her mother is some kind of fanatic about pure blood."

"I don't understand what that means?" Renya interrupted her husband.

"Apparently Cassandra's mother does not believe in adoption and she is so vehement about it that the younger Rualas, who all know this woman don't want her near any of the children in Gabriel's house."

"Do they think she will hurt them?" Renya gasped.

"I believe they are concerned about her words. This morning Cassandra and Elan told the team that they have given up their ties to their blood families and have chosen the team as their family. They even want Emeral and Maxwell to go on their wedding trip with them."

"Well, that is sweet, sad and unbelievable at the same time. Do not be shocked if I end up kicking that woman out of our home."

"I won't stand in your way."

"So are they adopting the boy?"

"They went to the orphanage to get him, while I was holding the meeting."

"Do you know anything about the child? I will want to buy gifts."

"A little boy about five or six, shy, his family was killed in a fire that apparently had suspicious circumstances. Oh and his name is Joey."

"Well how is our dance partner?" Annabelle asked as she and Vitomas walked into Thor's bedroom. Thor was sitting up in bed without a shirt on and blushed deeply when he saw the princesses. "Thor we are married; we see half naked men all of the time, don't worry," Annabelle said with a chuckle as both women kissed Thor on his cheeks.

"Are you done with this tray?" Vitomas asked as she looked at Thor's empty lunch tray.

"Yes, I have to admit I am surprised to see you," Thor said. Vitomas put Thor's tray on a table and both women sat down in the overstuffed chairs near his bed.

"We've been here before but this is the first time you are awake," Annabelle said. "So tell us how do you feel?"

"Frustrated I have never been laid up like this before. I hate lying around all day."

"I would say that is a sign you are getting better," Vitomas said. "The rest of your family is just finishing their lunch. Koby told me to tell you they would be up to take you walking soon."

"Yeah, yesterday they told me I was too grouchy, so they are trying to get me walking a couple of times a day," Thor said with a grin. "I do have to admit I feel better getting out of bed once in a while."

"Thor, Raul feels awful that he told you about Misha and Diana, he didn't mean to upset you," Vitomas said. "Misha is such a nice man that Raul thought you would be happy."

"I suppose they told you about me yelling at everyone."

"No," Vitomas said.

"Yes, I had Diana crying but the good thing out of that was Misha jumped in front of her and defended her; it let me get an idea of the kind of husband he would be."

"If I tell you something don't get mad," Annabelle said. "But Diana said that you and Misha are a lot alike so she is hoping you two will become friends some day."

"One night I am in battle at your castle and the next thing I know I can't walk, I've been adopted and my sister who I raised is married to a man I don't even know. I am afraid I have not handled it well and I am not saying I am fine yet but the people here are very nice and now that I am beginning to know some of them, I like them."

"Then you might stay?" Vitomas asked. "It sounded like you were adamant about leaving."

"Not sure yet; it will be a while before I can walk down those stairs alone, much less leave the kingdom."

"We hope you stay," Annabelle said. "Just so you know; Renya is downstairs talking with everyone because she wants to have a big celebration for all of the pregnant girls, and there are eight of them. So you better start healing fast because you've got a wedding and a baby celebration to attend."

"There are going to be men at the baby celebration?"

"When Renya throws a celebration people beat down the doors to get in. It will be a major event."

"Renya that is so gracious of you," Hannah said.

"I would like to have the celebration while Vivian's family is here, so when do you think would be a good time?"

"We are in the process of building chambers for them," Raphael said. "We are hoping they will stay here for a while."

"We've been keeping it as a surprise," Vivian said then looked at Raphael. "But perhaps we should tell Mother and Father about all of this in case they need to make arrangements."

"That is fine with me," said Raphael.

"Where are the children? We wanted to meet Joey." Renya said.

"Since Alexander gave them that fort, they never leave the playroom," said Natasha. "I will get him."

"No, we can walk into the playroom. Sudfad said the boy is shy."

"I'll get the gifts out of the boca," Laurel said.

"Do you need help?" Joao asked.

"Actually we will, there are gifts for Misha and Diana too," Renya said. "Are they here?"

Calen grinned. "They aren't up from their nap yet."

"Diana was so cute, she really thought that Misha was talking about sleeping," Natasha said.

Calen laughed, "I told you she sounds just like you." Then he turned to Renya and Laurel. "My new bride didn't know that people could make love when it was daylight." Everyone smiled.

"Well..." Natasha started to say.

"We all heard you say it," Dagon said. "You're not getting out of it."

"Actually I think we should start taking more afternoon naps," Calen said. "I would like to start working on the next baby."

"You are just trying to keep me out of the missions," Natasha said with a grin. "We are finally able to sleep through the night."

"I know I keep saying that but I do want a big family," Calen said then winked at Renya. "Besides I've got to catch up to Simon and Raul."

Natasha gave her husband a look of disbelief. "Calen if you want to catch up to those two, you had better plan on giving birth to a few babies yourself." Everyone roared with laughter.

Queen Rosa was pruning plants in her parlor when she heard footsteps. Turning Rosa saw Claudius and Mathas enter the room.

"Claudius I didn't know you were here. Were you able to eat lunch or I will gladly have something prepared for you."

"Thanks Rosa but I don't think I can eat."

"Honey where are the children?" asked Mathas.

"Why, what is wrong?" Rosa asked when she saw the solemn looks on the faces of the men.

"Please just tell us," Mathas asked.

"Margarit is playing with Sarah and Jacob in her room and Angelina is taking a nap with Alexas. Matthew is working. Mathas what is going on?"

"The body of a young mother and her two babies were found; they all had been stabbed dozens of times and the woman had been raped."

"Timothy," Rosa gasped with horror. "He killed the babies too?"

"I saw it myself," Claudius said grimly. "The family lived in the City of Tufold, so they are in Lenz and apparently on their way to Fahron's."

"I want one of us to know where the children are at all times," Mathas said to Rosa then he turned to Claudius. "I want those animals caught. Have the men work in shifts."

"Already done."

"Claudius, does Fahron know?"

"Yes, I stopped at his castle before coming here. It broke my heart to have to tell them. Isadore broke down."

"I wish they would have stayed here with us," Rosa said sadly.

"What kind of monster did we bring into this world?" Isadore sobbed. Fahron held his wife as he too was overwhelmed by the horrific acts Timothy had committed. "I thought we were good parents."

"We have two other children who are wonderful," Fahron said. "But you are right. We brought Timothy into this world. It is up to me to stop him."

"Fahron where are you going?" Isadore cried as Fahron walked out of the room.

"Father have you seen this?" Matthew asked as he rejoined the family as they ate their evening meal. "That was a soldier at the door. He said Fahron has a hundred men writing these posters and they are being handed out throughout the kingdom."

"Fahron put a bounty on Timothy's head," Mathas said in amazement as he read the poster.

"Just Timothy?" Angelina asked.

"No," Mathas said and handed her the poster. "There are bounties on all three men along with their descriptions and details of their crimes."

"He will pay the bounties if the men are captured or killed," Matthew said. "Father I don't think that is such a bad idea. All of our citizens are at risk from these men, the sooner they are stopped the better."

"I didn't say it was a bad idea," Mathas said. "But Fahron must have come to the realization that his son is beyond saving to do something like this. It is one thing to put a bounty on a stranger but to do so when it is your own flesh and blood it is quite another matter."

Fahron sent soldiers to all corners of the kingdom with the bounty posters. When the news spread among the troops that they too were eligible for the bounty a great enthusiasm arose in them, for the amount to be paid for the three convicts would change a man's life. Fahron sent a poster to Sudfad with a note saying that Sudfad could make the news public to his kingdom. Fahron was not a stupid man, he knew that greed would spur men quicker than a sense of righteousness and he wanted Timothy and the others caught as soon as possible.

The posters were displayed in every tavern in Lentz and even the coldest of hearts were angered when the men read that the escaped convicts were raping and butchering children. Fahron was unaware of the unspoken hierarchy of criminals; even the most vicious murderers now hated Timothy, Aaron and Jackson. The posters explained in great detail the crimes of these men because Fahron had hoped that information would inflame the hearts of people and warn them to protect their children.

What Fahron was not prepared for was the almost immediate response the posters received. Men and demons stopped what they were doing and took to the roads both in groups and as individuals. Citizens, who were not going to hunt the convicts held meetings to determine how to best protect their families and they traveled to farms to warn their neighbors.

Timothy, Jackson and Aaron had been incarcerated in the dungeons of Wetpr for a long time so the guards were able to provide extremely detailed descriptions of the men; descriptions that were included in the bounty posters. The soldiers of Lentz had one piece of information that the public did not; it was well known among the military that Timothy had threatened to kill members of the ruling families. With that information many soldiers devised traps for the convicts.

The following morning as Mathas was preparing for the morning meeting, Fahron and his family arrived at the castle. Rosa and Isadore immediately hugged and cried; no words had to be spoken between these longtime friends. "Rosa," Fahron said as his family entered the castle. "Isadore and the children will be staying with you until we catch the convicts. I will have the men carry in their belongings."

"I am so happy to hear that," Rosa said. "But Fahron aren't you staying also?"

"No," was all Fahron said and walked into Mathas' study. Within minutes Matthew, Claudius, Stephan and Thaos all entered the study and the first subject of business was the escaped convicts.

"Fahron you aren't staying there by yourself," Claudius said.

"It is me he wants, I will not endanger others," Fahron said. "I brought that monster into this world and it is my responsibility to save the world from him."

"We will all take turns staying with you," Matthew said to Fahron.

"What you think I need babysitters?" Fahron replied angrily.

"My dear friend," Mathas said. "You have proven yourself in battle as a leader and a warrior. But what man really knows if he can take the life of his own child, even to prevent such horror. Learn from my mistakes."

"Fahron you are a general," Claudius said. "You always consider a variety of scenarios before going into battle. Timothy is being helped by a demon."

"What if he kills you; he will still be free to terrorize others. You are emotional now, as we all are. But you should prepare for this battle as you have done for others."

Out of respect for their superiors Matthew, Stephan and Thaos had spoken little to this point of the meeting. "Fahron," Stephan said. "You are not the only one who Timothy has sworn to kill. We have been working out a variety of plans where we use one of us as bait. Let's draw him out of the shadows."

"Fahron we are going to speak honestly," Thaos said. "Understand there is no disrespect meant towards you. Unless Timothy has changed greatly in prison he has always been quick to react without thinking things through. His anger and impulsiveness should make him easy to trick unless he is still traveling with the other two convicts. Both of those men sound like they are seasoned in battle, more intelligent than Timothy and more devious."

"Fahron I am not telling you anything you don't already know," Matthew said. "Timothy is such an arrogant, whining fool that he is difficult to be around. So if these other two convicts stay with him it is not because they have developed a friendship, it is because they want your money. Our best bet would be to find a way to divide them up but they will probably stay together out of greed. We would like to show you some of the scenarios we have created."

Simultaneously in the Kingdom of Wetpr King Sudfad was holding his morning meeting with his leaders and their first topic of discussion was also the escaped convicts.

"I like it," Simon said as he finished reading the bounty poster and handed it to Jared. "The more men after those animals the faster they will be caught."

"Death is too good for them after what they did to those babies," Raul said angrily.

"It is my fault they got away," Misha said as he had been filled with guilt after his last mission. "I request permission to go to Lentz and help with the search."

"Misha you were under attack while you were searching for them," Sudfad said. "And a demon was hiding them. You are not at fault. And don't you think there are enough men after them?"

"But they are all humans; Rualas have the advantage of a higher perspective. I am not after the money I want to stop them. I saw what they did to those little girls."

"You know Sudfad, we can't ever let Misha go any place by himself because he gets into too much trouble then Mother yells at us," Calen said and started to grin. "If you could spare a few of us we would be happy to go to Lentz and help."

"I will need some of you here also," Gabriel said. "I am going to try and capture Shanksaw."

"Is that the mission you want Diana to work on?" Misha asked. "Because I don't want her in taverns, it's too dangerous."

"I feel the same. Actually Edward, Archetenus and Jared are going to work this one," Gabriel said.

"I thought Archetenus didn't want to work on the team anymore," Luca said. "He's a straight military man now."

"This one is just too much up my alley," Archetenus said with a grin. "Why, Jared and me grew up in taverns playing cards and dealing with mercenaries. Edward is the new face in town but he is kind of a goody two-shoes; we don't want him to get hurt."

Edward laughed, "Yeah my buddies are watching out for me."

"Misha you know Diana will follow you," Maxwell said.

"Take her with you," the Sanuri said. "She will fit in well with the ruling families and she knows demons better than any of you; she will be help not a hindrance. Besides with Misha and Diana gone, Thor will start to connect with your family on his own terms."

"I don't know," Misha started to say when Calen interrupted him.

"Misha you of all my brothers have been the most against me not wanting Natasha to work on the missions and listen to you now; it's not easy is it."

"He's right," Luca said. "And before you say anything I don't like Lila working on missions either but she is not a trained warrior like your wives."

"Calen I will make you a deal," Misha said with a grin. "Diana comes with us but you loosen your hold on Natasha and let her help. The girl needs it."

Calen stared angrily at Misha for a moment, "I know you are right." Then Calen grinned. "But we are working on another baby."

"Calen while everyone understands your fears, if you use your children to imprison Natasha even as good of a mother as she is, she will start to resent them," the Sanuri said. "And may I remind all of you again, The Great Ruler sent you the wives you were meant to have; they too have their roles to play."

"Is something wrong?" Emeral asked. "That we are having a meeting now?"

"We have missions," Gabriel said. "I would like Thor to join us if he is awake."

"He's awake," Vivian said. "I was just up in his room.

"We'll get him," Joao said.

"Joao we will have the meeting in the dining room since it is closer to Thor's room," Gabriel said. "We will meet in ten minutes."

"Gabriel; Edward, Archetenus and Jared are here," Natasha said as she led the men into the dining room.

"I know; they are here for the meeting."

"Lila, Natasha help me get a few refreshments ready," Hannah said and ran into the kitchen.

Once everyone gathered in the dining room Gabriel stood up and addressed the group. "We just had our meeting at the castle and we have two missions that we will be working on simultaneously starting today. Thor I wanted you here because you are a new face in this area and not associated with us or Sudfad's family yet. I would like you to eventually work on the mission that will start here in Salar. You will hear the details in a few minutes. Would you be willing to help us?"

"Of course," Thor said with a grin, as the idea of getting back to work greatly appealed to him.

"Elan and Cassandra please listen to the information presented here. Considering you just adopted Joey and your wedding is just weeks away I do not expect you to work on the missions but I want you to be aware of what is going on in case something goes wrong," said Gabriel.

"I am passing around a bounty poster that Sudfad received from Fahron," Raphael explained. "I want everyone to read it but I caution you some of the information is very upsetting. Lila, I would like you to make several copies of this poster for us."

"Hannah," Raphael continued. "Between your work for Sudfad, the orphanage and home we are not giving you an assignment. But if you do want to assist you will work on the mission in Salar, the decision is yours. Emeral we will be using all of the girls with possibly the two exceptions we have mentioned. If you don't mind, the responsibility for keeping the household functioning will be yours. Of course the others will help but if you need us to pull someone out of a mission Gabriel and I expect you to tell us."

"Oh my god!" Natasha gasped when she read the poster.

"Yes," Gabriel said. "And that is why there are two missions. For those of you who have not yet read the poster, Timothy and the other two convicts raped a young mother; they literally butchered her and her two babies. Fahron has put an incredibly large bounty on the heads of these monsters. Although he should not, Misha feels responsible for the prisoners getting away; so he will be leading a team into Lentz to assist the ruling families in trying to capture the prisoners before they kill anyone else. Sudfad has already sent a letter to Mathas telling him such."

131

Gabriel continued, "Misha's team will consist of Diana, Calen, Koby and Joao. Diana while you are the newest member of the team, the Sanuri said that you and Vivian know more about demons than the rest of us. Do not feel intimidated to share your experience and ideas."

"Now for the mission in Salar," Gabriel explained. "The attacks against Misha's and Maxwell's teams as they were searching for the prisoners were orchestrated by a man named Shanksaw. The attacker's knew the members of our team by name. All we know about this man is that he is a mercenary who spends most of his time in the Racing Horse Tavern in Salar. We need to find out more about him as well as who he is working for and who is working for him."

"The Racing Horse Tavern is a pretty dangerous place to spend time. Edward is fairly new to this area so we are hoping he is not yet identified as a member of the team. Edward, Archetenus and Jared are going to be making contact with Shanksaw and hopefully gain his trust," Gabriel walked around the room as he talked. "Obviously we plan to stop Shanksaw but we also need to get information from him."

"Natasha since you are the best we have at gathering information and disguises you will be in charge of those areas. Lila and Vivian will be working with you and while I am thinking about it, Diana has volunteered for this type of work but she needs help learning some of the mannerisms and dress of the people here. I would like the three of you to help Diana when she returns from Lentz. We need to find out where Shanksaw stays. If his taste in taverns is the same as his taste for hotels they might be dangerous places. Feel free to have Edward, Archetenus or Jared go with you."

"Unfortunately Gabriel and I are so well known here that our presence will be suspicious, so we will be running the mission from here," Raphael said. "At this point in our operation we are trying to gather information because it is extremely unlikely that Shanksaw is working alone. Besides the people we have already mentioned, Luca, Dagon and Dack will be on this mission. Maxwell will be available but his responsibilities will be at the fort since the rest of us are working on the team."

Raphael now turned his attention to the three Rualas, "Luca, Dack and Dagon, part of your responsibilities will be to watch over the other members working with you. If you need to pull someone off the street do so. But remember that your appearance is likely to alert Shanksaw and whoever he is working with that something is going on."

"We will have a meeting every morning and every night unless there is an emergency," Gabriel said. "Does anyone have any questions or concerns about your assignment?"

"I do," Thor said. "Please I have to do more. I think getting back to work will be the best medicine for me. Also what you said about Diana having to learn the mannerisms and dress of the people here, I will need to learn those things also."

"We are glad to hear your enthusiasm," Gabriel said. "You can work with Raphael and me until you are able to walk without assistance. And we can train you in the mannerisms and dress." Gabriel now looked at the others who were seated around the table. "While Salar is our home, we will treat this mission like we would any other. You don't really know who has given Shanksaw our information; so be careful who you trust."

Jared looked at Thor, "Kid do you know how to play cards or gamble?"

"No."

"Archetenus and I will teach you, it is kind of our expertise."

"Why do I need to learn?"

"Because it is a great excuse to spend long hours in a tavern listening to what is going on. But if you act like you don't understand the games you will stick out like a sore thumb."

"Misha your team leaves after lunch today," Gabriel said. "But before you go, stop at the castle because Sudfad and Renya probably have things they will want you to deliver. Do you all have your pouches of lynswood?"

"Yes, everyone has a pouch," Vivian said.

"I would like to work with Natasha and the others," Hannah said. "So I can learn more skills."

"That is fine," Gabriel said. "But I want all of you to remember that all of our identities may be exposed so be careful."

"Gabriel what do you want me to do?" Bekka asked. "I haven't been included in anything."

"We didn't over look you, but we know you aren't healed yet and still weak. We don't think you are ready to work with Luca and the other Rualas. And you are too weak to fly to Lentz. What would you like to do?"

"I feel the same as Thor. I will help with the household but I would like to do something for the missions. Why don't you give me that poster and I will start making copies and hopefully you can find something for me to do."

"Bekka come with us," Natasha said. "We will have to go shopping for things to make disguises."

"Gabriel, Cassandra and I would like to sit out these missions, but let us know if you need us," Elan said. "We want to help Joey feel like part of the family and of course we will help around the household."

"I understand completely," Gabriel said. "And one last word for those of you who are fairly new, sometimes even the smallest detail can be important, share all of your information with the group. And every question is important so ask them."

"I have a question," Natasha said. "Although I am almost afraid to ask it."

Gabriel smiled and said, "I was waiting for this; ask it."

"This is the kind of mission briefings we used to have before everyone had families, something has changed. What is it?"

"The Sanuri had a talk with all of us at the meeting," Gabriel said. "He told us that as warriors we have proven the strength of our faith again and again with one exception, our wives. The Sanuri has told us many times and when I say us I mean Sudfad's family also, that The Great Ruler has sent us the perfect wives."

"But I don't think any of us understood what he meant until today. The Sanuri said the heavens had brought all of us men together because our strengths and our differences make us strong. Now I am going to explain the rest using the Sanuri's words. He said that the heavens blessed us with the perfect wives to not only be the loves of our lives but to work with us. The Sanuri said the group of women that we have married is unique; they are strong, intelligent, warriors, healers, seers, teachers, artists and military strategists and they are all faithful and courageous."

"The Sanuri said imagine how the heavens feel when instead of honoring these gifts we have been given we hide them out of fear. He said that by us not allowing you to work with us because we are afraid for your safety is a lack of faith on our parts."

"Of course that doesn't mean any of our wives will be forced to work on missions that they don't want to," Raphael added. "We just can't hold any of you back because of our fears." The women at the table all looked at each other as Raphael and Gabriel spoke.

Gabriel continued, "The Sanuri said that every one of us was brought together to form this union. He said there is not one person working with us and that includes you Thor; who was not meant to be here in this place at this time. I believe as a group we work and live together more cohesively than most. But everyone will admit there are some issues that we have to work on and now that we know it was the heavens that brought us together I believe we need to reevaluate those issues."

"Well I know I am the issue you are talking about," Thor said. Gabriel interrupted Thor.

"You are one issue but there are others and everyone seated at this table is aware of what I am talking about. But since you brought it up; I do have two questions for you. I have already spoken with Vivian and Diana about one issue."

"We greatly admire the training and knowledge of the Venatores and we realize that we can learn a great deal from the three of you. But since childhood you have been trained to work alone. Our team is strong because we work together. Thor, I know you haven't had a chance to really work with us yet but do you think you can learn to work with a team?"

"I will be honest, this meeting gives me a much better idea of what you do and how you work, I will certainly try. And I know what the second question is because both Vivian and Natasha have talked to me at great length about controlling my anger. They have told me how uncontrolled emotions put everyone at risk and I truly understand what they are saying. Honestly I will try to contain my anger and if someone has an idea that could help me I will certainly listen to it."

Chapter IX
Confessions

That night Misha and his team made it almost to the border of the Kingdoms of Wetpr and Lentz before sunset. They found an area that they felt was defensible if attacked and made camp. There had been a strained silence between Misha, Joao and Dack as well as with Koby and these two young men since Dack and Joao returned to Salar. This tension was the reason that Misha chose Joao and Koby to be on his team. As they sat around the fire eating their dinner Misha looked at Joao.

"Joao, I chose you for this mission so we could get to know each other better and I want to take this time to apologize to you for the way I treated you and Dack when you returned home."

"I am glad you brought it up," Joao said with relief. "If I would have had any idea that you and Diana were a couple I would not have asked her out. Cassandra and Bekka wrote to us every week and told us everything that was going on in Salar. They never mentioned Thor or Diana and I didn't see a ring on her finger. It wasn't until the two of you started to talk that it was obvious you were a couple."

"Really?" Diana asked with surprise. "Misha and I didn't hardly know each other then."

"Joao is right," Calen said. "Now this is going to sound mean, but I rather enjoyed seeing Misha get jealous because he has always had women after him and he has never cared about anyone enough to get emotional and Koby you weren't much better."

"When I got jealous, it was a new feeling for me so I was surprised and that was when I realized that I really cared for Diana," Misha said. "Unfortunately I acted like an ass and she and I got into a fight later that night."

"Over me?"

"You and Dack, I thought she was interested in you."

"How could you?" Joao asked with surprise. "She made it pretty clear to us she had chosen you."

"And that is what I was trying to tell him," Diana said with a grin.

Joao turned to Koby. "Has Bekka told you about the history of all of us?"

"No."

"Bekka, Dack, Fala, Cassandra my other sister Melinda who you haven't met yet and I have been friends since we were little kids. Then Elan joined us because he had a crush on Cassandra. My sisters and I were raised by nurses because our mother never wanted to get her hands dirty taking care of children. It wasn't until we got older that we realized what a monster Mother is. So Cassandra, Melinda and I spent as much time out of our house as possible."

"We would take turns staying at the homes of our friends," Joao continued. "Just so we wouldn't have to go home. All of us, except for Elan and Cassandra have only felt like brothers and sisters. Then when Fala was murdered and we thought Bekka was killed too; it terrified me and Dack and brought the three of us closer. We are no threat to your relationship with Bekka in fact we are really glad she has you. We tried to help her get over her guilt about Fala's death but we couldn't. She is doing much better since she has been with you."

"Now don't you feel like an ass?" Calen asked Koby then laughed.

"Actually I do," Koby said. "And I apologize but I have to admit I was kind of in the same situation as Misha. I told Bekka that I didn't want to rush into marriage and she has told me many times that she feels like she is so young and has so much she wants to see and do that she didn't want to get married. We both have been content with our relationship, then you two showed up and things started to get really emotional."

"Marry the girl," Calen said. "Hell, none of us thought Misha would ever marry; if he can do it so can you."

"I don't think it is that simple," Koby said seriously. "Diana wanted to marry Misha; I don't think Bekka wants to marry me."

"Matthew," Mathas said as his son entered his study. "I just received word from Sudfad that Misha, three other Rualas and Misha's new wife, who is a Venator are on their way here to help us. We should expect them late tomorrow."

"Misha is married? When did that happen?"

"The letter doesn't say. But Sudfad said that Misha feels guilty because he couldn't stop the prisoners from crossing into our kingdom and they want to help."

"Does the letter say who Misha married?"

Mathas laughed. "That is your point of interest in this letter?"

"Father, Misha and Stephan are very similar; yes to hear that he is married is a shock. But also we spent so much time in the Village of Gesmal that I have met every villager and I never saw Misha act interested in any of the women."

"Well, you will find out the answers to your questions tomorrow. Sudfad instructed Misha to lead his team here first. Since you know Misha so well, I am putting you in charge of making arrangements for their stay and their assignments. Also they are bringing that herb that the Venatores use to disclose trails that have been hidden by demons."

"Father, the Clan of Gesmal was so good to all of us especially our wives that I know Claudius' family will want to meet Misha's wife. Under the circumstances do you think a small gathering is inappropriate?"

"No, it might be just what we need."

"Is it too late for a visit?" Maxwell called out as he knocked on Thor's bedroom door.

"No, please come in."

Maxwell and Emeral walked into Thor's room and sat down in the overstuffed chairs next to his bed. "We wanted to talk to you about the meeting today because we thought you may have felt singled out when Gabriel was talking about issues among us," Maxwell said.

"You mean I am not the only problem here?" Thor asked somewhat jokingly.

"It is obvious you don't really know our boys yet," Emeral said and laughed. "You cannot have this many people living and working together without some issues. If Gabriel would have thought you were the only person with issues he would have said that straight out."

"Which is another reason we wanted to talk to you," Maxwell said. "We were very proud of you today. You seem enthused to be part of the team and you stood up like a man and announced you had problems with your anger and you are willing for advice."

"Did you come here to give me advice?" Thor asked with a grin.

"No," Maxwell said. "I think you are already working on it."

"Sometimes I feel really isolated up here; can I ask what some of the other issues are?"

"A big one that Gabriel talked about is how the men treat their wives," Maxwell said. "First let me explain that after the Ruala race was almost wiped out by the Hutas we changed our way of thinking. We could not defend ourselves against the Hutas because our people were farmers but now we are a tribe of warriors and both men and women are trained to be warriors, which is similar to your clan. But in most of the kingdoms women are not trained as warriors."

"Gabriel's team consisted of Gabriel, Raphael, our sons and Natasha for years. Natasha has been trained to be a fierce warrior, she almost died twice on a mission and now Calen wants to keep her tied to the kitchen because he is so afraid of losing her. Honestly Calen's behavior surprised us all, but then as every man on the team married they all acted the same way, although not as passionately as Calen."

"We think they have all seen such horror that they don't want their wives exposed to it," Emeral said. "And all of the women here are so loving they don't argue a lot with their husbands."

"Is Raphael like that with Vivian?"

"Yes and Misha is becoming like that with Diana," Maxwell said. "Now all of us in this room know that the Venatores are some of the fiercest warriors in all of Opots. And Raphael and Misha are fierce warriors. We are glad the Sanuri talked to the men of our family and Sudfad's."

"And Thor you should know that Misha was not the only man on this team who was interested in Diana, there were others which caused some jealousies. And although Koby and Bekka live together they are not married. We are not sure of what is going on with them but we are seeing Koby becoming jealous and we think insecure in that relationship," Emeral explained.

"Is that why Diana and Misha got married so quickly?"

Maxwell and Emeral looked at each other then Emeral replied, "No Thor it was because of your temper. They wanted to wait until you were healed so you could be in their wedding but as members of the team were telling them how you were acting and the things you were saying, they decided to give up the wedding that they wanted because they didn't trust what you would do." Thor's eyes widened as he stared at Emeral.

"You are our son now too, so we are not saying this to stand up for Misha but he had you put into the room next to his so he could help you. And he and Diana planned to include you in everything. They even wanted you to have a room in their chambers but no one in the house believes that is a good idea at this time," Maxwell explained. Thor remained quiet.

"We didn't tell you this to make you feel badly," Emeral said as she saw the look on Thor's face. "We are simply telling you the truth."

"No I am glad you did, I didn't know any of this. I thought that Diana was just trying to get away from me. You see she and I used to fight all of the time about Joshua and Iris. She wanted me to let them adopt us but I just couldn't because I felt like I was betraying our parents. Then I wake up from these injuries and she has got a family and a husband I don't even know. I wondered if she was doing all this to get back at me."

"Thor that was not what happened at all," Emeral said. "Your sister loves you very much and she is loyal to you. Diana is such a sweet and charming girl that we all fell in love with her."

141

"She had a very difficult time watching you suffer. One night Diana became hysterical and Misha had to carry her out of your room. That was the night that we asked if we could adopt both of you. Thor we honestly didn't think you were going to live and we just couldn't bear the thought of that child all alone in the world. And as brave as Diana is I think she was afraid of being alone too."

"Thor do you think some of your anger was caused by your fear of being alone?" Maxwell asked. "We all have fears; it is not a sign of weakness to admit it."

"I never thought about it."

"When Diana comes back I wish you two would sit down and talk all of this out Thor because it is clear to us that both of you feel awful about the tension between you," Emeral said.

"Since you feel isolated up here do you think you are up to joining us for meals?" Maxwell asked. "Those are the times when all of us get together."

"I would like that."

"Then we will start with breakfast tomorrow, but if you feel too weak tell us because the girls can't pick you up if you collapse," Maxwell said.

Cassandra and Elan put Joey to bed together. Elan read a story until Joey fell asleep, then the new parents each kissed Joey on the forehead and left his bedroom.

"It is truly amazing how close I feel to Joey after only a couple of days," Elan said. "I am so glad we found him."

"Elan I just love Joey so much and now I am almost regretting we are having a large wedding," Cassandra said. "I don't want my parents to find out about him and you know somehow they will."

"Maybe we should just tell them and get it over with; instead of worrying about it. Perhaps we should send them a letter and tell them about Joey and give them the choice if they want to attend our wedding."

"I like that idea," Cassandra said with relief. "Actually I would prefer they didn't come. Do you think we should talk to Emeral and Maxwell about this idea because they always seem to know the answers?"

The next morning as the family was gathering around the breakfast table, Gabriel and Luca were measuring a corner of the dining room; while Dagon and Dack helped Thor to the table. "What are you two doing?" Natasha asked as she walked out of the kitchen with a large platter of potatoes.

"We'll tell you as soon as everyone sits down," Gabriel replied.

"Oh a mystery," Natasha said and laughed then returned to the kitchen.

"She seems so much happier since she is working on a mission again," Luca said to Gabriel.

"I noticed that too. Last night Hannah was telling me how pleased she was that all our wives are allowed to help with this mission. I think we may have been mistaken to put all those rules on them."

"Well it looks like everyone is here," Lila said. "Except for, oh here they come." Elan and Cassandra walked into the dining room; Joey was already seated at the table with the other children.

"Is something wrong?" Hannah asked when she saw the serious looks on their faces.

"We need advice," Cassandra said as they took their seats at the table. "I have been so worried about how my parents will act at the wedding and now that we have adopted Joey I can hardly sleep at night because I know my parents will find out about him. Elan suggested that we send them a letter telling them that we have adopted Joey then give my parents the choice as to whether they want to attend our wedding. But Dack thinks that might make Mother even wilder. What do all of you think we should do?"

"I know your mother," Bekka said. "She is going to be mad no matter what you do; you might as well be honest up front."

143

"So you think we should send the letter?"

"Perhaps you should wait and let them meet Joey and they will fall in love with him," Hannah suggested.

"Hannah, I don't think our mother ever fell in love with us," Cassandra said.

"Certainly you aren't serious," Hannah replied.

"Yes she is," Dack said. "All the years that I have been friends with Joao, Cassandra and Melinda I have never once seen Tina hug or kiss any of them. She acts like she thinks she will get some disease if she touches them."

"It's true," Bekka said. "They got more affection from our families than they ever did from their own."

"Understand we don't care what they say to us," Elan said. "It's the children and I mean all the children in this family that we are trying to protect from Tina's wrath. You really don't know what she is like."

"You are right, we don't," said Gabriel. "And it is difficult for me to understand a person like that."

"Well, you know Tina is already mad that Emeral and Maxwell helped to plan your wedding and are in your wedding; when she finds out they are going on the trip with you," Bekka said. "It will be a war as soon as she gets here."

Raphael looked across the table at Emeral and Maxwell. "You are both very quiet and you know Cassandra's parents what do you think they should do?"

"First of all while some of what the children are saying sounds so unbelievable that some of you might think they are exaggerating, they are not," Maxwell said. "We are quiet because we both are so angry at the fear that Tina creates. A wedding and an adoption should be greatly celebrated not thought of as elements that lead to war."

"Would you like us to speak to your parents?" Emeral asked.

144

"I don't think that is a good idea," Cassandra said. "They are very jealous of you two."

"I think you should stop worrying about Tina and start enjoying the changes in your lives," Raphael said. "I think everyone should just be themselves and if Tina and Charles act inappropriately, there are plenty of us here who can handle them."

"I agree with Raphael," Luca said.

"So we should bring Joey to the wedding?" Cassandra asked.

"Of course," Gabriel said. "He is part of the family now."

"You should have him at the altar with you like Luca and Lila did with Christopher," said Natasha. "That was such a beautiful wedding."

"I would really like that," Cassandra said and looked at Elan.

"So would I. We will have him fitted for an outfit today," Elan said and kissed Cassandra on the forehead.

Dack looked at Thor. "You will be walking down the aisle with Melinda; don't be surprised if she is really upset by everything that is going on. She's a nice person, not at all like her parents. We have been asking her to visit us, just so she can get away from them."

Bekka looked at Thor and winked. "She's really pretty too." Thor blushed which surprised Bekka.

"I want to say something," Thor said. "But it has nothing to do with what you have been talking about. I want to apologize to everyone for the way I have been acting. I am not trying to make excuses but after talking to Emeral and Maxwell last night I realized that I misread some things and I am sorry."

Vivian got a big smile on her face and squeezed Raphael's hand. "Thor I do believe that is the first time I have ever heard you apologize; I am really proud of you."

Natasha could see how embarrassed Thor looked so she changed the subject. "So when are you going to tell us the big mystery?" Natasha asked as she looked at Gabriel and Luca.

"Children," Gabriel said as he looked at Christopher, Nicholas, Cerey and Joey. "Would you like your own table with the smaller chairs like you sit at when we are at the castle?" Both Christopher and Nicholas smiled and nodded.

Christopher looked at Joey, "Joey say yes."

"Yes," Joey said shyly and everyone in the room laughed.

It was almost nightfall when Misha and his team landed in the front courtyard of the castle of King Mathas. Matthew had previously alerted the soldiers that the Ruala team would be arriving so as soon as Misha and the others landed they were escorted inside of the castle. The soldiers led the exhausted team into the parlor of the castle, which to the team's surprise was filled with people.

The families of Mathas, Sorren and Claudius were in the parlor as was Fahron's wife and children. After Matthew introduced everyone, Misha said. "We have letters for all of you from the Royal Family." Then he opened his pack and handed out envelopes.

"What a wonderful idea," exclaimed Rosa. "Renya is having a large baby celebration for all of the girls, oh my lord there are eight of them," Rosa said as she read farther down the letter. "This will be so much fun."

"We have more invitations," Calen said and proceeded to hand out envelopes. "Since so many people were injured in the last attack at the castle, Elan and Cassandra didn't pick a date for the wedding until last week."

"They also adopted a little boy this week so they have a lot to celebrate. You are all invited to the wedding which will be held in the new chapel that Sudfad has built and the celebration and banquet will be at the castle."

"Well my dear, I think we need to put on our dancing shoes," Sorren said kiddingly to Shara.

As the group talked about their invitations Matthew handed glasses of whiskey and wine to the team members. "Misha I just don't remember Diana from the village and I thought that we met everyone."

"Diana and her brother Thor hunt together, they had spent months in northern Ryed. As soon as they returned to their village and told Joshua of the things that they had seen he sent a letter to Gabriel. We will be going to northern Ryed for a mission and Diana and Thor gave us a lot of information about that area and offered to guide us. Then they were both injured in the attack at the castle and Emeral and Maxwell adopted both of them and Diana and I fell in love."

Bella smiled and said, "I think there is a lot more to those stories that we need to hear. Diana almost everyone in this room has spent time in your village except for a few of us. I don't think I am alone when I say I would like to hear all about your people. Our families were so impressed with them."

Diana smiled shyly she was feeling a little overwhelmed at the extravagance of the castle. "Of course," she said. "I hope you don't think me stupid, but we are dressed for travel and all of you look so nice, should I change my clothes?"

"You are just fine, dear," said Rosa.

"Ok I have to ask," Stephan said with a big grin. "Is this the girl who killed two demons with her shoes? Because I want to hear that story."

"Before we get into any stories," Mathas said. "Misha tonight we are all taking a well-deserved break from the madness here. Tonight we enjoy our friendships then tomorrow morning we return to work."

Chapter X
Madness

"What the hell is going on around here?" Jackson yelled as he ran into a small cave on the eastern bank of the River Shey. "Put out that fire Timothy!"

"Why?" demanded Timothy as Jackson kicked dirt onto the fire.

"See for yourself you moron," Jackson said angrily and picked Timothy up by the back of his collar and pushed him to the front of the cave.

"What is that?" gasped Timothy.

"Torches," Jackson said as they looked at over one hundred torches that were illuminating the dark night.

"I can see that," Timothy spat.

"You really are the stupidest man I have ever met," Jackson said with disgust. "That's a hunting party and I am willing to bet they are hunting us."

"Where's Aaron?" Timothy asked fearfully.

"He's trying to find a way out of here for us since there doesn't seem to be anything but farm fields between here and your daddy's place."

"The demon protected us the last time we were running through fields."

"Well Aaron and I ain't betting our lives on your demons."

Since the celebration of the previous evening ran late, all of the guests in Mathas' castle spent the night and now with the first rays of dawn they gathered around the breakfast table. King Mathas' started off the conversation, "I hope you all slept well last night, if there is anything you need for your rooms please let us know."

"Also our morning meetings usually consist of just the men but since everyone is here you are all invited; though the subjects we will discuss are not appropriate for the children to hear."

"I would like to attend," Bella said confidently which made Claudius and her sons smile. As she looked at their faces Bella stated, "Just because I am not a warrior doesn't mean I am not interested in what happens to our families."

"Dear you are more than welcome to join us," Claudius said and leaned over and kissed Bella on the cheek.

"I will stay with the children," Rosa said.

"So will I," Isadore said in almost a whisper. "I know I should attend but I just can't bear to hear the awful things that Timothy continues to do. I will be so glad when this nightmare is over."

"Last night just us girls were talking," Angelina said. "And we would like to take our guests to our village."

"I would prefer you stay here until we have a better idea of what is going on with the search for the prisoners," Mathas said.

"Of course," Ingr responded. "We want to help with the search also. If Diana can help we should be able to." Ingr looked at Stephan and smiled as she spoke.

"That's fine but you stay with me," Stephan said.

"I suppose you want to go too," Thaos said to Nikki.

"Actually I am not feeling that well today," Nikki said. "I don't know why I am sick so much more with this baby."

"Do I need to ask?" Matthew asked as he looked at Angelina. Who smiled and kissed him on the cheek.

Sorren looked across the table at Diana, "I believe you will feel at home in our village because I certainly felt at home in yours. Our tribes are very similar."

"My Lord," said a young soldier as he ran into the dining room. "Please excuse my poor manners but I really think you need to come outside and see this."

Most of the people quickly got up from the table and ran outside. "My Lord we got one of them murderous baby rapers," yelled a man proudly through a mouth full of broken teeth. Twenty men on horseback were in the front courtyard of the castle. As the man with the broken teeth spoke a second man got off his horse and walked up to a horse that had a man's body lying over it. The man untied the body and threw it to the ground. Then he squatted down and turned the body on its back, exposing the face.

"Yep its one of those sons of bitches," the second man said.

Misha was the first to run up to the body. "They're right that is Aaron," Misha said. Then he looked at the men. "You have done well."

"Where did you find him?" Claudius asked.

"East of the River Shey," the man with the broken teeth explained. "He was two maybe three miles east of the river hiding in an alferto field. "It was night but with the torches we could see the ground pretty well and we didn't see no sign of them other two but we's going right back out."

"Matthew go in and get these men their money," Mathas said. "While we are waiting tell us what happened."

"Well there were a lot more'n me and the boys out hunting these fellers. Why there is men everywhere even saw some demons looking to get that bounty. We was spread out walking in a line and found this one here crouching in the alferto. He didn't even try to run he stood up and pulled out a big ole knife and the fight was on. He killed one of our boys and cut two others before we put him down," said the man with the broken teeth.

"Did he say anything?" Stephan asked.

"Just that he would see us all in hell," the man with the broken teeth replied then spit a mouthful of tobacco onto the ground.

"Did you actually see his footprints?" Misha asked.

"Yep, he wasn't trying to hide them. Why'd you ask it like that?"

"Because they have been working with a demon that was covering their trail."

"The only demons we seen was looking for these bastards too but they stink so bad you would think the convicts would smell them coming."

Matthew walked out of the castle and handed the man with broken teeth three pouches of gold coins. "I assume you are the leader so I will let you divide this up as you see fit."

"Thanks it's a pleasure doing business with you; hopefully we will find the others." The men turned around and rode away from the castle leaving Aaron's body on the ground. Thaos immediately started to search the body.

"I am sure those men took anything of value but there might be some information," Thaos said as he tore Aaron's shirt open.

"Maybe the only reason that demon was helping them was to set a trap for you," Calen said to Misha.

"Either that or Aaron wasn't the one who made the deal with the demon," Misha replied.

"Nothing," Thaos said. "I'll have the men dispose of the body; the rest of you can go in and eat."

The morning meeting at Mathas castle was short and afterwards Claudius, Stephan, Thaos, Matthew, Ingr, Angelina and Diana rode to Fahron's castle; while the Rualas searched the area from the sky. Angelina and Ingr wore their tribal leather outfits which were very similar to the clothing worn by the female Venatores. The three women bonded quickly and enjoyed each other's company.

"We would like to return to your village someday," Ingr told Diana. "We made many friends and in particular we became very close to Joshua and Iris."

"Raphael is building a living area for them at Gabriel's house. You know the boys are going to be in Cassandra's and Elan's wedding. Vivian and Raphael are going to ask her family to stay in Wetpr for a while; you should come and visit them."

"Will they be in Wetpr for the baby celebration?" Angelina asked.

"Vivian hopes they will."

"Perhaps we can see them then. Mother, Rosa and Bella would very much like to meet them also," Angelina continued.

Ingr lowered her voice as she now spoke to Diana. "We will be at Fahron's castle soon. He is a good man but the knowledge of what his son has become is killing him. He remains alone in the castle hoping that Timothy will try to kill him."

"Then Fahron is prepared to kill his own son?" asked Diana.

"He thinks he is but we don't really know."

"One of us should do it so Fahron doesn't have to live with the guilt," said Angelina.

"Actually all of you seem like a very close family, we are the strangers here, we should kill him."

"Will you stop your damn whining," Jackson snarled at Timothy. "Yes they may have gotten Aaron or maybe he just left me with you because he couldn't stand you any longer. Either way, this is your kingdom; I need you to think. Timothy do you know of any places we could hide around here?"

"There are some more caves a little south of here; they are along the river too."

"So big man," Jackson said sarcastically as he watched for intruders from the front opening of the cave. "You never did tell us how you planned to kill your daddy."

"With a knife."

"You damn moron, you said he has thousands of soldiers at his castle. How the hell did you plan to get past them and get your father alone? I am willing to bet he is a lot better fighter than you are." Timothy was silent.

"Oh don't tell me you thought the soldiers would welcome you home with open arms," Jackson said with disgust. "If your father is any kind of man at all he must be so embarrassed to have you as a son."

Jackson heard movement behind him and quickly turned as Timothy lunged at him. Jackson already had a knife in his right hand, now he threw a handful of dirt into Timothy's eyes with his left hand then grabbed Timothy's shirt and threw him to the ground. Timothy was still blinded by the debris in his eyes when Jackson jumped on top of him and cut off Timothy's right ear. Then Jackson covered Timothy's mouth as he screamed in pain.

"I am sick of babysitting you boy, the next time you come at me will be your last," Jackson growled.

"Where are you two going?" Mathas asked as he saw Ryan and Tabeth, Fahron's daughter, walking out of the front door of the castle.

"We are just going into the gardens," Ryan said. "Tabeth wanted to pick some flowers for Isadore and I didn't think she should be outside alone."

"Very well but be careful."

The two young people walked out the front door of the castle then turned to the left towards the entrance to the beautiful gardens that surrounded the castle. "I want to go home," Tabeth confided in Ryan. "I want to kill Timothy myself for what he has done to our parents. I can hardly stand to look at either one of them anymore, they are just so sad."

"Do you even know how to fight?"

"It can't be that hard, Angelina and the others all do it."

"Angelina and the others have trained since they were small girls; it is hard and you will only make things worse if you leave here."

Tabeth was the youngest of Fahron's and Isadore's children. A headstrong girl of fifteen she was well educated and trained in the responsibilities of a woman of her station.

Like her mother, Tabeth was a pretty girl with large brown eyes and black hair, which she usually wore in one long braid down her back. Tabeth was not a warrior but none of Fahron's children were. Her brother Chaez was two years older than her and almost five years younger than Timothy. Chaez was a nobleman with a head for business. Fahron had given his children choices with their lives; he never spoke of his feelings but it hurt Fahron greatly that none of his children chose to become a warrior.

"My father is sitting alone in that castle waiting for Timothy to try and kill him. They never want us to hear what Timothy has done but everyone speaks of it. He is a monster and should be put down like any rabid dog. Mother is protected here; I want to go to Father."

"You can't protect him."

"I know; I just want to be with him; he must feel so alone."

Timothy crawled to the rear of the cave and whimpered as he held his hand to his bloody head. "Aaron should have been back by now," Jackson said. "I'm going to take a look outside. You keep your whiney ass in here until I come back, do you hear me?"

"Yes," Timothy spat. After Jackson left the cave Timothy was too afraid to move. He alternated between crying and talking to himself as was his normal behavior while in prison. Suddenly Timothy heard a voice that he recognized; he spun around and saw the same entity that visited him in prison. "How did you get here?" Timothy asked incredulously as he believed the entity to be another prisoner.

"You really are a fool. Haven't you figured out who I am yet?" Timothy did not respond.

"You aren't doing us any good hiding in here; you have promises to fulfill."

"What do you mean us?" Timothy asked fearfully.

"We are the voices you have listened to and fed for a very long time; we are the faces you have seen in the corners of your eyes."

"Well that doesn't tell me a damn thing," Timothy said with annoyance. "If you are a damn demon just say the hell so." Suddenly the campfire that long ago had been extinguished flared up so high that the flames touched the ceiling of the cave. Then just as quickly the flames were gone. "Alright you are a demon, how am I supposed to fulfill my promises when there are men everywhere searching for us?"

"Figure it out, our patience is fading."

Timothy sat in the darkness thinking about what he should do. He knew Jackson would kill him if he ran away and Timothy believed he needed Jackson's help to fulfill his promises to the demons.

"Come on moron, let's make a run for it," Jackson called into the cave. Timothy ran out of the cave and followed Jackson through an alferto field.

"You look awful," Claudius said to Fahron as the group walked into Fahron's study. "When was the last time that you slept?"

"I don't even know," Fahron said wearily.

"We will do introductions in a moment," Claudius said as he saw Fahron looking at Misha's team. "First we have some good news. Your bounty worked. Some men killed one of the prisoners and brought him to Mathas' castle."

"Any sign of Timothy and the other?" Fahron asked.

"No but they caught this one two to three miles east of the River Shey which means they are close," Claudius said. "And of this moment I am giving the orders, Fahron go upstairs and get some sleep and we will stay here. We will wake you if something happens."

"I can't sleep."

"Then drink a whiskey and go to bed, you know you are useless when you are this exhausted."

"Fahron when was the last time you ate?" asked Angelina.

"I don't know."

"I will bring a tray to your room."

"Alright," Fahron said and stood up from his desk then he looked at Matthew. "Did Mathas pay those men, I owe him money."

"We paid them and were glad to do it, just get some sleep, we will watch over things," Mathew replied.

"This reminds me of Duncan and Sampson," Diana said after Fahron left the room.

"Diana stay here," Misha said. "We are going to search the area from the air. If the prisoners get past us, don't hesitate just kill them."

"We'll go out and check the troops," Stephan said. "You girls are protecting Fahron."

"I'm going to check the doors and windows," Ingr said. "Diana why don't you come with me then Angelina can stay upstairs near Fahron."

Fahron was already sleeping when Angelina brought a tray of food into his chambers. After setting the tray near his bed, Angelina searched his room for any sign of an intruder then took a chair into the hallway and sat outside of Fahron's door.

"I've never been in such fancy places until I came to Wetpr," Diana said to Ingr as they walked through the castle checking the doors and windows. "I have to admit I don't feel like I fit in with all of this sometimes."

"My family was so poor that we often didn't have enough food," Ingr said. "So I understand how you feel. Bella and Claudius made me feel welcomed from the beginning so that helped a lot."

"Oh, Gabriel's team and your families are all wonderful; it's me I guess."

"Lila came from a really poor family too, did she tell you?"

"No, actually I haven't gotten to know her that well yet. We've been on missions pretty much since I started to heal from my injuries."

"I don't know Misha very well but Stephan does and he said that Misha is a great warrior and a good man."

"He is so good to me. We weren't planning on getting married this quickly but my brother was not handling anything very well and when he found out about me and Misha he was telling the family that he was going to take me back to Ryed. So Raphael married us on a mission, that way Thor couldn't force me to leave. Misha wanted a big wedding and says we will have one later on."

"I know Fahron sent his staff home for their safety but doesn't this place seem awfully empty to you?" Ingr asked as they walked through the chambers on the first floor of the house.

"Does Timothy still have chambers here? Maybe we can find some information."

"This must be Tabeth's room," Ingr said as they entered a room filled with stuffed toys and lace covered pillows. "The doors to her patio are unlocked." These were the first doors that Ingr and Diana found that were unsecured. They searched the room and the small patio garden then returned to the castle, locking the doors behind them.

Chaez's chambers were next to Tabeth's, nothing stood out of the ordinary in his rooms. Ingr and Diana completed the search of Chaez's chambers and walked back into the hallway. "I am surprised these rooms are all on the first floor because they are easier for an intruder to enter," Ingr said. Diana opened the door to the next chambers as Ingr was talking.

"Ingr get Claudius now, I will stay here." Diana said.

"What is it?"

"Just go get him."

157

When Ingr returned a few minutes later, Claudius, Stephan, Thaos and Matthew were with her. Diana stood in front of the closed door. "What is it?" Claudius asked.

"Step forward and give me your hand," Diana said. Claudius hesitated for a moment then did as she requested. Diana lightly pressed the palm of Claudius' hand against the thick wooden door.

"What is that?" Claudius asked of the pulsing energy he felt.

"I want all of you to feel this so you will recognize it," Diana said. "There is demonic energy in that room. Let me open the door when you are done."

Each person touched the door; Thaos was the last and after he felt the energy he stepped back. "We often feel that same thing when we come upon a lair of demons," Diana said as she pulled a knife from her sheath. Diana opened the door and sniffed the air. "The smell of demons lingers long after they have left an area, this room doesn't smell," Diana said and walked in. "That is what was giving off the energy," Diana explained and pointed to the walls.

The group entered the first room of the chambers which was a small parlor. The walls of this room were covered in writing that was moving and pulsating. None of them understood the words that they saw. "What the hell is that?" asked Claudius.

"I don't know but I have seen it before," Diana said. "Thor and I saw similar things several times in northern Ryed." As Diana started to walk through the parlor Matthew yelled for her to stop.

"Wouldn't now be a good time to call us in?" Miranda's voice rang out.

"Miranda help us," Ingr said as Diana looked confused by the voice they were hearing.

Miranda appeared in the center of the room directly in front of Diana, who stared in awe at the beautiful Angel. "Diana few people have seen this and lived to tell about it. You and Thor were protected from what you saw in Ryed so you could teach Gabriel's team and The Seven Sons of such evil."

"This is propilatry it is a form of demonic curse. Anyone who gazes upon it is cursed with the words it is written in."

"Was this for Fahron?" Claudius asked.

"No, it was for those of you who have fought and defied the demons."

"Misha," Diana said fearfully and started to turn to leave the room.

"Diana stop," Miranda said. "I have already called to them and they will be joining us soon. This is a lesson for all of you. Diana for you the lesson is to call upon the Angels, you have met Daniel and I am Miranda. People have free choice; we need you to call upon us for us to help you." Within moments Misha, Calen, Koby and Joao ran into the chambers.

"Diana are you alright?" Misha asked as he ran to his bride.

"What is this?" Koby asked as he looked around the room.

"This was a trap for all of you but fortunately a Venator came upon it first," Miranda said. "The Great Ruler has sent you three Venatores as well as three Angels to assist you and to protect you and The Seven Sons. Misha while you want to keep Diana safe her role is to be at your side, as is Vivian's role with Raphael."

"Diana felt the pulsating energy when she touched the door so she knew what she would see when she entered. This writing is a demonic curse that only the most powerful demons can deploy. The words indicate the type of curse that is placed upon the person. As you can see this room is filled with different words; none of you would have lived through this. But do not worry I am protecting you. Diana and Thor were protected when they have encountered the propilatry before so they could teach all of you."

"As you know the demons are using Timothy as a means to ambush you," Miranda continued. "Do not let your guards down. It is not just Gabriel's team that has bounties placed upon them. You must share this information with Sorren also. All of you who defied Baal and the other Old Ones have bounties."

"Our wives?" Thaos asked.

"All of you, yet here we are and you are being protected once again by an Angel. There are no demons in this room." Miranda waved her hand and the propilatry disappeared from the walls. "Fahron refuses to listen to our voices and he has never called upon us even after listening to all of you speak of us. Leave this room and tell him what you have witnessed. He needs to call upon the heavens."

"I'm not going to wake Fahron up," Claudius said to Stephan, Matthew, Thaos, Ingr, Diana and the Rualas. "The poor man has not slept in days. I will tell him what Miranda said when he wakes up."

"Claudius it might be too late by then," said Matthew.

"He has only slept a couple of hours, we will let him sleep longer," Claudius said with a tone of authority.

"Perhaps we should put our energies towards trying to figure out the next trap," Thaos said. "By now the demons know this one didn't work."

The midday meal was being served at the castle of Mathas. As everyone was taking their seats, Isadore looked around the room then asked, "Has anyone seen Tabeth? She's not in her room."

"I saw her a couple of hours ago with Ryan; they said they were picking you flowers," Mathas said. "They might still be in the gardens. I was wondering if there is a blooming romance there."

"Sorry we are late," Bella said as she carried Titus into the dining room and Ryan followed her, holding Ingr's twins. "Nikki isn't feeling well and won't be joining us."

"Ryan where is Tabeth?" Isadore asked with fear in her voice.

"She was bringing you flowers the last I saw her," Ryan said as he handed one of the twins to Shara.

"I never got the flowers," Isadore said and started to stand up.

Ryan's eyes suddenly grew wide, "Oh my god, I bet she went home."

"Tabeth said she wanted to be with Fahron because she didn't want him to feel alone. I made her promise me she wouldn't leave here."

Without saying a word Mathas quickly got up from the table and ran to the front door.

Ingr walked around Fahron's castle informing the men that lunch was being served. Diana was in the kitchen cooking and preparing a tray for Fahron. Ingr returned to the kitchen. "I am going to take this tray up stairs and change places with Angelina," Ingr said as she walked out of the kitchen.

"Fahron is still sleeping," Angelina announced as she joined everyone at the table. "Ingr told me about what you found." Before anyone could speak Angelina looked across the table at Diana and smiled, "I recognize this food."

"I only know how to cook the food of my people but Hannah and Natasha are going to teach me other recipes."

"You should have Emeral teach you some of hers," Koby said. "She is a fantastic cook too."

"He means he really likes your cooking too," Misha said to Diana as she handed him a platter.

"Excuse me My Lords," a soldier said as he entered the dining room.

"What is it Lieutenant?" asked Claudius.

"Some of the soldiers killed one of the prisoners, they are out front." Everyone stood up from the table and walked out the front door of the castle where they saw a bloody body lying on the ground.

"My Lord," said one of the soldiers we found him just a mile from here, he was coming in from the west."

Misha knelt down by the body. "It's Jackson." Misha said and started to search through Jackson's clothing.

"Was he alone?" Claudius asked.

"Yes, we searched the area and didn't find Timothy."

"There's nothing on his body," Misha said and stood up.

"Tell us what happened," Claudius said.

"We was doing our normal patrol and Brent here saw movement in the alferto grass. So we started riding in that direction and this one here," the soldier pointed at Jackson's body. "He stands up and starts to run. So we chased him down. We didn't want to kill him right away because we wanted information but he pulled a knife and stabbed Thronson. He got killed in the fight."

"So you didn't get any information?" Stephan asked.

"No My Lord, like I said we didn't want to kill him right away."

"You did well men," Claudius said. "You wait right here and I will get your reward." Claudius returned to the castle, he knew where Fahron stored his money. Long ago Claudius, Fahron and Mathas all swore oaths to each other that if something happened to one of them the other two would take care of the families; because of this oath all three men gave each other access to their money and personal papers.

"Something doesn't seem right about this," Thaos said. "I just have that feeling in my gut. I'm going back in and check the castle."

"We're staying here until Timothy is caught," Claudius said as he returned to the table. "I just sent word to Mathas about all of this. Where are Stephan and Thaos?"

"They decided to check the doors and windows again in case Jackson was a distraction," Matthew said. "We already checked on Fahron, he is still sleeping."

"Jackson where are you going?" Timothy asked in a loud whisper.

"Will you shut the hell up," Jackson yelled.

"I thought you wanted to go south to the caves."

"And I thought you wanted to visit your daddy," Jackson said sarcastically. Jackson moved quickly forward in the tall alferto grass with Timothy following him.

As Claudius and the others were finishing their midday meal several Enrops started scratching against the windows of the dining room. Joao was sitting the closest to the window and opened it allowing the birds in. All four birds flew around the room. "We have an important message for Fahron," one of the birds said.

"He is sleeping I will take it," Claudius said and stood up to take the note from the beak of one of the large birds. As Claudius read the note the color drained from his face.

"What is it Father?" asked Stephan.

"Tabeth is missing they think she is headed here to be with her father. Mathas has troops searching for her."

"I'll wake Fahron," Matthew said and quickly left the room.

"Will you keep up?" Jackson called back to Timothy. "You are just stinking worthless."

"Why are you moving so fast?"

"Because I am not a sissy."

Fahron ran into the dining room wide-eyed as he was not totally awake. "Let me see that note." Fahron said frantically and grabbed the paper from Claudius' hand.

"Fahron," Claudius said loudly. "We have alerted the soldiers here and Misha and the other Rualas have taken to the air. I need you to sit down so I can talk to you."

"I can't sit down."

"Fahron, let us tell you about what we found in your home," Matthew said as he and Ingr entered the dining room.

"Here? In the castle?" Fahron asked in disbelief.

Angelina handed Fahron a glass of whiskey. "Drink this to calm yourself," she said. "I will get you some food."

Claudius and Matthew told Fahron about what they found in Timothy's chambers and the message that Miranda had for him. But between exhaustion and fear for his daughter's safety, Fahron's mind was having difficulty processing their words. Claudius and Matthew repeated the story two more times.

"Fahron, we have told you many times how the Angels have helped us," Matthew said. "You need to let them in; call to them."

"I don't have time for this foolishness," Fahron scoffed. "I have to find my little girl."

"Listen to them," Angelina said. "We would all be dead if it wasn't for the Angels."

"I will not put my family's safety in the hands of something I do not understand," Fahron barked and quickly walked out of the dining room.

Tabeth hid her horse in one of the barns on her family's property. She crept up to the castle because she did not want the soldiers to stop her and send her back to Mathas' castle. Tabeth hid in the greenery that surrounded the small patio outside of her chambers. She had left her doors unlocked so she could return home. When Tabeth was convinced that she was alone, she ran across the patio and to the doors to her bedroom.

"Locked, how can they be locked?" Tabeth said out loud as she pulled on the door handles. Suddenly a hand covered Tabeth's mouth and an arm wrapped around her tiny waist and lifted her off the ground. Tabeth struggled and kicked as she was carried away from the castle.

Chapter XI
Rage

"My Lord we found Tabeth's horse in the lower stable," Lieutenant Powell told Fahron. "The horse looks well rested it is difficult to determine how long it has been there."

"It was over twelve hours ago that the King sent word that Tabeth was missing. She has to be here, keep looking," Fahron ordered tensely.

"I told you, I told you all I would prove to you I was a man," Timothy said as lifted himself from his sister's naked and mutilated body. "Isn't that right Jackson." Timothy looked around the shed when he didn't get a response from Jackson. "Now were the hell is he?" Timothy asked out loud as he fastened his pants. "Jackson where are you?"

"Well you showed your father now," Jackson said. Timothy quickly turned around and saw Jackson sitting on a tool bench.

"Where were you?"

"We've been right here."

"We? Jackson what are you talking about; did you find Aaron?"

"You really are a moron, Aaron's dead."

"How do you know that?"

"So Timothy what are you going to do now?" Your father is in the castle but so are a lot of others, you can't fight them all."

"Who is inside?"

"Claudius and his sons, Matthew and his wife, Ingr another girl and four Rualas from Wetpr. They are here to hunt you. You swore an oath to kill them all."

Timothy started to pace back and forth in the small tool shed. "Damn it," Timothy yelled when he slid in a pool of his sister's blood. "I can't fight them all."

"Hell you can't fight," Jackson said sarcastically.

"What do you think I should do?"

"You're gonna have to find a way to get your father alone."

"Yeah," Timothy said as he was waiting for Jackson to say more.

"Which means, you moron, you are going to have to get the others away from him."

"Ok?"

"Do I have to do everything for you?"

"Well I just don't understand how I am going to get the others away from him, unless I wait around until they all leave."

"Well that is one idea. Another would be to cause a distraction."

"Yeah?"

"You really are the stupidest person I have ever met. Do you think finding your sister's body will be a distraction?"

"Ok but what do you expect me to do, stand in the doorway and yell?"

"How about starting the shed on fire and when they come to put the fire out they will find Tabeth's body."

"Yeah that might work, then when everyone is out here I can sneak inside of the castle."

Timothy started a fire in the far corner of the shed away from his sister's body. There was only one door to the shed so Timothy quickly ran out before the soldiers could see the smoke. There was no moon in the night sky which aided Timothy as he ran to the next shed which held cut wood. "No one is coming, move," yelled Jackson and the two crouched down and ran to the next building which was a small barn.

Soldiers started to yell and run towards the burning shed. Timothy ran inside of the barn and watched the soldiers through the open slots between boards in the back wall of the barn.

166

A crowd was gathering around the shed. "Someone get the General," a voice rang out.

"Now, they're distracted run to the castle," Jackson said.

Timothy turned and started towards the door but in the darkness of the barn he tripped and fell. "Damn it," Timothy yelled. "Damn it my nose is bleeding." Timothy never looked at what he tripped over; he never saw the long dead body of Jackson that had been placed on the floor of that small barn earlier in the morning.

"Hurry," Jackson's voice rang in Timothy's ears.

"My Lords come quickly," said the breathless soldier as he ran inside of Fahron's castle. Claudius and Fahron were in the study and quickly stood up and ran out the door. Ingr, Angelina and Diana were in the kitchen washing dishes and preparing dough for the breakfast meal, they never heard the soldier's message.

Soldiers with lit torches were everywhere on the castle grounds. The soldier who was leading both generals grabbed a torch from another soldier and ran towards the shed. "What is it? Did you find Timothy?" Fahron asked.

"My Lord, Lieutenant Powell just told me to bring you back here as quickly as I could. I didn't see what was in the shed."

"Stop," Claudius said sternly. "What shed?"

"My Lords there was a fire in the tool shed, some men were putting it out then they called for the lieutenant. He walked inside and told me to drop my bucket of water and to get you as quickly as I could that is truly all I know." Fahron grabbed the torch out of the soldier's hand and ran towards the shed, with Claudius close behind him; both men were overwhelmed with feelings of doom.

Lieutenant Powell was standing before the closed door of the shed when Fahron and Claudius arrived. Fahron walked up to Powell, "My Lord," the young lieutenant said and tears started to well in his eyes. Fahron and Claudius pushed past the lieutenant and entered the shed.

In less than a moment Fahron had fallen to his knees and his cries of pain were heard for some distance outside of the shed. Stephan, Matthew and Thaos ran to the shed when they heard the screams. "You shouldn't go in there," Powell said to the men. Fahron and Claudius are in there now."

"Is it Tabeth?" Matthew asked as he held a torch up so he could see Powell's face.

"I've never seen anything like that," Powell said then he turned and vomited on the ground.

Claudius heard the voices outside of the shed and stepped out closing the door behind him. Claudius was so angry his face was red, his veins protruding and tears were running down his cheeks. "That vicious animal raped and butchered his own sister. You find him and you kill him." Claudius turned to Powell. "Lieutenant have some men bring blankets and allow no one in this shed without my permission."

"Angelina all the soldiers are running around with torches," Ingr said as she happened to glance out of the kitchen window. Both Angelina and Diana ran to the window.

"Something has happened," Angelina said and ran out of the kitchen.

"Timothy must be here," Diana said. "Because they seem to be looking for someone."

"Neither Fahron or Claudius are here," Angelina said as she returned to the kitchen.

All three women pulled knives from their sheaths when they heard a knock at the back kitchen door. "It's Stephan," Ingr said and ran to the door and unlocked it.

"What has happened?" Angelina asked when she saw the grave look on Stephan's face.

"Timothy raped and butchered Tabeth. Her body is in a tool shed which he set on fire. The fire is out but you know that was a distraction. Fahron is beside himself with grief and Father is with him."

"Did you see the body?" Ingr asked.

"No, but Lieutenant Powell did and he was crying and puking; I can only imagine. Thaos and Matthew are searching the outside of the castle then they are going to come in and search the inside again. We think Timothy will lay in wait until his father is alone and defenseless."

"You mean he will kill him in his sleep?" Diana asked.

"Timothy is a coward; he doesn't know how to fight like a warrior," Stephan responded with disgust.

"He seems to have a weakness for women," Angelina said. "Maybe we can draw him out."

"He knows you and Ingr could kill him in a heartbeat," Stephan said.

"But he doesn't know me," said Diana.

"But you are dressed like a warrior," Stephan replied. "And he might have already seen you here."

"I am sure we can find something for her to wear here," Angelina said. "We will change her clothes and have Diana work in the kitchen; perhaps Timothy will think she is one of the cooks. Ingr and I will hide close by."

"Diana are you willing to do this?" Stephan asked.

"Of course; Stephan I know all of you want to kill him but your families are as one. You should let me or one of the Rualas kill Timothy so your families aren't filled with guilt."

"First let's find the bastard then we will fight over who kills him," Stephan said. "Also Misha and the others have not returned yet. I would expect them soon because it is getting so dark."

Ingr locked the kitchen door after Stephan walked outside. Then the three women ran up the stairs to the chambers of Isadore and Fahron. Angelina started to search through Isadore's clothing for something that would fit Diana.

"Sergeant hold this torch while I write," Claudius said to a soldier who had just brought him paper and pen. When Claudius was done writing he folded the paper and handed it to the sergeant. "Take a detail of men and deliver this letter to King Mathas. No one else sees it; do you understand?"

"Yes, My Lord." The sergeant handed Claudius his torch and turned around. As he was walking away, the sergeant called to other soldiers to join him.

Fahron's grief was inconsolable. He was crippled by the vicious rape and murder of his daughter and Claudius knew that was exactly what Timothy had intended.

"Father," Stephan said and pulled Claudius away from the others. "The girls are dressing Diana as a cook hoping that Timothy will see her and expose himself."

"Is Diana alone?"

"No, Ingr and Angelina are waiting for Timothy."

"Very well but don't be surprised if Misha gets angry."

"I would too," Stephan said and walked away.

"I just can't get used to these shoes," Diana complained. "I am going barefoot."

"We were the same way," Ingr said. "Diana don't take any chances, Timothy is crazy."

Diana returned to the kitchen and put an apron on over her dress. She lit many more candles to illuminate the kitchen in the darkness of the night. Ingr got on the floor and crawled into the pantry so she would not be seen through the kitchen windows. The pantry did not have windows but Ingr had an unobstructed view of most of the large kitchen. Angelina hid behind the door that led from the kitchen into the dining room. The dining room was dark and when Angelina cracked the door open she had a view of the back kitchen door.

Diana started to wash and peel potatoes for the morning meal. She deliberately did not look out of the windows but every muscle in her body was on heightened alert as she listened for sounds.

Stephan found Thaos and Matthew and told them of the trap that their wives had set for Timothy.

"How can that little bastard just disappear like this?" Thaos asked. "There's no sign of him anywhere. Does Fahron have any secret tunnels or entrances that we don't know about?"

"Ask Father he might know," Stephan said. "I will stay near the castle with Matthew.

Misha, Joao, Calen and Koby returned to the castle. As soon as they landed one of the soldiers told them about Tabeth and the four Rualas returned to the air. As Misha was flying around the castle he saw Diana alone in a well-lit kitchen, wearing someone else's clothing and he knew exactly what she was doing. Misha landed in a large tree where he had a view of the kitchen and waited.

Koby and Joao started to dust the area immediately around the castle with dried lynswood to try and find Timothy's footprints. Calen returned to the tool shed and dusted the ground there.

"I got something," Joao said. "Look there are prints but then they just disappear."

Koby started to pat the ground, "Sometimes humans build cellars under their homes. They hide the outside openings so intruders can't find them. Suddenly Koby felt a latch and he pulled it. A door that lay flat against the ground opened. "Go tell Claudius and the others," Koby told Joao. "I'm going in."

"I will be back soon," Joao said and quickly ascended into the air. Koby started to feel his way down the dark wooden steps."

Timothy opened the cellar door just a crack and peered into the kitchen. This door was flush with the floor boards and not easily detected; neither Ingr nor Angelina had a clear view of the cellar opening.

Timothy's lust started to stir within him as he watched Diana working in the kitchen. He was so mesmerized by her beauty that he did not realize he wasn't hearing Jackson's voice anymore. Timothy watched Diana for several minutes. He heard no sounds in the castle other than Diana walking.

Diana had her back to the cellar door because she was unaware of its existence. Timothy lifted the door farther and Diana did not react. Misha tensed as he saw a slight movement in the corner of his left eye, but he didn't know what is was. Diana now heard the wooden door creek but she continued peeling potatoes. She was waiting until she heard footsteps.

Timothy felt bolder as he heard no sounds and Diana did not appear to hear him. He slithered onto the kitchen floor and stood up; now Misha was the only one who saw him. Timothy pulled a large knife out of the sheath on his belt and quietly moved towards Diana, who was now aware of a presence in the room. She grabbed the hilt of a knife and quickly spun around and threw it at Timothy but as soon as she released the weapon Misha flew in through the window causing glass and wood to implode in the kitchen. Ingr and Angelina both burst into the room.

Timothy was bleeding from the knife that was lodged in his shoulder. Misha was closest and ran towards Timothy who turned and ran back towards the cellar door. Koby was on the cellar steps and just about to climb up into the kitchen when Timothy ran towards him.

Koby reached up and grabbed Timothy's ankles and yanked them forward, causing Timothy to fall hard onto the floor. Misha grabbed Timothy's hair and pulled his head back exposing Timothy's neck. Just as Misha was about to cut Timothy's throat, Claudius, Thaos, Matthew, Stephan, Calen and Joao burst into the kitchen.

"Wait!" yelled Claudius. "He is mine."

"Jackson help me," Timothy screamed.

"Jackson is dead," Misha growled. "I saw what you did to that family in Wetpr," Misha said through clenched teeth as he maintained his hold on Timothy. "I saw what you did to those little girls."

"Claudius perhaps we should kill him," Calen said. "You are Fahron's friend."

"And that is why it must be me," Claudius said soberly. "This will not be a pretty death," Claudius said as he walked towards Timothy.

"No!" screamed Timothy as Claudius picked Timothy up by his hair and yanked him to a standing position. Misha handed Claudius his knife and Claudius plunged it into Timothy's groin. Timothy screamed in agony. Claudius still had his hold on Timothy's hair with his left hand and withdrew the knife handing it back to Misha.

"You rape children!" Claudius yelled and violently punched Timothy in the stomach. Claudius was considerably larger and more powerful than Timothy and Claudius was consumed with rage.

"You butcher babies!" Claudius yelled and punched Timothy in the face.

"You raped your own sister!" As Claudius yelled all of Timothy's crimes he beat Timothy with his massive fists. The others in the room now stepped back so they would not get hit with the blood splatter. Blow after blow Claudius assailed upon Timothy. When Timothy's limp body collapsed on the floor, Claudius jumped on top of it and continued to beat him.

No one in the room spoke. Exhausted, Claudius stood up; he was drenched in Timothy's blood. It was at that moment that everyone in the kitchen realized Fahron was standing in the doorway between the kitchen and the dining room. Claudius turned and faced his friend. The two men stared at each other for a moment, then Fahron nodded at Claudius.

"I need to talk to Isadore," Fahron said with a sadness that stirred the hearts of all. "Claudius will you come with me?"

"We will clean up," Stephan said.

Fahron quickly spun around. "That monster will not have a burial; throw him to the animals," Fahron said with rage. "My little girl, protect her body so we can bury her."

Chapter XII
Aftermath

"I'll get my medical bag," Angelina said when she saw Diana cleaning Misha's wounds.

"Diana get use to it," Koby kidded. "Misha always makes the dramatic entrances." Koby's comment made many laugh which was a welcomed relief from the tension they all felt.

Stephan and Thaos each grabbed one of Timothy's arms and dragged him across the kitchen floor and out the back door.

"You're getting blood on everything," Ingr scolded.

"Everything is already covered with blood," Thaos replied. "I wonder if they have any paint here."

"Are you mad at me?" Diana whispered as she cleaned glass out of one of Misha's wounds.

"No, I have been sitting in that tree outside the window watching you for some time. I wasn't going to let him touch you. Actually it was a pretty good idea."

"It was Angelina's idea," Diana said. "She and Ingr were hiding, waiting for Timothy to come."

"How did everyone know to come here?" asked Ingr.

"Joao found Timothy's tracks using that herb that Diana gave us," Koby explained. "But the tracts suddenly stopped and that is when we found the door to the cellar. I sent Joao to get the others while I searched the cellar."

Angelina proceeded to help Diana clean glass out of Misha's wounds. "I don't know if Isadore and Fahron should even live here anymore," Angelina said sadly. "I mean how could they not remember their children with everything they see?"

Suddenly a group of soldiers entered the kitchen. "We came to help clean," a young private said; his eyes widened as he saw the amount of blood splattered around the room. Matthew followed the soldiers into the kitchen.

"Lieutenant Powell himself is guarding the door to the shed," Matthew said. "I think we should take the body out of there but I don't know where to put it. Powell said Tabeth was naked."

"Angelina and I will wash and dress her," Ingr said.

"It's too dark in that shed," said Matthew. "We will have to bring her in here."

"Why don't you bring her in the kitchen?" Diana suggested. "This room is already full of blood. After we wash her we can move her to another room, maybe her bedroom."

"I like that idea," Ingr said. "But I don't want to lay her on this bloody floor; I am going to get some blankets and towels."

"Wait until we are done cleaning Misha's wounds," Angelina said "Then all of you men can leave."

"If she looks anything like those little girls he raped, it's going to be gruesome," warned Misha.

Claudius never cleaned Timothy's blood off from him; nor did Fahron clean Tabeth's blood off. The two men rode in silence. Stephan ordered two details of men to accompany Fahron and Claudius so they would not fall prey to a demonic trap. Fahron was in a daze, his grief consuming him. Claudius wanted desperately to take his friend's pain away. The two men rode in silence...

Although Tabeth's body was wrapped in a blanket, Lieutenant Powell made all of his men leave the area between the shed and the castle as Thaos carried the girl's body. Ingr had placed several blankets on the floor for Thaos to lay Tabeth on.

"It's time for all the men to leave," said Angelina.

"Are you sure you want to see this?" Thaos asked. "He cut her breasts off."

All three girls stared at Thaos in horror for a moment. "We can't let Isadore see her like this," Angelina said.

175

"I'm going into the parlor," Thaos said. "And I will stay there until you are done. You holler if you need me."

"I'll be with him," Misha said and kissed Diana on the forehead. The two men started to walk out of the room then Thaos turned. "When you are done we are going to clean and paint this room. Maybe you could put some coffee on for the men."

Although it was very late when Claudius and Fahron arrived at Mathas' castle all of the adults were still up. Mathas did not have the heart to tell Isadore that Tabeth had been murdered but as soon as Isadore saw Mathas' face after he received the letter she knew. Bella and Rosa were trying to console their longtime friend.

"Oh my," Rosa gasped loudly when she saw Fahron and Claudius standing in the doorway to the parlor, where everyone was seated. Both men were covered in blood and clearly exhausted.

Mathas stood up and poured glasses of whiskey for everyone as Claudius and Fahron walked over to the sofa where Isadore, Rosa and Bella were sitting. Chaez was sitting in a chair near the hearth.

"Chaez will you come here?" Fahron asked wearily.

Fahron got on his knees before his wife and started to cry. Isadore put her arms around his neck and they both cried and held each other. Then Chaez knelt down near his parents and Fahron put his arm around his son. After a few moments Claudius asked, "Fahron do you want me to tell it?"

Fahron nodded. Mathas handed Claudius a glass of whiskey which Claudius gulped down. "We had been searching for Tabeth all day," Claudius explained. "Late this evening some of the soldiers saw a fire in that tool shed at the back of your property, as they were putting the fire out they discovered Tabeth's body." Claudius hesitated. "She had been raped and butchered." Everyone in the room either started to cry or gasped at this revelation except for Mathas because he already knew.

"Two of the prisoners were already dead so we knew this was Timothy's work. And most of us realized Timothy wanted to cripple Fahron so he would be easier to kill. While we were searching for Timothy; Angelina, Ingr and Diana devised a plan. They dressed Diana up in some of your clothes Isadore because they had to get her out of her warrior's clothes." Isadore now looked up at Claudius as he spoke.

"The girls lit many candles so that Timothy would be able to see into the kitchen. Diana stayed in the kitchen preparing food while Ingr and Angelina waited in hiding. It was Angelina's idea that Timothy would not be able to resist his urges to attack another woman." Everyone in the room sat in silence and hung on to every word that Claudius was saying.

"As the girls were setting this trap, Koby and Joao found a door that led to the cellar under your castle. That is how Timothy had gained entrance to the castle. The trap worked. As Timothy crept up behind Diana with a knife, Misha suddenly threw himself through the window and landed in the kitchen. Koby was already climbing up that wooden ladder that led from the cellar to the kitchen."

Claudius took another gulp of whiskey and continued, "When Koby found the cellar door he sent Joao to get us. Me and the boys and Calen and Joao got to the kitchen just as Misha was about to cut Timothy's throat. I stopped him. Calen said they should kill Timothy because all of us are family. I told Calen that was why I had to kill him. Isadore forgive me but I did not let that monster die an easy death; I made him pay for his crimes."

Bella stood up and walked over to Claudius and hugged him tightly. "Are the girls alright?" she asked.

"I believe so, if they had injuries they were minor. Misha is all cut up from the window, but I think everyone else is fine. I would not expect any of them to come home tonight."

"Is everything all right?" Misha asked as Ingr ran out of the kitchen."

"I am just getting her clothes," Ingr said as she passed the parlor; then she stopped and retraced her steps, walking into the parlor where Stephan, Matthew, Calen, Koby and Joao had joined Thaos and Misha. Ingr picked up Stephan's glass of whiskey and took a sip, then started to cough. "I am so glad that Claudius killed him," Ingr said and walked out of the room.

Matthew stood up, "I am going to get a bottle of wine, I am sure those girls will want a drink when they are done."

It was another half of an hour before Angelina walked into the parlor. Could one of you carry Tabeth to her bedroom?" All of the men stood up and walked into the kitchen.

"She looks beautiful," Thaos said. "You really did a good job."

"I hope I never have to see anything like that again," Angelina said as Matthew put his arm around her.

"We are going to fill her room with flowers in the morning," Diana said. "Does anyone know when Fahron and Isadore will return?"

"We'll send him a message," Stephan said. "I am sure Fahron will be grateful that Isadore doesn't have to see what Tabeth looked like."

"Why don't you girls have some wine and go to bed," Matthew suggested. "We will clean up this mess."

Angelina, Ingr and Diana all looked at each other. "I doubt if any of us can sleep after all this," Angelina said.

"I was thinking about starting breakfast," said Diana.

"But we will take some wine," Ingr said wearily.

Midmorning the next day Fahron received a message from Matthew telling him it would be appropriate to bring family and friends to the castle to view Tabeth's body.

The note informed Fahron that the house had been cleaned and repainted and the tool shed burned. The bodies of both Jackson and Timothy were burned in the fire as well as any bloody clothing and linens. Soldiers had dug a grave in the family cemetery and were building a coffin for Tabeth. Angelina sent a note to her father Chief Sorren telling him of the murder of Tabeth and that her body was ready for viewing.

Enrops alerted Matthew and the others that King Mathas was leading a large procession to Fahron's castle that would arrive in mid-afternoon. Lieutenant Powell had his men form two lines on either side of the roadway leading to the castle. For two miles the procession rode past soldiers who were standing at attention. Trumpets announced the arrival of the procession once they entered the gates surrounding the castle.

Angelina, Diana and Ingr had prepared a feast for those coming to view the bodies. The men prepared the rooms and tables of whiskey and wine. While the arriving guests were dressed in finery, Matthew and the others who had stayed at the castle making preparations were still wearing their bloody clothing from the previous night.

King Mathas and Queen Rosa entered the house first and saw Matthew and the others standing in line to greet the guests. "Bella and I brought clean clothes for all of you," Rosa whispered to Matthew and Angelina who were standing at the head of the receiving line.

"You all look so exhausted," Bella said. "Has anyone slept?"

"No," Ingr said as she hugged her mother-in-law.

When Fahron, Isadore and Chaez walked into the castle; Fahron stopped the procession and turned to the hundreds of people waiting to enter. "The receiving line is made up of the brave warriors who did battle here last night. And in their graciousness they have not slept because they were preparing this showing. I am disbanding the receiving line so our friends can change into clean clothing."

Bella and Rosa both hurried back out of the castle and had soldiers help them carry in the changes of clothing they had brought for everyone. The Ruala warriors were amazed that Bella and Rosa had taken clothing that belonged to Matthew, Thaos and Stephan and had them altered so the clothing would fit around the wings of the warriors.

Fahron, Isadore and Chaez were the first to go into Tabeth's bedroom. Isadore's cries could be heard throughout the first floor of the castle. Since Fahron had sent his house staff home to protect them from Timothy; Mathas brought his own staff to help at the showing and the feast.

Fahron and Isadore were both well-liked and respected by the people of Lentz. All day long people came to the castle to pay their respects and to help with duties. Several women from the Nordes Tribe volunteered to help with the care of the children of the ruling families so they could focus on the showing.

The showing and the feast lasted all day and late into the night. Many guests spent the night at the castle so they could be present for the burial the following morning. The members of the ruling families as well as Misha, Diana, Calen, Koby and Joao were all exhausted and operating on energies their bodies could barely support.

Chapter XIII
Relationships

Misha and his team stayed in the Kingdom of Lentz for one more day after Tabeth's burial so they could rest before their journey home. The night before the team left, Fahron, Isadore and Chaez came to the castle of Mathas with gifts for everyone who had helped them. Fahron split the bounty between the members of Misha's team, Claudius, Thaos, Stephan, Ingr, Matthew and Angelina.

"After talking to all of you I am promoting Lieutenant Powell," Fahron said. "For his dedication and service to my family. And I have given bonuses to the soldiers who are stationed at my home."

"They deserve it," Stephan said. "That situation was difficult for everyone."

Diana handed her pouch of gold coins to Misha. "Keep it you earned it," he said to her.

"I don't know what to spend it on," Diana replied.

"You'll think of something and if you don't it can go towards our next wedding." After Misha said these words he and Diana explained the circumstances under which they got married and now told everyone about Thor and the lives that Thor and Diana had led prior to becoming members of Gabriel's team. After Misha finished talking and had invited everyone to their future wedding and celebration, Diana turned to Angelina, Nikki and Ingr.

"If you know any girls that we could match Thor up with bring them to the wedding." Everyone laughed at Diana's statement.

"You might be sorry you asked that?" Stephan said. "That's how Nikki and Thaos met but Angelina and Ingr invited a number of girls to meet him and well, let's just say that is another story."

"Dack and I wouldn't mind meeting some of the girls from your tribe too," Joao said and grinned.

"I can already see the wheels turning in their heads," Matthew said as he saw Angelina, Nikki and Ingr all smiling.

When Misha and his team returned home, both King Sudfad and Gabriel had already received letters from King Mathas, Claudius and Fahron detailing all of the events that had occurred in Lentz and thanking them for sending Misha, Diana, Calen, Koby and Joao to assist them.

It was almost dinner time when the exhausted team walked into the house. "Oh my lord Misha," Emeral gasped when she saw all of the cuts on her son's body.

"He flew through a window to help me," Diana said as she set her large pouch on the floor.

Natasha ran to the front foyer carrying Lily and flew into Calen's arms. Bekka was behind Natasha and put her arms around Koby's neck. "I really missed you," Bekka said and kissed him on the lips.

As the two couples embraced, Hannah saw the look on Joao's face and walked up to the young man and gave him a hug. "You were missed too," she said. Within moments the entire team realized that Misha and the others had returned and came to greet them.

"You all look so exhausted," Cassandra said.

"We are," Koby replied. "I would rather fight an army of Hutas than to go through something like that again. I felt so sorry for that family."

"Mathas, Claudius and Fahron all sent letters to Sudfad and me telling us what a great job you did."

"The entire thing sounded like a nightmare," said Natasha.

"The nightmare was seeing what Timothy did to his sister," Diana said. "I don't think I will ever get that sight out of my head." Misha put his arm around Diana and kissed her on top of the head.

"Diana, Angelina and Ingr cleaned and dressed Tabeth's body because they didn't want her mother to see the way that Timothy had left her," Misha explained. "Since Tabeth was naked, only a few men saw the body but the lieutenant who told us about her was puking and crying; if that gives you any idea of how bad it was."

"Welcome home," Thor said with a big smile as he slowly walked across the room towards Diana.

"Thor, you're walking," Diana gasped and ran up to her brother and hugged him. With his arm around Diana, Thor walked up to Misha and held his hand out to shake hands. Misha grinned and the two men shook hands, ending the tension between them.

"We all felt so sorry for you after we read about what you had been through," Bekka said. "That Emeral made her famous cakes for you."

"Elan, Cassandra," Calen called. When the couple looked at him, Calen said. "Expect a good number of people from Lentz at your wedding." Calen was holding Lily with his right arm and had his left arm around Natasha who looked up at her husband. "Not a good subject to bring up."

"Why?" Calen asked.

"We decided to send Tina and Charles a letter telling them about Joey and Emeral and Maxwell coming on the trip with us," Elan said. "We thought perhaps the fireworks would die down by time they got here. Tina has sent us, well I will just show you the letters."

"I hope they don't even come," said Cassandra.

Dack looked at Joao and said, "Your parents have disowned Cassandra and you are probably next because you knew about all this."

"Are you telling the truth?" Joao asked in disbelief.

"Yes," Bekka said. "We need to get Melinda away from them. I can't imagine what she is going through with all of this."

"I am going to send her a letter tonight," Joao said.

"Mother said she didn't want us to tarnish Melinda so she wasn't going to allow Melinda to come to the wedding so Gabriel sent Melinda a letter asking her if she wanted to try out for the team," Cassandra said.

"Did you really?" Joao asked as he quickly turned to Gabriel. "Thank you so much; that is probably the only reason our parents would let her leave home."

During dinner Misha and his team told everyone about their experiences in Lentz. They also talked about the graciousness of the ruling families and the members of the Nordes Tribe. They talked about their encounter with Miranda and repeated every word she said.

"It makes you wonder," Raphael said. "That if Fahron would have let the Angels in if there would have been a different outcome to all of that."

"I found it interesting," Calen said. "That Miranda told us The Great Ruler had sent us three Angels and three Venatores to help us and in each case she emphasized the word three."

"I noticed that too," Koby said. "But I didn't know why."

"Did anyone ask her?" Gabriel asked.

"No, she disappeared quickly," Calen said. "But she did say that both Vivian and Diana were sent here to work at their husband's sides." Calen now turned to Thor. "Miranda didn't say anything else about you. Have you decided if you are going to work with us or go back to Ryed?"

"At this point I am working with you," Thor said. "I am trying to get my strength back so I can be more useful. Also I have apologized to the others and I want to apologize to all of you for my behavior. Emeral and Maxwell made me realize that I had misinterpreted some things which I want to talk to Diana and Misha about later."

"Thor you wake up in a strange place, you can't walk and your entire world has changed, I think most of us would be pretty angry too," Koby said.

"There was a little more than that," Thor said. "Actually after listening to your stories I wish I could have gone to Lentz with you."

"Well, you will meet all those people because we invited them to our next wedding," Misha said. "Diana and I will have a regular ceremony after Elan and Cassandra return from their wedding trip. And Diana here has already been working on finding girls for all the single men."

"What?" Dagon asked with a laugh.

"Angelina, Ingr and Nikki are so incredibly beautiful," as Diana spoke she turned and looked at Thor. "And they are really nice and fierce warriors. I asked them to bring other girls from their tribe to our wedding to meet all of you."

"She did," Joao said grinning and looked at Dack. "And Diana is correct in her assessment. Wait until you meet them."

"I am not ready for a wife," Thor said and blushed.

"Thor you don't have to get married," Diana said and laughed. "You can have a girlfriend or just someone to dance with. The Nordes Tribe seems very similar to ours; I think you will like those people."

"One of the ruling families always has to remain in Lentz," Gabriel explained. "So, not everyone will be here for Elan's and Cassandra's wedding. But we work closely with them, so those of you who do not know them will meet them all eventually. While you were in Lentz we have been working on the mission here," Gabriel continued as me looked at the members of Misha's team. "But I don't want to discuss it now. Besides the fact that many of you look exhausted I would like Archetenus and Jared to join us; so plan for a meeting here tomorrow morning after we return from Sudfad's meeting."

After dinner Misha and Diana helped Thor walk up the stairs to his bedroom. "I just can't believe how well you are doing," Diana said happily. "Thor you are improving so quickly."

"I have been working on it but I get exhausted easily which angers me."

185

When they reached Thor's room it was apparent to both Misha and Diana that he was exhausted. "Thor we can have this talk some other time, you look pretty tired," Misha said.

"No, I want to tell you now. Misha will you close the door." Thor sat down on his bed and looked at both Diana and Misha. "I will admit that I was both angry and scared when I finally woke up and found myself here. I wasn't scared of the people; it was my own body that scared me. I have never been this injured before. Misha I don't know if Diana has told you that she and I have spent years fighting about letting Joshua and Iris adopt us. While I realized my little sister needed more than I could give her I just felt like we would be betraying our parents."

"You never told me that," Diana said and sat on the bed next to Thor.

"Granted I was unconscious for days but when I wake up I find out that you arranged to have us adopted and you took a husband. I did not understand why you rushed into these important decisions. The only thing that made any sense to me was that you were doing these things to get back at me and that hurt me and made me really angry. Our life has been hard but I have always taken care of you Diana." Diana started to cry and held her brother's hand.

"Thor," Diana said but he held up his hand for her to stop talking.

"Is it true that you got married so quickly because you were afraid of what I would do?"

"Yes," Misha said. "That was never our original intention. We weren't even going to start planning a wedding until you could be part of it with us."

"Then I am sorry," Thor said sincerely. "I thought Diana was trying to push me out of her life. When Maxwell and Emeral explained to me all of the things that had occurred while I was sick and the reasons for them I realized I had misunderstood a great deal. And it was during that conversation that I really understood that Diana was my life and Maxwell made me realize that I didn't want to be alone." Diana threw her arms around Thor's neck and hugged him tightly.

"So Thor what do your words mean?" Misha asked. "Are you going to become part of this family?" Before Thor could answer Misha continued. "Remember what we were talking about during dinner; Miranda said The Great Ruler sent you, Diana and Vivian to us. If I were you I wouldn't leave until I found out what role the heavens wanted me to play."

Calen was sitting up in bed waiting for Natasha to join him. "That is worth the wait," he said with a big smile as she walked towards him wearing a lace turquoise colored nightgown. "You are so beautiful."

Natasha sat on the bed next to Calen and kissed him passionately then she stopped and looked into his eyes. "Calen I want you to do something but you might get mad that I asked."

"After seeing you in this nightgown I can't imagine getting mad about anything."

"I've been spending a lot of time talking with Thor and he has never had a girlfriend."

"So?"

"He has never even kissed a girl."

"And what does that have to do with us?"

"We laugh about how innocent Diana was but I think Thor is the same way. I think you or one of the other boys need to explain things to him."

"What?" Calen said as he sat up straighter in bed.

Natasha laughed and put her hands on her hips. "After living with all of you, I have heard you and your brothers talk. How old were you the first time you kissed a girl? Well I will tell you, pretty young. And how old were you the first time you made love?" Natasha laughed again. "Well, I don't know the answer to that but I will imagine you were pretty young. Imagine being in Thor's place. I think you and the others need to take him under your wings," Natasha laughed again at the pun that she said.

"I think Misha should be the one who explains sex to him."

"He and Misha barely get along, it should be someone else."

"I don't want to."

"You have never had any problem talking about sex before," Natasha said with a grin.

"How would I even start?"

"You're a smart man I am sure you can think of something. I will make it up to you," Natasha said flirtatiously. "This isn't the only new gown that I bought." As Natasha spoke she opened a drawer in the nightstand next to Calen's side of the bed and took out several small jars of massage oils."

"How can I say no?" he asked and laughed loudly.

The following morning immediately after breakfast Calen took Maxwell by the arm and ushered him into Gabriel's study then closed the door. Gabriel, Raphael, Misha, Dagon, Elan, Koby, and Luca were all sitting in the study and smiling at Maxwell. "Something is going on," Maxwell said as he looked at everyone's faces.

"Calen the floor is yours," Gabriel said.

"Our wives plotted against us," said Calen.

But before Calen could finish his sentence Dagon interrupted, "I don't have a wife they just pulled me in here."

"As I was saying; last night all of our wives, except for Diana, came to bed in sexy night gowns with massage oils and after they got our attention they told us they wanted us to do something."

"You have my attention now," Maxwell said with a chuckle.

"Apparently Thor has absolutely no experience with women. Natasha said he has never even kissed a girl so they want us to teach him about sex," Calen said with a grin and Maxwell broke into laughter.

"So what are you going to do?" Maxwell asked.

"You're his new father we think you should explain these things to him," Calen continued.

"If I remember correctly I never even explained them to you." Maxwell said then looked at Gabriel and Raphael. "By time I got around to sitting the boys down to have that talk, not only did they already know everything, they taught me a few things." Everyone in the room laughed.

"Why do I believe that?" Gabriel joked.

"I believe Thor understands where babies come from," Maxwell continued with a big grin on his face. "I think it is the steps to the dance that he needs to learn and the way you boys have always talked you are great dancers." Raphael and Gabriel roared with laughter as they looked at the faces of Calen, Luca, Koby, Dagon and Misha.

"Actually Natasha said something very similar to that," Calen said. "I never realized we talked about sex that much."

"We need to learn to shut up," Koby said sarcastically.

"We all agree that Misha should not be the one to talk to Thor," Gabriel said. "Because they had their first non-hostile talk last night."

"How did you boys share all of that information?" Maxwell asked as he looked at his sons.

Luca sighed dramatically and said with a chuckle, "Well, I guess we need to get a couple of bottles of whiskey."

"Think of it as practice for your children," Maxwell said. "I have to tell Emeral she is going to really enjoy this."

"So you think we should have a guy's gathering?" asked Koby.

"That's what we did when we were young," Luca said.

"How do we start?" Calen asked Maxwell.

"I would just tell him the truth. He knows Diana is trying to match him up with girls. If he doesn't want to hear it you know he will tell you," Maxwell said.

"But I'll bet he wants to hear it and he is just too embarrassed to ask any questions. My only caution is don't say anything that would make him think you are talking about Diana."

"We would never say anything bad about Diana," said Luca.

"The joke about the honey," Calen reminded his brother. "But that was pretty funny."

"What are you talking about?" Elan asked.

"Misha walks into the dining room with a jar of honey in his hand and wants Diana to go upstairs so they can take a nap. It was the middle of the morning and she was so confused."

"I want to be part of this talk," Elan said with a grin. "Because I think I can learn a few things." All the men laughed.

"Who knows it might be fun," Gabriel said. "How about tonight after dinner, we will all meet in here and if Thor doesn't want to talk about sex we can talk about something else."

"So should I come?" Misha asked.

"Are you kidding?" Calen said. "You could teach classes."

"But would Thor approve of his baby sister being married to such a knowledgeable man?" Raphael asked. "At the same time you don't want Thor to think you are shunning him. Misha why don't you come and if things get uncomfortable leave? And the rest of you will have to stop teasing Misha about his single life, at least during tonight's talk."

"We should invite Joao and Dack too, just so they don't feel left out," Gabriel said. "I think they do at times because the rest of us are so close."

"That reminds me I need to have a talk with Dack," Misha said and stood up. "I already apologized to Joao for becoming so jealous."

"I'll go with you," Koby said. "I need to talk to him too."

Elan stood up and stopped the two men from leaving the room. "Koby I know this is not my place to interfere but Cassandra and Bekka and I have been friends since we were little kids. And while Bekka is beautiful and good at so many things she is also very insecure. You need to sit down and have a talk with her also."

"What do you mean?" Koby asked fearfully. "Is she leaving me?"

"You sound just like Bekka," Elan said. "Don't the two of you ever talk?"

"Does she think I am leaving her?"

"No."

"Is it about how I treated Dack and Joao?"

"No."

"Elan, I am getting really worried, tell me."

"Bekka will kill me," Elan said. "I have been after her to talk to you for a while."

"Alright Elan I am really getting worried just tell me."

"She's pregnant and she is afraid to tell you because she thinks you will leave her."

"What!" Koby said loudly and sat down in a chair as Elan continued. "Bekka feels that if the two of you break up she will have to leave the team and return to the Ice Caves. And like us; she has made this place and all of you her home and family." No one in the room made a comment while Elan talked.

"Elan, I am confused. Does she want to stay with me?"

"Koby you two really need to talk about your feelings," Elan scolded. "How can you have a relationship and not understand these things about each other?"

191

"We've tried but Bekka always tells me that she feels like she is so young and there are so many things she hasn't done or seen that I feel like she thinks our relationship is temporary."

"Bekka does want to see and do things. And she never considered she would get pregnant," Elan said. "Bekka and Cassandra talk about these things all of the time because Cassandra and I have been trying so hard to have a baby. I know that Bekka really cares for you and I know she is very scared by all of this. But Koby I shouldn't be the one telling you these things. The two of you have to learn to talk."

"Elan you are right about everything," Koby said in a daze.

"Son," Maxwell said. "You should collect your thoughts before you talk to her. How do you feel about all of this? Do you want a wife and family?"

"I know this must sound crazy because just about every woman in this household is pregnant but I never, I mean, I just didn't even consider that Bekka could get pregnant and we have sex all of the time so I can't even begin to explain this."

"Whether you decide to marry or not," Elan said. "Bekka is really scared right now and I don't think she knows what she wants."

Gabriel handed Koby a glass of whiskey. "You look like you need this." Koby emptied the glass with one gulp.

"Do you know what you are going to say to her?" Maxwell asked.

"No," Koby replied. "I really care about Bekka and I don't want to lose her. I don't want her going back to the Ice Caves."

"Do you care about her enough to marry her?" Maxwell asked.

"I think so," Koby said then he looked at the others in the room. "I am sure that sounded awful. You all married so fast and I just couldn't understand that. How do you know when the girl is the right one?"

"You just do," Misha said. "And the fact that you are asking that question makes me wonder if Bekka isn't the one for you."

"But there is a baby now, and you have to think about that child," Gabriel said. "Koby whether you and Bekka are ready for the responsibilities of marriage and parenthood I don't know. But I do know that both of you are good, loving people and would make great parents. Look how Bekka is with the children here. And we have all seen how you take care of her. Elan is right you both have a lot of talking to do. But tell Bekka that if you two break up over this, she doesn't have to leave the team. She is part of this family and we will welcome another baby."

Koby suddenly felt like a small boy. "Do you think I should talk with Emeral first?" Koby asked Maxwell. "I mean she just always seems to know the perfect things to say."

"I would look for her now because she was going to go to the castle and help Renya with the plans for the big baby celebration," Maxwell said. Koby stood up and quickly left the room.

Elan now looked at the others. "Do you think it was wrong of me to tell him?"

"No," Maxwell said. "If Bekka is scared now I think Koby's initial reaction would have upset her. I will be honest I don't know if either of them are ready for this."

"Maybe I shouldn't tell you this," Elan said. "But Cassandra told Bekka that if she and Koby don't want the baby that we would adopt it."

"What did Bekka say?" Maxwell asked.

"Cassandra said that Bekka just cried."

Emeral had already left the house by time Koby started to look for her. He was torn as to whether he should go to the castle or look for Bekka. When Koby realized that he wanted to talk to Emeral so she could help him organize his own thoughts, he left the house and flew to the castle.

Marie escorted Koby into the Great Hall where Emeral, Laurel and Renya were sitting at a table that was covered with lists and samples of material. "Emeral I am sorry to interrupt but can I talk to you for a moment?" asked Koby.

"Koby are you alright you look like you have seen a ghost?" Emeral asked as she stood up from the table.

"That's why I want to talk with you."

"You two can have this room," Renya said and she and Laurel each grabbed items from the table and left the room.

"I need your advice," Koby said as he sat down next to Emeral. "This morning most of the men in the house had a meeting in Gabriel's study because everyone's wife wants them to explain, well explain sex to Thor. As I was leaving the room, Elan stood up and gave me a talking to. He told me that Bekka is pregnant and is afraid to tell me. Elan said Bekka is afraid that I will break up with her and she will have to move back to the Ice Caves."

"I asked Elan a lot of questions and he scolded me and said that Bekka and I need to start talking things out, which is true. But when we do talk she always says there are so many things that she wants to see and do that I feel she doesn't want a permanent relationship; so I have been expecting her to break up with me. Maxwell was in the room and asked me how I felt about the news. Emeral I didn't know how I felt other than shocked."

Koby was talking very fast as he spoke to Emeral, "Then I asked the others how they knew their wives were the ones they should marry. Misha said you just do and if I had to ask that question that perhaps Bekka wasn't the one for me. Elan said that Bekka is really scared by all of this. I know I am just rambling but I need you to help me sort my head out before I talk to her."

"Do you love Bekka?"

"I think so, shouldn't I know for sure?"

"Does she love you?"

"I don't know."

"How do you feel about being a father?"

194

"In shock. I like children I guess I just didn't think about the possibility."

"Let's start from a different point of view. Do you want Bekka in your life?"

"Yes."

"Would you take care of her and the baby?"

"Of course, I wouldn't turn my back on them?"

"What if Bekka doesn't want to be a mother?"

"I don't understand what you are asking?"

"I am just trying to have you think about this situation from all sides. What if Bekka doesn't want the baby; would you still want it?"

"I can imagine her not wanting it; you know how she is with children."

"Koby now really think about this answer. What if Bekka said she was returning to the Ice Caves but she didn't want the baby; would you want it?"

"I'm not giving my child up for adoption but you know you would end up helping me raise it."

Emeral smiled. "Koby you and Bekka have been having so much fun that you haven't considered the responsibilities of your actions. She may be as unclear of many things as you are. But you know you want Bekka in your life and you know you want the baby; tell her these things and be honest about the rest. After you have talked why don't you and Bekka come and talk to Maxwell and me; you are our son and we will help you in whatever way we can."

"What's this?" Lila asked with a big smile when she looked up from playing with the children and saw Koby standing in the doorway of the playroom with a large bouquet of flowers in his hand. Bekka was sitting on the floor near Joey and looked up when she heard Lila speak.

195

"Bekka can I talk to you?" Koby asked. He was smiling but as soon as he spoke Bekka started to cry.

"Bekka what is wrong?" Christopher asked with concern.

"Nothing Honey; I will be back." Bekka stood up and walked out of the playroom with Koby.

"You know don't you?" Bekka asked as the tears were running down her face.

"Yes," Koby said and put his arm around her shoulders. "Let's go to our room to talk." Neither of them spoke as they walked through the house and up the stairs to their room. After they entered the room Koby closed the door and Bekka turned and looked at him without speaking.

"I'm not really sure where to begin," he said. "Even though we have been together for some time I realize now there is so much we never talked about. How could you even think that I would break up with you because you are pregnant?"

"Elan talked to you didn't he?"

"Yes and I am glad he did. I have always considered him like a little brother but he really gave me a talking to and he was right about everything but you haven't answered my question."

"I'm not sure I know the answer," Bekka said and sat down on their bed. "Koby don't misunderstand what I am going to say. You treat me wonderfully but I just never thought this was a permanent relationship. You're right maybe it's because we have never talked about things but I didn't think you wanted to be saddled down with a family."

"I am surprised to hear you say that; actually I thought you were the one who wanted a temporary relationship I think that is why I was starting to get jealous about your friends. Bekka I will admit I was shocked when Elan told me, both about the pregnancy and your fears."

"I wanted to have my thoughts straight before we talked so I talked to Emeral. She thinks you and I have been having so much fun that we haven't considered the consequences of what we have been doing, like falling in love and having a baby."

"I think she is right." Koby set the flowers on a dresser and sat down on the bed next to Bekka. "I know I want you in my life and I know I want the baby but I really need to hear how you feel?"

"Koby I don't want to lose you and I want the baby but I will be honest I have been so scared that I haven't thought a lot through."

"So we agree that we want to stay together and raise the baby?" Koby asked.

"Yes."

"Bekka would you want to stay with me if we weren't having a baby?"

"Yes," she whispered.

"You are always telling me about all of the things that you want to see and do," Koby said. "You can still do those things and Elan made it sound like you thought you would have to leave the team. This is your home, even if we would have decided to break up you wouldn't have to leave." Koby put his arms around Bekka and hugged her; she was crying on his shoulder.

"So the question is do you want to get married or continue living together?"

"I don't know," Bekka cried. "What do you want?"

"I will be honest I don't know and I have to admit I am still a little in shock by all of this; we probably should get married."

"I think you're right," Bekka said as she tried to stop crying. "You know I am already showing, so the question is do you want a wedding where everyone can see that I am pregnant or do you want to wait until after the baby is born?"

"Bekka first I don't care what other people think and second you aren't showing?"

"Yes I am," Bekka said with emphasis and stood up. She was wearing a loose fitting dress which she now pulled tight over her stomach.

Koby laughed. "You aren't showing very much. I don't care when we marry except that I think it should be after Elan and Cassandra because they have put so much time and planning into their wedding I don't want to take away from their day."

"Oh I agree," Bekka said sincerely and sat back down on the bed.

"You know how us boys are; we kind of let Emeral plan the weddings, maybe because we are lazy I don't know. I am trying to say that right this moment I don't know what I want for a wedding but I want to get us different living quarters and have a nursery built right away. Have you thought about what you want for a wedding?"

"No because I thought you were going to break up with me," Bekka was smiling and crying at the same time. "Should we wait until after Misha and Diana have their ceremony?"

"I don't know. Emeral said that we should talk to her and Maxwell after we decided what we wanted. Let's do that today. If we decide we want a big wedding Emeral will have some idea how long it takes to prepare things and that should help us figure out when we want to marry."

"Bekka, Elan really held a mirror up to me this morning and made me realize a lot of things. Just because we have made these decisions doesn't mean we don't have a lot of other things to talk about. Do you realize I know more about Cassandra's and Diana's families than I do yours? And I talked with Joao; both Misha and I apologized to him for acting jealous. He told me about all of you being friends since childhood, why didn't you ever tell me those things?"

"I don't know. It's not that I wanted to keep things from you." Bekka said thoughtfully and was quiet for a few moments. "You know Elan, Cassandra, Melinda, Joao, Dack and I have been friends for so long that I guess it is just easy because we don't have to explain ourselves but now that you are asking me these things I realize I haven't talked to anyone in the household about my life."

198

Then Bekka laughed, "Well except for Christopher he asks me a lot of questions. Sometimes that little boy seems so much older than he is. I don't know if I told you but when Luca and Lila first met, well, you know it was a horrible situation and Luca was wounded saving them. Christopher was so scared that he wouldn't leave Luca's side. So Luca would give him money and tell Christopher to take Fala and me into Nora and buy us things. We all had so much fun. Fala and I felt like Christopher's big sisters. Then when she was murdered; it was that little boy who spent so much time with me."

"Maybe we should have him in our wedding," Koby said with a grin.

"Really?" Bekka laughed. "I would like that."

"I am going to the castle to get Emeral," Koby said. "I wonder if Maxwell can leave the fort."

"They are both here; they walked in moments before you came home."

Koby stood up and held his hand out to Bekka. "Are you ready to talk to them?" he asked. And the young couple walked out of the bedroom.

Chapter XIV
Shanksaw

"I am sorry this meeting is starting late but it has been a very busy morning," Gabriel said. "Before we get started Koby wants to say a few words. The meeting was being held in Gabriel's study, Bekka and Koby were sitting next to each other and both stood up and were holding hands.

"I just wanted to tell everyone that Bekka and I are having a baby and getting married, yes in that order," Koby said and many laughed. "We haven't made any other decisions other than I need Calen to draw up some plans for chambers that include a nursery." Everyone in the room clapped as Koby and Bekka returned to their seats.

"Last night Misha's team returned from Lentz and they briefed us on their mission but since everyone was so exhausted I didn't want to brief them about the Shanksaw mission until today," Gabriel said.

"Archetenus and Jared are becoming regular patrons of the Racing Horse Tavern. The plan is for them to become recognizable faces there before they make contact with Shanksaw, who is in that tavern most days and every night. Shanksaw always sits at the same table that not only gives him a view of the front door and the front windows but also a view of the door that leads from behind the bar to what we believe is a store room. Jared and Archetenus why don't you tell the rest?"

Both men now walked to the front of the room. "Jared and me have had a lot of experience with men like Shanksaw. Most mercenaries are careful to the point of being paranoid. We want him to get used to seeing us around or we won't have any chance of getting information from him. So far Jared and me are entering and leaving the tavern separately and acting like we don't know each other."

Archetenus continued, "Edward walked into the tavern on the third day that we were watching Shanksaw. And as soon as Edward entered the place, Shanksaw and a couple other men tensed up and watched him real carefully. We believe they recognized him as one of Sudfad's men; so Edward won't be working the tavern portion of the mission anymore."

"But the good thing about what happened when Edward walked in," Jared said. "Is that Archetenus and I figured out who some of Shanksaw's men are. They enter the tavern and all sit separately and act like they are strangers. Shanksaw is very careful and if he motions to anyone it is very subtle."

"So far we haven't seen anyone sitting at Shanksaw's table to just talk to him but we have seen him handing pouches to men as they walk past his table. We believe these pouches are payoffs. Shanksaw likes to play cards but he doesn't do much talking when he is playing so we haven't figured out how he is passing information and we haven't seen him with any demons."

Archetenus looked at Gabriel, "Do you want us to continue?"

"Sure."

"Since we believe Edward was recognized, Natasha has gotten him a fake mustache, beard and hair piece to wear and bought him some different clothes. Edward and Natasha have been going to all of the hotels in the area trying to see if Shanksaw has registered a room anywhere. So far they have found four hotels where he has paid for rooms. We think he is so paranoid that he probably sleeps in different locations every night," Archetenus said.

"Hannah, Lila and Vivian wanted to either pretend they were patrons of these hotels or staff so they could gather information but the places that Edward and Natasha discovered are so seedy it wouldn't be safe for the girls to step foot in those places. We are hoping that Thor heals enough that he can help with this part of the mission," Jared explained.

"We've been wondering if Shanksaw has a room at the Racing Horse Tavern or if the tavern has some hidden tunnels because both Rualas and Enrops have been trying to follow him and no one see's Shanksaw going to the tavern but he is suddenly there," Jared said. "Natasha is trying to figure out a way to steal keys to some of Shanksaw's hotel rooms. But like Archetenus said, these are the kind of hotels that cater just to criminals so it really isn't safe for the girls and these ain't fancy rooms so there aren't any balcony doors for the Rualas to get into."

Archetenus spoke again, "We were thinking about asking some of the men from Lentz to help us but everyone has seen them at the big celebrations and weddings that Sudfad and Renya have. The problem we are having is everyone here knows most of us except for Diana and Thor."

"Do they serve food at the Racing Horse Tavern?" Vivian asked.

"Yes and the bartender usually brings it to the tables," Archetenus said. "We haven't seen the kitchen."

"I haven't talked this over with Raphael yet, but why don't Diana and I dress like we are peasants and see if we can get a job cooking or cleaning there. If nothing else perhaps we can find the rooms that you haven't been able to see yet."

"That's a good idea," Gabriel said. "Raphael, Misha what do you have to say?"

"Of course neither of us really want the girls doing this," Raphael said. "But both the Sanuri and Miranda had those messages for us so I am going to say yes."

"So am I," said Misha.

"But I think Vivian is going to need to change her appearance," Raphael said. "Our wives are all so beautiful that they draw attention."

"I can take care of that," Natasha said. "Sudfad and Renya routinely have groups of actors perform at the castle. There is a small room at the castle that is filled with outfits, wigs, makeup and all sorts of things for the plays and I am now the keeper of that room."

"My only concern," said Diana. "Is I still can't walk in the shoes women wear here and that will draw attention to me."

"Diana I will work with you after this meeting," Hannah said. "And if you really can't pick it up perhaps I can wrap one of your feet and you will just have to say you have an injury."

"Archetenus and Jared, you know we are going to want you watching over our wives," Misha said.

"Of course," Archetenus said. "But so far Jared and me haven't seen who cooks or cleans there so if the girls get hired they won't be walking around inside of the tavern."

"I want to do more," Thor said.

"And we want you to," Raphael said. "But you're just not healed enough." Raphael now stood up and addressed the group. Gabriel, Thor and I have been here trying to find out information about Shanksaw. Erebus is healed enough that he has also been helping us and we have found absolutely nothing. It is like Shanksaw didn't exist before he came here."

"Is he one of those demons wearing a human's body?" Joao asked.

"We'd have to splash a little blessed water on him to figure that out," Gabriel said.

"I have an idea," Hannah said excitedly. "Gabriel remember when we met I had an office with an apartment attached in Nora. Why don't I get another office, some place close to the Racing Horse Tavern? It doesn't matter if I am recognized because everyone should know I am a physician."

"That would give us a headquarters in the city so it wouldn't look suspicious if any of you were there. Also it is a great way to get information about what is going on in the city. And if one of you somehow hurts Shanksaw you can bring him to me as a patient then we can find out if he is a demon."

Gabriel stood up from his chair and walked over to Hannah and kissed her on the lips. "Raphael and I will go into the city today and look for a building."

"I can be Hannah's assistant," Lila said. "She will need one."

"For those of you who weren't in Nora with us," Gabriel explained. "Raul and I were looking for some men. We were walking down the main street of Nora asking people questions. This is when Roch still ruled Nora so everyone was afraid. Suddenly Hannah runs up to us and tells us to pretend we know her. She got us off the street and gave us sanctuary in her home and office."

"When we walked into her office it was filled with weapons. The apartment could be entered through the medical area or from a back door in an alley, so the Rualas could come and go without being seen. It was a perfect setup."

"Can I work in the office?" Thor asked. "I am sure I could help with something until I am better."

"He could spy on the tavern and we could say he is a patient," Hannah suggested. "And everyone can help with moving furniture and equipment so it won't be suspicious having all of the Rualas in an area."

"Calen, Luca and Dagon come with Raphael and me," Gabriel said. "We will want a place that you can easily access even if that means having some work done on the building. Calen you might be drawing up some more plans." Gabriel turned to Hannah. "After this mission we could probably use this building for other things but do you think you would like to have a practice in the city? It could be open as much as you are comfortable with."

"Hannah smiled, "I think I would like that. And I think now might be a good time to tell everyone of our idea."

"The other night Hannah and I were talking about educations for all of the children here and Sudfad's learning center. Hannah studied medicine at Cicero College which is just a short distance from here. But they also offer studies in many other fields. If any of you would like to go to college Hannah and I will pay for your educations. We aren't pressuring any of you but the offer is there and we will help you as much as we can."

"Honestly I would just love it if one of you wanted to become a physician too," Hannah said.

"You mean we could study anything we want?" Dack asked.

"If any of you would like to become a priest we will set you up with studies at the new learning center because that is not a field offered at Cicero," Gabriel said. "But we aren't putting any restrictions on what you want to study. Hannah and I are both big believers in education and we have more money than we need so we would like to share our good fortune with all of you."

"Every person in this room is bright enough to attend any college you want but understand there will be a lot of work involved so you will have to organize your time."

"Thor and I didn't go to a regular school, Joshua and Iris taught us," Diana said. "Would we be allowed to go to college?"

"Both you and Thor are extremely bright people," Gabriel said. "But all of you should know that both Raul and Simon attended Cicero College and Sudfad and Renya are benefactors of that school. We can get you accepted into college but you will have to do the work."

"Gabriel and Hannah did not tell Vivian and me about this idea, which I think is wonderful," Raphael said. "Vivian and I will also help any one of you. From the looks on your faces many of you seem interested in the idea. Gabriel and I will go to the college and get information for you after we look at buildings in Salar."

Vivian looked at Raphael, "I have never thought about it but I think I would like to go to college."

"Do you know what you would like to study?" he asked with a proud smile on his face.

"Some of the same courses that you and Gabriel did; history and ancient languages."

"I am very proud of you," Raphael said and hugged Vivian then he turned to the room. "We have our first student who will be next?"

Elan stood up but looked very embarrassed. "Hannah I would love to learn medicine but wouldn't I need two arms?" The entire room became quiet. "I've learned how to do a lot with one arm but I don't think it would be enough." Before Hannah could answer Cassandra stood up.

"Could I be his arms? I could study with him and help him when he needs it."

Hannah couldn't answer because she was crying so she looked at Gabriel for help. "The classes will be difficult and time consuming even with Hannah helping you. I want you to understand that since you are starting a family."

Hannah was trying to compose herself, "If you two want to learn medicine I will sponsor you; I can do that as an experienced physician. You can both work with me at my job for experience. In fact you can come with me starting tomorrow and see if you would like it."

"You should study medicine," Luca said to Lila. "You are a natural."

"But we are going to have a baby."

Luca looked at Gabriel and Raphael, "Would Cicero prevent her from taking classes because we have children?"

"Under normal circumstances I don't know," Gabriel said. "But I did mention this idea to Raul and all of you have the backing of the Royal Family. No college is going to turn you down. But I still want to stress there is a great deal of work involved."

"With all the babies coming maybe it's time we hired some nurses," Luca said. "Emeral we know you want to take care of the grandbabies but you only have two arms. Personally I am not interested in going to college, at least not now, but I don't think any of you should not go because you are starting families. We will figure things out." Lila threw her arms around Luca and kissed him on the lips. "I guess you've got another student," Luca said with a grin.

After the meeting Misha returned to the fort and told Edward and Maxwell everything that was said. Since Edward was recognized by Shanksaw it was decided that he and Maxwell would work at the fort so others could be free to work on the mission. Both Edward and Maxwell were pleased with the ideas that had come up during the meeting and Maxwell was particularly proud of those who he considered his new children wanting to attend college. "I will bet Emeral was not happy about the idea of hiring nurses," Maxwell said.

"Luca was right, there are a lot of babies coming, Emeral can't possibly take care of them all at once, besides she needs to enjoy life too," Misha said.

"I will bet you a bottle of whiskey that she wants to choose the nurses," Maxwell said then laughed.

Gabriel, Raphael, Calen, Luca and Dagon stopped at the castle before going into Salar so they could brief Sudfad about their plans. Sudfad gave them the names of land owners in the city and information about the men they would be dealing with. Both Sudfad and Renya were pleased to hear about Gabriel's and Raphael's offer to pay for the educations of the team members.

"I will personally write letters for every member of your team who wants to go to college," Sudfad said. "And I particularly like the idea that several of them are thinking about studying medicine. I need to have people I can trust and that entire affair with Philip put a bad taste in my mouth. You tell them that if they successfully complete their studies I will hire them; but of course they will still be members of your team."

"That will make them very happy," Gabriel said. "To say nothing about being a great motivator. Just so you are aware, once this mission is completed we will keep the building and Hannah will also see patients in the city. She will be sponsoring the members who want to study medicine so they will be working out of that building also."

Jared returned to the Racing Horse Tavern, it was late morning and most of the tables were open. He chose a table that gave him a view of the front door and Shanksaw's table. Shanksaw was sitting at his table boldly watching everyone who entered. There were dirty plates stacked on his table; enough for several men. Jared wondered if he missed something important while he was at the meeting at Gabriel's house.

Archetenus paid for rooms at each of the hotels where Shanksaw had rooms. It was common practice for people not to register under their real names in hotels such as these. While Archetenus was paying for his room at the Staghorne Hotel the clerk left the desk to break-up a fight in the lobby. Archetenus grabbed the ledger and to his surprise saw Shanksaw's name written on it. Shanksaw was in room seventeen while Archetenus was one floor above in room twenty-three. Archetenus was not so lucky at the next three hotels.

Jared was playing solitaire and sipping whiskey when he noticed that Shanksaw seemed to be watching the street intently.

Jared was sitting with his back to the windows so he stood up and walked to the bar and ordered some food. When Jared looked through the windows he saw Gabriel, Raphael, Calen and two men Jared didn't recognize walking along the street that was opposite the Racing Horse Tavern.

Jared glanced back at Shanksaw who was staring intently at Gabriel and the others. Jared remained at the bar until the bartender handed him a plate with meatloaf and potatoes. "This looks real good, you do the cookin?" asked Jared.

"No, my brother's wife cooks. Great cook she is but mean as a hornet."

"This morning I met two young girls looking for work, they said they were looking for cooking or cleaning jobs. I don't know if they can do either but I will tell you they sure were easy on the eyes. Real pretty little things even in their raggedy clothes. Hutas killed their family, I kind a felt sorry for them. Do you know any place they might find work?"

"You say they are pretty?"

"Like angels, one has white blonde hair and the other black, but they ain't no whores they are just down on their luck."

"Think you will be seeing them again?"

"Sure hoping to, hoping I can get on their good side if'n I help them find some work."

"Send them by tomorrow morning, I'll talk to them."

"Thank ya kindly." Jared said and returned to his table.

Shanksaw was a man who appeared to always be aware of every little thing that occurred in the tavern; so Jared was surprised at how mesmerized Shanksaw was by Gabriel and the men he was with. Shanksaw was staring so intently that Jared started to wonder if Shanksaw was uttering a spell.

Suddenly Shanksaw stood up and quickly left the tavern. Jared watched as Shanksaw crossed the street and walked past Gabriel and the men who had just exited a building and were now standing on the walkway looking at the front of the building.

Jared saw a movement in the corner of his left eye and saw Luca and Dagon moving on a roof top, they too were watching Shanksaw.

Jared watched as Shanksaw walked into a store then walked back out after a few minutes and was once again walking towards Gabriel and the others. Gabriel, Raphael and Calen were well aware of Shanksaw's movements even though they appeared to be concentrating on the building. As Shanksaw was walking past Gabriel he moved to his right and deliberately bumped into Gabriel.

"I am so sorry," Shanksaw said pleasantly. "I need to get my mind on what I am doing, please forgive me."

Gabriel turned and faced Shanksaw. "That's quite alright we were taking up the walkway. I'm buying a building for my wife."

"Buying your wife a whole building that's a strange gift," Shanksaw responded.

"She's a physician and will be opening a practice here in the city. She is very good at what she does so I am expecting she will have a lot of patients, so I want a large building for her."

"Well once she has opened shop, I will come and see her if I am ailing," Shanksaw said and returned to the Racing Horse Tavern.

The building that Gabriel purchased was not empty; there was a small tobacco store on the first floor. The owners of the building made arrangements to move this store to another building but Gabriel wasn't going to wait for the move before he started construction on the building. Calen returned to the house to work on diagrams while Luca and Dagon stayed in Salar and watched Shanksaw. Gabriel and Raphael rode to Cicero College.

"I was a little apprehensive when Shanksaw came by the second time I thought he was going to stab you," Raphael said.

"I thought the same thing, but he was just sizing us up. But we did find a weakness, he was so curious about what we were doing he couldn't contain himself. We can work with that."

"I think we should have Edward or one of the Rualas in Hannah's office all the time, just in case the girls need help," Raphael said.

"I agree. By the way this college thing, Hannah and I weren't keeping it from you we hadn't really finished discussing the idea before we presented it to the group. What Hannah originally asked me was if she could pay for the educations of all the children in the house; we started talking and it wasn't until today that the idea really took form."

"I figured as much. But I was pleasantly surprised when I watched the faces of our team as you were explaining your idea. I will bet more people will take you up on the offer but that might mean we are short on the team at times. So I was thinking; you know Vivian and I are building chambers for her family. I don't know how long or how often they might stay but I am sure we can talk Joshua and Vivian's brothers into helping us if we need them."

Gabriel laughed loudly, "I have been thinking about that too."

That evening Gabriel was holding his usual mission meeting before dinner. Both Archetenus and Jared attended and talked about what they had seen and done during the day then left to return to the Racing Horse Tavern.

"This will be easier than I thought," Vivian said. "Jared already got us in the door."

"Just be careful," Misha warned.

Gabriel told of the building he had purchased and Shanksaw's encounter with them. "After meeting Shanksaw both Raphael and I want someone in Hannah's office at all times as protection. If any of you would like we can take you to the building tomorrow so you can see it." Gabriel turned to Hannah and said, "Calen is drawing up plans similar to what you had in Nora, you should get together with him and work on those."

"We told Sudfad that some of you wanted to attend Cicero and he said he would personally write letters for each one of you," Raphael said then looked at Gabriel and smiled.

"Tell them the rest," Gabriel said.

"Sudfad said that any of you who will be studying medicine will have a job waiting for you once you successfully complete your studies. But you will be working on the team also." Lila, Elan and Cassandra all smiled.

"Tomorrow morning Jared plans to be at the tavern about seven, Vivian and Diana I want you to arrive there shortly after that," Gabriel said. "If you don't get hired try to study the layout of the building. And after dinner tonight all the men are meeting in my study." Natasha looked at Diana and smiled.

"Misha can you wait just a minute?" Natasha asked as he was walking into Gabriel's study after dinner. Natasha pulled Misha aside. "Diana would like you to go up to your chambers for a couple of minutes."

"Is she alright?"

"I think she just wants you to help her with something."

When Misha entered their chambers dozens of candles were lit and there was a fire in the hearth. Diana walked out of the bedroom wearing a light blue lace nightgown and carrying two glasses of wine. Misha looked at her and smiled then he turned around and locked the door.

"You look absolutely beautiful," Misha said as he walked up to Diana and kissed her.

"Do you like it because Natasha took me shopping and I bought quite a few."

"I love it," he said and kissed Diana again.

"I also bought massage oils."

Misha laughed. "Is this because of our conversation this morning?"

"Yes, I felt really bad because I had no idea what you were talking about," she said with a frown.

"I didn't say it to make you feel bad."

"I know, but Misha you have to remember there is a lot I don't know so instead of feeling hurt because I didn't do something you might have to tell me what you want me to do. After you left this morning I talked to Natasha and she explained a lot of things to me."

Misha laughed and kissed her again, "I promise I will do better at telling you things." Then he paused and looked seriously at Diana. "I am going to tell you something that I don't want you to repeat. This morning Elan was the one who told Koby that Bekka was pregnant."

"Koby didn't really handle it well at first and kept asking Elan all these questions about Bekka. Elan scolded Koby and said that he and Bekka should talk to each other more. Apparently neither Bekka nor Koby even considered she might get pregnant so it was a shock to both of them. After listening to Koby and Elan talk I realized there is a lot that you and I haven't discussed."

"Like what?"

"Do you want to have children?"

"I thought we talked about that."

"All I remember you saying is you wouldn't be able to catch flying babies," both Misha and Diana laughed.

"Of course I want babies, don't you?"

"Yes, when do you want to start a family?"

"I don't understand what you are asking me."

"When a couple is working on a baby they have sex a lot more frequently."

Diana laughed, "Then we must be working on a baby already."

"Luca and Lila and Vivian and Raphael wanted babies as soon as they married. Is that what you want?"

"I wouldn't be upset if I found out I was pregnant right away, but I would prefer to wait a little while. You and I need some time to get to know each other and this way of living here is all new to me. And I want to go on that mission to Ryed."

Misha smiled and brushed back a strand of Diana's hair. "Well my beautiful wife, you and I are of the exact same mind." Misha took the glasses out of Diana's hands and set them on a small table then he picked her up and carried her into their bedroom.

Chapter XV
Disguises

"Look at these beautiful morning cakes," Hannah gushed as the women were setting the table for breakfast.

"I was so excited about going to school that I couldn't sleep," Lila said. "So I got up and baked." Lila walked over and kissed Hannah on the cheek. "Thank you so much. I have always dreamed about going to college."

"This makes me so happy," Hannah said. "You will have to tell Gabriel and Raphael how excited you are because we really didn't know how anyone would react to our offer. What Gabriel hasn't told you yet is that we plan on paying for the educations of all the children; of course it will be their decisions if they want to attend college."

"Really!" Lila gasped. "You are wonderful, we must tell the others."

"I am sorry I am late," Diana said as she ran into the dining room. "What needs to be done?"

"You can pour coffee and milk," said Hannah.

Misha walked around the table to Natasha, who was setting down plates. He twirled Natasha around and kissed her on the cheek, which made her giggle. Calen was standing in the dining room holding baby Lily. "Why are you kissing my wife you have one of your own?" Calen asked and laughed loudly because he already knew the answer to his question.

"She knows," Misha said with a smile and walked over to his seat at the table.

The dining room was starting to fill with people as they took their seats at the table. "How is everyone feeling this morning?" Natasha asked with a laugh as she saw the faces of some of the men.

"We might have drank too much whiskey last night," Koby said. "Thank god you girls made those snacks up for us so we had something to soak up the alcohol."

214

Natasha laughed loudly. "Did you have a good time?"

"Yes," Dagon said. "We stopped getting together after everyone started to marry off. Last night we all kept saying we have to do that more often."

"Good," Natasha replied and giggled when she again looked at how white Koby's face was.

Gabriel and Raphael walked into the dining room and Lila kissed each of them on their cheeks. "I was so excited about going to school I couldn't sleep last night so I got up and baked. Thank you so much." Both Gabriel and Raphael smiled.

Luca was taking his seat at the table. "Honey if you wanted to go to school so badly why didn't you say something before?"

"My family was so poor that I just lost hope that I would ever be able to go to school and since I met you and moved here we always seem to have so much going on that I forgot about it."

"Where is Vivian?" Hannah asked Raphael.

"She is sick again and upset because this is the morning that she and Diana try to infiltrate that tavern."

"I'll get her something," Hannah said and quickly left the room.

Thor and Maxwell walked into the dining room together. "Thor are you alright?" Lila asked.

Thor laughed and sat down at the table, "I drank too much whiskey last night."

"Apparently the boys all had a good time," Maxwell said with a grin.

"Misha we missed you last night," said Luca.

"Diana had a nice surprise for me," Misha said with a smile as he held Diana's chair out for her to sit down.

"Misha I am not kidding about this," Natasha said. "You have changed since you got married. You used to be grumpy a lot, now you seem so calm and happy." Misha laughed.

"She's right," Maxwell said. "Marriage agrees with you."

"I'm not arguing with you. Maxwell I have heard you and Emeral talk over the years but I didn't really understand what you were saying before," Misha said. "There is a contentment when you find the right person." Diana kissed Misha on the cheek then quickly turned and looked at her brother.

"Thor that is exactly way I am going to find you a girlfriend and don't even think about arguing with me about the subject." Everyone at the table laughed including Thor.

"Speaking of Emeral, where is she?" Natasha asked.

"Out inspecting the structure of the house," Maxwell said with a grin.

"Why?" Gabriel asked.

"I will let her tell you."

Vivian and Hannah walked into the dining room and took their seats; within a moment Emeral entered the dining room and addressed the family. "Yesterday I wasn't too happy with Luca's comment about hiring nurses."

"I knew it," Luca said and laughed.

"But then I realized we will be having four babies born in a relatively short period of time. Now Gabriel and Raphael you put me in charge of the household while everyone is working on missions." Gabriel and Raphael both grinned as they watched Emeral walk around the room. "And don't get me wrong I personally think all of you should take advantage of the opportunity that is being offered to you to attend college. But this is what I am thinking." Emeral walked to the opposite side of the dining room.

"I want to take this wall out; on the other side of this wall is the hallway and the children's playroom. I want to add another large room for a nursery and make the play room bigger and connect those two rooms with a door."

216

"This house is so big and spread out but everyone gathers in the same three rooms. The kitchen, the dining room and Gabriel's study. This way all the babies and children will be in a central area when all of you are gone or god forbid we have an emergency."

"That is a wonderful idea," Hannah said.

"I like it too," said Natasha.

"There is more," Emeral said. "I believe Luca is right we do need to hire nurses but I would like to be in charge of that. Of course we will need at least one nurse that is Ruala and I would like them to have some warrior training after that horrible situation that happened at the castle. Gabriel that means we might need a couple of bedrooms for the nurses. So what do all of you think?"

Emeral smiled as everyone applauded her ideas, when the clapping stopped Emeral said. "I will be putting a few extra baby beds in the nursery since everyone you work with either has or will be having babies."

"Emeral after breakfast I will give you money and you just go ahead with whatever you want," Gabriel said. "Your ideas are smart and practical and we all appreciate everything you do to care for our families. I don't want you paying for any of this so just tell me or Hannah when you need more money."

Jared was sitting in the Racing Horse Tavern watching for Vivian and Diana. Shanksaw had not yet arrived at the tavern. When Jared saw the two girls walking on the street he stood up and walked out of the tavern and met them.

"Jared I am so sorry we are late," Vivian said. "I couldn't stop puking this morning."

"I understand, Zoya is going through the same thing, it hit her later. I didn't tell the bartender you would be here at any particular time so you really aren't late and you both look great. Remember Hutas killed your family, the rest of the story you can make up yourselves."

Jared escorted Vivian and Diana into the tavern; the three walked up to the bar. Since it was so early there were few patrons in the tavern and the bartender was busy stocking the bar. Jared slammed his fist on the bar a couple of times and the bartender walked out of the back room. "These are the two gals I told you about," Jared said. "I'll let you all talk." Jared turned around and returned to his table.

The bartender smiled exposing two broken front teeth. That fella was right you two are sure enough pretty. I'm Gus and I own this place. My sister-in-law Berta has been helping me out with the cooking but she is ornery as hell and wants to work less hours. That fella said you two wanted jobs cooking and cleaning?"

"Yes," Vivian said. "Our mother was a great cook and she taught us both. We are hard workers, you won't be disappointed."

"Have you girls got a place to stay cuz I got a few rooms in back that I rent out?"

"We met a nice family yesterday and they gave us a room until we get on our feet," Diana said.

"Well come on back here and meet Berta, she might bite your heads off but she will be glad to share the work."

Since the tavern was almost empty it was easy for Jared to listen to Gus, Diana and Vivian talking. The revelation that there were rooms in the back of the tavern explained how Shanksaw would suddenly appear at his table.

"Berta now be nice," Gus said as the three walked into the small kitchen behind the bar. "These two girls just lost their family to Hutas and need some work cooking and cleaning. You're always complaining that you want help, so don't scare them off."

Berta was large for a woman; in fact Berta was large for a man. She had large muscular arms from a life of hard work. Her brown hair was pulled tightly back exposing a face that once was pretty but now showed the signs of a difficult life. There was no nonsense about Berta; she was at the bar to work not to make friends. She didn't speak to either Diana or Vivian until Gus left the kitchen.

218

"He's a fool," Berta said then looked at Vivian. "Can you cook?"

"Berta our family was poor and we had nine brothers besides grandparents. Diana and I grew up doing the house chores. We are good cooks and we sure know how to clean and we will work real hard. Just tell us what you want us to do."

"Gus serves breakfast, lunch and dinner here. Every day he writes on a board what the meals will be for the next day so customers come back. I need about a dozen apple pies baked to start with.

"I can do that," Diana said. "Just show me where the supplies are."

"What do you want me to do?" asked Vivian.

"The lunch menu is ham, corn on the cob, mashed potatoes and apple pie. The hams are already in the oven, I need potatoes peeled and corn husked."

Vivian and Diana wanted to stay employed at the tavern so they worked hard to impress Berta. They spoke little except to ask Berta questions and they didn't take any breaks. When the first apple pies were done baking, Diana put a slice onto a plate and handed it to Berta to taste.

Berta took a bite and rolled the pastry around in her mouth for a moment. "It's good, it's real good." Both Vivian and Diana washed dishes and kept the kitchen clean as they worked; which made Berta happy although she didn't say anything."

After lunch Berta and Vivian started preparing the dinner meal while Diana cleaned the dishes. "Berta is every day this busy because I don't know how you kept up with this by yourself?" Diana asked.

"Tell that to Gus, he drinks as much whiskey as he pours but he does pay well." Berta was quiet for a moment then she turned and looked at both Vivian and Diana. "You seem like nice girls; if Gus ever gets out of line with you, just hit him over the head with a frying pan." Both Vivian and Diana laughed.

"Is Gus prone to such things?" Vivian asked.

"When a man is drunk who knows," Berta said with disgust.

It was late afternoon by time Archetenus walked into the tavern. He walked past Jared's table and bought a drink at the bar. As Archetenus sipped his drink he turned around and looked at everyone in the tavern. Shanksaw was seated at his usual table by himself. Jared was playing solitary and pretending not to pay attention to Archetenus. Up to this point, Archetenus and Jared had not spoken to each other when they were in the tavern. Now Archetenus bought a bottle of whiskey and walked up to Jared's table.

"Know how to play poker?" Archetenus asked loudly.

"Got any money?" Jared replied without looking up.

"Wouldn't ask if I didn't."

"Have a seat," Jared said and looked up at Archetenus.

While Shanksaw listened to Archetenus and Jared he did not find their words or actions suspicious. All day long Shanksaw's attention had been drawn to the crew that was working on the building that Gabriel had just purchased. Shanksaw suddenly stood up and walked over to a window and stared across the street. Jared did not have a view of that window so he did not look up but Archetenus could see what Shanksaw was watching. Gabriel, Raphael, Hannah and many members of the team were now standing in front of the building looking at it then they all walked inside.

Since Shanksaw already knew the identities of most of the team members, Gabriel was not going to waste resources by trying to hide the members. Gabriel's plan was to try and draw Shanksaw out of the shadows by allowing him to watch the members working on the building and hope that Shanksaw would reveal more of his personality and plans.

Raphael and Gabriel had several buildings to choose from when looking for one to purchase. They deliberately chose the building that sat directly across the street from the Racing Horse Tavern not only because it was a prime site for surveillance but it was close enough to the tavern that Archetenus, Jared, Vivian and Diana could take shelter there if needed.

220

Both Archetenus and Jared found Shanksaw's behavior curious. Shanksaw was the type of man who made a good poker player because he did not reveal much of himself in his words or actions except when Gabriel was within sight. Shanksaw made it obvious that he was watching Gabriel and the team, so obvious that Archetenus and Jared started to wonder if he was putting on a show for them. They didn't know much about Shanksaw but they suspected he was intelligent and cunning and perhaps he realized they were only in the tavern to spy on him.

That night at the evening mission meeting Jared appeared but not Archetenus. "I want to talk first then leave," Jared said. "Archetenus and me think Shanksaw has either made us or suspects us. That man plays everything so close to the vest that he is like a statue except when he sees Gabriel on the street then he almost puts on a show and we think the show is for us. We need some new eyes in there to see if he acts the same way when we aren't in the building. Can any of those priests of yours make themselves look like criminals?" Jared was referring to the Patronus priests at the Cicero Headquarters.

"I am sure they can," Raphael said.

"And further more we know you have Enrops watching for spies, but a man like Shanksaw has to have people watching us. So I don't think the new faces you get here should be coming to the house. Now me and Archetenus are the kind of guys that spend time in taverns like that so we are just going to keep going there even if he knows who we are. But we need more eyes."

"Can't I go in?" Thor asked.

"Kid you look like a warrior but not a criminal. The kind of men that frequent a place like that drink hard, play cards and kill the people they think are cheating. You and Edward both don't have the presence for a place like that no matter how we dress you up. Do any of you know any ex-criminals besides me and Archetenus?"

"Did Shanksaw see the girls today?" Raphael asked with concern.

"He wasn't in sight when they came in and they spent the entire time in the kitchen."

"Thaos is an ex-criminal," Natasha said. "But he was pretty notorious so Shanksaw might know him."

"Archetenus and me think we should stop coming to the meetings and communicate with you through Enrops."

"Fine," Gabriel said. "This will be your last meeting. But be careful and we will get more men."

"Did the girls tell you about the back rooms?"

"We will," Vivian said. "Do you want to stay for our part?"

"Might as well," Jared said.

Both Vivian and Diana stood up, Vivian walked around to the front of the group while Diana handed out drawings.

"The bartender is also the owner and his name is Gus and he drinks a lot. His sister-in-law is the size of Thor but a nice lady, her name is Berta. She really does need help so Diana and I are working really hard to get her to trust us. Today we only cooked. But Gus told us he had rooms in the back that he rented out. We didn't see any of the rooms today but Berta was quite behind in her work so we hope that if we can help her catch up that they will give us cleaning tasks and we can get into those rooms."

"Diana is handing out drawings of the areas that we did see; which is the kitchen, the backdoor to the kitchen where food is delivered and the supply rooms. We did not see any other doors leading to cellars."

"That reminds me," Jared interrupted. "Archetenus spent the entire day finding ways to break into Shanksaw's hotel rooms and everyone looked like no one was living there. He probably has a room at the tavern. I'll tell you this Gabriel; if Shanksaw isn't putting on a show for me and Archetenus then there is something else going on. Like he has something real personal against you because he is acting like he is obsessed."

"Yesterday when I talked to him, he didn't look familiar," Gabriel said. "But you are right he did single me out. Jared I want you to know that I am hesitant to use Wetprian soldiers for your eyes because anyone we could trust has probably been seen in uniform."

"The priests can dirty themselves up but your comment about the presence of a criminal concerns me. We can get bodies into the tavern but we won't have anyone to deal with Shanksaw. I am going to talk to Edward and see if there is anyone in the Guardians who will fit that description and I am going to send a letter to Thaos."

"I guess I don't understand why you need someone with the presence of a criminal?" asked Thor.

"Because we need someone to make contact with Shanksaw and to get information from him," Gabriel explained. "The plan was for Archetenus and Jared to become regular patrons of that tavern then work their way up to talking to Shanksaw and hopefully have him offer them jobs. A man like Shanksaw is too smart, he will figure out a trap."

Over the next three days members of the Patronus started arriving in Salar. These men paid for rooms at the same hotels where Shanksaw had rooms. They frequented the taverns and milled around on the streets; many of the stores and taverns put chairs in front of their businesses for people to sit on and the Patronus took advantage of them.

It was late afternoon when Thaos and Stephan, the sons of Claudius walked into the Racing Horse Tavern. Jared and Archetenus were already in the tavern, Jared was playing cards with three other men and Archetenus was standing at the bar drinking. Neither Thaos nor Stephan acknowledged the presence of these men as they walked up to the bar and bought a bottle of whiskey and ordered food.

Thaos and Stephan took a table in the back of the room that gave them a good view of the doors and windows. They recognized Shanksaw from his description. Archetenus and Jared were discretely watching Shanksaw to see his reaction to Thaos and Stephan; if Shanksaw knew who these men were he was not revealing it.

Vivian and Diana had not wasted any of their time over the three days. They worked incredibly hard to help Berta organize the kitchen and prepare meals.

223

Although Vivian and Diana had only worked at the tavern for four days they were beginning to know the farmers who delivered meat and produce to the tavern. Berta would send the women to one of the general stores to place orders for flour, sugar and other items and the store owners would have the groceries delivered to the tavern. After four days the women had not seen anything suspicious at the tavern but they never went into the bar area.

"I don't know what is going on back here," Gus said with a grin. "But Berta hasn't complained about anything since you girls started."

"Gus I hope you know Berta has been doing the work of three people," Vivian said. "You should appreciate her." Gus laughed and walked out of the room.

"He's a fool," said Berta.

"I was going to tell him to give you a raise," Vivian said. "But then I thought I better not."

Berta laughed at Vivian's comment; it was the first time the girls had heard her laugh. "Saturday mornings I come in a couple of hours earlier to clean the rooms but since there is three of us why don't we all come in one hour earlier tomorrow."

"Berta where are the rooms?" Diana asked. "Gus told us about them and I haven't even seen a staircase."

Berta motioned for both Vivian and Diana to come closer to her. "Do you know why you don't ever go out front?" Both Diana and Vivian shook their heads from side to side to indicate they did not. "The type of men who come to this tavern are dangerous and often wanted for crimes. Some of them pay Gus a great deal of money for him to hide them out."

"Now these men know I clean the rooms on Saturday mornings so they should be out of the rooms, but tomorrow if you girls have any trouble you let me know right away. And if you think something isn't right you just leave the room and come and get me." Vivian and Diana both looked at each other pretending they were scared of what Berta was saying.

"And for god's sake just clean the rooms and get out. Don't touch any of their things unless you have to."

"Why would we have to?" asked Diana.

"We will be changing the bedding, if they have things on the bed you will have to move them. But all of the men staying here have been renting the rooms for a while so they should know better than to leave their things out on cleaning day. That's why Gus pays me so well so I keep his secrets. Has he told you girls what he is paying you?"

"We never talked about it," said Vivian.

"Well, when he does pay you let me know because if it's not enough I will tell him."

"How many rooms are there?" Diana asked.

"Six, after this week I will have you two split them but for your first day I want to be with you because these fellas know not to mess with me."

Vivian and Diana knew there must be a secret entrance to the rented rooms because they had not seen any of the men around the kitchen area. And neither Diana nor Vivian had been in the bar room except for their first morning; they always entered the kitchen by the back door. On this evening as they left the tavern they were walking down the streets of Salar when Jared called to them, he was standing in an alley. The girls walked into the dark alley, looking around for observers.

"Is something wrong?" Vivian asked.

"It might be. First Thaos and Stephan are inside the tavern and Shanksaw doesn't act like he recognizes them. Did you girls learn anything?"

"Yes, Gus gets paid well to hide criminals. There are six bedrooms in that tavern that we will be cleaning every Saturday morning. We haven't figured out where they are yet, but we will find out tomorrow."

"How is Berta treating you?"

"She seems protective of us," Vivian said. "I think she likes us."

"You two have to be careful cuz Gus is really drunk tonight and he's been shooting his mouth off about the two beauties he has working for him in the back room. That's not the kind of tavern that he should be saying those things; you could have all the guys there coming in the kitchen after you."

"We'll have to carry more weapons," Diana said.

"If something happens just scream, instead of giving up your disguise. Half the men in there are working with us now. I'm going to walk you to your horses tonight cuz I just feel like something ain't right. In fact I may have someone walking with you every night. It can't always be me or it will look suspicious. If Gus says anything to either of you about me walking with you just tell him I am kind of sweet on one of you, then let me know what you said."

"Maybe we should change the places we keep our horses," Vivian said.

"Not a bad idea," Jared said as he looked both ways down the street as the three returned to the walkway. "I saw Dagon and told him to follow you two home; he's probably waiting by your horses."

"Jared you are being very sweet but Diana and I really can take care of ourselves."

"Well, that all depends on how many attackers you have and I don't want to scare you but its men like Timothy and those other two prisoners that frequent that tavern. Now you tell the others what I told you." Jared waited as Vivian and Diana mounted up and started riding westward. Jared heard a noise and saw Dagon fly out of a tree and follow the women."

"I don't think any of us like hearing what Jared had to say," Gabriel said at that evening's meeting. "But we can't pull you two out until after you find the rooms."

"We don't want to be pulled out," Vivian said. "We are in a great position to get information. Berta is being protective of us and telling us things. She said that Gus pays her well to keep quiet about his business dealings. We can get information and if something goes really bad in the barroom we can help out."

"I agree," Diana said. "And besides I like Berta and I'm starting to worry about her working there."

"Vivian knows Archetenus and Jared a little better than you do Diana," Luca said. "But we have worked with those men a great deal and neither of them are prone to exaggeration, if they are warning you things are most likely a lot worse then what they are telling you; and most of us in this room know that."

"Tomorrow I am escorting the two of you back and forth to work," Misha said.

"Dack and I will go with you too," Joao said.

"Also I am pulling Calen from the missions for a while. He has several construction projects to design then I want him in charge of the construction at the building we just bought," explained Gabriel.

"How are Thaos and Stephan going to communicate with us," asked Lila.

"We sent them all the information about our mission so they know who is working in the tavern and who is staying at the different hotels. So they may pass messages through people or Enrops but they are not going to be coming to the house or the castle," Raphael said.

"And when we need to get information to them?" Diana asked.

"At this point probably the same way," Raphael replied.

Natasha walked out of the study and returned a few minutes later holding two dresses. "Now that I am in charge of disguises I want to make outfits for all of you like I had for me. Diana and Vivian will you stand up?"

Natasha handed a dress to each woman. "Vivian the pink dress is for you because you are taller and Diana you have the blue one; please hold them in front of you so the others can see. The skirts are full with what looks like pockets on the sides, but they are actually openings so the girls can grab the knives they have sheathed to their thighs. And these little vests that go over the dresses have knife sheaths for the smaller throwing knives. Laurel made them and the only problem is the material is thin so she had to put buttons on the corners of the vests so they wouldn't reveal the knives."

"This is so fun," Diana said with a big smile.

"I love it," said Vivian.

"I am in the process of having a variety of outfits made up so we will have them on hand for the missions," Natasha said and returned to her seat.

"Anything else?" Gabriel asked.

"Tomorrow when we go into the rooms do you want us to just look for things or take them?" Vivian asked.

"If you take anything tomorrow they will know it was you," Gabriel said. "Once we know the locations of the rooms perhaps we can find different ways to access them. I would like you to really study the layout so you can draw the rooms, hallways and so on. Read things but only steal something if you think it is so important that it is worth compromising your disguises."

Chapter XVI
Saturday Morning

Vivian and Diana arrived an hour earlier than scheduled at the Racing Horse Tavern Saturday morning. Misha, Joao and Dack escorted the women into Salar then hid on rooftops and watched them. Berta was already working in the kitchen and surprised to see Vivian and Diana come in so early.

"Since it is our first day cleaning the rooms we want to make sure we have enough time to clean and cook," Diana said. "Do you need help with anything now?"

"I like you girls," Berta said genuinely. "Have some coffee and pastries. I want to make sure we give those men time to get out of the rooms. Not that I am afraid we are going to see anything bad but some of them wake up real cranky. Why, one morning I knocked on a door, nobody answers so I walk in and a knife flies past my head and sticks in the doorframe. Of course that man is dead now, got killed in a fight."

"Berta, Vivian and I worry about you when you are here alone," Diana said. "If one of these men got mean with you would Gus help you?"

"In case you haven't noticed I am more muscular than that old drunk," Berta said and laughed. "I'm afraid if there was a problem it would be me saving him." All three women laughed at this statement.

"Is Gus here?" Vivian asked. "It sounds pretty quiet out front."

"He's still sleeping; he has a room here too. When you girls finish your pastries I'll show you where the linens and supplies are."

"We're done," Vivian said and gulped down the last of her coffee.

Berta led the women to a closet in the back of the supply room. The closet was fairly large with shelves on both side walls but nothing on the back wall. The shelves were filled with things that would be needed in the rented rooms as well as cleaning supplies.

"Since we don't want to keep bothering the men in these rooms we will do an entire room at once," Berta explained. "We will change the linens, sweep and wash the floors, generally wash everything down and stock things they might need. As you can see I have those two large baskets already filled with things, just to get me a little ahead. Vivian why don't you fill that bucket with hot water while we gather more supplies?"

When Berta decided they had everything they needed she showed Vivian and Diana a latch on the back wall. The latch was difficult to see and once pulled the entire wall slid to the left and into a pocket that was made inside the wall. When the women walked through this doorway they were immediately in a hallway that was shaped like a 'T'.

"If you go to the left you will end up in the bar room," Berta explained. "If you go right you will come out in the back alley and the rooms are straight ahead; three rooms on each side of the hallway. This first room on the left is where Gus sleeps. We will clean his first because he usually gets up before the others."

Berta knocked on the door twice, when no one answered she pulled a small ring of keys from her apron pocket and showed the keys to the women. "There are only six keys and each key has a number scratched on it. That number is the same as the number on the door of the room."

"Are we supposed to know who is in each room?" Vivian whispered.

"No, it really doesn't matter unless the man has a special request for his room."

Berta unlocked the door to Gus' room and all three of the women wrinkled their noses. "It smells like whiskey in here," Diana said.

"Imagine that," Berta said sarcastically. "Gus spills a lot."

Berta started to pick up all of Gus' clothes and other things that he had thrown on the bed. Diana swept the floor and Vivian started to wash the furniture in the room. "If there was a window we could air this place out a little," Vivian said as the smell was making her nauseous.

"None of these rooms have windows," Berta said. "Except for Gus every man renting is probably hiding from someone."

Vivian and Diana worked quickly because they were both afraid that Vivian would start vomiting from the smell. Diana helped Berta change the bedding and finished washing the floor as Vivian and Berta moved on to room number 2. "I found three more empty bottles in Gus' room," Diana announced as she joined the other two women in room number 2."

"He drinks so much that he seems normal," Berta said. "Until he gets over his limit."

The second room was not much better than Gus'; making Vivian realize she might have to tell Berta that she was pregnant. Never before had Vivian been so sensitive to smells and now she was fighting with her body not to vomit.

"These men sure are sloppy," Diana commented as she cleaned.

"Not all of them," Berta said. "Wait until you see room number 5, not only will it be clean but that man arranges everything in his room. Everything is perfectly lined up, even the clothes in his drawers. And he is the only one here who could tell if anything is touched. The first time I cleaned his room I leaned the broom against his dresser, well the broom fell over and slightly moved a couple of things he had on top of the dresser and that same morning he hunted me down and asked me about it."

"Was he mad?" asked Diana.

"I think so," Berta said. "He is a real strange fella; not that they all aren't here." Berta laughed at her own comment. "He was very polite to me, he never yelled but he was so, let me think of the right word." Berta paused for a moment. "Intense, like he seemed like he could explode any second."

"He sounds scary," Diana said. "Point him out sometime."

"He's a big man with red hair and scars all over, I hate to think what he done to get all those scars," Berta said. "And he wears three gold earrings in each ear. I guess when you are that big and mean you can wear something like that without the other men putting you to shame."

When Berta opened the door to room number 3 a disgusting smell hit them in the face. Vivian immediately turned and vomited on the floor. "I know that smell," Diana said.

"So do I," said Berta and pushed the door open. The women had been carrying lit candles with them because the rooms were dark since they didn't have windows. "I'll go in first." Berta said. She returned to the hallway in a few seconds. "You girls stay here; we got a dead one in there. Wish I could tell you this wasn't normal. I'm going for Gus."

Vivian cleaned up her vomit while Diana walked into the room. A man's bloody body was lying crossways on top of the bed. There was blood on the floor and the furniture." Diana quickly looked around the room then returned to the hallway just as door number 5 opened. Shanksaw stood in the doorway and looked in both directions before he walked out of the room. He too recognized the smell that had now permeated the hallway.

"What's going on?" Shanksaw asked as he walked towards Diana and Vivian. Diana did the talking since Vivian was still nauseous.

"Berta is teaching us to clean the rooms and there is a dead man in there," Diana said. "She went to get Gus." Shanksaw took the candle out of Diana's hand and walked into the room and looked around. He returned to the women, handed Diana her candle and started to walk down the hallway.

"What do you think happened to him?" asked Diana.

Shanksaw turned around and said, "He wasn't attacked in there. He probably got into a fight someplace else and died hiding out in his room." Shanksaw turned around and started walking.

"That is really sad," Diana said.

Shanksaw again stopped and faced the women. "Not really," he said then continued walking down the hallway and entered the bar room.

After Berta told Gus about the dead man, he looked around the bar room for someone to help him carry out the body.

Since it was so early there were few patrons and none of them well known to Gus. Jared was the only face that Gus recognized so he walked up to Jared and whispered. "The cleaning girls just found a dead body. You can have free food and drinks all week if you help me get him out of here."

"Sounds like a good deal to me," Jared said and stood up. He followed Berta and Gus into the back hallway, they passed Shanksaw who boldly stared at Jared but didn't speak.

"He's helping me get rid of the body unless you want to," Gus said to Shanksaw who just continued walking.

When Gus, Berta and Jared walked up to Diana and Vivian; Diana quickly said, "The smell is making her sick, I'll go in with you." Diana took Vivian's candle and walked into the bedroom holding the two candles. Both Jared and Gus walked around the room and looked at the blood and body.

"Damn, I'm gonna have to get a new mattress in here," Gus complained. "I'll throw in some extras if'n you help me carry that out too."

"This guy's been dead for a while," Jared said. "Let's wrap him in this bedding before we start carrying him or we are gonna get full of shit."

The three women moved out of the way so Jared and Gus could carry the body out the back door and drop it in the alley. When they returned for the mattress, Berta was in the room. "Gus this rug is full of blood too."

"Damn it, this is gonna cost me," Gus growled.

"Why don't you girls start cleaning the next room?" Berta suggested. "This may take a while."

Vivian was grateful to somewhat get away from the smell of rotting flesh; she and Diana worked as fast as they could to clean room number 4 because they wanted to enter Shanksaw's room which was next.

In room number 3 the bloody carpet was large and all of the furniture in the room was setting on it. Jared and Gus had to move a great deal of the furniture into the hallway so they could roll up the carpet. Both Vivian and Diana were hoping they could enter Shanksaw's room while Jared was still in the back of the building with them.

"We're ready for the next room," Diana said as she reentered room number 3. This time Berta handed Diana the ring of keys instead of unlocking the door for the women. Diana showed the keys to Vivian and both girls were trying to figure out how they could steal that key. They entered Shanksaw's room and it was just as Berta had described. "I have never seen a man's room so clean," Diana said as she brought fresh linens into the room.

"Gus can you move this dresser?" Vivian said. "We can't get to our cleaning supplies."

"I'll get it," Jared said and walked out into the hallway that was now crowded with furniture from the dead man's room.

"We have the key but we don't dare steal it," Vivian whispered to Jared.

"Make a mold with the wax from your candles," Jared whispered as he moved a dresser down the hallway.

Vivian grabbed the cleaning supplies and quickly ran into room number 5. Diana cleaned the room and changed the bedding while Vivian dripped melted wax onto one of the plates that a candle had been on, then she pressed the key into the hot wax. After Vivian removed the key and cleaned the wax off she kept blowing on the wax to try and cool it. Diana wanted to give Vivian more time with the key so Diana walked back into room number 3.

"We are in that room you told us about. We've done everything except washed off the tops of the dressers. Can we move his things to clean?"

"Yes," Berta replied. "But put everything back exactly where you found it. It always takes me longer to clean that room."

Diana returned to the room and found Vivian looking through Shanksaw's things.

"Berta said we can clean but we have to put everything back exactly where it was," Diana said loudly as she closed the door to the room. "Have you found anything?" Diana whispered.

"No, but I have never seen anything so organized. He even lines up his socks." Vivian continued to search the room as Diana finished the cleaning. There wasn't a closet in the room but an old armoire which Vivian searched. She searched on the back and undersides of the furniture and between the mattresses. The carpet in this room was smaller than in some of the other rooms, the women looked under the carpet and checked the walls.

"We need to get out of here," Diana said. "Or they will be suspicious."

When Vivian and Diana walked out of Shanksaw's room Jared and Gus were trying to carry the large rolled up carpet out of the narrow hallway, which was made narrower because of the furniture now setting against the walls. Diana and Vivian had to wait for the men to walk past them before they could enter room number 6. Berta returned to the supply closet to get more cleaning supplies for room number three, leaving Diana and Vivian in the back of the building by themselves.

"I know we missed something in that room," Vivian whispered to Diana as they were cleaning the last bedroom. They could hear Jared and Gus talking as they walked back into the building. Vivian ran out into the hallway and deliberately bumped into Jared. "Oh I am so sorry," she said as she slipped the wax mold into his vest pocket. "I just need a little air this smell is still making me sick."

Vivian walked out the back door and took a few deep breaths; she could see the body, mattress and carpet in the alleyway. She took a small ball of warm wax out of her pocket and pushed it inside of the lock mechanism so the door to the alley would not lock properly. Vivian returned to room number 6. Jared and Gus had returned to the bar room.

When Diana and Vivian finished cleaning the last room they returned to room number 3. "Berta do you want us to clean in here or start breakfast?" Diana asked.

"The blood soaked through the floor, I'm never going to get these stains out," Berta said. "So we can all go back to the kitchen."

"Can't we put something in there to get rid of that smell?" Vivian asked.

"One of you girls run to the General Store and buy some dried ashta leaves, we'll cook then up and put the whole kettle in that room.

"I'll go, I could use some fresh air," Vivian said and walked out the back door to the alley, once outside she tested the lock to make sure the wax was preventing the mechanism from locking.

Berta showed Diana where to put the dirty linens then the women worked on the breakfast meal. Berta already had bread in the oven and sliced potatoes soaking. "That man that helped Gus is the man who told us to come here and ask for work," Diana said as she wanted to get Berta's reaction to Jared. Berta didn't say anything. "He's kind of scary looking but he seems nice."

"You girls would be wise not to talk to any of the men who come into this place," Berta warned. "These aren't good men here."

"Berta it's not my business but you seem so nice why do you work here with Gus?"

"Well you are."

"Yeah but we were really hungry we didn't have a lot of choices. But it is a good job. I guess I mean, well, you seem to put up with a lot with Gus."

"My husband used to own this place with Gus. One night there was a big fight in here and Harold tried to stop it. Someone put a knife through his back. He was crippled at first but I think he just gave up and died. All our money was tied up in this place. Like you, I needed work."

"But you should be part owner," Diana said.

"Gus said that's not how the paperwork reads."

236

"Have you read the paperwork?"

"I saw it but I don't read so well."

"Berta, Vivian and I read real well, if you show us the paperwork we can tell you what it says." Berta didn't say anything. "If the paperwork says that you are part owner would you challenge Gus?"

"I am going to have to think about that," Berta said. "Gus might get real mad at you girls for doing that for me."

"Berta you have been very kind to us but maybe you should wait until he pays us then if he fires us we have some money for food."

When Jared returned to the bar room he felt his vest pocket, trying to figure out what Vivian had put into it. Jared felt Shanksaw watching him. "That smells like a son of a bitch back there," Jared said loudly to Shanksaw. "No wonder those poor girls were puking," There were only three other patrons in the bar room and two of them were Patronus priests.

Shanksaw didn't respond to Jared's remark but walked up to Gus, within a moment the two men walked into the kitchen where Berta and Diana were cooking. "I pay you a lot of money for privacy," Shanksaw said to Gus. Shanksaw was not yelling but his manner of speaking was intense. "Do you know who that guy was you brought back there?"

"He's a customer and he seems alright. Is there something about him that I should know?" Shanksaw stared at Gus angrily. "So tell me, what's the problem, the guy is huge and strong and I needed help. It was either ask him or three or four other guys. We had to get that body out of there. So tell me did the guy do something to piss you off?"

"No, I just don't trust him," Shanksaw said through clenched teeth. Vivian returned to the kitchen and stopped abruptly when she saw the encounter between Gus and Shanksaw.

"Vivian put those herbs in a kettle of water and get it boiling," Berta said quickly.

"Hell you don't trust nobody," Gus said. "Did you want me to ask you to help move that body?"

"I might have to find other lodging now," Shanksaw said. Both Diana and Vivian were listening intently to the men's conversation.

"Well that would be up to you, I don't have no problem keeping them rooms filled. But I think you are wrong about that big guy he seems alright to me."

"Do you know what his name is or where he is from?"

"Nope but the girls do," Gus turned to Diana and Vivian. "Girls come here and tell us about your friend."

Both Diana and Vivian walked up to the men and acted like they were scared. "I don't know if you would call him a friend," Diana said. "Our family was killed by Hutas and Vivian and I thought we could find work in the city. The first night we came here we were sleeping on some chairs in front of that little bakery a couple of blocks down the street and some men started bothering us. We were scared and all of a sudden Jared, that's his name he comes up and punches one man in the face and another in the stomach and tells the rest to leave us alone."

"We were scared of him too," Vivian said. "But he was nice to us and sat and talked with us until the sun came up. We told him we were looking for work. And the very next day he finds us on the street and tells us to come here and talk to Gus. He's been really nice to me and Diana."

"That's a similar story to what the big guy told me," Gus said.

"Do you know where he is from?" Shanksaw asked.

"No," Diana said. "Me and Vivian did most of the talking. He didn't tell us much besides that his wife was killed by Hutas too and when he went after the Hutas one of them cut off his ear."

"Did he do something to make you mad?" Vivian asked. "Because he has been real nice to us."

"No, but there is something familiar about him."

238

"Hell that guy would stand out in any crowd," Gus said. "If you'd seen him before you sure as hell would remember him." When Gus and Shanksaw returned to the bar room, Thaos and Stephan were standing at the bar.

"Everything all right?" Stephan asked.

"Yes, what can I get you fellas?" asked Gus.

Shanksaw marched up to Jared's table. "Do I know you from some place?" Shanksaw asked gruffly.

"Maybe," Jared said as he slowly looked up from his game of solitary. "You might say I travel a lot for work."

"What kind of work do you do?"

"The kind that pays." Jared was staring intently into Shanksaw's eyes.

"Ever kill anyone?"

"Well I might have answered that question if you hadn't yelled it in the entire place," Jared said as Shanksaw sat down at Jared's table. "Are you asking cuz you think I killed someone you liked or are you asking cuz you need someone killed?"

Thaos and Stephan took two cups of coffee and a bottle of whiskey to a table and sat down. They picked a table that gave them a good view of both Jared's table and Shanksaw's usual table. Shanksaw stared at Jared as he tried to read him.

"Those two girls back there said you saved them from being attacked by some men, then sat and talked with them until the sun came up. They tell me you're a real nice man but you sure don't look like one," Shanksaw said trying to irritate Jared who just grinned.

"We'll some would say I am nice and others wouldn't. Actually that's not true; most of the ones who would say I'm not nice are dead. Those little girls are just good girls down on their luck; they've had enough bad happen to them lately they don't need no more."

239

"They said your wife was killed by Hutas and that you went after them and one cut off your ear."

"Yep."

"You tracked down Hutas?"

"Why you so interested in my personal business?"

"Just trying to find out what kind of guy you are."

"What the hell do you care?"

"I might have work for you but I have to know who I am hiring."

"I come home one day and my wife Mary; she wasn't much older than those two little girls. The best thing that ever happened to me. Well, I come home and I find her in the back outside of the house. She had been raped and skinned alive. It took me some time but I found every one of those bastards and I skinned each one of them alive."

"How did you know which ones were the right Hutas?"

"I just kept capturing Hutas until I found out."

"And they told you?" Shanksaw asked with disbelief.

"Look at me," Jared said. "Every scar on me is from a damned Huta."

Shanksaw sat back in his chair and stared at Jared. "How long are you going to be in Salar?"

"Not sure yet," Jared said. "People usually find me for jobs I don't go looking." Jared was staring back at Shanksaw. "Not that I am real particular but I don't kill women and children and I don't care for working with demons cuz them bastards stink." Shanksaw laughed and stood up and walked over to his regular table.

"Everyone's breakfast is ready," Gus announced as he set plates on the bar. Jared, Stephan and Thaos all stood up and walked up to the bar to get their meals.

240

"I'd be leery of him," Thaos said under his breath to Jared who just nodded and returned to his table.

Shanksaw walked up to the bar while Stephan and Thaos were still standing at it. Shanksaw ordered his breakfast and when Gus walked into the kitchen, Stephan and Thaos could see Diana and Vivian through the open kitchen door. While Stephan and Thaos had been listening to Shanksaw they wondered if he hurt Diana and Vivian, the men were relieved to see that the women were fine.

"Are you always so loud about your job interviews?" Thaos asked Shanksaw. "Because you really put on a show."

Shanksaw stared at Thaos and Stephan, "What's it to you?"

"Nothing, just thought you sounded like an ass," Thaos replied. Shanksaw quickly grabbed for the knife on his belt but before he had it out of the sheath Thaos had a knife blade against Shanksaw's throat. "My friend and I want to have a quiet breakfast so why don't you just keep your big mouth shut for a while." Shanksaw slowly returned his knife to its sheath and turned around and walked back to his table. Thaos and Stephan both expected Shanksaw to throw a knife as soon as their backs were turned but he did not.

"Now that's what I call a job interview," Stephan whispered and both men laughed.

Jared realized what Thaos was doing and Jared realized that Shanksaw was suspicious of him. Since Thaos and Stephan were in the tavern to protect the women, Jared ate a double breakfast then walked out of the tavern and down the street to a tobacco store. Once he was inside of the store Jared reached into his pocket and saw the wax mold of a key.

There were two Patronus priests sitting in chairs outside of the shop, Jared whistled and one of them walked inside. The owner of the shop was stocking the store so he kept walking into the back of the shop. Jared handed the priest the mold instructing him to have a key made and to get it to Gabriel as soon as possible.

241

"This is a key for Shanksaw's room in back of the tavern, room number 5. Tell Gabriel that Shanksaw is really suspicious of me but Thaos had a good first contact with him." After the priest left the store, Jared purchased some tobacco and returned to the Racing Horse Tavern.

Chapter XVII
Answers

"I'm worried that Shanksaw will become suspicious of Vivian and Diana too, now that he knows there is a connection between them and Jared," Hannah said at the evening meeting about the mission.

"I think Jared is in a lot more danger than we are," Diana said. "People really seem to believe our story."

"Gus likes Jared and defended him," Vivian said. "And Gus brought up an interesting point. Shanksaw says there is something familiar about Jared and Gus said that Jared is so different looking that he would be hard to forget. Gus told Shanksaw he was imagining things because he doesn't trust anyone."

"This has nothing to really do with the mission," Diana said. "But both Vivian and I like Berta and worry about her. Today she told me that your husband used to own the tavern with Gus. Her husband was killed in a bar fight and Gus told Berta the legal papers don't give her any right to the business. I asked Berta if she read the papers herself and she said she can't read well; so I said Vivian and I would read them for her if she liked."

"While that is a very nice thing you are suggesting that could cause enough conflict to affect our mission," Gabriel said.

"Berta is thinking about it and we decided that we should wait until after Vivian and I get paid in case Gus fires us, so we could put it off for a while."

"If Berta owned that place I am sure she would kick out all those criminals and run a decent business," Vivian said. "Maybe when this mission is over, Diana and I can help her with some things." Both Gabriel and Raphael smiled at Vivian's statement.

Diana got a mischievous look on her face and said, "Well wouldn't you rather have a less dangerous place near Hannah's office?"

Gabriel laughed. "You have a good point. I'll tell you what."

"Don't do anything to compromise this mission and when it is over I will help you help Berta."

Vivian and Diana were pleased with Gabriel's statement. "We agree," Diana said.

Raphael stood up and addressed the team. "The business in the lower portion of our building has moved out so starting tomorrow morning Calen will be at the building every day to run the construction project. Thor you seem to be going crazy staying in the house so starting tomorrow tell everyone you are Hannah's nephew and you will be helping her set up the new business. We don't want you hurting yourself, rather we want you watching the tavern; but you can't make that too obvious to the workers, we never know who is connected to Shanksaw."

"Great, but what should I do?"

"You can start making lists of all the things we will need and you can purchase them, just don't lift anything heavy," Hannah said. "I can always find things for you to do."

"Raphael why don't you pull Archetenus and Jared out of there since Shanksaw suspects them?" Vivian asked. "Thaos and Stephan should be able to make contact with him."

"We've talked to Jared and Archetenus about that and they want to stay to protect the two of you," Raphael replied.

"Seriously it's Jared who might need protecting," said Diana.

"We'll make sure he is safe," Raphael responded. "That is one reason we are putting Thor in the building. But we need to find out about this key and Shanksaw's room."

"Diana already handed out drawings of the back of the building. Shanksaw is in room number 5. There are no windows and only one door. Jared told me to make a wax mold of the key to Shanksaw's room, which I did and slipped it into his pocket. Then I took a small ball of wax and stuck it in the lock of the door that leads to the alley so the lock doesn't work." Several people smiled as Vivian spoke.

"We searched his room and found absolutely nothing. He is very obsessive about his things," Vivian continued.

"Everything and I mean everything even his socks are lined up exactly. Because of the way he displays his belongings he can easily tell if anything as been moved."

"We looked underneath and behind the furniture, under the carpet, between the mattresses," Diana said. "We both feel that we missed something but we have no idea where he could be hiding things."

"Is it possible he is a dark lord?" Dagon asked. "He could be using magics to hide his things."

"I was thinking the same thing," Gabriel said. He turned and looked at Vivian and Diana. "You two have done very well but don't let your feelings for Berta or your enthusiasm put you in danger." Gabriel now addressed the entire group again. "I think Raphael and I need to sneak into Shanksaw's room. If there are demonic magics we should be able to tell."

"Oh I don't like that idea at all," Vivian said. "You two are known to more than Shanksaw. Remember we never saw the other men who pay for rooms there; they might work for Shanksaw too. If the two of you don't get hurt you might still tip off Shanksaw that something is going on. Isn't there some other way? Diana and I have a reason to go into his room; can't you teach us how to do what needs to be done?"

"In Nora when I was pretending to be a cleaning woman I felt the presence of a demon when I entered Meekos' room," Hannah said to Vivian and Diana. "Did you feel anything?"

"No and we really expected to," Diana replied.

"You make a good point," Gabriel said. "Let Raphael and I think about this further.

"In the meantime one of us needs to keep an eye on that alley incase Shanksaw decides to move," Luca said. "Joao and Dack are there now."

Thaos and Stephan left the Racing Horse Tavern periodically during the day and frequented other taverns; they did not want it to seem obvious to Shanksaw that they were watching him.

Jared spent the day in the Racing Horse without speaking to Shanksaw again. After Jared ate his dinner he left the tavern. Since Shanksaw was suspicious of Jared and Archetenus they and Thaos and Stephan decided to alternate their times in that tavern but they all agreed that someone needed to be in there when Diana and Vivian were working. And that is where the addition of the Patronus priests became invaluable. The priests drew less attention than Jared, Archetenus, Stephan and Thaos and daily four to five different priests would sit in or just outside of the Racing Horse Tavern.

Jared was concerned about putting Diana and Vivian in danger so he was going to avoid contact with them unless necessary. That evening Archetenus found Thaos and Stephan in another tavern and joined them for a game of poker. The men pretended they were strangers but they were able to exchange information during the game. All of the people working on this mission understood that if Shanksaw was as paranoid as they believed, he probably had his men frequenting other taverns to gather information.

The one thing that surprised every member of the team was how little information they were able to acquire about Shanksaw and his men. Either Shanksaw was very good at keeping his work covert or he was greatly intimidating the people of Salar.

After the evening meeting Gabriel and Raphael rode to Sudfad's castle to visit Erebus. They found him sitting in an overstuffed chair in his chambers. Erebus was reading before a roaring fire.

"You certainly look at home," Gabriel joked as he and Raphael entered the room.

"I certainly can't complain about how I have been treated," Erebus said as he set down his book. "If I only had a glass of whiskey I would say it was a perfect night."

"Well then you are fortunate that we came to visit," Raphael said as he set a basket on top of a small table. Hannah sent you some apple pie and we brought some whiskey and glasses. Do you want the pie now?"

"I will wait on that treat but I will have a little whiskey."

"We were planning on visiting you tonight..." Gabriel said.

Erebus interrupted him, "I know Hannah told me. Gabriel I don't need to tell you what a wonderful physician she is and a sweet woman. Hannah has the ability to scold me and make me end up thanking her." All three men laughed at this comment.

"Some things have come up so we are also here for some advice," Gabriel continued.

"Advice from me, this should be interesting."

"As you know we are watching Shanksaw. I don't know if Hannah told you but Vivian and Diana have acquired jobs in the Racing Horse Tavern as cooks and cleaning women. While all of us are concerned for their safety they are the only ones on this mission who are finding out any information. We have men working in every tavern of the city and they have not found one single thing about Shanksaw," Gabriel said.

Raphael now took a folded drawing out of his shirt pocket and handed it to Erebus. "There are six secret rooms in the back of that tavern that the owner rents out. Every Saturday morning those rooms are cleaned. This morning there was a dead body in one room which distracted the owner and his sister-in-law long enough that the girls could search Shanksaw's room. Vivian made a mold of the key to that room and sabotaged the lock to this door here," Raphael explained.

Raphael was pointing things out on the drawing as he spoke. "That door leads to the alley. The girls said Shanksaw is obsessive about his belongings and everything is lined up and appears to be measured out. They thoroughly searched his room, checking for secret compartments in the walls and floor and couldn't find anything."

"Raphael and I want to go into that room to see if we can sense demons or dark magics," Gabriel said. "But the girls raised a valid point. They said we are well known by many and the other men who rent those rooms could work for Shanksaw. The girls have not seen the other renters because all the men know to be out of their rooms so they can be cleaned. As you know Vivian and Diana are both Venatores and knowledgeable about demons."

247

"They said they did not feel the presence of demons but we feel Shanksaw has to be hiding things even if it is just the money to pay his hired killers."

"I agree with your thoughts about Shanksaw and I agree with the girls that you two should not enter that building. What is it you would like me to do?" Erebus asked.

"We are wondering if you could tell us of any magics that could be hiding things from us that are in plain sight," Raphael said.

Erebus looked back at the drawing. "There does not appear to be windows in these rooms is that true?"

"Yes, why?"

"Actually that might be of significance," Erebus said. "I will need you to go to my cottage. The cottage has three rooms. In the room containing the bed I have stacks of books and scrolls would you please bring them to me. They will not bring any evil into this house; but I must do some research."

"Could Gabriel and I help you with the research we both speak a variety of ancient languages."

"Yes you can but there will be some things you shouldn't read and I am saying that for your own good; but I will sort those things out. The cottage is unlocked. Gala has already been in there to bring me clean clothes but no one else should have entered; so if you see anything unusual tell me."

The chambers that Erebus was staying in were located in the same hallway as Sudfad's study and the family dining room. Both of the high priests stopped into the study before they left the castle for Erebus' cottage.

Edward was in the study talking with Sudfad. Gabriel told Sudfad and Edward all of the information that had been brought up during the evening mission meeting. Then Gabriel explained that he and Raphael approached Erebus for help and the three men would be doing research in Erebus' chambers.

"I'm not doing anything this evening," Edward said. "I will gladly help you."

248

"Tell the soldiers at the front door where you are going, just so they are aware of it. They can also give you torches," Sudfad said. "Do you want me to have Marie bring you something to eat and drink?"

"We brought a bottle of whiskey," Gabriel said. "And we never turn down food."

As Gabriel, Raphael and Edward walked across the grounds towards the cottages Edward asked, "So do you want to hear the castle gossip?" Then he laughed. "I am not much into gossip but this is unusual."

"You have our attention," Raphael said.

"All the women in the castle think that Gala and Erebus are getting interested in each other which is startling because she believes in The Great Ruler and he is a sorcerer."

"I am sure they are both lonely people," Gabriel said. "For them to actually have a relationship one of them would have to change their ways. If that was Erebus, I would be happy. If Gala chooses darkness; that will be another matter."

The three men found nothing out of the ordinary in Erebus' cottage. Each man gathered an armful of books and scrolls and returned to Erebus' chambers; where they saw several platters of food on a small table which had been moved closer to the hearth.

"I'm glad I volunteered to join you," Edward said. "Your cottage didn't look like anything was out of place." Edward turned to Erebus. "If you have valuable things in there we could station a soldier outside."

"I had a considerable amount of money but Gala brought it to me. Now trust what I am to tell you. There are writings here that would be dangerous for you to read. Let me sort through the books first and I will pull out the ones you shouldn't open."

"What will happen if we read those books?" Edward asked.

"Well there is a variety of things, some have cursed pages but others contain such evil content that once the words enter your mind they remain there and sort of fester."

"How do you protect yourself?" Raphael asked.

"Maybe I haven't," Erebus replied then laughed. Then when he saw the looks on the faces of Edward, Gabriel and Raphael, Erebus added, "Protection spells."

Thaos and Stephan entered the Racing Horse Tavern shortly before closing time. The two men were sober but acted as if they were slightly drunk. Shanksaw was sitting in his usual spot but there were four men sitting at his table with him playing cards. Shanksaw stared coldly at Thaos and Stephan when they entered the tavern and both men laughed.

"Yep, you should see them," Gus was drunk and talking to five men who were standing at the bar. "They both are as pretty as the day is long. Why Shanksaw saw them." Shanksaw heard his name mentioned but did not respond in any way. "Hey Shanksaw didn't you think my little cleaning girls are beautiful?"

Shanksaw quickly left his table and grabbed the neck of Gus' dirty shirt with his left hand and held a knife to Gus' throat with his right and said angrily, "Don't yell my name around here."

Both Thaos and Stephan felt that Shanksaw's actions were meant as a show for them. Neither man said anything because they were more concerned with what Gus was saying about Vivian and Diana. Shanksaw let go of Gus and pushed him backwards, then Shanksaw returned to his table. Gus stopped talking and started to clean the bar.

Thaos and Stephan slowly drank their glasses of whiskey then walked out of the bar. They had only walked a few yards from the tavern when eight men suddenly surrounded them.

"Did Shanksaw send you?" Thaos asked as he was sizing-up his attackers.

"The big fella ain't as stupid as he looks," one of the men said and spit a wad of tobacco on the ground.

"So what's his beef?" Thaos asked as Stephan moved so he was standing with his back to Thaos' back.

"Not our business," the same man replied then spit another wad of tobacco on the ground.

"What the hell!" yelled another of Shanksaw's men as three of the eight men suddenly fell to the ground with Ruala arrows in their backs. The remaining five men jumped and looked up at the roof tops but didn't see anyone. With the momentary distraction, Stephan lunged forward and rammed his knife into the stomach of one of the attackers, who instantly fell to the ground.

Thaos kicked the man who had been doing the talking in the groin, that man fell to the ground and Thaos grabbed two knives from his belt simultaneously. Both of Thaos' knives landed in their marks. As Stephan was fighting with one of the assailants, a group of Patronus priests joined the fight.

"Keep that one alive," Thaos said of the man who he had kicked in the groin. "And take him to Gabriel. Pull those arrows out of the others; we have some business with Shanksaw." Thaos and Stephan looked around to see if they were being watched then they both marched into the Racing Horse Tavern.

Shanksaw screamed when one of Thaos' knives flew past his head but cut his ear. Before Shanksaw could stand up, Stephan was behind him with a knife pressed against his throat. "The next time you want us taken out have enough balls to do it yourself," Stephan growled.

One of the men sitting at the table with Shanksaw reached for his knife but Thaos grabbed the man's arm and hand and broke the man's wrist. The man screamed in pain. "Are these some more of your worthless men? After the show you put on today I expected professionals," Thaos said and took the weapons from all of the men who were sitting at Shanksaw's table.

Stephan waited for Thaos to finish collecting the weapons then he slammed Shanksaw's head onto the table top. Thaos and Stephan walked up to the bar where they piled the weapons. "Two whiskeys," Thaos ordered. Then he turned and stared at Shanksaw.

Koby quickly entered Erebus' chambers. "Sorry to interrupt but the Patronus just brought eight of Shanksaw's men to the house, seven are dead. They tried to attack Thaos and Stephan."

"The one that is alive appeared to be the ringleader of the group." Gabriel, Raphael and Edward followed Koby out of the castle.

With his company gone, Erebus poured himself another drink. He picked up one of the books that he would not allow the others to read and his hands began to shake.

When Gabriel, Raphael, Edward and Koby reached Gabriel's house, six Patronus priests were standing outside next to an uncovered boca. Seven bodies were laid side by side on the ground so that their faces were exposed. The eighth man had his hands tied behind his back; his ankles were tied together and he had a gag in his mouth. A row of lit torches illuminated the grizzly scene.

"Luca, Misha and Father flew to Salar to watch over Thaos and Stephan since they went back into the Racing Horse Tavern and confronted Shanksaw," Calen explained. "The priests said they saw these men hiding around the tavern and as soon as Stephan and Thaos walked out this group surrounded them. Dagon, Joao and Dack must have been watching these men also because apparently they killed the first three with arrows.

"We searched the bodies," Padre Arches said. "We found little, some money but not even much of that. We don't know how Shanksaw communicated with these men because we have all been watching him."

"The children didn't see any of this did they?" Gabriel asked Calen.

"No they are all in bed, and we told the girls to stay out of sight," Calen said.

Gabriel looked at Thor who had been quietly standing near Calen. "Thor you are going to have a new experience tonight. Go in and ask Hannah for a vial of truth potion, some paper and pen and meet us at that shed over there." Gabriel pointed at a small shed about twenty yards to the left of the barn.

By the time Thor entered the shed the eighth man was tied to a chair in the middle of the shed. Thor was surprised that the shed contained little besides chairs. Candles lit the inside of the small building.

Calen pulled down on the man's chin at the same time he was pulling the man's forehead back to open his mouth. Gabriel poured the contents of the vial down the man's throat which made him cough and choke.

"Thor we are going to interview this man," Raphael explained. "We want you to write down everything that is said. The Patronus priests stood inside of the shed; none of them had ever witnessed someone who was given the truth potion before. After a few minutes the man tied to the chair started to grin and sway back and forth. "They act like they are drunk when the potion takes effect," Raphael told the observers.

"What is your name?" Gabriel asked.

"Swenson."

"Why did you attack those two men tonight?"

"Orders from the boss."

"Who is the boss?"

"Well we got a couple."

"Who told you to attack those men?"

"Berta."

"Berta who cooks at the Racing Horse Tavern?"

"That's the one, big ugly woman."

"Berta is your boss?"

"She's one of them."

"Who are the others?"

"Shanksaw is Berta's boss and Shanksaw takes orders from someone but I don't know who."

"Have you ever seen the person who Shanksaw takes orders from?"

"Can't say that I have."

"How do Shanksaw and Berta communicate?"

"Notes in the plates of food."

"Have you worked for Shanksaw long?"

"About six months. He pays well but his men are always getting killed off."

"Tell me everything you know about the bounties that are on members of Gabriel's team."

"Actually I don't know much about that stuff, Shanksaw has had me working on other things but I know he has sent men after that team."

"Who put the bounties on Gabriel's team?"

"The King of Stordt."

"Are you sure?"

"That is what I was told."

"Why?"

"It has something to do with Nora but he wants them out of the way because he has some big plans and he's afraid the team will stop him."

"Which king are you talking about?"

"The one there now."

"You mean Hamond?"

"No, from what Shanksaw said Hamond wasn't around long enough to even get his bearings. He was killed and another is king."

"What is his name?"

"Zieman."

"What do you know about Zieman?"

"Just that he had the other king killed and he isn't making it public that he runs the kingdom. I guess he wants it to be a surprise." Swenson laughed at his own comment.

"Is there anything else you can tell us about Zieman?"

"No."

"Is Zieman Shanksaw's boss?"

"Don't think so, Shanksaw called him a client."

"So what has Shanksaw been having you do?"

"There's a couple of fellas that have been hanging around the tavern, Shanksaw thinks he knows them but he can't remember from where. They make him nervous, so he has us watching them."

"What have you seen them do?"

"Eat, drink and play cards but the one with one ear met those two girls one night when they were done working. He walked them to their horses."

"What else do you know about those two men?"

"For some reason they really get under Shanksaw's skin. He thinks they are spying on him."

"Who would they be spying for?"

"Shanksaw has a lot of enemies. He didn't say."

"So you have talked to Shanksaw?"

"Yeah, he meets us in the alley behind the tavern early in the mornings."

"Tell us about Shanksaw's enemies."

"Shanksaw is mean as hell but he usually hires his dirty work done. He has arranged for a whole lot of men to be killed over the years as well as gold shipments stolen and other things. Now when you have people killed, course you're gonna piss people off but I think Shanksaw cheats a lot of his clients as he calls them."

"I know he has some demons really pissed at him that's why he has been so edgy."

"Do you know what demons?"

"Hell no, I don't want to even go near no demon."

"Do you know any of his enemies by name?"

"There's a fella out of Port Friada name Tehtfote, he used to work for a dark lord down there and hired Shanksaw for some kind of job that Shanksaw never completed but took the money. Then not too long ago Shanksaw was working for a couple of demons but from what I heard neither of the demons knew he was working for the other and Shanksaw wanted to keep it that way cuz those demons was enemies. Shanksaw screwed up on both jobs after the demons paid him."

"What were the jobs?"

"Helping some men escape from Wetpr and killing some of those team members."

"Has Shanksaw been in Wetpr long?"

"About a year I think."

"What other work has he done in Wetpr?"

"What do you mean?"

"How does he make his money?"

"Mostly extortion, he has most of the shop and tavern owners in Salar paying him not to hurt their families. In fact he's got a place outside of the city where he keeps people that his men kidnap. If a family doesn't pay up, Shanksaw has the person killed. And if Shanksaw is in one of his moods hell he will just have the person killed anyways. Shanksaw is kinda crazy."

"Tell us where this place is that he keeps the hostages?"

"About ten miles north of the city, just across the River Toba before you get to Elba."

"Describe the place."

"It's an old farmhouse in a valley."

"What security measures does he have?"

"The valley is surrounded by hills. Shanksaw's men are on all the hills and if anyone rides up that isn't one of Shanksaw's men they are supposed to kill the people in the house."

"How many men does Shanksaw have working for him?"

"About fifty. He lost a bunch a couple of weeks ago."

"How many people are being held in that farmhouse now?"

"I don't know maybe a couple of dozen."

"Are they all men?"

"Don't think so but I haven't been inside for a few months."

"What have you been doing?"

"I do collections."

"What?"

"I collect the money from the businesses."

"And if they can't pay you grab someone from their family?"

"Yep."

"Tell us about Berta."

"She's as big as a man and as mean as a mule."

"I mean tell us about her involvement with Shanksaw."

"He's got her husband. She'll get him back when Shanksaw doesn't need her anymore but between you and me that guy will never last that long."

"What guy are you talking about?"

"Berta's husband, he's a cripple and you don't think those guys guarding the house are taking care of him."

"How long has he been a prisoner?"

"I don't know maybe a month. Shanksaw doesn't trust Gus cuz Gus drinks too much and when he drinks he can't keep his damned mouth shut. The only reason Shanksaw hasn't killed Gus is because he has a good setup at that tavern. Gus hides all of Shanksaw's money for him and he's got those secret rooms in the back. And hell no one thinks nothing about all the guys getting together in one place like that."

"What all does Berta do for Shanksaw?"

"He passes notes to her to tell us stuff."

"Does Gus know Berta works for Shanksaw?"

"Naw, Gus is an idiot."

"What about those two girls that work in the kitchen with Berta, do they work for Shanksaw too?"

"No they just started there. Shanksaw doesn't think they will be there long?"

"Why not?"

"Cuz Gus is trying to sell them. Guess those girls don't have no family and the only person they know is that big guy that Shanksaw doesn't' like."

"Do you know who Gus is thinking of selling them to?"

"I think he is taking bids."

"Does Berta know about this?"

"Don't think so; she seems to like those girls."

"So is something planned for that big guy so he doesn't stop Gus from selling the girls?"

"Not that I know of but that doesn't mean nutin."

"Is Shanksaw a demon or dark lord?"

"Hell no, what kind of guy do you think I am? I wouldn't work for no demon or dark lord."

"But Shanksaw has clients that are demons and dark lords."

"Well yeah."

"Then I guess you do work for them."

"How did Shanksaw get information about Gabriel's team?"

"The demon that hired him."

"I thought you said the King of Stordt hired him."

"You fool the King of Stordt is a demon."

Chapter XVIII
Hostages

It was almost two o'clock in the morning when Gabriel's team met with Sudfad, Simon and Raul in the Great Hall of the castle. Marie was serving an early breakfast as the men and women took their seats. Prior to the meeting, Gabriel had Patronus priests bring Jared, Archetenus, Thaos and Stephan to the castle. All of the Rualas who were working in Salar were at the castle for the meeting.

Dozens of Patronus priests were scattered around the City of Salar monitoring Shanksaw. Archetenus was asked to wake Delilah and bring her to the meeting. Even though Sudfad told Renya to return to sleep, she was one of the last people to walk into the Great Hall.

Gabriel and Raphael stood before the group and apologized for the late hour. They shared with the group all of the information that they had gotten from Swenson. Since Gabriel and Raphael had so much information to share they had asked that all questions wait until they were done speaking.

"There are just so many things that you brought up," Sudfad said. "But the fact that Stordt now has a king that is a demon and he wants your team out of the way of his plans is extremely disturbing."

Raul stood up and interrupted his father. "I am sorry I am just so angry I can barely control it. How can Shanksaw have been kidnapping and terrorizing our citizens for a year without us hearing about it. After we stop him we have to put something in place to ensure this never happens again."

"Shanksaw is an opportunist," Raphael said. "We have been focused on other threats which allowed him to take a hold on the city."

"But our men patrol the city daily," Simon said. "Wouldn't you think that someone would have passed them a note or something?"

"They are terrorizing families at their core," Sudfad said. "And I will bet they are victimizing the most helpless, that is how terrorists operate; they don't have the balls to fight like warriors."

Before we work on any plans I want to explain that I had everyone returned from the city because the mission as originally planned is off. Archetenus, Jared, Thaos and Stephan I wanted you to find out who hired Shanksaw. I will no longer put you at risk now that we have an answer," Gabriel said.

Stephan and Thaos looked at each other then Stephan spoke. "We are already here and I don't think either of us want to go home until you stop Shanksaw. Besides we were just getting warmed up." Both Stephan and Thaos smiled.

"Archetenus I believe Shanksaw thinks you look familiar because he worked for Dieter. I don't know the connection with Jared unless Shanksaw saw a list of the men who were created to be vessels. Delilah this is the reason I asked you to join us. Do you recognize either Shanksaw's name or Tehtfote?" Gabriel asked.

"Tehtfote was one of Dieter's lieutenants. I don't recognize Shanksaw but you must understand that the type of criminals that Dieter associated with often did not use their real names. Can you tell me what he looks like?"

"A large man with red hair, reddish face with lots of scars on his face and neck," Archetenus explained. "He wears three gold earrings in each ear."

"Is he really paranoid and I don't know how to describe it," Delilah said but was interrupted by Vivian.

"Obsessive." Vivian said loudly.

"Yes," Delilah said. "I know him but when he worked for Dieter he went by the name of Caulder."

"That's why we haven't been able to find any information about him," Gabriel said.

"Dieter used to hire him for special jobs, like assassinations or large robberies of gold shipments that Dieter did not want his men tied to. From what I know of him he acts as a middle man. People come to Caulder when they want a job done and he makes it happen. I don't believe he usually takes part in the jobs but my impression of him was that he was a dangerous man just the same," Delilah explained.

"Is it possible Dieter told him about the men he was going to sell to the demons as vessels?" asked Raphael.

"I don't know the answer to that question; understand I was not allowed to hear most business matters. I was supposed to provide lavish celebrations and dinners and that is how I heard most of the information about Dieter's work," Delilah said. "But even if Caulder doesn't know about Archetenus and Jared directly, they certainly fit the descriptions of most of the vessels. Caulder might recognize them as vessels but he doesn't know yet if the demons still control them."

Delilah paused. "I know Caulder would recognize me," then she laughed and looked at her protruding stomach. "Even like this. I could walk past a window and let him see me; that might distract him for a while."

Gabriel started to speak but Archetenus interrupted him. "If you want to use Delilah in the manner that she suggested I would not argue as long as one of the Rualas takes her off the street. Remember that stunt you pulled on Roch when you kept having women who looked like Vitomas walk around, it drove him crazy."

Diana quickly stood up and looked at Misha who had been telling her to wait to speak, "Can I talk now?" she asked him with obvious irritation in her voice. Misha grinned and nodded his head. "I am sorry but I am so damn mad. I think tomorrow Vivian and I should go to work like always and pull Berta out of that place; you guys take her and let me and Vivian deal with Gus. We could keep him and Shanksaw and whoever else busy while you raid that farmhouse and save those people."

Both Gabriel and Raphael smiled, "Actually we were thinking along those lines," Gabriel said. "But we want more than just you and Vivian in that tavern."

262

"Gabriel don't pull us out until we've had a chance at those guys," Diana said angrily which made everyone in the room grin.

"When the baby lioness wakes up," Thor said. "There's no stopping her."

"Raul, Simon why don't you plan the attack on the farmhouse while the team takes out Shanksaw and his men in the city." Gabriel said. "The Rualas should go with you so they can eliminate the guards on the hill tops. And remember the people inside probably need medical care and maybe food and water."

"While I think this is a good plan, I'm staying close to Diana," Misha said.

"That's fine," Raphael said.

"Before we go any further," Sudfad said. "The Sanuri and Erebus have been sitting in the back of the room listening to all of this. They represent two very different points of view. I would like to hear what they have to say."

"I am not unhappy with your plans thus far," the Sanuri said as he stood up to address the room. "I can tell you that Simon and Raul are correct in saying that you have to develop some type of system to prevent another Shanksaw from infiltrating your kingdom because I am speculating that there will be many distractions in your future. As for Zieman, I have been confused by some of the visions I have had, now they make more sense. I will find out information about him."

"Is Shanksaw a member of the Insidiae?" Erebus asked.

"Yes," Delilah said. "He attended many functions with them."

"Why?" Sudfad asked.

"Because of their blood oath, all the members feel some kind of energy when one of them is destroyed. Sophie used to tell me about it although she wouldn't know exactly what happened to whom. So you should be prepared for retribution."

"I agree," replied Gabriel, is anyone opposed to the way we are planning things now?" No one spoke so Gabriel continued.

"Vivian, Diana do you think you can get Berta out of that kitchen and into the building we just bought?"

"We will have to tell her the truth," Vivian said. "But I think she will come with us. Remember Berta's as big as Thor so you will need a couple of people in that building to watch her because we are going back to the tavern."

"I've never seen you two this mad before," Misha said to Vivian and Diana then laughed.

"I have," Thor said. "And Misha you'll just want to stand out of their way. I know, in fact I still might have the scars."

Renya now stood up. "As usual I am proud of all of you; you are so dedicated and such people of integrity. But I will tell you I am just as mad as Vivian and Diana. Our capital city, the city we live near, people are being kidnapped, families terrorized and apparently young girls sold."

"I am so very angry and so filled with shame that I can hardly talk. Sudfad we can have soldiers walking up and down every street, but unless the citizens know they can come to us and trust us it does no good. After all of you clean this mess up we are going to apologize to the citizens of Salar and explain to them that we need their cooperation in order to protect them."

Vivian and Diana walked into the kitchen of the Racing Horse Tavern earlier than expected this morning. When they arrived they heard voices towards the front of the kitchen. Gus was sitting at a table holding a piece of raw meat against his bruised face and Berta was standing near him. Diana and Vivian did not see anyone else in the kitchen.

"Gus you have to stop drinking so much, one of these nights someone is going to kill you," Berta scolded with frustration in her voice. Neither Berta nor Gus heard the women in the kitchen until Diana spoke.

"Gus what happened to you?"

"One of the customers got mad because I yelled his name across the bar room is what he said but I think he was really mad because two strangers showed him up." Both Diana and Vivian realized that Gus was talking about Shanksaw because they knew of the confrontations between Shanksaw and Thaos and Stephan.

"Why are you girls here so early?" asked Berta.

"You always have so much work we wanted to get an early start," Vivian said as she was desperately trying to maintain her disguise in front of Gus. Both Diana and Vivian where fighting urges to hit Gus.

"I'm gonna get me a drink," Gus said and walked out of the kitchen and into the bar room.

Vivian and Diana quickly walked up to Berta. Diana whispered, "Berta we need you to come with us, now."

"Where?"

"Berta we know about your husband and the others that Shanksaw has kidnapped. We are here to help you. Your husband will be freed today but you must leave here now."

Berta paused, "How do you know these things? Who are you?"

"We are Venatores, warriors of the Clan of Gesmal," Diana said. "And we truly are here to help you. Berta you have to trust us. Please, we will explain everything later."

"My Harold is going to be freed?" Berta asked with tears coming to her eyes.

"Yes, but you need to leave with us now," Vivian said and took Berta's arm leading her towards the back door of the kitchen. Vivian and Diana wanted to get Berta out of the tavern before Shanksaw got up and had his usual morning meeting in the back alley with his men. Diana walked out of the door first and looked both ways in the alley before motioning for Vivian and Berta to follow her.

The three women walked down the alley and onto a walkway, they crossed the street and walked on another walkway until they were within feet of the building that Gabriel owned. Then they walked into an alley and entered the building from the back.

Dack had a full view of the alleyway behind the Racing Horse Tavern. After the women left the building Dack called out the song of the yellow mandeze bird as a signal for the others on the team. At that early hour most of the businesses on the streets of Salar were not yet open. Dozens of Patronus priests took positions on the streets and in the alleys that were located near the Racing Horse Tavern.

Jared pounded on the front door of the tavern, "Gus open up!" Gus walked to the door still holding the raw meat against his face; when he unlocked the door Jared, Archetenus, Thaos and Stephan all entered the bar room. "Gus we would be obliged if you would just stay in here," Jared said as he took a seat at his usual table. Gus felt there was going to be trouble when he saw these four men together. He walked behind the bar so that he could hide behind it when the trouble started.

As soon as the meeting at the castle ended which was around four o'clock in the morning, Raul and Simon led two hundred men to the farmhouse where Shanksaw was holding kidnapped citizens. The Rualas flew in advance of the army and hid in trees on the hills that surrounded the farmhouse as they looked for the men who stood guard on top of the hills.

Calen was the first warrior to see one of Shanksaw's men walking along a hilltop. The man did not hear Calen land behind him nor did he hear Calen creeping up to him with knife drawn. There was no fight, Calen slit the man's throat then looked for another. The Rualas had to kill the men on the hills before they saw the Wetprian army and alerted the men in the farmhouse to kill the hostages.

Luca was getting off from a man he had just killed when one of Shanksaw's men hit Luca over the head with a rock. Luca fell face forward into the dirt. The man pulled a large knife from its sheath on his belt and straddled Luca's unconscious body.

As the man lowered himself onto Luca, Maxwell flew down towards the ground. Maxwell did not slow down on his descent as he flew into the man, hitting the man from his right side. Both Maxwell and the man rolled off Luca and down the hill as they punched and gouged each other. The man had dropped his knife with the impact of Maxwell colliding into him. At one point the man was on top of Maxwell and grabbed a rock. Maxwell blocked the man's arm as he tried to hit Maxwell with the rock. Maxwell shifted his weight, throwing the man off balance and the two started to roll down the hill again.

The two men kept rolling downwards until they landed against a fallen tree. The hired killer grabbed for a knife that was in a sheath in his boot but Maxwell jumped on top of the man and started to choke the life out of him. All Maxwell kept thinking about was Luca lying unconscious at the top of the hill as Maxwell crushed the man's larynx.

"You'll be safe here," Vivian said to Berta as they walked up the back steps of the building. Berta this is Emeral, Lila and Diana's brother, Thor. You stay here until we return."

"I don't understand what is going on," Berta said.

"We really will explain everything later," Diana said as she and Vivian took off their work dresses and exposed their leather Venator outfits. "Your husband will be brought to this building as will the other hostages. A physician is traveling with the soldiers who are going to rescue the hostages. And anyone who is injured in Salar will be brought here for care also."

"Is there going to be a battle?" Berta asked as she was feeling overwhelmed by the situation.

"Berta the girls speak highly of you," Emeral said kindly. "For now you must know that there are a group of us who work with the King. We have found out how Shanksaw has been terrorizing the city and it will stop today."

"Are you Gabriel's team?" Berta asked fearfully.

"Yes and we know that Shanksaw was forcing you to work for him and we know why," Emeral said.

"Are you girls going after Shanksaw?" Berta asked as the information was slowly becoming real for her.

"Yes and Gus," Vivian said. "Did you know Gus was trying to sell us?"

"What!" Berta gasped. The girls turned to leave but Berta called to them. "Stop, I have to tell you some things. Shanksaw booby traps his room when he is gone, except for cleaning mornings."

"How? Arrows?" Diana asked.

"No snakes, large red snakes the likes I have never seen before."

"We didn't see any snakes in his room yesterday," Vivian said. "How did he hide them?"

"He puts them behind the bar with Gus."

"How come they don't attack Gus?" asked Diana.

"They are in a cage then."

"Berta while we are gone think about where you want us to take you and your husband," Vivian said. "Do you have a home nearby?"

"Yes."

"We'll work all that out," Emeral said. "You girls should go."

When Shanksaw walked into the bar room and saw Jared, Archetenus, Thaos and Stephan in the tavern, he sensed something was wrong although the four men were not acting suspicious. Shanksaw momentarily stopped in the doorway before he entered the bar and sat down at his usual table. Shanksaw looked over at Gus but Gus was pretending to clean the bar and would not look at Shanksaw.

Gabriel's team still did not know the men who were working for Shanksaw so they were waiting for the men to enter the tavern. Five Patronus priests walked into the tavern and took seats at different tables.

268

Gabriel and Raphael walked into the tavern and looked around until they saw Shanksaw then they boldly walked up to his table. Shanksaw thought about escaping but he saw Jared now blocking the doorway to the rented rooms and Stephan and Thaos blocking the front door.

"We won't bother with introductions since you already know us," Gabriel said as he and Raphael sat down at Shanksaw's table. Shanksaw was breathing fast as he was trying to decide if he wanted to fight or to run.

"Just relax," Raphael said. "You aren't going anyplace."

Suddenly there was a loud noise in the kitchen then the sound of furniture being knocked over and people running. Archetenus quickly walked towards the kitchen door when it suddenly swung open and a man flew out and landed on the floor.

"We're fine," Vivian called out. "He had six of them in the back alley."

"This one's dead," Archetenus said with a grin as he checked the body on the floor. "You girls holler if you need help," he called out then laughed.

Diana peaked her head out of the kitchen door, "Gabriel he booby traps his room with those red demon snakes so be careful."

"What the hell?" Gus yelled when he saw Diana. "Who are you girls?"

"The girls you were going to sell," Diana said and ran up to Gus and kicked him in the groin. Gus yelped and collapsed on the floor. "We're not done with you," Diana said and ran back into the kitchen to help Vivian tie up the men they had captured. The bar room was filled with laughter after Diana kicked Gus; everyone was laughing except for Shanksaw."

"How did you find out about me?" Shanksaw asked.

"You must not pay your men well enough," Gabriel said. "They talk a lot. And that is what we want you to do also."

"Why the hell should I tell you anything?"

"Because you are finished here," Gabriel started to say but was interrupted by the sound of fighting in the street. "As I was saying, this morning the King's men are attacking your farmhouse and freeing the hostages. Your reign of terror here is over. And we have a small army in the streets of Salar so don't think your men are going to rescue you. You can hear the fighting now."

"So what do you want?" Shanksaw asked. "You could have just killed me."

"We want to know more about the bounties that have been put on us," Gabriel said.

Shanksaw smiled because he now felt like he was in a position of power. "And what do I get if I tell you?"

"What do you want?" Gabriel asked.

"To ride away with my money."

"You mean the money you extorted from the business owners here or the money you took to have us killed?" Shanksaw stopped smiling because he felt like he was walking into a trap.

Both Thaos and Stephan jumped out of the way as two men fell into the tavern fighting, one was a Patronus priest and the other was one of Shanksaw's men.

"We've got five tied up in the kitchen," Vivian said as the women ran into the bar room. "The building is surrounded with his men and ours."

A man threw himself through the front window; Diana's knife impaled his chest before he hit the floor. Two more of Shanksaw's men barged through the front door, Thaos grabbed one and Stephan the other. As Stephan and Thaos were fighting, three more of Shanksaw's men ran through the front door.

Archetenus swung his sword in a slicing motion and struck the first man through the door with such force that the man was dead before he hit the ground. Jared's knife penetrated the throat of the second attacker as Archetenus stabbed the third.

The men in the tavern could see arrows flying through the air as Misha, Dagon, Joao and Dack shot Shanksaw's men from the roof tops."

Edward drove a covered boca with Hannah, Elan and Cassandra in the back. Two more covered bocas followed Edward's. The bocas were brought to transport the hostages and Hannah, Elan and Cassandra came along to provide medical care. Raul and Simon had ordered the bocas to the rear of the convoy as they traveled to Shanksaw's farmhouse.

The sun had been up for an hour when Raul stopped the convoy, three scouts were sent ahead of the troops. When the scouts returned Maxwell was flying with them and carrying Luca. Maxwell flew to the first boca and Edward helped him put Luca in the back. Luca was conscious but dizzy and disoriented. "I'll be back," Maxwell said to Hannah then he flew to the front of the convoy.

"We killed eighteen men, all of them standing guard on the hills," Maxwell said. "Our men only received minor wounds with the exception of Luca who was hit on the head with a rock. Koby and Calen are close to the house, they tried to look inside but there are blankets over the windows. There is a back door but I would assume it is locked from the inside. There are two windows in back, one either side of the door. One window on each side of the house and two windows in the front, one on either side of the door.

"Is it just the one road leading to the house?" Simon asked.

"Yes but the hills are not treacherous, the bocas would have difficulty but your men could easily ride across the hills and attack the house from different sides."

"Once we start moving it will have to be fast so we don't give them time to kill the hostages," Raul said as he addressed the soldiers. "The bocas stay where they are for now. Everyone else we are going with our secondary plan. Everyone knows what they need to do, so move out."

The convoy separated into four groups, Raul was leading the frontal attack, while Simon was leading the attack on the rear of the farm house.

Lieutenant Markus was leading troops from the east and Lieutenant Tanner was leading the attack from the west. Enrops were flying over the area and would tell Raul when the other troops were in place.

"Edward," Hannah yelled from the boca I need your help. Edward quickly climbed into the back of the boca as he could hear Luca arguing with Cassandra and Elan. "Edward hold him still," Hannah said as she mixed a mild sedative. "He is disoriented from his head wound and he wants to go out and fight."

Edward held Luca down while Hannah poured the liquid sedative down his throat. "I didn't give him a lot but it should be enough to settle him down," Hannah said to everyone in the boca, then she turned to Edward. "Would you stay here while we clean his wound?"

Shanksaw had many more men than Gabriel and his team expected. While the Patronus priests were in the midst of battle dozens of Shanksaw's hired killers stormed the Racing Horse Tavern to rescue their boss. Raphael and Gabriel quickly tied Shanksaw to his chair so they could join the fight since the attackers were filling the bar room.

Vivian, then Diana yelled the war cry of the Venatores as they joined the melee. Initially Shanksaw's men were not attacking the women but going after the men. Diana and Vivian proceeded to attack many of the hired killers from behind as they went after other team members. As Shanksaw's men realized that Vivian and Diana were dangerous they directed their attacks towards them also.

Citizens of Salar who would normally be starting their days were running and hiding to avoid being caught up in the battle. The streets of this large city were vacant except for the battle between Shanksaw's hired killers and Gabriel's team.

No one emitted war cries as Raul led the charge on the farmhouse. Once Raul started the attack the three other leaders led their men down the hills that surrounded the farmhouse.

Koby, Calen and Maxwell were hiding close to the house and tried to enter through the back door but it was either locked or blocked. They heard a woman scream inside of the farmhouse, with their adrenaline pumping the three Ruala warriors ran to the windows and tore the blankets down.

"Stop your damn screaming," a man's voice yelled inside of the farmhouse as he pushed a woman aside so he could get to the window where Calen was tearing down the blanket. "What the hell is going on here?" the man yelled as he saw the blanket fall away but did not see an animal or a man at the window.

The hired killer stopped and looked at the window then slowly moved towards it; he stuck his head out of the window but didn't see anything because Calen had flown above the window. Calen grabbed the man by the head and broke his neck. Calen pulled the body through the window then entered the farmhouse, where Maxwell and Koby were already fighting with the guards.

"Untie me," Shanksaw screamed as one of his men ran towards him but the man fell dead to the floor with one of Stephan's knives in his back. Gus was on his hands and knees trying to crawl out of the bar room and into the kitchen when Vivian saw him, she ran up to Gus and kicked him in the head; Gus fell unconscious onto the floor.

A man hit Archetenus across the back with a wooden chair; the chair shattered. Archetenus grabbed one of the chair legs and rammed it through the man's chest. Thaos threw a man off from his back and ducked as a knife flew past his head. Then Thaos spun around and stabbed the man who had been on his back. When Thaos came back to a standing position he did so with such power that he punched another assailant and knocked him out. Jared had a huge knife in each hand and was going through the crowd stabbing Shanksaw's men. "Give em hell Archetenus, give em hell," Jared yelled.

Raphael tried to make it through the fighting crowd so that he could be closer to Vivian but both Gabriel and Raphael drew the attention of the hired killers.

Every man and woman in that tavern was bruised and bleeding when they heard the Horn of Cass being blown.

Now some of Shanksaw's men tried to turn and run because they knew the horn indicated the army was coming.

Adrenalin spurred all of the soldiers riding towards the farmhouse because unlike most battles the lives of hostages were at stake.

Koby was rolling around on the floor of the farmhouse with one of the hired killers. The man got on top of Koby and punched him twice in the face. Koby was gouging the man's eyes when the man collapsed on top of him. Koby quickly threw the man off him and saw one of the female hostages holding a frying pan in her hand. "Thanks," Koby said with a grin. "But all of you need to get out of here; the soldiers are coming to help."

"Get out of here," yelled Maxwell after he pulled his knife from the chest of one of the guards. "Get everyone out of here."

As Raul and his men rode up to the house men, women and children were running out. "Sergeant Dresden round up the hostages and get them to the bocas," Raul ordered as he jumped off from his horse and ran inside of the house.

As one of Shanksaw's men tried to run out of the tavern, Misha thrust his sword through the man then pushed him out of the doorway. "Diana," Misha yelled into the crowd.

"I'm near the bar," Diana's voice rang out but Misha could not see her so he pushed his way towards the back of the room.

A man threw a punch at Diana and she ducked down so the punch missed her. Vivian ran up behind the man and kicked him in the side of the knee. As the man started to stumble, Diana kicked him in his other knee then turned quickly and kicked the man in the stomach with a roundhouse kick. Vivian grabbed the man's head and broke his neck.

The stench from dozens of people imprisoned in a small house overwhelmed the senses of the soldiers as they fought their way inside of the farmhouse.

"Sergeant Crater have the ones who can't walk carried out of here," Simon yelled as he dodged a knife that was thrown at him.

Once the soldiers arrived the fight ended quickly. The bocas were brought down to the house. Soldiers were handing out food and water to the hostages and helping with the medical care. Lieutenant Markus walked up to Raul and Simon. "All of Shanksaw's men are dead; we've got thirty-six bodies and that is just from the farmhouse. There were forty-four hostages crammed in this place and some are in pretty bad shape; we should have brought more bocas."

"Some can ride with the men," Raul said. "How about our men, what is their status?"

"I think the only ones who got hurt were the Rualas," Markus said. "They were inside fighting when the rest of us rode up."

"This is unbelievable," Simon said angrily. "Forty-four people kidnapped from Salar and no one said anything to us. Didn't they think we would help them?"

King Sudfad led the troops that rode through the streets of Salar that morning ending Shanksaw's reign of terror. By the time Sudfad walked into the Racing Horse Tavern the fighting was over. Stephan was behind the bar opening bottles of whiskey and pouring drinks for everyone. The wounded were being taken to Gabriel's building where Lila, Emeral and Thor were providing medical care.

"Glad to see you, but why did you come?" Raphael asked Sudfad.

"The Enrops told me your men were greatly outnumbered here. Is that Shanksaw tied to the chair?" Sudfad asked.

"Yes," Gabriel said as he joined the two men.

Sudfad walked up to Shanksaw. "When you hang it will be in the center of the city so that all those you victimized can see justice done. Nothing is more despicable than someone who preys upon the weak."

"So does that mean I can't work a deal with you?" Shanksaw asked with a grin. Sudfad punched Shanksaw in the jaw, throwing him back against the wall.

Sudfad turned to Gabriel and Raphael, "Use the truth potion on him before we execute him."

Soldiers pulled the five men from the kitchen who Vivian and Diana captured and dragged them out of the tavern. "What are they going to do with them?" Diana asked.

"They're going to the dungeons," Thaos said. "Then after that probably hanged."

"There's still the rented rooms," Vivian said. "There might be men hiding in them. And room five has the demon snakes."

"What do you want to do with Gus?" Jared asked when he heard Gus moaning.

"Is he the one who was going to sell the girls?" Sudfad asked.

"Yes, and he has been hiding criminals in here for years," Gabriel said.

As more soldiers entered the tavern Sudfad ordered, "The one on the floor there goes to the dungeons too. I should just burn this place down."

"Wait," Gabriel said. "Gus has been hiding all of the extortion money we may need him to open safes. Someone throw some cold water on Gus and wake him up."

"Gladly," Diana said and ran into the kitchen.

Vivian walked up to Sudfad, Gabriel and Raphael. "Before you burn this place down perhaps you should talk to Berta. She is a good woman and her husband is part owner. They might clean this place up."

Gus yelled as Diana threw a bucket of water on him. "You're lucky it wasn't scalding," she said loudly. "Gus you were trying to sell me and Vivian and what I want to know is how many other girls have you sold?" Suddenly the entire room became quiet as everyone turned and looked at Gus.

276

Chapter XIX
Responsibilities

Sudfad sent one of the soldiers back to the castle to get some truth potion from Gala. All of Shanksaw's men were being taken to the dungeons at Fort Salar except for Shanksaw, because Gabriel and Raphael planned to interrogate him before they moved him from the tavern.

Archetenus led a search of the rented rooms. Archetenus and the soldiers found men hiding in rooms numbered 2, 4 and 6. These men were also taken to the dungeons. Archetenus saved room number 5 for last since Berta had warned them about the snakes. Shanksaw refused to tell the men how many snakes were in his room and Gus didn't know because the snakes scared him so he didn't look at them when they were caged. Jared and Archetenus burst into room 5 and two huge snakes immediately lunged at the men. Since both men were prepared for the attack they quickly killed the snakes, then searched the room for more.

"The snakes are dead if you want to search his room," Archetenus said when he and Jared returned to the bar room.

"I'll wait for Raphael," Gabriel said. "He is having Gus open the safes."

Suddenly everyone heard Gus yelling, "You can't take all of the money. Some of that is mine."

"Then you will get it back after we figure out the amounts of money the store owners were forced to pay," Raphael said. "Sudfad can you come here?" Raphael called from a small room behind the bar.

"Look at this," Raphael said. "We are going to need a boca to transport it."

Sudfad returned to the bar room. "Thaos and Stephan would you mind supervising the transport of this money to the castle?"

"If you don't mind we wanted to talk to Gus about how many girls he may have sold," Stephan said.

"Good idea," Sudfad said. "I don't think any of us considered that until Diana said it."

"Me and Jared will take the money to the castle," Archetenus said.

"Actually I would prefer that you remain here while we interrogate Shanksaw and search his room. I don't believe this is over yet. Where are Misha and the girls?" Sudfad asked.

"Vivian and Diana went across the street to help with the wounded," Raphael said. "I don't know if Misha went with them."

"We'll go out and find Misha," Stephan said and he and Thaos left the tavern. Thaos returned about two minutes later.

"Raul, Simon and the others are just riding into the city," Thaos said. "Stephan is going to tell Raul and Simon to come here. I thought I would help with a few of the wounded."

"We should have gotten more supplies," Emeral said as she was overwhelmed with the number of wounded people in the building.

"Now that the fighting is done the stores should be opening up," Berta said as she was cleaning the wound of a Patronus priest. "Vivian, Diana why don't you run to the General Store and put everything on Gus's account, serves him good."

Both Vivian and Diana laughed, "Gladly," Vivian said. She looked around the room and saw all of the soldiers and priests who were helping with the wounded. "Emeral can Thor come with us, he has never seen any of the city before?"

"That's fine, just hurry back with the supplies."

"Thor I forgot the steps are hard for you," Vivian said as they walked out of the back of the building.

"I'm fine and after seeing what all of you look like I have nothing to complain about."

"I didn't want to say this in front of the others but Thor it was so much fun," Diana said then laughed. "I haven't been in a good fight like that since the first night we arrived here."

"Next time I will be fighting with you," Thor said. "Later take me to that tavern just so I can see where you were working. I heard everyone talking about it but I want to see it for myself."

"Well it's not fancy," Vivian said. "Here we are," The three stopped in front of a store about one half block from the Racing Horse Tavern. "Thor there are several General Stores in this city, but Gus only has accounts at two of them."

"And we are going to buy the store out and make Gus pay for it," Diana said with a giggle.

Thor, Diana and Vivian returned to the makeshift hospital with arm loads of supplies, two of the storeowner's sons also carried supplies into the building. The sons of the storeowner looked at all of the wounded fighters and hostages as they carried supplies through the rooms.

"We're telling Pa you need a whole lot more," the oldest boy said. "We'll be back." The boys put down their sacks and ran out of the building.

"Emeral we didn't have to pay for anything," Diana yelled above the din. "The people already know that we stopped Shanksaw."

Dagon ran into the building. "Hannah, Emeral, now that the fighting is done other physicians are opening their offices and want to help with the patients."

"Thank god," Hannah said. "Dagon can I put you in charge of having some of these people taken to other physicians?"

"Of course. Does it matter who goes first?"

"Cassandra can you take over here?" Hannah called out. "Dagon as soon as Cassandra gets here I will walk with you and decide."

"Harold, oh my god Harold!" Berta screamed as two men carried her husband into the building.

Berta was screaming and crying when she saw how her crippled husband had deteriorated while being held as a hostage.

"Follow me," Hannah said to the two men and took them to a small bed in the same room that Luca was in.

Berta fell to her knees at the side of her husband's bed. "Harold what did they do to you?" she asked. But Harold didn't answer her question. Hannah looked at Emeral who had followed Berta into the room.

"Berta, come with me Honey," Emeral said soothingly. "Hannah is a great physician let her work on Harold."

"Calen," Lila called as she saw her brother-in-law walking past the door. "Calen come in here." Calen quickly entered the room. "Calen I need you to stay with Luca while I tend to other patients. He wants to keep getting out of bed and fight."

"Does he know where he is?" Calen asked with concern as he knelt down beside his brother's small bed.

"No, but Hannah said that between the head wound and the medicine he might be a little disoriented but if he gets up he might start bleeding again."

"Lila help the others I will stay with him," Calen said as he sat on the side of Luca's bed.

"Vivian, Diana, Thor," Emeral yelled. "I need you." Within moments the three Venatores surrounded Emeral. "Dack just told me that people are lining up on the street bringing food and supplies for us but we can't let them all up here there just isn't enough room. I need you to organize areas up here for the food and supplies then have the things brought up. I am sure many people want to visit with the hostages but this just is not the time."

"Thor you can't keep running up and down those stairs," Diana said. "You find space up here and I will be back in a few minutes." Both Vivian and Diana ran down to the street.

"The King is here, the King is here," voices yelled out as Sudfad walked through the chaos. Sudfad stopped to talk with many of the patients.

"Thank you so much for saving us," one woman called out.

Sudfad stood up and started to speak but the noise in the rooms was overwhelming. "The King is trying to talk," a man yelled and soon there was silence.

"We did not find out about the extortion or the hostages until early this morning and within hours we had troops on their way to find you. It breaks my heart that my citizens were terrorized in such a manner. And it angers me that no one told us about your plight. Know that the men who did this to you will be hanged in Salar for all to see." Some people cheered and others cried over Sudfad's words.

Hannah ran out of the room that Harold and Luca were in and bumped into Sudfad. "Oh Sudfad I am so sorry," Hannah said then she paused. "This is why we need a hospital."

"I agree; you and I had talked about a hospital at the fort, after seeing this I believe we need one here too. After this madness has ended come and talk to me," Sudfad said and left the building.

Sudfad returned to the Racing Horse Tavern where Gabriel and Raphael were interrogating Shanksaw in one of the rented bedrooms. Simon, Raul, Archetenus and Jared were also in the room. Thaos and Stephan had taken Gus out of the tavern without saying where they were going. As soon as Sudfad entered the interrogation room, Simon whispered to him, "Lieutenant Markus is transporting the money to the castle and Lieutenant Tanner is in charge of the construction of the gallows."

"Shanksaw was kidnapping people and charging their families five-hundred dollars a month to keep the hostages alive," Raul whispered to his father. "There was just the one place that they held the hostages. That's as far as we've gotten with the questions."

"I want Shanksaw hung today," Sudfad whispered to his sons. "I talked with some of the hostages; Shanksaw's men were starving them and beating them. I am so damn angry I can hardly talk."

"Tell us all the names you use," Gabriel asked Shanksaw who was under the influence of the truth potion.

Shanksaw gave half a laugh, "I don't know if I can remember them all."

Raphael was writing down the questions and answers of the interrogation. "Tell us the ones you do remember," Raphael said.

"Shanksaw, Blatrman, Caulder, Lucene, Williams and Montingham."

"What is your real name?"

"Montingham."

"Did you help the prisoners escape from the dungeons a few weeks ago?"

"I didn't break them out if that is what you mean a demon did that and he had other demons in the dungeons to keep the soldiers busy while some of the prisoners escaped."

"Who was the demon who opened the doors to the cells?"

"I heard it was Petorus."

"Did Petorus hire you to help with the escape?"

"I told you I didn't help with the escape. Petorus is an Old One he doesn't hire men like me he has his underlings do it. Everyone knew the soldiers would go after the prisoners I was just hired to cause diversions to give the prisoners time to escape."

"What kind of diversions?'

"Anything I could think of."

"Is that why you paid men and demons to attack the soldiers who were following the prisoners?"

"You got everything all mixed up and I didn't pay any demons to work, Zieman sent them after my men were killed."

"Why don't you explain it to me so I can understand?"

"I had two jobs going concerning those prisoners a man named Hobart hired me to cause distractions so the prisoners could escape, then by my good fortune that same day a demon hires me to attack the troops that are looking for the prisoners but the only people that the demon was interested in me having killed was Misha and Maxwell who would be leading the troops. I was told they were part of Gabriel's team."

"I didn't know what Gabriel's team was so the demon gave me names and descriptions. So you see it worked out well because I could use the attacks against the troops as the distractions for the prisoner's escape from Wetpr."

"Who is Hobart?"

"Never met him before, I got a message from Berta that there was a man at the alley door to see me."

"Did he tell you who he worked for?"

"Well that is kind of another story," Shanksaw said and grinned.

"Tell us the story."

"Hobart was a mousy fella, the kind I just don't trust. He gives me five bags of gold and tells me there is considerably more in it for me if I cause distractions to help the prisoners escape. Hobart wouldn't answer any of my damn questions. Now, everyone knows the army would be hunting those men so I didn't know if this was some kind of set up for me."

"So I had Hobart followed. He leaves me and goes directly to the Half Horse Tavern but he doesn't go inside of the tavern he walks around behind the building. My men watch him just standing there for a while then a demon shows up. My men never saw where the demon came from, they said he just appeared."

Shanksaw continued, "After the demon leaves my men grab Hobart and take him to an abandoned farmhouse about a mile out of the city. I met them and let's just say that when we got done with Hobart he couldn't tell us enough." Shanksaw started to laugh.

"Tell us what he said."

"He was hired by a demon named Botis, who works for a demon named Vuall who apparently is a lieutenant for Petorus. Hobart didn't know why any of the demons wanted the prisoners to escape and I believed him cuz that guy was too scared to ask questions."

"I told Hobart that I wanted him to set up a meeting between me and Botis but Hobart just drops over dead. And guess who suddenly appears in the room. Botis, an ugly son of a bitch, but he pays well. I told him I didn't want to work with any middle men. Botis doubled the money of his original offer but he wouldn't tell me why he wanted the job done."

"Did you see Botis again?"

"Yeah, he sent me a message to meet him at that same farmhouse. Me and the boys went out there and that damn demon was yelling at me and cursing; he said he wasn't going to pay me because I took that other job too. I told him that if he wanted me exclusively he should have said so. Then I reminded him that the prisoners did escape the kingdom. I asked him why he was so damn mad and he said things didn't work out the way he wanted. I said they did too, the prisoners got away."

"He said that wasn't what he was talking about, then he just disappeared but there were seven bags of gold left on the floor where he had been standing."

"Have you seen Botis since then?"

"No."

"Tell us about the other job you took, the one to kill Misha and Maxwell."

"Like I said that same day, one of my boys comes into the tavern and tells me there is a real smelly demon that wants to talk to me in the alley. So some of my boys come with me. I'll tell you I don't know what kind of demon this was but you could smell him for a mile and he looked like he had slime running down his body. Well, this demon tells me about the prison escape like he thinks I don't know nothing so I figured he wasn't working with Botis."

"He tells me about the troops that are looking for the prisoners and he wants me to kill the leaders. Like I said he had to explain to me who the members of the team were that he was talking about. He said that if I completed my job that they wanted all of the team killed. He gives me ten bags of gold as a sign of good faith and leaves."

"What was his name?"

"Crocell."

"Who does he work for?"

"Now that was damn funny, he said he works for the King of Stordt. I said Hamond is hiring demons now. Because I have done some work for Hamond and he never had time for demons. Crocell says no, Hamond is dead and Zieman is the King. I asked him if Zieman was a demon, because of the name. He said yes, a very powerful demon so I shouldn't think about double crossing him."

"I asked Crocell why the new King of Stordt was so concerned about a few humans in the Kingdom of Wetpr. And Crocell says Zieman's got a lot of plans and he doesn't want Gabriel's team interfering. I asked him who Zieman worked for and Crocell said he didn't work for anyone."

"What day was this that these demons came to you?"

"The same morning of the prison break."

"How were your men able to get soldier uniforms so quickly and join the troops?"

"Oh we already had the uniforms, I like to be prepared.

"How did you get the uniforms?"

"There's a sergeant there that can get me anything I want for the right price."

"What is this sergeant's name?"

"Sattleman he works with the supplies."

As soon as Shanksaw said Sattleman's name, Simon walked out of the room to have Sattleman arrested.

"How were your men able to join the troops?"

"The fort was in chaos, they just blended in."

Raul stepped forward and spoke to Shanksaw. "The prison break happened in the middle of the night, so Hobart and Crocell couldn't have come to you on the day of the escape. They had to know about it ahead of time, but how would they know who would be leading the troops?" Shanksaw started to sweat profusely.

"Raul you have to ask one question at a time," Gabriel said then turned to Shanksaw. "What day did Hobart and Crocell come to you?"

"I told you."

"But your story doesn't make sense." Gabriel now looked at the others because previously no one had been able to lie while under the influence of the truth potion.

"I need some water bad," Shanksaw said as the sweat was pouring out of him. Jared left the room.

"We're getting you water. Did you know about the prison break in advance?"

"Yeah that's what I told you."

"No you said you were told the morning of the prison break."

"No, I said the morning before the prison break."

"So how did Crocell know that Maxwell and Misha would be leading troops?"

"I don't remember," Shanksaw said. "Oh my god I am burning up."

Jared returned to the room with a cup of water as he was walking towards Shanksaw, Raphael suddenly yelled for Jared to stop. Now all of the men saw smoke rising from Shanksaw's body.

286

"What is happening to him?" Sudfad asked

Shanksaw burst into flames. Both Jared and Archetenus ran out of the room and returned with buckets of water from the kitchen. Raul and Raphael were stomping our areas where the fire had spread to the carpet while Gabriel was smothering flames on the bedding. Both Jared and Archetenus threw their buckets of water on Shanksaw's body then left the room to get more.

Hannah walked out of the room where Luca and Harold had been put into beds. She had been tending to Harold's many wounds for a while and now that she was in the hallway Hannah realized things were less chaotic. She could see that there were considerably less people in the building and the noise level had decreased significantly. Hannah walked around until she found Berta.

"Berta, you should see Harold now," Hannah said as she put her hand on Berta's arm.

The solemn look on Hannah's face made Berta break into tears. "Is he dead?" Berta asked.

"No, but I won't lie to you he is not doing well. Some of his wounds got infected and the infection has spread throughout his body. Right now I can't tell you if he will make it. If you are a praying person I would pray."

Berta tried to compose herself as she walked to Harold's room. When she reached the doorway of the room, Berta took a deep breath and patted down her hair before she entered.

"Obviously a demon shut Shanksaw up," Raul said after all of the men returned to the bar room because they didn't want to talk in the rented rooms. "But now I am suspicious of what Shanksaw did tell us. Did the demon think it was alright for us to find out that information or is that information false?"

"Or maybe it took the demon a while to find and kill Shanksaw," Archetenus suggested.

"You all know it was one of the Old Ones to have the power to kill him like that," said Gabriel.

"That is the first time I saw anyone give false information or at the very least get confused about the answers to the questions," Raphael said.

"It sounds like Shanksaw always took men with him when he had meetings with demons. Hopefully some of them are still alive so we can question them," Jared said. "Does anyone know how many were rounded up?"

"The last I heard it was twenty-four," Sudfad said. "I want these men put to death quickly so the citizens feel safe and as a message to others of the consequences of preying on our people. I would suggest you start interrogating those prisoners soon then we will hang each one as you finish with them."

"Hannah, Hannah," Calen called from the doorway of Luca's room.

"Is Luca alright?" Hannah asked as she and Lila both ran to the room.

"Yes, but..." Calen did not finish his sentence but nodded towards Berta who was crying over the body of her now dead husband. Hannah ran to Harold to check him.

"He died a couple of minutes ago," Berta said through sobs.

"Do you have any other family?" Lila asked. "Someone we could send for?"

"No it was just me and Harold," Berta said as she stood up and wiped the tears from her cheeks. "I am going to make arrangements for his funeral."

"That can wait a little while," Hannah said softly.

"No, I have to keep busy," Berta said. "You know I heard what the King said. Harold would probably be alive if one of us would have told the soldiers what was going on. But we were all so afraid. Where are Vivian and Diana?"

"They are helping with patients," Hannah said.

"I don't know how I can ever thank all of you; at least I got to see Harold before he died," Suddenly Berta's demeanor changed. "And Gus that piece of scum, did you know he was trying to sell those girls? He's lucky I don't kill him." Berta paused as she was trying to compose herself. "Hannah when I finish with arrangements I am going back to the tavern and make all of you a wonderful meal. Would some of the men here be able to help me carry the food over?"

"Just let us know when you want them," Hannah said then hugged Berta.

Berta left the room and walked around the building until she found Vivian and Diana. "Harold's dead, but thanks to all of you I got to see him before he died," Berta said as tears ran down her face. "I hope you girls know I didn't know anything about Gus trying to sell you and if I had I would have put a stop to it. I'm going to make the funeral arrangements then I'm going back to the tavern and fix food for everyone here. Tell the men they can come and take all the whiskey they want."

"Berta, King Sudfad is having Gus locked up in the dungeons for hiding criminals and for trying to sell us. That tavern is yours now you might not want to give everything away," Vivian said.

"Mine? I'll have to think about that. I don't know if I want it because there is so much evil there."

"You could clean it up and turn it into a restaurant or at least a different kind of tavern," Diana suggested.

"I just can't think about that now," Berta said. "Tell the men they can have the whiskey and I will fix them food." Both Vivian and Diana hugged Berta before she left the building.

Thor was standing nearby and heard the conversation between Berta, Diana and Vivian. After Berta walked away Thor walked up to Diana and Vivian. "Is this what the missions are like?" he asked.

"What do you mean?" asked Vivian.

"All of these people have been thanking us."

"The people in Lentz were like that too," Diana said. "It makes me feel good to help people. Thor that is why you should stay here on the team; we get to help people and fight demons." Thor smiled but quickly became serious.

Vivian saw the look on his face. "What is wrong?"

"That first night that Misha and I talked he told me I had responsibilities in this family but we started arguing and he never finished telling me what the responsibilities are. I think I understand now."

Chapter XX
Berta

When Berta walked into the Racing Horse Tavern she entered through the alley door as was her habit. She immediately smelled something burning and ran to the stove but could not find the source of the stench. Berta was peeling potatoes and jumped when Thaos entered the kitchen from the bar room.

"Sorry to scare you," he said. "We thought the place was empty then I heard you back here."

"Are you part of Gabriel's team?"

"Yes and you must be Berta, why are you here?"

"My Harold just died and I have to keep busy so I am making food to take over to Hannah and the others. Are you hungry?"

"Sure, there's a few of us out here."

"How many?"

"Seven."

"Would steaks be alright?"

"I don't think any of us would turn down a steak."

As Thaos was leaving the kitchen Berta asked, "What is your name?"

"Thaos."

"Thaos you and your friends are welcome to the whiskey and anything else behind the bar, I'll be out with your food shortly.

"Thank you Berta."

Berta was consumed with her grief and didn't hear the men in the bar room. She was determined to cook all of the food in the tavern because she didn't know what the future held and she didn't want the food to go to waste. When Berta carried the first tray into the bar room she stopped abruptly. "Thaos why didn't you tell me the King was here?" she scolded. Everyone laughed.

"Berta don't be upset," Sudfad said kindly.

"Well, I would have fixed something better if I had known you were here My Lord," she said as she put a platter in front of him.

"This looks good to me," Sudfad said as he looked at the large steak, mashed potatoes and corn on the cob."

Berta brought out four more trays of food and coffee, when she was satisfied there was enough food for the men she said, "There is cherry pie for dessert. I am cooking food to take over to Hannah and the others so I will be in the kitchen if you need me."

"Berta," Thaos said. "I believe the only members of the team that you know are Vivian and Diana…"

Berta quickly interrupted Thaos. "I didn't know that Gus was trying to sell those sweet girls until they told me this morning. You have to believe that I would have stopped him if I would have known."

"Berta, Vivian and Diana speak very highly of you. I believe Thaos just wanted to introduce you to us. You obviously know King Sudfad. I will just go around the table. Next to Sudfad is Raphael, Vivian's husband, Archetenus, Jared, Stephan and Thaos are brothers and sons of one of the ruling families of the Kingdom of Lentz and I am Gabriel, Hannah's husband."

"I didn't know Vivian was married," Berta said with a slight smile.

"She is pregnant with our first child and because of that she was puking a lot when you found that dead body. She was afraid you would see through her disguise," Raphael said.

"I felt so sorry for her but it was getting to us all," Berta said then looked at Jared. "That's where I know you from you helped Gus carry out that body. Where is Gus anyways?"

"First I want to tell you this food is delicious," Stephan said. "And second, Gus is in the dungeons. Thaos and I kind of had a talk with him and he confessed to selling three other young girls."

292

"What! What girls?"

"He said one of them worked here for a short time."

"Oh my god please don't tell me it was that little Sally, she was so sweet and so young."

"She was one of them," Thaos said.

"Can you find those girls and get them back?"

"We were just discussing that," Gabriel said. "But there are some things we want to talk to you about. Diana and Vivian told us Gus had some legal documents that stated who owned this place. I promised the girls I would help you figure that out."

"My husband Harold was Gus' brother." Berta stopped talking so she could compose herself. "Harold just died and thanks to all of you at least I got to be with him in his final moments and he wasn't buried some place where I would never find him. Anyways, Harold and Gus bought this place together but after Harold got hurt who knows what that low down Gus did."

"Do you want to keep this place?" asked Gabriel.

"Vivian and Diana asked me the same thing. Diana thinks I should open a restaurant here. But to be honest there has been just so much evil here, well I don't know. I will have to think about it."

"Find that paperwork and I will help you with it," Gabriel said.

Berta took several steps towards the kitchen then returned to the table, "My Lord," Berta said as she looked at the King. "I was in that building across the street when you came in and talked to everyone. We should have told you about Shanksaw but everyone was just so afraid. He and his men would walk into places and beat people up and they even killed a couple of people."

"What!" Sudfad said angrily. "Who?"

"All I know of is a couple, but that blacksmith shop on Main Street; they killed his brother and they killed a couple of guys in Dillon's Tavern."

"You know we could have saved lives if we would have known about all of this sooner," Sudfad said with frustration.

"I think we all realize that now," Berta said and returned to the kitchen.

After a few minutes Gabriel got up from the table and peeked his head into the kitchen. "Berta can you come out here?"

"Just give me a minute and I will bring the pies."

Berta carried a tray with plates of pie and another pot of coffee to the table. "Berta we are still trying to get information about Shanksaw," Gabriel said. "Did he have any hiding places in this building? We searched his room and didn't find anything. We did get the money that Gus had in safes but I would guess some of that money is yours now."

"Did you look in the cellar, he was always going down there and I never knew why."

"We didn't know there was a cellar."

"The door is in the kitchen, I will show you when you finish eating."

"We know you passed messages for him did you do anything else?"

Berta got a guilty look on her face. "Sometimes he had me pass his orders along to some of his men; they usually came to the alley door."

"We know he was doing business with demons as well as humans do you remember the names of any of these men?"

"Most the time they just came to the back door and told me to get Shanksaw, I wasn't told their names but I would recognize them again, if that would help."

"Berta the reason I am asking is because Shanksaw put bounties out on many people including my team and we want to prevent people from being killed. Sometimes the smallest detail can turn out to be very important."

"Do you remember anything about Shanksaw or his visitors that you could tell us?" asked Gabriel.

Berta started to cry. "Come with me," she said and walked out of the bar room but instead of going into the kitchen Berta turned and walked into Gus's office. To Berta's surprise every one of the men followed her. "Gus was always drunk and shooting off his mouth; he would say things that made Shanksaw mad and more than once Shanksaw beat Gus up after the bar closed."

"One morning I come in and I hear all of this noise coming from Gus' office so I run in here thinking he is getting killed and I see him and Shanksaw. Shanksaw was yelling and hitting Gus but when I walked in they both grabbed things from the desk and put them in the wall and closed it up. I never knew that compartment was there before."

Berta made a fist and started to pound on the wall above Gus' desk. The wall appeared to be made of wood. In less than a minute they all heard a click and a panel opened in the wall. Berta stepped back so the men could look in the hiding place. Gus' office was small and cramped; there wasn't enough room for all of the men to fit in the office. Gabriel was the closest and pulled the items out of the hiding place and handed them to the other men. "Was everything in here Shanksaw's?" Raphael asked as he was looking through a ledger.

"I honestly don't know," Berta said. "I wouldn't even have known about that if I wouldn't have seen it that morning."

"As paranoid as Shanksaw was I find it curious that he would trust his things in Gus's care," Raphael commented.

"Are you thinking Gus might have had more of a role in all of this?" Stephan asked.

"I got along with Gus," Jared said. "But he sure seemed like a drunken fool most of the time. But I am sure there wasn't anything he wouldn't do for money."

Berta jumped, "I got to get to the kitchen and check the roasts," she said and ran out of the office.

"What do you think about her?" asked Archetenus.

"Do you think she is more involved than she says?" asked Gabriel.

"Don't know, just don't trust her; for all we know she could have been the brains behind this operation because Gus sure wasn't."

The next morning everyone wearily gathered around the breakfast table in Gabriel's home. "Where has the Sanuri been lately?" Dagon asked anyone at the table.

"He's been doing research and trying to translate the plyogram," Raphael said.

"I don't understand how he didn't know about Shanksaw and the others," Elan said as he brought Joey to the table.

"He can do a lot of incredible things," Gabriel said. "But remember he is just a man. When he has unusual insight into things it is because the heavens send him the information."

"I heard he is going after those girls Gus sold," Emeral said as she sat down at the table.

"He is returning to Lentz with Thaos and Stephan," Raphael said. "They have some information about where one of the girls might be and are going to look for her."

"That is so disgusting I can't even believe it," Hannah said as she was filling coffee cups.

"Diana, Vivian," Gabriel said. "After breakfast Raphael and I would like to talk to you for a few minutes. Yesterday we spent time with Berta. She fixed a great meal for Sudfad, Thaos, Stephan, Archetenus, Jared, Raphael and me. After we spoke with her half of us thought she was a victim of Shanksaw's and the other half thought she was the brains behind a lot of things."

"Really!" Vivian exclaimed. "She certainly seemed like a victim to us."

"I think that is how we all felt at first but the more we talked to her it was evident that someone at that bar was working more directly with Shanksaw than we originally thought."

"Some of the men think that Gus is too much of a foolish drunk to be the person," Gabriel said. "We are just trying to figure things out and thought you might be able to give us a little more insight."

"Why, I thought she was a lovely person," Emeral said.

"Feeling better?" Calen said as Luca came to the table. "You were really wild yesterday."

"That's what Lila told me," Luca replied. "I honestly don't remember some of it." Then Luca looked at Hannah. "My head is killing me do you have something I can take that won't put me to sleep."

"Sleep might be just what you need," Emeral said as Hannah left the room to get medicine.

Hannah gave Luca some pain medicine then was the last person to sit down at the breakfast table. Misha was waiting for Hannah to sit then he addressed everyone at the table. "I would like to talk about something that is probably going to make some of you mad but it is a subject we should discuss." Misha had everyone's attention.

"Last night," Misha continued. "My bride asked me if we could make love earlier in the morning so she could get to work in the kitchen earlier."

"Misha!" Diana gasped. "I can't believe you are telling that." People smiled as they watched Diana turning several shades of red.

"That's what we all do," said Natasha.

"And that is my point. No matter what time of the day or night at least one of you is working in the kitchen. We have five children in the house now with four babies on the way. All of the women want to be more involved with missions and many of you are going to start college. I think it is time we considered hiring kitchen staff or at least staff to help with the cleaning."

Gabriel, Calen, Luca and Raphael all started to grin when they saw the angry looks on the faces of their wives. "I really don't think that is necessary Misha," Hannah said coldly.

"Vivian, I know you have been sick a lot but every day you look so exhausted," Misha continued to support his argument. "Natasha how many months was it before you could sleep at all after Lily was born? And Hannah with all the projects you are working on for Sudfad, the orphanage and now a hospital when are you going to have time to enjoy that baby you've wanted so badly? You are all doing too much and honestly you can be dangerous on missions if you are too exhausted. I am just saying we should think about it."

"Thank you Misha," Calen said with emphasis. "Some of us have discussed that same thing but we didn't want to bring it up because we knew all the girls would get mad at us. So while everyone is mad at you I just want to say I agree with every word you said."

"Gabriel, Luca and I have been discussing that too," Raphael said. "Misha is right. You are all doing too much and it's not like we can't afford to hire someone."

Luca looked at Misha and laughed, "Boy, you have really changed and you've only been married what, two or three weeks?"

There was a strained silence at the table so Gabriel spoke, "We have options, if you girls really can't tolerate the idea of someone else cooking our food, we could hire someone part time or to help with other duties. I know I have said this so many times, but for those of you who will be starting college you have no idea how time consuming your studies will be and all of you have chosen difficult subjects."

"Vivian," Raphael said. "I worry about you every day because Misha is right you do look exhausted. We could hire some staff and if it doesn't work out we can let them go."

"Emeral what do you think?" Hannah asked.

"That is not an easy answer for me because like all of you I wanted to take care of my family without assistance. Yes I had a house full of children but I wasn't working on missions and all of the other projects and going to school. I believe I am going to agree with Misha on this."

"We can't just hire anyone," Natasha said. "Not with all of the threats against us."

"Honey we all agree on that," Calen said. "All of you need to seriously think about how much time every day you spend cooking and cleaning for a family this big. Think of other ways you could spend that time."

"I know what you are up to Calen you want to work on another baby," Natasha said and laughed.

"You're right but if you give up some of these responsibilities you would have time for another baby and still work on missions."

"Well for my part," Diana said. "If you find out that Berta was only a victim of Shanksaw's I think we should consider her. She is a really hard worker and a good cook."

Later that afternoon the Sanuri, Thaos and Stephan left Salar and rode north. Thaos and Stephan had forced information from Gus about the three girls he had sold over the last two years. The last girl that was victimized by Gus was an orphan named Sally. Sally was fourteen when she came to the Racing Horse Tavern looking for work. Gus sold her six months earlier to a man named Tyrone who lived in the Village of Telmark in Wetpr. Telmark was almost a day and a half ride northeast from Salar. The Sanuri was driving his boca while Stephan and Thaos rode on either side of the wagon.

"I'll tell you I really wanted to kill Gus when he was talking about those poor girls," Stephan said.

"I thought I was angry," Thaos said to the Sanuri. "I had to pull Stephan off that piece of slime."

"It's just a matter of time now," the Sanuri replied. "Did Sudfad tell you he is going to have Gus hanged with the rest of Shanksaw's men?"

"Good!" Stephan said.

"Edward has been in charge of interrogating the prisoners before they are put to death." The Sanuri explained. "Raul told me that Edward tried to interrogate Gus this morning but Gus' face was so swollen from the beating you gave him that he couldn't talk. So he might be the last to hang."

"It will be interesting to hear what he has to say," Thaos said. "While I thought Berta seemed sincere I agree with Archetenus that Gus does not have the brains to have been actively working with Shanksaw."

"If we discover that Berta was a partner of Shanksaw's do you think Sudfad will have her hanged?" asked Stephan.

"That is an interesting question," the Sanuri replied.

Lila walked into the dining room in Gabriel's home where most of the members of the family had gathered. "The children are in the play room I told them to stay there until I returned."

"Before they start," Misha said with a grin. "Diana and I went into Salar this afternoon to look for things for our wedding and this is what we came home with. Misha nodded at a blanket that was spread over the table.

"You bought a blanket?" Luca joked.

"We want to tell you what we are thinking before we show you these things," Diana said. "Joey hasn't really been talking to me or Thor but Christopher and Nicholas have because they know our parents were murdered too. I hope no one gets mad, but that night when I gave Emeral and Maxwell the lamsmans; remember you were all talking about when you should start training the children?"

"Well, I told Vivian and Thor what was said. And Vivian came up with this idea that we hope will help the children heal as well as train them." Diana looked at Vivian who started talking.

"We all come from different backgrounds and will have to make decisions about many things with the children but for now this is what Diana, Thor and I would like to try. Thor will you lift the blanket?" Vivian asked.

"Oh how cute," Natasha gushed when she saw four small sets of moccasins, leather belts, pouches, compasses and other items for the children.

"I didn't know they made canteens this small," Elan said as he picked one up.

"The children are so excited about the map classes that Diana and Thor have been teaching them that we thought we could start teaching them some basic skills. Like how to use a compass and how to walk without leaving tracks, how to build a fire, what berries they can eat. And when all of you decide we can start teaching the children more advanced things. Now for Thor's idea." Vivian said.

Thor placed four tiny lamsmans on the table. "As you know a Venator earns every stone in their lamsman. I thought that for the children every time they learn one of the basic skills that Vivian was naming that we would put a stone on a lamsman for them. As you can see now, each lamsman has one red stone already and that signifies they had to face a great darkness; which all of these children have."

"Diana, Thor and I are proposing this but of course all of you can join in with teaching these skills. The children really look up to all of you and want to be like you, so we thought if we started this training it might help them to heal from the loss of their original families too. But of course, they are not our children so we won't teach anything unless all of you approve," Vivian said.

"I think it is an absolutely wonderful idea," Emeral said.

"So do I," said Gabriel as he was looking at the many items on the table.

"The only thing that worries me are those little knives you bought. I am not sure the children are ready for them yet," Hannah said with concern.

"I wondered about that too, when we bought them," Misha said.

"There will be times when they could use a knife and maybe we only let them have the knives at those times," Diana suggested.

"I very much like this idea, as you know I have been really concerned about all the nightmares that Christopher has been having," Luca said. "But I want to participate with this also. And I am sure that Gabriel and Elan feel the same way."

"Actually we were hoping you would feel that way," Thor said. "Because we think part of what will help them to heal is becoming closer to their new parents."

"If you all agree on this," Diana said. "We want to have a little ceremony and have the parents of each child put the lamsman on them and present them with their equipment."

"I never even thought about this before," Gabriel said. "But after we teach some of the skills we should take the children camping overnight."

"Is this for fishing?" Cassandra asked as she was looking through the items.

"Yes, right now we are thinking about teaching basic skills for being in the wilderness," Vivian said. "We aren't going to teach anything about hunting demons until all of you think the children are ready."

Raphael put his arm around Vivian, "So you aren't mad at me because I don't want to teach the children to hunt until they are a little older?"

"I didn't think about that until Diana told me what all of you were discussing."

Calen asked, "Is there anyone here who thinks this is a bad idea?" No one responded. "Then everyone likes the idea? Unfortunately Lily is too small but as an uncle I want to participate too."

"Let's bring the children in," Diana said excitedly. "We are going to present these things like we do for Venatores so the children should line up with their parents next to them."

"Let me get the others," Cassandra said. "They didn't come because they aren't parents. It will just take a moment."

"As grandparents can we be involved?" Maxwell asked with a smile.

"Of course," Diana said.

Within minutes the entire team was gathered in the dining room which had been slightly rearranged. The four children, their new parents and grandparents all stood in front of the room. Thor did the presentation.

"In our tribe when the children are your ages they start to train to be warriors. Your fathers and mothers are warriors and would like you to be with them on their missions but there are many skills which you must learn first. So we are going to start teaching you those skills." Christopher and Nicholas started to smile and jump up and down.

"To begin, your parents are now going to put a lamsmans on your right ankle. Every time you master a skill we will put another stone on that lamsman. You are all starting with the red stone. For a Venator the red stone signifies they have stood up to a great darkness or evil. All of you have lost your parents as we did; you have all bravely stood up to that darkness and have earned your first stone."

The family applauded as the parents fastened the lamsmans to the children's ankles. Every child was then awarded a leather belt. Vivian and Diana handed each item to the parents or to Maxwell and Emeral to give to the children as Thor explained what the items were and what they would be used for.

The members of the team who were observing this simple ceremony all witnessed a transformation, small as it was it set a pattern for the future of the families of the team and their children. With every item that was awarded to the children their pride and confidence could be seen on their faces. Later the proud parents would say that with every item they presented to the children they felt the bond strengthen between them all.

The following evening the Sanuri, Thaos and Stephan entered the small Village of Telmark. They did not have a lot of information about Tyrone or Sally other than brief descriptions. The three men decided to split up and ask for information.

Thaos and Stephan each entered a tavern while the Sanuri walked into the General Store. An hour later they met back at their horses.

"Either Gus lied to us or people just don't want to tell us anything because we are strangers," Thaos said with frustration.

"There is the possibility that Tyrone lied to Gus also," the Sanuri said. "It's getting late, let's get rooms and resume the search in the morning."

Sudfad called an evening meeting at the castle which he held in the Great Hall because his study was too small. Most of Gabriel's team was in attendance besides, Archetenus, Jared, Edward, Simon and Raul. This was the first time they had gathered as a group since the battle with Shanksaw and his men. They started out the meeting by sharing the bits and pieces of information that each of them had so they could build a picture of what Shanksaw really was up to.

After an hour Edward stood up and addressed the group. "Many of us in this room have spent the last two days interrogating Shanksaw's men. We used the truth potion on all of them and to our surprise we learned very little new information. I believe that Shanksaw was so paranoid that he was very careful who he shared information with. Most of his men basically told us as much as Shanksaw did but we got a few more descriptions of demons and men who are probably members of the Insidiae."

"Thaos and Stephan beat Gus up pretty badly so we had to wait for some of the swelling on his face to go down so he could talk. He told us that Shanksaw paid him to hide things. Gus hid Shanksaw's money in a hidden safe and hid Shanksaw's ledgers in a hidden compartment in his office."

"Now I had almost no contact with Gus during the mission," Edward continued. "But almost everyone who did said he was a drunken idiot who talked too much which makes one wonder why a man as paranoid as Shanksaw would trust Gus. So far I have not found an answer to that question unless one of you has some additional information. I suspect there might be more of a connection between Shanksaw and Gus than we are aware of like perhaps they are distant family."

Edward paused before continuing, "Then there is the matter of Berta; one of Shanksaw's men referred to her as his boss. Berta admits to performing certain tasks for Shanksaw because he held her husband hostage. While we really have no solid information that her involvement was more than what Berta admitted to; many in this room suspect it was. Which raises the question do we want to interrogate her with the truth potion?"

"I had everyone hanged right after the interrogations because after Vivian's experience we don't really know the long term effects of that potion. I wanted the men hanged so the citizens would feel safer and as a deterrent to other criminals," Sudfad explained. "The quandary here is that I don't want to risk Berta's life with the potion if she truly was nothing more than a victim in all of this. Apparently Gus did not know about Berta's involvement or even that his brother was being held as a hostage which I find most unusual."

"While I agree with many of you that something just doesn't seem right about the connections between Berta, Gus and Shanksaw at this time we have no proof of Berta's involvement in a more sinister way. Unless you have objections I would like to wait until the Sanuri returns and have him talk to Berta, perhaps he can read her mind," Sudfad suggested.

"As Edward said we found ledgers," Raphael said. "But not surprisingly they are written in some type of code which Gabriel and I are still trying to decipher. If anyone wants to help break the code you are more than welcomed to join us."

Berta quickly sat up in bed; her heart racing as she tried to figure out what woke her. Silence was all she heard. After a few moments Berta lay back down and as soon as she closed her eyes she heard it again, movement she heard movement in her empty house.

Berta always slept with a large knife under her pillow which she now grabbed. Slowly she lifted the covers off from her body. Berta strained to hear any sound but heard nothing. Ever so slowly she got out of bed. Her eyes were accustomed to the darkness of her room. She moved slowly and quietly crossing the floor of her bedroom. Berta gently lifted the latch to her bedroom door which opened to the kitchen.

"Shanksaw," she gasped. "They told me you were dead."
Shanksaw's image did not speak but started to move towards the
frightened woman.

"I didn't tell them," Berta said fearfully. "I didn't say nothing."

Berta heard movement and looked down towards the floor and
screamed in terror when she saw two large red snakes coming
towards her.

Chapter XXI
Family Matters

"Luca are you awake?" Lila whispered softly. Luca smiled and rolled over on his side so that he was facing her. Without opening his eyes, Luca started to kiss her passionately.

After they had kissed for several moments Lila asked, "Can we talk for a few minutes? I haven't been able to sleep I have so much on my mind." Luca propped his head on his right hand and looked at his wife.

"Is something wrong?"

"Not really," Lila said as she sat up in bed. "Luca are you really alright with me going to school?"

"You have asked me this several times, Honey as long as all of you girls agree to let us hire some help around here, yes I am. In fact I am proud that you want to be a physician. But why do you keep asking me is there something else going on?"

Lila hesitated a moment, "I know I shouldn't say anything and I don't want to be a gossip but you know that Bekka and I are close friends. Luca yesterday she asked me if you and I ever tell each other that we love each other. And I told her the truth and said we say it all of the time. Luca neither Bekka nor Koby have ever said that to each other. And there are just so many other things they never talk about or say to each other. I know that I have a lot to learn but I just don't want us to become like them, so Luca promise me that we will always talk things out."

Luca pulled Lila towards him and kissed her on the lips. "I promise and I expect the same out of you."

"Oh I promise; I like both Bekka and Koby so much but Luca if I tell you something you can't repeat it."

Luca looked at Lila and said seriously, "Tell me." Because the tone of Lila's voice was worrying him.

"Bekka doesn't think she loves Koby and now, well, she doesn't know if she wants to go through with the marriage."

"She is thinking about going back to the Ice Caves and live with her family." Now Luca sat up in bed.

"I thought they were working things out, I know they have been having long talks with Emeral and Maxwell."

"And that brings up something else that I want to talk to you about later. Bekka loves everyone here so much and she is afraid that if she doesn't marry Koby we will hate her and she will never see any of us again."

"I think I should talk to Maxwell and Emeral about this."

"Luca, Bekka made me promise not to tell anyone."

"But Honey you don't want to lose your friend or have then have miserable lives. I haven't talked to Koby but I was there when he found out that Bekka was pregnant. Let's just say it was a different reaction than I had when you told me. I am not sure he is ready for all of this either."

"Well, what if they didn't get married and everything just stayed the way it is?"

"No one in the family is going to hate them if that is what you are asking but what happens when one of them finally meets someone they do fall in love with?"

"Did you know that Cassandra and Elan said they would raise the baby if Koby and Bekka didn't want it?"

"Yes and I think that is very generous of them but I think that too would cause problems with all of us living under the same roof."

"Luca I love Bekka and I want to help her but I just don't know how."

"Let me see what I can do; I love them both too."

"Luca, Bekka might feel really betrayed if she finds out that I told you all of this."

"We don't have to tell her. I mean I think everyone in the household is concerned about them. Let me take it from here."

"Alright, I just feel so bad for them."

"Honey they are adults they both knew she could get pregnant and the fact that they don't talk to each other about anything important is also their choices but I too want the best for both of them. I am glad that you told me. Now what was that other thing you wanted to talk about with Emeral and Maxwell?"

"Did you know that before Vitomas and Annabelle got married that they had a celebration for Sudfad and Renya just to show them how much they appreciated everything they did for them?"

"I wasn't there but I heard about it," Luca said and smiled. "Let me guess you think we should do the same for Emeral and Maxwell?"

"Yes, or something else that is wonderful. Luca all of you boys grew up with them and I don't think you always appreciate them. You know most of the rest of us in this house don't have parents or grandparents and I can't tell you how many times one of us girls goes to Emeral for advice. They do so much for us and the children that I think we should do something for them."

"I like your idea have you talked it over with anyone else?"

"No because between the weddings, the baby celebration, the missions and everything else it might not be the right time."

"Honey our team or I should say our family now is growing so fast I think we will always have a lot going on so we will have to make time for this, but I really do like your idea."

"I thought that if you didn't think a celebration was the right gift that we could remodel their chambers or send them on a trip or something."

Luca kissed Lila then asked, "Do you want me to say something to the family or do you want to?"

"Maybe you should talk to your brothers first before we tell everyone."

※

"Where were you?" Diana asked groggily as Misha returned to bed.

"Did you miss me?" he asked.

"Yes," Diana said as she put her arms around Misha's neck and kissed him on the lips. He pulled her closer to him and held her tightly as they kissed passionately for several minutes.

"Diana before we make love I have something for you," Misha said with a big smile. As Diana sat up in bed, Misha picked a box up that was on the table next to their bed. "Thor told Raphael and me that in your tribe Venatores exchange lamsmans when they marry. So Raphael and I got the idea to have something made up from us for you and Vivian." Misha handed Diana the box and kept talking. "Of course the ones we designed are different."

"Oh Misha! This is so beautiful I am almost afraid to wear it."

"Nonsense, now I will have to put it on you when you are done looking at it."

"Seriously Misha what if this breaks or I lose it? It is just so beautiful."

"If that happens I will just get you another. So do you like it?"

"I love it," Diana said and moved close to Misha and kissed him on the lips.

"I will be honest, both Raphael and I had trouble deciding on the stones so we decided to have them match our wedding rings."

"Can I show the others or should I wait?" Diana asked excitedly.

"No you can show them, Raphael is giving Vivian hers this morning too."

"I am sorry to wake you, I know it's early," Luca said as Maxwell opened the door to his and Emeral's chambers.

"Actually we were up and getting dressed, come in," Maxwell said as he stepped to the side so Luca could enter the room. "Is anything wrong?"

"Yes, but not with my family. I wanted to talk to the two of you before breakfast; it's about Koby and Bekka."

"I can hear you and I will be there in a few moments," Emeral called out from the bedroom. "The coffee should be ready by now." Maxwell poured three cups of coffee as the two men waited for Emeral. "I suppose it really didn't matter that you would have seen me in my robe," Emeral said with half a laugh as she entered the parlor.

"I may have seen you in it once or twice before," Luca said with a grin. "And I apologize again for the hour. Lila couldn't sleep last night because she had a lot on her mind; so she woke me this morning and talked to me about Koby and Bekka. You know how close Lila and Bekka are; and while Lila feels like she is betraying Bekka's confidence she is so worried about Bekka that Lila had to say something. And I am glad she did. Bekka has been asking Lila all kinds of questions like do Lila and I ever tell each other that we love each other."

"Already this doesn't sound good," said Maxwell.

"Apparently neither Bekka nor Koby have ever said that to each other. Bekka doesn't know if she loves Koby and is thinking about backing out of the marriage and returning to the Ice Caves to live with her parents. And from what Lila says it sounds like Bekka and Koby still don't really discuss important things. Lila also said that Bekka loves everyone here as her family and is afraid that we will all hate her and never want to see her again."

"This breaks my heart, yet it doesn't totally surprise me," Emeral said.

"Lila would like them to just keep their relationship as it is instead of Bekka leaving, but that brings up other problems," Luca said. "What if one of them falls in love with someone else?"

"And then there is the matter of Elan and Cassandra possibly raising the baby but personally I think that could cause problems if we all continue to live together. Lila doesn't want Bekka to find out that she is the one who told these things because she promised Bekka that she wouldn't say anything. I have not discussed this matter with anyone else."

311

"Well, I am glad you came to us," Maxwell said as he stood up to refill his cup with coffee. "Your mother has talked to Koby about what he would want to do with the child if Bekka didn't want it and Koby said he would raise it but he would need our help."

"I am not sure if that surprises me or not," Luca said. "But do you think Bekka would go to the Ice Caves and leave the baby here?"

"I don't' think either of them have any idea of what they are going to do," Emeral said. "Your father and I have discussed this matter; it is like both Bekka and Koby are in a panic. They know the proper thing to do is to marry and raise the child but honestly I don't think either of them want to marry."

"And Koby feels there is something wrong with him," Maxwell explained. "Because all of us have always considered Misha the, how should I say, wild card among you boys. And Koby sees how Misha has changed since he married Diana and how happy he is now; so Koby is really afraid that he and Bekka are not right for each other."

"Don't get me wrong," Luca said. "I love them both but I don't think either of them is right for the other. Koby helped Bekka a great deal with her guilt over Fala's death. And they are good to each other but it seems like they are simply friends who have sex. And from what Lila said I think both Bekka and Koby are looking at the rest of our marriages and comparing them to their relationship. So do you think I should talk to Koby or do you want to?"

"It should be us," Maxwell said. "That way we can say we have observed things instead of telling them we got our information from Lila; we don't want to damage Lila's and Bekka's friendship."

"I appreciate you saying that. But too, I am willing to help in any way."

"Look at what Misha gave me," Diana said excitedly as she ran into the kitchen to help prepare breakfast. Diana pulled her skirt up exposing the sapphire and diamond bracelet on her ankle. "Is Vivian here because she got one too?"

"Put your leg up so we can see it better," Natasha said as she laughed.

"It's really beautiful," said Hannah.

"Misha said that Thor told him and Raphael that Venatores exchange lamsmans when they marry so this is Misha's lamsman to me. I love it but I am so worried that I will break it." Diana was so excited that she was talking very fast.

"I like the idea of wearing a bracelet on your ankle," Lila said. "It is very pretty."

"It matches your rings. I might have to suggest to Calen that he should get me one also," Natasha said and winked at Diana.

"Where is everyone? The dining room was empty when I came in?" Diana asked.

"Luca is meeting with the men and I think Emeral and Maxwell are talking with Koby and Bekka," Hannah replied.

"Hannah do you feel alright?" Lila asked.

"No, the smell of the eggs is bothering me; I am going to set the table."

"Thank god all of you pregnant girls don't get sick at the same time," Natasha said and laughed.

Cassandra and Vivian walked into the kitchen together. "Let's see it," Natasha said. "Show them yours Diana."

"Oh I don't know which I like better," Cassandra said as the woman compared Vivian's emerald and diamond ankle bracelet with Diana's sapphire and diamond bracelet.

"They are both so beautiful," Lila said.

"Let's all tell our husbands we want one too?" Natasha said. "Things seem to work well when we all work together." Everyone in the room laughed.

"We didn't say this to hurt your feelings," Emeral said sweetly as Koby and Bekka stared at her and Maxwell. "It's just that Maxwell and I feel that while the two of you care about each other you just don't seem ready for marriage. And we wanted to talk about your options."

"As I said you don't have to come up with any decisions today but think about what we said," Maxwell explained. "Everyone in the family loves the both of you dearly so no one is going to judge you. Do what the two of you feel is right for yourselves."

Koby and Bekka looked at each other then back at Emeral and Maxwell but did not speak. "You both admit that you have difficulty talking to each other about your feelings. Is it possible that you two are afraid of hurting each other if you speak the truth?" Emeral asked. Bekka burst into tears.

Koby put his arm around her and asked, "Did Emeral hit a chord?"

"Yes," Bekka said as she sobbed.

"Do you want us to leave the two of you alone?" Maxwell asked.

"I don't know," Koby said. "It seems like the only time that Bekka and I can talk is when we are with you. Bekka what do you want?"

"Stay," Bekka said as she wiped the tears from her face. Bekka tried to talk but started to cough.

"I know it is early but would you like a little whiskey?" Maxwell asked. "Just to calm you a little?"

Bekka nodded. Maxwell poured two small glasses of whiskey and handed them to Koby and Bekka. It was clear to everyone in the room that Koby did not want to speak first.

Bekka took a couple of sips of her drink then gathered all of her strength. She turned and looked at Koby. "Koby you are my best friend and I do love you but when I look at all the other couples here, I don't, oh please don't get mad." Tears were pouring down Bekka's cheeks. "I don't think I love you the right way. I mean the way I should for us to get married. I just feel so confused."

314

Koby took the glass out of Bekka's hand and then took both of her hands in his. "Bekka I am not mad because that is exactly how I have been feeling too. And I didn't know if there is something wrong with me, because there certainly isn't anything wrong with you." Bekka leaned forward, putting her head on his chest."

"Koby there isn't anything wrong with you; you are a wonderful man," Bekka said softly.

"There isn't anything wrong with either one of you," Maxwell said. "You are best friends who were having sex. And now you are in a situation that you didn't plan for. What you just admitted was obvious to Emeral and me. So now there are things that you have to think about. You certainly don't have to get married. Actually you can just keep things the way they are if that is what you want but you should think about what will happen if one of you falls in love with someone else; because that is a real possibility."

"If you don't marry I hope you both understand this is still your home," Emeral said. "But what about the baby? Do you want to raise it together? Do you want to let Elan and Cassandra adopt the baby? The one thing you should think about is if you don't marry and you both fall in love with other people, who will take care of the child."

"What do you think we should do?" Bekka asked. Both Maxwell and Emeral hesitated.

"Understand this has to be your decision but during my life the marriages I have seen where the people didn't love each other were very painful for both of them," Emeral said. "You both respect each other and care about each other deeply. And you are both wonderful people who will find the loves of your lives someday but since you are responsible for that baby you have to make some hard decisions now."

"Now that you have admitted how you both really feel; do you think you can talk things out now?" Maxwell asked. Bekka and Koby looked at each other and both nodded.

"Koby I am so emotional and it may be because of the baby too, do you want your parents to stay while we talk?"

"We certainly can help you think through things," Emeral said.

"That might be for the best," Koby admitted.

"Then I am going downstairs and bring our breakfast up here," Emeral said. "Maxwell why don't you arrange the table."

"Emeral is everything alright?" Lila asked when Emeral joined the women in the kitchen.

"It will be," Emeral said and patted Lila's arm. "Koby, Bekka, Maxwell and I are going to eat breakfast in our chambers. They are finally able to talk about some things."

"Good," Natasha said with emphasis. "I have been so worried about them. I will help you carry the trays."

Fifteen minutes later the family was gathering around the dining room table for breakfast. "Koby, Bekka, Emeral and Maxwell are eating upstairs," Natasha announced. "So we won't be waiting for them."

"Well then this is the perfect opportunity to tell you about Lila's idea," Luca said with pride. "She wants to do something big for Emeral and Maxwell to show them how much we all appreciate everything they do for us."

"Oh I like that idea," Hannah said before Luca was finished talking.

"Lila suggested a big celebration like Vitomas and Annabelle had for Sudfad and Renya or sending Emeral and Maxwell on a trip or we could remodel their chambers. So what do all of you think?"

"Is that what you men were talking about this morning?" asked Natasha.

"Yes, Lila thought I should run the idea past my brothers before we suggested anything."

"Is there anyone here who doesn't think doing something for them is a good idea?" Gabriel asked. No one responded.

"That's what I thought. And for my thoughts I think we should do everything you suggested. We can have a celebration, you know Renya will want to have it at the castle then we can remodel their chambers while they are on a trip."

Natasha looked at Calen who was smiling proudly. "Remember how worried you were that your parents wouldn't fit in here?"

"Were you?" Hannah asked with surprise.

"Yes," Calen joked. "Guess a guy can be wrong once in his life." Natasha leaned over and kissed Calen on the cheek.

"Speaking of gifts," Natasha said with a coy smile. "I don't know if all of you men saw what Misha and Raphael bought for Diana and Vivian but I am pretty confident that every one of us women would like one too."

"What did you get?" Elan asked.

"Thor told us that Venatores exchange lamsmans when they marry," Raphael explained. "So we had Andrew make lamsmans for us but instead of leather and stones they are made of gold with the same stones as our wedding rings."

"And we just love them," Vivian said and kissed Raphael on the cheek.

"Girls show them," Natasha said. Both Vivian and Diana stood up and walked around the table showing everyone their new gifts.

"You must really like them," Calen said. "Because you have never asked for any jewelry before. Do you want the same stones as our wedding rings or something different?"

"As our wedding rings," Natasha said happily.

"Is there any woman at this table that doesn't want one of those?" Luca asked as he watched everyone's faces as they looked at the jeweled lamsmans. Hannah, Lila and Cassandra all smiled. "Lila why don't you write down the stones that each woman wants and I can take it to Andrews; I have to go into the city today anyways.

"We should get one for Emeral and Bekka too," Natasha said. "I know Emeral has rubies in her wedding band does anyone know what stones Bekka was going to pick out?" Everyone at the table became quiet.

"We might want to wait on that," said Luca.

"Why?" Natasha asked. "Then she looked at Luca accusingly. "Luca what aren't you telling us?"

"They haven't decided on their rings yet."

"Why don't I believe you?" Natasha replied.

The small Village of Telmark only had one hotel named Martha's. This hotel consisted of five rooms for renters, the living quarters for Martha and her three children, a small dining room and kitchen. Martha was very happy when Thaos, Stephan and the Sanuri rented rooms the night before because Telmark didn't get a lot of visitors. There was only one other man staying at the hotel and his name was Frank. All four men were told to be in the dining room at sunrise for breakfast.

"Martha I must compliment you on the fine food here," the Sanuri said as he poured syrup on his second plate of pancakes. "Tell me was this your family home before you turned it into a hotel?"

"Yes, after my husband James died, well I had to do something to feed the family," Martha said as she walked around the table pouring coffee into all the men's cups. "It's not a bad way to make a living but we don't get a lot of strangers here. Frank there," Martha nodded towards the fourth man sitting at the table.

"Why, he lives here in the hotel because his house burned down in a storm." As Martha talked Frank raised his cup of coffee to the other men as a sort of salute but continued to eat. "I must say you gentlemen came as an answer to a prayer."

"What do you mean?" asked the Sanuri.

"Well I was running out of money for food and I prayed that The Great Ruler would send me a renter and a couple of hours later the three of you walk in. I guess I didn't realize he worked that fast."

The Sanuri smiled at Martha's words. "My friends and I are here on some rather unsavory business and I wonder if either you or Frank might help us."

"What kind of help do you need?" Frank asked as he wiped his mouth with a napkin.

"We are here on behalf of King Sudfad," the Sanuri continued. Both Martha and Frank stared at the three men with this revelation. "The King's men rounded up a group of dangerous outlaws recently, my friends here were involved with that. While interrogating some of the men, Thaos and Stephan here learned that one of the men had sold three young girls against their wills. We are trying to find those girls now."

To the surprise of the men; Martha abruptly turned to Thaos and Stephan. "I hope you beat the hell out of the man who did that. I have two young daughters myself."

"Yes My Lady, we sure did," Stephan said with a grin.

"How can we help you?" Frank asked.

"About six months ago a fourteen year old girl named Sally was sold to a man named Tyrone who said he lived in this village," Thaos explained. "By any chance do you know these people?"

"This village ain't that big," Frank said. "And I never heard the name Tyrone before."

"Neither have I," Martha said. Then she turned to Frank. "But I heard that Sal suddenly showed up with a young wife, did you ever see her?"

"No, but now that you mention it I did hear the same thing," Frank said to Martha then turned to Thaos. "Sal is an old farmer; he lives about ten miles north of the village. If he's your man be prepared for a fight because he is nasty as hell. In fact if he isn't your man and you step on his property be prepared for a fight.

319

"Can you draw us a map to his place?" Stephan asked.

"I'll do better than that," Martha said as she took off her apron. "I'll take you there myself. Why, I have known Sal all my life and if he bought that girl, shame on him and I will tell him so." The men smiled as Martha talked. She turned to Frank. "Can you mind the place while I am gone?"

"Of course," Frank replied then he turned to the other men. "Actually Sal might be a whole lot nicer if you do take Martha along. She kinda has a way with people."

"Just let me hitch my boca and we can go," Martha said and turned to leave the room.

"I'll help you," Stephan said and followed her out of the hotel.

Sal's farmhouse was extremely secluded, a faint dirt road led to his home. Twice the men thought they would have to tell Martha to ride on one of their horses because the road was too rough and narrow for the small boca, but she persevered.

"What are you going to do to Sal if he has the girl?" Martha asked.

"Take him back to Salar and the King can decide his fate," Stephan responded.

"What do you think the King will do?"

"Well he hung the guy who sold the girls; I am willing to guess he will do the same to Sal. From what the guy who sold her said; Sally did not go willingly."

"And the other two girls, what about them?"

"They were sold over a year ago and the man who sold them was a drunk so he just didn't remember some things. He thought he might have sold them all to the same guy but he wasn't really sure."

"What would Sal do with three young girls?"

No one answered Martha's question and after a moment she became silent too as she realized the answer to her own question. "We will be there in a few minutes," Martha said. "I am not trying to tell you what to do but I do know Sal and he will be nice to me. So I am thinking you just let me drive up to his place and get him outside then you can do whatever you want. I am afraid that if he sees you riding up he will hurt the girl, he is kinda crazy."

"Sounds like a plan, My Lady," Thaos said. "And we appreciate your help."

"The whole business just makes me sick. If Sal has that girl I hope you beat the hell out of him too."

"Yes, My Lady," Stephan said and laughed.

Martha stopped the boca. "As soon as we past that turn up ahead Sal will be able to see the road. So you should hide now. The farmhouse is only a few hundred yards past the turn. Unless things have changed there, the area around the house is real open so I will try to keep Sal distracted," Martha said then waited until the three men rode into the woods that surrounded the roadway before she moved the boca. Martha drove up to the front door of the farmhouse. "Sal, Sal it's Martha, I got some news you will want to hear."

A moment later the front door of the farmhouse opened up and a large man with a protruding stomach and filthy clothes stood in the doorway. "Hello Martha, what brings you out this way?"

"Well, I am afraid it's not good news Sal, I came out to warn you." As Martha talked she was climbing down from the front seat of the boca.

"Warn me about what?"

"Sal I went and got my shoe caught could you help me?"

"Warn me about what?" Sal repeated as he walked around the boca to help her.

"Why thank you," Martha said as Sal helped her to the ground.

321

Sal did not notice that Martha was backing up from him as she spoke. "There's strangers in town asking everyone if they know you?"

"Strangers, why?"

"Well, when they talked to me they said you kidnapped one of their daughters and I said Sal wouldn't do that."

"Where are they from?"

"Salar," Martha was watching Thaos, Stephan and the Sanuri surrounding Sal but he did not hear the men.

"Did you get their names?"

"Why, Sal are you in some kind of trouble?"

"Well, I was gambling in Salar I may owe some people money."

"Sal you didn't take that girl did you?"

"Now Martha, that ain't really your business now is it."

"But it is ours," Thaos said as he grabbed Sal from behind and threw him to the ground. Both Stephan and Thaos jumped on top of Sal as they tied his wrists and ankles. The Sanuri and Martha both ran inside of the filthy farmhouse.

"Sally are you here?" the Sanuri called out. "We are here to help."

"I'm here," a girl's voice yelled as she crawled out from under the bed.

"Oh my god!" said Martha as she ran to the girl who was filthy and covered with bruises.

Suddenly the Sanuri stopped as he was getting a vision that was filled with fleeting glimpses. "Are there other girls here?" he asked.

"Yes, April come out they are going to help us," Sally yelled. "A girl that looked perhaps a year older than Sally slowly walked out from behind a large cupboard, she too was filthy and covered with bruises.

"Amy is in the cellar. He put her down there to punish her," Sally cried as Martha put her arms around both of the girls.

"Where is the cellar door?" the Sanuri asked.

"Here I will show you," Sally said as she ran into the kitchen and pointed to a large wooden cupboard. "The door is behind here."

"Help me move this," the Sanuri said to Thaos and Stephan as they walked into the farmhouse. "We have two so far and a third is locked in the cellar."

Stephan looked at Sally while Thaos and the Sanuri moved the cupboard. "Are there others?" Stephan asked.

"He killed Margo, so there's just the three of us. He just stole Amy and she is real little. She wouldn't stop crying so he locked her down there." As the Sanuri and Thaos climbed down the wooden ladder to the cellar, Sally yelled. "Amy these men are here to help us."

"I'm here," a little girl's voice screamed hysterically. "Get me out of here. I'm here, I'm here."

The Sanuri lit a torch as Thaos ran towards the little girl's voice. "I have her," Thaos yelled. "But that bastard tied her up." Then Thaos turned to Amy. "Honey hold still while I cut these ropes because I don't want to cut you. Then we will get you out of here." The Sanuri walked over with the torch and they now saw a girl of about seven years of age who was crying and covered with bruises. As soon as Thaos cut through the ropes, Amy jumped into his arms and hugged him tightly. Thaos hugged the child back and said in a low voice to the Sanuri. "I'm gonna hang him right here."

Both Stephan and Martha stared when they saw how young Amy was. When Thaos and the Sanuri climbed out of the cellar, Thaos tried to set Amy down but she wouldn't let go of his neck. "These poor children," Martha said as tears were filling her eyes. "Amy do you have a family that we can take you to?" Martha asked softly.

"He killed them," Amy said as she buried her head in Thaos' shoulder. "None of them have families," said Martha.

"What are you going to do with them?" Before Martha had completed her question Stephan said angrily.

"We will take them home; our mother will know what to do."

"I think that is a wise idea," the Sanuri said.

"Martha, why don't you and the Sanuri take the girls back to the hotel, while Thaos and I take care of Sal," Stephan said with a flat coldness to his voice.

Martha held her arms out for Amy but the little girl clung onto Thaos tighter and yelled, "No."

"Amy, Stephan and I are going to make sure that Sal never hurts another little girl again," Thaos said softly. "Now you go with Martha and the Sanuri and we will catch up with you shortly."

"Promise?" Amy asked as she was crying.

"I promise."

Martha carried Amy as April and Sally held onto the Sanuri's hands. "We'll get you a hot meal and a bath as soon as we get home," Martha said as the Sanuri helped the girls into the boca. When the boca was out of sight Stephan and Thaos walked up to Sal who was tied to a tree.

"What are you gonna do?" Sal yelled.

As Thaos untied Sal, Stephan said, "This is not going to be an easy death, you are going to pay for your crimes."

Chapter XXII
Healing

When Thaos and Stephan entered the hotel, Amy, April and Sally were sitting at the dining room table eating. Martha, Frank and the Sanuri were also sitting at the table. "Did you kill him?" Sally asked when she saw the blood on Stephan's and Thaos' clothes.

"Yes," Stephan replied.

"Good," Sally said solemnly.

"Martha, Thaos and I need to clean up. Would you make a list of clothes the girls will need so we can buy them?" Stephan asked.

"Have either of you ever bought clothes for little girls before?" she asked in a motherly manner.

"No," Thaos replied with a grin.

"Perhaps I should get the things," Martha said.

Stephan and Thaos both took pouches of gold coins from their pockets. Stephan handed the pouches to Martha. "Get the girls what they need and whatever you need; the rest is yours."

"This is a lot of money," Martha gasped.

"We couldn't have saved these little girls without you," Stephan said. "And don't forget to buy some candy."

Koby and Bekka did not join the family for the midday meal. Emeral and Maxwell had informed everyone that morning that Koby and Bekka would need some time to work out their future. Now at dinner time, some of the family members were becoming concerned because they had not seen Koby and Bekka all day.

"Do you think we should check on them?" Natasha asked as she was setting dishes on the table.

"I think we should just leave them alone," Emeral said. "They finally started talking to each other I hate to interrupt that."

"But they have been in their room all day," Lila said.

"They have a lot to work out," Emeral replied. "So did you girls have fun today?"

"Yes and thank you again for watching the children," Hannah said and smiled because the women had met secretly with Renya to plan a celebration for Emeral and Maxwell."

"Joey is certainly feeling more comfortable here," Emeral said as she prepared a sauce. "He was laughing and playing with the other children."

"I know," Cassandra said happily, then Cassandra's demeanor changed. "Emeral did Bekka and Koby say if they were going to keep the baby?"

"They had not made any decisions at all when I last spoke with them."

"Bella," Claudius yelled as he walked out of his study.

"What is it dear?" Bella said as she ran down the hallway towards him.

"I just got a letter from Stephan and Thaos; we need to gather the family for this."

As the Royal Family of Wetpr gathered around the dining room table for their evening meal Sudfad said, "I just received a letter from the Sanuri. They found Sally and two other little girls that a man named Sal had stolen. Since there are young ears at the table I will let all of you read this for the details. This Sal had a fourth girl but he killed her. The youngest of the girls is only seven. When Thaos and Stephan saw what this man had done to those girls they decided not to bring him back here but killed him at his home.

"Let me read that," Renya said as Sudfad handed her the letter.

326

"Sal killed the parents of the youngest girl and the other two were orphans before he took them. Stephan decided to take the girls home; hoping that Bella would find them good homes."

"Were all these girls from Salar?" Raul asked as Renya handed him the letter.

"They were all from Wetpr," Sudfad said. "While I certainly understand what Thaos and Stephan did I rather wish they would have let me make an example out of Sal. I will not tolerate anyone selling and raping children."

"Why don't we post notices around the kingdom that anyone who committees these crimes will be put to death?" Simon suggested.

"Well, I am just proud of the boys for thinking to bring those little girls home instead of putting them in an orphanage," Bella said as she handed the letter to Ingr.

"I'm proud that they cared enough to hunt for them," Claudius said.

"I'll prepare a couple of rooms," said Bella.

"Bella it sounds like they are pretty scared, you might want to put them all in one room at least for the first night," Ingr said then she turned to Nikki who was sitting on her left. "The littlest one won't let go of Thaos, she's so scared." Ingr finished reading the letter then handed it to Nikki.

"They will be here in two days," Bella said. "I would like to have Mathas' and Fahron's families here for dinner that night. They might be helpful in finding homes for these children."

"You mean you haven't already decided to adopt them?" Claudius asked and grinned.

"I think we should meet the children first," Bella said. "Before we decide if we will adopt them."

"The way you said that, do you think Isadore and Fahron might want to adopt them?" Nikki asked.

327

"It is probably too soon," Bella said. "But I think we should let them have first choice. It might be just what they need to heal."

"If Thaos wants to adopt this little one," Nikki said as she reread the letter. "I would not be opposed to it."

"I think we should wait until they are all back home," Claudius said. "But I do like all of your suggestions."

"What took you so long?" Hannah asked as Gabriel, Raphael, Misha and Calen walked into the house.

"Are Vivian and Diana in the kitchen?" Gabriel asked without answering Hannah's question.

"Yes, something is wrong isn't it?"

"Honey will you call the girls and we will tell you."

As soon as Hannah walked into the kitchen Cassandra entered the dining room with Nicholas, Joey, Christopher and Cerey. "Cassandra could you take the children back to the play room for a few minutes?" Gabriel asked. "We have to talk about something we don't want them to hear."

"Of course," Cassandra said. "We get to play a little longer," she said enthusiastically to the children.

Hannah, Lila, Emeral, Natasha, Diana and Vivian all walked out of the kitchen and into the dining room. "Earlier this afternoon we went to Berta's house," Gabriel explained. "While I wanted to ask her a few more questions I also wanted to see if there was anything in her home that might indicate she was involved with demons. When we got there we found Berta in the kitchen, she had been ripped to shreds." Both Diana and Vivian gasped.

"We didn't find any unholy altars or other demonic objects but there was writing on the wall of the kitchen. The words were written in Berta's blood. The words were *Cursed are those who stand against us*. Obviously the demons are trying to scare us off."

"Well does that mean that Berta was standing against them or working with them?" Vivian asked.

"We all suspected that she knew more than what she was telling us," Raphael replied. "Which is probably why they killed her. Now whether she had this information because she worked with them or if she was just a victim in all of this we will never know."

"I liked her and I think she was a victim in all of this," Vivian said. "Would it be possible for us to bury her next to her husband?"

"You and I can make the arrangements tomorrow," Raphael said.

"Thank you," Vivian said and kissed Raphael.

"You're awfully quiet," Misha said to Diana.

"I am really mad; I think Berta was a victim too. I hope we are going after those demons."

"First we have to find out who they are," Gabriel said.

"Well, you have the message," Diana said.

"Yes but what do you mean?"

"Demons are so arrogant they always leave their names in their messages," Diana said. "Really didn't you know that?"

"I don't think any of us have ever heard of that," Raphael said while Vivian ran to a table and grabbed paper and a pen.

"Now if it is just one word that is usually a curse they are putting on you but with messages especially in a language that you can read they insert their names. It's kind of like a taunt they throw at you," Diana continued to explain as Vivian wrote down the message.

"The demon's name is Cronn do you recognize it," Vivian asked.

329

"Wait how did you come to that conclusion?" Gabriel asked as he walked closer to Vivian and looked at the piece of paper.

"Write the words of the message backwards. Then take the first letter of the first word, the second letter of the second word and so on. But if a word is too short for example in this message 'who' was the fourth word but did not have four letters then you skip it and take the fourth letter from the next word."

"And you are sure this is correct?" Raphael asked. "Because I have never heard of this either."

Diana got a mischievous look in her eyes. "We are so sure it is the correct name that we are willing to make a bet on it. What do you want to bet?"

"Maybe I better get in on this," Misha said with a grin. "Let's make it more interesting than money."

"Well then perhaps Natasha and I should get in on this too," Hannah said as she smiled. "How about if the girls are right, our husbands take us out for dinner and dancing."

"And if they are wrong?" Calen asked.

"Then we each get a wild card so to speak," Misha said. "And each of us can decide what that card is."

"I bet I already know," Diana said with a sly smile.

"I'll bet you don't," Misha replied. "Are you willing to chance it?"

"Yes," Diana said immediately.

"So am I," Vivian said.

"Me too," both Hannah and Natasha said almost in unison.

"I really hope you girls are wrong," Calen said and started to laugh.

Within fifteen minutes everyone was seated at the dining room table except for Koby and Bekka.

"Should we get them?" Natasha asked just as Koby and Bekka entered the dining room. They both looked as if they had been crying and both looked solemn. They took their seats at the table without speaking. Everyone in the room was quiet for a moment then Natasha decided to break the silence. "Misha are you still trying to teach Diana to dance?"

"Yes, couldn't you hear me screaming in pain?" Misha teased. Diana turned and slapped Misha's arm.

"Well now that Thor is doing so much better I am going to teach him to dance for the wedding. Maybe we should teach them together?"

"That's fine with me if it's fine with them," Misha said as he glanced at Diana. "Her main problem is that she won't let me lead."

"Imagine that," Vivian said sarcastically. Which made many laugh.

Natasha paused for a second and gave a warm look to Calen. "The first time that Calen and I danced we were in that small bedroom in the hideout we had in that abandoned Taperian hotel. There wasn't much room and we were dancing and I suddenly realized we were both in the air. Actually it was very romantic but maybe if you tried that with Diana it would be easier for her to learn to follow you."

Misha and Diana smiled at each other. "Thank you we will try that tonight," Misha said. The room became quiet again and Koby stood up.

"Bekka and I have been in our room all day because for the first time since we have known each other we are really talking about our thoughts and feelings and I will tell you it hasn't been easy. Although Bekka and I care about each other a great deal we have decided to call off the wedding."

"We look at the rest of you and every couple in this room just knew who was right for them and that getting married was what you wanted. Neither Bekka nor I can say the same thing."

"We enjoy each other's company and care about each other but we don't have what the rest of you do and we don't think we will ever get it." Everyone listened to Koby in silence.

"Bekka and I don't have any bad feelings for each other but we are afraid we might if we marry when we aren't in love. So at least for the near future we are going to continue to live together until we can make more decisions. Bekka told me she was thinking about returning to the Ice Caves because she thought all of you would hate her if we didn't marry. I assured her that would never happen. But Maxwell and Emeral brought up some things that we have to think about seriously."

"If Bekka and I both remain on the team and living here, what are we going to do if one of us falls in love with someone else? And just say Bekka and I both marry other people, what about our child? Right now we are both so exhausted that we can't think anymore tonight. But if any of you have suggestions for us we are more than willing to listen. Bekka and I would like to remain the close friends that we are now, without any ill will towards each other, so, well I guess that is all I have to say tonight. Oh except that Misha you and Diana can set a date now and not wait for us."

"Are you sure?" Misha asked. "Because we certainly can wait."

"No, go ahead."

"I can only imagine how painful this must be for the both of you," Hannah said. "And while I know these are tough decisions that you have to make, know that all of us love the two of you for the people you are. You are part of this giant crazy family we have formed and this is your home."

"And you are both valued members of the team," Gabriel said. "I guess the real question that you both have to answer is; how are you going to handle it when you both start to see other people. Will you be able to live under the same roof? I am bringing this up because we are building an apartment in our medical building so if one of you needs to get out of the house you can always stay there."

332

"Thank you, we appreciate that," Koby said then he turned to Elan and Cassandra. "Both Bekka and I would like to keep our baby but that in a way is part of the problem because if we separate, we don't know how we are going to share the child. If for any reason we change our minds you will be the first to know."

The next morning Claudius read Stephan's letter to Mathas, Fahron, and Matthew during their usual morning meeting. "The boys will be home tomorrow night; of course the Sanuri is also with them. Bella would like to have all of your families over for dinner so you can meet these girls and perhaps help Bella find homes for them. Bella was also thinking that it might be easier on the girls if you all brought your children.

"While I commend them for saving those children I don't know if Isadore is up for something like that," Fahron said.

"Bella and I had that same discussion," Claudius said. "And Bella thinks that Isadore is such a natural mother that meeting these children might actually be healing for her."

"I honestly don't see how," said Fahron.

"These little girls have been brutalized. They are going to need a lot of love and attention to get over what has happened to them. Bella and the girls are prepared to help these children and Bella thinks that if Isadore helped too it might bring the life back to her."

"Fahron, I agree with Claudius," Mathas said. "Although I would not be surprised if Bella didn't end up adopting them all herself."

"Nikki is going to talk to Thaos about the youngest girl. Here you can read the letter but Thaos found the seven year old tied up in a dark cellar and when he brought her upstairs she was covered with bruises. Because Thaos is the one who first helped the child apparently she won't let go of him."

"Seven years old," Matthew said with disgust. "I assume Stephan and Thaos killed the bastard."

"Stephan says in the letter that they made him pay for his crimes."

"Claudius, Sorren, Shara and the boys were planning on coming over for dinner tomorrow night," Mathas said. "Would it be alright if we brought them along?"

"Of course, they are family too. And perhaps the more children in the castle the better."

"Do you think having these girls in your home will help Ryan?" Matthew asked.

"I certainly hope so," Claudius said solemnly. "That boy is so filled with guilt that he didn't stop Tabeth from leaving the castle that he still can't eat or sleep."

"Perhaps tomorrow night Isadore and I should talk to him," Fahron said. "None of this was his fault."

"I would appreciate that Fahron. Wait until you see what he looks like now. Ryan was never really big but he has lost so much weight that Bella is really quite worried about him."

"We will be there," Fahron said. "But if it is too difficult for Isadore we might leave early."

"I understand," Claudius said.

Bella, Ingr and Nikki spent two days preparing rooms and buying things for Sally, April and Amy. "I can't believe I am nervous," Bella said as they were finishing the last details before the dinner guests were to arrive. Both Ingr and Nikki hugged Bella. "Bella everything is perfect you can't do any more," Nikki said.

Ryan walked into the dining room and said, "There you are, the guests are arriving."

"Are our husbands home yet?" Ingr asked.

"I didn't see them."

"Well then," Ingr said as she took Ryan's arm. "I guess you will have to be my escort." Ryan blushed and Ingr kissed him on the cheek.

Claudius was in the parlor pouring drinks when Bella entered. Nikki, Ryan and Ingr entered the parlor moments later and both Fahron and Isadore were shocked when they saw Ryan. Isadore put her hand on Fahron's arm and whispered into his ear, "Dear we have to talk to him; why don't we do it before the girls arrive."

"Claudius may we use your study?" Fahron asked as he nodded towards Ryan.

"Absolutely."

Ryan's face was filled with guilt when Fahron and Isadore walked up to him. "Ryan can we speak with you for a moment?" Fahron asked. Ryan did not say a word but his eyes filled with tears. Fahron put his arm around the young man's shoulders and led him into Claudius' study. As soon as Isadore closed the door to the study Ryan started to cry loudly.

"I am so sorry I know I should have stopped her." Isadore immediately put her arms around Ryan as he spoke.

"Ryan you have no reason to feel guilty," Fahron said softly. "You did the right thing by making Tabeth promise not to leave the castle. She was a headstrong young woman and made her own choice to leave. If you would have known our daughter better you would know there was nothing you could do once she made up her mind. No one could have stopped her."

"Honey we don't blame you for anything," Isadore said as she stroked Ryan's hair. "You have a good heart don't let it be filled with the darkness that Timothy brought upon us. If you do then you are just letting the monster that was within him win."

Ryan had been crying on Isadore's shoulder now he turned and looked at Fahron. "Do you forgive me?" Ryan asked as his voice quivered.

"My son there is nothing to forgive," Fahron said and hugged Ryan.

335

"My dear wife and I have been searching our souls to understand how we could have brought such a monster into this world. We have been trying to figure out what we could have done differently. If there is blame to be had, it is upon us."

"Tabeth told me that she wanted to kill Timothy herself because of the pain he brought to both of you. She loved you very much and thought you were wonderful parents. I don't know Chaez that well but he seems like a good person and he is never disrespectful towards either of you. You are good parents you can't blame yourselves for Timothy." Isadore, Fahron and Ryan all cried and held each other in their grief.

Within moments they heard Bella call out, "They're here. They're here."

Fahron, Isadore and Ryan all wiped the tears from their faces and walked out of the study and towards the front foyer of the castle where Claudius, Bella, Ingr and Nikki were standing. The Sanuri walked into the castle first, two young girls were holding his hands. Stephan followed the Sanuri and Thaos walked in last carrying a little girl. All three girls were very clean and wearing fancy new dresses.

"Girls this is our family," Stephan said. "This is our father Claudius, our mother Bella, this beautiful blonde woman is my wife Ingr and the other beautiful woman is Thaos' wife Nikki. This is Sally," Stephan said as he put his hand on the shoulder of a pretty fourteen year old girl with long blonde hair and blue eyes. Sally curtsied. "And this is April," Stephan continued. April was a year older than Sally and very shy. April had long curly auburn hair and large brown eyes; she too was a pretty girl although the life seemed to be drained from her. April also curtsied.

"And this is Amy," Thaos said of the little girl who had her face buried in his shoulder. "Amy can you say hello to my family?" Amy turned her head revealing large brown eyes and dimples; her long hair was black and curly.

"Hello," Amy said softly.

Tears filled Bella's eyes as she saw the numerous cuts and bruises on all three of the girls. "We have been looking forward to meeting you," Bella said. "In fact we are having a little party in your honor. Please come in and make yourselves at home." Neither April nor Sally let go of the Sanuri's hands and Amy wouldn't let Thaos put her down. Stephan kissed Bella on the cheek then he kissed Ingr. Thaos kissed Bella on the cheek and kissed Nikki with Amy in his arms. They all walked into the parlor together.

"You're safe here," the Sanuri said to the girls. "You have nothing to fear here."

Bella introduced the girls to all the guests. Like Bella, Isadore, Shara and Rosa all fought the urge to immediately hug the girls because they looked so frightened. After the introductions Ingr spoke to the girls while Stephan picked up his son and daughter. "We prepared rooms for you but we didn't know if you all wanted to stay together or have your own rooms. Why don't we look at them now and you can decide." Ingr held out her hands and Sally and April each grasped one.

Nikki was standing close to Thaos as he had his arm around her shoulders. "Amy, why don't you come with me and we can look at the rooms and let Thaos hold his son? We'll come right back." To Thaos' surprise Amy held her arms out for Nikki to take her.

"Are you going to have a baby?" Amy asked softly.

"Yes," Thaos and I are having another son," Nikki said as Amy clung to her. Angelina held Margarit's hand as they followed the girls to the rooms.

As soon as the girls left the parlor Sorren said angrily. "I hope you killed the bastard that hurt them."

"We did," said Stephan. "And they look a lot better now than they did when we found them."

"We are all very proud of the three of you for hunting for those little girls," Claudius said.

"There's more," Stephan said angrily. "I wrote and told you that Gus admitted to selling three little girls. Sally is the only one that Gus sold to Sal. We don't know how to find the other two."

"Oh my god," Bella gasped. "Do you mean to tell us you just happened on these three?"

"Yes," Thaos said. "At first we thought we had the three that Gus sold. The girls were so upset that it took us a while to find out how Sal got them."

"We think the fourth girl, the one that Sal killed might have been one of the girls that Gus sold," the Sanuri said. "Bella you would have been so proud of your sons. As we wrote to you, a woman from the village helped us find the girls and when she asked what we were going to do with them. Your sons said we'll take them home; our mother will know what to do."

"Really?" Bella was deeply touched by this comment and kissed both Stephan and Thaos on the cheek.

"This is the room we fixed up in case you all want to stay together," Ingr said as the three girls looked at a beautiful room containing three beds and filled with flowers and toys. "You can look around," Ingr said. "We bought clothes for you but we weren't really sure of your sizes." April and Sally let go of Ingr's hands and started to walk around the room.

"I'll show Amy around," Margarit announced and held her hand out to the little girl. Nikki set Amy on the floor and Margarit grabbed Amy's hand and started to walk around the room.

"You're so quiet," Nikki said to Angelina.

"I am so angry I can hardly speak. They are such cute little girls I hope that monster rots in hell."

"Do you mean we can wear these things?" Sally asked as she looked at a dress that was hanging beside one of the beds.

"They are yours to keep," Ingr explained. "But like I said we had to guess at your sizes, so you can figure out what fits each of you and we will buy you more."

Amy walked over to one of the beds and started to pet a stuffed toy dog. "You can have that," Margarit said and handed the toy to Amy who hugged it tightly.

"Do you want to look at the other rooms?" Nikki suggested. "Each one is a different color so you can pick out which one you want." The girls walked through all of the bedrooms with wide eyes as they looked at the many beautiful things but they didn't say anything until they were in the last room.

"Are you adopting us?" Sally asked.

"We haven't really figured that out yet," Ingr replied. "We want you to have a choice in the matter also."

"Then why did you buy us so many things?"

"Claudius and Bella are wealthy and very generous; in fact all the families here are wealthy. Nikki, Angelina and I grew up poor so we know how you feel when you first walk in and see all of these things."

"Did you girls decide which rooms you want?" Angelina asked as she was trying to sound cheery.

"Where do you and Thaos stay?" Amy asked Nikki.

Nikki smiled, "Our rooms are in a different area of the castle."

"I can stay with you if you are scared," Margarit said to Amy. "I got stolen once too and I was afraid to sleep by myself for a while."

"Well you girls don't have to decide now," Ingr said. "Why don't we go back with the others?" Margarit and Amy walked back to the parlor holding hands. Sally and April walked behind them. Suddenly Sally turned and looked at Angelina, Nikki and Ingr.

"I hope you don't think we are rude, this is all so new and we just don't know what to think."

"We understand," Angelina said. "We just want you to feel comfortable and know that no one can hurt you here."

Margarit turned around and said with a proud smile, "Angelina, Ingr and Nikki are all warrior princesses. They will protect you. They helped save me when I got stolen."

"You are?" Sally asked in awe. "Will you tell us about it?"

"Yes," Angelina said and laughed for the first time since the girls arrived at the castle. "I will tell you after dinner." Everyone in the parlor looked up and smiled as the women and girls entered.

"The girls haven't decided on their rooms yet," Ingr announced. "But Amy wanted to know where Thaos and Nikki live." Ingr smiled as she said this.

Nikki sat on the arm of the chair that Thaos was sitting in holding their son. "If you want to adopt Amy; I would agree," Nikki whispered into Thaos' ear. He smiled and squeezed her hand. "I have thought about it but I am not sure if we should separate the girls. Let's talk about it later."

Margarit was reintroducing Amy to all of the children, while Bella put her arms around Sally and April and led them to a sofa where Rosa, Isadore and Shara were sitting. "Why don't you sit with my friends and tell them about yourselves while I make sure dinner is ready," Bella said.

"We could help you," Sally offered.

"This is your party. I will be back soon."

"So what do you think?" Claudius asked the Sanuri.

"You mean about the girls?"

"Yes."

"They are good girls but very overwhelmed. They have had nightmares every night but they dreamt about a real monster. He had April the longest so she has been more severely affected. I think it is very gracious that you are helping them."

340

"Bella believes these girls might help Isadore and Fahron to heal."

"Your wife is a wise woman," the Sanuri said then paused. "I have to smile. For two such powerful warriors, both Stephan and Thaos have been very gentle with these girls. I think fatherhood has changed them greatly."

All three of the girls began to relax and to talk more as the night wore on. Unknown to them, all of the older couples at the party were considering adopting the girls. Margarit assumed the role of big sister to Amy and proceeded to pass all of the information she had about everything to the little girl. As the guests were leaving, Margarit started to protest.

"Papa can't I stay here with Amy?"

"I think the girls are exhausted. But I will let you play tomorrow."

"When the men come over for the morning meeting, why don't all of you come and we can have breakfast and the children can play?" Rosa suggested.

"That sounds like fun," Bella said. "We will all be there."

Rosa turned to Isadore, "Will you come?"

"Yes."

When Rosa looked at Sorren and Shara, Sorren replied, "It is so late that we will be staying at the castle tonight."

"Wonderful," Rosa said happily.

Isadore and Fahron were the last to leave and they both hugged Ryan tightly before they left. With the last of the guests gone, Claudius' entire family and the girls were standing in the front foyer of the castle.

"Have you girls decided on your rooms?" Bella asked.

Sally looked at April as if she was worried about her. "Perhaps we should all stay together, at least for tonight," Sally said.

"That's fine." Bella replied.

But before Bella could finish talking Amy marched up to Nikki and grabbed her hand. "I'm staying with Nikki and Thaos and Titus," the little girl announced which made everyone smile. Nikki looked at Thaos who nodded and smiled. Thaos and his family said good night to everyone and started to walk towards their chambers. "What is that baby's name?" Amy asked Nikki as she looked at Nikki's very pregnant stomach.

"James," Nikki said with a warm smile.

"I like that name," Amy replied.

The rest of the family could hear Amy talking. "I think she just adopted them," Stephan said with a grin.

"That is the first time I have seen her act normally," said Sally. "She must really like them. I hope they take her."

"I have a feeling they just did," the Sanuri said. "But how do you girls feel about being separated?"

Sally glanced at April before speaking. "Sal just stole Amy so she hasn't been with us long. I am just happy if she gets a good home. April was taken when Margo was and she saw Sal kill her. April was with Sal the longest; he bought me about six months ago. For now I think I should stay with April. Will that be a problem?"

"Of course not dear," Bella said. "We want to do what makes you feel comfortable. Oh, I just thought I should take some of the clothes we bought for Amy to them."

"I will," Ryan said. "If you want to stay with the girls?"

"Do you know where it is?"

"I should, I helped move everything about a dozen times," Ryan said with a laugh and left the room.

"That is the first time I have heard him laugh since..." Bella didn't finish her sentence.

"Since what?" Sally asked.

No one spoke for a moment then Claudius said. "Fahron and Isadore just had their daughter murdered by a monster. Ryan was friends with the girl and has been filled with guilt that he didn't stop her from riding alone; that's when the man grabbed her."

"Ryan has no reason to feel guilty," Ingr said. "He just is such a gentle person."

"Does one of us look like their daughter?" asked Sally.

"No but she was about your age," Bella said. "Why?"

"Just the way they looked at us sometimes. They looked so sad."

"Their daughter was murdered just a few weeks ago so they are still healing," Bella explained. "They are really good people and I will be honest with you. I hoped that being around a couple of girls Tabeth's age would bring the life back to them."

"Do you want me to talk to them?" Sally asked to everyone's surprise.

"What would you say to them?" Claudius asked.

"I don't know, but it sounds like we have seen some of the same darkness."

"Amy, Ryan just brought some clothes for you," Nikki said. "Why don't you put on this nightgown?" Amy put down the cookie she was eating and took the gown. "You can change in that room," Nikki said and pointed to Nikki's and Thaos' bedroom. Thaos was rocking Titus to sleep, when Amy came out of the bedroom, Thaos walked into the bedroom and put Titus in his bed. Amy watched Thaos as Nikki changed into a nightgown.

"Where am I going to sleep?" Amy asked as Nikki walked up to them.

Thaos picked Amy up and stood her on their bed. Then he looked into her eyes. "Tonight you can sleep with us but after that you will need to sleep in your own room. Do you understand?" Amy got a huge smile on her face and she jumped up and threw her arms around Thaos' neck and kissed him.

"Daddy does that mean her room will be here with us?" Nikki asked happily.

Thaos smiled and nodded. Amy let go of Thaos and turned and hugged and kissed Nikki.

Chapter XXIII
Little Warriors

The next morning as Claudius' family was preparing to go to the castle of King Mathas, Thaos said with a coy smile. "Bella would you like to help Nikki prepare a room for our new daughter?"

Bella clapped her hands. "I am so happy."

"Amy, Bella is your grandmother now and Claudius is your grandfather," Nikki explained. Amy looked at them both and smiled happily. Then Amy looked at Stephan and asked, "What is he?"

"Stephan is an uncle and so is Ryan," Nikki continued. "Ingr is your aunt and their babies are your cousins." Amy's happiness shone on her face.

"And him?" Amy pointed to the Sanuri.

"I am a family friend," the Sanuri said warmly.

"And what about April and Sally?" Amy asked.

Claudius looked at the two girls then spoke, "Last night there were several families here who are interested in adopting the girls but we want everyone to spend time together so they can get to know each other."

"Who?" asked Sally with surprise.

To Bella's surprise Claudius said, "Well besides us, there is Sorren and Shara, Fahron and Isadore and even Mathas and Rosa." This was the first time Claudius had stated that he was interested in adopting April and Sally.

"You all want us? I can't believe that," Sally said happily.

"You two will have a choice in this matter," Claudius said. "But we all think the wisest thing is for you to get to know all of the families first. So you might spend a couple of days with each family. Sorren is the chief of the Nordes Tribe so you will spend a couple of days with his tribe."

345

Amy gasped and looked at Nikki, "Is that where I am going to learn to be a warrior?"

"Yes," Nikki said then spoke to the family. "Thaos said it was alright for her to train with Sorren and the others."

Amy looked at Sally and April. "Nikki, Ingr and Angelina are all warrior princesses and I can train to be one too. Then when I become a warrior I won't have to be afraid of anyone."

"Joey will you hold still?" Cassandra asked and laughed as she and Hannah were trying to put the small Venator belts on all of the children, who were lined up in the dining room.

"Your canteens all have water in them," Natasha said as she carried four tiny canteens out of the kitchen.

"Are you and Papa coming with us?" Joey asked. Cassandra, Hannah and Natasha all turned and looked at Joey because this was the first time that he referred to Elan and Cassandra as his parents.

"Thor wants just the fathers to come this morning, so yes Papa is going with you and I will go on a different day," Cassandra said happily. "But I want you to tell me all about it."

"Grandpa is coming too," Christopher said proudly.

"So am I," Calen said as he walked from the kitchen into the dining room.

"You aren't their father," Natasha teased.

"I am close enough and besides I am carrying the food," Calen said and kissed Natasha on the cheek. "I think this will be fun."

"I can see it now, next week you will have Lily in the class," Natasha joked.

"You tease," Calen said. "But I am starting her as soon as I can."

"Well you might want to wait until she can walk," Hannah said with a grin then she added.

346

"Calen I don't want Thor carrying anything heavy on his back, he is not completely healed yet.

"Don't worry Luca and I already told him we are carrying everything."

"Just how much stuff are you taking?" asked Natasha.

"We decided to fix lunch in the woods after the training, so don't expect any of us back until later in the afternoon."

The door to King Mathas' study suddenly flew open during their morning meeting. Margarit was trying to come into the study while Rosa was holding her back.

"Papa, Papa," Margarit called.

"You can talk to Papa after his meeting," Rosa said loudly.

"But Papa it's important."

"You can let her in," Mathas said with a grin.

Margarit ran up to Mathas. "Papa, Amy is going to train to be a warrior princess like Angelina can I too? Please Papa please. I promise I will work really hard. Please." Mathas smiled at his daughter then looked at all of the other men in the room who were grinning at him. Suddenly Margarit stepped back and looked at her father as she decided to change her strategy. "Papa, Amy is pretty little you know I have to watch over her."

Everyone in the room broke into laughter. "She is getting more like Angelina every day," Matthew said.

"It is alright with me but Sorren does the training you will have to ask him," Mathas said. Margarit hugged her father then ran up to Sorren.

"Uncle Sorren will you train me too? Please, I want to be just like Angelina."

"I would be honored to have you in the classes," Sorren said. Margarit jumped up and hugged Sorren.

347

"Thank you, thank you." Margarit ran out of the study but before the door closed completely the men could hear her yelling, "Amy, Angelina they said yes."

"Sorren, Nikki and I were going to tell you after the meeting that we adopted Amy and she wants to be a warrior princess," Thaos said with a grin. "So you are a grandpa again."

"Well indeed, this is a very good day," Sorren said with a big smile.

"Actually I believe Amy told them she was going to be their daughter," Stephan said and chuckled.

"That's pretty close to the truth," Thaos said. "She was so different this morning. All the child did was cry before and this morning she was running around the chambers talking non-stop. The only thing that worries us is that she wants to carry Titus and we don't trust that yet."

"No kidding," Matthew said. "Titus is huge. But as small as Amy is she might not be able to pick him up if she tries."

"We just don't want her to try and then drop him."

Mathas, Claudius, Fahron and Sorren were all smiling. "What's so funny?" Stephan asked.

"We just enjoy listening to our children talk about their children," Mathas said. "You know it wasn't all that long ago when we were talking about you like that."

"Mama, Mama," Nicholas yelled as he ran into the house. "Mama you have to come outside."

Hannah was in the kitchen and quickly ran to the front foyer when she heard Nicholas calling. "Is someone hurt? Why are you by yourself?"

"Just come outside," Nicholas said and grabbed Hannah's hand. Hannah and Nicholas walked out of the front door of the house and saw all of the men lined up in the yard smiling.

Christopher, Cerey and Joey were playing with a large white dog that badly needed a bath and a brushing.

"Mama can we keep him?" Nicholas asked as they walked towards the group. "We found him in the woods and he was real hungry."

"I was so worried I thought someone was hurt," Hannah said with relief.

"Well, Gabriel thought you might hurt him if he walked in with the dog so he sent Nicholas in," Calen said then laughed loudly.

When Nicholas and Hannah were close to the group, the dog ran up to Nicholas and licked his face then ran up to Hannah who knelt down and petted it. "The dog must have heard the children and came running out of nowhere to play with them. From the way he looks he can't belong to anyone," Gabriel explained. "So Mama can we keep him?"

"We love him," Christopher said before Hannah could answer.

Hannah started laughing, "Of course but he needs a good bath before he comes in the house. And actually the rest of you look like you could use one too, what were you doing?"

"Thor was teaching the children how to hide from enemies and we all learned a few things," Luca said. "I was lying in a pond breathing through a reed."

"What!"

"The children didn't go into the water," Gabriel said quickly. "That is what Thor was teaching us."

Thor was grinning proudly, "We all had fun. And the men want to come along for the next class too."

Hannah laughed and shook her head then she looked at her daughter, "Cerey do you want to keep going to these classes?"

"Yes, Mama," Cerey said happily. Cerey was covered with dirt.

"Come on children," Elan said. "You are going to learn how to wash a dog."

"Luca and I can help," offered Calen.

"You're all so excited about this dog," Hannah said. "Thor I think you have more kids here than you thought." Thor laughed.

"The children are already arguing over which room the dog is going to sleep in tonight," Gabriel said. "Maybe we should let them all camp out in the playroom."

"Where is Ryan?" Bella asked. "He disappeared after we returned from Rosa's."

"He is in his workshop," Ingr replied. "He's so shy I don't know if he is hiding out from the girls or working on something."

"Well, let's hope he is working on something. After Tabeth's death he couldn't work. This could be a really good sign."

Bella and Ingr were gathering some of the things they had put in the room they first set up for Amy and were going to take the items to Thaos' and Nikki's chambers. "I am so glad they adopted little Amy, she is so sweet." Bella said. "If they wouldn't have I was going to talk to Claudius about her."

"After I saw her I thought maybe Stephan and I should adopt her too. But Amy is so attached to Thaos I think everything worked out just fine."

Ingr walked closer to Bella and whispered, "Are you and Claudius considering adopting Sally and April?"

"I will tell you I was so shocked when he said that this morning, of course you know me; I would take them in a heartbeat. But between you and me I would be so happy if Fahron and Isadore adopted them. Not that I couldn't love the girls but Claudius and I are blessed with a wonderful family."

"I understand what you are saying," Ingr said. "And I feel the same way. Although I was surprised to hear that Sorren and Shara were interested in adopting them also. I guess I really shouldn't have been."

"All the families have good hearts and it is just so sad what happened to these girls that everyone wants to help."

"Oh my god who is this?" Natasha asked as she knelt down to play with the white dog as he was being brought into the house for the first time.

"We named him Jasper," Christopher said. "And we just gave him a bath."

"He found us in the woods," Nicholas said. "And Mama said we could keep him if we gave him a bath."

Calen walked up to Natasha and kissed her on the cheek. "I think you should have taken a bath with Jasper," she said kiddingly. "Did you have fun?"

"I think we had more fun than the children," Luca said. "Thor taught us a lot of really good things. We are going along on the next class too."

"I am thinking about having them work on lamsmans too," Thor said with a big grin as he now felt considerably closer to the men on the team.

"We're all going to sleep in the playroom with Jasper tonight," Joey said happily. Natasha looked at Gabriel who smiled and nodded.

"Christopher go to the cupboard and grab a big towel," Natasha said. "Joey, Nicholas and Cerey come with me into the kitchen so we can choose dishes for Jasper's food and water."

"Ok," Nicholas said as he, Joey and Cerey ran into the kitchen with Jasper running behind him.

"We fed him a lot at lunch, he was starving," Calen said of the dog.

"This is going to be fun," Natasha said. "Did Gabriel tell you that he wouldn't buy me a dog when I was little because we were always working on missions?"

"No," Calen said. "If you wanted a dog you should have said something."

"Well, we have one now."

"A dog!" Lila said loudly as she entered the dining room with Christopher. "I love dogs, where is it."

"In the kitchen," Luca said and laughed. After Lila and Christopher entered the kitchen Luca turned to Gabriel and Calen. "I've never seen Lila that happy about a piece of jewelry. We should have gotten a dog before this."

"I don't think any of us thought about it until we saw Jasper," Gabriel replied. "Where did Elan go?"

"I think he and Thor went to get things to set up a little camp in the playroom," Luca replied.

"Ryan it's been three days and we've hardly seen you. Are you hiding out from the girls?" Ingr asked and laughed as she walked into his woodworking shop.

"Careful I just painted some things," Ryan called out.

"Oh Ryan these are wonderful," Ingr gushed as she looked at a small table with four chairs and a matching cupboard. The furniture was sized for children.

"There's more over here," Ryan said as he showed Ingr three little cradles and matching dressers for dolls.

"Amy is going to love these. Do Nikki and Thaos know you are making these?"

"No, I probably should have asked them if it was alright."

"Oh, they are going to love them. Ryan can I get Bella?"

"Yes, but warn her that I just painted all of the furniture."

Within minutes Ingr returned to the workshop with Bella. "Oh Ryan these are adorable how did you ever think of something like this?"

"I was watching Amy and Margarit playing and the idea just came to me."

"I want you to make the same things for Sicily when she is old enough," Ingr said. "Bella do you think we can find some small dishes for this cupboard?"

"Why don't we get April and Sally and go into the city to shop?" Bella suggested to Ingr then Bella turned to Ryan. "When are you planning on giving these to Amy?"

"It will take all day for the paint to dry. I haven't told Thaos and Nikki about them yet."

"Let's set everything up in the parlor tonight and it will be a surprise for the family," Bella said. "Ryan do you want to go shopping with us?"

"No, I am thinking that Margarit is going to want the same things when she sees them so I am starting on a set for her."

Later that evening, Sally, April, Ingr and Ryan carried all of the furniture and toys into the parlor. Bella had bought little dishes, dolls and doll clothing and now the four young people prepared all of these gifts for the grand showing. Thaos and Stephan were in the study with Claudius while Nikki, Amy, Bella and all three of the babies were in the kitchen.

Ingr walked into the kitchen and smiled at Bella. "Ingr can you send Ryan after the men?" Bella asked. "Nikki we have to show you something so we will need to bring the babies." Nikki picked up Titus, while Ingr picked up Marcus and Bella carried Sicily. Everyone met at the closed doors that led into the parlor.

"Today we found out why no one has seen Ryan for the last three days," Bella said. "Ryan will you open the doors?"

"Amy look," Nikki said as they all entered the parlor. "Look what Uncle Ryan made for you."

"They're for me?" the little girl asked with awe.

"Yes," Thaos said smiling. "Thank Ryan for all the work he did."

Amy ran up to Ryan who now knelt down. Amy threw her arms around his neck and hugged Ryan tightly. "Thank you Uncle Ryan I love them all."

"Look at these little dishes," Stephan said with a grin.

"I asked Ryan to make these same things for Sicily when she is older," Ingr said as they all watched Amy touching her new gifts.

"I probably should have asked you first," Ryan said to Thaos.

"Do you really think I would say no? This was very thoughtful of you Ryan. Can I pay you for these?"

"No, it's my way to welcome Amy into the family."

"Ryan thinks, and rightfully so," Bella explained. "That Margarit will want the same things so he has already started building her furniture."

Claudius smiled. "Well done Ryan and I am sure that Mathas and Rosa will be just as pleased as we are."

Nikki and Ingr were sitting on the small chairs looking at all of the things that Bella bought. Nikki looked at Thaos and said, "I might have fun with some of this too." Thaos laughed.

"I am trying to decide if we should put all of these things in her bedroom or start making a playroom for all of the children," Thaos said.

The following morning at the regular meeting in King Sudfad's study, Renya waited until Edward, Archetenus, Jared, Calen, Luca, Gabriel, Raphael and Misha had joined Sudfad, Raul and Simon before she entered the room.

"Before we discuss normal business," Sudfad said as he stood up when Renya entered. "Renya has special business to talk to you about. And this special business is why everyone in my castle is crazy right now."

"We were wondering if you were preparing for war," Calen kidded. "The courtyard is filled with workmen."

"It's only going to get worse," Sudfad said with a grin. "So all of you are invited to hide out in my study until all of the ceremonies are over."

"Where is Maxwell?" Renya asked.

"At the fort," Edward replied. "We rather made up some work for him to do."

"First of all I think your idea to honor Emeral and Maxwell is absolutely wonderful," Renya said as she walked among the men and handed each of them invitations and slips of paper. Hannah has an excuse to come to the castle everyday so we have been trying to work on things without Emeral and Maxwell getting suspicious. Now gentlemen, Elan's and Cassandra's wedding is less than two weeks away so please read the things I am giving you because we are running short on time for changes."

"As you will see these are different invitations than you saw before. They have all been mailed out. First we will have the wedding. Then I have the baby celebration scheduled for four days later and have asked all the guests to stay with us during that time. Of course I will have plenty of activities planned. And I am so happy Ibula and Thedes changed their minds and will be attending the celebrations."

"Thedes is really protective of the baby and just thought it was too early to travel with him," Calen explained.

"Oh I understand but I am very happy they are coming." Renya said. "Now for the big secret; of course we will have balls every night but on the second night after the wedding instead of a ball it will be the celebration for Emeral and Maxwell. Ibula has been helping me and she decided to inform all of the Ruala guests except for Cassandra's parents, who may not even attended their own daughter's wedding," Renya said with obvious disapproval.

"The sheets of paper I gave you have the head table arrangements for every ceremony and well, you can read the rest. Raphael I didn't know where you wanted to seat Vivian's family for the surprise celebration so all of you please look these things over and get back to me."

"Calen, Luca and Misha, I need you to read the guests lists and the things that will be presented during the ceremony for your parents. If you want to make changes or add anything could you get that information to me by tomorrow's meeting?"

"Of course," said Luca as he was reading some of the paperwork. "Renya you are really going all out for this, I hope you plan to let us pay for everything."

"You do know that all of your wives are buying gifts and I believe they are having a new dress made for Emeral also."

"Really?" Misha asked. "Honestly I didn't think the celebration would be so soon so I haven't been involved." Then Misha looked at his brothers, "Right after this meeting I am going to Andrew's. When Diana and I were picking out our rings I saw Emeral eyeing some jewelry. I'm going to buy it for her."

"Well, let us come too," Calen said. "We are all in the same situation."

"Gabriel the reason you have so many more papers is that Hannah has been the courier between our families. Most of that is for her and the other girls.

"Good because I didn't know what you wanted me to do with this material," Gabriel said and laughed.

"Raphael I just love Vivian and I have not deliberately left her family out of things; it's that I need to talk to you about the celebrations. Can you stay for a little while after the meeting?"

"Would it be alright if I went home and brought Vivian right back?"

"That would be even better," Renya said to Raphael then she turned to the Rualas. "Every time I organize a celebration Ibula is my right arm with your tribe. But she said there might be some people that you want invited that are not on that list so please look it over tonight. Archetenus, Jared and Edward, while you are not immediately involved with the celebration for Emeral and Maxwell you are with the others, so please tell me if I have omitted anyone from the guest lists."

"Since, I am not getting married or having a baby or related to Emeral and Maxwell I don't think I have much to contribute," Edward said and started laughing.

356

"Nonsense, you are part of this family now Edward," Renya said in a scolding tone. "Your family and friends are more than welcomed. And if you have a lady friend please invite her."

"You do realize that last question had several meanings don't you?" Raul asked and grinned. Edward gave Raul a blank look.

"Mother is probably going to invite women for you to meet," Simon said.

"Oh I am fine with that," Edward said with a big smile.

"Really," Renya said happily. "After the meeting why don't we talk?"

"Careful Edward or the next celebration will be your wedding," Raul joked.

Archetenus waited for everyone to stop speaking before he said anything, "Renya, Sudfad, I know I speak for Jared also, we are overwhelmed with all that you are doing for us, especially considering our histories. But neither Delilah nor Zoya or for that matter Jared and I have any family or friends other than all of you and the people in Lentz. And while that is not an issue with me and Jared, I think the girls feel a little badly that they don't have mothers to celebrate the babies with."

"He's right," Jared said. "Do you have any ideas of what we can do to make them feel better? And don't get us wrong the girls are just so happy with everything that you are doing for them. It must be a woman thing that they want their mothers around when they have babies."

"Emeral will be their mother," Calen kidded.

"Actually I was thinking of something like that," Renya said. "Because we don't know Delilah and Zoya all that well, I guess; let me think about this. I mean many of us can certainly make an attempt to get closer to them."

"The reason our wives aren't closer to the rest of you is because of us," Archetenus said. "I know Delilah kind of lives in the shadow of my past."

As King Sudfad was holding his morning meeting in Wetpr, simultaneously King Mathas was holding his meeting in Lentz. "What's all of this?" Mathas asked when he saw two large, covered baskets on his desk.

"Ryan made children's and doll furniture for Amy and he is making the same things for Margarit," Claudius explained. "Bella bought little dishes and things for Amy and apparently a second of everything for Margarit."

"Very nice, thank you. Let me pay you for these things"

"Mathas don't insult us," Claudius said. "We should be able to bring the furniture over day after tomorrow; Ryan has to paint the pieces after he makes them."

"Well then let me pay Ryan."

"No, we were just glad to see him go back to work. I don't know what Fahron and Isadore said to him but it worked," Claudius said.

"I am glad to hear that," Fahron said. "Both Isadore and I were shocked to see how much weight Ryan had lost. And honestly he told us some things that helped us to heal also."

"Speaking of healing," Claudius said. "There is one more thing I would like to discuss. Amy has already become a part of our family. Sally is a strong girl with a good head on her shoulders and she feels the need to protect April. April is having difficulty getting over the horror she saw. She finally has started talking although not much."

"I already told the girls that all of you are interested in adopting them and that pleased them a great deal. I said they should spend a few days with each of your families. But I want you to understand about April. And that is why we haven't brought them to any of your homes yet. So let Bella and I know when you would like to have the girls stay with you or if you change your minds."

"I think we all expected that," Mathas said. "Actually I am surprised at how well Amy and Sally seem to be recovering."

"All three of the girls have been healing since we found them," the Sanuri said. "And that is because of the love that Stephan and Thaos showed them and now the love that all of you are showing them. I will tell you I was more than pleased as I watched Thaos and Stephan because they made those girls feel safe and loved."

"Do you think April will get better?" Stephan asked.

"Yes, but the rate in which she heals depends on all of you but she will never be as bold as Sally or Amy."

"This morning Nikki and I were talking about Amy. That little girl has worked her way into our hearts so quickly that it seems like we have had her for a much longer period of time," said Thaos.

"Tomorrow why don't Shara and I come over and get the girls, they can stay with us for a few days" Sorren said. "Amy can certainly come too if she wants."

"Ingr and Nikki have been telling the girls about you and your tribe, I think they all will want to visit," Thaos said.

"And this brings up another thing, normally I wouldn't care," Claudius said. "Did all of you receive the new invitations from Renya?"

"Yes, we got them last night," Mathas said.

"Isadore and I already discussed this," Fahron explained. "Neither of us are ready for those big celebrations so we will stay home and watch over things."

"Then will you take April and Sally?" Claudius asked. "Sally doesn't think that April is up for them either but she won't leave April behind."

"Of course, we would love to take them. I will tell Isadore to prepare rooms."

"Those girls have a lot of nightmares," Stephan said. "I don't think they are ready for separate rooms yet."

Chapter XXIV
Freedom

The following morning at the regular morning meeting in King Mathas' study Stephan asked, "Guess who was puking this morning?" Claudius quickly swung his head around and looked at his son who was smiling proudly.

"Do you think Ingr is pregnant?"

"We have been trying for another child but we didn't want to say anything in case she couldn't have any more children after that attack."

"Did I just hear my friend say he was trying for another child?" Matthew asked and laughed. "Stephan you sure have changed."

"Have you told your mother?" Claudius asked.

"Ingr is going to tell her this morning."

"Son this makes me very happy," Claudius said with a huge smile.

"I know it is early but we are going to have a toast," Mathas said. "Matthew will you do the honors?"

"Father did you forget those things under your desk?" Matthew asked as he walked over to a table in the study and started to pour small glasses of whiskey for everyone. Mathas moved his huge chair back and proceeded to lift packages from under his desk and pile them on top of the desk.

"Thaos most of these gifts are for you, Nikki and Amy," Mathas said. "We are all so proud of you for adopting little Amy. There are gifts from all of us here but I would like you to open the one from Sorren and Shara now." Mathas handed one of the packages to Thaos.

"Are you sure?"

"You have got to see it," Matthew said as he handed out glasses of whiskey. All of the men roared with laughter as Thaos held up a tiny leather warrior's dress and sandals.

"I've never seen anything so cute," Stephan said. "It makes me look forward to when the twins start training."

"There is a little belt and some other things in one of the other packages," Matthew said. "Sorren gave Margarit her outfit this morning."

"This will make both Nikki and Amy very happy," Thaos said as he continued to laugh.

"We didn't want Sally and April to feel left out so there are some gifts for them also," Mathas said. "I believe their names are written on the packages."

"Sorren when you pick the girls up after the meeting, Nikki and I are going to ride along," Thaos said. "Because Nikki's family hasn't met Amy yet."

"Glad to have you and we are looking forward to the girls' visit."

"Sorren, Ingr told me that Sally is very curious about the warrior training but she is afraid to leave April for any periods of time," Stephan explained. "April just isn't ready for something like that yet. So is there something else April could learn while Sally is training? Even though Sally knows April is safe with any of our families I think she feels that she must stay with April always."

"I am glad you told me this," Sorren said. "This is the first that I have heard that Sally was interested in training and I am sure there are a variety of things Shara can do with April to keep her busy. But first I want to ask; since neither of those girls are officially adopted yet is there anyone here who would be opposed to Sally going through the training?"

"It was never something that Isadore or I would have thought about before," Fahron said. "I always let the children decide what they wanted to do. But I can't help but think that Tabeth might be alive today if she was trained to defend herself."

"Fahron," Claudius said. "I am sure that you realize by now that although any of our families would take those girls we rather hope that you and Isadore adopt them. We know they won't bring Tabeth back but they will certainly bring you some joy."

"Both Isadore and I suspected that. Honestly I am just not sure we are ready."

The next several days were hectic at both the castle of Sudfad and the home of Gabriel. All of the families worked hard at preparing for Elan's and Cassandra's wedding, the baby celebration and the secret celebration for Emeral and Maxwell.

"We're going to have to tell them," Natasha whispered to Vivian and Hannah who were in the kitchen with her preparing lunch.

"I think we should tell them the afternoon of their party that will give them time to prepare," Hannah said. "Then we can tell the children also; those little ears are everywhere I can't believe they haven't figured it out."

Bekka entered the kitchen. "Hannah, Cassandra and Joao just received an awful letter from her mother and Cassandra is so upset, is there something you can give her."

"I hate Cassandra's mother already," Natasha said as the women marched out of the kitchen.

"Where is she?" Hannah asked as she was going to her medical office that was inside of their house.

"In the playroom."

Natasha, Bekka and Vivian walked into the playroom and saw Cassandra sitting on the floor crying. All of the children were standing around her and Jasper the dog, was sitting on Cassandra's lap and licking her face. Joao was standing behind his sister and his face was red from anger.

"I just want to hit your mother," Natasha said as she knelt down and hugged Cassandra.

"You're going to have to stand in line," Joao said through clenched teeth.

"What is wrong?" asked Misha as he and Diana followed Hannah into the playroom. Cassandra held up a letter for Misha to take.

"Honey drink this," Hannah said. "It won't make you sleep but it will calm you down." Misha started to read the letter as Cassandra drank the medicine.

"Your mother is really a..." Misha stopped himself and looked at the children. "Joao perhaps it is time some of us took a trip to the Ice Caves."

"What do you mean?" Vivian asked.

"After Tina says really awful things about Joao, Cassandra and her family she writes that she is forbidding Melinda from coming for the wedding. Do you think that if we flew to the Ice Caves and got Melinda she would return with us?"

Joao and Cassandra looked at each other. "Melinda has never been out of the Ice Caves, she believes she has no place to escape to," Joao said.

"Well she does now, even if she doesn't want to be on the team," Misha said angrily as he handed the letter to Hannah.

"Are you serious about that?" Cassandra asked.

"I certainly am," Misha replied. "We need to devise a plan."

"I can't believe this woman," Hannah gasped as she handed the letter to Natasha. "She threatened..." Hannah stopped talking and looked at Joey then the others.

"Can I go with you Misha? I would love to see the Ice Caves," Diana asked.

"Certainly but it might not be a pleasant visit."

"I don't care; I want to see your home."

"Joao, you and Cassandra discuss this and at dinner tonight we will talk with the others," Misha said.

"Your mother is a horrible person," Natasha said as she handed the letter to Vivian.

"Would her parents try and stop Melinda from leaving? I mean are you going to get into trouble for taking her?" Hannah asked.

"Oh, Melinda will gladly come with us," Joao said. "And our parents will yell but they aren't warriors, there won't be anyone to stop us."

"The only thing is that Melinda will probably be disowned," Cassandra said.

"Does that mean you can't go back to the Ice Caves?" Natasha asked.

"Well we can," Joao said. "We just don't have any place to stay."

"Emeral and Maxwell built Calen and me a home that I have never even seen," Natasha said. "You are always welcome to stay there."

At sunrise the following morning, Dack, Joao, Dagon, Elan, Misha, Koby, Diana and Thor left for the Ice Caves. Both Diana and Thor were elated at the new adventure and both loved to fly. Elan, Joao and Dack were unusually quiet the first day and night of their journey; because all three men were so filled with anger over Tina's behavior. They got an early start on the morning of the second day.

"Misha I didn't want to say anything in front of the others," Diana said as they were in flight. "But this is really a good thing you are doing. I am always so proud of you."

"What Tina is doing is horrible but to do it to Elan and Cassandra; I mean they are the two nicest people," Misha said with disgust. "And the things she said about little Joey. What kind of a mother says things like that? All of you girls are right we should appreciate Emeral and Maxwell more."

"Did you see their faces when they read the letter? I have never seen either Emeral or Maxwell mad before."

"They have every reason to be mad," Misha said. "I am just glad that Calen talked them out of coming with us. I think their presence would make things much worse."

Renya knocked on the door to Sudfad's study while his morning meeting was in process. "I am sorry to interrupt," she said.

"No please come in dear," Sudfad said. "Calen was just showing me something you should see." Sudfad handed Tina's letter to Renya who turned red in the face as she read it."

"This is unspeakable," Renya sputtered.

"Misha and some of the others left for the Ice Caves yesterday to bring Cassandra's sister here. She will be living with us from now on," Luca explained.

"Sudfad I don't want that evil woman under our roof," Renya said angrily then she turned to Calen and Luca. "Would I get any of your family in trouble if I sent a letter to Tina telling her she may attend the wedding but she will not be a guest in the castle."

Both Calen and Luca laughed, "Renya, all Tina cares about is status and money that would be a great blow to her."

"Then it is alright with you?"

"Yes." Calen said. "I only wish I could see Tina's face when she gets the letter."

"Well then I am going to send it out this morning," Renya said and turned to leave the room then stopped. "I almost forgot what I came in here for. I received a letter from Bella, Thaos and Nikki adopted the youngest girl that was saved. The other two girls are staying with Claudius' family but Fahron, Mathas, Sorren and Claudius have all expressed interest in adopting them so that is a wonderful thing. And Gabriel tell Hannah that Ingr is pregnant so we will be adding one more to the baby celebration."

"Renya, I don't know if anyone has told you but Bekka and Koby decided not to get married. Bekka is wondering if she should still come to the celebration," Calen said.

"Why aren't they getting married?"

"Because they realized they are not in love."

"Well, I suppose that is a good reason but they are still having a baby. Tell Bekka that nothing has changed as far as we are concerned."

The second night into their journey Misha and the others made camp late. Diana prepared the meal while Koby and Dagon set up the campsite, the other men went hunting.

"Koby please don't get mad at me," Diana said. "But you look so sad, if you want to talk I will listen but I am not an expert on relationships."

"I don't think any of us are," Dagon said.

"Actually I don't know if I am sad, I just feel really confused," Koby replied.

"Well for what it is worth I think that you and Bekka are doing the right thing," Diana continued. "I never thought about marriage, I don't know why I just didn't. And that first night that I met Misha, I can't even explain it. It was like my heart melted and I just knew. Koby that feeling is worth waiting for. You and Bekka are both wonderful people and you will be good parents whether you marry or not."

"You think so?" Koby asked.

"We all know you will be good parents," Dagon said. "I don't know why you doubt it."

"So your heart melted," Misha said with a grin as he walked into the campsite. Misha bent down and kissed Diana. "Diana is right about everything she said," Misha said to Koby. "And from now on Thor is doing all the hunting."

Everyone now turned and saw Dack, and Joao carrying a large ekel beast. "He shot this with one arrow before the rest of us even saw anything," Joao said. "And Thor is mad that we won't let him carry it."

"Thor," Diana scolded. "You know what Hannah said."

"Well, I think we need to cut some steaks," Dagon said as he pulled out his knife.

The next morning, two hours after sunrise, Misha and the others were flying towards the secret entrances to the Ice Caves. "Misha!" Diana screamed, "You are flying into the side of the mountain."

"The Sanuri made the openings so only the Rualas can see them. Just hang on," Misha said and flew into the mountain.

"Oh my god!" Diana gasped as she looked at the scenery and the tall pillars of holy energy. "This is the most incredible place."

"Honey I will take you through the caves on our next visit. Right now we need to get Melinda and leave."

Once inside of the mountain, Elan, Joao and Dack took the lead. Both Thor and Diana were overwhelmed with the beauty of the Ice Caves as they flew through a series of caves and tunnels.

"There," Joao yelled and started to descend. They all landed in front of a large wooden home that was surrounded with gardens. Joao, Dack and Elan marched inside as the others followed.

"Joao," Tina gasped when she saw her son.

"Where is Melinda?" Joao demanded.

"Don't talk to me in that tone of voice. I am still your mother."

"No you aren't we all disowned you, now where is Melinda?"

"I'm here," Melinda yelled as she ran down the stairs. Melinda was an extremely beautiful young woman with large hazel eyes and long curly reddish blonde hair. Dagon, Koby and Thor all stared at her.

"Pack your things you are coming to live with us," Joao said.

"Really! Oh thank you," Melinda yelled and turned and ran up the stairs.

"Melinda don't you dare leave this house, you are just as worthless as the rest of them," Tina yelled.

"Diana why don't you help her pack?" Misha said angrily.

"Why don't I stay down here," Diana said coldly as she walked towards Tina. "The rest of you won't hit a woman." Diana's comment made all of the men smile. Thor and Koby were the closest to the stairs and ran up to help Melinda. Diana walked up to Tina and got very, very close to her.

"Joao maybe you should leave your mother and me alone for a few minutes," Diana said in a voice none of them had ever heard her use before.

"Actually if you hit her I want to see it," Joao said coldly.

Diana took a step closer to Tina, who backed up. "We all read your letter; you are nothing but a vicious viper. Cassandra, Elan and Joao are wonderful people who any real mother would be proud of and Joey the grandson who you disowned and threatened is a little angel. I don't know why you are so miserable but you won't hurt our friends anymore. You will not send them hateful letters and you will not come to see them. Because if you do Tina I will come back and hurt you. Do you understand me?"

Tina turned red as the anger surged through her. "You can't talk to me like that."

"I can talk to you any way I want, you disgust me. And another thing; I am the adopted daughter of Emeral and Maxwell the most wonderful people in the world."

"We've got everything," Koby said as he, Thor and Melinda ran down the stairs. Melinda had packed her things in the typical large back packs that the Rualas used to carry items. Dack, Koby and Dagon each put a pack on their backs and walked out the door. Misha and Diana were the last two to leave the house.

Misha grabbed Diana and kissed her, before they ascended into the air. "Now I know what Thor is talking about when he says the baby lioness wakes up. You were wonderful."

"Misha I really wanted to hit her."

"We all did."

"I can't believe this is happening," Melinda said loudly as the group flew out of the Ice Caves. "Thank you all so much."

368

"Joao are you going to introduce us?" Dagon asked.

"Melinda." Joao pointed the people out as he called out their names. "Dagon, Koby and Misha are sons of Emeral and Maxwell. Diana is Misha's wife and Thor's sister. Emeral and Maxwell also adopted them." Then Joao turned to Misha and yelled, "Misha can I kiss Diana on the cheek when we land?"

"Certainly," Misha replied and laughed. "Thor the baby lioness roared."

"What did she do?" Thor asked.

"I can't remember what I said I was so mad," said Diana.

"I'll never forget," Elan said then flew to his left so he would be closer to Koby, Thor and Melinda. "When Elan finished telling them of Diana's encounter with Tina, both Thor and Koby laughed loudly.

"Did she really say that?" Melinda asked. Elan nodded. "Diana I love you," Melinda yelled then laughed.

"I love you too," Misha said to Diana who smiled warmly at him.

"Koby are you Bekka's fiancé?" Melinda asked. Everyone in the group became quiet.

After a few moments Koby said, "It's complicated."

"I don't understand," Melinda said.

"I don't really know how to explain it," Koby replied.

"Koby can I?" Dack asked and Koby nodded.

"Melinda think if we kept our relationship the way it always has been then we started to have sex and suddenly you found out you were pregnant," Dack explained.

Melinda looked at Koby, "What are you going to do?"

"We started to plan a wedding but realized that as much as we care about each other we aren't in love with each other."

"We called off the wedding because we are both afraid that if we have a marriage without love we might start to hate each other. We want to remain friends; so for now we are still living together and trying to figure things out."

"That sounds really difficult," Melinda said. "But I think as long as you can stay friends you will be alright."

Melinda turned to Thor. "Cassandra wrote to me that we are walking down the aisle together, that is you right?"

"Yes," Thor replied. "But I have to warn you I am learning how to dance and I am not very good."

"I love to dance," Melinda said. "I can help you." Diana smiled as she listened to Thor and Melinda talk.

"Cassandra writes to me often," Melinda said. "She has told me about all of you and the others. I am so looking forward to meeting everyone. I will have to admit I never heard of a Venator warrior until Cassandra started to write about Vivian. Your tribe sounds very fierce."

"They're impressive warriors," Misha said. "We are glad to have them on the team."

"I just remembered," Diana said. "Vivian's family will be at the house by time we return. Misha can we stop in Salar so I can buy them a gift of some type?"

"I want to get them something too," Elan said.

"Thor do you want to go too?" Misha asked.

"I wouldn't mind."

"We can either divide up or Melinda can see the City of Salar with us."

"I am just so excited I can barely breathe," Vivian said to Raphael as they put the finishing touches on the chambers they had built for her family. "What is this?" Vivian asked as Lila, Bekka and Emeral all walked into the chambers carrying huge bouquets of flowers. "They are beautiful."

"Where do you want them?" Lila asked.

. "We should put one in the master bedroom, one in the parlor and the third on the dining table," Emeral said.

"Vivian, wait until you see all of the gifts Cassandra and Elan bought for your brothers, they bought so many that they decided to buy gifts for the other children too so no one would get jealous," Bekka said.

"And Hannah and Natasha are going all out on the meal tonight," Emeral said. "This is beautiful, they will love it." Emeral was speaking of the chambers.

"My family has always been so poor they might be a little overwhelmed," Vivian said. "I just can't believe how nervous I am."

"Honey you weren't this nervous when I met your family," Raphael said and kissed Vivian on the forehead.

"I know, do you think I am just being strange because I am pregnant?" Everyone laughed.

"I know I am," Bekka said and grinned.

"Now remember, tomorrow night Renya wants us all over for dinner so they can meet your family," Emeral said to Vivian.

"They're here, they're here," Christopher screamed as he ran up the stairs with Jasper running beside him.

By the time Vivian and the others got to the front foyer, Joshua, Iris and their sons were surrounded with people. "Here they are," Gabriel said as Vivian and Raphael walked towards the group. Vivian flew into her parent's arms hugging them both over and over.

"Calen why don't you and Luca take their things upstairs?" Maxwell suggested.

"Raphael let's show them their chambers now," Vivian said excitedly. The entire team followed Vivian and her family up to their new chambers.

"It was Raphael's idea, he built this for you," Vivian said with great pride as her family looked in awe at their home.

"I'll show you your bedroom," Christopher said to Paul and Adrone. "It's full of toys."

"Micha and Thomas you each have your own room," Vivian said. She was so proud of the chambers that Raphael had built that Vivian could hardly contain her excitement.

"And wait until you see your room," Emeral said to Iris and Joshua.

"I don't know what to say, everything is so beautiful," Iris said. "When you said you were building us a place to stay; why, we never imagined anything like this."

"This is your home in Wetpr," Raphael said. "We are hoping you can stay for a while. Now is not the time to talk business but we might try to recruit Micha and Thomas to help us on our next mission. We are a little shorthanded since so many of the women are pregnant."

"Really?" Micha asked excitedly. "I am saying yes now."

"You don't even know what it is yet," Vivian said with a laugh.

"I don't care; it is an honor to be asked to work with all of you. Thomas come out here."

"Micha wait until you see our rooms," Thomas said as he returned to the group.

"Raphael and Gabriel want us to work with them on their next mission."

"Yes," Thomas replied without hesitation.

"That was easier than I thought it would be," Gabriel said and grinned.

"Paul, Adrone you've got to come downstairs and open your presents," Nicholas said.

"Because we can't open ours until you open yours," Joey added.

"Well, I guess we are all going back downstairs," Emeral said and led the group back to the dining room.

"Where are Diana and Thor?" Joshua asked as they watched the children opening gifts.

"You might say they are on a mission," Raphael said. "We can explain it when the children are in the playroom."

"Mother, and wait until you hear the story you will never believe it," Vivian said. "I am still angry." Then Vivian looked at Cassandra. "Do you still have that letter?"

"Yes, Elan told me to tear it up but I want to show it to Melinda."

"Would you mind showing it to my parents later? Because they will never believe parents can act like that."

"Luca, Hannah, Gabriel," Christopher said loudly as he ran to them. "Now that Paul and Adrone are here can we all camp in the playroom again?" Paul and Adrone turned and looked excitedly at their parents.

"It's fine with me," Luca said.

"Hannah and Gabriel looked at each other and smiled. "That's fine," Gabriel said. "But don't keep running to the kitchen so you can feed Jasper all night."

"He was hungry," Nicholas said.

"I think he will keep eating as long as you keep giving him food," Gabriel said with a smile then looked at Joshua and Iris. "Thor has started the children on Venator training and the fathers went along last week and we found a dog. Needless to say Jasper is now the most popular member of the family."

After their dinner, Gabriel's team and guests sat up most of the night talking and drinking wine. Iris and Emeral became friends immediately as Maxwell thought they would. After the children were asleep, Cassandra went to her chambers and got her mother's letter.

While Cassandra was gone, Vivian and the others were explaining the situation with Cassandra's family to Joshua and Iris.

"This is so embarrassing," Cassandra said as she handed the letter to Iris.

"Oh my gosh," Iris repeated several times as she read the venomous letter then handed it to Joshua.

"Misha and some of the others flew to the Ice Caves to bring Melinda back here," Vivian explained. "We expect them back tomorrow."

"She's living here with us," Natasha said. "We aren't letting her go back to that."

"To say such things not only about your children but your grandchild is your mother crazy?" Iris asked Cassandra.

"No she is just a very hateful person. I hope she doesn't come to the wedding."

Calen looked at Gabriel, "Maybe we should tell her," Calen said then he looked at Cassandra. "We showed Renya the letter and she wrote to your mother and said..."

"And said what Calen?" Cassandra interrupted.

"Renya said that any woman who could say such awful things about her family was not welcomed in the castle. Renya said that if your parents came for the wedding they would have to stay in a hotel in Salar. Then she told your mother that three of their sons are adopted and are blessings to their family."

"Really?" Hannah gasped.

"Good for Renya," Natasha said.

"Speaking of the Queen," Raphael said. "We are all having dinner at the castle tomorrow so she can meet you."

"What!" Iris gasped. "I don't have anything to wear before the King and Queen."

"The girls are taking all of you shopping tomorrow and Gabriel and I are paying for everything."

"Raphael, Gabriel, I protest," Joshua said. "Your friends left us some money I can pay for the clothes."

"Absolutely not," Raphael said. "We are all just so happy to have you here that you aren't paying for anything."

"I don't feel right about it," Joshua said.

"Joshua you and Iris took us all in, fed us and cared for us when we were at war," Gabriel said. "This is the very least we can do."

That night as Misha and Diana cuddled in their blankets before the camp fire, Diana whispered, "I think Thor is interested in Melinda and that makes me happy."

"I think Dagon and Koby are both interested in her too and I don't want to get in the middle of it."

"Koby, are you sure?"

"They are my brothers, I know them. Like I said I don't want to get caught in the middle of this but there is something you should explain to Thor tomorrow. Just because he and Melinda are walking down the aisle together doesn't mean she is his date for the wedding. If he wants her to be his date he will have to ask her before someone else does."

"Is that why you asked me right after we met?" Diana asked with a grin.

"Of course, your heart wasn't the only one that was melting that night."

375

Chapter XXV
Appreciation

The next afternoon Misha and the others walked into Gabriel's house. The entire group had remained together and went shopping in Salar before coming home.

"Melinda," Cassandra yelled and ran to her sister, the two women hugged tightly.

"Are Iris and Joshua here?" Diana asked.

"Yes they are in the dining room," Cassandra replied.

Diana ran into the dining room and hugged Iris then Joshua. Thor was close behind his sister and he also hugged Vivian's parents. Then Diana hugged Micha and Thomas. "Where are Paul and Adrone?" Diana asked.

"In the playroom," Lila said.

"Here, Thor, Misha and I got you these gifts," Diana said as she handed packages to Vivian's family. But before they could open them Cassandra and Melinda walked into the dining room with their arms around each other.

"Everyone I would like you to meet my sister Melinda," Cassandra said with a proud smile and was in the process of making introductions when Emeral walked into the room.

"We are all having dinner with the King and Queen tonight so everyone has to be ready to leave in one hour," Emeral said. As everyone jumped up from the table Emeral added, "Diana here this came for you from the girls in Lentz." Emeral handed an envelope to Diana who tore it open.

Diana started to giggle. "Wait before everyone leaves the room. All you single men listen to me." Diana's comment brought laughter. "Angelina, Ingr and Nikki are bringing eight single girls to Elan's and Cassandra's wedding. They said all of the girls are beautiful and are warriors and if you don't like these eight they have plenty more friends."

"You are becoming my favorite sister-in-law," Dagon said with a grin.

"Are they only for the single men?" Calen asked kiddingly and immediately Natasha punched his arm.

Renya had dinner served in the Great Hall because there was more room than in the family dining room. "I really meant for this to be a family gathering, not anything special," Renya said as everyone was seated. "Raul and Simon have told us so much about your tribe and we just love Vivian, Diana and Thor so Sudfad and I wanted to get to know you," Renya said to Iris and Joshua.

"We are more than proud to be here," Joshua replied.

"Did Vivian tell you that she and Renya fought spies that had infiltrated our castle, then later Diana, Thor and Vivian fought at our sides when the castle was attacked?" Sudfad asked.

"Vivian wrote to us about the battle where Thor and Diana were injured but not the other one," Joshua said.

"Vivian's brothers are going to join us on the next mission," Gabriel said. "Although we haven't had time to explain it to them yet."

"Excellent," Sudfad replied.

"Simon and I have been talking and we think one of us should go with you too," Raul said.

"Raul, you have been gone so much," Vitomas said with frustration.

"Raphael and I have been discussing that and we think it might be better if Edward goes as a representative from the military. We fear if they see either of you they will suspect something is going on." Gabriel now turned to the others at the table. "I am sorry to sound so vague but we cannot let the details out yet."

Vivian's family as well as Melinda soon felt at ease and became more comfortable around the Royal Family. Although Bekka and Koby were sitting together, Koby kept staring at Melinda. Several people at the table watched Bekka watching Koby look at Melinda and the situation was making others feel uncomfortable. Finally Emeral took control of the situation.

"Melinda I know you just got here but have any of the boys asked you to the wedding yet?"

"No," Melinda said shyly.

"Then I am going to be an interfering mother will you go to the wedding with Thor? He is not used to our customs and it will be his first celebration. Perhaps you could show him around." Then Emeral looked at Thor. "I don't mean to embarrass you but you are shy and Melinda is a nice girl. It's just for one night."

Although Thor looked embarrassed he said, "Actually I was planning on asking her." Then Thor looked at Melinda. "Will you go to the dance with me?"

It was obvious to everyone that Melinda was embarrassed by the situation. "Yes," she said sweetly.

"Good," Emeral said then gave Koby a disapproving look which was noticed by everyone at the table.

"Melinda," Dagon said loudly. "Will you go to the next dance with me, which is for the baby celebration?"

"Yes," Melinda said slowly. Then she looked at both Thor and Dagon then at Emeral. "Dagon and Thor I think you are both very nice men but I am feeling uncomfortable is something going on here?"

"We just both want to get a chance to know you better," Dagon said as he too gave Koby a disapproving look.

"I don't want to cause any conflicts," Melinda said.

"The boys will be gentlemen," Emeral assured Melinda.

After Gabriel's team returned home, Misha asked both Dagon and Thor to come to his chambers for a drink.

"Do you want me to leave?" Diana asked when she saw the three men walk in. "I can go to bed?"

"No you can stay, we are just going to have a drink and a man's talk," Misha said as he poured three glasses of whiskey.

"If this is about Melinda, Dagon can go to the wedding with her," Thor said. "She is nice but I don't have feelings for her."

"When I asked her out it wasn't to start a fight with you Thor," Dagon said. "I was so damn mad at Koby I could have punched him. I mean a week ago he and Bekka are planning a wedding; fine now that they don't want to get married. But he doesn't have to sit next to Bekka, who is pregnant with his baby, with his tongue hanging out for another girl. I asked her out so Koby couldn't."

"Thor I hope you realize that was the same reason that Emeral embarrassed you tonight. I think all of us were pretty disgusted with Koby," Misha said. "And I am glad you two aren't going to fight about this."

"Actually I was trying to get the nerve up to ask Melinda to the wedding but like I said I don't have feelings for her."

"So what are you going to do about the secret celebration for Emeral and Maxwell?" Diana asked. "If you want to keep Koby away from Melinda someone is going to have to ask her to that too."

"What if Melinda would like to go out with Koby?" Thor asked.

"She seemed really uncomfortable with the way he was staring at her," Dagon said.

"I don't know if I feel comfortable trying to keep Melinda and Koby apart, I mean it really isn't my business," said Thor.

"Koby is a great guy with a good head on his shoulders," Dagon said. "But he is so confused right now that I don't think he has any idea of what he wants. I am not trying to keep Melinda away from Koby forever; I just think he needs some time to think things through."

"I agree with Dagon," Misha said.

"I felt sorry for Bekka," Diana said. "Misha I hope you don't ever do that to me."

Misha put his arm around Diana and kissed her on top of her head. "Thor if I ever treat your sister like that I hope you kick my ass."

"Gladly," Thor said then laughed.

"We all felt sorry for Bekka," Dagon said. "She's a really nice girl."

"Where is everyone?" Natasha asked the next morning as the team was sitting down to breakfast.

"I don't have a good feeling about this," Dagon said and stood up and started to leave the room but Elan, Cassandra, Melinda and Joey met him in the doorway. "Has something happened?" Dagon asked when he saw the looks on their faces. Cassandra handed Dagon a note. Dagon became visibly angry as he read the note. "Damn it! Does Koby know?"

"We didn't stop in his room," Elan said.

"What is going on?" Emeral asked.

"Last night Bekka asked Joao and Dack to take her back to the Ice Caves. She doesn't want any of us to follow her," Cassandra answered.

"I feel awful," Melinda said. "Is this because he was looking at me?"

"You didn't do anything wrong," Dagon said. "Koby is just going through a bad time right now. I'm going to his room." Dagon handed the note back to Cassandra and left the room.

"May I see that?" Emeral asked. Cassandra handed Emeral the note and the team ate breakfast in silence.

Koby and Dagon never returned to the dining room for breakfast so when Maxwell finished eating he announced, "I am going upstairs to talk to Koby." Maxwell looked at Emeral who had not spoken through the entire meal. "Do you want to come along?"

"No I am too angry; I need to clean something," Emeral said and stood up and walked into the kitchen.

As Maxwell was leaving the dining room he heard someone at the front door. "Misha, Diana there are some deliveries for you," Maxwell called out.

Misha smiled. "Well come on," he said to Diana and they walked out of the dining room.

Everyone in the dining room could hear Diana gasp, "Misha!" Then she called for Thor to come to the front door. In a few moments Misha, Diana, Maxwell and Thor all entered the dining room with their arms filled with packages.

"What is all of that?" Hannah asked as she was grateful to think about something else besides Bekka and Koby.

Misha didn't answer Hannah's question he looked at Diana and said, "Open the big ones first." The children all got up from the table and gathered around Diana.

"You can help me open them," Diana said to the children. Diana opened the first large package and held up an emerald colored gown. "Misha it is beautiful, thank you but..."

Before Diana could complete her sentence Nicholas said. "There's another dress here." Diana draped the emerald dress over a chair and now held up a dark sapphire blue gown.

"There's red shoes here," Adrone said

"Diana there is a red dress here," Christopher said as he opened the last of the large packages. Emeral heard the commotion and walked into the dining room. The children continued to open the smaller packages and call out the contents. The women all stood up from the table and walked over to examine Diana's gifts.

"Thanks for making the rest of us look bad Brother," Luca said and laughed.

"Misha these are all so beautiful but you already bought me dresses," Diana said as she stretched up and kissed him on the lips.

Misha put his arms around Diana, "Elan's and Cassandra's wedding will be the first time I get to show you off to the rest of my family and friends; I wanted to get some special things."

"You want to show me off?" Diana said emotionally and kissed Misha again.

"Misha that was really sweet of you," Hannah said. "And these gowns are gorgeous."

"Diana try these on right away and I can make any alterations," Lila said.

Emeral was looking at the gifts which Diana received. "Misha this was very thoughtful but why three dresses?"

No one said anything for a moment, then Misha replied. "I couldn't make up my mind."

"Really?" Emeral asked in a way that made the rest of the family suspect she knew about the secret party.

Everyone became quiet again and then Gabriel spoke, "Perhaps now would be a good time for us all to think more pleasant thoughts."

Natasha smiled and grabbed both Emeral and Maxwell by the hand and led them back to the table. Cassandra quickly cleared the breakfast dishes while Vivian and Hannah called to the children to follow them out of the room. Luca Lila, Misha, Diana and Thor suddenly disappeared and everyone else looked at Maxwell and Emeral and smiled.

"Calen perhaps someone should ask Koby and Dagon if they want to join us," Natasha suggested.

"Gabriel, Raphael can you help me?" Elan called from the kitchen.

"I am not sure what is going on but I want to help," Iris said and grabbed some dishes from the table and walked into the kitchen.

"What is going on here?" Emeral asked with a smile.

"I have no idea," Maxwell said.

"You two stay just where you are," Natasha said as she quickly rearranged some furniture in the dining room. "Oh I forgot something," Natasha said and ran out of the room, then Natasha peaked her head back into the dining room. "Micha, Thomas don't let them move," Natasha said then laughed and disappeared behind the door. Micha and Thomas looked at Maxwell and Emeral and grinned.

"We have no idea either," Micha said. "But it seems fun."

Joshua came out of the kitchen laughing, "Can one of you boys come in here and help?" Thomas stood up and walked into the kitchen. Soon whispering could be heard all around the dining room as well as children giggling. "Is everyone ready?" Luca called out.

"Luca you start while we pour the wine," Hannah said and ran into the kitchen; within moments Gabriel, Raphael and Thomas carried out trays filled with glasses and bottles of wine. Iris and Joshua each carried out a tray filled with plates and forks. Hannah and Cassandra carried a huge cake out of the kitchen and set it on the table. "We baked this for Vivian's family but Iris said now would be a good time to cut it," Hannah said.

Some commotion was heard by the kitchen door and Vivian and Diana were giggling. Elan came out of the kitchen holding a giant bouquet of flowers. "The girls just picked these and I dropped them on the floor," Elan said and laughed.

While the items were being brought out from the kitchen all of the adults in the family gathered around Emeral and Maxwell, including Koby and Dagon. "Move up here with us," Diana said to Vivian's family.

"Our wives don't think we appreciate you two as much as we should and they are right," Luca said. "You have adopted everyone here as either your child or grandchild and you bring so much love to this home that the family wanted to show you how much we appreciate you and everything you do."

Calen handed Maxwell a beautiful white and gold envelope then he kissed his mother on the cheek. No one spoke until Maxwell and Emeral had finished reading the invitation.

"For once I don't know what to say," Maxwell said with great emotion.

Emeral started to cry. Elan handed Emeral the flowers and kissed her on the cheek. "We weren't going to tell you about the celebration until just before it started," Calen said. "So we are a little unorganized right now."

"Oh this looks wonderful," Emeral said.

Gabriel picked up a glass of wine, "Let's have a toast." As soon as everyone held a glass Gabriel said, "To Maxwell and Emeral." Everyone repeated the toast and took a drink of their wine.

"Alright children," Luca called. Christopher was in the lead as the children formed a line, each child presented Emeral and Maxwell with a gift. As soon as the gift was opened that child ran back to Lila and Vivian for more gifts. Although Adrone and Paul didn't know Emeral and Maxwell very well they had fun delivering presents.

"Where's Natasha?" Gabriel asked.

"We forgot something," Hannah said.

Emeral and Maxwell were overwhelmed as they opened both extravagant gifts as well as gifts made by the children. Emeral kept crying so Hannah brought her a handkerchief. "Mother this is incredible," Calen said jokingly. "I have never seen you speechless before." Everyone laughed.

Misha stepped forward and kissed Emeral on the cheek, "Since we hadn't planned to do this today, Natasha is getting something that is very important and we would like to wait with the rest of the gifts until she returns."

"More gifts," Emeral gasped.

"So while we wait," Lila said as she lined the children in front of Emeral and Maxwell. "The children have a song they want to sing for you." Hannah sat down at the piano which was in the far corner of the dining room and started to play while Lila led the children in the song. Emeral started to cry again and grabbed Maxwell's hand. "That is our wedding song," she said.

After the children finished singing they all ran up to Emeral and Maxwell and hugged them.

"We might as well have cake while we wait," Cassandra said as she and Iris cut and served the cake.

"Seriously, we just don't know what to say," Maxwell said. "This is all so wonderful and unexpected."

Elan, Koby and Dagon suddenly left the room. A few moments later Natasha peaked into the dining room. "I have everything."

"Since the celebration is to honor both of you," Calen said with a big grin. "You have to be dressed for the event. Koby walked up to Emeral and handed her a purple silk dress with just a hint of gold trim. Christopher ran up to Emeral with the shoes for the dress. Koby kissed Emeral on the cheek.

"Oh my, this is beautiful," Emeral said as she stood up and held the dress in front of her. Dagon walked in carrying a silk black suit for Maxwell. Nicholas ran up to Maxwell with the matching shoes. Elan followed Dagon. Elan carried a silk white shirt and a tie which he presented to Maxwell while Joey ran up and handed Maxwell a box which contained amethyst and diamond cuff links and tie pin. Diana and Thor handed a velvet box to Emeral which contained an amethyst and diamond necklace, earrings and bracelet.

Misha stepped forward and handed a large box to Emeral, "Since your best friend is the Queen we thought you should have one of these."

"Maxwell look," Emeral gasped as she lifted a small diamond tiara from the box.

"And in case the night is cold," Gabriel said as he and Raphael presented Emeral and Maxwell with fur coats.

Maxwell stood up, "We are so overwhelmed that we are speechless. How can we ever thank you enough?"

"Oh we aren't done," Calen said. "While you are on your trip with Elan and Cassandra we are going to redecorate your chambers so you need to let us know what you would like."

"And your daughters here made something very special for you," Luca said. All of the women in the house now gathered around Emeral and Maxwell. Natasha stepped forward and handed them a huge leather bound book.

"Hannah did all that fancy writing," Natasha explained as Maxwell and Emeral opened the book. "That is not the history of your family in the Ice Caves but the history of your family here. As you can see we left blank pages that Hannah will fill in. Lila, Vivian, Diana and I drew portraits of all the family members and there are blank pages left for more. Cassandra and Bekka did the art work and wrote the poems."

"This is so incredibly wonderful," Emeral sobbed then held out her arms to hug the women.

Elan stepped forward. "I was saving the best for last. When we went to get Melinda, Tina well, was herself. And Diana got really close to Tina's face and yelled at her and when Diana was done she said, 'And one more thing, I am the adopted daughter of Emeral and Maxwell, the two most wonderful people in the world.'"

Chapter XXVI
Before the Wedding

The next five days before the wedding of Elan and Cassandra were both exciting and sad for the people living in Gabriel's home. No one had received word from Bekka, Joao or Dack and now the morning of the day before the wedding, Cassandra and Elan were becoming concerned that Joao and Dack might not make it back for the wedding.

Koby and Bekka were supposed to be attendants for Elan and Cassandra. Since Bekka was gone, Koby asked to be excused from his role in the wedding ceremony. This request brought mixed reactions from the family members since many of them were angry at Koby for his actions towards Bekka. When Thor heard of Koby's request he told Elan and Cassandra they should take him out of the ceremony and have Koby in the wedding instead. Now the morning before the day of the wedding Koby finally agreed to be in the wedding ceremony.

Earlier in the week, Emeral and Maxwell had a private luncheon with Sudfad, Renya, Alexander and Laurel. Emeral and Maxwell showed the other couples many of the gifts they had received from their children and grandchildren in Wetpr. As everyone was looking at the beautiful drawings contained in the book that had been given to Maxwell and Emeral, Maxwell looked at his wife then spoke emotionally.

"One of the reasons this meant so very much to Emeral and me is, well, we have three grown daughters who have families of their own in the Ice Caves. The girls are nothing like our sons or our new daughters. Our blood daughters don't have time for us and we rarely see their children. Our sons told us it was their wives who had the ideas to do these wonderful things for us."

"What Maxwell is saying is that our own blood daughters have never said or done anything to make us feel like part of their families. And look at what our newly adopted children have done. Our lives have changed so much since we came here. Honestly, both Maxwell and I were feeling rather useless at home, you know once all of the children moved out. We just don't know how we are ever going to repay the children for all they have done for us."

"Emeral, Maxwell this was the children repaying you for all you have done for them," Sudfad said. "While all the members of Gabriel's team are strong people and powerful warriors, except for your original sons most of them had no families. Because they didn't have families they could devote all of their time to the missions. But that is no life and they started to realize that when the members started to fall in love and marry. While they are all adults you two bring a presence that unifies them all and really makes them feel like a family. They all tell us how much you mean to them, this time they told you."

"Iris and Joshua," Raphael said as they were walking down the stairs for breakfast. "While we appreciate all of the help, know it is not expected; you are our guests."

"Raphael, we are your family," Joshua corrected. "And Iris and I have never felt comfortable sitting around watching others work."

"Besides this is so much fun," Iris said. "Everyone is so excited and well, it is pretty crazy here which is fun."

"It's always a little crazy but this is by far the worse I have seen," Raphael said then laughed.

"Also, Raphael I know I have said it before but I just don't feel comfortable with all of the clothes and other things that you and Gabriel have bought us."

"Joshua, Vivian isn't always good at expressing her feelings so I don't know if she has told you how much she misses all of you. And you are my family also, my parents died long ago. It makes both Vivian and me very happy to have you here. And as for Gabriel, you already gave him a great gift. You took care of Hannah when she was in Ryed. Gabriel is a different man since he met her. I fear that if anything ever happened to Hannah my friend would die of a broken heart."

"We are having fine wine with breakfast this morning," Gabriel announced. "To celebrate Elan's and Cassandra's wedding tomorrow." Gabriel held up his glass, "To Elan and Cassandra may they have a life filled with love."

388

Everyone at the table repeated the toast then took a drink of their wine. Emeral stood up. "Cassandra while I am not your mother,"

Calen interrupted Emeral by loudly saying, "Thank god!" Which made everyone laugh.

"As I was saying," Emeral said with a grin. "Every bride should have something borrowed to wear at her wedding. This locket belonged to my grandmother who gave it to my mother who gave it to me. I would be honored if you would wear at for your wedding."

"Oh Emeral," Cassandra said. "This means so much to me. It's beautiful. Thank you so much." Cassandra hugged and kissed Emeral. But the gaiety of the moment was shattered when an angry voice filled the dining room.

"Koby will you step outside?" Joao asked as he and Dack stood in the doorway of the dining room.

Without speaking Koby stood up and walked outside, Lila stayed with the children while the rest of the team followed the three men out the front door. As soon as they were off the front steps, Joao punched Koby in the jaw so hard that Koby fell backwards and landed on his back.

"Joao I am not going to fight you," Koby said. "I deserved that and more. You can hit me again if you want." Koby said as he stood up.

Both Joao and Dack looked angry and Joao was clenching and unclenching his fists but he did not strike Koby again. "She never stopped crying," Joao yelled. "You were so jealous of us when Bekka is like a sister to me and Dack then you flirt with Melinda right in front of her when she is pregnant with your child. You don't deserve Bekka. I am glad she left you!"

"You're right," Koby said. "I feel awful. Is she staying with her family?"

"Yes," Dack said. "But don't think about going there. Bekka really doesn't want to see you."

"But..." Koby started to say.

"Really just leave her alone," Dack said. "You two are not in love. You both realized you could have feelings for other people. Bekka does not want to watch you with other women and I don't think you could watch her around other men. Let her have her own life. She has a good family and they are glad to have her home and they are excited about the baby." Koby stared at Dack and Joao without speaking. There was a great deal of tension between the three young men.

"Joao, Dack," Emeral said as she walked between them and Koby. "Bekka was a part of this family and we all miss her. Will she allow the rest of us to write to her?"

"I think she would like that," Dack said. "She felt sad leaving all of you."

Emeral turned to the rest of the family. "Many Rualas will be here at the ceremonies. I am sure we could ask some of them to take packages to Bekka. You are all so good at making thoughtful gifts, let's let Bekka know she is still part of the family." Emeral paused for a moment. "And Koby is still family. Many of us have been angry with him but my son is also confused and hurting. We cannot change the past but I hope all of you learn from the mistakes that Koby and Bekka made as you move forward. Now Elan and Cassandra deserve to have a wonderful wedding. Let's turn our thoughts to their happiness."

Emeral turned to Luca. "Why don't you let me explain to Christopher that his friend is not coming back?"

Later that morning after the men on Gabriel's team returned from a meeting at the castle they all met in Gabriel's study. Joshua and his sons were also invited to the meeting. Moments after Gabriel closed the door to the study the door burst open and Christopher ran into the room with Lila running behind him. Christopher ran up to Koby and started punching him. "She was my friend," Christopher yelled angrily then he started to cry. Koby put his arms around Christopher and hugged him tightly. As Koby was carrying Christopher out of the study the other men could see that Koby too was crying.

Many of the wedding guests had to travel great distances to come to Wetpr. The day before the wedding was exceptionally busy as guests arrived at the castle. Renya, always the perfect hostess, had many events planned to entertain her guests and this evening there would be what Renya called a pre-wedding celebration. Sudfad sent carriages to Gabriel's home to bring the members of his team to the ball. Everyone was dressed in their finest clothing. The situation between Koby and Bekka put a damper on any romantic interests between Melinda and any of the men on Gabriel's team.

Renya made sure that Elan and Cassandra were the last couple to enter the ballroom, so that all the guests could applaud them. The young couple walked in with Joey and all three were overwhelmed by their reception. Renya led Elan, Cassandra and Joey to the head table in the front of the room.

"Dinner will not be served for a while," Sudfad said as he addressed the room full of people, so we have a variety of musicians to entertain you. Please enjoy this night." As soon as Sudfad had finished speaking, Angelina, Ingr and Nikki found Iris and Joshua in the crowd and hugged them. Then the girls pulled Vivian's parents through the room so they could introduce them to their families.

"Oh I am so very glad to finally meet you," Bella said as she hugged both Iris and Joshua. "I have heard so much about you." After the families were properly introduced, Ingr, Angelina and Nikki walked through the crowd looking for Diana.

Luca was walking with Christopher when they met Thaos who was carrying his baby son in his left arm and holding Amy's hand with his right. "Luca meet our new daughter Amy," Thaos said proudly. Luca looked at Thaos who nodded to Luca's unspoken question, if Amy was one of the young girls they rescued. Luca knelt down to shake hands with her.

"It is very nice to meet you. I want to introduce you to my son." When Luca turned around both he and Thaos started laughing when they saw the look on Christopher's face. Christopher was staring at Amy with his mouth open. "Amy this is Christopher." Luca had to push Christopher forward so he would shake hands with Amy.

"How come your daddy has wings and you don't?" Amy asked.

"He's my second daddy. Luca saved me and my sister from Hutas."

"Thaos is my second daddy too; he saved me, Sally and April from a monster."

"Do you want to go to the playroom?" Christopher asked Amy.

"Renya has a huge room set up for all the children through those doors," Luca said and pointed to two side by side doors on the wall near to where the men were standing."

"You can play but stay there until either Nikki or I come to get you," Thaos said. Christopher grabbed Amy's hand and they ran to the playroom.

"I think Christopher is in love," Luca said and laughed.

"I do too," Thaos said. "It is amazing Amy hasn't been with us long but both Nikki and I feel like she is our real daughter."

"I felt like that about Christopher right away too," Luca said. "Speaking of Nikki; she, Ingr, Angelina and Diana are busy playing matchmaker with the men on our team, I am trying to stay away from it."

"Well join us," Thaos said and led Luca to the tables occupied by the families from Lentz.

"I am not really sure how we should do this," Angelina said as she had Misha, Dagon, Joao and Dack moving tables together.

"Well decide soon," Misha said with a laugh. "This is the third time we have rearranged these tables."

"Let's leave them in this kind of circle," Angelina said. Then she called to Ingr and Nikki who escorted eight beautiful women to the table. "Everyone take a seat," Angelina said. "Diana will be here in a minute with the men."

As soon as Angelina said these words Diana escorted the men to the table. The young women were all seated on one side of the table and the men on the other.

Angelina, Ingr, Nikki and Diana stood at the head of the table; Misha stood behind Diana and grinned. "You all look so nervous," Angelina said. "Since there are so many of you we didn't know how to introduce all of you. So we decided to just set you all at the same table, make introductions then leave you to the rest. All of the women are warriors from the Nordes Tribe. In our tribe women have the choice as to whether they want to become a warrior or not. If they choose to be a warrior the training starts very early."

"My seven year old adopted daughter just started her training," Nikki said with obvious pride.

"After I introduce the women, Diana will introduce the men," Angelina continued. "Before we begin, this is just something fun we are doing, there are no expectations here. No one is going to be forced to be a couple and honestly there are many other single men and women at this party also. So everyone should stop looking nervous." Angelina laughed. "I am going to start at the head of the table.

"This is Bianca." Angelina pointed to a beautiful woman with brown eyes and brown curly hair. "Next to her is Sasha." Sasha had red straight hair and large blue eyes. "Then is Valerie." Valerie had long straight blonde hair and blue eyes. "Corina." Corina had raven black straight hair and brown eyes.

"Toni." Toni was taller than the rest of the girls with long straight hair that was almost white and green eyes. "Darla." Darla's long red hair was very curly and she had large brown eyes. "Jasmine." Jasmine had long curly dark hair and hazel eyes. "And last we have Batina." Batina had dark curly hair and large blue eyes that seemed to dance.

Diana looked at Misha and asked, "Do you want to do the introductions?"

"Oh no, I am staying out of this," he replied with a laugh.

"All of these men are part of a very special team," Diana said. "I am very proud to be on that team but I am also a new member so I don't know a great deal about some of the men at this table besides that they are all great warriors and honorable men. Two tribes are represented here, the Ruala Tribe and the Clan of Gesmal, both tribes are known to be fierce warriors."

"I will let the men explain the rest to you. I will start out like Angelina did. Edward is from the Kingdom of Puntd and is now a general in charge of King Sudfad's army. And I am sorry to say Edward is one of the men I don't know very well so he can tell you about himself. Next to him is Dagon, who is from the Ruala Tribe and one of my brothers-in-law," Diana said with a giggle.

"Next to Dagon is Koby, also a Ruala and also my brother-in-law. Joao and Dack are both Rualas and relatively newer members of the team. Next to Dack is my brother Thor who is of the Clan of Gesmal. The two men next to Thor are both brothers of Vivian, for those of you who know her. Micha and Thomas are also members of the Clan of Gesmal."

"We are sorry if we have made you feel awkward," Ingr said. "But all of you have some things in common. You all are mighty warriors and good people who have dedicated much of your lives to your training and your missions. So we hope you have fun. All of us from Lentz will be here for at least a week, in case you don't get the chance to talk to everyone tonight."

"So what did you think?" Ingr asked Misha as he, Diana, Angelina, Nikki and Ingr left all of the single people to mingle.

"All of your friends are beautiful," Misha said then looked at Diana. "Don't get mad."

"I'm not mad, I thought they were beautiful too."

"I was surprised how nervous everyone seemed. Maybe we should send some bottles of wine to their table," Misha suggested.

Renya had the tables in the Great Hall rearranged before the dinner was served. She now had two head tables positioned diagonally in the front of the room. The Royal Families were seated at one head table and the wedding party at the other. Diana smiled when she saw Joao, Dack, Koby and Dagon each approach the head table with one of the Nordes warriors as their companions.

Diana looked down the table and saw Emeral looking at Melinda who was sitting without a companion. Emeral left the head table and walked through the crowded room until she found Thor sitting at a table with Edward, Micha, Thomas and four Nordes warriors.

"I truly apologize," Emeral said. "But we need Thor at the head table, he will return after the meal."

Without saying anything Thor stood up and walked with Emeral towards the head of the room. "If any of those women are angry with you because of this I will talk to them," Emeral said. "Melinda is sitting alone which must be very embarrassing for her. I am sorry to ask you to leave your friends."

"That's alright. The truth is that after all of that business with Koby, I have tried to stay away from Melinda."

"Why?"

"Emeral I am just getting to know the family I don't want to step on anyone's toes."

Emeral did not respond to Thor's comment because they had reached the head table. Thor sat down next to Melinda who looked embarrassed. After the many toasts to start the dinner Melinda leaned over and whispered to Thor, "I am so sorry you keep being forced to be with me. This is embarrassing."

"I'm not being forced."

"I know Diana wanted you to meet one of those girls tonight."

"There are eight girls and eight of us; we are all just getting to know each other and they will be here for a week." Melinda had a sad look in her eyes when she smiled at Thor. "Melinda, I don't know if anyone told you how I became a part of this family. I was badly injured for weeks and when I woke up I found out I couldn't walk, I was adopted and my sister who I had raised was married. I was filled with rage and took it out it out on everyone. I am just getting to know the family and I don't want to do any further damage because they are good people."

"What do you mean further damage?"

"I had planned to ask you to the wedding but after Koby and Dagon," Thor hesitated. "I don't want to ask you out if they are interested in you or you in them. I don't want to hurt your feelings, I am just being honest."

"Thor I don't know either you or Dagon and he hasn't spoken to me any more than you have. You have to understand that Bekka and I have been friends since we were small. Even if I was interested in Koby I would never act on it because I love Bekka. And I feel so awful about what happened."

"I was there, you didn't do anything wrong."

"They would probably still be together if I hadn't come."

"I don't think that is true. They had decided they didn't love each other, although that was no excuse for how Koby acted. He could have at least waited to flirt with you when Bekka wasn't sitting there watching."

"And your whole family saw it."

"No one blames you, Melinda."

"I already sent Bekka a long letter but I haven't heard from her yet."

Melinda and Thor stopped talking and watched the crowd. "Life here is so different," Thor said. "I feel very out of place at times."

"I am not used to all of this either," Melinda said. "Thor after we eat Elan and Cassandra are going to be called out on the dance floor to lead a dance. Then everyone from the head tables is supposed to join them before the rest of the guests do. If you don't want to dance with me you should probably leave as soon as you finish eating."

"I don't think a dance would hurt," Thor said then started to laugh. "Actually it might if I step on your feet."

Chapter XXVII
A Wedding Affair

"Where is everyone?" Natasha asked as she was putting breakfast on the table the next morning. "I hope they aren't all hung-over."

"I don't know if everyone made it home last night," Misha said as he sat down at the table.

"Well they better be ready for the wedding," Cassandra said. "I am so nervous I am not sure I can eat." Cassandra was putting plates of sausages on the table when Elan and Joey walked into the room.

Joey ran up to Cassandra, "Mama we got you this." Joey said as he handed Cassandra a small box. Cassandra knelt down and kissed Joey then opened the box.

"This is so beautiful," Cassandra said as she slipped a ring on her finger that had tiny rubies and diamonds. "Thank you so much." Cassandra kissed Joey again then walked around the table to kiss Elan.

"It has tiny stones so it will fit under your wedding rings," Elan explained.

"I love it; thank you."

"Tina are you sure you want to go through with this?" Charles asked as he and his wife were having breakfast in their hotel in Salar.

"Charles what will people think if we don't attend our own daughter's wedding?" Tina said curtly. "And besides I am not going to let that queen tell me how to be a mother."

"I know your feathers are ruffled but Sudfad and Renya are not only the most powerful King and Queen in Opots but they are personal friends of our Royal Family. I would suggest you try to improve your temperament. It could benefit us greatly to have such rich and powerful friends."

"Charles if you remember that was my plan all along that is until all the rest of this nasty business came up."

"Tina you have always been able to turn on the charm when it benefits you; I would suggest today would be one of those times."

"You mean when it benefits both of us," Tina snapped.

"Might I remind you that you are the one who compromised our plans by sending those hateful letters to the children?"

"How did I know they were going to show them to others, what on earth were they thinking?"

Dagon, Joao, Koby, Thor, Micha, Thomas and Dack walked into the dining room together laughing and wearing the same clothes they had worn the night before.

"Are you all drunk?" Cassandra asked with concern.

"We might be a little," Dagon replied and laughed.

"Thor did you have sex?" Diana asked in a scolding manner which made all seven of the men roar with laughter."

"No," Thor answered as he sat down at the table still laughing.

"Well what were you doing then?" Natasha asked.

"We were with the girls," Dagon said. "They showed us this game they have where you shoot arrows and throw knives into targets."

"And are we supposed to believe that is what you were doing all night?" Natasha asked with a grin.

"We were," Joao said defensively. "Of course we were drinking too."

Natasha grabbed a pot of coffee and filled the cups of the seven young men, "You need to sober up the wedding is in a couple of hours." All seven of the men started to laugh again.

Lila brought all the children into the dining room. "They were so busy playing they forgot about breakfast," she said. "It sounds like someone is having fun in here," Lila added as she looked at the drunken young men sitting around the table.

Luca and Calen walked into the room and took their seats, "Emeral, Maxwell, Raphael and Gabriel already left for the chapel." Luca said then looked at Dagon and the others and grinned. "Did you have fun?"

"Yes," Dack said. "But we didn't have sex." Calen and Luca both laughed.

"Yes we were worried about that," Calen replied sarcastically.

There was silence for a moment then Nicholas said, "Christopher has a girlfriend." Christopher smiled and nodded as everyone at the table looked at him.

"Is it Amy?" Luca asked with a grin. Christopher smiled and nodded again.

"Does Amy know she is your girlfriend?" asked Calen.

"No," Christopher said with a mischievous look.

"Who is Amy?" Cassandra asked.

"One of the little girls that Thaos and Stephan rescued after the last mission," Luca said. "Thaos and Nikki adopted Amy; she is only seven and really a pretty little thing."

"One of those girls was only seven?" Hannah gasped. "I thought they were older."

"The other two are fourteen and fifteen," Luca replied. "You know I have only been with Thaos when we are on missions and he is such a savage fighter and last night he is walking around with his son in one arm and holding Amy's hand with his other. I saw a whole different side of him."

Emeral and Maxwell had left the house for the castle long before the other members of Gabriel's team were awake. Maxwell left a note on Luca's door, telling him where they would be.

Neither Emeral nor Maxwell wanted to alarm the children, but Emeral had received a letter the evening before from a close friend of hers in the Ice Caves. Greta warned Emeral that Tina and Charles had left the Ice Caves to attend Cassandra's wedding. Emeral showed the letter to Renya and Sudfad immediately after she read it. Renya told Emeral and Maxwell to meet them for an early breakfast the following morning.

When Emeral and Maxwell arrived at the castle they were extremely surprised when Marie led them to the private chambers of the King and Queen. Sudfad and Renya were both sitting at a table on their balcony drinking coffee.

"This is where we hide out when the castle is filled with people," Sudfad said with a smile to Maxwell and Emeral then Sudfad turned to Marie. "They will be joining us for breakfast."

"Yes My Lord," Marie said and left the chambers.

"We thought we would have more privacy here," Renya said as she poured two more cups of coffee.

"We really didn't mean to impose upon you," said Maxwell.

"Nonsense," Sudfad replied. "Elan and Cassandra are sweet young people and don't deserve the heartache her family has been imposing upon them. And besides we are responsible for the ceremonies and don't want terrorists disrupting them and honestly we consider Tina and Charles terrorists."

"Last night Emeral and I were talking and we realized that you have only really met the honorable people in our tribe," Maxwell explained. "Like any community there are all types of personalities among the Ruala people. There are many Ruualas who are not warriors and many who are not honorable."

"Tina and Charles are not good people. They are opportunists who try to turn every situation into something which can benefit them either with power or money. I know you have not visited the Ice Caves but they are like an entire world, there are cities and villages. The Ruala people have flourished since the Sanuri gave us sanctuary in the Ice Caves."

"I am going to interrupt a moment," Emeral said. "You two have been so gracious to our people and you have no idea how well known and honored you are among our tribe. We would very much like to take you to the Ice Caves someday for a holiday. I can guarantee you will be amazed at the caves and greatly welcomed by our people."

"Sudfad I would just love that." Renya's face lit up with excitement as she spoke.

"I would also love to visit your people. Our sons are old enough to run the kingdom without us. Let's seriously talk about this after all of these ceremonies."

"Excellent!" Maxwell said. "But back to Tina and Charles. The more that Emeral and I talked last night the more we wondered if perhaps Tina and Charles had other motives besides terrorizing their children."

"What do you mean?" asked Sudfad.

"As Emeral said, you and Renya are very well known among our people. Tina and Charles are aware of your wealth and your power, two things they covet. Of course we have no proof that they have ulterior motives we just wanted to warn you."

"This year has been like no other for me," Sudfad said sadly. "Never in my life have I had terrorists infiltrate my military and my home. And many of these people were people I knew who betrayed us for money. From the way you describe Tina and Charles they sound like they could be easily swayed by demons. I know demons cannot enter the Ice Caves but down here they walk among us."

Vivian arrived at the chapel early so she could help Raphael and Gabriel prepare for the wedding. Both priests had been asked to conduct the ceremony. "I am just so proud that my family will be able to hear the two of you speak," Vivian said. "Gabriel did I ever tell you that the first time I heard Raphael conduct a ceremony I felt like the Angels were singing to me. That's when I knew I had to marry him." Raphael smiled brightly as Vivian spoke. "This is a beautiful chapel," Vivian continued as she brought in vases of flowers from her boca.

"Honey did you bring your dress here or are you going back home to change?" Raphael asked. "Because it is getting late. I can put the flowers out."

"Oh I have everything with me. Is there a room where I can change?"

As soon as the sun had risen guests upon guests arrived at the castle. An hour before the ceremony was to start the front court yard of the castle filled with Ruala and Shettee families.

"My Lady," Marie said excitedly as she ran into the Great Hall. "My Lady, Ibula is here with the baby."

"Oh I am so glad they made it," Renya said and quickly went to the front courtyard where she found most of her family talking to the newly arrived guests. "Ibula," Renya called out and hugged her adopted daughter. "Let me see him." Ibula handed her infant son to Renya.

"He is a beautiful baby," Renya said. "I am just so happy you could come."

"My husband is rather over protective," Ibula said with a smile as she glanced over at Thedes who was talking with Raul and Simon.

"We have fixed up permanent chambers for you that include a nursery and they are filled with everything you could want, so when you come to visit you don't have to worry about transporting so many things."

"You are so good to us," Ibula said. "Let's tell Thedes."

"The carriages are here," Lila called out as carriages were lining up in front of Gabriel's house.

"Can we take Jasper with us?" Nicholas asked Hannah as she once again straightened his tie.

"No, I gave Jasper a large bone which should keep him busy while we are gone."

Melinda, Natasha and Lila hurried Cassandra through the house and into the first carriage so no one could see her dress. The three women also got into the carriage as it was the first to leave the house. Elan, Joey, Joao, Dack and Thor climbed into the second carriage.

Joshua and his family rode in the third carriage. Adrone and Paul were both nervous and proud about their roles in the wedding. Diana was carrying baby Lily as Hannah ushered all of the children into the next carriage. Luca, Calen, Dagon, Koby and Misha rode in the last carriage.

"Next time we do this it is going to be you," Calen said and winked at Misha.

"You know before I met Diana a comment like that would have scared the hell out of me. Now I am looking forward to it."

"I keep saying it," Luca said. "I just can't believe how much you have changed since you got married. You used to be such a rebel and now you are reminding me of Maxwell." All of the brothers laughed loudly as the carriage sped towards the castle.

Elan led his groomsmen to the altar of the chapel. Elan was holding Joey's hand and the small boy was dressed exactly like his new father. When the men turned to face the guests the very first thing they all noticed was that the church was filled past capacity. The doors to the chapel were open and people were standing near the entrances.

The second thing that Elan, Maxwell, Joao and Dack noticed was Tina and Charles sitting in one of the front seats. Tina did not smile at her son or soon to be son-in-law. Elan held Joey's hand tighter as if he was afraid that Tina would rush the altar and attack the boy. Dack turned to Luca who was to his right and told him about Tina and Charles. Luca in turned told his brothers. Unknown to Elan all the groomsmen know stared hostilely at Tina and her husband, who stared back at the young men.

The music changed and within moments Emeral was walking down the aisle followed by Melinda, Vivian and the rest of the bridesmaids.

Iris was in a front row holding baby Lily; she could not help but notice that all the groomsmen seemed tense. Melinda gasped when she saw her parents, a sound that was heard by many.

The altar was designed in a semi-circle that had four aisles leading to it and four sections of seating. The Royal Family sat in a section to the left of the groom's family placing them two sections away from Tina and Charles. Sudfad had increased the guards around the chapel after he was informed that Cassandra's parents had arrived.

Diana was the last bridesmaid to walk down the aisle and she dropped white rose petals on the carpet before Cassandra. Elan caught his breath when he saw his bride walking towards him. "Look at Mama," Elan whispered to Joey. Behind Cassandra walked Paul and Adrone dressed in the same suits as the groomsmen. Paul carried the rings and Adrone carried two long stemmed white roses. Cassandra's eyes were on Elan and Joey she did not see the glances she was receiving from members of the wedding party.

Gabriel and Raphael were aware of Tina's and Charles presence in the chapel so they made some last minute changes to the ceremony. As soon as Cassandra reached the altar, the priests made sure her back was to the guests at all times. Tina sat stoned face as she watched the ceremony that brought tears to the eyes of others.

Raphael had Adrone and Paul come forward when they handed the wedding couple the rings and roses so that Cassandra would not turn and see her parents. Like Luca's wedding ceremony, Elan and Cassandra presented Joey with a ring also to show their love for him.

When the ceremony was completed and the couple turned to face their guests, Cassandra froze as terror filled her being. Tina was staring coldly at her daughter. Elan let go of Joey's hand and grabbed Cassandra's and they walked down the aisle. Once outside of the chapel they climbed inside of a carriage and were driven to the castle.

Renya had scheduled a luncheon meal immediately after the wedding ceremony. Then a variety of different types of games, competitions and entertainment filled the afternoon until the grand ball in the evening.

It was obvious to Tina and Charles that they were not welcomed at the wedding ceremony. Charles knew his wife well and knew she would regard their cold reception as a sign of war. As soon as they walked out of the chapel, Charles forced Tina to get into a carriage and they returned to their hotel.

"Tina I know you, you are not going to get us removed from the reception tonight. We are going back to the hotel so you can cool off." Tina's face was bright red and the veins were protruding from her neck. "Your little temper tantrums are not going to ruin any possibilities we might garner tonight. Set your priorities straight woman!" Tina did not speak until they were in the city.

"You are right Charles. I need to have a glass of wine and calm down. Then we are going to make our presence known at the ball."

"Are you alright?" Thor asked Melinda as she rode next to him in a carriage. Diana and Misha were riding in the same carriage.

"I can't believe they came," Melinda said. "You don't know my mother; I have a really bad feeling about this."

"Melinda stay close to Thor he will protect you," Diana said.

"It's not me I am worried about, its little Joey."

"Are you saying your parents might do something to Joey?" Misha asked angrily.

"If they really want to hurt Cassandra and Elan, Joey would be the means."

"This is getting out of control," Misha said. "We are having a family meeting when we return to the castle." Misha waited until Gabriel and Raphael had returned from the chapel then he had all of the adults except for Elan and Cassandra meet in a small room of the castle.

They all agreed that Elan and Cassandra should be able to enjoy their wedding without any added distress. The team decided they would all take turns guarding Elan, Cassandra and Joey. "We can't make it obvious," Gabriel said. "So we will change positions often."

"If she touches that child I will kill her," Vivian said.

"I think we all will," Luca replied. "If Joey goes to the playroom one of us should stay in there."

Gabriel's team as well as Elan and Cassandra were relieved that Tina and Charles did not attend the luncheon or the entertainment that immediately followed. But the fact that Tina and Charles were not present at these events also raised suspicions. After the luncheon the members of Gabriel's team took turns going home so they could change their clothes. Misha and Diana were the last of the team to arrive at the ball, because Diana was afraid to leave Cassandra and Elan at the castle.

Misha had asked Diana to wear the emerald silk dress that he bought her, which was strapless and very form fitting. After Diana was dressed Misha presented her with an emerald and diamond necklace, earrings and bracelet. Diana got tears in her eyes and kissed Misha over and over. She continued to kiss him in the carriage ride to the castle.

As soon as Misha and Diana entered the Great Hall they headed towards the table where Gabriel's team was sitting, so Diana could show her gifts to the others. Just as they were within feet of the team, Dagon called Misha's name but the warning did not come soon enough because instantly a beautiful blonde Ruala woman was standing in front of Misha and Diana. The woman stared angrily at Misha and when the woman realized that Misha and Diana were holding hands the women became enraged.

"You never answered any of my letters," the woman said accusingly.

"Diana this is Mia, Mia this is my wife Diana."

"Your wife!" roared Mia and she slapped Misha across the face which made the members of Gabriel's team roar with laughter.

406

Misha, Diana and Mia were close enough to the tables that the team members could hear every word that was being said. Misha smiled but did not say anything. Mia pulled her hand back to slap Misha again but in an instant Diana had crossed in front of Misha and grabbed Mia's wrist.

"You will not hit my husband again," Diana said seriously. Suddenly Misha's brothers started saying very loudly that they were placing bets on who would win if Diana and Mia fought. Misha was trying very hard not to laugh. "I understand why you are angry but you hit him once," Diana continued and let go of Mia's wrist.

"You understand!" Mia said to Diana then turned to Misha. "You told her?"

"Of course she is my wife."

"Were you married to her when you slept with me?"

"Of course not; I would never do that to Diana." This comment infuriated Mia as Misha knew it would. Mia pulled her arm back again to strike Misha. Once again Diana grabbed Mia's wrist but this time Diana twisted it causing Mia to yelp in pain.

"I warn you I am a warrior," Mia said angrily. Misha grinned as his brothers once again roared with laughter.

"And I told you to stop slapping my husband," Diana said calmly as she slipped off her shoes. An act that wasn't noticed by Mia but it was by everyone on Gabriel's team.

"As much as I would like to see you girls fight over me," Misha joked. "Diana is a Venator warrior while you Mia are no warrior at all. For your own good I would suggest you leave us."

"I just can't believe you would rather have that little human instead of me," Mia said and with a toss of her hair she quickly walked away. Diana picked up her shoes and she and Misha walked to the table where everyone was laughing about the encounter.

As Misha held Diana's chair for her, she looked at him angrily. "I can't believe she called me a little human!"

407

Now everyone at the table stopped laughing and grinned at Misha and Diana. Misha sat down and looked at Diana because he wasn't sure if she was really angry or kidding.

"Honey you are. You are a human and you are considerably smaller than Mia." Diana glared at Misha as she thought about his words.

"Well alright then," Diana said with indignation. "But she didn't have to say it like I had the plague or something." Now everyone at the table roared with laughter again.

"Oh my god, I am crying," Vivian said as she laughed uncontrollably. Misha put his arm around Diana and kissed her.

"Melinda I wish you would quit talking like that," Thor said. "That is unless you are trying to get rid of me so you can be with someone else?"

"No, I just feel like you are being forced to accompany me when there are so many girls here who can't take their eyes off from you."

"You do realize there are men looking at you too? I know you have been through a lot lately but let's just start all over and enjoy the evening. It's the only time your sister will marry and she and Elan have enough on their minds."

"You're right. I am sorry about all this. I am still so upset about Bekka and then Mother. But you are right Thor. Let's dance."

"I warn you I might step on your feet," he said with a grin.

"See that's an advantage to being Ruala, I could just float off the floor if I had to," Melinda laughed as they walked to the dance floor.

"Gabriel," Claudius called out and started to stand up. "It is good to see you."

"I wanted to bring my family over to meet you," Gabriel said as he carried Cerey and held hands with Hannah.

Nicholas and Christopher walked next to Gabriel and the two little boys were directed to hold hands so they wouldn't get lost in the crowded room. All of the families from Lentz were seated together at adjoining tables. Claudius and Gabriel made all of the introductions. Angelina, Ingr and Nikki all stood up and hugged Hannah.

"Nikki when is your baby due," Hannah asked as she looked at the young woman's stomach.

"I'm not really sure but soon," Nikki said as she smiled brightly.

"Tomorrow morning would you mind if I examined you?" Hannah asked. "Because I believe that baby will come very soon."

"Really," Thaos said excitedly. "How can you tell?"

"The position of her stomach and this is her second child so it should come more quickly."

"Hannah when you say soon, just how soon are you talking about?" Bella asked.

"Now, I am just guessing but you might be holding another grandbaby at the baby ceremony." Bella and Claudius both got huge smiles on their faces. Hannah turned to Shara and asked, "What do you think?"

"She has dropped considerably in the last twenty-four hours." Everyone at the table looked at Shara since this is the first she had said anything. "I have been watching her and I would rather deliver a baby here than on the road."

"If you don't mind I am going to speak with Renya so we have a room prepared for you," Hannah said.

"Claudius if Nikki doesn't have the baby in the next few days we may want to stay longer so she doesn't give birth as we travel," Bella said.

"I was just thinking the same thing."

Thaos started to laugh as Christopher and Nicholas walked up to him and stared at Amy, who was sitting on Thaos' lap.

"You are going to spend the rest of your life beating the boys away," Stephan said with a grin.

Gabriel winked and nodded towards the two little boys, "Christopher is quite enamored."

"Luca was telling us about her," Hannah said. "She is a beautiful little girl. But I was..." Hannah paused to think about her words in front of the children. "I was shocked at her age."

"We will tell you about it when the children aren't around," Claudius said.

Ingr had been watching Christopher, Nicholas and Amy with a big smile on her face. "Why don't I take all of you to the playroom for a while?" Nicholas and Christopher swung their heads around and looked at Gabriel for approval, while Amy looked up at Thaos.

"You can go but stay with Ingr," Gabriel said.

"You have the same instructions," Thaos said with a smile. Amy hugged Thaos then jumped off his lap. Christopher took one of Amy's hands and Nicholas the other.

"Give me Cerey she can play too," Ingr said and took the little girl from Gabriel.

"Where are your babies?" Hannah asked.

"We wanted the girls to enjoy the celebrations so Claudius brought nurses along. They are all upstairs in our chambers," Bella explained.

Luca and Lila were accompanying Elan, Cassandra and Joey when Luca saw Tina and Charles enter the Great Hall. "Your parents just walked in," Luca said. "Cassandra this is your night, they have no power over you unless you allow them to. You are a mother and a wife now and you have your own family which Tina and Charles are not a part of."

"You're right," Cassandra said nervously. "I don't know why I let them upset me so."

"They have taken a position to be your enemy you may have to view them as such," Luca continued. "You are a courageous and intelligent warrior you would never let a demon or a Huta affect you like this."

"Elan did your parents come?" Lila asked as she was trying to change the subject.

"Yes, would you like to meet them?"

"Very much."

As Elan led the small group to a table across the room, Luca watched as Tina and Charles walked directly to the table where Sudfad and Renya were sitting with Mathas and Rosa. All during the day people had been talking about Tina and Charles and many were now watching the couple walk through the Great Hall. As Mathas saw Cassandra's parents approaching he turned to Ryan who was also sitting at their table. "Ryan would you take Margarit for a dance?"

"Of course," Ryan said as he looked at the couple approaching the table. Ryan stood up and bowed before Margarit. "My Lady could I have this dance?" Margarit started to giggle and jumped out of her chair and grabbed Ryan's hand and pulled him onto the dance floor.

"Mathas looked at Sudfad and said with a grin, "I may owe Ryan for this."

"My Lord, My Lady I am Charles father of the bride and this is my lovely wife Tina," Charles said to Sudfad and Renya. "We feel that we may have made a bad impression on you and very much want to correct any thoughts you may have about us."

Sudfad and Renya stared coldly at Charles and Tina, after a moment Sudfad turned and introduced King Mathas and Queen Rosa to Cassandra's parents.

"And how would you have us correct our thoughts?" Renya asked as she boldly stared at Charles and Tina.

Charles paused before speaking, "My wife wasn't herself when she wrote that letter to Cassandra and Joao, and she would very much like to apologize for it."

"Then wouldn't it be more appropriate to apologize to your children?" Sudfad smiled as Renya questioned Charles.

"We were going to find them in just a moment," Charles said as he realized his charm was not warming up the Queen.

"I personally read the letter that Tina wrote as did the King," Renya said. "Since it is obvious you have no idea who your children are." Tina's face was turning red as Renya spoke. "I will tell you; they work for the King and this kingdom. Your children have bravely risked their lives on more than one occasion to protect the people of Wetpr and in case you didn't know, that is how Elan lost his arm. And even with that injury he continues to be a courageous warrior and a man of integrity."

Unknown to Tina and Charles, Gabriel and Hannah as well as other members of Gabriel's team and other guests were gathering around the couple so they could hear the exchange between Cassandra's parents and Sudfad and Renya. Raul and Simon saw the crowd gathering and instructed some of the soldiers guarding the doors to stand near the King and Queen.

"Your daughter who you said was so worthless that you should never have brought her into this world, has fought Hutas," Renya continued. "Demons, dark lords and criminals with integrity and great courage as has Joao. And through everything they have been exposed to; they are kind and loving people. Tell me Tina can you say as much for yourself?"

"Why you pompous bitch!" Tina screamed. "I know my children and you can't tell me how to be a mother." Soldiers now ran through the crowd and grabbed Tina and Charles.

"Charles, Tina there is a darkness inside of you that we have never seen in a member of your tribe. A darkness that unfortunately we recognize. You will leave my castle and you will leave my kingdom and you will never return." Sudfad now looked past Charles at the soldiers, take them to their hotel and make sure they pack and leave tonight and if they refuse throw them in the dungeons."

"You can't do this to us," Tina shrieked. "Who the hell do you think you are?"

"The Queen my dear."

Sudfad and Renya were so focused on Tina and Charles that they did not realize the music had stopped playing and all eyes were upon them. As the soldiers started to remove Tina and Charles from the presence of the King and Queen, Calen yelled loudly, "All hail the King and Queen!" Within moments everyone in the room was loudly repeating the tribute and continued to repeat the words until Tina and Charles were taken out of the Great Hall.

Erebus had been standing close by and now walked up to Sudfad and Renya. "I too applaud you for standing up for your people, but I believe there is more to those two than meets the eye. I have a feeling they will come back and if they do; don't underestimate them."

"What did you sense?" Sudfad asked.

"It is what I saw," Erebus said then looked at Mathas and Rosa who were listening to the conversation. "I am a warlock," Erebus explained."

"Sudfad has told us about you," Mathas replied and honestly I find that very interesting. "Perhaps you would have a drink with us?"

"Thank you but the reason I announced myself was so you would understand what I was about to say. I have always been able to see things that others do not, except for the Sanuri. Every person gives off a type of energy that is a projection of who they are. And as difficult as it may be to believe some people have spirits around them. For example the first time I met Roch I was stunned at the whispering demons that were circling him which no one else was aware of. The energy around Cassandra's parents is black as night."

"What exactly does that mean?" Renya asked. "Are they demons?"

413

"I can tell you at this time they are not demons but that type of darkness calls to demons and dark lords. I would not be surprised if they make some very unwise choices in the future. Now I am going to share something with you because I am continuously overwhelmed by your kindness and acceptance of me."

"The energy that surrounds the Sanuri is like sunshine, it can hurt my eyes. The other day when I was taking a walk your son Petra and his friend Kyra asked me if I wanted to meet their pets. Charming children. Petra's energy is brilliant also. Do not be surprised if someday he follows in the steps of the Sanuri."

"Really?" gasped Renya. "How wonderful."

"Do you believe the Sanuri can see that also?" Sudfad asked.

"As powerful as he is I would be very surprised if he could not."

As Erebus was speaking with the two Royal Couples, Cassandra, Elan, Joey, Joao and Melinda all approached the table. As soon as Renya looked at them, Cassandra flew to the Queen and hugged her tightly. "I am sorry that was probably inappropriate but thank you so much," Cassandra said.

"Nonsense child," Renya said.

"May I hug the King?" Cassandra asked.

"Of course," replied Sudfad with a big smile.

"No one has ever stood up for us before," Joao said. "We are very grateful to you."

"I knew they set Renya off when they tried to charm us instead of apologizing to all of you," Sudfad said and chuckled.

"We will never forget what you have done," Elan said. "Cassandra hasn't been able to sleep for weeks she has been so upset."

414

Gabriel and Hannah were now standing at the table. "We didn't want to say anything before but the team feared Cassandra's parents would do something to Joey to hurt Elan and Cassandra so we have been taking turns guarding them all night," Gabriel explained.

"Is that what has been going on?" Elan asked. "I suspected something."

Renya's face became red as she listened to Gabriel speak. "I will not say your fears are not valid but I just cannot understand a mother or grandmother being so heartless."

"You always have a home in Wetpr," Sudfad said to Elan and the other young Rualas. "I hope you realize that."

Chapter XXVIII
James Duran

The celebration for Cassandra's and Elan's wedding went late into the night. "Come on I want to introduce you to a few more people before we leave," Misha said to Diana.

"Am I going to be fending off any more of your old girlfriends?" Diana teased.

"You might but I am confident you will win," Misha joked and took Diana's hand as they pushed through the crowd.

"Ryan please just one more dance," Margarit pleaded.

"You're wearing me out," Ryan kidded.

"Margarit let Ryan be," Rosa scolded. "Aren't there any boys your own age here?" A mischievous light filled Margarit's eyes which made everyone at the table laugh.

"I'll go look," Margarit said exuberantly.

"Perhaps I better dance with you," Ryan said and stood up.

"Thank you Ryan," Mathas said with a grin. "I appreciate this."

Gabriel and Hannah walked up to the table where Mathas and Rosa and Sudfad and Renya were sitting. Gabriel was carrying Nicholas and Hannah carried Cerey; both children were sleeping. "We just wanted to say goodnight before we left," Gabriel said. "And thank you for everything."

"Renya as usual is was a wonderful celebration," Hannah added.

"Marie prepared a room for Nikki," Renya said. "You think the baby might come in the next few days?"

"I would not be surprised if you send someone for me tonight."

"This is going to be so exciting, I love it when babies are born," Rosa said. "Hannah if I am not there when Nikki goes into labor would you have someone get me?"

"Of course," then as an afterthought Hannah asked with a smile. "Renya how many of those women did you set Edward up with?"

Both Sudfad and Renya started laughing, "The tall blonde is a Nordes warrior and the other three I asked here so Edward could meet them. I think we are all surprised that all four women have not left his side a moment."

"And I am sure that is quite the hardship for him," Sudfad said sarcastically.

"I can't believe how much you have changed since your parents were kicked out of here," Thor said to Melinda as they danced.

"And I can't believe how much your dancing has improved now that you've relaxed," Melinda said with a small laugh. "I may have been dramatic but I don't trust my parents at all and I was really frightened that they would do something awful to get back at all of us."

"Well you are all safe from them now. Would you like to go for a walk in one of the gardens?" Thor asked and took Melinda's hand.

"You just couldn't keep your big mouth shut; could you?" Charles screamed at Tina as they were flying out of Salar. "You do realize that you ruined everything. And not only were we in the presence of one wealthy king but two. Tina that vicious temper of yours just cost us a fortune. You better find some way to make this up to me."

Tina was so angry and humiliated that she couldn't speak. "Are you listening to me?" Charles screamed.

"Don't worry I will think of something!"

"Emeral and Maxwell certainly seem to be enjoying themselves," Lila said as she and Luca walked up to Sudfad and Renya to say goodnight. Christopher was soundly asleep in Luca's arms.

"They have been talking with old friends of theirs from the Ice Caves. My parents are very well liked by our tribe and have many friends."

"I am so very glad that Renya and Sudfad threw Cassandra's parents out of the castle," Lila said. "I just love Renya, she told them off but with her usual graciousness."

"I don't really know Tina and Charles but I have a very bad feeling about them," Luca replied. "Don't say anything to the others but I bet we will all hear from them again."

"It's a beautiful night, let's fly home instead of taking the carriage," Misha said to Diana after they said goodbye to the Royal Family. Misha and Diana walked out of a side door to the Great Hall and entered a garden. "This is the same garden where we fought those demons the first night that we met," Misha reminded her. As they strolled across the stone patio they stopped to kiss in the moonlight; as they embraced they both heard a sound. Standing perfectly still they listened into the darkness.

"Sorry, didn't mean to disturb you," Thor said with a laugh as he and Melinda walked out from behind some bushes, hand in hand.

"Thor what are you doing out here?" Diana asked with a grin.

"The same as you."

"Well we can move," Misha said.

"Actually if you walk around the garden you will find a lot of members of the household," Thor said with a smirk.

"Are they enjoying the moonlight too?" Misha asked with a grin.

"I don't think some of them are aware of the moonlight," Thor said and Melinda laughed.

"Who are they with?" Diana asked seriously.

"Diana do you think I stopped and asked for names?" Diana giggled at Thor's remark.

"We're heading home since it is crowded in the gardens," Misha said. "We'll see you later." Misha picked Diana up and ascended into the air.

"I was so glad to see Thor with Melinda," Diana said and giggled again. "I like her."

"Just because they were in the garden doesn't mean they are a couple so don't jump to conclusions. Thor is just beginning to meet girls."

"I know, I didn't say they were getting married but that is the first time I ever saw him holding hands with a girl."

"Really?"

"Well not everyone started dating with they were six years old like you," Diana said jokingly and laughed.

"Seriously I do appreciate your attitude with my former life and former girlfriends," Misha said as they soared through the cool night air. "I hope you realize you will never have to be jealous of anyone because you have my heart."

"That is so sweet," Diana cooed. "And you have mine. Misha look there are soldiers down there."

"They look like they are heading to our house?"

"Why?"

"We'll find out," Misha said as he descended. When they were considerably closer to the four soldiers Misha called out, "Its Misha are you going to Gabriel's house?"

"Yes," yelled one of the soldiers. "Queen Renya sent us for Hannah; Archetenus' wife is having the babies."

"I'll get her and bring her to the castle," Misha said and sped away. Within minutes Misha and Diana walked into the house, Misha went directly to Gabriel's and Hannah's bedroom door and knocked loudly. "Hannah they need you at the castle."

"I'm awake," Hannah called out. "Is it Nikki?"

"No Delilah, I will take you there." Misha could hear the sounds of Hannah running around her room; within minutes the door opened.

"Let me just get my bag. You know I don't remember seeing Delilah and Archetenus at that wedding ceremony now that I think about it; I wonder how long she has been in labor."

"I don't know the soldiers just said to get you." Misha kissed Diana goodbye before he and Hannah walked out the door.

When Hannah arrived at the castle Jared was waiting by the front door and led her to the room that had been set up for Delilah to give birth in. Hannah could still hear guests in the Great Hall celebrating the marriage of Elan and Cassandra.

"I didn't see any of you at the celebration," Hannah said as she followed Jared. "How long has Delilah been in labor?"

"All I know is she hasn't felt good all day and Zoya has been with her and wait until you see Archetenus, he is a wreck."

"Jared I am going to need you to keep him occupied. Is Shara or Angelina up here?"

"No."

"After we get to the room would you go down to the Great Hall and get them, this might be an unusual birth."

"Do you mean because he is so large and she is so tiny?"

"That and she is carrying more than one baby."

420

"You're here," Archetenus said with relief as he grabbed Hannah by the hand and led her into a bedroom where Delilah was in bed with Zoya standing beside her."

Before Hannah entered the room she turned to Jared, "Jared please get Shara and Angelina and if Elan or Cassandra want to come they are both studying to be physicians."

"Delilah how long have you been in labor?" Hannah asked as she started the examination.

"I wasn't feeling well all day I guess I didn't realize it was labor."

"She's been having contractions for a while," Zoya said.

"I've been downstairs all night," Hannah said you should have gotten me.

"Zoya, will you bring Delilah a pitcher of cold water and a glass. Then I will need extra towels and some really hot water."

"What do you want me to do?" Archetenus asked.

"Perhaps you should have a whiskey; you are as white as a sheet."

"I don't want to leave her," Archetenus said nervously.

"How many cradles do you have here?"

"Two do you think that will be enough?"

"I certainly hope so," Hannah said and laughed.

Ingr ran into the room as Archetenus was reluctantly walking out. "Hannah everyone is changing and will be here in a minute. Is there anything I can do?" Ingr asked.

"Do you know how to make that pain tonic of your tribe?"

"Yes, I will go down to the kitchen anything else?"

421

"We know she is carrying more than one baby so this is going to be a long night, perhaps a couple of the men from downstairs could keep Archetenus company; he is really nervous."

"I'll be back," Ingr said and ran from the room.

"Thanks Hannah, I am worried about Archetenus."

"There is nothing to be worried about Delilah. The Nordes Tribe makes a tonic that is absolutely wonderful for women having babies. It makes them feel energized while it greatly lessens the pain. But they have to boil some herbs which is why I wanted to get that started. Now I am going to close the door so I can finish examining you."

"Hannah I think Archetenus is so scared because you know he was created to be a vessel but Miranda said that wouldn't affect the babies."

"He loves you very much Delilah, now don't worry about Archetenus. This night may not be as long as I thought, you have dilated considerably. Tell me have you picked out names?"

"After all this time we still haven't decided," Delilah said and laughed then gritted her teeth in pain. Within moments voices were heard outside of the bedroom door. Then there was a knock.

"It's Shara."

"Come in," Hannah called.

"All the men are coming up to make Archetenus play cards," Shara said and laughed. "When I walked in he said she is having more than one baby."

"Yes, we just don't know how many so I appreciate you coming. Ingr is in the kitchen making that wonderful tonic you always give the women and Zoya is getting some supplies."

"I can hear Sorren's voice," Delilah said and laughed.

"Oh yes, well first of all he likes Archetenus but I think Sorren likes being around when babies are born. It makes him happy."

Zoya and Angelina entered the bedroom together. Angelina carried a tray with coffee and biscuits. "So many men came up they are setting up three card tables," Angelina said and laughed. "And Marie is bringing them things to eat and drink."

"She hasn't eaten all day," Zoya said.

"You will feel much better after you drink the tonic," Shara said as she was examining Delilah. "Can we bring you some food?"

"Maybe after I have the tonic."

Shara looked at Hannah, "Thaos and Nikki went to their room early. I wouldn't be surprised if we don't deliver another baby tonight."

"Really?" Delilah asked.

There was another knock on the door, "Its Cassandra and Elan." Hannah opened the door for them to enter the room.

"I know it is your celebration but Delilah is going to give birth to more than one baby which is an experience you won't often get. So you are welcomed to help." Then Hannah turned to the other women in the room. "I am sponsoring Elan and Cassandra; they both want to be physicians. Shara, Angelina perhaps you can teach them some things also."

"Joao has Joey," Elan said. "Let us change and we will be back."

"Delilah I hope you don't mind," Hannah said. "I should have asked you first."

"That is fine."

"I don't know what Edward did with his four dates but he is up here playing cards," Angelina said and laughed. "And Jared doesn't look much better than Archetenus and Zoya isn't even in labor yet."

"He is looking at this as our practice," Zoya said. "Both Jared and Archetenus worry because they are such huge men that the babies will be too big for us."

"Both of you will be just fine," Hannah said as Ingr walked into the room with a pitcher of tonic.

After half an hour, Hannah walked out of the bedroom and was surprised to see the parlor filled with men. "Hannah we already have bets going on how many babies will be delivered in the next twenty-four hours," Claudius said with a huge grin.

"He's just anxious to be a grandpa again," Stephan said as he dealt cards.

"Archetenus, Delilah is doing much better she's had some tonic for the pain," Hannah said as she put her hand on his shoulder. "If you want to see her you can." Archetenus left the card game and went into the bedroom.

It was almost sunrise when Ryan ran into the parlor. He ran up to Claudius. "Thaos woke me and said I should get Hannah, the baby is coming. Is Hannah here?" Claudius quickly stood up and knocked at the door. "Nikki is in labor," Claudius yelled through the closed door." Shara, Angelina and Ingr came out of the bedroom.

"Where is she?" Shara asked. Ryan was so nervous that he just grabbed Shara's hand and pulled her out of the room.

"Son, we better check on Thaos," Claudius said as he and Sorren stood up from their table.

"I was thinking the same thing," Stephan said. "Too bad these rooms weren't closer."

After Sorren, Matthew, Stephan and Claudius left the room; Raul stood up. "I will be right back; I am going to tell Marie we have two rooms that will need breakfast."

For the next six hours Hannah, Shara, Angelina, Ingr, Cassandra and Elan ran back and forth between Delilah's room and Nikki's room which were two hallways apart. It was just afternoon when Delilah delivered a son and then a daughter. Shara walked out into the parlor.

"Archetenus would you like to meet your son and daughter?" Shara asked with a smile. "And Delilah is just fine."

Archetenus quickly stood up but then froze in place as reality hit home. "You're not going to pass out are ya?" Edward joked.

"I have a son and a daughter," he said in a dazed manner.

Shara started laughing and took Archetenus by the hand and led him into the bedroom. Delilah was sitting up in bed, holding one baby and Hannah was holding the other. "Your husband is in shock," Shara said.

"Are you alright Honey?" Archetenus asked as he knelt down next to the bed and kissed Delilah.

Delilah and Zoya both laughed when they saw the dazed look on Archetenus' face. "You really are in shock," Delilah said. "Would you like to hold your son?" Delilah helped Archetenus hold the infant and to everyone's surprise Archetenus started to cry.

Shara and Hannah had delivered Delilah's babies while Cassandra and Elan assisted. After everything was cleaned they all walked down the two hallways to Nikki's room. "You two don't have to help with this delivery," Hannah said to Cassandra and Elan.

"We want to," Cassandra said that was incredible.

"Although my stomach jumped a couple of times," Elan said and the three women laughed.

When they entered the parlor directly outside of Nikki's bedroom Bella said. "Angelina told us all to leave the bedroom about ten minutes ago."

"That means the time is close," Shara said to Elan and Cassandra as they all entered the bedroom.

Amy had been sitting on Bella's lap watching Thaos nervously pace back and forth. After Hannah and the others entered the bedroom Thaos sat down. Amy jumped off from Bella's lap and climbed onto Thaos' lap but instead of sitting down she knelt facing him and reached up and put her arms around Thaos neck. "It will be alright Papa," Amy said.

Thaos stared at the little girl for a moment then hugged her tightly. "That is the first time you have called me Papa, I like it." Everyone in the room smiled as they watched Thaos and Amy.

For the next two hours people were walking in and out of the parlor visiting Claudius' and Sorren's families including Gabriel who came to visit Hannah. Then mid-afternoon the cry of a baby caused everyone in the parlor to stop talking. Thaos picked up Amy and quickly ran to the bedroom door.

"They will tell you when to go in," Sorren said as he too waited impatiently to see his newest grandson.

A few minutes later the door opened and Shara walked out, "You have a beautiful boy and wait until you see all that hair." Thaos ran into the room while the rest of the family congregated outside the bedroom door. Thaos kissed Nikki then set Amy on the bed.

"How are you doing?" he asked.

"I'm just fine but James was bigger than Titus; do you want to hold your son?"

Thaos took the baby and stared at it in awe as Nikki said to Amy, "Amy you have a new baby brother." Amy kissed the baby on the forehead then Thaos turned and introduced James Duran to the rest of the family.

Chapter XXIX
Paths

The Sanuri had chosen to stay in Lentz instead of returning to Wetpr for the wedding of Elan and Cassandra. Since both the families of Mathas and Claudius were in Wetpr, Fahron and Isadore invited the Sanuri to stay at their castle. Sally and April were also staying with Fahron, Isadore and their son Chaez. The Sanuri thought this would be the perfect time to help all of those people to heal from the horrors they had encountered.

"Some of our friends tell us to move to a different home," Isadore was telling the Sanuri as they were having coffee. "While there has been so much tragedy here, this is still our home."

"Isadore if you and your family do not heal it does not matter where you live, that darkness will be with you."

"I believe talking about healing is considerably easier than the actual healing," Isadore said as she refilled their cups. "Sanuri one reason that I asked you to have coffee with me was that Fahron and I are not only trying to heal from the death of Tabeth at her brother's hands but, well I am not sure how to say it. Fahron and I have always tried to be the best parents that we could and both of us are so overwhelmed and filled with guilt about how Timothy could have turned into such a monster. Sanuri what did we do wrong?" Isadore started to cry.

"Isadore before I answer that question can we bring Fahron in here?"

"I believe he is still in his study, I will get him."

A few moments later Fahron followed Isadore into the parlor. He looked at the Sanuri apprehensively. "Fahron the reason I asked you to join us is that Isadore asked me a question that I believe you both need to hear the answer to."

"Sanuri I am not sure I am ready to talk about my feelings," Fahron said.

"That is fine then just listen. Isadore asked me what the two of you did wrong to have Timothy turn out as he did."

"You are both good and loving people who did nothing wrong. The Great Ruler gives all of mankind freedom of choice; Timothy made his own choices. And he knew what he was doing when he made those choices. Timothy called to demons and enjoyed their company. You cannot make choices for another person. The best you can do is to help guide them. You can also pray to The Great Ruler to be with that person and to help that person with their choices."

Fahron suddenly started to sob loudly; he buried his head in his hands. Isadore put her arms around her husband to comfort him. "Isadore there is something I have not told you," Fahron said brokenly as he sobbed.

"Fahron you will need to bring that out to the light," the Sanuri said warmly.

Fahron tried to compose himself then he took his hands from his face and looked at Isadore. The morning before Tabeth was killed; Claudius and the others came here to see me. I had not slept or eaten in days and they all realized that when they saw me. Claudius ordered me to bed and Angelina brought a tray of food to my room then she sat outside of my door to protect me. In the meantime, the men searched outside of the castle and Ingr and Diana searched the inside."

Fahron started to choke-up so he paused for a few moments before he continued. "The girls were about to enter Timothy's room when Diana felt the door pulsating; she knew what this meant so she had Ingr get Claudius and the boys. Diana opened the door and showed everyone demonic writing on the walls of Timothy's chambers, the writing was alive and moving."

"Diana had seen this before although she did not understand what it really was. Diana started to enter the room and the Angel Miranda stopped her. They told me Miranda appeared to them all and explained the writing as powerful demon curses that would have killed them but she was protecting them. Then they said that Miranda told everyone that I had not asked The Great Ruler or the Angels to help us and that I must do so."

"Later Claudius, Matthew and Angelina all came to me and pleaded with me to call to the Angels and I told them I would not put my trust in something I could not see."

Fahron started to sob loudly again for a few minutes before he continued. "Isadore if I would have called to the Angels; Tabeth might still be alive." Isadore sat in shock and looked at her husband.

"Fahron I don't know if Tabeth would have lived," the Sanuri said. "Claudius told me of this incident because he was worried that you were filled with guilt. It is never too late to call to the heavens. You still have a family to care for and I have watched you two with Sally and April and I know you are becoming attached to those young girls. But you cannot help them or your son to heal if you, yourselves are broken."

Fahron stopped crying as he and Isadore listened to the Sanuri. "Many people pray to The Great Ruler for help or guidance. But when He sends them help or an Angel the people don't recognize the gift because for whatever reasons they thought the gift would appear in a different form. So they dismiss the gift and believe The Great Ruler isn't listening to them. Fahron you had an Angel appear in your home in a form you would recognize. I don't know what Miranda was going to tell you but I am willing to bet it was important. Of course the choice is yours but I would suggest you call to Miranda."

"Fahron you have always taken care of us," Isadore said. "But this is different. The Sanuri is right we are both so broken. If you do not call out to Miranda I will, if nothing else we owe it to the children."

"I am going to leave the two of you to discuss this," the Sanuri said as he stood up. "Just call her name."

Now the second day after the birth of Archetenus' and Thaos' babies the castle was preparing for the celebration for Emeral and Maxwell which was to take place that evening. Bella walked into Nikki's bedroom and watched as Amy seemed to imitate everything that Nikki did. "Have you noticed that Amy does exactly everything that you do?" Bella asked.

"Yes," Nikki replied. "She is my little shadow."

"Amy do you like living with Nikki and Thaos?" Bella asked. No one in the family had spoken to Amy about her life before she was rescued.

Amy was helping Nikki fold baby clothes and replied nonchalantly, "Yes, Thaos doesn't drink like my other daddy used to and I didn't have a mommy, my grandma took care of me." Both Bella and Nikki now watched Amy as the little girl continued to fold clothes."

"How else are Thaos and Nikki different from your other family?" Bella asked.

"They are nice. My daddy would drink a lot and yell and throw things."

"Did you have any brothers or sisters?" asked Nikki.

"No daddy said that mommy died when I was born, sometimes I didn't think he liked me very much."

Nikki knelt down and looked at Amy, "Well we all love you very much and we are glad you are part of our family." Nikki hugged Amy tightly.

"Hannah I think you should take the day off and sleep," Natasha said as the women were preparing the breakfast meal, you look exhausted."

"I did get some sleep, I think I am just more tired because I am pregnant."

"That and you were up for almost two days delivering babies," Lila said.

"Tonight is Emeral's and Maxwell's party, there is a lot to do," Hannah said.

"And we will get it done, you need to get some sleep," Natasha said as she carried platters of scrambled eggs into the dining room.

Within minutes the entire family was gathered at the dining room table. Gabriel and Raphael poured everyone a glass of wine and led a toast to Emeral and Maxwell.

"I don't want to spoil the festive mood," Natasha said after everyone returned to their seats. "But Gabriel make Hannah get some sleep. Look at her she is just exhausted."

"Natasha!" Hannah scolded. "I can't believe you said that."

Before Gabriel could speak, Emeral stood up. "Now would be a good time to bring up this subject. As you know I will be hiring nurses and with all the Rualas here for the ceremonies I was going to start interviews tomorrow. But I had my first interview this morning and I would like your opinions." Emeral looked at Melinda who stood up.

"I don't know why I am nervous," Melinda said with a shy smile. "Hannah when you allowed Cassandra and Elan to help you deliver those babies, you woke something up in them that they didn't understand. They truly want to become physicians. And I know that Lila and Vivian are just as passionate about wanting to attend college."

Melinda turned to Gabriel, "It is such an honor that you are allowing me to try out for the team but, well, I feel like I owe you all so much so I am proposing that until everyone finishes their studies that I will take care of the children and do the housekeeping. I am not as good of a cook as everyone here but I am certainly willing to learn. I am a warrior so I can protect the children, I know that is a concern. Gabriel I will certainly help with anything else that you need me for."

"She's got my vote," Luca said before Melinda returned to her seat.

"Melinda are you sure this is what you want?" Gabriel asked.

"Gabriel I felt like a prisoner and all of you gave me my freedom. I know with all of the attacks against your family that everyone is concerned about bringing strangers in to help with the workload. I promise to do a really good job so the rest of you can have the freedom to concentrate on the missions. Yes this is what I would like to do."

431

Gabriel looked around the table, "Is there anyone who has an objection or would like to speak with me in private about this matter?"

"I think we all like the idea," Calen said. "And the girls certainly could use the help."

"Ladies you were the ones opposed to hiring anyone," Gabriel said as he looked at his wife.

"Melinda is family now so it doesn't seem like hiring a stranger. I think she would be perfect but I feel we should pay her for these duties," Hannah replied.

"Of course," Gabriel said. "Melinda you are hired and thank you."

"I didn't want to interrupt," Joshua said sternly. "But what is going on here? Are you concerned about attacks against the children?"

"Father we wanted you to enjoy your visit," Vivian explained. "But there already have been attacks. The battle where Thor and Diana were injured a group of men went after the children. The Queen got stabbed trying to protect the babies."

Joshua looked angry. He looked at his wife and sons then back at his daughter. "And what is this about studies?"

"Gabriel and Raphael will pay for any one of us to attend college and the King will write letters to get us accepted. Lila, Elan and Cassandra want to become physicians and I want to take the same studies as Raphael and Gabriel so I can be more help on the team," Vivian replied.

"We will pay for your son's educations also if they are interested," Raphael said.

"That is a great gift that my children will need to think about," Joshua said. "But I have to tell you I am really angry at what I am hearing. Iris and I are thrilled about our first grandchild and to know the demons are going after the children fills me with rage. We are family too, if you need help you should tell us."

432

"Joshua, we weren't keeping things from you," Raphael explained. "This is your holiday and we want all of you to enjoy it."

"Well as far as I am concerned the holiday is over," Joshua said angrily.

"Father are you leaving?" Vivian gasped.

"No, we are helping. You need help on the missions and you need help in the home. And I will be damned if a demon is going to hurt our grandchild. Gabriel, Raphael, put us to work and that is an order."

Everyone at the table smiled.

"Well you have to think of something," Zoya said and laughed. "The babies are two days old; they need names."

"I don't want to name them after my parents because they sold me to a monster and Archetenus doesn't want to name them after his parents," Delilah explained. "He wanted to name our daughter after Miranda but Raul is naming their daughter Miranda. Archetenus says that if it wasn't for Miranda he would not have me and the children. And Gabriel is naming their son after the Angel Daniel."

"Well how about yours' and Archetenus' names?"

"Archetenus is so afraid that the darkness that plagued him before will be passed on to the children that he doesn't want to name our son after him."

"What about middle names of people?" Zoya suggested. "I know the Angels take different names when they come to this world but maybe they take middle names too. Why don't you call to Miranda and ask?"

"I like that idea. Have you and Jarrod picked out a name?"

"There are two names we both like," Zoya said. "Alexander and William."

"I like both of those names too. Would you be naming him after Laurel's husband?"

"Partially."

"Sanuri we wanted to talk with you when the children were not around," Fahron said as Isadore filled their cups with coffee. "It has been almost two days since you talked to us about Miranda. I will admit that it was me not Isadore who was afraid to talk to the Angel. But last night after everyone retired we called to Miranda."

"I am pleased to hear that," the Sanuri said then took a sip of his coffee.

"Oh Sanuri, she was so beautiful, it was the most incredible thing," Isadore burst out. Then she looked at Fahron. "I am sorry to interrupt, I just couldn't contain it any longer."

"Not that we didn't believe you but we really didn't think she would appear to us," Fahron said. "It was an incredible encounter. But I am ashamed to say that I could have protected my family more if I would have spoken to her sooner." Tears were running down Fahron's cheeks as he spoke. Fahron was trying to contain his emotions. "She told us the same thing that you did; that Timothy was an adult and made his own choices. But she also told us that Timothy had sold himself to the demons many years ago and that we blinded ourselves when he gave us glimpses of his true self."

Fahron paused for a few moments then continued, "Our son committed many crimes during his short life; crimes that could have been prevented if I would have been willing to see Timothy for what he was."

"Fahron you are not alone in this," Isadore scolded. "I am equally as guilty."

"Fortunately Chaez has not been touched by the same darkness," Fahron said. "But Miranda told us that we too do not see Chaez for who he is or the man he will become."

434

"Honestly we have been so consumed with Timothy's actions and Tabeth that Chaez has not received our attention for some time. We plan to speak with him after we talk with you."

"I have been talking with Chaez a great deal since my arrival in Lentz and while I will tell you about that in just a moment I do have some questions for you," the Sanuri said. "Have you learned now that you should be talking to the heavens and are you willing to do such a thing?"

"Yes to both of your questions," Fahron said. "Although I still don't understand why The Great Ruler sent an Angel to us."

"Miranda did not tell you?"

"No, we had so many questions for her and suddenly she was gone," Fahron said.

"While I do not have an answer to your question I can venture to guess," the Sanuri explained. "Fahron you are a powerful man and a leader of one of the wealthiest kingdoms in Opots. Darkness of great proportions is upon this world, darkness that will be conquered by faith, not swords alone. I hope you realize the gift you have been given." Neither Fahron nor Isadore spoke so the Sanuri continued.

"As I said I have spent a great deal of time with your son. He too has been overwhelmed by the horror of Timothy's choices. He loves both of you very much and it breaks his heart to see the pain you have been in. Everyone handles devastation differently. You two have protected your children; shielded them from the darkness of this world until it broke your door down. Your son is young and has been speaking to me because he wants to make a difference in this world, now that his eyes have been opened in many ways."

"Sanuri what are you saying?" Isadore asked fearfully.

"Chaez wants to return to Wetpr with me and study to become a Patronus priest. It was his idea but he is afraid to leave home because he knows how broken the two of you are. He does not want to leave you, yet you do not reach out to him for comfort."

"As you know Sudfad is building a great learning center which will also be a training site for the Patronus. I am sure that Sudfad and Renya would bring Chaez into their home if you allow him to follow this path."

"He wants to be a warrior priest?" Fahron asked incredulously. "He has never taken any interest in such matters before."

"He is a bright boy who has taken more interest in Mathas' and Claudius' families and their activities than you realize. He will succeed if you but give him the chance."

Fahron looked at Isadore then at the Sanuri, "I would be very proud to have my son become a member of the Patronus."

"Good, but there is more and that is the reason that I am telling you about this before Chaez speaks with you. He does not want to leave you alone. Last night he told me he is going to ask you to adopt Sally and April. So you have many things to think about before you speak with Chaez."

"Miranda, Daniel," Archetenus called as he stood next to Delilah's bed in Sudfad's castle. "This isn't an emergency we would like to talk to you."

"It's good that you know you can talk to us any time," Miranda said as she and Daniel materialized in the bedroom. Both Angels walked over to the cradles that held the sleeping son and daughter of Archetenus and Delilah. "Your children are beautiful," Miranda said.

"They are why we called you," Archetenus said. "And I want to thank you again."

"We wanted to name the babies after both of you," Delilah said. "Archetenus said that if it wasn't for you we wouldn't have them. But Raul and Gabriel are already naming their children after you. We know you take different names when you are in this world. Do you take middle names also?"

"Truly we have never been asked that question before," Miranda said as she and Daniel smiled. "The answer is that we have not."

436

"Well then do you have some suggestions?" Archetenus asked. "Or can you take middle names now?"

"Do you realize that by naming the children after us that you could be affecting the paths they take in this lifetime?" Daniel asked.

"We figured as much," Archetenus said. "Which is great but..." he paused.

"But what Archetenus?" Miranda asked.

"I know you are probably already reading my mind. But we don't want to name the children after our families and other than Jared and Zoya you are our closest friends. Can I say an Angel is a friend?"

"Of course you can," Miranda said. "You have come so far Archetenus, it makes me happy." Miranda and Daniel looked at each other and smiled.

"Ava and Benjamin," Daniel said and the two Angels disappeared.

Chapter XXX
Pasts and Futures

"Emeral I am glad that we told you about the party," Natasha said and laughed. "Because you both have been a lot of help." Natasha, Lila, Vivian, Diana and Cassandra were putting bouquets of flowers on each table in the Great Hall of Sudfad's castle, while Renya and Emeral were setting up a table to display the many gifts that Emeral and Maxwell had received from their children and grandchildren. Laurel and Iris were performing last minute alterations on clothing.

"So Emeral have you and Maxwell decided where you want to go for a trip?" Vivian asked.

Emeral and Renya looked at each other and smiled. "You can tell them," Renya said.

Emeral turned around. "Renya and Sudfad haven't told their children yet but Maxwell and I are taking them to the Ice Caves for a holiday."

"And I am just so excited," Renya said happily.

"Really?" Vivian asked. "Diana and Thor were only there long enough to get Melinda but they both said the Ice Caves were incredible."

"I have never seen anything as beautiful before," Diana said. "I asked Misha to take me there again."

"I want to go there sometime," Lila said.

"I think we all do," said Natasha.

"Have you told the boys this?" Emeral asked.

"I think Diana is the only one who has said anything," Vivian replied.

"Well, say something to your husbands girls," Emeral said with a grin.

"Did you get any sleep?" Gabriel asked as Hannah walked into his study.

"A couple of hours but it really made a difference."

"I have everyone doing the things on your list. While Maxwell and Joshua were at the castle, Alexander told them he had finished the table and chairs for our children. Now that Vivian's family will be with us a while I am glad we had extra children's chairs made. The furniture is in a boca in front of the house, I didn't want to bring it in until you were awake."

"Oh Gabriel this will be fun, give me a few minutes then we can bring it in."

"Hannah wait a moment. Now that Joshua and his family will help on the mission in Ryed we may be leaving sooner than I had originally planned. There have been so many delays to this mission that I am feeling anxious and I want to make sure we are all back home when the babies are born. I know Thor will be upset if he can't come and I would like to use Erebus also. When will they be ready?"

"How soon are you thinking about leaving?"

"Two or three weeks."

"Oh Gabriel I just hate to think of you leaving again; but I do want you home for the baby," Hannah said with frustration. "Erebus doesn't strike me as the kind of person who does anything really physically strenuous. He will be able to travel in that time. Thor is healing quickly because the Sanuri gave some of his essence to heal him; so I really don't know what to say. Thor will be able to travel but I would prefer he not carry anything really heavy or fight; but I know he will probably do both."

"Perhaps I will tell Thor he must follow your orders if he wants to come along."

"Gabriel, I know you have been planning this mission for a long time but I hope you plan to stay home for a while after the baby is born."

"Actually Honey that is why I am trying to get things caught up now. I already spoke with Misha and Diana, they will plan their wedding ceremony after we return from Ryed. Diana wanted Iris and Joshua here for the wedding and now that Vivian's family is staying longer there isn't such a rush."

"Gabriel, we are going to need to get ready for the celebration soon, we can discuss this later."

"Girls come in," Fahron said with a big smile as Sally and April stood in the doorway to the parlor.

"Is everything alright?" Sally asked. "All of you have been in here so long."

"Well, we have been discussing some very important things but very good things," Fahron said.

"Jackie said to tell you she would be right in with the refreshments," Sally said as she and April sat next to each other on one of the sofas. April and Sally looked at Chaez, the Sanuri, Isadore and Fahron and everyone was smiling at them. "All of you are looking at us so strangely," Sally continued. "Are you going to adopt us?"

"That is one of the things we would like to talk to you about," Fahron said. "Isadore and I would very much like to have you as our daughters but we want you to have a say in the matter. You've been able to spend a few days with all of the families that want to adopt you. Have you made any decisions about who you would like to live with?"

"Everyone has been so kind to us," Sally said then stopped talking when the housekeeper brought in a tray of refreshments. "April and I both like you very much but..."

"But what Sally?" Isadore asked.

"What I need to ask you is important but you may not want us after I ask the question," said Sally.

"Sally ask your question," the Sanuri said.

"You know that neither April or I will ever be Tabeth, don't you?" Both Fahron and Isadore were taken back by Sally's question.

"Isadore and I have been so overwhelmed with Timothy and Tabeth that we realized last night we have not really seen anything else that has been going on around us," Fahron said. "We just apologized to Chaez and I am very proud to say that our son will be going to Wetpr to study to be a Patronus priest. But girls we didn't even realize that Chaez wanted to do this because we weren't paying attention to him because of our grief. Have we been making you feel like we want you to be Tabeth?"

"No, but when you look at us you always look so sad. Do we make you miss her more?"

"Oh Sally," Isadore said and sat down on the sofa between the girls. Isadore put her arms around both girls and hugged them. "I am sorry if our grief has made you feel badly. We enjoy both of you girls for the people you are; we don't want to pretend that you are someone else."

Fahron looked at both of the girls then at the Sanuri then back at girls. "Sally, April I am so sorry if we have made you feel badly. Your presence here does not make us miss Tabeth more on the contrary you have brought us joy. I don't know how much you really know about what happened. But besides grieving for our children both Isadore and I have been filled with guilt that Timothy turned out the way he did and that we couldn't have protected Tabeth and others from him."

"I wish I could tell you that Isadore and I will be over our grief and guilt soon; but I don't know if that is true. But I will promise both of you that we will try to be good parents and will give you a loving home," Fahron continued. "You girls don't have to give us an answer now."

"Girls you have four wonderful families that want to adopt you," the Sanuri said. "Has anyone asked you what you want?"

441

"What do you mean?" asked Sally.

"All four of these families will give you love and will protect you. They are all good people. You will never want or go hungry. But what would you girls like?"

"We would like the things that you said but you see part of the problem for April and me now is that we really like all of the families so much and we don't want to hurt anyone's feelings. We are so grateful that everyone wants us but it is hard."

"Would you like to go to college or train to be a warrior or anything else?" Chaez asked with a knowing smile. "You can tell them."

"Chaez told us he wanted to study to be a warrior priest," Sally said. "I would love to go to school but I too want to train to be a warrior. I would like to train with the Nordes Tribe."

Isadore and Fahron looked at each other and smiled. "We always let our children make their own decisions about their futures," Fahron explained. "But I never told any of them that I was always disappointed that none of them wanted to be warriors. Today Chaez has made me very happy. If you want to be our children, we will provide you with educations and we would be proud to have you become warriors. April you have not spoken, please tell us what you want."

"A dog," April said and everyone smiled. "I have always dreamed about having my very own pet. I love animals." Then April turned to Sally. "Don't not go to training because of me."

"Well we can certainly get you some pets," Isadore said.

"Do you girls know how to ride horses?" asked Fahron.

Sally and April looked at each other and both shook their heads from side to side to indicate 'no'.

"Would you like lessons? We can get you your own horses too," Fahron asked. "Would you like that?"

Both Sally and April got big smiles on their faces.

"Do you think your sisters will really come?" Diana asked as Misha buttoned the back of her red gown.

"I hope so; they weren't at the castle when I left a couple of hours ago," Misha said. "If they don't come it will hurt Maxwell and Emeral a great deal."

"I don't believe they could be that cold," Diana said with disgust. "I love Emeral and Maxwell and want to name our children after them."

Misha laughed loudly. "His first grandson is named Maxwell and Lily is Emeral's middle name."

"Are you saying we can't name our children after them?"

"No, but we will have to ask them if they have other middle names. I am sorry to say I don't know. Now hold still."

"Misha what are you doing?"

"Putting a necklace on you. Alright now you can look in the mirror."

"Misha this is beautiful," Diana gasped when she saw the ruby and diamond choker around her neck. She turned and kissed him. He then handed her a box with matching earrings and a bracelet. "You are so good to me," Diana said and kissed Misha again. "But I didn't get you anything."

"I don't want anything, besides I told you I am going to show you off tonight. You will be meeting a lot of my family and it might not be pleasant."

"Hurry everyone the carriages will be here soon," Natasha said as she ushered the family into the parlor. "Who are we missing?"

"Maxwell and Emeral," Calen said. "I'll get them."

"We're here," Maxwell said as he and Emeral walked into the parlor wearing the clothes their children had made for them.

"You look beautiful," Hannah said and hugged both Emeral and Maxwell.

"Everyone looks beautiful," Emeral said emotionally.

"We want to have a quick toast before the carriages arrive," Luca said as he and Raphael were pouring wine into glasses. Vivian and Lila were handing the glasses to the family members.

"To Maxwell and Emeral," Gabriel said. "This is your night." Everyone raised their glasses for the toast.

"I don't think Emeral and I will ever be able to tell you what this means to us," Maxwell said.

There was a knock at the door. "That must be the carriages," Gabriel said.

Renya personally met Gabriel's team when they entered the castle. "I hope you don't mind but we have made a few changes," she said with a coy smile. "Is everyone from your team here now?"

"Yes," Gabriel said and nodded to the Queen because he was aware of the new surprises that were to come.

"I will escort Emeral and Maxwell into the ballroom and the rest of you should follow two at a time.

"Renya what are you up to?" Emeral asked.

"Just come with me," Renya said.

The doors to the Great Hall were closed with two soldiers standing in front of them. When the soldiers saw the Queen approaching them one of the soldiers knocked on the door and within moments trumpets were heard from inside of the ballroom.

The soldiers opened the doors and Renya led the procession down a long white carpet. Hundreds of people filled the room which was also filled with huge bouquets of white roses.

444

"White roses," Emeral gasped. "My favorite flower."

The crowd applauded as Renya led Maxwell and Emeral to the front of the hall where two large head tables were erected on a raised platform. "This is so beautiful," Emeral whispered to her friend. Sudfad was standing on the platform smiling as they approached. Renya, Emeral and Maxwell walked up the platform and turned to face the audience. It was then that Maxwell and Emeral saw that Gabriel and the others were no longer behind them but had disappeared into the crowd.

The trumpets stopped playing and King Sudfad addressed the people. "This celebration was the idea of the children and adopted children of Maxwell and Emeral. Their children wanted to show them how much they love them and how much they appreciate all that Maxwell and Emeral do."

"But Renya and I wanted to also take the opportunity to honor these two courageous warriors for their service to our Kingdom and to our family. During a time of great conflict both Emeral and Maxwell have served in my military. Maxwell still retains the rank of Colonel and many of his sons also hold leadership positions in the Army of Wetpr."

"Now I would like to introduce some of the special guests who have arrived for this celebration," Sudfad said. "It is with great honor that I introduce King Manu and Queen Delilia of the Rualas." The crowd applauded as King Manu greeted his brother and sister-in-law. After King Manu said a few words, Maxwell's brothers Zeman, Segal and Gunnel all came on stage with their wives and spoke. Other guests took the stage to speak and to present Maxwell and Emeral with gifts.

"Are your sisters here?" Natasha asked Calen.

"Yes, it looks like they are in line to go up on the stage. I'm glad they showed up." Calen paused then asked, "Where's Misha?"

"Misha is that you?" a woman's voice asked. Both Misha and Diana turned around and saw a beautiful Ruala woman who appeared to be in her forties. Misha and the woman stared at each other without speaking. Diana saw that the color drained from Misha's face and realized the woman must be Misha's mother.

"Hello, I am Diana, Misha's wife," Diana held her hand out to the woman. "And who are you?"

"Diana this is my mother Nada," Misha said in almost a whisper. Diana could see that Misha was upset and she was trying to figure out what to do. Diana grasped Misha's hand and held it tightly as she spoke to Nada.

"It is very nice to meet you," Diana said sweetly.

"It is nice to meet you too," Nada said. "You are such a pretty girl and Misha has grown into such a handsome man. I had heard he was married. Misha and I haven't seen each other in some time."

"I am surprised to see you here," Misha said. "You were never close to Emeral and Maxwell."

"Misha our entire family is here for this celebration, all of your brothers and sisters are here, you should talk to them."

Misha was trying to control his feeling to flee his mother. He suddenly felt like that five year old boy again so filled with pain and rage. For the only time in Diana's life she saw panic in her husband's eyes.

"Nada would you excuse us, Misha and I have to prepare something for the presentations. We can meet with you later," Diana said and pulled Misha towards the back of the hall before Nada could speak. Misha was silent as Diana led him out of the Great Hall and into one of the royal gardens. "You look like you needed some air." Diana said. Misha grabbed Diana and hugged her tightly. "Misha you looked so upset I didn't know what to do for you." He did not speak but kept hugging Diana. "Misha you don't have to tell me what she did to you, but for tonight do you want me to tell her to leave you alone?"

"This is the first time that I have seen her since I left home; I can't believe how my emotions were going crazy," Misha said. "I suddenly felt like a little boy again."

"Misha what can I do for you?"

"You're doing it. I love you so much Diana."

After the presentations by the guests, a feast was served, followed by dancing. Two additional tables had to be set up to hold gifts. While Maxwell and Emeral were overwhelmed they were also radiant. Calen and Natasha were leaving the ballroom when they saw Misha and Diana.

"We're taking Lily home," Natasha said.

"We can take her if you want to stay at the party," Misha said. "We're going home."

Natasha was about to speak when Calen said, "I saw Nada but it was too late to warn you."

"Who's Nada?" Natasha asked when she saw the looks on the faces of Diana, Misha and Calen.

"Misha's mother," Diana said. "It's the first time he has seen her since he left home."

"Seriously we can take Lily if you want to stay," said Misha.

Calen searched Misha's eyes. "No you two probably have a lot to talk about," Calen said. "But we can all fly home together."

Most of the members of Gabriel's team never got close to Maxwell and Emeral that evening because the two were surrounded with friends and family from the Ice Caves.

Raphael and Vivian were sitting at a table with her parents. Vivian's two older brothers were not shy about asking women to dance and had spent most of the night on the dance floor. Vivian's two younger brothers were in the extravagant playroom that Renya had set up for all of the children.

"I have never seen you dance like that before," Vivian said with a warm smile as her parents returned to the table. "Are you becoming more comfortable in these surroundings?"

447

"You certainly do lead a different life here," Joshua said as he held out a chair for Iris.

"What surprises your father the most is how down to earth most of these people are for being kings and queens and chiefs."

"They are also warriors and I believe that makes a difference," Raphael said then smiled and looked past Joshua and Iris. Both Raphael and Vivian stood up so Joshua and Iris turned to see who was behind them.

"Father, Mother I would like you to meet the wonderful people who took me in like their daughter," Ibula said as she led her parents to the table. Thedes was carrying baby Tamas. "This is Joshua and Iris and these are my parents King Manu and Queen Delilia." Both Joshua and Iris stood up and to their surprise Manu and Delilia hugged them.

"Ibula and Thedes have told us so much about you," Delilia said.

"How can we ever repay you for what you did for our family?" Manu asked.

"Honestly they became our family too," Joshua said. "They are wonderful people it was the least we could do. Did they tell you they saved our daughter from the Valdees?"

"This is High Priest Raphael and his wife Vivian who is the daughter of Joshua and Iris," Ibula explained.

"Please would you all join us at our table?" Manu asked.

"We should stay here so the children can find us," Raphael said. "Joshua and Iris you go and enjoy yourselves."

As Joshua and Iris walked away with the Royal Family of the Rualas Raphael said, "I think your parent's lives are changing rather quickly."

Thor, Dack and Joao were becoming close friends. Thor was a little older than the two Rualas but their similarities and interests were building a strong bond between them. These three handsome young men were surprised when women were coming up to them and asking them to dance and they were very flattered by the attention.

"You should ask Melinda to dance," Dack said as he and Thor poured themselves a drink from the bottle of whiskey on their table.

"She has been on the dance floor all night," Thor said. "And besides I don't want to make any more waves than I already have."

"What do you mean?"

"I was such an ass to everyone in the beginning that I am greatly embarrassed. Dagon asked Melinda to the next celebration and I don't know how Koby feels about her," Thor said.

"Well she isn't spoken for yet and I know that like you she is embarrassed about her start here. You do realize that everyone she has been dancing with is from the Ice Caves, no one from the team has asked her."

"What difference does that make?"

"I think everyone is afraid to go near her and that just makes her feel worse," Dack said. "I know Melinda and even if she was in love with Koby she would never act on it because she is so close to Bekka. Why don't you ask her to dance if nothing else so she feels a little more accepted by the team?"

"You and Joao haven't asked her?"

"It's not the same we are like her brothers," Dack laughed when he realized what he said. "Joao is her brother. Go on; one dance won't kill you and it might make her feel better."

"So are you saying this because you are trying to push us together or to make her feel better?" Thor asked and laughed.

449

"Maybe a little of both," Dack said. "I think she got put in an unfair situation. I've known her since we were little and she is really self-conscious around the team because of what Koby did."

As soon as the music stopped playing, Thor got up from the table and moved quickly across the dance floor as he watched another young Ruala man walking towards Melinda. Melinda saw the man walking towards her but she walked towards her table to get some water. "Can I tear you away from your friends long enough for a dance?" Thor asked.

Melinda smiled brightly at Thor, "Just let me get a drink of water then I would love to." Melinda took Thor's arm as they walked towards her table. "You, Dack and Joao have been busy tonight," she said with a grin. I could barely see you with that crowd of women surrounding you."

"I was surprised that the women are asking us to dance. But it has been fun. I am starting to feel more comfortable at these things."

"Where's Diana? I haven't seen her for a while?" Melinda asked then drank a glass of water.

"They left early, Misha looked like he was sick."

That night Diana cried and hugged Misha as he told her about the abuse that he and his siblings had suffered not only at the hands of his mother but also from her string of boyfriends. Diana lay awake long after Misha had fallen asleep and held her husband.

When Diana opened her eyes in the morning Misha had been watching her sleep. "Thank you for taking care of me last night," he said. "No one has ever done that, well, except for Emeral and Maxwell."

"Misha I will always take care of you," Diana said and kissed him on the lips. She pulled away so she could look Misha in the eyes. "Would you get mad at me if I had a talk with your mother?"

"Talk or fight?" Misha asked with a grin.

"I really want to beat the hell out of her," Diana said angrily.

"My past are my demons to face," Misha said and put his arms around Diana. "But I will admit I do feel better after telling you everything."

Chapter XXXI
Nada

"I thought you were getting Maxwell and Emeral," Natasha said to Calen as Gabriel's team was sitting down to breakfast.

"They weren't in their chambers," Calen said as he sat down at the table while holding Lily. "I don't think they ever came home last night. I just don't know what we are going to do with those two," Calen said then laughed loudly which caused everyone at the table to laugh.

"Children do you like your new table and chairs?" Natasha asked. All the children had their mouths full so they nodded their heads. "That was a great idea," Natasha said and looked at Gabriel.

"Misha are you feeling better?" Thor asked. "You didn't look so good last night."

Misha and Diana looked at each other. "You can tell them," Misha said to his wife.

"Misha's mother came up to us and had the nerve to act like a sweet little mother," Diana said angrily. "I cried all night while Misha was telling me how she went crazy after his father was killed. You can't believe the things she did to Misha and his brothers and sisters then," Diana's voice kept rising because of her anger. "Then she lets her many boyfriends hurt the children too. I just want to kill her." No one at the table spoke as they stared at Misha.

"It's amazing I would rather face an army of Hutas than my own mother," Misha said softly.

"Does Emeral and Maxwell know?" Luca asked.

"Yes, that night that I got so jealous over Dack and Joao, Diana and I got into a fight. She ended up holding a mirror up to me and telling me why I was doing the things that I do. Well, she made me mad but she was right. After I left Diana's room I told Emeral and Maxwell, it was the first time I ever told anybody."

Diana looked at Misha, "I am going to tell you something but don't get mad. I think all of you should know this. Emeral came to check on me the morning after Misha talked to them. Suddenly she starts crying. Misha she didn't tell me what you said because Emeral said she would never betray your trust but she said you had told them about your past. Emeral said that she and Maxwell have been filled with guilt that they didn't stop Nada and take in all of your brothers and sisters."

"I'll talk to them," Misha said in a hoarse whisper.

"I told her that she and Maxwell should be proud of all their children and the people they touch and not beat themselves up because they couldn't save more," Diana said. Everyone remained silent at the table for several moments.

"I am going to change the subject," Gabriel said as he could see how embarrassed Misha looked. "This afternoon, Raphael and I are going to christen Thaos' baby and Archetenus' twins. There is going to be a small celebration and everyone here is invited."

"Did they finally name the babies," Natasha asked.

"Archetenus said that they wanted to name them Miranda and Daniel but those names are taken so they called to the Angels and asked if they had taken middle names in this world. Miranda said they had not but when the Angels left Daniel said Ava and Benjamin. So those are the names of the twins."

"He called to Angels to name his children?" Joshua asked in disbelief.

"Archetenus was one of the men created to be a vessel for a demon and he was a pretty bad guy. Miranda told us that not every vessel had the same purpose and if Archetenus died he would turn into a monster that would kill many people," Raphael explained.

"Well according to Archetenus, Miranda pretty much started to haunt him. You really should have him explain it. You see he didn't believe in The Great Ruler or Angels and he and Miranda would fight then one day he realizes she is the only one he has ever trusted and his only friend. Once he started doing what she said his entire life changed for the better."

"Raphael is right, any of you should just ask Archetenus he will tell you the story because it is incredible. But he knows he would not have Delilah or the babies if it wasn't for Miranda. Archetenus feels that he owes the Angels a great debt," Gabriel added.

Natasha looked at Iris and Joshua and said, "Before Archetenus was good he kidnapped Vitomas."

"Raul's wife," Joshua gasped. "But they all seem to be friends now."

"Like I said it is an incredible story," said Raphael.

"What I want to know," Vivian's brother Micha said with a grin. "Is it always like this here? Battles and celebrations?" Everyone laughed.

Because of the previous night's events, Sudfad's morning meeting was held later in the morning. This was the first morning that Gabriel and Raphael brought Joshua to the meeting. Sudfad had previously suggested that Joshua's knowledge of Ryed and the Teivel Clan might be invaluable. Sudfad moved the meeting to the family dining room so there would be more room. Just as the men were taking their seats a small flock of Enrops flew through the open dining room window and delivered letters to most of the men.

"These are from Fahron and the Sanuri," one of the birds announced.

"Is anything wrong?" Mathas asked with concern.

"They did not say," the bird said and left the room.

"Fahron said that he sent almost identical letters to me, Claudius and Sorren," Mathas explained to the group. "Fahron says that the Sanuri and Miranda are helping him and Isadore to heal. He says that they want to adopt Sally and April and although the girls are willing they have become so attached to all of our families that they don't want to hurt anyone's feelings so he would like to have us all over for dinner when we return. He also said that Sally wants to train with Sorren to be a warrior."

Mathas paused, "The next part of the letter concerns Gabriel, Raphael and Sudfad. Fahron said that he and Isadore have been so consumed with grief that they have not paid any attention to Chaez," Mathas looked up from the letter. "That is Fahron's teenage son and their only remaining blood child. Chaez has been spending a lot of time with the Sanuri." Mathas now looked up from the letter and spoke to the group.

"Fahron and Isadore are good people and tried to protect their children from the horrors of the world. Chaez is a bright young man who also was overwhelmed by the actions of Timothy. Chaez asked the Sanuri how he could make a difference in the world; to stop monsters like his brother. Chaez has requested that Fahron allow him to study to be a Patronus priest. While Fahron is very proud of his son's decision he doesn't know if Timothy's actions will prevent Chaez from being allowed to study to be a priest."

"Chaez is a really good boy," Claudius said. "But he has always been interested in his studies, I don't think he has ever been in a fight."

"Well we can certainly train him," Raphael said. "I would not hold his brother's transgressions against him. How do the rest of you feel?"

"My letter is from the Sanuri," Sudfad said. "And he says everything that all of you have said. But the Sanuri says that Chaez has never been away from his family before and is wondering if Renya and I can watch over him." Sudfad looked at Simon and Raul. "I will direct this question to you."

Simon was quiet for a moment then said. "Father you and your brother were as different as day and night. I think we give the kid a chance but if he turns out like Timothy we will deal with him accordingly."

"Chaez is a good kid," Matthew said. "I can see him as a priest, but I don't know about a warrior."

"Fahron says that Chaez never told him how much he admired you boys and apparently wanted to be like you," Claudius said. "This all surprises me too."

"So are we in agreement that Chaez will be allowed in the first class of Patronus priests to be trained here?" Raphael asked. After all of the men agreed, Raphael said. "If you would like I will be the contact for Fahron and Chaez on this matter."

"I think that is appropriate," said Sudfad.

The small ceremony for the christening of babies James Duran, Ava and Benjamin had over one hundred people in attendance. The christenings were performed in the new chapel and the ceremony was held in the Great Hall of the castle. Several tables had been erected for gifts and each was piled high. Renya had a late lunch served to the guests.

In other areas of the castle grounds, competitions and entertainment were held for the guests who were staying at the castle until the next big celebration. Gabriel gave the members of his team time off from their duties so they could enjoy the festivities. Diana found Emeral and Maxwell at the luncheon and told them about Misha's encounter with his mother. Neither Emeral nor Maxwell discouraged Diana when she said she wanted to talk to Nada; but they did remind her that they were all guests of Sudfad and Renya.

Later that afternoon, while Misha was participating in a weapons competition, Diana slipped away and searched the crowd for Nada. She found Misha's mother sitting at a small table with three men all of whom seemed enamored with Nada. The sight before Diana only fueled her anger. She had great respect for Sudfad and Renya and did not want to disrespect them by causing a scene.

"Why Diana how nice to see you," Nada said. Then she turned to the men, "Diana is married to my son Misha."

"Nada could I speak with you in private?" Diana asked.

Although Diana's tone was not threatening the hair on Nada's neck was standing on end. "We can talk in front of my friends," Nada said; thinking that would be a deterrent for Diana.

Diana stared at Nada for a moment then walked a couple of steps closer to the woman. Diana smiled sweetly but spoke with confidence and anger. "I know how you hurt and abused your children," Diana said loud enough for the men at the table to hear. "And I know that you allowed your many drunken boyfriends to hurt them also. Nada you stay away from Misha, you are poison to his soul. I will not allow you to hurt him again."

Nada looked embarrassed as she turned to see if her admirers were listening to the conversation. Nada turned back to Diana, "Did Misha send you?"

"No, he doesn't know I am here. Your son is a courageous and honorable warrior; he would not let someone else fight his battles. But I am his wife and I think you are despicable."

"You can't keep me from my son," Nada said curtly.

"I heard how you like to gamble," Diana said with a forced smile. "You and I will compete for Misha and if I win you never come near him again."

"What sort of competition?" Nada asked smugly.

"You choose," Diana said with confidence. At that moment in time there were two things that Diana did not know, the first was that Nada was well known as a cheat. And the second that Dack and Joao were standing behind her and now turned to tell the rest of the team.

Nada looked at the various competition arenas and said, "Let's do the Trimoth." This was a competition played on a long field that had lanes. All along the lanes were targets of different sizes and shapes. The contestants had to run down the lanes and give a killing blow of any type to every target.

When the contestants reached the end of the lane they had to turn around and repeat the attacks on the targets. To win, the contestant had to deliver the most kill strikes besides having the fastest time. The kill strikes could be delivered with any variety of weapon or the physical strength of the contestant.

457

There were two contestants on the site when Diana and Nada arrived. Diana was so focused on Nada as they waited for their turn that she did not realize the crowd that had formed behind them. Although all of the competitions had spectators this crowd was told the reason for the competition. At the starting line of the lanes, there were extra weapons for the contestants.

As Diana and Nada were choosing weapons, Nada asked, "Do you want to sweeten the pot? Do you have any money on you?"

Before Diana could speak a large hand reached over Diana's shoulder and handed her a pouch of gold coins. Diana looked up and smiled at Stephan and at that moment Diana realized the crowd behind them.

"If you win you get the money," Diana said loudly. "If I win you admit to everyone here the atrocities you committed against your children."

"What the hell is going on here?" Misha asked angrily as he pushed through the crowd. Dagon and Calen both grabbed Misha.

"Let them be son," Maxwell said. "Then in a loud voice Maxwell yelled. "Diana everyone knows that Nada always cheats."

"I don't want her fighting my fights," Misha said.

"I'm not sure if that is what Diana is doing," Emeral said with a proud smile. "I think she wants justice for all of you."

Angelina pushed through the crowd and walked up to Diana. "My lucky knife," Angelina said with a grin and handed a small throwing knife to Diana. While Diana had enough weapons this act was a sign of support.

"Who will judge this competition?" Maxwell asked loudly.

"I will," said King Manu and walked up to the line. "Let there be another." Manu too had heard the reason for the competition.

"I will," said Sorren and took his place near the lanes.

A flag was dropped and the two woman started the competition. Nada was fast and powerful. Diana was a Venator. Within feet of the starting line was the first target on the right side of each lane; both women stabbed their target. As they both did the next target on the left side of each lane. Each women attacked two additional targets before they came upon one in the middle of each of their lanes.

Diana flew through the air and struck her target with her foot, a blow that would crush a throat. Nada stabbed her target and now realized that Diana was a worthy opponent. Nada acted like she tripped and picked up a handful of dirt. She ran ahead of Diana and threw the dirt into Diana's eyes.

"Did you see that?" Vivian screamed with rage.

King Manu was going to stop the game until Thor yelled, "Let them keep going; she's my sister." Only the Venators in the crowd knew that part of their training was to find threats when the Venator was blindfolded. People in the crowd were betting on the two women. As badly as Diana wanted to stop and punch Nada she wanted to expose her more. Diana kept running.

"I bet that Diana beats the hell out of her when this is over," Thaos said with a grin.

Diana suddenly ducked as she saw movement out of the corner of her eye. Nada had thrown one of the targets at Diana which flew over the warrior's head. Diana was not as much surprised that Nada cheated as she was at how fast and powerful the older woman was. The last target in the lane was also positioned in the middle of the lane. Diana jumped into the air and punched the target so hard it fell over, when Diana landed she was already facing the crowd and running back towards the finish line.

Now fear gripped Nada's heart. Diana was as powerful and as fast as Nada and Nada did not want her secrets exposed. As Nada started to panic she pulled a small knife from her sheath.

Erebus did not hear about the competition until after it had started. He arrived later and was standing alongside of the lanes instead of with the crowd at the finish line.

"Diana knife!" Erebus yelled. Diana threw herself forward and the knife landed in her shoulder instead of her neck. She did not stop nor did she pull the knife out. Diana raced forward, attacking every target and reached the finish line seconds before Nada.

The crowd was in an uproar. King Manu turned to the crowd and yelled, "This is not the way of our people; Nada's actions bring dishonor to us all." Misha tried to push towards Diana but his brothers maintained their hold on him.

Manu was going to speak again when Diana said loudly. "This woman has done more to bring dishonor to your people than you know. I won now she must admit to her crimes."

Nada did not speak. "What are you talking about?" Manu demanded.

"If you don't tell them I will," Diana said to Nada.

"No one will believe you," Nada screamed.

"I demand to know what is going on here," King Manu said angrily.

"This woman tortured and molested her own children and allowed others to do the same," Diana yelled angrily and the crowd became silent. "She should never be allowed near children again."

"She lies," Nada screamed and jumped towards Diana but Sorren grabbed Nada and held her tightly.

"My wife does not lie," Misha said loudly and pushed through the crowd until he was standing at Diana's side.

"This is true Misha?" King Manu asked.

"Yes."

Manu now addressed Sudfad who was standing in the crowd with his family. "King Sudfad could we put her in one of your dungeons until we leave? We do not tolerate such crimes and will deal with Nada accordingly."

460

"Of course," Sudfad said and was about to call some soldiers when Calen said. "We will deliver her to the dungeons." Calen, Luca, Dagon and Koby all stepped forward and took Nada from Sorren's grasp. Nada screamed, cursed and fought the men.

"Misha I am so sorry to embarrass you, that was never my intent," Diana said emotionally. "Do you hate me now?"

"I could never hate you," he said and kissed Diana.

"You two can do that later," Hannah scolded. "I need to take care of this wound."

"Misha what did I tell you about the baby lioness?" Thor yelled then laughed.

The crowd remained as Hannah cleaned and dressed Diana's wound. "Thanks to Erebus this is minor," Hannah said. "She was trying to kill you."

"Where is he I have to thank him," Diana said as she looked around.

"If you weren't so short you could see through the crowd," Misha said teasingly and waved to Erebus to join them.

"Thank you Erebus," Diana said when he approached them.

"It happened so fast I didn't have time to do a spell to protect you," Erebus said. "I am glad you are alright."

"Thank you," Misha said and shook Erebus' hand.

Maxwell and Emeral walked up to Diana and Misha just as Hannah finished bandaging Diana's arm. "Diana the integrity that you showed in that game only held up a mirror for others to see Nada for who she is. I am proud of you," Maxwell said and hugged Diana. As Emeral hugged Diana Maxwell spoke to Misha, "And I am proud of you son for bringing this nightmare out into the light." Maxwell hugged Misha as he talked, "I hope you don't think what Diana did was wrong. Nada is a monster and needed to be stopped. If either of you want to talk about this you know you can always come to Emeral and me."

A young woman walked up to Diana and said angrily, "Now everyone knows our shame, you had no right."

"But Lea, now you can all start to heal," Emeral said warmly.

Emeral pulled Lea, one of Misha's older sisters aside and talked to her for some time. Misha and Diana returned the pouch of gold to Stephan and the knife to Angelina. While people congratulated Diana some of them felt awkward, not really knowing what to say to Misha. But the tension was broken when Calen's voice thundered through the crowd, "Misha I've got a bag of coins that you can't do that course as well as your wife." The crowd laughed and Thaos walked up to the starting line to challenge Misha.

Diana turned and saw Sudfad and his family looking at her. She walked up to them and said sincerely, "I am very sorry to make such a scene; that was never my intent. Renya you always have such wonderful celebrations I hope this didn't ruin things."

"Doesn't look like anything was ruined to me," Raul said with a grin.

"You don't have to apologize for anything," Sudfad said. "You performed well."

"It took courage to do what you did," said Renya.

"I don't want to pry," Annabelle asked. "But how did you find out?"

"You all know how fierce and brave Misha is. Last night we turned around and Nada was standing behind us. You should have seen what happened to him. I can't really describe it but it broke my heart. That's why we left the celebration so early. I cried all night as he told me about what Nada did to him and the other children. I will be honest I wanted to kill her but for the monster she is I couldn't kill my husband's mother."

"You made a wise choice," Sudfad said. "Now her tribe knows and it should be up to them to administer justice not you."

"One of his sister's already yelled at me for telling everyone about their shame, Emeral is talking to her now."

"I can't even imagine what those children have lived through," Renya said. "Some of them may never heal."

Chapter XXXII
Bonds

"Tonight is the baby celebration, so I don't expect you to read this today," Sudfad said as he handed Gabriel an envelope of papers. "But you will need to read it before you leave for Ryed."

Before Gabriel could speak Raul asked, "What is it Father?"

"Well, our old friends Padre Thomas and Padre Bartholomew don't like to have idle time on their hands," Sudfad said with a grin. "With building a new monastery, teaching and administering to the people in Nora they still find time to do research. It turns out that the citizens of Nora have been hiding books, scrolls and all manner of religious items for years so that Roch's men would not destroy them. The people are now giving all of these items to the priests. While some of the information in their notes may not be useful for your mission in Ryed, it is still fascinating."

Sudfad continued as he addressed the men at his morning meeting, "Of course others can read that material, but I only have one copy of these notes. The priests also add information that they have been told by people. There are apparently several stories about strange occurrences in Ryed that have been told and retold so many times that there may not be any truth to them. The reasons I mention these stories is that they all involve the Teivel Clan."

"Sudfad did the Sanuri receive a copy of these notes?" Gabriel asked.

"Not to my knowledge."

"If it is alright with you, I will have some of the members of my team make more copies; unless there is something so sensitive that you don't want them to see it."

"No they can certainly read the notes," Sudfad replied. "I just wanted to get them into your hands as soon as possible since you will be leaving soon."

"When are you leaving?" Archetenus asked.

"Hopefully in two weeks. I want Thor on the mission and Erebus has volunteered to help us and to allow us to stay in his castle; Hannah wants them both to have a little more time to heal from their wounds. While I do not totally trust Erebus he could be extremely helpful to us," Gabriel said. "Unless something comes up in the next two weeks I have the list of people I will need. Archetenus and Jared of course you are staying home with your wives. Raul and Simon I would prefer that you remain here; I am afraid that your presence will give us away."

"Our wives certainly prefer that we stay home," Raul said. "But if you need us please let us know."

"I want to take Raphael and Edward; as generals they will be inspecting Fort Polta. Misha, Koby, Dagon, Joao, Dack, Thor, Diana, Joshua, Micha and Thomas will be going on the mission. Maxwell will remain here to work at the fort and to watch over our families. We will need more Rualas, if for no other reason than to transport us. I have already spoken to Lakin and he will get volunteers."

"I hope you know that we will watch over your families also," Simon said.

"We appreciate that especially with so many of our wives being pregnant," Raphael said. "Vivian wants to come with us but she has been so much sicker than Hannah and Lila that it worries me."

"If you are going to have Raphael and Edward inspect Fort Polta you will need some of our troops to escort them," Sudfad said.

"Raphael and I have been talking that over," Gabriel said. "We are actually considering taking Patrons priests with us because we expect to be fighting more dark lords than criminals. The priests at the Cicero headquarters still have the military uniforms that we took up there before that big attack on Fort Salar."

"So you will be traveling in two groups then?" Jared asked.

"Yes, Raphael and Edward will be leading troops from Fort Salar while Rualas fly the rest of us to Ryed. Erebus' castle is north of the Village of the Clan of Gesmal, yet considerably south of the lands owned by the Teivel Clan."

"You might also have problems with Hecate and Sampson," Sorren warned.

"Actually I am expecting as much," Gabriel said. "Last night I sent a letter to the Sanuri telling him of our mission."

"I am going to send a letter to Generals Colter and Orlan also in case you need help," Sudfad said. "Have you notified High Priest Rueben that you will be in the area?"

"Not yet," Raphael said. "I was planning on writing the letter today. Also here are some maps that Diana drew of Ryed. Her maps are very different from the ones we previously had." Raphael continued to talk as he handed the maps out. "As you can see she has indicated all manner of traps, both natural and man-made. When I say man-made I am also referring to those made of dark magics. Diana and Thor found a lot of bodies as they hunted in northern Ryed. Many of the bodies had died because of some type of trap."

"What will you need from us?" asked Sudfad.

"Actually I will need some letters with your seal on them. Natasha has been forging other papers for us."

"You will also need supplies and money; I don't want you paying for this mission," Sudfad said.

"Gabriel I couldn't help but notice that Diana is the only female on your mission. If you need more we did bring eight female warriors with us to meet your boys. Of course I don't know if there are any romances going and if that would be a problem," as Sorren spoke he looked at Edward and grinned. "They are all fierce warriors and smart. I could ask for volunteers if you would like."

"So why did you look at me?" Edward asked then started to laugh.

"Because you have women flocking around you like flies to honey," Jared said and laughed. "I'm just waiting for a couple of them to start fighting over you."

"They are all beautiful women," Edward said with a grin.

"Let me talk to my team," Gabriel said. "I appreciate the offer but with so many young men going with us it might be too much of a distraction."

"But they all know this is an important mission and they want to prove themselves also," Calen said. "Just tell them to keep their hormones in check."

"That evening as Gabriel's team was sitting down at the dining room table, Calen walked into the room holding Lily and smiling broadly. "Where's Natasha?" Calen asked. Hannah was coming out of the kitchen at that moment and was holding the door open. Natasha was in the kitchen and heard Calen.

"I'm in here," she called out.

"You need to come out here," Calen said excitedly.

"What's the matter?" Natasha asked as she was wiping her hands on her apron and walking towards her husband.

"I was upstairs trying to finish up all of these building plans before we leave when I heard a sound, I turned around and Lily was flying in the parlor," Calen said with a huge smile.

"No!" Natasha gasped then she started to smile. "I wish I could have seen that."

"Once they start you can't keep them down," Emeral said happily. "You're going to have to be careful about open windows."

"Oh my god," Hannah said. "I always keep at least one window wide open for the Enrops," then she too started to laugh.

"Make her fly now," Christopher said excitedly.

"I don't know if she understands the word yet," Emeral explained to Christopher. "Just keep an eye on her and she will be flying all over before she walks."

Many people at the table talked about Ruala babies flying for several minutes. When there was a lull in the conversation Gabriel spoke. "I am sorry to talk business at the dinner table but time is short and there is much to prepare before the next mission. Raphael and I had another meeting with Sudfad this afternoon and these are the changes: It had already been decided that Raphael and Edward would ride in full military uniform and lead a contingent of men made up of both Wetprian soldiers and Patronus priests. Raphael and Edward will be travelling under the guise that they are performing inspections for the King."

Gabriel continued, "So as not to raise suspicion Raphael and Edward are to actually inspect Fort Stanus, which should be near completion. While Fort Stanus is a considerable distance from Fort Polta it is close to the border of Ryed. The commanding general at Stanus is named Craven and he is a close friend of Sudfad's. Sudfad wants Raphael and Edward to deliver a letter to Craven telling him that our team will be working in Ryed. If we need help Craven is ordered to dispatch troops to help us."

"Well, that certainly makes me feel better," Hannah said.

"If our suspicions are correct about General Kretcher, we will be relieving him of his position at Fort Polta. General Ridon and Captain Malard are to replace Kretcher, of course they do not know this yet," Raphael said. "Now Gabriel and I have some things to discuss especially with the newer members of the team. In Gabriel's original plans he and Hannah were going in disguise as a wealthy couple who needed protection. Currently Diana is the only woman coming with us. The Rualas cannot be seen so we have been working out a variety of scenarios."

"Today Sorren suggested that we use the eight young female warriors that they brought along to meet all of you and that is what we need to talk about," Gabriel said. "Before any of you speak I want you to really think about what Raphael and I are saying."

"First Raphael and I don't know anything about these women and secondly we don't know if there are romantic relationships or jealousies among all of you. These things are very important because people get hurt when they are distracted and emotional."

"Learn from my mistake," Elan said, referring to the loss of his arm.

"For those of you who actually know these woman I want you to decide who you think will be appropriate for this mission. And don't decide because of your personal attraction to someone. You can always visit their tribe after the mission. This is a task of responsibility I am assigning to you," Gabriel concluded.

"All of us that Diana set up with these girls have been spending a lot of time with them," Dagon said. "I am not saying there aren't romances going on but we have also been entering competitions with them. As a group they are well trained and proficient with weapons," Dagon said. "But, well, I will wait until the rest of us talk as a group."

"I think you and I are thinking the same thing," Thor said seriously as he looked across the long table at Dagon.

"Do you care to share your thoughts?" asked Raphael.

"Everyone here knows that I have the least experience romantically with woman," Thor said then laughed. "But maybe because of that I look at them a little differently. They are all beautiful and they can all fight but..." Thor now looked at Micha. "Micha don't get mad because I know you have spent a lot of time with Corina but she is trouble."

"Everyone has spent a lot of time with Corina," Micha said. "And you are right she plays games and tries to get us all jealous of each other."

"That is exactly the kind of information we need," Raphael said. "I hope you all understand that your personal relationships are your business but this is work."

"I think we all understand that," Joao said. "Raphael do you have the names of the girls?"

"Not yet."

"I'll get some paper," Vivian said and left the table.

Everyone waited for Vivian to return to the table with paper and pen before they continued. "We could discuss this now unless someone is concerned because the children are in the room," Koby said. No one protested so Koby continued. "Their names are Corina, Toni, Jasmine, Darla, Batina, Valerie, Sasha and Bianca. We all agree we don't want Corina on the mission. Toni has it bad for Edward and seems jealous of the other women around him, so I don't know if that will be an issue."

"I will talk to Edward tomorrow," Gabriel said. "But I think no for Toni also."

"Dack you and Valerie spend a lot of time together," Dagon said. "Do you think you two can work together?"

Before Dack could answer Joao said, "No, they can't keep their hands off from each other, they would both be distracted."

"He's right," said Dack.

Micha turned and looked at his brother Thomas who then said, "Sasha and I have been spending a lot of time together but it's not like with Dack; I really like her. I think she and I could work together well, but let me talk to her first.

"Thomas are you saying you have a girlfriend?" Vivian teased.

"Thomas, Sasha really likes you," Diana said. "She was asking me questions about you and our clan."

"Well, he brought her to meet Joshua and me," Iris said with a smile.

"So this is serious?" Vivian asked happily.

"Gabriel, Raphael, Sasha is a dedicated warrior and I believe that the two of us can work together but I want to talk to her because I don't want to do anything to jeopardize this mission," Thomas said.

Vivian handed Raphael the list. "So we have Bianca, Darla, Jasmine, Batina and Sasha as possibles and Valerie, Corina and Toni as no's. "Unless anyone else has comments, Gabriel and I will talk with the five girls before we make a final determination.

"I know I am going to start the war of the year," Natasha said and stood up at the table. "This is an incredibly dangerous mission and I have had a bad feeling about it for some time. While we have plenty of warriors, there are few who have been trained in the clandestine work that needs to be done and most of them are Rualas and can't be seen. I want to come along or should I say I think you need to have me on this mission. Lily is almost seven months old and Cassandra and Elan said they would care for her. Alright Calen you can start yelling."

"I agree with Natasha and I would feel better if she went," Hannah said.

"No one is yelling because we all agree with you," Luca said then he turned to Calen.

"As much as I want to tell her she can't go," Calen said. "I have worked on these missions for years and I agree. I think the people who will be doing the direct contact are in a very dangerous situation and have to know what they are doing."

"I am so happy to hear all of this," Gabriel said. "For all of the rest of you who are new on the team, what Natasha and Calen are talking about are things we have not had a chance to train you in yet. I promise you will learn a great deal on this mission but I want us all to return."

"Calen I am so happy," Natasha said as she kissed him on the cheek. "When we return we can start working on that second baby." Calen grinned.

The following day was the morning of the grand baby celebration which would end almost a week of celebrations, balls and competitions at the castle of King Sudfad and Queen Renya. This also meant that the following day most of the visitors would be leaving which caused sadness for some since both friendships and romantic relationships had developed over the week.

The visitors from Lentz decided to stay another week until baby James Duran was a little older before making the journey home.

This morning at Sudfad's daily meeting, Gabriel and Raphael stood before the group and talked about updated plans for the mission to Ryed. They completed their portion of the meeting by repeating the discussion from the night before about the female warriors from the Nordes Tribe.

"Our intent is not to insult anyone nor to put anyone on the spot," Gabriel said. "But we need your honest feedback about these warriors. Edward as we told the rest of the team last night, personal relationships are just that, personal but this is work."

"Gabriel I know we have not spent a great deal of time together but I too am a man of mission and I have the same concerns as you and Raphael. Actually I think your team was on target with their assessments of personalities and relationships. I agree with everything they said."

"Sorren, we don't want to insult anyone from your tribe," Raphael said. "What are your opinions on these matters?

Sorren turned and looked at Joshua, "Sasha is a fine girl and a fierce warrior. It makes me happy that she and Thomas seem to be falling in love. A marriage would bind our tribes. As for the others, I agree with Edward and your team on their perspectives but I will tell you that all the girls will want to go and will be angry that they were not chosen."

"Do you think we should not take any of them?" Gabriel asked.

"No, they will be of great help to you and it will be a good training experience for them. I have not mentioned anything to them yet," Sorren replied.

"Raphael and I wondered if you would like to join us when we speak with them," Gabriel said. "Your insight is invaluable."

"I would like that and perhaps the girls will feel more comfortable with me there."

"Would ten o clock this morning work for you?" Gabriel asked. "Sudfad said we could meet in one of the rooms here."

"Fine."

"Archetenus this is for you," Raphael said and walked over to Archetenus and handed him a large packet of drawings. "Calen didn't come because he is not only trying to complete all of the design drawings but teach Elan how to read them. Elan will be overseeing many projects while we are gone. What I handed you are the plans for your house, Calen would like you to look them over and let him know what changes you want."

"For those of you who may not know," Sudfad said. "Next week we are starting construction on a hospital inside of Fort Salar. And that building that Gabriel bought for Hannah's medical office in the city is being converted into an office and a hospital. I bought the building next to it and the buildings will be combined. It has been decades since we have had attacks on our soil, and my eyes have been opened to the need for medical facilities."

Sudfad continued, "Calen has been helping with the designs of these buildings also. And the healers among all of your tribes have helped with ideas in a variety of areas. Because of this we will be combining the knowledge and experience of all our peoples to provide medical care in these facilities. And of course they are open to all of your peoples as well. And now this brings me to another matter," Sudfad said. "But I will let Raul and Simon present this information."

"When Petra was kidnapped our family fell apart. My father in his wisdom came up with an idea to keep us occupied. And this idea has taken on a life of its own. I am talking about the Learning Center that we are building. The other day you heard us talking about providing a training site for Patronus priests. But this is so much more," Raul said proudly. "We wanted a place where our children could receive the best educations possible without fear of attack. So this center contains a university as well as a building to house all of our children of any age."

"We are near completion of the buildings," Simon said. "But we are still determining courses and instructors. We will teach the courses offered in a university along with other subjects like woodworking, cooking, medicines, military strategies, various types of fighting and anything else all of you can think of; because we are offering this to all of your peoples as well."

473

"Father is building extra housing for the students. And we all believe that the shared knowledge and experiences of our peoples make us stronger. So we are asking for instructors from all of you. After this meeting Raul and I will take you to the building site."

"Well, I must say I very much like this idea," Sorren said with a huge smile.

"As do I," Mathas said.

"Does this mean our tribe also?" King Neputa asked.

"Of course," Sudfad said. "Manu is smiling because Emeral and Maxwell already told him about the center."

"We are going to train our team members in these buildings," Gabriel said. "And the Sanuri will also be teaching."

"Renya and I were going to have the students stay in the castle but then our sons reminded us that the students may want to feel less supervised so I am building additional lodging. But for any of you who would prefer your children live in the castle we will provide accommodations," Sudfad said. "The soldiers who guard these premises and our children will be handpicked. What I would like to do is to form a group of us to oversee the learning center and the studies. I would like representatives from each of your peoples to be in that group."

"Thor is so enjoying training the children of the team members that he said he would like to train the ways of our people in your school," Joshua said.

"And we would welcome that," Raul replied. "Tell Thor to meet with us."

"Sudfad I also like this idea but are you saying our family members or people of our kingdom are invited?" Claudius asked.

"We at first thought the family members," Simon said. "But as Raul said this has really taken on a life of its own. And that is why Father would like representatives of all your people to help run this center. At this point we have no idea how many people will want to come here."

"Well, the reason I asked," Claudius said. "Is you could very well have more people then you can hold and how will you choose?"

"Those are the decisions that the group of representatives will have to make," Simon replied.

"I am telling you right now you will have all of our grandchildren attending," Claudius said and the group laughed.

"Ignorance feeds fear and fuels hatred," Sudfad said. "I believe that not only will we provide our children with wonderful educations in a safe setting but we will strengthen the bonds between all of our peoples."

Chapter XXXIII
Unexpected Visitors

To the surprise of Sudfad and his family, the news of the Learning Center spread among their guests with great enthusiasm. Raul and Simon spent most of the day giving tours of the site. Another surprise was the excellent suggestions that surfaced during these tours; the Princes wrote down every suggestion for future discussion. By time the Baby Celebration started, a list of advisors for the Learning Center had been established.

The celebration started with dinner and entertainment and would end with the gift opening. As soon as the dinner dishes were cleared from the tables, Luca, Lila, Christopher, Emeral, Maxwell, Gabriel and Hannah walked up to the tables that had been pushed together to seat the visitors from Lentz.

"Please join us," Claudius said happily. "We will get more chairs."

Luca and the other adults from Gabriel's team were all smiling as Luca said, "We will join you but first Christopher has a gift for Amy." Christopher walked up to Amy proudly and handed her a box that was decorated with golden ribbon. Amy was sitting on Thaos' lap and now jumped down so that she was facing Christopher.

"Why did you get me a present?" she asked.

"Because I like you," Christopher said with a big smile.

All the adults at the table grinned as they watched Amy open her gift. "Oh Mama, Papa look," Amy said and handed the box to Thaos.

"Christopher this is beautiful," Nikki said as she showed everyone the golden necklace that held a single locket. Christopher smiled brighter as he listened to the comments. After everyone looked at the necklace, Nikki took it. "Amy come here and I will put it on you."

476

After Nikki clasped the necklace, Shara said, "Let's see it." Amy proudly showed off her new gift. Then she walked over to Christopher and hugged him.

"Thank you Christopher, I love it," Amy said.

"Christopher would you like to join us at the table?" Thaos asked with a grin and pulled out a chair. Christopher nodded and sat down at the table; Amy sat in the chair next to Christopher.

"I am afraid that Christopher is going to miss Amy after you leave," Lila said as she sat down at the table.

"Well Sorren, Shara, Bella and I are going to be representatives for the Learning Center so perhaps we can bring Amy to visit when we come for meetings," Claudius said with a grin he couldn't contain. Amy and Christopher both looked at Claudius and smiled.

Renya now stood on the platform in the front of the Great Hall and addressed her guests. "Unfortunately there is not enough room on the platform to set up the tables for our guests of honor as I would like. So I am going to ask those of you in the front tables to please leave your tables while the staff quickly rearranges the room."

"The staff will put screens up so you can't see what we are arranging until the proper time. The husbands of all of the women who are either pregnant or recently had babies will be asked to come to the front also and to make it a real family affair please bring your children with you. If there are any young men with strong backs who would be willing to help, I would appreciate it."

Renya started to walk off the stage when Sudfad spoke to her. Renya now addressed the audience again. So that you won't mind the inconvenience, staff will be bringing trays of wine and whiskey for your pleasure." As soon as Renya walked off the platform, staff started to divide the room with huge wooden screens. At least thirty young men walked up to the Queen to volunteer their services and Renya put them all to work. Many of the families had their children napping so they would be awake for this portion of the ceremony. The many couples now left the Great Hall.

All manner of noise as well as laughing could be heard from behind the screens. "Archetenus and Delilah just walked in with the babies, let's give them their gifts now," Misha said to Diana as they pushed through the crowd.

"I want to hold a baby," Diana cooed as soon as they reached the couple. Delilah handed Diana baby Ava.

"Your dress is beautiful," Delilah said to Diana who was wearing a dark sapphire dress with sapphire and diamond jewelry.

"Thank you Misha bought me everything but I am afraid this big bandage on my shoulder doesn't go with the dress," Diana said with a laugh. "And you look beautiful too."

"We are all warriors here; no one cares about the bandage," Archetenus said.

"We brought baby gifts earlier but Diana and I wanted to give you a little gift before the chaos starts," Misha said and handed Archetenus and Delilah each a small box.

"This is wonderful, thank you so much," Delilah said and kissed both Misha and Diana on their cheeks. Delilah showed Archetenus a delicate gold chain containing three disks, one with Archetenus' name and the other two with the names of their babies. "Oh let me open that for you," Delilah said with a laugh as she watched Archetenus try to open his gift while holding his son. Archetenus' gift was the same but with a large masculine chain and larger disks.

"Thank you," Archetenus said. "But why the extra gifts?"

"First I have to tell you we have similar gifts for Thaos and Nikki," Misha said. "I had never worked with either of you until the last few missions. You and Thaos are both good men and I am glad that you and Delilah decided to make your home in Wetpr." Archetenus was very touched by Misha's words since he always felt that he had to live down his past. Misha now turned and looked at Diana as she was holding baby Ava. Archetenus saw the smile on Misha's face and laughed.

"Thaos and Nikki just walked in with their babies," Diana said as she handed Ava back to Delilah.

478

"We'll have a drink later," Misha said to Archetenus as Misha and Diana disappeared into the crowd. Thaos and Nikki were equally surprised and pleased with their gifts.

As Diana and Misha walked back to their table Diana gushed, "I just love all of these babies."

Misha stopped walking and turned and faced Diana, "I know we decided to wait to start a family; but I've been thinking that perhaps we should work on having a baby when we return from Ryed."

Diana smiled and kissed Misha, "I agree, I think we are ready now."

"We have a few announcements while we wait," Sudfad said as he and Emeral stood in front of the screens. "The group of advisors for the Learning Center are: Claudius and Bella from the Kingdom of Lentz, Sorren and Shara from the Nordes Tribe, Ibula and Thedes representing the Rualas and Shettees, Maxwell and Emeral representing the Rualas, Joshua and Iris representing the Clan of Gesmal, Gabriel and Raphael representing the Patronus, and my lovely wife and I and Raul and Simon representing Wetpr. Of course others are also welcomed to participate in this group." The audience applauded.

"We originally had another mother-to-be who was going to be honored here but she had to return to the Ice Caves. We have a great deal of gifts for Bekka and her baby that need to be transported to the Ice Caves, if anyone is willing to carry these items will you meet with me after the ceremony?" Emeral asked.

Suddenly music started to play and staff carried the wooden screens out of the room. The audience laughed and applauded when they saw the front of the Great Hall. There were ten beautifully decorated tables set up with chairs in front of each table that were facing the audience. In front of the tables was a huge sand box that was surrounded with toys. Pink and blue drapes hung behind the tables. Renya called each family forward and they were escorted to one of the tables. When all the families were seated Renya spoke again.

"Any children in the room who would like to hand out gifts please walk up to Emeral." A group of children of all ages ran up to Emeral and she led them behind the curtains.

"I think this is going to be a long night," Calen said with a laugh as he poured whiskey into his brothers' glasses.

"Dack is that a black eye?" Cassandra asked when Dack and Joao walked into the dining room for breakfast the following morning. Several of the young men in the dining room started laughing hysterically.

"Ok, what did you do?" Natasha asked as she too laughed.

"I didn't do anything," Dack said as he sat down at the table.

"Valerie wasn't happy that she didn't get chosen for the mission," Thor said with a grin.

"And none of us are going near Corina," Joao said. "She's the real mean one."

"You should have done like Edward," Koby said with a smirk. "He asked Toni if they could continue to see each other after he returns from the mission; so she is all happy now."

"Well, it certainly sounds like we made the right decisions," Gabriel said as he held out Hannah's chair for her.

"So did you pick the other five girls?" Emeral asked.

"No," Raphael replied. "Actually having Sorren talk to the girls with us was very helpful. Raphael and Gabriel now looked at Thomas. "Did Sasha tell you what she told us?"

"Yes," Thomas said and smiled a smile that lit up his face.

"Well?" Micha asked.

"She told them she was in love with me and didn't want to be distracted on such an important mission," Thomas said.

"So how do you feel about her?" Joshua asked.

"Father I think I love her too but we haven't known each other long and now I am leaving and she will return to Lentz. And I don't know how long we will stay here in Wetpr. I don't want to ask her to marry me after only a week."

"It's been done," Calen said with a grin.

"Son do you think Sasha is the one?" Joshua asked.

"Yes, I feel differently for her than any other girl I have dated," Thomas said with both pride and frustration. "But I think we need more time together before we make any decisions and I don't know if we will ever see each other again."

"Sorren speaks highly of Sasha," Gabriel said. "You do have options. After the mission you can go to Lentz and visit her tribe or you could ask her to stay here with us until you return. But we would put her to work."

"Really?" Thomas asked hopefully.

"There has been so much going on since all of you came here," Raphael said and looked at Joshua and Iris. "Gabriel and I were talking. You certainly are welcomed to stay here for as long as you would like. Actually we all wish you would stay for a long time. And now with the Learning Center opening perhaps some of the boys want to stay here for an education."

"Iris and I were talking about this very subject," Joshua said. "Diana wants us here for her wedding and Vivian wants us to stay until the baby is born. Honestly it is such a different life here but we are enjoying it. But we started to enjoy it more when we could be useful."

"Emeral and I can certainly understand that," Maxwell said. "Although you still have children at home. We were feeling quite useless until we came here, now we both feel alive again."

"I have been talking to the girls and I know how upset they have been at the idea of bringing outsiders in to help with the chores. I would be happy to cook, clean and take care of children," Iris said. "We would all rather be working than sitting around."

"Joshua you said your family would help us during this mission," Gabriel said. "And we really need the help. But it seems like there is always a mission and as fast as our family is growing we are going to need help for a long time, so think about staying here with us."

Joshua looked at his two oldest sons who were sitting to his left. "Micha, Thomas I don't want to put you on the spot but what are your thoughts?"

"I really like it here," Micha said exuberantly. "It's fun and exciting and I like everyone we have met. And if we stay I would like to go to the Learning Center."

"I really like it here too and I'm not just saying that because of Sasha," Thomas said. "I too would like to go to the Learning Center but I don't know what I want to study yet."

Joshua looked over to the children's table. "Paul and Adrone have you been listening to what we are discussing?"

"Yes," Paul said.

"Would you like to live here for a while or go back home?"

"Would Elan be coming back with us?" Adrone asked which made everyone laugh.

"No, Elan and his family live here," Joshua said with a smile. "So you only want to stay here because of Elan?"

"No," Adrone said as he put a forkful of pancakes into his mouth. "It's because of what that lady said."

"What lady?" Joshua asked.

"The lady at the competitions, you know the day that Diana got stabbed," Adrone said.

"What did she say to you," Joshua asked with concern in his voice.

"She was asking me about how long we were going to be here. Then she said that Gabriel's team wasn't going to be here long."

"Did she say anything else?" Gabriel asked.

"Not really because everyone started to run over to see Diana and that girl fight so I went too," Adrone said.

"Adrone, what did this woman look like," Raphael asked.

"Like Vivian, that's who I thought it was at first when I went up to her." Everyone at the table now tensed up at Adrone's comment because they knew the woman was the demon Hecate.

"So you went up to her, she didn't call you or anything?" Gabriel asked.

"No, I was looking for Christopher, Nicholas and Joey and I was going to ask Vivian if she had seen them."

"What did she say to you?" Gabriel asked.

"She said she didn't know who they were and asked me my name, she was nice."

"Adrone this is important," Joshua said. "Did the woman touch you or give you anything?"

"No, I only talked to her for a minute."

"Why didn't you tell us about her?" Joshua asked.

"Because I didn't think anything was wrong. I thought she was here for the Baby Celebration," Adrone said nonchalantly.

"Why, did she say she was going there?" Raphael asked.

"No, cuz she had a baby in her," Adrone said and the room fell silent.

Before anyone spoke again, horses were heard outside of the house, Dagon and Joao were sitting closest to the front foyer and both got up and walked to the front door. Within moments familiar voices were heard.

"I hope you don't mind," Thaos said with a grin as he led many of the visitors from Lentz into the dining room. "This morning Amy was asking where Christopher lives and we realized that only Stephan and I have been to your house. So we decided to visit."

"And we have gifts," Bella said as she carried a large basket into the room.

"We are so pleased to have you," Gabriel said as he and Hannah walked up to their guests to greet them. "And your timing couldn't be better."

"Children why don't you take Sorren's sons and Amy into the playroom and show them your fort," Gabriel said. Before Gabriel finished his sentence the children were running out of the room.

Natasha, Lila, Diana and Vivian were all setting extra place settings on the table while Koby and Thor put more chairs around the table.

"I thought our dining room table was large but this certainly is not one table is it?" Bella asked.

"It's three tables," Hannah said. "And we had the dining room enlarged. The house is huge but everyone gathers in the dining room, kitchen and Gabriel's study. We are always having more work done on the house. Please have a seat."

"We ate," Sorren said. "But I will take a piece of that morning cake."

There was a knock at the door. "That's probably Matthew and Angelina, I told them we were going to visit you," Stephan said. Within moments, Matthew and Angelina walked in with their children and Margarit.

Before everyone was seated Amy ran into the dining room and yelled, "Margarit you have to see this," and held out her hand to her friend. After the little girls left the dining room Dack asked.

"So is that the Amy that Christopher says he is going to marry some day?"

"I've never seen anything so cute as when Christopher gave her that golden locket last night," Ingr said. "And then they just sat next to each other smiling."

"He gave her a locket?" Dack asked.

"Yes and my son has expensive taste," Luca said with a grin. "He picked it out himself. I was impressed."

"Dack you should try that and maybe the girls won't punch you," Joao said and laughed.

"Did one of my girls give you that shiner?" Sorren asked with a grin.

"Yeah, Valerie wasn't pleased that she wasn't coming on the mission," Dack said and laughed.

"But half an hour later they were kissing again," Dagon said and everyone laughed.

"Now that the children are out of the room," Gabriel said. "I want to tell you what Adrone just told us."

Chapter XXXIV
Sightings

The realization that the demon Hecate had been on the castle grounds during the competitions with the families and the children was a shock to everyone. That morning before Gabriel and the others left to go to the castle they formed the team into shifts to guard the house. Only Gabriel, Raphael and Joshua left the house with the families of Lentz to attend King Sudfad's morning meeting.

Iris and Hannah did not want to scare Adrone but they examined him to ensure that Hecate did not harm the boy in any way.

"You know Adrone you told us that lady asked you how long you were going to be here," Iris said. "How did she know you weren't from Wetpr?"

"I told her, why?"

Iris looked her young son in the eyes. "Adrone you have started your Venator training to become a warrior and you will be a fine warrior someday. None of us wanted to scare you but we all believe that lady you spoke with is a demon; so it is very important that you tell us everything that was said." As Iris spoke, Vivian and Diana joined them in the small room.

"She seemed awfully nice for a demon," Adrone said.

"Some demons go in disguise," Iris said. "Can you remember exactly the words you both said?"

Adrone paused for a moment and looked at all four women. "Like I said I was looking for my friends when I saw the lady. I yelled, 'Vivian' and ran up to her but once I got close I could see it wasn't my sister. The lady smiled at me and said that Vivian was a friend of her husband's and asked how I knew her. I said Vivian was my sister."

"Then the lady said you are a long way from home. I said we were visiting Raphael and Vivian then she asked me how long we were going to stay? I told her I didn't' know. Then she said Gabriel's team isn't going to be here long."

"She started to say something else but I saw everyone running to see Diana and that girl fight so I ran too."

"Was that all that was said?" Vivian asked.

"Once I stared running I yelled 'bye' to her and she yelled the same to me."

"Adrone what was she doing when you saw her?" Diana asked.

"She was just standing and watching everyone."

"Was she alone?" asked Vivian.

"No one was near her the whole time I saw her."

"Adrone, Venators are trained for their observation skills and I am going to test you on this lady. So far you have done well. I just have a few more questions," Vivian said. "Do you remember what she was wearing?"

"Yes she wore sandals and a light pink dress with no sleeves. The dress was tight around her stomach."

"Very good!" Vivian said. "You know that Hannah, Lila and I are all going to have babies, did this lady's stomach look like any of ours?"

"Almost as big as Lila's."

"You are doing so well," Vivian said. "You have observed the person and the words now for the last part of the test. Do you remember exactly where she was standing?"

"Near one of the flower gardens, I could show you," Adrone said excitedly.

Diana left the room and when she returned, Misha, Luca, Calen, Koby and Thor were with her. "Thor has some pouches in case we find anything," Diana said.

"Well, she did exactly what would scare us the most," Sudfad said after being told about Adrone's encounter with Hecate. "She showed up around our families and spoke to one of our children. Raul and Simon, most of our guests are still here please call a meeting in the Great Hall and find out if anyone else saw or spoke to the demon." Before Raul and Simon could leave the room there was a knock at the door. Jared was sitting the closest to the door and opened it.

Calen, Luca, Koby, Misha, Thor, Diana, Vivian and Adrone walked in. "Mother told Adrone our concerns about the lady he spoke with," Vivian explained. "Adrone is in Venator training and he is now being tested on his observation skills. He said Hecate wore a light pink dress that was tight around her stomach and sandals. He said her stomach was about the size of Lila's and he is going to take us where he saw her. He said she was alone."

"Joshua, tonight I am putting a new stone on Adrone's lamsman so we can celebrate," Thor said. "He did very well."

"Adrone that is good information; I am proud of you," Sudfad said. "Is there anything you want to say?"

"She was awfully nice to me and she didn't stink like a demon that's why I didn't think anything was wrong," said Adrone.

"That's interesting," Raphael said.

"Not really," Thor explained. "Demons walk among people all of the time and to maintain their disguises they mask their smell. I don't know how they do it."

"We're going to search the area now," Vivian said.

"I'll go with ya," Jared said and stood up. "An extra pair of eyes can't hurt."

"I don't know if this is important," Diana said. "But Adrone ran up to Hecate calling Vivian's name. Hecate said that Vivian was a friend of her husband's and that the family was a long way from home. Adrone told her they were visiting Vivian and Raphael."

After Vivian and the others left Claudius spoke, "Hecate is cunning I would assume everything she said and did was well planned. She wanted to scare us to prove her power and you know what she said to Adrone about her husband and Gabriel's team was planned. The Sanuri told us in Ryed that Hecate took an appearance similar to Vivian's to entice Sampson, but why here and now?"

"Maybe to get information or more likely to let us know it was her," Gabriel said.

"Perhaps Sampson was here too," Sudfad suggested.

"No that guy sticks out in a crowd and not just because of his nasty personality," Sorren said. "He's a big muscular guy who never wears a shirt so he can show off his tattoos. His body is covered with tattoos including his bald head."

"Could he have been in disguise?" asked Mathas.

"He would have to have completed his trials to change his appearance," Joshua said. "And even if he was in disguise I would think he would still have exposed himself in some way because of his anger. What concerns me is that she appears to be pregnant with Sampson's child, can you imagine what kind of monster that will be? I will send a letter to Duncan as soon as this meeting is over."

"Right here is were I saw her, I remember because of that bush, there's a bird's nest in it," Adrone said proudly.

"You have done so well," Diana said. "We are all so very proud of you Adrone."

"What exactly are we looking for?" Koby asked.

"She seemed to want to leave us messages," Vivian said. "I would imagine something we would recognize."

"Maybe it wasn' that she left something maybe the spot is important," Calen said as he stood in the same spot that Hecate had stood.

"If she was Vivian's size she wouldn't be that tall and this entire area was filled with people; so I would expect that some of her view was blocked." As Calen slowly turned around he said, "You can see the west side of the castle, part of the back wall and the wooded area. Adrone where was she facing when you saw her?"

"Straight ahead, where the crowd was forming around Diana."

Renya knocked on the door then walked into Sudfad's study, "I spoke with Petra and Kyra and they remembered seeing a woman they thought was Vivian but it wasn't the same day. It was two days earilier also at the competitions. They were walking up to her but when they realized she wasn't Vivian they walked away without speaking to her."

"When Adrone saw her, Hecate was wearing a pink dress and sandals and was very pregnant," Raphael said. "Did Petra or Kyra say what she looked like."

"Petra doesn't seem to notice a lot," Renya said. "But Kyra said she was wearing a light blue dress and sandals."

Raul walked into the study, "Why don't all of you join us in the Great Hall, it appears there were some sightings."

Vivian and the others returned to Sudfad's study without finding anything of significance. "We didn't find anything and it appeared she was watching the crowd form around Diana and Nada," Calen said to Sudfad and the group of leaders who had returned to Sudfad's study from the Great Hall.

"We found out that Kyra and Petra saw her two days earilier also walking around the competitions but she was wearing a blue dress," Sudfad explained. "Simon and Raul called a meeting of our guests and it appears there were several sightings of Hecate walking around the competitions but she only spoke to Adrone and that maybe because he initiated it."

Before anyone else could speak Archetenus called out, "Miranda, Daniel would you talk to us?"

"We were wondering when some one would call to us," Miranda said as the Angels materialized in the study.

490

"So what do you think Hecate was doing here?" Miranda asked.

"Getting information?" Matthew suggested.

"She has minions for that," Miranda said. "She appeared to some of you in a form you would recognize."

"She was trying to scare us," said Raul.

"Now the question to ask is why would this powerful demon come here herself to scare you," Miranda said. "She knows many of you call to us and have the power and courage to fight her."

"She wants us to know about the baby," Vivian gasped. "This is a trick for Duncan and his sons."

"Vivian you have done well," Miranda said. "Sampson still needs to complete his trials and she is hoping that news of their child will force Duncan and his sons to come after Sampson."

"And she was hoping that by filling you with fear she could get some of you to go after her," Daniel added. "Claudius was right, Hecate is cunning but you should know there is much more to this. Hecate has collaborated with her old lover Orbus and they are trying to build an army of demons to take over one of the hell demensions and that is her primary focus now. If they are successful she will obtain the powers of an Old One. She is keeping Sampson in his human form because he is more useful to her because demons can not touch holy things or enter holy places."

"If her main focus is to take over a hell demension she must want something from us,"Gabriel said.

"And that is exactly how you should be thinking," Miranda said. "She has lost every battle with you but once she takes over a hell demension she will be a more formidable opponent."

"Does Sampson know about her lover?" Vivian asked. "Because he would kill him."

"And Hecate knows that," Daniel said. "So far Sampson does not know but he is starting to suspect."

"I'm confused by what you just said," Jared said. "Is she trying to get Sampson to complete his trials or not?"

"Sampson badly wants the power of a demon, he is not comfortable with having a wife so much more powerful than he is. Hecate will help him with the trials but for now she is trying to keep him appeased."

"So Sampson thinks Hecate is working on what he needs but she really isn't?" Sorren asked.

"Hecate is ambious and has a lot of private agendas," Daniel replied.

"Why was she nice to me?" Adrone asked.

"Because you are a smart boy and if she would have tried anything you would have called for help," Miranda said. "We were protecting you." Miranda looked at the group. "There are many questions you should be asking us."

"Did Hecate do anything here other than appear to some of us?" Simon asked.

"She was looking through the crowd, demons can see the darkness in the hearts of men. She was watching the competiton between Diana and Nada because she was watching Nada. A woman after her own heart. Misha I know you don't want to hear this but you can no longer ignore the monster your mother is. Her crimes have been exposed. Nada has choices to make and I will tell you she is making the wrong choices," Daniel said.

"Also Hecate knows that someone who is powerful in the arts of dark magics severed her connection with the demons she sent to attack your castle and fort. It was the sorcerer she was looking for and because Erebus does not hide himself she now knows he is helping you. You would be wise to warn him," said Miranda.

"Rapahel and I were going to call to you because of the mission we are planning against the Insidiae in northern Ryed," Gabriel said. "Do you want to talk about that now?"

"I believe everyone in this room has an interest in that mission," Miranda said. "You would be fools to go on it without us. There is more darkness there than you can imagine." Miranda turned, "Renya have you not been researching the Insidiae?"

"Yes," Renya replied hoarsely. "I am sorry but this is my first time meeting the two of you and it is quite overwhelming."

"Before Gabriel's team leaves for this mission; you must share with them the findings you have at that point," Daniel said. "Sudfad, Erebus gave you a great gift when he warned you about two of the Grand Masters. Erebus was correct in his assessments of their agendas and their actions are causing additional conflicts in the underworlds. Emeric and his sister Banaka started the Teivel Clan although they go by different names now. Emeric uses the name Valdus and Banaka is called Oriah. Teivel was the name of their father."

"You are correct in your suspicions that Cedrick Kretcher is a dark lord and you will need to remove him from your military. But while he seems powerful he is merely a puppet of Emeric and Banaka. Removing him alone will not protect your families. So tell us what you hope to accomplish on this mission," Miranda said.

Gabriel smiled, "Miranda what would you like us to accomplish on this mission?"

"Thank you and I am making you phrase these words for a reason. And in the future you should be asking the same questions because for all of your research and your resources you really have no idea of what you are walking into. Almost everyone of you in this room fought in the battle of Ogg, think of being on that mission without the help of the heavens. Without our help none of you will make it back alive and you will accomplish nothing. Once Hecate realizes you are returning to Ryed she will warn the Teivel Clan and they will be waiting for you."

"We sent Thor and Diana to you, to tell you of the horrors they saw and yet you are planning a mission with a handful of warriors, many of whom are young and inexperienced. Are you planning on freeing the people of northern Ryed and destroying the monsters or are you traveling that far to committee suicide?"

"Gabriel my words are harsh but gone are the days when your team could operate without detection; there are eyes upon you that you cannot even imagine. If you want Daniel and me to help you we will but you must re-think this mission."

"I gave Gabriel the mission to find out if Tievel was a spy and traitor in my military," Sudfad said. "And now you confirm that he is. But you are saying that the real threats to my family come from the Grand Masters?"

"Yes, but it is not just your family," Daniel said. "All the people in this castle now consider themselves part of one incredible family. Many of you refer to each other as family. This is the Prophesy of The Seven Sons unfolding. Good and courageous people standing up to the demons, the dark lords and the criminals."

"Every person in this room and in this castle is now feared by darkness and darkness will strike out. Some of you are so humble you have no idea of the power you possess; power that the darkness wants to take from you."

Daniel deliberately paused and looked into the eyes of every person in the study. "Claudius you led an army into hell. Sorren you called forth an army of Angels. Sudfad you defied an attack by thousands of demons and every one of you has been threatened and have failed to bow to the demons; don't you realize how truly different you are from most of mankind?" And Archetenus and Jared, you delivered blows to the hell regions which will be felt for decades."

Daniel continued, "One voice can cry out from the darkness and call The Great Ruler's Spirit in. What do you think all of you can accomplish especially when you work together. All of you can leave the battles and return to your homes but that does not mean the threats against you have ended."

"Mathas your daughter and Fahron's son called out to demons but the most powerful demons answered their calls because they wanted to stop all of you. You see the dark ones have been trying to prevent the Prophesy of The Seven Sons from unfolding for centuries, so they have been speculating on the players and trying to kill them off."

"Miranda, I have more experience with you than the others here and I know there is always so much more to your words than I often hear," Archetenus said. "There is a reason you are telling all of us this instead of just Sudfad and Gabriel's team isn't there?"

"Yes, we know that the people from Lentz are staying here another week. King Manu and King Neputa I would ask you to have your people stay but one more day. Gabriel and Sudfad I would like you to have all of your guests assemble in the Great Hall. We would like you to present them with the information that we have shared with you in addition to your plans for this mission."

"Have your people come together as they did when strategizing for the mission to stop Roch. Have Erebus join you. We are protecting your families you do not need guards at your homes, have them come to the meeting instead," Miranda said and she and Daniel dissappeared.

Within moments of the depature of the Angels everyone left Sudfad's study. The visiting leaders went in search of their people to tell them not to leave the castle. Renya immediately met with staff to make arrangements for food and lodging for the guests who were now staying longer. Then Renya went to her chambers to review her research.

Gabriel and Calen returned to the house to get the others and Gabriel's research for the mission in Ryed. Archetenus had an overwhelming feeling to bring Delilah to the meeting so he went to their chambers. Raul looked for Vitomas and Annabelle, while Simon spoke with Erebus and Sudfad quickly wrote a letter to the Sanuri. Joshua also wrote a letter to his dear friend Duncan and the words Joshua wrote brought great sadness to his heart.

Within an hour the meeting started in the Great Hall. Misha had not commented on what the Angels said about Nada; the horror and pain of his childhood were filling his being. He was glad when the meeting started so he could focus on something else.

Daniel's comments about Nada were vague; Misha knew he would have to ask the Angels for clarification. But not today; Misha knew he could not handle that much truth today. When Daniel spoke about Nada, Diana tightly grasped Misha's hand and she did not let go.

The meeting lasted the entire day and into the night. The most revealing information came from both Erebus and Renya because of their individual research into the Insidiae.

Commanding General Cedrick T. Kretcher was actually Cedrick Teivel, a dark lord and a Master in the Insidiae organization. Teivel's territory covered the Kingdom of Ryed and a small portion of western Wetpr. He ruled his territory with an iron fist.

King Nehmota of Ryed was merely a figurehead, Teivel held the real power in that kingdom and had for hundreds of years. Generations of kings were allowed to sit on the throne in Ryed as a diversion for Teivel's activities.

Under the rule of Teivel, Ryed became a haven for every manner of criminal and for those who worshipped the darkness. While the peoples of Ryed had revolted on occasion the uprisings were easily suppressed but a small group of freedom fighters remained. This group was hunted by Teivel's people, so they maintained a secrecy that rivaled that of the Insidiae itself.

The freedom fighters became heroes who were larger than life for the people of Ryed. Because of the status they achieved the number of freedom fighters increased. Many villagers and city dwellers became the eyes and the ears for this organization; while not members themselves. But there were those who believed this clandestine group was nothing more than the illusions of a people who were without hope.

All of the guests remained at Sudfad's castle that night and the next morning. They were instructed by their leaders not to leave until after King's Manu and Neputa had news from the morning meeting. As soon as the leaders gathered in Sudfad's study, King Sudfad did something he had never done before; he started the meeting by calling to Miranda and Daniel.

"Thank you for coming," Sudfad said when the Angels appeared instantly. "Investigating Teivel was an assignment that I gave to Gabriel's' team I do not want innocent men sent to their deaths. We need your guidance on this matter."

"You show your wisdom," Miranda said to the King. "I have overheard some of the men in this room previously say that Daniel and I tend to play down the dangerousness of situations. Sudfad I tell you this so you understand how dangerous the mission you contemplate is."

"Before we discuss the details of this mission," Daniel said. "I have a question for Archetenus. You brought Delilah to part of yesterday's meeting. She was too shy to speak in front of the group. What did she tell you last night?"

"Well, she said some of the same things that Erebus said. That the Insidiae are spread throughout this world and that each continent is divided into regions. Each region is run by an Insidiae Master and that Master is in full control of how he runs his region. To her knowledge, Delilah has never met Teivel but she heard his name mentioned often. Delilah said that Dieter and others would refer to Teivel as a barbarian. Which I think says a lot if you knew Dieter."

"And we agree, which is why I had you say that." Daniel said. "Delilah possess more knowledge about the Insidiae than she realizes; it would be wise for you to bring her to more meetings. Now before we say anything else I want every man and woman in this room to have some questions in their head as we proceed. "Why would a powerful dark lord and a Master of the Insidiae first work at a job and secondly work as a Commanding General in the military of Wetpr?"

"Raphael and Edward you would have been butchered trying to arrest Teivel," Miranda said. "Fort Polta is filled with members of the Insidiae. And the Kingdom of Ryed is a hell dimension on earth. The Clan of Gesmal is truly the brightest light in that kingdom. But there are other lights, whose flames have not yet been extinguished. Gabriel not only would your team have been killed but you would have been responsible for extinguishing those lights had you proceeded as planned."

"I don't mean to interrupt," Simon said. "But you told us before that there is a monastery in Ryed. The one that Sampson was supposed to steal from. Is that monastery run by dark lords too?"

"No, that monastery harbors the lights that Miranda spoke of," Daniel said. "Certainly not every citizen of Ryed is evil and the good citizens have revolted over the years but these are not trained soldiers and they have been slaughtered an imprisoned. But their desire to rid themselves from evil is still alive."

"There is a small group of men and women who call themselves the Libertas, in the old language liberta means freedom. They are as their name suggests a group of freedom fighters. They have been forced to become a clandestine group; but the people of Ryed are their eyes and ears."

Daniel continued, "This group is led by three brothers the oldest is Dominic, Fennel and Asher. They are good men who are sick of seeing their people tortured and killed by Teivel's regime. The monastery at Rubar is run by High Priest Othnial, a faithful servant who calls to The Great Ruler to help his people. Othnial protects the Libertas. For you to successfully combat the Teivel Clan in Ryed you would need to work with the Libertas."

"But there are several issues that all of you must ponder here," Miranda said. "Obviously Sudfad must cleanse Fort Polta of the Insidiae and the demonic presence there. But then there is the question, do you want to return to battle and loose more of your men and women to save the people of Ryed; a battle that really isn't yours."

King Mathas stood as he spoke, "The Insidiae is a threat to everyone in this world. The Teivel Clan is run by two Grand Masters and yesterday you said they were a threat to us all; did you not?"

Miranda said, "They are threats to all of you but you could say they are not yet on my doorstep."

"Ogg wasn't on our doorsteps either," Sorren said passionately.

"There is a much greater challenge in attacking the Teivel Clan than King Douma. Douma housed all of his prisoners in one area. That is not the case with the Teivel Clan," Daniel said and turned to the Princes of Wetpr.

"When you freed the hostages of Shanksaw, you knew that if Shanksaw's men saw any of you they would kill the victims. That is also what you would face in Ryed."

"How would we find out where the victims are?" Gabriel asked.

"The Libertas," Daniel replied. "But this group of freedom fighters are hunted men and will not trust easily. If you want to fight the Teivel Clan in Wetpr and Ryed you obviously have more than one battle front. To minimize the number of innocent people who are killed you have a great deal more planning and research to do. But you must decide what you are willing to do."

"You have many things to think about," Miranda said. "And I have to tell you I was disappointed that a subject was not brought up in your meeting yesterday. We told you that the Prophesy of The Seven Sons was unfolding and some of you are those sons. And while you know this you do not fully understand the power or importance of your positions. The Seven Sons together are a formidable force. You must realize that you must stand together to overcome great evil."

"Petra is not yet ready. But there are five who are and the Seventh Son is almost on your doorstep. But initially his presence will not be what you expect and for many of you your worlds will change."

"The Sanuri told us that the Seventh Son has been fighting demons and we will know him when we see him," Sudfad said. "Does this man know of his destiny?"

"No," Miranda replied. "He is not a priest or a nobleman." Miranda turned to Gabriel. "Remember when you were pulled into hell?"

"Vividly," Gabriel said. "I was fighting the thirteen demons."

"While it seemed like an eternity to you," Miranda explained. "It was but a few days in this world. Yet that is the existence the Seventh Son has had all of his days in this world."

"Can't we help him?" asked Matthew.

"Simon, your experience was different but Gabriel, Archetenus and Jared, what were you like when you first escaped the hell dimensions?" Miranda asked.

"Disoriented," Gabriel said.

"Felt like I was still fighting," Archetenus said.

"Didn't trust my surroundings," Jared added.

"Remember these words and that is how you will help him," Miranda said. "The Seventh Son is escaping from the hell dimension again."

"Again?" Sorren asked. "Did the demons pull him back in?"

"No, he returned to protect those who could not escape," Miranda said.

Chapter XXXV
At Our Doorstep

King Manu and King Neputa decided to keep their people at Sudfad's castle one more day as they discussed the information they received from the Angels. There was another large meeting in the Great Hall where the leaders shared the words of the Angels with their people. All of the Venatores were asked to come in front of the group and to share information they had. While some of them had heard of the Libertas, they thought the stories were legends. But it was when Joshua revealed the names the Angels had given them that Thor and Diana paused.

"We helped a man named Asher," Thor said. "I don't know if he is the same man that you speak of, but he said he was in our debt. In northern Ryed there is an enormous swamp that covers many, many miles. It lies east of the City of Rubar and west of the City of Teivel and the castle of King Nehmota. This swamp is also south of the castle of Teivel but it extends to the very back of Teivel's castle."

"Diana and I hunted there often. One day we heard the sounds of a fight and found one man surrounded and fighting with monsters the kind we had never seen before. Diana and I joined the fight and killed the monsters. The man asked our names and gave us his before he left."

"He recognized our outfits and knew of Venatores," Diana added. "Which surprised us both."

"By any chance did this man tell you a way that you could find him again?" Gabriel asked hopefully.

"Yes," Thor said. "But it would require us to return to that swamp. He gave us something that looked like a talisman and told us to hang it on a tree in the area where we helped him fight the monsters. He said he would find us."

"He didn't tell you to stay in a specific area so he could find you?" Gabriel asked.

"No, but I asked him how he would know it was me and Diana that wanted to talk to him and he responded he would know."

"The Angels said that many people are the eyes and ears for the Libertas," Sorren said. "I'll bet Asher and his brothers knew when you entered the territory."

"Where is this talisman?" asked Raphael.

"In my room at the house," Thor said. "Diana and I brought all that we owned with us."

"Thor you and Diana are very perceptive," Thaos said. "What were your opinions of Asher?"

"He dressed like a poor man," Thor said. "But he fought like a warrior and he carried a well-made sword. He was in his early twenties with curly dark reddish hair. He did seem grateful when we joined the fight," Thor added then laughed.

Claudius stood up and spoke to the group with his normal air of authority. "I know we have not made any decisions and I do believe there is much preparation in what I am proposing. I think our best chances to win would be to attack the Insidiae at Fort Polta and in Ryed simultaneously. We need to keep the Grand Masters from helping their people at the fort."

"Which means my team needs to make contact and get an offensive in place in Ryed before we attack Teivel at Fort Polta," Gabriel said.

"While I agree with what has been said," Raul stood up and said to the group. "Teivel is in a real position of power at that fort, we need to find some way to stop him from doing more damage before we attack him."

Joshua now stood up. "I find myself in such awe around the Angels that perhaps I don't always hear everything they say but do they want us to wait until the Seventh Son comes before we attack the Teivels?"

"Joshua I too have that same question," Sudfad said.

"I have had more experience with Miranda than the rest of you," Archetenus said. "And trust me if she took the time to explain to us the condition that poor bastard is going to be in after being tortured, it may be some time before he is in any condition to help us."

502

"Especially if he doesn't know about the prophesy or hasn't met the Angels."

"You are all speaking as if you have already decided to attack Ryed," the Sanuri said as he walk towards the front of the room."

"When did you get here?" Sudfad asked.

"A short time ago; the Angels hastened my journey. Before you ask me any questions I probably know less than you do about Ryed and Teivel. But I have seen the names of Emeric and Banaka in some writings and I believe them to be exceptionally dangerous," the Sanuri said then looked at Gabriel. "I found some very old scrolls that you missed in the library of Hannah's house. I would like to come to your home tonight and show them to you."

"Of course," Gabriel said. "Please join us for dinner."

"I received Sudfad's letter about the first encounter with the Angels talking to you about Ryed, I have heard much in this meeting about your second conversation with the Angels. You are all courageous warriors but have you ever had the Angels warn you in such a manner? Take it to heart. If you decide to infiltrate or attack Ryed it will be a very dangerous proposition," the Sanuri warned.

King Neputa stood up and addressed the group. "As you know it was the tradition of my people to separate ourselves from others who were not our kind. When the Hutas left Marba and started persecuting and murdering humans we heard of it but we did nothing because the humans were not our kind. Then when the Hutas went after the Rualas, we heard of it but again we did nothing because the Rualas were not our kind. When the Hutas came after us there was no one left to be our ally."

Neputa paused as it was obvious to everyone he was becoming overwhelmed with emotion. "We did not worship The Great Ruler then; but when my kingdom was destroyed and my people without hope, The Great Ruler sent us Angels, humans and Rualas to rescue us. Those who we would not stand before, stood before us. Our swords are few but they are swords we will go to Ryed to help free those people."

King Manu stood up and looked kindly upon Neputa. "My brother and I are of the same heart," Manu said. "We too will fight."

"Considering my son-in-law is one of The Seven Sons," Sorren said with great pride. "The Nordes Tribe will also throw down their swords."

"Sudfad it is now up to you and me," Mathas said as he stood up. "My heart is heavy because of all of the battle the people in this room have been involved in over the last two years. Is there no peace in the hearts of men? I sincerely hope that our sacrifices will make this a better world for our children and grandchildren. We will not forsake our allies in this unholy war. The swords of Lentz will fight also."

"The deaths of our soldiers and our citizens too weigh heavily upon me," Sudfad said solemnly as he stood before the group. The Insidiae are in my kingdom, attacking my people, attacking my family. I do not delight in war, but war it must be." Sudfad took his sword from its sheath and thrust it into the floor. Without hesitation every warrior in the room did the same.

Now to the surprise of many Erebus stood up. "While we have many differences we have the same enemies. My home is Ryed and I have many contacts there although I knew nothing of the Insidiae until my late wife Sophie told me. I am offering my help and my castle but now that Hecate may be coming after me that may be a danger you don't want to risk. But the offer is there."

"Hecate is always coming after us," Sorren said sarcastically. "You are in good company. Where is your castle?"

"Northwest of the Village of Gesmal. And directly south of the monastery at Rubar. The monastery is on the southern-most outskirts of the City of Rubar. On a map it is a straight line from my castle to the monastery to the castle of Teivel. But there is a great deal of dangerous land in between our castles."

"And we believe that Hecate's lair is south of the Village of Gesmal in the mines," Simon said. "We need to keep her distracted until we get everything in place."

Luca stood up. "We know the King of Ryed is merely a puppet for Teivel's Clan. And from what Erebus told us yesterday if we kill Teivel the Insidiae will be fighting among themselves to put another leader over that territory. We are talking about freeing those people but who will be their leader when we leave?"

"Hopefully the Libertas can answer that," the Sanuri said.

That evening the Sanuri joined Gabriel's team for dinner. "We are just so proud to have you here," Hannah said as she showed the Sanuri to a seat at the head of the table. "I don't know why we never thought to ask you here before?"

"I hope you didn't go to a lot of trouble," the Sanuri said and was interrupted by the sounds of children laughing and a dog barking.

"We found a dog," Gabriel explained. "And he has become the most popular member of the family."

"The children adore him and he is very protective of them," Natasha said as she filled wine glasses at the table.

"I have known most of you for such a long time," the Sanuri said as people were taking their seats around the table. "You have all been in battle far too long; it warms my heart to now see you with families. Even those of you who are not married; this used to be a military team, now it is a huge family of warriors."

"When Maxwell and I first came to visit," Emeral said. "We were very excited to see our children and to learn of their lives in this world but we really didn't know what to expect. We weren't prepared to find the kinship and unity that we found here. It is crazy a great deal of the time but it works and we are so happy here."

"And you and Maxwell make it so much more of a family," Hannah said sincerely.

"Joshua how long are you and your family staying?" the Sanuri asked.

"Hopefully until Raphael and I are done having children," Vivian said with a grin.

"We really don't know; while it is such a different lifestyle we are all enjoying it here," said Joshua.

"You all seem to fit so well together," the Sanuri said. "And I can't help but believe you are here at exactly the right time."

After the dinner meal was eaten the Sanuri said, "Gabriel why don't you Raphael and Hannah meet with me in the study, then you can decide if you want others to join us."

"Me?" Hannah asked with surprise.

"The papers we will be reviewing were your father's," the Sanuri said and Hannah's face turned white.

"You don't have to join us," Gabriel said to Hannah when he saw the look on her face.

"No, no that is alright," Hannah said as she composed herself.

"Hannah go, we'll take care of things," Natasha said as she cleared dishes from the table.

Gabriel led the small group into his study and closed the door. He poured everyone a drink while the Sanuri spoke. "I spent a great deal of time at the Patronus Headquarters in Nora trying to translate writing that was on the outside of the mausoleum as well as research information for the blood moon ceremonies."

"I often went into your father's library Hannah and one evening I found these old scrolls on the top of a dusty bookshelf." The Sanuri opened a pouch he had been carrying and removed several scrolls and books; the Sanuri handed one of the scrolls to Gabriel as he spoke. "This scroll contains the names, identities, family information and locations of many of the members of the Insidiae as well as Grand Masters. Note there is also other personal information written near some of the names, like weaknesses of that individual."

"The reason I wanted to talk to the three of you first, is this is not the type of information just anyone in the Insidiae can see. Hannah I believe your father was either a very high ranking member in that organization or he was planning some type of takeover."

Hannah's hands shook as she listened to the Sanuri. "Hannah if Arthur had this information to gain more power within the Insidiae his death may not have been a suicide." Hannah gasped and the tears started to run down her cheeks.

"Both of my parents were devastated after Laurabelle's murder, but I could never see my father killing himself," Hannah paused and then said sadly. "Of course I could never see him as a member of the Insidiae or a murderer either."

"There is no personal information about your family in any of these writings," the Sanuri said. "But they contain a great deal of information that members of the Insidiae would not want brought out to the light of day. Gabriel, Raphael while I believe this information will aid you greatly in your work, for the Insidiae to know you have it would put all of you in even greater danger."

"Hannah had several safes built into this home," Gabriel said. "We could lock them up and perhaps when we are done reading them we could lock them in the holy vault."

"I think you would have to ask the Angels if such items could be put into the holy vault," the Sanuri suggested. "But I would assume that Sudfad has other places where such things could be locked away. It is up to you as to whether you want other members of your team to read these; I wanted to talk to the three of you first as a courtesy."

"And you say there is no personal information about my family?" Hannah asked.

"Not in what I have read but I will admit I have not read all of this," the Sanuri said. "I had an overwhelming feeling that I should give these texts to you."

"You are more than welcomed to come here and read them," Gabriel said. "Our home is always open to you. But I notice that these are written in different languages, most of which our team cannot read."

"Vivian might be able to read some of this and perhaps Joshua," Raphael said. "Hannah if it alright with you perhaps we can ask them to help, there is a lot of material here."

"I believe everyone on the team knows about my family," Hannah said. "It's not that I want to keep it a secret, it is just so upsetting to me to keep learning what a monster my father was. I really did love him."

"Actually only those of us who were in Nora know about your father," Gabriel said.

"Then we should tell them all; it is only fair," Hannah said. "But would you mind telling them?"

Gabriel, Raphael, Hannah and the Sanuri walked into the dining room where everyone except the children had remained. The four stood in front of the table. "The Sanuri asked us to leave the room as a courtesy to Hannah," Gabriel said as he held his wife's hand. "While the Sanuri was at the Patronus Headquarters in Nora, which was the home that Hannah grew up in, he discovered some manuscripts. While some of you understand the significance of this statement most of you do not."

Gabriel paused and looked at Hannah. "My wife believed she grew up in a loving home with two wonderful parents. On the mission in Nora when we stopped the priests from raising Omnibus; we discovered that Hannah's father Arthur Marcus was a member of the Insidiae. The papers that the Sanuri just brought us would indicate that perhaps Arthur was a very high ranking member or that he held this sensitive information to orchestrate a power play within the organization. If that was the situation then perhaps Arthur's death was not a suicide."

Raphael now spoke, "Hannah does not want to keep secrets from you although it breaks her heart to discover the man her father really was. The Sanuri brought us a great deal of information to read. The scrolls and books are written in a variety of languages. If any of you would be interested in helping us translate the texts we would welcome the help."

The following morning Sudfad again started out his meeting by calling to Miranda and Daniel. "We have decided to attack the Teivels at both Fort Polta and in Ryed," Sudfad told the Angels. "Other than it would be to our advantage to attack both sites simultaneously we have worked out little else."

"The Teivels are a great darkness in this world," Daniel said. "We will stand with you but you will not like some of what we say. Now is not the time for the attacks because Emeric and Banaka are causing such conflict in the underworlds that it is to your advantage."

"Take this time to research your opponents and to work out your strategies because this mission is different from what you have done in the past." Daniel turned to Gabriel and Raphael. "You need to intensify your research because your team has much to do before any attacks are launched. You will need to get the people of Ryed on your side before the Teivel's are attacked and you will do this with the Libertas."

"The people of Ryed have known nothing but cruel dictators, if the hearts and minds of these people are not prepared they will be easy prey for another dictator to rule them, no matter how much they say they want freedom. The Libertas must play a significant role in determining the people of power in Ryed," Miranda explained.

"The man named Asher that Thor and Diana saved, is he one of the Libertas?" Raphael asked.

"Yes," Daniel replied. "But Sudfad remember when you could trust no one but a core group of your people? That is what it is like for the Libertas always. You will have to prove your sincerity and willingness to help their cause. And you need to prove yourselves to High Priest Othnial for he knows too well the evil that surrounds his monastery."

"While I understand what you say," Raul said. "How do we prevent Commanding General Teivel from doing any further damage until the time is right to unseat him?"

"A majority of your soldiers at Fort Polta are members of the Insidiae or work for the Insidiae," Miranda said. "It would be wise for you to figure out ways to weaken those forces before you attack."

"We get them to fight with each other, or other members of the Insidiae," Simon suggested.

"That or other demons and Grand Masters," Miranda said. "Erebus figured out what Emeric and Banaka were up to. What if that information was leaked to the underworlds?"

"Could Erebus help us with that?" Gabriel asked.

"Yes," the Sanuri replied. "Sudfad did Delilah ever draw you the picture of the seal of the Insidiae?"

"Yes and I had a replica made."

"Have several more replicas made, because we are going to be causing confusion in those ranks."

Chapter XXXVI
Holiday

Over the next two weeks the majority of guests left the castle of King Sudfad and returned to their homes; except for a small contingent of Ruala warriors. These Rualas remained to help work on the mission for Ryed since Gabriel's team would be starting the mission well in advance of any other troops. With the information from the Angels that the mission against the Teivel Clan would be much greater in proportion than originally thought, it was decided that Elan, Cassandra, Emeral and Maxwell should take their trip to the Kingdom of Lentz at this time.

As preparations were being made for the trip to Lentz, Elan and Cassandra decided they could not bear to be away from Joey for several weeks. Christopher had been moping around the house since Amy returned to Lentz as had Thomas because Sasha returned to the Nordes Tribe. After almost two weeks of correspondence between Gabriel's team and their friends in Lentz, the trip that was to be a honeymoon for Elan and Cassandra took on a life of its own.

Joshua, Iris and Thomas were corresponding with Sorren and Shara. Joshua and his family were going to visit the Nordes Tribe so they could meet Sasha's family and so Thomas could propose marriage. Sorren and Shara were making arrangements for a celebration that would be a surprise for Sasha and her family. Since Joshua's two young sons and Joey were going to Lentz, Emeral and Maxwell felt guilty about leaving the other children behind and made arrangements to take all of the children to Lentz except for baby Lily.

Almost two weeks to the day that the families of Lentz had returned to their home kingdom, the majority of Gabriel's team arrived at the castle of King Mathas, where their holiday was to begin. Only Hannah, Gabriel, Natasha, Calen, Lily, Diana and Misha remained in Wetpr to finalize the mission plans. Raphael initially did not want to leave Wetpr but he realized he was now part of Joshua's family and his place was with them to celebrate Thomas' engagement.

Natasha was normally a vivacious person but now that she was working on the Teivel mission she was filled with even more life and gaiety; something that was noticed by others in the household.

Shortly after Raphael and the others crossed the border into Lentz a company of soldiers met the group and escorted them to the castle of King Mathas. Some of the team members were flying while others were on horseback. Joshua and Iris were driving a small boca which was filled with gifts for Sasha's family and items for the engagement ceremony.

It was mid-afternoon when the caravan arrived at the King's castle and they were surprised that the grounds were filled with people who were awaiting their arrival. Mathas and Rosa had prepared a feast for their guests. They had entertainment and competitions organized. Many members of the Nordes Tribe were at the castle as well as the ruling families and other citizens of the kingdom.

"We are just so happy to have you all here," Queen Rosa gushed as she hugged every one of the new guests. While the families of Mathas, Claudius, Fahron and Sorren were greeting their guests Margarit and Amy ran up to the group.

"Papa can we take them to the play area?" Margarit asked excitedly.

"Yes but keep an eye on Cerey," Mathas replied with a grin. Then Mathas turned to Raphael. "Raphael I don't believe you have met Fahron yet, although you have corresponded with him. This is Fahron, his beautiful wife Isadore and their son Chaez who has many questions of you. And this is Sally and April, soon to be the adopted daughters of Fahron and Isadore."

As soon as all of the introductions were made, Bella, Rosa, Isadore, Shara, Angelina, Nikki and Ingr all surrounded Thomas, Joshua and Iris.

"Watch out Thomas they all love weddings," Matthew yelled then laughed.

"He is right," Rosa said and giggled. "Sorren and Shara told us that Thomas wants to propose and we think that is wonderful. If you decide to have the wedding here we would all like to help you."

Thomas was clearly overwhelmed by the women. "I don't know if Sasha will say yes," he said shyly.

"That girl has done nothing but sulk since she returned home," Shara said. "Trust me she will say yes."

Angelina turned and looked at Micha, Thor, Joao, Dack, Dagon and Koby who were standing together. "And we invited lots of friends to meet the rest of you. Maybe we can have more than one marriage," Angelina said teasingly.

"You're scaring us," Dagon joked.

"Are you too scared to meet the girls?" Ingr asked.

"Never," Joao replied.

"Sorren is getting Sasha and her parents now," Shara said. "We wanted a chance to talk to you first about the wedding."

"Of course it is up to the children," Joshua said. "But I believe Thomas realizes what an honor this would be."

"Actually I don't think Thomas has been able to think about anything since Sasha left," Iris said with a warm smile. "Our family would be very honored to have you help with the wedding."

"Here they come," Nikki warned the women.

When Sasha saw Thomas she ran up to him and the two young lovers hugged. They were both too embarrassed to kiss in front of the others. Sasha turned towards her parents and said with loving pride, "Father, Mother this is Thomas, Thomas my parents Hugo and Greta." Thomas stepped forward and shook hands with Hugo. When Thomas put out his hand to shake with Greta she grabbed Thomas and hugged him. "We have heard so much about you," Greta said.

"That's because Sasha can't speak of anything else," Hugo said and laughed heartily.

"This is my father Joshua, my mother Iris, my brother Micha, my sister Vivian and her husband Raphael and I am afraid my two younger brothers are playing with the other children." After everyone greeted each other all the parents smiled as they watched how Sasha and Thomas were staring at each other.

"Why don't you two enjoy the festivities and let the rest of us get to know each other," Hugo suggested then he turned to Joshua and Iris. "Sorren and Shara have told us a great deal about you and your tribe, we are honored. For Thomas to bring his entire family on this visit should we assume it is of some importance?"

"Not to interrupt," Luca said. "But Hugo you look and sound so much like Sorren are you two related?"

Both Sorren and Hugo laughed. "Hugo's my little brother," Sorren said. "I didn't want to tell Thomas that Sasha was my niece because I was afraid it might scare him off."

"Well then our son will be marrying into a noble family," Joshua said. Which made both Greta and Hugo smile. "Thomas plans to ask Sasha while we are here. He was originally just going to come and visit so you could all get to know each other but as the days passed he realized he couldn't live without her. In our tribe any warrior who has completed the trials to become a Venator can make their own decisions without family approval. We realize that your ways are different and that you will need to give your blessing for a marriage. Thomas is planning to ask you for Sasha's hand first."

"Thomas is a brave and courageous warrior and a leader," Iris said. "But he is so in love he just can't think straight right now so please bear with him."

"Our daughter too," Hugo replied. "It was like she was a different person when she returned from Wetpr."

"Come, let us all get to know each other better," Hugo said and nodded towards the festivities.

"First," Joshua said. "Since we traveled some distance to come here, this boca is filled with gifts for your family as well as food, wine and whiskey for any celebrations. What would you like us to do with these things?"

"We really should move some of the food to a cooler spot," Iris suggested.

"Why don't you let Shara and me take care of that?" Sorren said. "While the rest of you spend some time together."

Raphael and Vivian spent the first portion of the afternoon talking with Fahron and his family. While Fahron, Isadore and Chaez spoke with Raphael about the Patronus, Sally and April had many questions for Vivian about female warriors.

Late afternoon an announcement was made that the feast was to be served in the Great Hall. Angelina and Matthew were detaining Elan and Cassandra while Claudius and Bella were detaining Maxwell and Emeral until all of the other guests had entered the Great Hall. When Elan, Cassandra, Maxwell and Emeral entered the hall they were surprised to see it decorated for a wedding.

"I hope you didn't think we forgot you are on your wedding holiday," Mathas announced and asked the four Rualas to join the Royal Family at the head table. "And we might have one or two gifts for you." Mathas pointed to a table filled with gifts. Everyone in the room laughed and applauded and Mathas said a toast to Elan and Cassandra, then the King said a second toast to family and friends.

After the meal, the guests remained in their seats as a variety of musicians and performers provided entertainment. Thomas could no longer contain himself and walked over to Sorren and asked to speak with him in private. The two men walked into the children's playroom to speak. Cerey squealed with delight when she saw Sorren and ran up to him. Sorren picked Cerey up and held her as he spoke with Thomas.

"I am sorry to take you away from the celebration," Thomas said. "I just don't want to make any mistakes."

"I want to ask Sasha's father for her hand in marriage but we don't really know each other. When do you think I should ask him?" Thomas was visibly nervous and didn't wait for Sorren to answer before he asked another question.

"I am going to give Sasha my lamsman but Raphael said I should also give her an engagement ring. He took me shopping but I couldn't make up my mind so Raphael bought two rings and said I could return one later. Of course I will pay Raphael back." Thomas pulled two small pouches from his pocket and showed both rings to Sorren who smiled broadly. "Which one do you think I should give her?"

"Perhaps you should let Sasha choose," Sorren said. "They are both beautiful."

"Can we see?" Adrone asked as some of the children were gathering around the two men.

"Don't lose them," Thomas said as he handed the rings to his little brothers.

"Thomas, Hugo and Greta know you better that you think," Sorren said with a grin. "Hugo is my brother and many of us have told him and Greta about you and your family. I think you should speak to Hugo whenever you feel the time is right. Are you afraid he will say no if you speak to him so soon?"

"Yes," Thomas said anxiously. "I have never done anything like this before and I want to do it right."

"What haven't you done before?" Christopher asked as he too was looking at the rings.

"I want to marry Sasha and I have to ask her father for permission before I can ask her to marry me."

"We'll go with you if you want," Adrone offered. Both Sorren and Thomas laughed.

"Thanks but I think I should meet with Sasha's father by myself," Thomas said.

"Give her this one," Paul said as he handed the ruby engagement ring to Thomas. "And give the other one to Mother. I heard mother tell Vivian that those green stones are her very favorite."

"I didn't know that but I am not sure that Mother would want a ring I bought for someone else," Thomas said. "Besides it will take me a while to pay Raphael for one ring." Then Thomas returned his attention to Sorren. "Why didn't you tell me you were Sasha's uncle?"

"I didn't want to scare you off son," Sorren replied. "I think you are a fine young man and I am happy that you and Sasha fell in love. Remember many of us here got to know you and your family when we all fought at each other's sides in Ryed and Ogg. Everyone from Lentz has told Hugo and Greta only good things about you. Now since Sasha is sitting with her parents would you like me to get Hugo for you?"

"Yes, if you wouldn't mind, but perhaps I should speak to him outside, away from the children."

Sorren started to leave the room then turned back to Thomas and said with a big smile, "Show Hugo both of the rings that you bought."

"Luca," Christopher said as he walked up to Luca and Lila as they were sitting at one of the tables in the Great Hall. "Luca I need to buy a ring."

"A ring!" Lila asked. "For who?"

"For Amy," Christopher said.

Luca picked Christopher up and set Christopher on his lap. "Now tell us what all of this is about," Luca said warmly.

"Thomas and Sorren were talking in the playroom. Thomas wants to marry Sasha but he has to ask her father for permission and he is kinda scared. He showed us the two rings he bought for her cuz he didn't know which one she would like."

"So you want to ask Amy to marry you?" Luca asked.

517

"Yes, but not until we are old like you," Christopher said with a smile.

"You know if you buy her a ring now it won't fit her when she is grown," Luca said. "But I will take you to get her another kind of ring that will fit her now. But you still have to ask Thaos."

"When should I ask him?" Christopher asked excitedly.

"Why don't you ask him now," Luca said with a grin. "Lila and I will come with you."

Christopher held Luca's hand as Lila, Luca and Christopher walked across the Great Hall to a long table where the family of Claudius was seated. Amy was also at the table sitting on Claudius' lap. "Please join us," said Claudius jubilantly.

"Thank you we will but Christopher wants to talk to Thaos," Luca said with a grin and winked at Claudius.

Christopher marched up to Thaos who was taking a swallow from his glass of whiskey. "Thaos I would like your permission to ask Amy to marry me when we get old," Christopher said loudly; causing Thaos to choke on his whiskey. Christopher didn't take a breath but kept talking. "Luca said if I bought an engagement ring now it wouldn't fit Amy when she is bigger but he said I could get her another kind of ring now."

Everyone at the table wanted to laugh but they didn't want to embarrass Christopher. "Christopher I don't think I have ever seen my brother speechless before," Stephan said with a smirk.

Nikki composed herself before Thaos could. "Christopher have you asked Amy to marry you?" Nikki asked.

"No, cuz Sorren told Thomas he had to ask Sasha's father first."

Thaos looked at Luca who was grinning at him. "Christopher, I will admit you took me by surprise because you both are so young but we all like you very much and think you will be a fine warrior someday."

"But people change when they grow older and you and Amy may not want to marry when you are grown up so I will make you a deal. You can give Amy a ring now if you want but it will only be for friendship and when you two are older if you both want to marry Nikki and I will approve."

Christopher turned and smiled proudly at Luca and Lila then he turned back to Thaos and jumped into his arms and hugged Thaos tightly then Christopher walked up to Nikki and hugged her also. "Christopher why don't you give Bella and Claudius a hug too," Luca suggested when he saw that Bella was crying. Christopher hugged Bella tightly which made her cry harder then Christopher climbed onto Claudius' lap to hug him.

"I have plenty of room for both of you on my lap," Claudius said to Christopher. "If you want to join us." Christopher and Amy sat next to each other and smiled.

"Are you crying too?" Stephan asked as he looked at Ingr.

"That was just the cutest thing I have ever seen," Ingr said.

"So who wants to go shopping with us tomorrow?" Luca asked with a grin as he held a chair out for Lila to sit on.

"Since you asked I would like to go," Bella said. "And I am sure that Nikki and Ingr would like to go also."

Nikki turned to Thaos who was grinning and asked, "Why don't you and Stephan come too and we can show Lila and Luca the city."

Hugo smiled as Thomas nervously asked him for Sasha's hand in marriage. Before Hugo could answer, Thomas pulled out the two engagement rings, "Sorren said I should show these to you. I couldn't decide which one to give her." Sorren had already told Hugo about his conversation with Thomas.

"Thomas you entered a hell dimension and fought alongside of my brother besides your experiences in Ogg. I know that you are a courageous warrior and a man of honor. I will be proud to call you my son."

Thomas was so anxious that he stared at Hugo, "Does that mean yes?"

"Yes my son," Hugo said and laughed then pulled Thomas to him and hugged him. "Now why don't you find my daughter? And Thomas she will want the ruby ring."

Paul and Adrone were waiting by the garden door for Thomas. "What did he say?" Adrone asked loudly while Hugo and Thomas were walking into the Great Hall.

"I said yes," Hugo said and laughed heartily.

"Which ring are you gonna give her?" Paul asked.

"Hugo said she would like the ruby ring, why?"

"We'll be back," Paul said and he and Adrone ran to the middle of the Great Hall and looked for Raphael and Vivian who were talking with Matthew and Angelina. Both boys ran up to Raphael and stared at him. Raphael was standing and grinned as he looked down at Vivian's little brothers. "Raphael can we ask you a question?" Paul asked.

"Certainly," Raphael replied as the four adults now looked at the boys.

"Sasha's father said yes," Adrone said excitedly. "And Thomas is giving her the red ring. Mother said her favorite stone is the green one. Paul and I want to pay you for it so we can give it to her."

"But it might take us a while to pay it all," Paul said as he pulled two gold coins from his pocket.

"What are you talking about?" Vivian asked her brothers.

"Raphael took Thomas shopping for a ring for Sasha," Paul explained before Raphael could speak. "Thomas couldn't decide so Raphael bough two rings and told Thomas he could take one back to the store, but Adrone and me want to buy it and give it to Mother."

520

Vivian looked at Raphael and smiled. "Why didn't you tell me?"

"Thomas asked me not to. I think he was embarrassed when he saw the prices. One is a ruby and the other an emerald," Raphael said. "The rings are already paid for; I don't know why the boys couldn't give the emerald to Iris."

"We want to pay you for it so it will be from us," Adrone said with a proud smile.

Raphael looked at Vivian and said, "I think there are enough chores around the house to pay off that ring don't you?"

"Bend down so I can kiss you," Vivian said. After Raphael and Vivian kissed she turned to her brothers. "Raphael and I would like to be with you when you give Mother the ring. Does Thomas still have it?"

"Yes, but he is asking Sasha to marry him now," Paul said. "We should wait."

"I agree," Raphael said and laughed.

"So what do you want us to do for chores?" Adrone asked.

"Well first of all, I am going to be doing the Venator training while Thor is on the next mission, you can help me with that," Vivian said. "Then you can help me paint the nursery and I am sure we can find other things."

Suddenly the music stopped and Sorren stood in the front of the Great Hall. "I want to make an announcement," Sorren yelled. "I am proud to tell you that Thomas son of Joshua and Iris and my niece Sasha, daughter of Hugo and Greta will be married. Besides the fact that they are both fine young people and brave warriors this wedding will bind the Nordes Tribe and the Clan of Gesmal from this day forward. Will the families please come forward?"

Thomas and Sasha held hands as they walked to the front of the room with their parents and stood next to Sorren and Shara. Loud applause filled the Great Hall.

Mathas joined the group in the front of the room and said to the families, "Please remain up here." Mathas turned to the room of guests and said. "Servers are bringing more wine to the tables so we can have a toast. "This is a great day for us all. Our family is one with the Nordes Tribe so we too are now united with the Clan of Gesmal."

After a series of toasts were given, Sorren turned to Thomas and Sasha and said, "Yes we are interfering," and laughed loudly. "But it would bring great joy to us all if we could celebrate your wedding while everyone is here. What do you say?"

Thomas and Sasha shyly looked at each other then at their parents. "They say yes," Greta said and everyone laughed.

As soon as Thomas, Sasha and their families joined the other guests in the Great Hall, Paul and Adrone ran up to Thomas. Raphael, Vivian and now Micha followed the small boys. Paul and Adrone had pulled Thomas away from Sasha and were whispering to him when Raphael, Vivian and Micha reached them.

"Is what they say true?" Thomas asked Raphael.

"Yes," Raphael replied.

Thomas took a pouch from his pocket and handed it to Paul. Raphael walked up to Thomas and whispered to him as Paul and Adrone showed Vivian and Micha the ring. "Raphael are you sure?" Thomas asked with surprise.

"Yes, it's only fair," Raphael said and walked up to Vivian.

"What did you tell him?" she asked.

"That he could pay off his ring in the same manner," Raphael replied.

"You are the most generous man," Vivian said with admiration and squeezed Raphael's hand.

Iris and Joshua had just sat down at their table, when all of their children including Raphael and Sasha walked up to them.

522

"This is from me and Adrone," Paul said excitedly as he handed Iris the pouch.

"Raphael said we could pay for it by doing chores," Adrone said proudly as they watched their mother take the emerald and diamond ring from the pouch. Iris got a look of shock on her face as Adrone kept talking. "Raphael bought two rings for Thomas and we wanted to give this one to you."

"I loaned Thomas the money for his engagement ring," Raphael said quickly so that Thomas would not be embarrassed. "Thomas picked out two rings and couldn't decide, so we bought them both. Paul and Adrone were adamant that they wanted to give you the emerald ring."

"Mother I hope you don't think badly because the ring was originally bought as an engagement ring," said Thomas.

"Think badly, why no," Iris said as tears filled her eyes. "This is absolutely beautiful. But I can't let you boys pay for something like this."

"We already have the chores set up," Raphael said.

"I dare say the boys may be doing chores for a very long time," Joshua said with a warm smile.

As Iris hugged and kissed Adrone and Paul, Thomas turned to Sasha and explained. "Your father told me you liked rubies after the rings were bought."

"You wouldn't even have had to give me a ring," Sasha said and kissed Thomas. "I am proud to wear your lamsman."

"Luca granted it is cute, but I don't think you should encourage Christopher," Emeral scolded the next morning after Lila and Luca asked Emeral and Maxwell to join them on their shopping trip.

"They're six and seven, what can it hurt?" Luca asked with a grin. "Besides Christopher hasn't had any nightmares since he started spending his time daydreaming about Amy."

523

"Honey I agree with Luca," Maxwell said. "And remember all of our boys got interested in girls at a young age."

"That may be what bothers me," Emeral said sarcastically.

"Please come," Lila said. "It will be fun."

"Your mother and I have an announcement to make," Sudfad said to his family and guests who were gathered around the breakfast table. Both Sudfad and Renya had bright smiles on their faces. "Renya and I are going to do something we have not done since before Raul was born. We are talking a holiday to the Ice Caves with Maxwell and Emeral."

"Good for you," Simon said before the words were even out of Sudfad's mouth.

"We are just so excited," Renya gushed.

"I guess I never realized it but you really don't ever leave Salar," Raul said. "You two deserve to take holidays, Simon and I and the girls can certainly take care of things while you are gone."

"Actually your mother and I were talking about that too," Sudfad said. "While we both plan to live long lives we must also prepare you for the roles you will someday assume. After breakfast we will be holding a family meeting and among us we will decide which of our responsibilities the four of you will now take on. Of course we will be rotating the responsibilities so that you can all learn these things."

"You should have gone to Lentz with Gabriel's team," Raul said.

"Believe me Renya and I were thinking about it. We will go at another time. And there is another matter we wanted to bring up as we talk about families," Sudfad said. "Archetenus and Delilah, while we understand how excited you are to start building your new home, we want you to know we don't want you to be in any hurry to leave."

"Trust us we know how crazy things are with twins," Annabelle said. "You really should stay here longer so we can all help you with the babies. Simon and I never would have gotten any sleep if the rest of the family hadn't helped us so."

"We really do mean this," Vitomas said.

Archetenus and Delilah looked at each other and smiled. "Just last night we were talking about how much help all of you have been," Archetenus said. "And even with all of your help sometimes it is a little overwhelming with the babies. We really appreciate your offer and may very well take you up on it."

"You have all been so kind to us," Delilah said emotionally. "You have treated us just like family and we appreciate that so."

"Luca don't spend a lot of money," Nikki said as Bella, Ingr, Nikki, Luca, Lila, Emeral, Maxwell, Christopher and Amy walked inside of a large jewelry store.

"Do you have any children's rings?" Luca asked the store clerk. "My son wants to buy his friend a ring."

The old clerk grinned when he looked down at Christopher and Amy. "I am sure I can find something, I will be right back."

"Are you bothered by this?" Stephan asked with a grin as he and Thaos walked towards the jewelry store.

"I think I am still in shock," Thaos replied. "I didn't think I would have to deal with something like this for a long time."

"They're little kids with crushes on each other," Stephan said. "You don't need to start worrying for a few years yet."

"Just wait until boys start getting interested in Sicily," Thaos said and laughed.

"Papa, Uncle Stephan look!" Amy yelled and ran up to the men as they entered the jewelry store. Amy held out her hand and showed them the gold ring with a pink stone that she was wearing.

"Amy that is really pretty," Stephan said then saw the look on Thaos' face and laughed loudly.

Chapter XXXVII
Dishonor

King Mathas as King Sudfad always invited the leaders of his guests to attend his morning meetings. On this morning Raphael, Luca and Maxwell joined the Ruling Families of Lentz. Joshua and his family were staying in the village of the Nordes Tribe with their new family. Within moments of everyone taking a seat several Enrops flew through the open window behind Mathas' desk; one bird carried a note. "This is from King Sudfad," the lead Enrop announced as Mathas took the envelope and pulled out a long letter.

"Thank you," Mathas said to the Enrops. "There is a garden in back if you are hungry."

As Mathas started to read the letter a smile took over his entire face and he walked over to the door to the study, opened it and called to his wife several times.

"Mathas is something wrong?" Rosa asked as she ran into the study.

Mathas now addressed everyone in the room. "Sudfad, Renya and the rest of Gabriel's team are coming for the wedding and expect to be here in two days."

"Really?" Rosa gasped. "This is wonderful!"

Mathas turned to the men in his study. "My sister has been home only once since she married. Sudfad says Renya is acting like a school girl because she is so excited. Sudfad says they don't want a lot of fanfare but they would like to visit the homes of Claudius, Sorren, Fahron and Isabella."

"Who is Isabella?" Luca asked.

While Stephan laughed loudly, Matthew replied, "My aunt and she is a retch of a person." Mathas gave Matthew a stern look which made Stephan laugh louder. "Well she is Father," Matthew said defensively. "We don't have to invite Isabella here do we?"

"Matthew!" Rosa scolded then turned back to Mathas and said, "Honey let me see that letter."

Mathas held his hand up for a moment as he read a few more lines then handed the letter to his wife. "Maxwell, Sudfad says that Hannah is so lost with the children gone that they will probably take Nicholas and Cerey home with them."

"I don't think that surprises any of us," Raphael said.

"You know that Gabriel is the same way but he just won't admit it," Luca said with a grin.

"Well, I hope they don't get angry," Mathas said as he continued to smile. "But we are going to have a bit of fanfare."

"Renya you can't stop smiling," Natasha said as she was seated in the royal carriage with Lily, Renya and Hannah.

"I know, I am sorry to be acting like this but I am just so excited. The last time I went home for a visit Raul was almost a year old. I grew up in the castle Mathas and Rosa live in. There are still a lot of things of our parents in that castle, oh I know I am being sentimental." Renya now looked out of the side window of the carriage so Hannah and Natasha wouldn't see the tears in her eyes.

"Renya don't apologize, it is understandable," Hannah said. "I'm glad we can be with you."

"So am I," Renya said as she continued to look out of the window. "Does Diana know she can ride in here with us?" Renya asked as she watched Diana riding on a horse beside the carriage.

"You know what a warrior she is," Natasha explained. "She and Thor came here to protect you and Sudfad and she still feels that is her duty."

Renya smiled, "We have a small army travelling with us, besides the Rualas flying overhead."

"And she is a Venator with a strong sense of responsibility," Natasha replied.

"I like her," Renya said as she turned to Hannah and Natasha. "Don't get me wrong because I have always liked Misha but has he changed since he married?" Both Natasha and Hannah laughed loudly.

"I came as soon as I got your message," Sorren said as he entered Mathas' study, where the King was alone sitting at his desk.

"Did Shara come?" Mathas asked.

"No, as soon as I told her Sudfad and Renya were going to visit us she went crazy," Sorren said with a hearty laugh. "When I left she was gathering all of the women in the village for a meeting."

"Claudius and Fahron should be here soon, they went home to get their wives. I wanted us all to sit down and work out a schedule for the visit. Renya hasn't been home since Raul was a baby so we are just so very excited."

"And I feel it is a great honor for my people to have them visit our village," Sorren said. "Since they are both warriors I was thinking about having some of the competitions that my people use for training."

"Knowing Sudfad and Renya they will want to take part, so you should have extra weapons for them," Mathas said as he leaned back into his chair. "Sudfad said they didn't want a lot of fanfare but I want to do something special."

Claudius walked into the study and poured himself a cup of coffee, "Bella is here, she is talking to Rosa."

"Is she acting crazy too?" Sorren asked with a grin.

Claudius laughed loudly, "I thought she was going to faint when I told her. I am just glad I went home and told her in person."

"I have a feeling none of us are going to get any sleep until Sudfad and Renya get here," Sorren said and laughed again.

The next two days went quickly for the ruling families of Lentz although they seemed to drag on for Renya, who was anxious to go home. A couple of days before their arrival in Lentz, Hannah had slipped a note to Gabriel who in turn sent it to Mathas via Enrops. Mathas and Rosa were happy to get the information and immediately made a few changes to their plans.

A company of soldiers wearing their dress uniforms met Sudfad's caravan at the border and escorted them to the castle of King Mathas. Tears ran down Renya's cheeks as they traveled towards the castle; she pointed out many sites and places to Hannah and Natasha. The sounds of trumpets carried far in the cool morning air as they approached the castle of the King of Lentz. "I can't believe that I am nervous," Renya gasped and Hannah put her arm around Renya and kissed the Queen on the cheek.

As soon as the caravan rode through the gates of the wall that surrounded Mathas' castle they found the roadway lined with both people and flowers. "Why are they cheering us?" Renya asked.

"You were once their princess," Hannah said. "And I see a lot of Nordes tribesman in the crowd also."

Sudfad was riding in the lead of the caravan which stopped in front of the castle where the ruling families as well as Sorren's family were waiting. Sudfad shook his head and smiled when he dismounted. "I said no fanfare," Sudfad said as he hugged Mathas. Gabriel helped the Queen out of the carriage and escorted her to the King then Gabriel returned to the carriage for Hannah and Natasha.

"Where is Petra?" Rosa asked as Sudfad's party was going through the receiving line.

"Gabriel gave him a pouch of gold to take care of their dog," Sudfad said and laughed. "Knowing Petra they will never get their dog back."

Gabriel and Hannah could hear the children calling to them as they walked through the receiving line. Emeral and Maxwell were standing at the end of the line with Nicholas, Cerey, Christopher and Joey.

Both Gabriel and Hannah maintained professional demeanors until they got to their children; they hugged and kissed all four of the children over and over.

Maxwell and Emeral were the only two members of Gabriel's team who were in the receiving line, everyone else was inside of the castle finishing preparations. "Oh I hope they like this," Lila said anxiously.

"They will love it," Luca said and put his arm around Lila's shoulder. "Is everyone ready to go outside?"

"Wait," Cassandra yelled as she and Elan carried a gift into the Great Hall. "This is the last one."

"They are going to need a boca to take all of this stuff home," Dack said as he and Joao arranged some of the gifts.

"Come on," Luca called and they all hurried to the receiving line on the front lawn of the castle.

After everyone was through the receiving line Mathas and Rosa led all of their guests into the Great Hall which was set up for a feast. As soon as everyone was in the room Mathas turned to the group. "Before the meal is served we have some things to present to Renya and Sudfad so you may want to remain standing." A portion of the room was obscured by thick red drapes which Dagon and Koby now pulled open. Renya gasped and took Sudfad's hand.

"Hannah sent us a note," Mathas explained loudly. "Saying that Renya was sentimental and if we were considering a gift we might want to give her a family memento. Well, Rosa took everyone through storage rooms that we had forgotten about and as you can see we found a variety of things from the history of our family." Renya started to cry as she and Sudfad walked towards the display of furniture, toys, clothing and paintings.

"Sudfad these are my old toys," Renya gasped as she lovingly picked up a doll. "And my bed when I was little."

"We have extra bocas for you to take these things home," Mathas said with a laugh as Sudfad and Renya walked through the history of her family.

"You mean we can take these things?" Renya turned and asked.

"Of course," Mathas said.

"Oh this is so wonderful," Renya said as she cried. Everyone in the room was touched by Renya's reaction since she was always doing so much for others.

"Aunt Renya the girls made you something too," Matthew said.

Angelina walked up to a table and motioned for others to join her. "Renya this was so much fun for all of us as we discovered these things. Then Lila and Cassandra suggested we make a book for you like they did for Maxwell and Emeral; Ingr, Nikki and Melinda helped us." Angelina lifted a cloth from a large leather bound book. "We hope you like it."

Renya's hand was shaking as she opened the book and saw a letter from her father to her mother. Renya started to cry again and tightly hugged Angelina, Cassandra, Lila, Melinda, Ingr and Nikki.

"Get your hands off from me!" Nada screamed to the two Ruala warriors who were presenting her before the Grand Council of the Ruala and Shettee peoples. Nada had been locked in a cage since her return to the Ice Caves. No one had visited Nada during the time of her incarceration nor did anyone tell her that the Grand Council was investigating the allegations that Diana brought to light.

The Ruala warriors who were in attendance at Sudfad's castle when Diana and Misha exposed Nada; had immediately told their friends and families about Nada upon their return to the Ice Caves. Now this day that Nada was brought before the Grand Council; huge crowds of Rualas and Shettees filled the Hall of Light as well as the immediate area around the building. "Misha and his tramp of a wife are liars!" Nada screamed.

"Nada let King Manu speak," Thedes said sternly. The tone of Thedes' voice scared Nada.

As soon as the King started to speak the crowds became silent. "Nada as you know you are being held because of the allegations that your son Misha and his wife Diana made against you."

"They are stinking liars," Nada yelled as she tried to pull away from the two warriors who held her arms.

"Nada if you do not allow the King to speak you will be gaged," Thedes warned.

King Manu waited until Nada calmed herself down before he spoke again. "Nada the allegations against you were so horrendous that many of us did not want to believe them. While we were still in Wetpr I started an investigation into the matter. The reason I started it while we were in Wetpr was so I could hold Misha and his wife accountable if we discovered the allegations were false."

"What we found was that both Misha and his wife Diana are held in high regard as honorable warriors. King Sudfad and his family as well as King Mathas and his family were but a few who we spoke to."

Manu stared coldly at Nada as he spoke, "Upon our return to the Ice Caves we have spoken with all of your children as well as many, many other Rualas. The information we received disgusts me as well as breaks my heart."

"How anyone could abuse children as you did much less their own flesh and blood is quite literally beyond my comprehension. Never in the history of our people have we heard of such things and this council will make sure that this diabolical behavior never again darkens our peoples."

The members of the Grand Council were sitting around a horseshoe shaped table with Nada and her two guards standing in the middle. King Manu now stood up. "Nada from this day forward you are no longer a member of the Ruala Tribe. You have brought such shame and darkness upon us all. You will be cast out of the Ice Caves never to return. You will no longer wear the robe and trappings of a Ruala warrior. You will leave here with nothing, no weapons, jewels or money."

"But where will I go?" Nada asked in astonishment for no member of the Ruala Tribe had ever before been banned from their people or the Ice Caves.

"You must have some demon in you to have committed the crimes that you did," Manu replied. "Perhaps you can find a home among them."

Nada was suddenly filled with rage and again struggled against the two warriors who restrained her. "You can't kick me out of my home," she screamed.

"The Sanuri has already prohibited your entrance into the caves," Manu said. "Ibula and several other female warriors will now strip you of your warrior's robe and you will be removed from the Ice Caves. Two female warriors now replaced the two male warriors who had been restraining Nada. Six more female warriors now circled Nada and spread their wings so that none could look upon her.

Ibula removed Nada's sword and knife sheaths that were empty and handed them to a female warrior who now walked around the outer circle of female warriors and showed the crowd what she was holding. This warrior then placed the sheaths on the table of the Grand Council. The same was done with Nada's golden belt, golden sandals and white robe. Ibula would not allow Nada to put on the pants and shirt that had been brought from Nada's house. The female warriors dressed Nada then moved so the crowd could witness Nada's disgrace.

"Nada as dark as your heart is I am sure you will plan some type of revenge," King Manu said then he looked at the crowd. "By order of the Grand Council; any Ruala or Shettee warrior will kill you on sight if you pose any kind of threat to our peoples or the humans we protect." Manu paused then in a voice of great authority he loudly ordered, "Cast this demon from our home."

Two Ruala warriors dragged Nada from the Hall of Light, then flew with her to the entrance to the Ice Caves. The crowd followed. Rualas carried their Shettee brothers and sisters as they flew solemnly through the beauty of the Ice Caves. The two warriors threw Nada into the world outside of the Ice Caves and the entrance immediately closed to her. Nada screamed and pounded on the rock wall that contained the secret entrance to this magical world. But the entrance would never again open to her.

The investigation that King Manu had ordered revealed the names of the men who Nada allowed to molest and torture her children. There had been three men, one of whom was killed in battle. Unknown to Nada the other two men had also been incarcerated and now individually they were brought before the Grand Council to receive a similar fate.

The emotional start of this day for Renya turned into a day of great levity. Mathas and Rosa had many activities organized and as another surprise for Renya, Rosa invited many of Renya's old friends and childhood playmates to the castle.

Since Sudfad and Renya were staying at the castle of Mathas and Rosa, it had been decided that the wedding of Thomas and Sasha would be held at the castle of Claudius and Bella. The particular honors being bestowed on this young couple was because their marriage was uniting the Nordes Tribe and the Clan of Gesmal. But three days of feasts, entertainment and competitions were being held at the village of Sorren and Shara.

All of the events that were planned for the visit of Sudfad and Renya and the wedding of Thomas and Sasha did not overshadow the fact that Elan and Cassandra were on their wedding trip. The ruling families as well as the Nordes Tribe had special activities and events to celebrate the wedding of the young Ruala couple.

King Manu in his wisdom, did not trust Nada and immediately after the trials Manu sent a group of Ruala warriors to Wetpr to tell Misha and his family about Nada and the two men who were banished from the tribe. The group of eight Ruala warriors were led by Ratri an old friend of Misha's and his brothers. Ratri had also worked on numerous missions with Gabriel's team and knew the team members well. In addition to warning Misha, Ratri was told to tell King Sudfad and his family about the trials.

Three days after the arrival of King Sudfad and Queen Renya to Lentz and the day before the wedding of Thomas and Sasha eight Ruala warriors landed on the front courtyard of the castle of King Mathas. The soldiers stationed at Mathas' castle were now accustomed to seeing Ruala warriors and simply led the men to Mathas' study where the morning meeting was just ending.

Maxwell, Calen, Luca and Misha were among the men who attended the Kings' meeting on this morning and they were quite surprised when a soldier led the eight Ruala warriors into the study. "Is something wrong?" Maxwell immediately asked.

"We have messages for Misha and Sudfad," Ratri explained. "I am not sure if they want everyone to hear this information."

"Is it about Nada?" Misha asked.

"Most of it," Ratri replied.

"You can tell us all," Misha said as he feared the news would affect the security of others. "But first let me introduce you."

After the introductions, the eight Ruala warriors remained standing and Ratri spoke to the group. "Misha after Diana made those accusations about Nada the Grand Council did an investigation as they have never done before. People from Wetpr and Lentz were asked about you and Diana and perhaps hundreds of Rualas, including your brothers and sisters were asked about the allegations. As it should be; no one could say anything about you or Diana that would darken your reputations."

Ratri paused and looked uncomfortable. "But the things they found out about Nada shocked our tribe. The truth was greatly worse than the allegations. So the Grand Council took actions which never before have been done in our tribe. Nada, Morgan and Bruno had trials that were witnessed by hundreds."

"They were stripped of their warrior robes and weapons and thrown out of the Ice Caves with only the clothes on their backs. They have no weapons or money. They have been banished from our tribe for the remainder of their lives and the Sanuri has made it so they can no longer enter the Ice Caves."

Ratri had been addressing the group of men in Mathas' study in an official manner, now his voice softened and he spoke to Misha, "Misha you should know there were many, many more victims than you may have been aware of. I do not know all of the results of the investigations but it appears that Nada, Morgan and Bruno have never stopped their attacks upon others. How so many people could have been attacked without saying anything is beyond my comprehension."

535

"Shame," Misha said in almost a whisper. "They did not speak out because of shame and fear."

After Misha's answer Ratri paused for a few moments before continuing. "Many members of the Grand Council fear that at least Nada may act in retribution for exposing the monster that she is. Nada knows that all of the people from Wetpr and Lentz stood behind you and Diana," Ratri said as he looked again at Misha. "So that is why we were also told to warn Sudfad. In addition, the Grand Council called Charles and Tina before them, they were not banished but publically humiliated for their behavior in Wetpr and their treatment of their children."

"Sudfad, you should know that we stopped at your castle first and told Raul and Simon what we are telling you now," Ratri added.

Misha sat in silence so Maxwell stood up and addressed the group. "The actions of the Grand Council for both Nada and her boyfriends and Charles and Tina have never before been done by our people. It shows how seriously they take these crimes against our children. While I commend the Grand Council for their actions I too fear retribution. Without weapons and money Nada, Morgan and Bruno will be desperate and as dark as their souls are I would assume they will become criminals in this world."

"If you will excuse me I need to tell Diana," Misha said as he stood up.

"We need to tell Cassandra and the others also," Luca said as he and Calen both stood up.

As his sons left the room Maxwell looked at Ratri, "Have you eaten?"

"We are hungry," Ratri said. "We wanted to get the messages to everyone as soon as possible."

"Matthew will you make arrangements for rooms and meals for these men?" King Mathas asked his son then he turned to the Rualas. "We are having a week of celebrations and a wedding tomorrow you are more than welcome to stay and celebrate with us."

536

Diana was on a morning ride with Vivian and Thor when Misha found them. His face was pale and drawn as he told them about the trials in the Ice Caves and the fears of members of the Grand Council that Nada, Morgan and Bruno would seek revenge. "Diana I want you to be careful," Misha said. "You are the one that Nada would come after."

"Misha she will come after you also," Vivian said. "I can't imagine viewing my mother as an adversary but that is what you will have to do. Don't let your emotions weaken you because I don't believe Nada has any compassion."

"I'll do what I have to do," Misha said almost in a whisper then he looked at Thor and Vivian. "Watch over Diana."

"Always do," Thor replied. Misha kissed Diana and flew back to the castle.

Diana looked at Thor and Vivian as anger filled her being. "It's Misha we have to watch out for. He is such a huge, strong man and such a vicious warrior and yet when he was around Nada, oh I don't even know how to explain it," Diana said with frustration. "It was almost like he turned back into that tortured little boy. I don't know if he would defend himself from her. I need both of you to help me watch over him."

"No one should be put into a position where they have to kill a parent," Thor said. "Vivian and I will watch over both of you."

"Are you going to say anything to his brothers?" Vivian asked.

"I don't know, Misha might get really mad."

"Well, you should tell Emeral and Maxwell what you told us," Thor advised.

Tina, mother of Melinda, Cassandra and Joao, had spent her life trying to be held in high esteem by others. Her desire for status among her people was only overshadowed by her driven desire for riches and the power that comes with wealth. Tina was a beautiful woman who learned at a very early age how to use her looks to her advantage.

Tina was a fortunate woman in that her beauty did not seem to fade with age. Her husband Charles, on the other hand had lost the handsomeness and physical strength of his youth.

There were those who believed that Tina and Charles were not in love because of the ways they spoke and treated each other. But these people were wrong. Tina and Charles were so similar in personalities that they often clashed. Although they were self-absorbed, selfish people they did love each other very much. In fact they had so much love for each other that there was little love left for anyone else, including their children.

Charles and Tina were both horrified and frightened when they were ordered to appear before the Grand Council. Their fears were intensified because the three Rualas who had appeared before the Grand Council on that same day had been banished from the Ice Caves. Tina and Charles were brought before the council together; they were not bound as Nada, Morgan and Bruno had been. The Hall of Light was still filled with the people who had witnessed the trials and were curious as to why Charles and Tina were now being judged.

Thedes and Ibula acted as the representatives of the Royal Family of Wetpr and the members of Gabriel's team. It was Thedes and Ibula who originally brought complaints against Charles and Tina to the Grand Council but once the door was opened many others also came to the council with complaints about this couple.

Thedes and Ibula told the Grand Council and the large crowd of the ways that Charles and Tina treated their own children. Ibula described Tina's strong belief in something Tina called 'pure blood' and Tina's letters to her children in which she threatened the lives of her children and Joey.

Thedes then talked about Gabriel's team and how these battle savvy men and women sought to protect, Cassandra, Elan, Joao and Joey from Tina and Charles. Thedes talked about members of Gabriel's team taking Melinda from the house of Tina and Charles because they were concerned for Melinda's safety.

Ibula again took the floor and talked about Tina's and Charles' characters and actions of their past that they took for power and money. Once the Grand Council and the crowd had an understanding of Tina and Charles and their motivations.

538

Thedes spoke and detailed Tina's and Charles encounter with the King and Queen of Wetpr which resulted in Tina and Charles being banned from that kingdom. "As a father of three sons, two of whom are adopted and as a member of the Grand Council it brings me great shame to tell you what many of us witnessed next," Thedes continued.

"Tina was screaming threats and obscenities as Wetprian soldiers dragged her and Charles from the castle. And their own children ran to the arms of King Sudfad and Queen Renya and said for all to hear, that no one had ever stood up for them before. While it is inconceivable to most of us that anyone could hurt their own child; I believe we have learned today that we must do a better job of protecting our children."

Tina was starting to speak when Charles turned and said angrily, "Tina just keep your damn mouth shut before you get us in more trouble. Charles words were overheard by many in the room.

King Manu stood up and addressed Tina and Charles. "I have been told by many that King Sudfad told the two of you that he saw a darkness in you that he has never before seen in a member of our tribe. And Sudfad said he recognized this darkness because he has seen it in his world; a world where demons walk freely. I speak for myself as well as the Grand Council when I say that we see that same darkness in both of you. This will be your first as well as your final warning; if you are brought before the Grand Council again you will be banished from the Ice Caves."

Both Charles and Tina stared at King Manu and the other members of the Grand Council with horror. "In addition you are stripped of all honors that you possess. Your words no longer have any value for the members of the Ruala and Shettee tribes so you no longer have any say in the matters of our tribes. You have brought great dishonor upon us and you would be wise to change your ways," King Manu said then he looked at the Ruala warriors who were standing behind Tina and Charles. "Take them from our sight," Manu ordered.

"Emeral are you alright?" Maxwell asked as he walked into the chambers he and Emeral shared in the castle of King Mathas.

"Yes dear, Diana wanted to meet with us in private," Emeral said. Diana and Emeral were seated in the small parlor of the chambers.

"Is this about Nada and the trials?" Maxwell asked as he sat down in one of the overstuffed chairs near the hearth.

"Yes," Diana replied. "The reason I wanted to meet with you in private is that I do not want to bring dishonor to Misha but there is something that concerns me greatly. I was with Misha when he encountered Nada and you will think me crazy but I watched him transform before my eyes. That woman is poison to him."

"What do you mean he transformed?" Maxwell asked with concern.

"It's hard to explain," Diana said. "But we all know Misha for the strong man and courageous warrior he is but when he saw Nada," Diana paused. "It was like he became that little boy again. And the reason I tell you this is for all the pain she caused him, it is like Nada has some kind of hold on Misha. I am afraid that if she tries to hurt him, he will not defend himself or at least not well. I was with Thor and Vivian when Misha told us about the trials and I told them my concerns. They will tell no one else, but they will help me watch out for him."

"Nada brought such terror into Misha's life when he was a child that perhaps that is the response she ignites in him," Emeral said. "I am glad you told us."

"I didn't tell his brothers because you know how they all tease each other," Diana explained. "But I don't think this is something they should tease Misha about."

"We agree," Maxwell said. "But Diana you should know that after that competition where you exposed Nada, every one of our boys came to us to talk about Misha. They were horrified to find out what had happened to him. I do think they will use good judgment when it comes to teasing him about this matter."

"So does that mean you are going to tell them?" Diana asked.

"Not at this time," Maxwell replied. "But if Misha is truly threatened by Nada and those men we may have to tell his brothers."

"Diana you do understand that she will probably come after you, don't you?" Emeral asked.

"It may sound awful for me to say this but I hope she does. I see her as any other monster I would kill."

Charles and Tina were now shunned by many of the members of their tribe. Filled with anger and humiliation they strategized their next moves. They had heard the stories about how honored Rualas were by the people of Nora. In addition Tina and Charles had heard about all of the gifts the people of Nora bestowed upon the Ruala warriors who saved their city from the Hutas; gifts which included land and money.

In the middle of the night, Charles and Tina flew out of their beloved Ice Caves to start new lives in the City of Nora, the city of gold. They told no one of their plans they simply left their tribe.

"Sudfad owns Nora," Tina said as they flew across the Safer Mountain Range. "What if he finds out we are living there?"

"Really Tina, how will he find out?" Charles asked with disgust.

Chapter XXXVIII
Predators

Morgan and Bruno were together the evening that their tribesmen took them into custody and both men had already heard that Nada was in trouble. But Nada did not know that Morgan and Bruno were also going to trial until she overheard someone say it as she was being escorted from the Ice Caves. After Nada tried unsuccessfully to enter the Ice Caves she sat on a cliff waiting to see if Morgan and Bruno would be expelled also.

Within an hour Morgan was thrown out of the Ice Caves. Nada called to him and they both decided to wait and see if Bruno would be banished too. Bruno was a man with a quick temper, he fought the other Rualas when they stripped him of his warrior's robe and he cursed at and threatened the members of the Grand Council as he was being dragged from the building. Nada and Morgan laughed as they watched Bruno kick and pound on the rock wall that concealed the entrance from him.

"We've been waiting for you," Morgan called.

Bruno's rage gave him such tunnel vision that he did not realize his two friends were sitting on a cliff just feet away from him. Bruno turned and stared at Morgan and Nada angrily then all three of them burst into laughter. While all three of these Rualas were angry and horrified to be turned away from their tribe, at least they had each other and were not alone.

"Right now we need to focus on getting some weapons and money," Morgan said. "And there is a storm coming; without our robes to protect us we can't fly in that so we need shelter; we can worry about the other things later."

While the Ice Caves ran throughout the Safer Mountain Range, there was but one opening and that was located near Mount Petrov. From this opening the Kingdom of Norkv lay to the south and the Kingdom of Ganz to the North. Norkv was a poor kingdom, the original home of the Rualas that was often overrun with Hutas. Morgan, Bruno and Nada decided to travel north. Just fifteen miles northwest from the base of the Safer Mountain Range was the small Village of Czar. The three decided to take shelter near this village; they knew they were going to have to steal what they needed.

Rualas were a tall, muscular race of people; but Bruno was considerably larger than most Rualas in both height and build. He was a savage fighter with a mean constitution; he liked to fight and he liked to push others around. Bruno had short dark hair and brown eyes, his body was covered with scars from battle; scars which he wore proudly.

Morgan was a fighter also but his temperament was easy-going. He and Bruno had been friends since childhood and their differences in personality traits formed a unique balance for them. Morgan strategized situations while Bruno was reactionary. Morgan was shorter than Bruno with light brown hair and blue eyes. Unlike Bruno, Morgan did not look dangerous; Morgan looked very mundane, a trait that helped him in enticing his victims.

Nada was a beautiful woman with long white-blonde hair and blue eyes which were inherited by all of her children. Nada married her childhood sweetheart Adwell at a very young age; they had baby after baby which overwhelmed them both.

Adwell, the father of Misha, was a good man who died in battle with the Hutas. Adwell was a strong man who had always taken care of Nada. When Adwell died Nada realized she was not equipped to provide for ten children. She was filled with both grief and fear for the first few months after Adwell's death.

After only a few months Nada realized she was experiencing something she had never felt before, a sense of freedom. Nada was filled with the wild desires of youth. Desires other young Rualas acted on when Nada was home having babies. As these desires grew within her, Nada resented her children more and more and felt that they prevented her from having a wonderful life. As this darkness grew in Nada's heart she listened more often to her personal demons until they were the only voices that she heard.

Within six months after Adwell's death Nada had a string of boyfriends, the attention of men thrilled her. She wanted to experience all of the things she felt she had missed in her youth. Unlike many, Nada never learned from her mistakes. In fact, Nada never wanted to learn any lessons; she only wanted thrills; thrills that were being driven by her unholy appetite.

Nada's desire for thrills quickly turned into sadistic cravings. She soon became addicted to these cravings and needed more and more to get the same heightened sense of exhilaration. It was Nada's sadistic cravings that brought her to Bruno and Morgan for the three shared the same dark desires. From their first encounter, Nada, Bruno and Morgan became lovers. They turned every type of sexual adventure into a form that would fulfill their sadistic desires. Many of the adults and children who joined the three in their bed, did so unwillingly; which only increased the satisfaction for Nada and her two lovers.

Diana had barely walked out of the chambers of Maxwell and Emeral when there was another knock on the door. Maxwell opened the door and saw Elan, Cassandra, Melinda, Joao and Dack standing in the hallway; both Cassandra and Melinda looked as if they had been crying.

"Did you hear about our parents?" Joao asked when Maxwell opened the door.

"Yes, come in," Maxwell said. "You all look like you could use a drink."

"I think we could," Elan replied as he held Cassandra's hand.

"Oh my," Emeral said and hugged every one of their visitors. "Please have a seat. Where is Joey?"

"Hannah has him," Elan said. "We didn't want to upset him."

"I think that was a wise decision," Maxwell said as he handed everyone a glass of wine.

"Maxwell told me what Ratri said," Emeral explained as the young Rualas all took seats in the parlor. "How do you feel about what happened?"

"Shocked," Cassandra replied.

"Personally I think it was a good thing," Dack said. "But they aren't my parents."

"I think we all feel relieved, embarrassed and afraid," Melinda said.

544

"I'm not sure afraid is the right word," Joao said indignantly. "We will have to watch out for their retribution."

"Charles and Tina are not allowed to return to Wetpr," Maxwell reminded Joao. "And after what happened I doubt if anyone from the Ice Caves would work on their behalf. I don't think there is any way they can hurt you."

"Maxwell is right," Cassandra said as she wiped the tears from her cheeks.

"I don't know if we told you but Diana threatened to return to the Ice Caves and hurt Tina if she sent us anymore hateful letters and Tina hasn't written anything since," Elan said hopefully. "Maybe we are free of them now."

"I believe you are," Emeral said soothingly. "But it must still hurt because they are your parents."

"It's strange I feel happy and sad at the same time," Cassandra said. "But now I don't feel like I have to be afraid they will come after Joey."

After the morning meeting, most of the guests of King Mathas and the ruling families traveled to Sorren's village for a day of competitions and a feast. All four of Misha's adopted brothers dragged him to the village and persuaded him to participate in the games. While Vivian, Diana and Thor went to the castle of Claudius to help Bella, Greta and Iris with the wedding preparations.

Calen, Luca, Dagon and Koby decided among themselves that at least one of them would stay close to Misha at all times; they did not share this information with Misha. Only Natasha and Lila knew what the brothers were doing and both women agreed with their husbands. Natasha and Lila were both independent enough that they did not need their husbands constantly at their sides at the festivities.

Shara was beside herself with the anticipation that King Sudfad and Queen Renya would be visiting her home after the morning meeting. To the surprise of many Sudfad and Renya rode into the Village of Tyger with no fanfare. Both the King and Queen were on horseback wearing clothing appropriate for the competitions.

Sorren was filled with pride when he saw Sudfad and Renya riding down the main street of his village and immediately greeted his friends. "Shara is going crazy," Sorren said with a laugh as he led Sudfad and Renya into his home.

"Well I certainly hope she didn't go to any trouble," Renya said. "She already has her hands full with preparations for the wedding."

"Something smells really good," Sudfad commented as they walked through the front door of Sorren's house.

"Shara our guests are here," Sorren called then laughed when he could hear commotion in the kitchen.

Shara ran out of the kitchen still wearing her apron and hugged both Renya and Sudfad. "I am so glad you could come. Are you hungry?"

"I wasn't until I smelled whatever that is you are cooking," Sudfad said with a smile.

"Shara is a great cook," Sorren said with pride. "Please have a seat."

Sudfad was carrying a set of saddlebags and Sorren carried the pouch that Renya had been holding. "We brought a few gifts," Renya said.

"I know it is early but let's have a drink," Sorren offered joyfully.

"Wait," Sudfad said as he opened one of the saddlebags. "Mathas went through his wine cellar and sent some bottles of his finest whiskey and wine for you. He thought you might want to toast the wedding but I grabbed a couple of extra bottles in case we wanted to make a toast now." Sorren laughed.

"Shara I bought a couple of things and now tell me if you don't like them," Renya said as she started to pull items from her large pouch. Rosa took me shopping in Langer and I found the most wonderful things. What great markets and stores in that city."

"I know your dresses for the wedding will be light pink, so I got some shawls for you and Greta but I found so many beautiful ones that I couldn't make up my mind, so I bought both of you several of them."

"What!" Shara said as Renya handed her a stack of beautifully colored silk shawls.

"And look at these I have never seen such things, I bought every set the man had; to give as gifts," Renya said excitedly as she handed Shara a pouch that contained a pearl necklace and earrings. "They are a light pink," Renya continued.

"I may be borrowing an extra boca from Mathas to take home all of the things that Renya bought," Sudfad joked.

"Bella told us that the men will be wearing suits instead of the warriors clothing," Renya continued. "So Sorren I picked these up for you." Renya handed Sorren two pouches.

"She couldn't decide which she liked best," Sudfad said as Sorren emptied the contents of both pouches on top of the table.

"Renya really you shouldn't have gotten us so much," Sorren said as he looked at the two sets of gold and jeweled cufflinks and tie bars.

"Seriously Sorren if you don't like them I will get you something else," Renya said.

"These are beautiful," Shara said as she looked at her husband's gifts. "But really this is too much."

"You and Sorren bring us gifts every time you visit," said Renya. "It is not too much."

"After we eat I was wondering if you would like to take a ride and see some of our lands," Sorren said. "Or would you rather join the competitions now?"

"I think we would like to see your lands," Sudfad replied. "Matthew and Angelina have told us so much about your villages and lands that we are eager to see everything."

Although Ratri and the seven Ruala warriors that he led were exhausted they decided to go to the Village of Tyger and join the festivities. Ratri was a handsome young man, with dark brown curly hair and blue eyes. He had grown up playing with Misha and his brothers and felt a strong bond to their family. Ratri had volunteered to go to Wetpr and Lentz to warn Misha and the others although giving Misha the message saddened Ratri's heart.

There was so much more that Ratri could have told Misha about the trials but the words would not come from his mouth. Ratri was trying to decide if he should tell Misha's brothers or Maxwell and Emeral before he and the others returned to the Ice Caves. The Rualas received a warm welcome when they landed in the Village of Tyger; Matthew and Angelina acted as their tour guides and introduced the Rualas to everyone they met.

"Well, all the girls now realize there are eight new warriors in the village," Matthew said with a laugh as he saw the attention the Rualas were getting.

As Matthew spoke, Angelina winked at Ratri. "We have many beautiful women in this tribe," Angelina said with a grin. "If any of you would like me to make introductions just say so." The Rualas all laughed.

"Maybe we will join a few competitions," Ratri said.

In the few days following their expulsion from the Ice Caves, Morgan, Bruno and Nada terrorized the small Village of Czar. The villagers had never before thought of the Rualas as their enemies so they welcomed the three with open arms. The villagers of Czar were a poor people but the three rogue Rualas were without compassion.

Nada, Bruno and Morgan took what they wanted from the people of Czar. The terrorized looks of many of the victims only ignited the sadistic lust within their attackers. For the first time in their lives, Bruno, Morgan and Nada felt they could do anything; they were no longer bound by laws and oaths. There was no one to stop them and they showed no mercy.

"You could come and join us instead of just standing there staring at the girls," Dagon said with a grin as he walked up to Ratri.

"I'm staring at one girl," Ratri said with half a laugh and shook hands with Dagon.

"Which one," Dagon asked as both men faced the line where several members of Gabriel's team were standing with a group of Nordes female warriors.

"The one with the blue features in her hair, she is talking with Dack."

"That's Batina, do you want me to introduce you?" Dagon asked. "She's really nice and funny." Dagon changed his tone of voice as he teased Ratri. "And she is single."

"How do you know so much about her?" Ratri asked as he blushed.

"Diana became good friends with Angelina, Ingr and Nikki on a mission. Diana is always looking for a girl for Thor and jokingly asked Angelina and the others to bring some single women to Elan and Cassandra's wedding. Well they bring eight Nordes warriors to the wedding and everyone of them is gorgeous."

"They weren't looking for husbands just some fun. But after Sorren finds out how short handed we are for our next mission he tells Gabriel and Raphael to talk to the girls. They all volunteered but only four made the cut and now they are too scared to even hold hands with any of us," Dagon said and laughed.

"Why? What did you tell them?"

"Have you met Thomas and Sasha yet?"

"I already knew Thomas and I just met Sasha."

"Well, they fell in love hard and fast. Neither of them can think straight; they are both so distracted that they can't come on the mission and the other girls are afraid of something like that happening to them."

"That's interesting," Ratri said. "So who made the cut?"

"Batina, Bianca that's the girl with Micha, I think they are kind of sweet on each other. Darla, she's competing against Koby and Jasmine, she's the girl with the pink ribbons in her hair talking to Joao. Come on I will introduce you."

"First, are any of you interested in Batina? I don't want to step on any toes?"

"I think a lot of the guys are kind of interested in her but nothing more than that. You have to understand the reason most of the girls didn't make the cut was because they were jealous or playing games with the guys. And this was an eye opener for the younger men on our team too. Gabriel and Raphael don't care who we date, they didn't want issues on the misson and we all agreed. In fact they let us help choose who came because this is going to be a bad one."

"So tell me about this mission," Ratri said.

"Thaos I'll hold Titus if you want to compete," Lila offered. "I'm just watching the children anyways."

"Are you sure?" Thaos asked as he really wanted to join the competitions.

"You had Christopher all yesterday, you know we could take turns watching the children. Here give him to me; you look like you really want to play."

"Where's Luca?" Thaos asked as he handed Titus to her.

"With Misha, everyone's worried about him. But they don't want to make him feel embarrassed. I don't know the details but Diana and Emeral do and they couldn't stop crying when Misha told them. It is difficult for me to even imagine such things."

"Did you see the competition between Nada and Diana?" Thaos asked.

"I couldn't see much in the crowd."

"I was up close and Misha's mother cheated every chance she could get, then she tries to kill Diana. I couldn't understand why Diana didn't just let her have it until the end when Diana exposed Nada's crimes. I lived on the streets when I was a kid and I met people like that; I'll tell you I wanted to go after Nada myself."

"If I tell you something you can't repeat it, promise?"

"Yep."

"Like I said I don't know the details, but Diana said that Misha really changes when he is around his mother and that is what worries her. I am not sure what she means but I know that Diana is scared for Misha."

"I know exactly what she means," Thaos said solemnly.

Chaez spent a great deal of time with Gabriel and Raphael who were happy with the young man's enthusiasm but concerned because Chaez had no training or experience as a warrior. This afternoon, Gabriel and Raphael met with Fahron, Isadore and Chaez at their castle.

"The reason we wanted to meet was to talk about Chaez's desire to train to become a Patronus priest," Gabriel said as Isadore served them all coffee in the parlor. "We have spent a great deal of time with Chaez and he is a bright and enthusiastic young man. And we believe he is dedicated to becoming a Patronus priest. And both Raphael and I will be honored to sponsor him on one condition; Chaez needs to start training as a warrior before the school opens."

"You must understand that traditionally there is a great difference between the Patronus priests and other priests. While many men apply for such training only the most faithful warriors complete the training. And because there are so many who apply they compete with each other in many areas," Raphael explained.

"Of course we can teach Chaez a great deal but the fact that he not only has no training but has never even been in a fight puts him at a great disadvantage. Fahron you are a warrior surely you can understand."

"Actually Chaez and I have already spoken about this," Fahron said. "But we didn't know what qualifications he would need to enter training."

"As you know Sudfad is building a second training site for the Patronus priests," Raphael continued. "Both Gabriel and I recommend that is the site where Chaez should train because we will all be close by to assist him. The buildings are near completion but the site won't open for two to three months. And Gabriel and I will be on a mission at that time. Now we have already spoken with Sudfad and Renya and Chaez is welcomed to stay in the castle instead of the barracks."

"Chaez and I agree that he would concentrate more on his studies if he stayed in the barracks," said Fahron.

"Your options are to start Chaez on a rigorous training program here or he can return to Wetpr with us and train with Raul and Simon, as I said we expect to be gone a long time on this mission," Raphael said.

"You should know that if you feel Chaez is not ready for the training he can certainly take it later on," Gabriel offered. "Chaez I don't want to scare you but the reality is that if you can't hold your own in the arena the first few weeks you will wash out."

"The choice is yours Chaez," Raphael said. "Gabriel and I knew we wanted to become Patronus priests and we worked very hard. Now if you want to study to become a priest first then decide if you want to be a warrior priest that is certainly an option too."

"So I can understand," Chaez said. "You have fought and worked with many people from Lentz, who would you say has the qualifications to past the trials to become a Patronus priest?"

"Well we have never worked with your father but we have heard he has such skills," Raphael said. "Thaos, Stephan, Matthew, Claudius and of course the Nordes Tribe. Fahron I believe you now understand the skill level required. Of course Chaez would not have to be at that level to enter the training."

"Son, the men that Raphael mentioned are not just fighters they are exceptional fighters," Fahron said. "We will not feel badly if you change your mind."

Chaez did not hesitate before he spoke, "Father I will be honest I could not fight with you but I have money and will ask the others to train me. I would like to train with both the Nordes Tribe and Matthew and the others."

"I doubt if anyone will take your money," Fahron said. "We are going to Sorren's village today for the festivities we will speak with him and the others there." Fahron was made very proud by Chaez's comments.

"Fahron, you know Sally wants to train with Sorren; if you make arrangements for Chaez it is only fair that you do so for her too," Isadore said in a scolding manner.

Fahron smiled, "Do you want to tell her now or surprise her?"

"Batina I want you to meet our friend Ratri," Dagon said with a smirk. "He can't keep his eyes off from you but I warned him you girls are giving us the cold shoulder so you don't get kicked off the mission." Both Batina and Ratri blushed as they looked at each other.

"Dagon you are awful," Jasmine scolded then she looked at Ratri and said, "He's just mad because the girls that didn't make the team won't talk to any of these guys anymore. But there are plenty of other girls for him to meet."

"So let's meet them," Dagon joked.

"Are you too shy to introduce yourself?" Jasmine asked with a grin.

"That's me," Dagon said and laughed.

"Come on," Jasmine said; rolled her eyes and grabbed Dagon's hand leading him away from the group.

"Those two always act like brother and sister," Joao said to Ratri. "Come join us this game is fun."

"We've got a mission coming up and we are pretty short-handed," Koby said to Ratri. "You should join us."

"Actually Dagon was just telling me about it," Ratri replied. "I am going to talk to Gabriel and Raphael when they get here."

"Are you volunteering?" Batina asked shyly.

"Yes, I have been on missions with Gabriel's team before so I know the ropes," Ratri said then paused. "I know Dagon was teasing all of you about giving the guys a cold shoulder but what you are doing is smart and that goes for all of you," Ratri said as he looked at Joao and Dack. "Sometimes timing alone is crucial and if you're distracted it can be dangerous. Now that Koby is off the front line I need to talk to him for just a moment." Ratri looked directly at Batina, "When I return perhaps you can teach me this game?"

Batina blushed and nodded but did not speak, she was surprised at herself at how nervous she was in Ratri's presence. As Koby and Ratri walked a few feet away from the group Darla said, "Batina he is really cute, you should get to know him."

"Dack, Batina must not think we are cute because she is never speechless around us," Joao joked. Batina turned and punched Joao on the arm as the others laughed.

"Bekka asked me to give this to you," Ratri said as he handed Koby an envelope.

"How does she look?" Koby asked. "I mean does she seem happy?"

"She looks very pregnant and she looks happy," Ratri replied. "You know Bekka always was a popular girl and has lots of friends and she said her family is really happy about the baby." Ratri paused. "Koby I had heard you and Bekka were getting married, is the baby yours?"

"Yes, it's kind of a long story which I will tell you more about later, but basically we spent all of our time together had a lot of sex and both fell apart when she got pregnant. I know it sounds insane but we never thought about that possibility."

"Immediately we decided to get married, but the more we talked about things and the more we watched the married couples in the house; Bekka and I realized we weren't in love with each other. We love each other as friends but nothing more. While we were trying to figure out our future; like what we would do if one of us fell in love with someone else, well I did something bad and she left."

"She didn't seem angry when she gave me that letter," Ratri said. "In fact she was asking me how you were doing. Everyone in the Ice Caves knows about Misha's mother now and how Diana exposed her so your family is kind of the talk of the town; and I mean that in a good way."

"Cassandra's sister Melinda came to live with us and one night I was making a fool of myself with Bekka watching. She left that night and the whole family was mad at me and I couldn't blame them. Joao even punched me and told me not to contact Bekka. But I sent her a letter and gifts for her and the baby. I apologized for hurting her but of course I couldn't take back what I did."

"Why don't you open the letter," Ratri urged. Koby paused as he was somewhat hesitant to open it. "I don't know if you noticed but the envelope smells like perfume." When Koby realized this he quickly opened the letter which was several pages long.

"Bekka is apologizing for the way she left and she said she was glad to get my letter," Koby explained as he kept reading. "She said she told her parents everything." Koby paused and re-read the words as they sunk in.

"Her father said a baby is never a mistake and he understands that Bekka's feelings were hurt but that doesn't change the fact that I am the baby's father. He said it would be wrong for her to keep me from the baby so she wants me to help name it. And if I am back from the mission in time; she wants to know if I want to come for the birth of the baby," Koby said excitedly. I certainly didn't expect this."

"So are you happy?" asked Ratri.

"Yes and I am going to tell Gabriel that I want to be at the birth whether we are done with the mission or not. Ratri I am going to find Emeral and Maxwell and show them this letter."

"Why don't you join the others? Batina is a really nice girl if you are interested in her. But if you compete against her she has a wicked throwing arm." Both Koby and Ratri laughed and walked in different directions.

As soon as Ratri joined Joao and the others, Dack asked. "It's not my business but was that a letter from Bekka you gave him?" Is she doing better?"

"Bekka seems happy and Koby can tell you about the letter."

"Are they getting back together?" Melinda asked hopefully.

"That really is Koby's place to tell you."

"Please, I have been so filled with guilt that I am afraid to even talk to him," Melinda said emotionally.

"Melinda didn't do anything wrong," Joao said. "It was all Koby."

"That's what he just told me," Ratri paused. "Koby sent Bekka a letter and gifts. So it sounds like they are talking again and plan to share responsibilities with the baby. They both seem happy about that. I have known Koby most of my life. He is a good and honorable man, although he admits he made some mistakes."

"I am glad she is doing better," Joao said. "She never stopped crying the entire way home."

Ratri noticed that Batina, Darla and Bianca were listening to the conversation. "I don't mean to be rude but this is Koby's business so I am not going to say anymore."

"They already know," Micha said.

"Does Koby know this?"

"He's the one who told them," Joao replied. "Ratri we wouldn't have talked about it in front of them if Koby wanted to keep it a secret."

Ratri spent the rest of the afternoon with Joao, Dack and their friends, who were teasing Batina because she was acting so shy around Ratri. While Batina stayed near Ratri during the various competitions she spoke little, something that was uncharacteristic for her.

Just before the dinner feast was to commence Koby walked up to Ratri and said, "Gabriel and Raphael just rode into the village if you want to talk to them." Koby had a smile on his face as he had been showing Bekka's letter to everyone in the family. To Joao and Dack's surprise Koby handed them the letter to read.

Ratri took Batina's hand and led her a few feet from the group. "I am going to talk to Gabriel about going on your mission," Ratri explained. "Would it be alright if I joined you afterwards?"

"I would like that," Batina said. "I will stay right here until you return."

"Or you could come with me."

"I don't know if that is a good idea. I really don't want to get kicked off the mission," Batina said seriously.

Ratri smiled and took a step closer to Batina. "Why are you afraid about getting kicked off the mission?"

"Because Joao and Dack are right I am acting differently around you and I don't want Gabriel to see that; I really want to go on that mission, it would be such an honor."

"Why are you acting differently around me?" Ratri asked teasingly.

Batina stared at Ratri then she blushed. After a few moments she said, "I'll wait here for you." Ratri laughed and started to walk away but changed his mind and turning he gently grabbed Batina and softly kissed her on the lips. Batina kissed him back. Ratri smiled and walked away. When Batina turned around her group of friends were watching her and smiling. Batina walked up to them and said, "Oh, I think I am going to get into so much trouble."

Dack, Joao and Koby roared with laughter. "Ratri is a good man he will treat you honorably," Koby said.

"That's not what I am afraid of," Batina said seriously.

As the evening wore on huge bonfires were set ablaze throughout the Village of Tyger. Music was playing and people were dancing. The families of Thomas and Sasha were honored that evening, not only for the pending marriage but also for uniting the tribes.

During the toasts Hugo made an announcement, "I am proud to say that after the wedding Thomas and Sasha will be living with us for several months so Thomas can learn the ways of our people. He is already showing wisdom in his decisions."

"This has been such a nice day," Renya said as she and Sudfad danced together in the light of one of the bonfires. "It is nice just to act like normal people."

"I agree," Sudfad said as he kissed Renya on the forehead. "You know now that the boys are older we should take little trips every so often. We certainly shouldn't wait another twenty years before coming back here." Renya smiled and laid her head against Sudfad's chest.

"I am so glad you came," Vivian said as she and Raphael danced. "I know you just did it to please my parents but it has been so nice having you here."

"It wasn't that I didn't want to come, I thought I should work on the mission," Raphael said as he held his wife close. "But I am glad I came too. And besides everything else I have learned more about your family and tribe."

"Are you going to the wedding tomorrow?" Ratri asked Batina as they danced.

"Yes are you?"

"I was thinking about it but I didn't bring anything to wear besides my warrior's robe."

"That doesn't matter," Batina said. "You should come; it will be fun."

"Are you going with anyone?"

"Do you mean a date?" Batina asked and smiled. "No I was going with my friends."

"Would you like to go as my date?"

Batina looked up into Ratri's face and smiled, "Yes I would like that very much." Then as an afterthought she asked, "Where are you staying?"

"At the King's castle."

"The wedding is at Claudius' castle which isn't far from here. Should we just meet at the wedding?"

"I would prefer to come here and get you unless you take issue with that. I would like to meet your family."

Batina was both pleased and surprised by Ratri's statement but she tried to maintain a nonchalant composure. "No, I just thought it would be easier for you. I was going to change into a nice dress when I got to the castle so I wouldn't get it dusty riding there."

"Show me where you live and I will come and get you and fly you to the wedding. You won't get dusty flying."

Batina smiled brightly. "Come I will show you now," she said as she took Ratri's hand and led him away from the dance area.

"You look so incredibly beautiful tonight," Gabriel said as he and Hannah danced near one of the bonfires.

"And you look so handsome my husband," Hannah said happily. "I never stop thinking about what a lucky girl I am."

As Nada, Morgan and Bruno sat around a campfire outside of the Village of Czar they passed around a bottle of whiskey. "I'm going to kill that little bitch," Nada said angrily. "She ruined everything for us."

"And you think you are just going to fly into Wetpr without any other Rualas seeing you? Do you even know where she and Misha live?"

"No but I can find out," Nada said defiantly. The whiskey was adding fuel to her hatred of Diana.

"From what I heard you made quite the spectacle of yourself in Wetpr," Bruno said as he wiped his mouth on his sleeve. "I wouldn't be surprised if people remember you."

"Oh Bruno just shut up," Nada snapped.

Bruno looked at Morgan and winked then he said teasingly, "From what I've heard Misha's wife is a rare beauty perhaps you shouldn't be so quick to think about killing her. I mean we could share her for a while."

Chapter XXXIX
Wedding Day

Like Renya, Bella loved to host celebrations so the wedding for Thomas and Sasha was held in the splendor befitting a ruling family. Both Gabriel and Raphael preformed the wedding ceremony which was held mid-morning. Sasha and Thomas grew up in poor families and both were overwhelmed with the extravagance of the event. As was becoming typical of warrior weddings, competitions and events were held in the afternoon and a ball was scheduled for the evening.

When one of the guests asked Claudius why his family would hold such a celebration for two young people they barely knew Claudius' only reply was, "As long as it makes Bella happy." What Claudius did not say was that the extravagance of the wedding was also meant to show honor to Sorren and his family. Which is exactly how Sorren's family and village interpreted the lavishness.

It had not gone unnoticed by Sorren that every unmarried visiting warrior had a Nordes warrior as their companion for the wedding with the exception of Thor and Melinda who attended the wedding together. As a young chief, Sorren separated his tribe from what he referred to as 'outsiders', but now he was pleased to see the interaction of his tribe with these honored warriors.

Earlier in the morning when Ratri arrived at the modest home of Batina he found her waiting excitedly at the door. Batina had dark curly hair and brilliant blue eyes and she looked radiant in the blue dress her mother had made her for the wedding. Batina introduced Ratri to her parents and brothers and sisters, all of whom were also going to the wedding. Ruala warriors were held in high esteem by the Nordes Tribe and Batina's parents were proud that Ratri was escorting their daughter to the wedding.

As Ratri and Batina started to walk out of the house, she grabbed a small bag and a bow and quiver of arrows. Ratri laughed, "Are those wedding gifts?"

"No," Batina replied and blushed. "There will be competitions all day."

"Let me take the bow and arrows," Ratri said. "It will be easier for me to carry you that way." As he slung these items over his shoulder he asked Batina, "Have you flown with any of the others?"

"Yes, they took us all flying so we could see what it was like, it was very exciting."

"Good, I am going to put my arms around you from behind," Ratri explained.

"That's what Dagon did when he took me up," Batina said, then gasped as they quickly ascended into the air. "This really is fun."

"I am sure that Dagon explained that the tighter I hang on to you, the less movement you experience and you are less likely to get sick. If you start feeling sick close your eyes and tell me." Ratri paused then said. "You look very beautiful, you took my breath away again when I saw you."

"Thank you," Batina said shyly and blushed. "What do you mean again?"

"Yesterday you had the same effect on me."

"Ratri are we going to get into trouble?" Batina asked earnestly.

He laughed loudly, "What do you mean?"

"I couldn't sleep all night because I kept thinking about you and I was so excited to be going to the wedding with you."

"And how is that going to get us into trouble?"

"Well, maybe that wasn't the right word," Batina said. "Besides the fact that I want so very much to go on that mission with Gabriel's team it is also an honor for my family. I'm afraid that if Gabriel knows..." Batina paused.

"Knows what?"

Batina hesitated, "That I like you that he won't let me on the mission."

"I like you very much also," Ratri said warmly. "And I too thought about you last night. But let me explain something."

"We can have feelings for each other and still go on the mission. The problem is when a person gets so distracted that they can't think or react properly, that's when mistakes are made and people are put in danger. You have told me repeatedly how important this mission is to you and I have been on many missions with Gabriel's team. We just have to make sure that we don't lose our focus on the mission. So you don't have to be so worried."

Batina did not speak for several moments as she thought about his words. "While that makes me feel better it might not be as easy as you make it sound."

"I like what you are saying."

"What, that I might not be able to focus on the mission!"

"That your thoughts are on me and I will let you in on a secret; there are always missions."

After the wedding ceremony there were two hours of events scheduled before the midday feast. Thor and Melinda had changed into clothing more appropriate for the competitions and were walking around the grounds, holding hands.

"You haven't stopped smiling, what is going on?" Thor asked.

"I just feel so much better knowing that Bekka and Koby are doing better," Melinda said jubilantly. "I was feeling so guilty."

"How do you know this?"

"Koby let me read a letter he got from Bekka yesterday. He had written to her and this letter was her response. They are going to try and remain friends and share the responsibilities of the baby. Koby is very happy."

"So does that mean you would feel free to date Koby now?"

Melinda stopped walking and turned and looked at Thor. "I can't believe you asked me that. I am so happy that my friend's heart isn't broken and you want to know if I am thinking about dating her boyfriend. Thor you can just be an ass sometimes." Thor laughed which made Melinda angrier.

"Besides what do you care anyways we aren't dating. In fact I am not really sure what our relationship is. Are we friends who hold hands once in a while?"

As Melinda was yelling at Thor, Vivian walked up to Diana and Misha. "You might want to stand closer to Thor because Melinda is really mad and yelling at him," Vivian said with a grin.

"Come on," Diana said as she led Misha towards her brother. "This might be fun."

"You girls have a strange idea of fun," Misha said and laughed.

"Why aren't you answering me? And stop laughing, what are you laughing at anyways?" Melinda now had her hands on her hips and her head was bobbing back and forth as she yelled at Thor.

"I'm not answering you because I don't know the answer to your question and I am laughing because you look so cute when you are mad," Thor said with a big grin.

"Cute!"

"Melinda just hit him that always makes me feel better when he makes me mad," Diana said and laughed.

"I'm not even sure what I said to make her so mad," Thor said and chuckled.

"Thor you never are," Diana said as Misha stood back; he did not want to get involved in the situation.

"I was telling him how happy I am that Bekka and Koby aren't mad at each other anymore and are trying to work things out and all your brother can say is do I want to date Koby. So I asked him why he cares and all he can do is laugh," Melinda said angrily. Now Misha was grinning too.

"Well, there was a little more to it than that," Thor said.

"Melinda you are the only girl I have ever seen my brother hold hands with," Diana said. "I know he likes you but he is just too pigheaded to tell you."

564

"Thankfully I have a little sister for that," Thor said and he and Misha both laughed.

Misha took Diana's hand and started to pull her away from Thor and Melinda, "Honey why don't we let them work this out," Misha suggested and laughed again.

Melinda wasn't the only one who was elated about the news of Bekka and Koby, a weight seemed lifted from the entire family that now made up Gabriel's team. Koby was asking everyone for suggestions for baby names and made arrangements to return to the Ice Caves with Ratri and the other Rualas. Koby planned to have a short visit with Bekka before he left for the mission in Ryed. Several of the warriors with Ratri also volunteered for Gabriel's mission and they needed to return to the Ice Caves to get their belongings.

Batina had just finished taking part in a game where the players kicked a ball around the field. She looked at the faces of the small crowd that had gathered around the players and did not see Ratri. She suddenly had a feeling like her heart was sinking which she mentally chastised herself for. "Have you seen Ratri?" Batina asked Micha and Bianca as they walked past.

"Yes, he's over there talking to your father," Bianca said and pointed to the two men.

"Talking to my father!" Batina gasped. "This might not be good." As Batina ran towards Ratri and her father, Micha and Bianca watched her and laughed. Batina stopped running when she was a few feet from the two men and walked towards them hesitantly. Both Ratri and Batina's father laughed when they saw the concerned look on her face.

"What do you think we are talking about?" her father asked.

"I don't know," Batina said slowly.

"Ratri promised me he would watch over you on the mission."

"Father I am a warrior," Batina said somewhat indignantly.

"And you are still a young girl on a dangerous mission far from home," her father replied with a voice of authority. Batina did not respond so her father Edgar continued. "After the ceremonies Ratri and the others will be returning to the Ice Caves to get the things they will need for the mission. He has asked me permission to take you with him to meet his parents. I know he hasn't asked you yet but I did give my permission." Although Edgar sounded stern as he spoke he was smiling.

Batina looked back and forth at the two men in disbelief. "You want me to meet your parents?" she asked Ratri.

"Yes," he said with an amused smile.

"And you gave us permission?" Batina asked her father.

"That's what I said."

"I really don't know which of this surprises me the most," Batina said then her demeanor changed. "Are you both telling me the truth?"

"Yes," Ratri replied. "Koby will be joining us because he is going to visit Bekka. Without any major storms it will take three days each way to travel to the Ice Caves and back. That would give us almost two days for you to meet my family and see the Ice Caves. Then I will bring you home. Do you know when Gabriel want's you in Wetpr?"

"No, but I will ask him," Batina said excitedly. "When do we leave?"

"Daybreak tomorrow," Ratri replied.

Batina's eyes grew wide. "I am going to find Gabriel now," she said excitedly then turned to leave but turned back and hugged her father then Batina hugged Ratri and ran into the crowd of guests searching for Gabriel.

"Kid, all I want you to do is watch the participants," Thaos said to Chaez as the two walked around the various competitions being held on the grounds of Claudius' castle.

"And I mean really study them. Watch how they hold their bodies, when they breathe and how they focus. Everyone is different and what works for one person may not work so well for someone else. But to get at the level you want you have to be able to focus on your target and still be aware of your surroundings."

"The fighting competitions aren't going to be until later this afternoon and I will show you what I am talking about. The Rualas have this fighting competition where they put a bunch of guys in an area and the last one standing is the winner."

"Are you having that competition here?" Chaez asked.

"Yeah, but we had to tone it down for Bella, so there won't be any fighting with weapons," Thaos said. "I really want you to watch that one for the various fighting styles."

"Thaos I want you to know I appreciate this."

"Kid this isn't going to be easy. I've got a couple of months to teach you what I learned over years. If it gets too much for you tell me. Today you watch, tomorrow we go hands on."

After all of the appropriate toasts were made before the mid-day feast. Fahron and Isadore stood in front of the wedding guests. "We know many of you planned to leave tomorrow but we would like you to stay one more day so we can entertain you at our home. We have adopted two daughters and as of yesterday Sally will be training with the Nordes Tribe to become a warrior. And as of today our son Chaez is starting his training to prepare him for his studies to become a Patronus priest."

"Isadore and I couldn't be prouder of our children and would like you to share in our happiness." Many of the guests knew that Fahron and Isadore had not held festivities at their home for several years because of their shame over Timothy's crimes. It touched the hearts of many to see Fahron and Isadore so happy again. Claudius immediately started a round of applause which was emulated by all of the guests. The Rualas who would return to the Ice Caves were the only guests who did not change their travel plans.

Lila held Christopher's hand as they walked up to Luca and Koby; Lila could not contain the smile on her face. "Christopher, Koby is leaving in the morning with some other warriors for the Ice Caves. Koby is going to visit Bekka and wants to know if you want to go along," Luca said. Christopher's eyes widened and his mouth fell open. "But if you go you have to promise to stay with Koby and to do what he tells you."

"Yes, I want to go; I promise, I promise," Christopher said excitedly and started to jump up and down, then he ran up to Koby and hugged his legs, then ran to Luca and hugged his legs and ran back to Lila. "I've got to tell Nicholas and Joey," Christopher said excitedly.

"Go tell them," Koby said. "Then come back here and we'll go into town and buy Bekka some gifts."

Christopher ran through the crowd yelling, "Nicholas, Joey you'll never guess what."

"That's very nice of you to take him," Lila said.

"Bekka and Christopher love each other," Koby replied. "She will be just as excited as he is."

"You can't do this," a woman screamed as Nada, Morgan and Bruno landed in the middle of an outdoor wedding and drew swords on the guests.

"You see there you are wrong," Bruno said with a grin. "We can do anything we want." As Bruno talked Nada grabbed a basket off a table. "Now why don't you good folks just put all of your valuables in that basket and me and my friends might not hurt anyone."

"I protest," a man yelled moments before Morgan ran his sword through the man.

"Father!" screamed the bride and knelt down by the dying man.

"As I was saying, all of your valuables in the basket," Bruno said with a sadistic grin.

Chapter XXXL
Nemesis

"I still can't believe my father is letting me go to the Ice Caves with you," Batina said as they flew southward towards the Safer Mountain Range. Ratri and his group started their journey just before dawn.

"I promised him that I would take care of you and act honorably," Ratri replied.

"Well, he must really like you because he doesn't let me do anything alone with the boys in the village. I can do things in groups but certainly nothing like this."

"He let you go to Wetpr to meet the single men on Gabriel's team."

"Yes, but there was a group of us and Sorren and Shara watched over us like our parents," Batina said. "Besides most of us girls just wanted to go to Wetpr to attend the celebrations, we weren't looking for husbands or anything. That's why we were so surprised when Sasha fell in love with Thomas. Ratri it was the strangest thing, I don't know how to explain it. It's like Sasha and Thomas fell in love the minute they were introduced. Everyone was teasing them, we really didn't think they would get married."

"So you don't believe in love at first sight?"

Batina did not answer the question. "Ratri I have to admit I am nervous about meeting your family. I wish I would have brought a gift for them. What will they think when you tell them we only met a few days ago?"

"Well, first you have nothing to be nervous about, I wasn't nervous about meeting your parents."

"That's different you're a man."

"Batina it's not different at all and besides your father is considerably more protective of you than my parents are of me. And your father should be; you are a beautiful young woman."

"Besides it's not like we live near each other. We have to take advantage of the time we have together; your father understood that. We will have another eight days together, I hope by that time we have a better idea of our relationship."

"What do you mean?"

"Well, you may say you don't want to spend time with me anymore," Ratri was grinning as he spoke. "Or we may decide we want a more serious relationship."

"I can't imagine I am going to not want to spend time with you," Batina said hesitantly. "Why do we have to make those decisions in the next eight days?"

"We don't, but I would like to be honest with Gabriel about us."

"Ratri! You know he will keep you on the mission; it's me he will send home."

"There have been couples on the missions who fell in love, in fact Gabriel met his wife on a mission. The issue is whether we can keep our focus. And besides Gabriel is not the kind of man you keep things from, sometimes it's like he can read your mind. If we tell him we have feelings for each other but are determined to focus on the mission, he will respect that. And worse case if he sends us home that doesn't mean we can't work on other missions."

"Really?"

"Yes, if you really want to work with Gabriel, Raphael and the others you have to be honest and forthcoming with them all. And before I forget your parents did send gifts along for my parents, they are in my pack."

"What! Ratri they must think we are getting married. Do you know what the gifts are?"

"I don't know what is inside the packages and who knows perhaps we will marry some day." Batina didn't speak. "Is your silence a good thing or a bad thing?" he asked.

"Neither," Batina said slowly. "Everything is happening so fast I feel like my head is spinning. It's like I am excited and scared at the same time."

"Before I scare you too much can you cook or hunt?"

"Of course; why are you asking?"

"Because the group we are travelling with as well as Gabriel's team divides up work duties, it's expected."

"I can cook, hunt, fish and set up a defensible camp; all of our warriors are trained to do such things. I know we have only been going to competitions and dancing since we met but I am a hard worker, I will pull my weight."

"Good that will be important for Gabriel's team. They all work hard and expect others to also. And speaking of camps when we sleep I want you to stay close enough to me so I can keep an eye on you," Ratri said then smiled. "Now how close you want to sleep to me will be your decision."

"My decision?" Batina asked with a coy smile. "What if I get cold and want to sleep close to you?"

"I will certainly keep you warm, but remember I made promises to your father," Ratri paused. "But that doesn't mean we can't kiss."

The festivities started early in the morning at the castle of Fahron and Isadore. When guests arrived pigs were already roasting over large pits. Tables and platforms for entertainers were set up in both the Great Hall and the yard. Games and competitions were offered and a horse race was scheduled as part of the afternoon events.

"Chaez today you are entering the competitions that require skill, not fighting," Thaos instructed. "Remember what you saw yesterday and what I told you and remember this is training, no one expects you to excel at any of this yet."

"Thaos do you mind if Nikki and I give Chaez a little practice at knife throwing, just so he is warmed up for the competitions?" Ingr asked.

"That's probably a good idea," Thaos said and looked at Stephan.

As Ingr was leading Chaez towards some targets, Nikki said to Thaos and Stephan. "This all comes so easy for you. Ingr and I are afraid that if Chaez feels humiliated in front of all these people he might give up."

"Honey the reason I wanted him to enter the competitions is because I think Stephan and I intimidate him some."

"Let's try this," Nikki suggested. "Ingr, Angelina and I will work with him at least today. He doesn't seem intimidated by us and once he builds up his confidence a little he should perform better when he trains with you."

"If you girls want to have a go with him first that is fine with us," Thaos said. "Hopefully it will work."

"Lila has Amy and Titus and Cassandra has James so you are free to enter competitions," Nikki said. "And my mother and Bella have the twins," Nikki added as she looked at Stephan. "We told them we wanted to help Chaez train." Nikki paused. "I wasn't sure if I was going to tell you this but last night Ryan said that he and Chaez have been talking and Chaez really looks up to the two of you and Matthew; so much so that he is nervous around you."

"I don't know if that makes me feel good or bad," Stephan said. "Is that when you girls decided to help him?"

"Yes, we'll let you know how it goes," Nikki said and walked away then she stopped and turned back towards the men. "Thaos tell Stephan about Amy this morning."

Thaos looked at Stephan and grinned. "Amy cried when she found out that Christopher had already left."

"Watch if those two don't get married some day," Stephan said and slapped Thaos on the back.

"It's just so wonderful to see Fahron and Isadore happy again," Rosa said to Mathas, Sudfad and Renya. Rosa was holding baby Sarah, while Mathas held Jacob and Renya carried Alexas Rose.

"I am going to miss you both so much," Rosa said to Sudfad and Renya. "I wish you didn't have to leave."

"This is the first time we have left the boys in charge of everything," Sudfad said. "But Renya and I have been talking and we want to come back here for a visit very soon. Of course how soon might depend on what we find when we get home," he said and chuckled.

"I should start doing that with Mathew," Mathas said. "Put him in charge every now and then for the experience."

"At least you have Fahron and Claudius to fall back on if something happens to you," Sudfad said. "As wild as our boys were I didn't think they would ever be ready for the responsibilities of the throne but since they married they have really changed."

"I'm surprised you let Batina go to the Ice Caves with Ratri," Sorren said to Edgar with a broad grin.

"So were Cora and Batina," Edgar said and laughed. "Of course I asked around about the boy first and everyone said what a good man he is. And I like him."

"He is a good man and a great warrior," Sorren said. "So do you think a wedding is on the horizon?"

"Batina is so focused on that mission with Gabriel's team that I don't know. But Ratri wanted to meet me and Cora and wants Batina to meet his parents so I know he is thinking seriously. He came out and told me that he lives so far from here and with the missions and such, that time and distance were working against them."

"He is hoping that by time they return they will have a better understanding of where their relationship is heading. He promised me he would act honorably and I believed him. Batina has been acting so shy around him. He will have a surprise when he gets to know her," Edgar said with a grin.

"It would be nice to have our tribe bonded with the Rualas," Sorren said. "Of course I'm just thinking out loud." Sorren laughed loudly.

"Misha everyone's just watching out for you," Diana argued. "You should be happy that so many people love you."

"I'm not that helpless little boy anymore I don't need everyone hovering over me," Misha said with frustration.

Misha and Diana were walking in the yard at Fahron's castle. Diana now pulled Misha away from the crowd and turned and stared into his eyes. "Misha remember when we came here to stop Timothy?" Diana said in a low voice but did not wait for him to answer the question. "Remember how we all said that it should be one of us who killed him and not his own father or his father's friends. Well, there are many who feel the same way about you and Nada. I don't care what a monster that woman is; you have suffered enough and should not be put into that position."

"I appreciate the sentiment and I agree that Nada, Bruno and Morgan are coming after us. But they are all fighters, dishonorable fighters, but fighters all the same. They're not stupid; they won't attack us when we are surrounded by everyone in the family. They will stalk us and attack when they can outnumber us."

"Misha you look me in the eyes and tell me you could kill your mother if you had to."

"If she attacked you, yes."

"And you?" Misha momentarily hesitated in answering Diana's question.

"See that is what we all understand, personally I would prefer to turn the tables on them and we hunt them. But I don't think there is enough time before we have to leave for Ryed."

"Elan I will be so happy when we have a baby," Cassandra cooed as she held the young son of Thaos and Nikki.

"So will I," Elan said as he lovingly looked at his wife, then Elan chuckled.

"I think Nikki thought it would be an imposition for us to watch the baby. I think you startled her when you grabbed him out of her arms."

"I know, that's why I felt I had to explain how badly you and I want more children."

"Well, there isn't any reason why we can't adopt more," Elan said then looked down at Joey who was holding his hand. "Joey how would you feel if we adopted another child?"

"Would I get to help pick?" Joey asked.

"Of course you would," Cassandra said.

"Then I already know," Joey said with a huge smile.

Both Elan and Cassandra stopped walking and now turned to Joey. "Joey who are you talking about?" Cassandra asked.

Joey took a deep breath and looked at Cassandra and Elan seriously. "Before you adopted me sometimes I would get really homesick and one day I walked into the nursery at the orphanage. And I found a girl that reminded me of my little sister that died in the fire. I would go visit her a lot. She likes me and then I wouldn't feel so sad."

"I don't think I was ever in that area," Cassandra said. "She is a little baby?"

"Not like him," Joey said and looked at baby James Duran. "She's older more like Cerey."

"What is her name?" Elan asked.

"Cicely,"

"So you would like it if we adopted Cicely?" Elan asked. Joey grinned and nodded. "Let's find Hannah and ask her about Cicely."

Ratri and his group only stopped for small breaks this first day of their travel but they decided to make an early camp. Batina wanted to prove her worth and called out that she would do the cooking before their feet touched the ground.

"Batina would you watch Christopher while I gather wood?" Koby asked.

"Sure he can help me," Batina said then turned to Ratri. "Which packs have the food?"

"There is some in my pack," Ratri answered as he took it off and handed it to Batina. "I'll get the rest."

As Christopher ran towards Batina he was already talking in his normally loud and exuberant style. "Batina we're going to visit Bekka, she's my friend. Who are you going to visit?"

"Ratri's parent's," Batina replied but then thought that Christopher might not know who Ratri was. "That's Ratri carrying the packs towards us."

"Is he your boyfriend?" Christopher asked.

Ratri stared at Batina and grinned as he was waiting to hear her answer. "Yes Christopher, Ratri is my boyfriend," she said with a smile to Christopher but she was looking at Ratri.

"Right answer," Ratri said as he put the packs down and kissed her on the forehead."

"I have a girlfriend," Christopher announced loudly which made the warriors in the area smile.

"You do," Batina said. "What is her name?"

"Amy."

"Is that the Amy that Nikki and Thaos adopted," Batina asked.

"Yes," Christopher said and grinned.

"She's really pretty," Batina said.

"I know," Christopher said then took a deep breath. "I already asked her daddy for permission to marry Amy when we get old." Everyone started to laugh at Christopher's comment.

"What did he say?" Ratri asked.

"He said that sometimes people change as they get older but if Amy and I want to marry each other when we are big he will give us permission."

"Christopher tell them how Thaos reacted when you asked him," Koby said with a grin.

Christopher got a mischievous look on his face and leaned close to Batina as if he was going to tell her a secret but he talked loudly. "Thaos started choking on his whiskey and his face turned colors. Then he kept looking at Luca but I don't know why." Everyone now roared with laughter.

All of the warriors were setting up the campsite while Batina prepared dinner. Christopher was sitting next to her when Ratri walked up to the campfire. "I'm putting out the blankets, where do you want me to put yours?" Ratri asked Batina.

Without looking up Batina replied, "I think it's going to be a cold night, a really, really cold night." The men, who were gathering around the fire all grinned.

"Well, if it's going to be that cold perhaps I should build us a second fire," Ratri suggested and smiled.

"That might be a good idea," she said with a grin.

"Cold," Christopher said in disbelief. "I think it's really hot. Koby is it going to get really cold tonight?"

"You'll understand when you get older," Koby said and smiled. Christopher gave Koby a confused look which again brought laughter from the group.

After talking with Hannah and Gabriel about the little girl Cicely, Elan and Cassandra decided to return to Wetpr with the rest of Gabriel's team the next day. Although they had originally planned to stay in Lentz two more weeks, the royal families said they understood. Maxwell and Emeral were given the opportunity to stay in Lentz longer but they too decided to return to Wetpr.

The journey from Lentz to Wetpr took three days for those on horseback and in carriages but the Rualas could travel much faster. Elan, Cassandra and Joey were so excited about possibly adopting Cicely that they flew ahead of the main group. Melinda, Dack and Joao joined them.

The people from Wetpr added two additional bocas to the caravan to carry all of the items they had either bought or received. Joshua and Iris were melancholy because they were leaving Thomas behind in the Village of Tyger, even though it was only for three months. After three months Thomas and Sasha were going to live in Wetpr for a while. Joshua and Iris had quickly bonded with many members of the Nordes Tribe and had become close friends with Sasha's parents.

Renya was sad to leave her home kingdom of Lentz and Mathas and Rosa. Sudfad could see the sadness in his wife's eyes and promised her another holiday in Lentz in the near future. But Renya's sadness only lasted for a few hours as she was getting excited about returning home to her children and grandchildren.

Nicholas was lost without Christopher and Joey so Gabriel let Nicholas ride in Joshua's boca with Paul and Adrone. Now that the festivities were over, the minds of many of Gabriel's team returned to the upcoming mission. While Gabriel enjoyed the time with his family in Lentz, the entire holiday he was plagued with an overwhelming feeling that something was not right with his preparations for the mission in Ryed. Gabriel was convinced he had over looked something of great importance.

Ratri's group once again made an early camp on the evening of the second day of their journey to the Ice Caves. Batina had received so many compliments about her cooking that she volunteered to cook all the meals of their journey.

On this evening after the wood was gathered and the fire made, the men went hunting while Batina and Christopher set up the campsite.

"Well what have we here?" Bruno asked with a grin as he, Morgan and Nada landed in the campsite. The three Rualas landed several yards behind Batina, she turned expecting to see her traveling companions. Batina stared at Nada because she recognized Misha's mother from her competition with Diana. Within seconds of the three Rualas landing Christopher charged at Nada yelling, "You're the girl that hurt Diana."

"Christopher!" Batina screamed and ran towards the child but she couldn't grab him before he reached Nada. Christopher kicked and punched Nada while Morgan and Bruno howled with laughter.

"Why you little bastard!" Nada screamed and lunged at Christopher who bit her arm.

"Christopher run to me," Batina yelled as she saw Nada lunge at Christopher a second time. Nada was furious and cursing the boy. Batina grabbed one of her knives from a sheath on her belt and threw it. The knife impaled Nada's right shoulder preventing her from grabbing Christopher, who was now running to Batina and screaming for Koby.

"Koby, Koby help us," Christopher screamed loudly as Batina threw a second knife at Morgan as he jumped towards her. Morgan saw the knife coming and quickly jumped to the left avoiding the blade. Bruno started to circle behind Batina who had her third knife in her right hand while she was pushing Christopher behind her with her left hand. Batina slowly backed up and screamed a war cry as the three Rualas moved towards her.

Although Koby and the others were hunting in two separate groups they heard Christopher's screams and flew back to the campsite, their adrenaline surging through them. It was only seconds from the time they heard Christopher's first screams until they heard Batina's war cry but for Koby, Ratri and the others it seemed like hours since they feared the worse.

"You touch him and I will kill you," Batina said with confidence and authority. "I know who you are."

579

"It ain't the boy that I want," Bruno said with a salacious grin.

"Christopher run and hide!" Batina said sternly and let go of him. Batina could hear Christopher running as she kept her eyes on the three who were coming towards her. Bruno lunged at Batina from her right side, she jumped into the air and kicked him in the chest, although it was a powerful kick, Bruno was a big man and it only knocked him backwards.

Batina landed on her feet and immediately did a forward roll as Morgan reached for her. Batina came to her feet behind Bruno. She kicked the back of Bruno's knees causing him to stumble, when he did Batina jumped up and grabbed his hair pulling his head backwards and pulling him off balance. She held onto Bruno's hair with her left hand and pressed the blade of her knife against his throat with her right. "Stop or he dies," Batina said through clenched teeth.

Nada was so filled with rage and focused on Batina that she did not realize that Koby had grabbed her until his knife was tightly pressed against her throat. "There is nothing I would enjoy more than to cut your throat," Koby whispered into Nada's ear as three Rualas grabbed Morgan and wrestled him to the ground.

"Batina!" Christopher yelled and in the instant Batina was distracted Bruno threw himself upwards and forward with all of his weight, breaking her hold on him. Bruno quickly turned and grabbed Batina by the throat with his left hand and swung his right arm back to punch her. But before his fist made contact with Batina's face Ratri kicked Bruno in the head as he flew over him. Ratri landed in front of Bruno and punched him in the face causing Bruno to release his hold on Batina. Ratri punched Bruno in the stomach with his left fist and an uppercut to Bruno's jaw with his right fist.

Bruno took a couple of steps backwards to put distance between him and Ratri as he pulled a large knife from its sheath on his belt. Ratri too pulled a knife but the second hunting party now flew into camp and two of the men grabbed each of Bruno's arms forcing him to drop the knife. Christopher ran up to Batina and she picked him up and hugged him.

"Are either of you hurt?" Ratri asked of Batina without taking his eyes off from Bruno.

580

"We're alright. I didn't kill her because she is part of your tribe, but I should have," Batina said angrily as she watched her companions tie Nada, Morgan and Bruno to separate trees. Cage and Eilig, two of the Ruala warriors searched the pouches of their three attackers.

"They must be robbing people," Cage said as he dumped the contents of Morgan's pouch onto the ground. "These are full of money and jewels."

"I need something to stop this bleeding," Nada yelled now that her anger was subsiding and she realized the seriousness of her wound.

"You raped your own children you can just bleed," Batina said with disgust while she still held Christopher.

"So what are you going to do with us?" Morgan asked with a grin. "Gonna kill us? Kill your own kind?"

"We're trying to figure that out now," Koby said. "We should take you back to the Ice Caves."

"You can try but I don't think we're allowed through the doors anymore," Morgan said and laughed.

Bruno had not taken his eyes off from Batina. "Ratri," Bruno yelled. "If that little beauty ain't your wife I would like to buy her. How much you want?" Ratri knew that Bruno was trying to bait him.

"Bruno you're just lucky I don't let her kill you," Ratri said.

"Damn fine way to go," Bruno replied with a laugh.

"We're getting company," Sauer said as he and Milo landed back in camp. Both of the Rualas were searching the area to make sure Nada and the others didn't have friends hiding in the shadows. "Hutas, maybe twenty riding this way."

"Well I guess we know what we are going to do with you," Koby said with a grin. "Throw all the wood on the fire so we can make sure the Hutas find the camp."

"You can't just leave us," Nada screamed as Ratri and the others were quickly packing their things.

"Nada you would kill us all in our sleep. Why should we save you?" Milo yelled.

"Notice they aren't grinning anymore," Koby said loudly. "I never thought I would be glad to see Hutas."

The entire camp was packed up in minutes. Koby and Cage walked up to Nada, Morgan and Bruno who were all struggling to free themselves from the ropes that bound them to the trees. "We'll give you a little fighting chance," Cage said sarcastically and he and Koby threw a knife into the ground at the feet of each of the criminals.

"You know what Hutas do to women," Nada screamed fearfully.

"Rape and torture," Koby said. "You mean like you did to our brother and your other children. Seems like justice to me." Milo was carrying Christopher and was already in the air. Koby and Cage were the last two to leave the campsite.

"If we survive this I am going to kill all of you," Nada screamed.

"Shut the hell up and see if you can push that knife over here," Morgan yelled.

As Koby and the others sped through the cool evening sky, Batina and Christopher told the men what had happened in the camp. "I was so afraid they were going to hurt Christopher," Batina kept saying.

"I was afraid they were going to hurt both of you," Ratri said as he flew with Batina in his arms. "Batina they didn't just rape and torture children; they are animals."

The sun had not completely set and there were still orange and pink streaks cutting through the skyline. "If we hadn't been fighting with them," Sauer said. "The Hutas may have attacked us. So there is some good out of this."

"Sauer you are always so damn positive you make me sick," Cage joked. Then he changed the subject. "Did all of you see the treasures Bruno and the others were carrying? They have probably been robbing and killing people which means people are going to look at all Rualas as threats. We need to meet with the Grand Council when we get home."

"Tonight I wish I hadn't made those promises to your father," Ratri whispered into Batina's ear. Ratri had been filled with terror when he heard Christopher's screams and now he was overwhelmed with the desire to make love to Batina.

Chapter XLI
Introductions

"Bekka, Bekka," Christopher screamed as Koby was landing at the front door of Bekka's parents' house. Bekka didn't know that Koby and Christopher were coming for a visit. "Bekka, Bekka." Christopher was so excited he couldn't contain himself. The front door of the house flew open as Bekka stood in the doorway in amazement.

"Christopher? Oh my god it is you," Bekka knelt down and Christopher flew into her arms. The two hugged and kissed as Bekka's parents stood behind her smiling. Koby was also all smiles as he walked up behind Christopher.

"We probably should have told you we were coming," Koby said and to his surprise Bekka stood up, put her arms around his neck and kissed him on the lips.

"Christopher, Bekka has told us so much about you," Bekka's mother said warmly as she knelt down and shook hands with the boy.

"I'm so excited," Bekka said breathlessly and took Koby's arm.

"Christopher, Koby these are my parents Sam and Ella. Mother, Father this is Koby and Christopher." Koby stepped forward and shook hands with Sam.

"We've heard so much about you too," Ella said and hugged Koby and kissed him on the cheek. "What a pleasant surprise. How long can you stay?"

"We came here with Ratri and others and plan to return to Wetpr in two days for a mission," Koby said as Sam led them all inside of the house.

"Well, you will stay here with us," Ella said with determination.

Sam was holding Christopher's hand. "We got attacked," Christopher announced.

"What!" Sam said and looked at Koby.

"Nada, Bruno and Morgan," Koby replied.

"What!" Bekka cried. "Did anyone get hurt? You have to tell us what happened."

"Ratri has a girlfriend, a warrior from the Nordes Tribe, her name is Batina. Night before last Batina and Christopher were setting up the campsite while the rest of us went hunting," Koby explained as they all sat down around the kitchen table. Nada and the others land in the camp and immediately Christopher attacks Nada because she had previously hurt Diana."

"We heard about that," Sam said as Ella set plates of breakfast food on the table.

"Batina recognized Nada and was terrified she would hurt Christopher. We heard Christopher screaming for help when Batina started to fight with the three of them. Batina tells Christopher to run and hide so she could fight."

"Batina is young and inexperienced but by time we got there she had stabbed Nada and was holding a knife to Bruno's throat. But he got out of that hold and was turning on Batina while I got Nada and others were fighting with Morgan. Ratri stopped Bruno from hurting Batina. We tied them to trees and while we were deciding what to do with them Sauer saw Hutas riding our way. So we left, hopefully the Hutas got those monsters."

"Christopher I can't believe you attacked Nada," Bekka said with surprise.

"He attacked me after you left," Koby said with a grin.

Christopher nodded and smiled while he pushed a forkful of pancakes into his mouth.

"He did?" Bekka asked with disbelief.

"I think everyone in the house wanted to, but Christopher was the only one with enough guts," Koby said. "That is until Joao came home." Now Koby looked at Sam and Ella and said. "And I deserved it."

"Bekka when are you coming home?" Christopher asked.

"Well Honey this is my home. These are my parents."

"I know but you have a home with us too. Everyone misses you. They talk about you all of the time."

Bekka looked like she was going to cry so Koby changed the subject. "Cage and Milo are trying to call a meeting of the Grand Council for tonight so we can tell everyone what happened," Koby explained. "Nada and the others were carrying pouches of money and jewels so we know they are robbing people."

"We will certainly attend," Sam said. "Never did any of us realize that such monsters lived among us."

Koby looked at Bekka's parents and asked, "Perhaps later would you mind watching Christopher for a little while so Bekka and I can talk?"

"Of course," Ella said happily.

"Thank you," Koby replied.

"Mother, Father I would like you to meet Batina," Ratri said as they all stood in the parlor of Ratri's home. "She is a warrior of the Nordes Tribe in Lentz. Batina this is my Mother Clair and my Father Joseph." Batina was visibly nervous as she stepped forward and extended her hand. But Clair pulled Batina to her and hugged her and Joseph followed suit.

"I am sorry I am so nervous," Batina said self-consciously. "Ratri wasn't nervous at all when he met my parents." Now both Clair and Joseph looked at their son and their smiles broadened. "My parents sent you some gifts, I don't know what is in the packages," Batina said as she removed several packages from Ratri's pouch that was setting on a chair. Both Clair and Joseph looked at each other and smiled brighter as they now realized what kind of an introduction this was.

"Batina there is no need to feel nervous," Clair said soothingly as she took one of the packages that Batina was handing them.

"We can only stay for two days," Ratri said. "We are both going with Gabriel's team on their next mission. I have to tell you that Batina and I have only known each other for six days but since we live so far apart and have the mission coming up I asked her to come here to meet you and so she and I could get to know each other better."

"I see," Joseph said as he placed one of the packages on the table. "Batina's parents must approve if they sent us gifts."

"They really like Ratri," Batina said as she blushed. "My father is strict; I couldn't believe he let me come here."

"I know it's early but let's have a little wine while we open these gifts," Joseph said.

"Should I prepare a room for Batina or will she be staying in your room?" Clair asked Ratri as she was trying to get information about his relationship with Batina.

Ratri and Batina looked at each other then Ratri looked at his mother, "She will need her own room. I promised her father I would act honorably and it is getting more difficult every night that we spend together; we've been sharing the same blankets as we traveled."

"Ratri, I can't believe you said that," Batina gasped and blushed.

"Which part?" Ratri said and put his arm around Batina's shoulders.

"All of it."

"Honey I am very forthcoming, you are going to have to get used to it."

Batina looked at Clair and Joseph and said, "I think I am going to be embarrassed a lot." Which made everyone laugh.

After Joseph poured four glasses of wine he held up his glass and toasted, "To Ratri and Batina."

"My family isn't wealthy," Batina explained as Joseph and Clair opened the first package together. "So I don't know what they sent."

The first package contained two finely decorated leather sheaths, each containing a well-made knife. Under the knives lay a finely woven table cloth with three smaller clothes that all matched in design. "These are beautiful did your mother weave these?" Clair asked.

"Yes, like with your tribe the women are warriors and homemakers too," Batina said.

The second package was larger and contained a finely decorated quiver filled with arrows and a woven shawl. The third package was the heaviest and contained jars of canned food. The fourth package contained homemade candy and cookies. "These are fine gifts, we are very pleased," Joseph said. "From these gifts are we to assume that the two of you are considering marriage?"

"Ratri did you tell my father we were getting married?" Batina asked with surprise.

"No, but he could tell," Ratri said. "Your father is no fool."

"We didn't even know each other two days when Ratri asked Father if I could go on this trip," Batina explained.

"You haven't answered my question," Joseph said with a smile.

Ratri and Batina looked at each other and smiled, then Batina nodded. "Batina has been nervous because things are going so fast," Ratri explained. "The first time I brought the word up I thought she was going to run."

"I couldn't we were flying," Batina said with a shy smile.

"Well, we are very pleased," Joseph said. "Tomorrow we will have a celebration and a feast."

As soon as Cage and Milo told King Manu about Nada, Morgan and Bruno, the King called a meeting of the Grand Council before lunch. Messengers were sent throughout the Ice Caves to announce an emergency meeting.

The Hall of Light was filled with both Rualas and Shettees even with the short notice. Christopher sat on Bekka's father's lap while Koby, Ratri and their group stood in front of the room to address the Grand Council. Ratri wasn't sure if Batina should go in front of the council so his parents sat in the front of the room with her.

After the Rualas told of their encounter with Nada and her boyfriends King Manu asked Batina and Christopher to approach the council. Sam took Christopher's hand and walked with him up to the large table. Batina blushed as she walked to the front of the room. She stood next to Ratri and curtsied before the King which made him smile. "Since the two of you had initial contact with the criminals is there anything that you didn't tell Koby and the others or anything they forgot to tell us?"

"It all happened so fast," Batina said shyly. "Once Christopher started kicking Nada all she did was swear while the men laughed. Nada kept trying to grab Christopher and as I ran to help him the shorter man tried to grab me. The big man just kept laughing. Then when I told them I knew who they were and I would kill them if they touched Christopher the big man said it wasn't Christopher they wanted."

"You didn't tell me that," Ratri said.

"I didn't think it was important," Batina said to him then turned back to the Grand Council. "But I must confess to something. In my tribe we are trained to kill when we throw our knives. I deliberately threw to wound them because they were members of Ratri's tribe and I didn't know if I should kill them. Now I know I should have."

"You did well, you faced three vicious killers and you live to tell of it," King Manu said. "We should have ordered their deaths but we have never put to death one of our own. So we ended up unleashing monsters onto the world below. After the meeting I will be asking for volunteers to hunt down Nada, Morgan and Bruno and kill them if the Hutas didn't."

Ibula stood up and walked before the council. "We know they have been robbing people, but with their histories they have probably been raping and killing people too."

"We should send warriors to the villages below so they understand that Nada, Morgan and Bruno do not represent our people and that we will stop them."

"I agree," King Manu said.

"I will volunteer to go with one of the groups," Ibula said.

"Ibula why don't you organize those groups and volunteers," King Manu suggested. "While the council organizes the death squads. Then Manu turned to Christopher who was standing next to Sam, holding his hand. "Christopher do you remember anything else that happened?"

"No one said anything about that other lady," Christopher said. Now everyone who was standing before the council looked at Christopher.

"What lady?" Batina asked.

Christopher took a deep breath and explained, "When Batina told me to hide I didn't run far and I hid behind a tree and watched. Koby grabbed Nada while Milo, Sauer and Eilig fought with the smaller man. Batina was fighting with that big man and as soon as she pulled his hair back and put a knife on his throat that other lady appeared behind her. That's why I yelled at Batina but then Batina looked at me and that man started to hurt her."

"What happened to the woman?" Manu asked.

"Ratri and the others came and when I looked again she was gone."

Now King Manu was fearing the worse as he asked, "Christopher what did this woman look like."

"Like Vivian only her stomach was really big with a baby."

"This is worse than I thought," King Manu said as he looked at the crowd then at the other members of the Grand Council who knew what Manu was about to say. "That was the same form the demon Hecate took when she appeared at the celebration at King Sudfad's castle. Later one of the Angels told us that Hecate was watching Nada because Nada's soul is so dark."

590

Manu turned to Ratri and his group. "Draw us a map of where you left Nada and the men. The demon might have helped them escape."

At the very end of the meeting Joseph and Clair stood up, "I would like to make a small announcement," Joseph said to King Manu who nodded. "Most of that group standing before you will be leaving in two days for Wetpr because they will be working with Gabriel's team on a very dangerous mission."

"Although Ratri and Batina have not known each other long they are considering marriage and are trying to meet all of the parents before they leave on that mission. Clair and I will be having a pig roast tomorrow to celebrate and to see the warriors off. Everyone is invited, but depending on the size of the crowd you may have to bring a dish."

As soon as King Manu announced the end of the meeting, people crowded around the young warriors standing before the Grand Council and around Ratri's parents. To work with Gabriel's team was a great honor among the Rualas so people were congratulating the warriors on the mission in addition to congratulating Ratri and Batina. People surrounded Joseph and Clair to talk about preparations for the pig roast. Bekka's father had fallen in love with Christopher and now carried him as Sam approached Joseph and Clair.

"I never expected all of this," Batina said to Ratri.

"Are you scared?"

"A little," then Batina paused. "Ratri if we decide to marry where will the wedding be? It doesn't matter to me but it will to our parents."

"So you are thinking about the wedding now?" he asked with a big grin. "We will need to include our families in the preparations. We can talk with my parents today."

Batina shook her head and said in amazement, "I just can't believe that we have known each other for a week and now we are talking about a wedding." Ratri laughed loudly and kissed Batina on the forehead.

591

"Mind you," Ratri said to his parents with a big grin on his face. "Batina and I haven't decided if we will marry but if we do we have a lot of questions about the wedding plans. We feel there are more concerns because our tribes live so far apart."

"First," Joseph asked. "If you were to marry are you thinking after the mission or before?"

"Before," gasped Batina. "That gives us no time to prepare."

"You two need to think this out," Joseph said. "Believe me I understand your fears that you have only known each other such a short period of time but Ratri you told us that it is getting harder for you to keep your promises to Edgar. What are you going to do if you are on that mission for months like you are considering? Are you not going to share the same blankets? Ratri are you going to break your promise? Batina you are turning red but the truth is you two are healthy young people who both look in love."

"You do have options," Clair said soothingly as she could see how nervous Batina was. "You could get married before or during the mission then have the celebrations when you return. We could have two big celebrations, one here and the other in Lentz or one big celebration. Or you could not go on the mission and take your time getting to know each other and planning a wedding."

"Everything you both have said makes so much sense but I feel like my head is spinning," Batina said as she held Ratri's hand.

Bekka took Koby into the room that was prepared for the baby. As he looked around the room the reality of their situation struck him. "This makes it so real, we are really going to have a baby," Koby said almost in awe.

Bekka laughed, "The look on your face Koby; you look in shock."

"I've been thinking so much about you and me and I know we are having a baby but it just didn't seem real before." He said and took Bekka's hand in his.

"Bekka I am so sorry for what I did and how I hurt you. If I could do it all over again I would. And I'm not making excuses but I can't even explain it."

"Koby we both panicked and we were both fools not to consider the fact that I could get pregnant. I can't tell you how many times I came close to leaving the team and coming back here. And in my mind I planned to leave just as I did, in the middle of the night without telling anyone. I could run away from all of you but I couldn't run away from the fact that I was pregnant. My parents have helped me think through a lot and they think you and I were fools too."

"Why were you thinking of leaving all of the time?"

"I was so scared and I couldn't think about anything but running away. I can't explain it, I have never felt like that before."

"You still have a home in Wetpr and a place on the team. I can't tell you how upset everyone was that you left. Lila cried for days. Your parents seem wonderful and you have so many things prepared for the baby but consider coming back to Wetpr when you are ready."

"I miss everyone there too but I get letters from someone on the team every day; which is really nice. But Koby the issue is still us and our feelings for each other. You are a much more jealous person than I am and I don't want to watch you with other women; it is probably best that I stay here."

Late that night Ratri heard a knock at his bedroom door. He got out of bed and put on some trousers before opening the door. "I can't sleep," Batina said. "I have so much on my mind. Ratri we have so many decisions to make; I feel like I can't think anymore."

"Come in," Ratri said as he moved so Batina could enter. She had a blanket wrapped around her shoulders. "Do you have anything on under that blanket?"

"Yes," Batina said indignantly. "Do you think I would walk around in your parent's house naked?"

He laughed. "Ratri why don't you seem as nervous about all of this or aren't you showing it?"

"By the end of the first day I knew I wanted to marry you, the rest is just details." Ratri took Batina's hand and walked towards his bed and they both sat down. "You know my father made some good points about us getting married before or during the mission."

"I know," Batina said. "Both of my parents are warriors too. I think they would be alright with us getting married and having the celebrations later but you have to ask my father permission to marry me. It is our custom."

"I haven't asked you yet because you seem so scared. Batina if I ask you to marry me tonight what are you going to do?"

"What do you mean?" Batina asked as she laughed.

"Well, are you going to slap me, kiss me or run out of the room?"

"Ratri I have spent the last couple of hours thinking about our wedding plans, what do you think?" Batina asked with a grin.

Ratri walked over to a table and grabbed something then returned to the bed, as he sat down he said, "I've been with you almost every moment since we met and you know I haven't had time to buy a ring. After our conversation today, Mother gave me this, it belonged to my grandmother. Mother said you could keep it or wear it until I got you another one." Ratri handed Batina a wide golden band with tiny little rubies embedded in it.

"Ratri this is so beautiful," Batina gushed and slipped the ring on her finger.

"Does it fit?"

"It's a little big but I love it; I don't want another one."

"Batina will you be my wife?" Ratri asked as he held her hands.

"Yes," she said excitedly and kissed him on the lips.

"This is what I am planning," Ratri said. "We will go to your village and I will ask Edgar for your hand. Then we will go to Wetpr, have the ring adjusted and ask Gabriel to marry us. Then we can have a big celebration when we return. I think the celebration should be at your village because it is easier for my family to travel there. So what do you think?"

"I think it sounds perfect," Batina said then she joked, "I wasted all of that time worrying about it." Batina stood up as she spoke.

"Where are you going?"

"Back to my room."

"Now that you have pledged yourself to be my wife we can make love," Ratri said as he stood up and gently took the blanket from Batina's shoulders.

"But what about your promises to my father?" she asked with a coy grin.

"Edgar and I talked about many things that I did not tell you," Ratri said and bent down and kissed his bride.

The next morning Joseph and Clair were having their morning coffee when Ratri and Batina joined them. "We were wondering when you two were getting up," Joseph kidded. "It's going to be a big day and we have a lot to do." Joseph paused. "You two are all smiles is there something you want to tell us?"

"Batina you're wearing the ring," Clair said happily and walked around the kitchen table and hugged her new daughter-in-law and her son. Joseph also hugged his children.

"Clair and I are both very happy about this, we have much to celebrate."

"First let me tell you what Batina and I decided on and tell me what you think," Ratri said happily as they all sat down at the kitchen table.

Koby rolled over and realized that Christopher wasn't next to him. Koby quickly got dressed; as soon as he opened his bedroom door he heard voices. Koby found Christopher in the kitchen with Sam and Ella.

"Christopher you worried me," Koby said as he joined them at the kitchen table. "I didn't know where you were."

"I am sorry but I didn't want to wake you," Christopher said. "I could smell the food in here."

"I got up early to start preparing food for the feast tonight," Ella said as she poured Koby a cup of coffee.

"Where's Bekka?" Koby asked.

"Still sleeping," Ella replied. "She sleeps more now since she is closer to having the baby."

"So did you have your talk?" Sam asked.

"Yes, but I don't know if anything has really changed," Koby said. "We care about each other, but in our house everyone who got married was sure they were marrying the right person. Bekka and I have never felt like that and are afraid that if we get married and don't love each other we will end up hating each other and we don't' want that. What was it like when you two met? Did you know right away that you should be together?"

Sam and Ella looked at each other. "I would say we knew right away," Ella said to Koby then looked at Sam. "Would you say?"

"Oh yeah, I saw her at a ceremony and knew I wanted to marry that girl," Sam said with a smile. "You two are in a difficult situation and we understand that. Ella and I think that part of the reason you and Bekka got so close is that you were helping her get over Fala's death and we appreciate that."

"What Sam is trying to say," Ella explained. "Is we think you were helping Bekka through the most emotional time of her life and it had to be very emotional for you also. You both seem like bright and responsible young people but we think you got caught up in all of the emotions. Bekka told us the same things Koby and just so you know she has never said a bad word about you. We know she misses you."

596

"I miss her too."

"So do I," Christopher added as he was eating a biscuit.

Sam smiled, "And this one we could keep as a grandson. We just love him." Both Koby and Christopher smiled.

"You know Ella, I hadn't thought about things the way you just explained them; you might be right," said Koby pensively. "I am not making excuses here, but both Bekka and I have been really confused by so many things."

"Koby, if you and Bekka decide not to marry you are always welcome here as family," Sam said. "Honestly Ella and I are really excited about having our first grandchild."

Ella laughed, "Bekka thought we would be mad; she was shocked at how happy we were."

"They're home, they're home," Melinda called out as Gabriel and the rest of his team rode up the driveway. Melinda let Jasper out of the door and the dog ran happily towards his family, barking all the way.

"Joao, Dack quick put these on the table," Cassandra said excitedly as she handed platters of breakfast food to the two young men.

Melinda quickly ran into the kitchen and grabbed two more platters of food and put them on the dining room table. Then Melinda, Cassandra, Joao and Dack met Elan at the front door. Elan was holding Cicely with Joey at his side. Cicely was a two year old blonde girl with huge blue eyes and dimples. The small group walked out of the front door to greet the rest of their family.

"Oh my god!" Natasha said loudly. "Calen look at her; what a cutie." Natasha handed Lily to Calen so Elan could put Cicely into her arms. "Emeral you have to see her," Natasha called and within moments Emeral and Maxwell were landing near their newest adopted grandchild. "I don't ever remember seeing her at the orphanage," Natasha said as she handed Cicely to Emeral.

"I know," Cassandra said excitedly. "There was an entire wing of younger children that I never saw before."

"Nicholas I have a sister too," Joey said with pride as Nicholas and Jasper ran up to them. Gabriel, Hannah and Cerey were following Nicholas.

"Isn't she adorable?" Emeral gushed and handed Cicely to Maxwell.

"Everyone come in; we have breakfast on the table," Cassandra said happily. She had not stopped smiling since they brought Cicely home.

Chapter XLII
Messages

The pig roast at the home of Joseph and Clair took on immense proportions. People started to arrive while Ratri's family was still eating breakfast.

"What are they doing here so early?" Batina asked as she walked outside and stood next to Ratri.

"They are digging more pits for cooking and setting up areas for competitions. Good thing my parents don't have any close neighbors," Ratri replied and chuckled. "Father is planning the different areas, I am just waiting for him to finish."

"What should I do?"

"For now, why don't you help Mother," Ratri said and kissed Batina on the forehead.

While many Rualas and Shettees were preparing for the celebration, King Manu and the other members of the Grand Council were meeting with a dozen Ruala and Shettee warriors who were being sent to the location where Nada, Morgan and Bruno had been left, tied to trees. The group was led by a seasoned Ruala warrior named Soto.

"If you find the bodies, return here," Manu said. "And if the Hutas left the pouches of stolen money and jewels bring those back and we will return them to their owners. If you can't find any trace of the bodies send us word by Enrop and continue looking for the criminals. Let us know what areas you will be searching so we can send other teams to different locations. This morning I sent letters to King Sudfad, King Mathas, Chief Sorren, Chief Duncan and Gabriel with as much information as we have. You can always go to any of these men for help or shelter."

"Batina, Batina," Christopher yelled as he ran through the crowd at Ratri's parents home. Batina and Ratri were walking between competitions when they heard Christopher.

"Batina, I want you to meet my friend," Christopher said excitedly when he caught up with the couple.

"Where is she?" Batina asked.

"This way," Christopher said as he grabbed Batina's hand and started to pull her. Both Ratri and Batina laughed as they followed Christopher. Within moments Koby and Bekka walked up to the three. "Batina this is my friend Bekka," Christopher said with pride.

Batina hugged Bekka and said, "I have heard so much about you, it is good to finally meet you."

"Christopher has talked about you a lot too," Bekka replied.

"Oh, I have heard more people than Christopher talk about you." Then with a smirk Batina looked at Koby. "Koby isn't that right?" Koby laughed. "Koby look, isn't it beautiful," Batina said excitedly as she showed Koby her ring.

"So you two are getting married?" Koby asked.

"She finally said yes," Ratri said with a grin.

Koby shook his head and looked at Bekka, "They have only known each other a week," Koby said then he turned back to Ratri and Batina. "It's people like you that confuse Bekka and me. The first time you look at each other you know you are going to marry."

"If we lived closer and didn't have the mission we would have taken things slower," Ratri said then looked at Batina who was smiling at him. "Or maybe not." Ratri saw that Koby and Bekka were holding hands. "You both look so content and happy, you two might have more together than you think."

Koby and Bekka looked at each other and smiled. "Actually we have been trying to figure that out," Koby said.

It was a tearful goodbye for many when Ratri, Koby and their small group of warriors left the Ice Caves the following morning. Christopher stopped crying when Koby promised they would visit Bekka and her parents again.

"You know all of you are welcomed to visit us too," Koby said. "The house is huge, there is plenty of room for guests."

Sam and Ella looked at each other. "Maybe we will," Sam said.

Bekka and Koby kissed goodbye. "Let me know when the baby is coming," Koby said. "I will probably be in Ryed but I told Gabriel I will be leaving as soon as I hear from you."

"Your parents sent so many gifts for my family," Batina said as they flew to meet the others.

"They like you and they are very happy about our marriage," Ratri said. "They meant it when they said they will fly to your village while we are gone so they can meet your family and plan the wedding celebration."

"I think they will all get along don't you?" Batina asked.

"I know they will," Ratri said with a smile and soared higher in the sky.

This first day returning from Lentz was chaotic at both Gabriel's house and the castle of Sudfad. Vitomas, Annabelle and Laurel had great fun sorting through all of the things that Mathas and Rosa had sent home with Renya. After a meeting with Raul and Simon, Sudfad was pleased with how his sons had run the kingdom in his absence. "You two did such a fine job that your mother and I might just take more holidays."

"Well you both deserve it," Raul said. "But I will admit it really seemed empty around here without you. I even think Marie felt lost."

Everyone in Gabriel's household fell in love with Cicely. And it amused many to see how excited Cerey was to have another little girl in the house. Elan and Cassandra asked Gabriel to christen Cicely the following day. Hannah and Emeral decided they should have a small party to celebrate the adoption and the christening.

After breakfast, Elan and Cassandra flew with their children to the castle to invite the Royal Family to the party. As they all sat in the parlor, Marie escorted Joao, Dack and Melinda into the room. A moment later Enrops flew into the castle with a message for Sudfad.

"Is something wrong?" Cassandra asked when she saw the look on her brother's face.

"This came for you and Elan; it probably says the same thing that our letters did," as Joao spoke he handed an envelope to Cassandra. "Mother and Father have not been seen since they were forced to appear before the Grand Council. It is believed that they left the Ice Caves."

"My letter states the same thing," Sudfad said and handed the letter to Renya.

"Where would they go?" Cassandra asked in shock.

"That's one reason we came," Joao said. "The three of us believe they would go to Nora. Melinda said they spoke often of the gifts the people of Nora are always giving to our warriors. And Sudfad they know you rule Nora."

The following morning as Hannah, Natasha and Emeral were in the kitchen preparing breakfast, Gabriel barged through the door with a serious look on his face.

"What's wrong?" asked Hannah.

"We need to have a meeting at once," Gabriel said. "Where are Luca and Misha?

"They are all outside setting up the area for the party," Emeral said as she put down the potato she was peeling. "I'll bring everyone in. Where do you want to meet?"

"My study but someone will have to stay with the children," Gabriel said and left the room. In less than five minutes all of the adults except for Melinda were gathered in Gabriel's study. Melinda was in the playroom with the children.

"Dagon would you shut the door," Gabriel asked as everyone took seats. Raphael walked to the front of the room and stood near Gabriel. "I just received a letter from both King Manu and Thedes. Before I tell you the contents of this letter I want you to know that both Koby and Christopher are alright."

Lila gasped at Gabriel's words. "As you know Koby and Christopher were flying to the Ice Caves with Ratri, Batina and a small group of Ruala warriors. On the second night of their journey Batina and Christopher were setting up the camp while the men formed two hunting groups."

Gabriel continued, "After the men left the camp, Nada, Morgan and Bruno landed behind Batina. Apparently as soon as Nada landed Christopher attacked her because he remembered Nada had hurt Diana. Batina was here when Diana and Nada had that competition so she also recognized Nada."

"I will let you read the letter for the fine details but basically Batina ended up fighting with all three of the invaders in an effort to protect Christopher. The hunting parties heard Christopher screaming for help and when the first group arrived Batina had stabbed Nada and was holding a knife to Bruno's throat. Christopher yelled at Batina which distracted her and Bruno got the advantage."

The first hunting party was already fighting with Nada and Morgan and the second hunting party arrived in time to stop Bruno from seriously hurting Batina. Nada, Morgan and Bruno were all captured and tied to trees."

"As Koby and the others were trying to figure out what to do with the three, one of the other Ruala warriors warned that a war party of Hutas was approaching. Koby gave the orders to leave the three tied to trees and to build up the fires so the Hutas would find the camp. When Koby and the others reached the Ice Caves they asked King Manu if they could appear before the Grand Council."

"Some of the men with Koby had searched the pouches that Nada and the men were carrying and found them filled with money and jewels. That was the information Koby and the others wanted to tell the Grand Council because they suspect that Nada and her friends are robbing and probably raping and killing people."

"After the men spoke before the council, King Manu called Batina and Christopher forward to see if they wanted to add any information. Christopher wanted to know why no one talked about the second woman who appeared behind Batina when she was fighting with Bruno. No one from Koby's group knew what Christopher was talking about."

"It turns out the reason Christopher had yelled at Batina was because Hecate appeared behind Batina but then disappeared as the hunting parties arrived. Christopher described the woman as looking like Vivian but very pregnant. The Grand Council is sending warriors out to see if the Hutas killed Nada and the men or if Hecate set the three free. They will keep us informed. The Grand Council is also sending warriors to the neighboring villages to explain that Nada and the others are not typical of their tribe and will be stopped."

"So Batina is alright?" Dack asked.

"Yes, apparently she fought well but she apologized to the Grand Council because she threw her knifes to wound instead of kill. Batina said at the time she didn't know if she should kill members of Ratri's tribe and now she regrets her decision. Also it sounds like Ratri and Batina are getting married."

"So that you know," Calen said. "Morgan and Bruno are both Nada's boyfriends and..." Calen glanced at Misha.

"And they commit their crimes as a group," Misha said. "All Rualas are taller than most humans but Bruno is huge even for a Ruala. Morgan is not a small man but is smaller than Bruno but they are all well trained warriors. They are also sadistic. Honestly I am amazed that Batina could hold her own that long with the three of them. I know Batina is well trained but I don't think she has ever seen battle."

"Batina was so scared that Nada and the others were going to hurt Christopher that was all she could think about," Gabriel said as he handed the letter to Raphael to read. "Later when she was before the Grand Council she told them that Bruno said it was her that they wanted, and understandably this disturbed Ratri a great deal."

"It sounds like Batina was acting like a mother protecting her young," Emeral said.

"We owe her greatly but all of this is so disturbing. Gabriel you told us that the Angels said Hecate was at the competitions here, watching Nada because Nada's heart is so black. I know Nada, Morgan and Bruno and I don't think it would take much for them to align with a demon. To say nothing about Nada and the others coming after Diana and Misha."

Maxwell stood up, "And the crimes that Nada and those men committed against the humans could cause a war between our peoples."

As Raphael handed the letter to Maxwell he asked, "It isn't my place to judge but why did the Grand Council let those three go?"

"We have no prisons in the Ice Caves and never have we put our own to death," Luca explained. "Our tribe has sworn allegiance to The Great Ruler so few crimes are committed among our people. Sadly I think that is why Nada and her boyfriends got away with their crimes for so long because our people couldn't consider anyone in our tribe doing such things."

"You said the Grand Council said Nada and the others will be stopped," Hannah asked. "How?"

Maxwell was reading the letter and now spoke, "If Nada and the men were not killed by the Hutas; Manu is sending death squads after them."

"We all expect Nada to come after Diana and Misha," Thor said. "But did any of those three make comments or threats?"

"Nada threatened to kill Koby and the others for leaving them to the Hutas," Raphael said. "There was no mention of Diana or Misha."

"You said Christopher wasn't hurt but did any of them touch him or threaten him?" Luca asked.

"Batina told the Grand Council that while Christopher was punching and kicking Nada, Morgan and Bruno just stood by laughing. When Nada reached for Christopher, Batina's knife landed in Nada's right shoulder, so Nada couldn't grab him," Maxwell said.

"I find it very curious that Hecate would appear then disappear," Gabriel said. "She is so powerful that the hunting parties would not scare her off. I think she wanted us to know she was there. She is trying to fill us with fear. I will speak with the Angels to see if this makes any difference to the plans for our mission."

"Edgar, I know it is early but there is something I need to show you," Sorren said as he stood in the doorway of Edgar's home.

"Join us for breakfast," Edgar said as he moved so Sorren could enter the house. Sorren immediately saw the children sitting around the table as Cora was getting another plate for Sorren.

"I received this letter from King Manu and Thedes," Sorren explained. "I don't think I want to talk about it in front of the children but you should read it right away?"

"Is Batina alright?" Cora asked fearfully.

"Yes and you will be proud of her when you read this," Sorren said as he took a seat at the table.

Soto was a seasoned Ruala warrior in his early thirties. He was a handsome man with brilliant blue eyes and long straight blonde hair that he wore in a ponytail which hung halfway down his back. Soto was leading a dozen Ruala and Shettee warriors as they searched for the bodies of Nada, Bruno and Morgan.

Never before had his tribe sent death squads after their own kind and the responsibility weighed heavily on Soto and his men. But the crimes committed by Nada, Morgan and Bruno had so horrified the Ruala and Shettee tribes that these three were no longer looked upon as Rualas. In fact many who dwelled in the Ice Caves considered these three more despicable than the Hutas.

After two days of traveling Ratri and Batina turned east towards the Kingdom of Lentz while Koby and the others turned west towards Salar.

Koby had promised Ratri that he would explain to Gabriel and Raphael why Ratri and Batina had left the group. The evening before Ratri had composed a letter for Gabriel and Raphael which he had given to Koby to deliver. The plan was for Ratri and Batina to join them in Wetpr in three days.

"This is not good," Soto said as he and his men walked around the shredded bodies of twenty Huta warriors. Some of the horses of the Hutas had remained in the area. The Rualas took the saddles and bridles off from these creatures and set them free. Three sets of ropes lay at the base of three trees. Any footprints were obliterated by the ocean of blood that pooled from the Huta bodies. "Check the area," Soto ordered some of his men. "I have many messages to write."

Ratri and Batina landed at her parent's house just before dinner. One of her brothers saw them land and the entire family came out of the house to greet them. "We have so much to tell you," Batina said as she hugged both of her parents.

"We read the letter from King Manu about your experiences with Nada and those men," Edgar said approvingly. "You did well my daughter. But I have to ask why did you throw your knives to wound and not kill?"

"Never have I heard of any of us killing Rualas and they were members of Ratri's tribe; everything happened so fast it was a decision I made and I should have made a different one," Batina said. "I will tell you I have never felt fear like that before; I was so frightened they would get Christopher from me. I heard what those people do to children."

"She did well," Ratri said proudly then changed the subject. "Edgar, Cora my parents were extremely pleased with the gifts that you sent them and my pack is filled with gifts for you also but before we open them; Edgar I would like to speak with you in private."

Edgar smiled and said, "Would it have anything to do with that ring on my daughter's hand?"

"It has everything to do with that," Ratri said happily as he removed his pack from his back and handed it to Batina.

"Everyone go into the house and we will be in shortly," Edgar said then when he saw the worried look on his daughter's face Edgar laughed. "Batina don't look like that, in fact why don't you open some wine and pour us all a glass."

As soon as they entered the house Batina showed her mother and her brothers and sisters her ring and started to tell them about the Ice Caves when Edgar and Ratri entered the house. "Well, that certainly didn't take long," Cora teased.

"It doesn't take long to give them my blessing," Edgar said with a grin and Batina flew into his arms and hugged Edgar tightly.

"Thank you Father, wait until you meet Ratri's parents they are so nice." Batina stopped talking and looked back and forth at her parents then she turned to Ratri and said, "I just realized how much alike our parents are, I didn't see that before."

"I know that is why I know they will get along when they come to visit," Ratri said with a grin.

"Visit!" Cora said. "When?"

"Perhaps we should sit and discuss our plans and see what you think," Ratri said. "You know we have to be in Wetpr in a few days and the mission may take months. Batina and I have been trying to figure out our wedding plans and this is what we would like to do. We want to ask Gabriel to marry us when we start the mission because we don't want to be distracted with planning everything."

"Then when we return we would like to have a second wedding and a ceremony here in your village. My Father and Mother love Batina and are very excited about the wedding. They want to come here and get to know your family and all of you can plan the ceremonies together." Ratri paused, "Now that I am explaining it, I didn't realize that Batina and I are asking all of you to plan everything. We don't mean to burden you."

"Nonsense," Edgar said happily. "You do realize that your wedding bonds our two tribes so it should be a big celebration. We will need time to plan it."

"Here is a letter from my parents with their names and the location of their home so you can send Enrops back and forth with messages," Ratri said.

"Are these all gifts?" Batina's little brother asked as he was taking packages out of Ratri's bag.

"Dano don't open those," Edgar scolded.

"There are gifts in there for the children too," Ratri said.

"Father can we open them?" asked Dano.

"Bring them here and we will open them all together," Edgar said.

"Ratri when your parents come will they be bringing children?" Cora asked.

"I am the youngest of four sons. My brothers are all married. I will be honest I don't know if my parents will make the trip alone, but anyone they bring with them can make camps."

"They will not," Edgar said indignantly. "We will provide lodging for everyone. I hope you realize that besides having our children marry, uniting the tribes is a great honor. I am sure the entire village will open their homes to guests."

"Dano will you bring the biggest gift here first?' Ratri asked. "But be careful it is sharp."

"Can we open another one first?" Batina asked excitedly and sorted through the large pile of gifts until she found a specific box. "The Ice Caves are the most beautiful place," Batina gushed as she returned to her parents. There are giant crystal pillars everywhere that provide light and healing energy. The Ice Caves are blessed by The Great Ruler. All of the Rualas wear necklaces with pieces of the crystals. When they get injured they put the crystals in the wounds and it heals them." Batina handed a box to her mother containing seven necklaces for their family.

"They are beautiful," Cora said.

"Sorren has told us of those crystals," Edgar said as he too looked at the necklaces.

"Before we open the other gifts Edgar I have one for you from my father and I must explain what it is because among my people it is a great honor to receive such a weapon." Ratri took the heavy material off the weapon and handed it to Edgar. "As you know the Shettee Tribe have become our brothers and live with us in the caves. The Shettees are mighty warriors. This is a Gafet; it is an ancient Shettee weapon. It is made out of the metal Taluth; it is light in weight yet well balanced no matter where you hold it. It takes a long time to make each weapon."

Ratri continued, "The Shettees had never heard of The Great Ruler before they came to us so they used to worship the sun, moon and stars. The crescent shape of the weapon represents the moon. That long blade in the middle represents the rays of the sun and the blades on each end represent the stars. If you would like my father will teach you how to use this weapon when he visits."

"I would like that very much," Edgar said with a proud smile as he examined his prized gift.

Ratri and Batina had already left for Wetpr when Sorren received a message from Soto about the twenty dead Hutas. As Soto, Sorren too realized that only a demon could have shredded the Huta bodies. Sorren immediately took the letter to Edgars' house.

When Gabriel received his message from Soto he sent Joao, Dack, Dagon and Koby to find Ratri and Batina and to escort them back to Gabriel's house. Not only was Gabriel worried about Ratri and Batina but he was anxious to start the mission so he and Raphael could be home in time for the births of their children. Luca had decided not to go on the mission to Ryed because Lila was so close to her delivery date.

As soon as Gabriel dispatched Joao and the others to find Ratri and Batina he rode to the home of Jared and Zoya where Hannah and Cassandra had been all night to deliver Zoya's baby.

"Come in and see our son," Jared said with great pride as Gabriel entered the house.

"We were just coming home," Hannah said when Jared led Gabriel into the bedroom where Zoya was sitting up in bed holding her baby.

"We are naming him William after Jared's father," Zoya said as Gabriel bent down to look at the baby.

"I can't believe how much hair he has," Gabriel said. "He is a beautiful boy."

"Archetenus, Edward and Simon came out to keep Jared company," Zoya continued. "And Jared did so much better than Archetenus did when his babies were born. This comment made everyone laugh. "Raul didn't come because Vitomas is going to give birth any day."

"He didn't come to the meeting this morning either so I would not be surprised if she gives birth today or tomorrow," Gabriel said.

"Maybe I should stop at the castle before we go home," Hannah said with concern.

"You need to get some sleep too," Gabriel said to Hannah. "They will send someone when they need you."

"Gabriel I won't be able to sleep until I know how Vitomas is. She always comes early with every baby."

As Gabriel, Hannah and Cassandra walked through the front door of the castle, Marie ran up to them and said excitedly, "Raul just told me to send a soldier for you Vitomas is having the baby."

"Marie, Hannah and Cassandra have been up all night delivering Zoya's baby would you make them some coffee and something to eat?" Gabriel asked.

"Most certainly," Marie said then turned and quickly walked to the west wing with Hannah and Cassandra.

Gabriel knocked on the door to Sudfad's study, when no one answered he turned and walked to the living quarters of Raul and Vitomas in the west wing of the castle.

As was typical for a royal birth the entire family including the Sanuri were seated in the parlor. Gabriel sat next to the Sanuri and handed him the note from Soto. "Did you receive one of these?" Gabriel asked.

The Sanuri read the note and handed it back to Gabriel. "I read Sudfad's which is almost identical to yours."

"I sent some of the Rualas to meet Ratri and Batina and bring them back here," Gabriel said then paused. "I don't know if I am being paranoid but for a couple of weeks I have had this nagging feeling that I have overlooked something really important. I just have a bad feeling about this mission. Have you had any visions about it?"

"Gabriel when was the last time you omitted something important on a mission?" the Sanuri asked. "You are an incredibly detailed person. Usually when I feel like that I have to ask for clarification."

Gabriel paused, "I have been meaning to call to the Angels but things have been so crazy lately."

"That might be the exact reason you should call to them."

"You are right. I will go home now and call to Miranda and Daniel," Gabriel said as he started to stand up.

"My old bones are telling me you should probably call to The Lion first, I don't know why; it is just a feeling."

"You did what?" Sampson asked loudly.

"Sampson now don't get upset," Hecate said as she handed him a glass of wine. "I did it for you so let me explain. You know I am monitoring the battles going on in the hell regions. Well, I have formed an alliance with an old friend and we are in the process of raising an army. When all of the armies are done fighting and exhausted we plan to attack. If I can take over a hell region I will have the same powers as an Old One and I can help you complete your transformation. Which means I can help you gain your power."

"So you haven't been able to find another demon to sponsor me?" Sampson asked as he gulped his glass of wine and poured another.

"Sampson there has never been anything like these wars in the history of this world. All of the Old Ones are fighting against each other and against demons from other worlds. None of them are going to be distracted from battle to help you. At first I thought you could be more help to my cause as a human because you can go into places and touch things which I cannot. But since you have been having such difficulty maintaining your human form I no longer believe that is an option."

"As you know the Ruala race worships The Great Ruler and works on His behalf. Well, I have found three Rualas with souls darker than yours my dear and that is saying a lot," Hecate said and leaned forward, kissing Sampson on the lips.

"These Rualas have been banished from their tribe because of their crimes. They can no longer enter the Ice Caves so they have no sanctuary. They were recently in a situation that I helped them out of but the price was their souls. Think of it Sampson no one suspects a Ruala of being evil, their usefulness to me is unlimited."

"But you sent them into my village?"

"No, I said I have them getting me some items I need then I am sending them to your village to grab your brothers. I cannot change what Baal has put into motion. You still have to kill them to complete your transformation."

As Gabriel was riding home from Sudfad's castle he was deep in thought when he realized a great lion was standing in the roadway before him.

"Gabriel you are working on a mission with implications that you cannot even imagine and yet you put off asking the heavens for advice because what? You do not want to bother us? Gabriel I am disappointed. Speaking with us should become routine for you."

"I am sorry you are right. I do realize this mission is different from any other I have worked on and it causes me concern."

"There are so many variables and so many ways innocent people could be hurt."

"You have battled demons and dark lords before and you have overthrown tyrants before what about this mission worries you so?"

"That's part of the problem, I can't really tell you. I feel like I am missing something right before my eyes."

"You are," The Lion stated. "You are successful partially because of your understanding of the human mind. You know how people will react but the goodness within you makes you ill prepared for this mission. You need to understand the motivations and agendas of darkness. I find it curious that two incredibly powerful priests live in a home with someone who has been a victim of demons yet you do not offer him comfort or have allowed him to unburden his soul, why is that?"

"Misha!" Gabriel gasped as the words of the Angel brought great realization to him. "You are right, I don't have an answer except that Misha doesn't seem like a victim."

"His wife has seen the victim in him and that is why she will stop at nothing to protect him. You need to see what Misha has seen before you can lead your team on this mission. You and Raphael would be wise to speak with Misha and expect to spend a great deal of time together. Really listen to what he has to say. You have not spoken to Misha of the abuse because you did not want to embarrass him. Gabriel you should be helping him heal. He will heal as he gives you what you need but you will have to tell him and Diana that I told you to speak with him."

Chapter XLIII
The Cry of a Baby

The cry of a new born baby is often viewed as a miracle by mankind; it is always celebrated as a miracle in the heavens. When baby Miranda announced to the world that she was born Angels sang. Within moments of holding his new granddaughter, King Sudfad sent messengers throughout the kingdom to announce the birth of a baby princess. There was no mistaking the heritage of this child with her black hair and aqua eyes she looked like her father and grandfather.

After the members of the Royal Family had each held the baby, Raul asked that they leave the bedroom for a few moments. Raul put the baby back into the arms of his beautiful wife and closed the door. "Miranda, Daniel we know you are watching," Raul called out to the heavens. "Miranda would you like to meet your namesake?" In an instant two glorious Angels appeared near the bed. Vitomas handed the baby to Miranda.

"She has dark hair like you and Raul," Vitomas said as the Angel smiled upon the baby.

"She is most beautiful," Daniel said as he stood near Miranda. Vitomas and Raul thought they were imagining it, but the room seemed to become warmer and brighter.

"We know she is human," Raul said. "But Vitomas and I hope she takes after you."

"Oh Raul," Miranda said lovingly. "You really have no idea what you just said." And the Angel kissed the baby on her forehead.

Later that afternoon, Gabriel and Raphael met with Misha and Diana in Gabriel's study. "This morning as I was riding home from the castle, The Lion blocked my passage. He knew I had planned to call to him when I got home. For weeks I have been overwhelmed with not only feelings of dread concerning our next mission but feelings that I was overlooking something of great importance." Both Misha and Diana were taken by surprise at the words that Gabriel was saying.

"The Lion told me my feelings were valid because I was not yet ready to lead my team on such a mission. He said that although I am gifted in understanding the minds and motivations of men I do not understand the same traits in darkness and until I do I cannot safely lead my mission."

Gabriel continued, "Then he told me something that has brought both Raphael and I great shame. The Lion said he could not understand how two powerful priests could live in the same home with someone who had been victimized by demons and not offer comfort or confession."

"Neither Raphael nor I have acted as friends and we certainly have not acted as priests. The Lion said that you can give me the information I need to lead the next mission and in so doing you will be healed. He said we had to carefully listen to your words and to tell you exactly what he said."

"Misha we both apologize to you," Raphael said sincerely. "We have no excuses. The Lion said we did not comfort you because we didn't want to embarrass you but Gabriel and I think some place deep within us we didn't want to see that horror. We should have been there for you and we hope you will forgive us."

Misha sat motionless while Diana held his hand and cried. "Misha you are such an incredibly strong man to have endured what you did and yet turn out as such a fine person. The Lion also said that Diana has seen the victim within you and will stop at nothing to protect you. I am telling you this because I was to repeat his words."

Diana left the men alone to talk. Both Hannah and Cassandra had returned from the castle and were now sleeping. Lila and Melinda were watching the children so Diana walked into the kitchen to help Natasha and Emeral with the evening meal. Diana knew she had to keep busy and she had no intention of sharing with anyone the words that Gabriel said. But the moment that Diana walked into the kitchen she was crying in Emeral's arms and telling Emeral and Natasha everything.

Jared and Zoya wanted their baby christened immediately because of Jared's fear that the darkness that once owned him would touch his child. The Sanuri came out to their home and christened the baby that afternoon.

"Thank you so much," Jared said. "We will have a celebration later but with my past I didn't want to take any chances."

"Jared, the curse that was placed upon you has been broken by your choice and cannot be passed to your children. But they have free will to make their own choices. You and Zoya should not live in fear; the key is to teach your children well."

"I think you need to have this same talk with Archetenus and Delilah too," Jared said.

Gabriel, Raphael and Misha did not leave the study for dinner so Diana and Natasha served the meal in the study. Few words were said as the women set up one of the tables with the evening meal. Diana kissed Misha on the cheek as she left the room.

"They all look like they have been crying," Natasha whispered to Diana and put her arm around her friend's shoulders.

Two days later, Koby and members of the team returned to the house with Ratri and Batina. "Batina, Batina," Christopher screamed as he watched the group land on the front yard. As soon as Batina's feet were on the ground she squatted down and Christopher jumped into her arms and they hugged and kissed.

"Christopher always gets the girls," Joao joked.

"Batina and I fought those bad people," Christopher said proudly and took Batina's hand.

"That we did," she said as the rest of the team came out of the house to greet them.

"And we owe you a great deal," Luca said and hugged Batina.

"You owe me nothing," Batina said. "I told Ratri I have never been that scared before. I was so afraid those monsters would get Christopher."

Lila hugged Batina and handed her a gift saying, "We have no idea what you like so this is just a small token." Simultaneously Luca handed Ratri a small box.

"Open them now," Christopher said excitedly.

Everyone from the household smiled as Batina opened a small box containing a single white flower. Then they laughed at the look of confusion on her face. "Ratri open yours and we will explain," Maxwell said.

Ratri opened the small box and held up a key for Batina to see. He smiled and said, "I am sorry I really don't understand."

"Sorren sent us a message that you were on your way and wanted me to marry you before the mission so you would not be distracted thinking about wedding plans," Gabriel explained. "He said you wanted something very simple because his village will host the celebrations when the team returns. Not only does Sorren like both of you but he is ecstatic that your tribes are uniting. He also told us that you could have put off the mission but you both considered it a priority over your personal lives. That kind of dedication should be rewarded."

"The flower symbolizes the wedding we are going to have for you here," Emeral said and hugged both Batina and Ratri.

"And the key is to the chambers you will have in this house," Gabriel said. "It is our understanding that you have not taken the time to decide where you will live after the mission and although you both have homes you will have a home here with us also."

Both Ratri and Batina stared at Gabriel without speaking. "You both look in shock," Calen said with a grin.

"We are," Ratri said. "Batina has been terrified that once we asked you to marry us that you would not allow her on the mission. In fact her fear of being removed from the mission was her main concern when we discussed marriage. We really did not expect anything like this."

"Come inside," Hannah said sweetly and we can take you to your chambers and show you the house. "Your other friends from the Ice Caves are in Salar but they will be back this afternoon."

Batina's eyes widened when they entered the house. "This is so beautiful, I have never seen a home like this before."

"We have to warn you we always have some kind of construction project going on since our family just keeps growing. We can introduce everyone in a moment but let's go to your chambers," Natasha said.

"I really am in shock," Batina said as she and Ratri walked with Calen and Natasha up the stairs, the others followed. Calen proudly opened a door which opened into a small parlor.

"There are two bedrooms here," Calen said. "If you decide you want to live here permanently we will move you to larger chambers. The girls decorated the rooms and picked the furniture but if you want something else just say so."

Ratri and Batina were quiet as they walked around the chambers. "Don't you like them?" Nicholas asked.

"We love them," Ratri said. "We are just so very overwhelmed. We planned to camp in your yard. Thank you so very much."

"Yes thank you," Batina said. "It is not only your generosity that is overwhelming but I grew up poor, I have never even been in chambers like this, well, except when we stayed at Sudfad's castle for the wedding."

"We understand how you feel," Lila said. "Several of us grew up poor."

"She wouldn't even pick out a wedding dress because she was afraid to spend the money," Luca said and laughed. "So I picked it out."

"And you did a fine job," Emeral said with a warm smile.

"The key is symbolic," Misha said and grinned. "We don't lock the doors here although we probably should to stop people from walking in when we are making love." Misha looked at Thor and everyone laughed.

"You two are always making love, you need to put a sign on the door," Thor said with a grin.

Upon the return of Gabriel's team to Wetpr, Iris and Laurel started spending a great deal of time together. Both women loved to sew and knit. They were making many baby gifts which they put aside to make some gifts for Ratri's and Batina's wedding.

The morning that Ratri and Batina arrived at the house, Vivian, Diana and Ratri's friends were in Salar purchasing items for the wedding. Ratri was a childhood playmate of Maxwell's and Emeral's sons. The boys had all grown up together and spent a great deal of time at each other's homes.

Ratri's parents sent several letters to Emeral and Maxwell updating the news of Ratri and Batina. Joseph and Clair were also making arrangements to visit with Emeral and Maxwell when they came to visit Batina's family. Emeral and Maxwell felt like one of their own sons was getting married.

A week and a day after Ratri and Batina were married, Gabriel's team started its journey towards Ryed. This mission was planned with two fronts, Gabriel was leading a team into the Kingdom of Ryed to initially gather information about the Teivel Clan and to make contact with a clandestine group of freedom fighters. Gabriel hoped to talk the freedom fighters into combining their forces and launching an attack against the Teivel Clan.

With or without the assistance of the freedom fighters Gabriel's team was going to attack the Teivel Clan which owned most of the Kingdom of Ryed. It was understood by all that launching an attack would start a war. The priority for Sudfad was to remove the members of the Teivel Clan and the Insidiae from Fort Polta and the Kingdom of Wetpr. The members of the Teivel Clan were known for their powerful dark magics. Gabriel's team was going to provide a distraction for the clan so they could not help their members as Fort Polta was being attacked by Raphael's team.

If the freedom fighters of Ryed would agree to assist Gabriel's team then the second plan was to destroy the Teivel Clan's reign of terror in Ryed. Raphael, Edward and their troops would join Gabriel's team after the situation at Fort Polta was stabilized.

The initial group to leave for Ryed was small; it consisted of Gabriel, Misha, Diana, Thor, Ratri, Batina, Calen, Natasha, Joao, Joshua and his son Micha, Dack, Milo, Eilig and Sauer. These last three men were Ruala warriors who had never worked on one of the small clandestine operations before.

Erebus also traveled with this group and was allowing them to use his castle for the base of their operations, but his castle was a considerable distance from the castle of Teivel.

A week after Gabriel's team left Wetpr, Raphael and Edward led troops on what was to appear to be an annual inspection of the forts. In truth Raphael and Edward were inspecting the forts to maintain their covers. Many of the men they led were Patronus priests who were dressed in the uniforms of the Wetprian Military. Darla, Jasmine and Bianca, all female Nordes warriors were assigned to this group. These women did not ride with the soldiers but were carried by Rualas.

Natasha and Vivian had worked intensively with all the female Nordes warriors to train them in covert operations and to provide them with a variety of disguises. Other Ruala warriors who volunteered to help were Cage, Asher, Apel, Betu, Daz and Eli all of these warriors had participated in large battles that were led either by Gabriel's team or the combined armies led by General Claudius.

The members of Gabriel's team who remained in Wetpr were Maxwell, Emeral, Luca, Lila, Elan, Cassandra, Vivian and Hannah. Melinda and Iris had volunteered to help with the children and household duties.

While Raul, Simon and Sudfad were the generals on duty at Fort Salar they were closely monitoring both Raphael's and Gabriel's teams and were prepared to give assistance. The Sanuri remained at Sudfad's castle to try and translate the plyogram but intended to join one of the two teams once they were closer to going into battle.

King Mathas, King Manu, King Neputa and Chief Sorren all pledged troops if Sudfad needed them. Sudfad assumed that Hecate was watching the teams and he knew the new King of Stordt was a demon who had put bounties on the heads of Gabriel's team.

621

Sudfad understood that if he moved large groups of troops it would alert these demons that some kind of mission was at hand. For several weeks before Gabriel's team left Wetpr, Sudfad started having troops cross the border at various locations and enter the Kingdom of Stordt.

These troops traveled in small groups and wore civilian clothing. The groups of soldiers had orders to report to either the Patronus Headquarters at Nora or to Fort Nora. So far the Taperian border guards were not acting suspicious of these small groups of Wetprian soldiers. Sudfad planned to keep sending additional forces to Nora, in this manner, until the missions were completed.

Sudfad was paranoid about spies within his military and he had every right to be. Over the past two years Sudfad had two new forts constructed on Wetprian soil and he put two of his most trusted generals in charge of these forts. Besides Fort Nora, these were the only forts that were currently receiving additional troops.

General Craven was the commanding general of Fort Stanus which was located on the southern border of Wetpr and General Farnsworth was commanding Fort Serpha which was located in northern Wetpr. Raphael and Edward carried papers for these generals with information about the missions.

Sudfad did not want to send the information by messengers. In fact, both Raphael and Edward were ordered not to give the letters to either general if they felt something was suspicious at the forts. General Ridon and Captain Malard were now stationed at Fort Stanus. Sudfad planned to have these two men assume command of Fort Polta once General Kretcher was removed from power. But neither Ridon nor Malard were aware of the missions or the new orders. Raphael and Edward carried letters for these two men also.

Gabriel's team was flying from Wetpr to Erebus' castle. Every Ruala warrior carried a human and a pack of supplies on their back. This was the last evening of the journey; tomorrow they would reach Erebus' castle and the mission would begin. This group of people interacted well and this night they were particularly light-hearted.

Erebus was considerably older than most of the people in this group but he enjoyed the youthful exuberance. After dinner the group was sitting around the fires laughing as Joao collected wagers he had just won. All of the men had placed bets on how long it would take Micha to realize he missed Bianca. As everyone was laughing and joking, Natasha suddenly announced with great sadness that she missed Lily.

Calen put his arm around Natasha and everyone was silent for a moment. Diana decided to lighten the mood. "Misha and I decided to start working on a family after this mission," she announced. But before the words were out of Diana's mouth Thor was roaring with laughter.

"Start! You two barely come up for air, how much more can you start?" Thor's laughter infected everyone in the group.

"Thor!" Diana scolded and slapped her brother's arm as she turned a deep shade of red but within moments she was laughing too. "Well, you are kind of right," Diana said and looked at Misha who was laughing.

"Misha did Diana warn you that we have twins in our family?" Thor asked.

"So do I," Misha replied with a grin and the entire group laughed again at the comic look that overtook Diana's face.

"Well it's a good thing then that I have picked out two boy's names," Diana said.

"Let's hear them," said Misha.

"You said that Maxwell already had a grandson with that name, so I thought our first son would be named Maximus Bartholomew. Bartholomew was our father's name and is Thor's middle name. Then I thought our second son should be named after your birth father, I thought Adwell Thor or Thor Adwell. So what do you think?"

"I really like them," Misha said sincerely.

"They are good strong warrior names," Joshua said with approval.

"I think the second son should be Thor Adwell," Joao said with a grin. "Then we could have a big Thor and a little Thor in the house."

"Actually I like that," Misha said then he turned to Diana. "What did you pick out for girl's names?"

"I was thinking that you and Thor could pick out those names," Diana said with a big smile. Both Misha and Thor looked stunned for a moment. "Oh come on," Diana joked. "You've had hundreds of girlfriends you must know a lot of names." The group again roared with laughter.

"She got you," Calen said as he continued to laugh.

Batina was sitting on the ground between Ratri's legs; she now looked up at him and said, "We haven't even discussed having a family." Ratri smiled and kissed her.

"You mean in the whole two weeks..." Dack was saying but was interrupted when Erebus suddenly jumped to a standing position. Erebus had been sitting on a log between Gabriel and Joshua.

"What is happening?" Gabriel asked as he too jumped up.

Erebus routinely wore a long leather necklace on the outside of his robes. There was an unusually shaped medallion hanging from the necklace which now was glowing bright red. "Someone just broke into my castle," Erebus announced then decided to explain his comment when he saw the confused looks on everyone's faces.

"I have a powerful protection spell on my castle," Erebus explained. "Besides me, there are only two other people who should be at the castle and I made exceptions for them in the spell. They are an older couple and only work during the daytime. Gabriel, I have never had intruders before; this is no coincidence someone is setting a trap for us."

624

Chief Duncan of the Clan of Gesmal had been receiving messages from Gabriel, King Manu and the Ruala warriors who were hunting Nada, Morgan and Bruno. While Duncan appreciated the information he rather dismissed it because he could not understand how three rogue Ruala warriors could be a threat to his tribe of fierce Venatores.

But this night Duncan's heart was filled with both fear and grief as he led one of the search parties that were looking for Duncan's two sons. Both of his sons, George and Ivan had simply disappeared earlier in the day.

Both of these men were fierce warriors who would have fought any attackers. But the Venatores, who were trained to be exceptional trackers, found no sign of a fight anywhere they searched. The mystery was that there was absolutely no trail or tracks of any kind.

The entire village knew that Sampson had sworn to kill his younger brothers in order to complete his trials to become a demon. Venatores rarely felt fear but the hearts of every man and woman in the search parties were heavy. Both George and Ivan were loved and admired by their clan while Sampson was feared and despised. It was beyond the comprehension of many of the villagers that one brother could kill another, yet alone for such a diabolical reason. And what would their futures hold if Sampson did complete the trials.

Luca ran into the parlor of Gabriel's house where Hannah, Iris, Vivian, Maxwell and Emeral were sitting.

"Good you're not in bed yet," Luca said frantically. "Lila is having the baby."

"When did she start having contractions?" Hannah asked. "She didn't say anything today."

"I don't know but she looks like she is in a lot of pain." Luca replied and quickly ran back to his chambers.

Vivian woke the other members of the family as Hannah, Emeral and Maxwell went to Luca's chambers. Iris ran into the kitchen and started to prepare tonics and coffee. Christopher was sitting on the bed next to Lila looking scared. "She's bleeding," Christopher screamed as everyone ran into the room.

"Maxwell take Christopher," Hannah said as she ran to the bed where blood was oozing through the blankets.

"Lila, Lila," Christopher screamed as Maxwell carried him out of the bedroom.

Luca stood paralyzed as he watched Hannah and Emeral working on Lila. "She wasn't bleeding when I left," Luca said in almost a whisper.

Iris entered the bedroom, her eyes widened when she saw the scene before her. "What do you need me to do?"

"Get my medical bag; it's on the chair in my bedroom," Hannah said as she wiped the tears from her eyes.

The women worked frantically to try and stop the bleeding. "Luca tell Elan or Cassandra to get the Sanuri," Emeral ordered.

Vivian ran into the bedroom and stopped and stared at the blood soaked bed. "Luca is crying," she stammered.

"Vivian we need you to stay with Luca right now," Emeral said through her tears.

Elan and Cassandra were awake and in the parlor with their children when Luca ran up to them crying. "Get the Sanuri," Luca could barely get the words out then his knees started to buckle. Cassandra helped Luca to a chair as Elan ran out into the night.

After ten minutes Hannah and Emeral looked at each other. "I'm going to have to take the baby," Hannah whispered.

The sound of a baby crying greeted the Sanuri and Elan as they ran into Gabriel's house. "Upstairs," Melinda yelled frantically as the men ran through the house. Christopher was screaming hysterically as Maxwell tried to calm him.

626

Maxwell was carrying Christopher into the hallway as Elan and the Sanuri sped past them. Both Hannah and Emeral were covered with blood. Emeral was holding a tiny baby wrapped in a towel. Neither of the women said anything as the Sanuri and Elan ran into the bedroom and saw Luca holding the lifeless body of Lila and sobbing.

Hold the hand that is offered

Wipe away the tears

Love the ones discarded

Dissolve the darkest fears

If I Had Wings © 2008

By

Sandra J Yearman

Glossary of Characters

Aaron: an escaped prisoner from Wetpr

Aaryan: a male Grand Master of the Insidiae

Abaddon: an ancient demon/one of the Old Ones

Abella: daughter of Prince Lakin and Princess Zada/Ruala

Abigail: sister of Marie/ nurse for grandchildren of King Sudfad

Adi: son of Elen and Batya/ Ruala

Adrone: youngest son of Joshua and Iris/younger brother of Vivian/Clan of Gesmal

Adwell: Prince/ son of King Zachariah and Queen Noella of New Samona/husband of Nada/father of Misha/ Adwell was killed in battle leaving Nada to raise ten children/Ruala/

Ael: an ancient demon/ one of the Old Ones

Aetes: Shettee warrior

Ahriman: an ancient demon/ one of the Old Ones

Aiden: five year old Ruala boy/son of Artis and Jenna/nephew of Ratri

Akasha: former king of Ryed/grandfather of Nehmota

Alexander: former servant of King Roch's parents/ father of Annabelle

Alexander: one of the twin sons of Simon and Annabelle

Alexandras: King of Wetpr/brother of Jaretta/uncle of Sudfad and Roch

Alexas Rose: daughter of Matthew and Angelina

Alexis: son of Usman, the leader of the Valdore Tribe

Alice: and her husband find Jorge near death in Nora

Aloeus: Shettee warrior

Amiee: sister of Marie/ nurse for grandchildren of King Sudfad

Amundsen: Commanding General of Fort Friada in the Kingdom of Ganz

Amy: a young girl who was kidnapped by Sal

Ana: eleven year old Nordes girl/daughter of Edgar and Cora/younger sister of Batina

Ana: Princess/daughter of Zeman and Oda/niece of King Manu of New Samona/Ruala

Anda: one of Chief Romogi's three wives/Huta

Andrea: female Ruala warrior/ sister of Bekka

Andres: Princess of Ryed/daughter of Oren and Astrel/ has twin sister Jorga

Andrew: jeweler in Salar

Andrus: father of Rabi/Ruala

Angelina: daughter of Sorren, Chief of the Nordes Tribe/female warrior

Annabar: daughter of King Sharonne

Annabelle: handmaid and best friend to Queen Vitomas of the Kingdom of Stordt

Anthony: one of the twin sons of Simon and Annabelle

April: a young girl who was kidnapped by Sal

Arca: Enrop leader who protects King Mathas' family

Arches: a Patronus priest

Archetenus The Brave: Captain in the Taperian Army

Arianna: daughter of Simon and Annabelle

Ariel: daughter of Raul and Vitomas

Arlene: housekeeper and cook for Erebus/wife of Theodore

Armstrong: soldier and scout in the army of Wetpr

Arthur Marcus: father of Hannah

Artis: male Ruala warrior/oldest brother of Ratri/husband of Jenna

Asher: male Ruala warrior

Asher: youngest of three brothers who formed the Libertas in Ryed

Asmodeus: an ancient demon/ one of the Old Ones

Astrel: former princess of Ryed/daughter of Akasha and Norah

Atomos: Elder of the Centras and Keeper of the Box of Itifer

Augustus Endleson: a wealthy businessman who owned part of the City of Nora

Ava: twin of Benjamin/daughter of Archetenus and Delilah

Baal: an ancient demon/ one of the Old Ones

Babu: Enrop

Bac: male Ruala warrior

Bachnenus: warrior guarding refugees/Shettee

Bali: Enrop leader of the flock that does battle at Juleta's castle

Balin: Prince of Norkv/son of Thaddius and Omara/grandson of Benjeman and Esther

Balius: Shettee warrior/brother of King Neputa

Banacus: General in the army of King Tobias of Puntd

Banaka: a female Grand Master of the Insidiae

Barak: Prince of Norkv/grandson of Benjeman and Esther

Barak: Prince/son of King Neputa and Queen Tiara/Shettee

Barid: Prince of Ogg

Barid: Prince of Ryed/son of Nehmota and Vasart

Bart: male Ruala warrior/ married to Bekka's sister Andrea

Bastra: Huta captain

Batina: young female Nordes warrior

Batya: wife of Elen/Ruala

Beatrice Endleson: wife of Augustus

Becca: Princess of Norkv/daughter of Thaddius and Omara/granddaughter of Benjeman and Esther

Behtay: Princess/daughter of Segal and Cahina/niece of King Manu of New Samona/Ruala

Bekka: female Ruala warrior

Bella: wife of Claudius and mother of Stephan

Benedict: Prince of Norkv/son of Benjeman and Esther

Benjamin: twin of Ava/son of Archetenus and Delilah

Benjeman: vicious rebel leader who overthrew the government of Samona

Benson: a Private in the Wetprian military

Bentra: an ancient demon/ one of the Old Ones

Berta: cook at Racing Horse Tavern

Berta: Queen of Stordt/wife of Micha/grandmother of Roch and Sudfad

Bertha: an elderly woman from Nora

Betty: a woman from Nora

Betu: male Ruala warrior

Bianca: young female Nordes warrior

Black Jack: a regular patron at the Ghost Ship Tavern in Port Friada

Bode: Shettee warrior

Botis: a demon

Brik: son of Prince Lakin and Princess Zada /Ruala

Brina: Princess of Norkv/daughter of Valor and Cai/granddaughter of Benjeman and Esther

Bruce: male Nordes warrior/eldest son of Edgar and Cora/older brother of Batina

Cabal: son of Karzman and Nadia

Cacu: Enrop leader that joined Raul and Simon on a mission

Cade: son of King Pergo and Queen Vinus/ Kingdom of Gandt

Cadi: daughter of Prince Hadar and Princess Paj/ granddaughter of Manu/Ruala

Cael: Shettee boy who is adopted by Thedes and Ibula

Cage: male Ruala warrior

Cahina: Princess/ married to Segal son of King Zachariah and Queen Noella of New Samona/Ruala

Cai: Princess of Norkv/wife of Valor who was the son of Benjeman and Esther

Calen: male Ruala warrior/cousin of Luca/son of Maxwell and Emeral/

Calla: female Ruala warrior

Calvin: a desk clerk at The Captain's Retreat Hotel in Port Friada

Campbell: one of the spies at the Castle at Wetpr

Canton: Cisero's second in command

Cara: Princess of Ogg

Carlsman: a Lieutenant in the Army of Lentz

Carson Dormors: a wealthy landowner in the Kingdom of Ganz

Carston: member of the governing body of Nora

Casey: male Ruala warrior/father of Melanie/husband of Tasha

Cassandra: female Ruala warrior

Cassandra: daughter of King Friada and Queen Marla of the Kingdom of Ganz

Cedrick Teivel: a ruthless, powerful man in the Kingdom of Ryed

633

Celo: Prince of Ryed/son of Oren and Astrel

Cere: daughter of Tristt/Shettee

Cerephus: General in the Taperian Army

Cerey: orphan girl/sister of Nicholas/adopted daughter of Gabriel and Hannah

Ceria: Princess/daughter of Gunnel and Uma/niece of King Manu of New Samona/ sister of Elan/Ruala

Chaez: son of Fahron

Chaladrone: an ancient demon/ one of the Old Ones

Chalice: hired fighter for Dieter

Chalta: daughter of King Pergo and Queen Vinus/ Kingdom of Gandt

Chance: works with the Patronus

Chara: three year old Ruala girl/ daughter of Orin and Rene/niece of Ratri

Charlene: a woman from Nora

Charles: Father of Cassandra, Joao and Melinda

Charles: hired farmhand of Arthur Marcus

Chief Romogi: leader of the Hutas/ Kingdom of Marba

Christopher: six year old boy who Luca saves from the Hutas/brother of Lila

Ciao: female Ruala warrior

Cicely: adopted daughter of Elan and Cassandra

Cisero: a member of the Insidiae

Clair: a woman from Nora

Clair: female Ruala warrior/mother of Ratri/wife of Joseph

Claudius: General in the Army of Lentz

Cleo: a man who works for Cicero/a vessel

Cobren: Prince of Norkv/son of Grace and Makalo/Grandson of Benjeman and Esther

Compro: Taperian soldier injured at Wall of Dorath

Cora: mother of Batina/wife of Edgar/Nordes warrior

Corina: young female Nordes warrior

Corwin: son of King Fahra and Queen Sitha of Zorta

Crater: a Sergeant in the Wetprian army

Crater: a soldier in the army of Wetpr

Crispus: a guard at King Roch's castle

Crocell: a demon

Cronn: a demon

Cronos: Shettee warrior

Dack: male Ruala warrior

Dacron: former prince of Ryed/is murdered by his younger brother Nehmota for the throne

Dael: an ancient demon/ one of the Old Ones

Dagon: a male Ruala warrior

Dagor: son of King Fahra and Queen Sitha of Zorta

Dai: son of Gael, grandson of Manu/Ruala

Daisy: nine year old Nordes girl/ daughter of Edgar and Cora/younger sister of Batina

Damas: an ancient demon/ one of the Old Ones

Danar: a man created to be a vessel for demons

Daniel: an emissary of The Great Ruler who takes on the disguise of a human man

Danilla: mother of King Mathas

Dano: seven year old Nordes boy/son of Edgar and Cora/youngest brother of Batina

Darius: Prince of Samona/son of Thomas and Rewel/brother of Varden

Darla: young female Nordes warrior

Darlah: sister of Marie/ nurse for grandchildren of King Sudfad

Delilah: wife of Dieter

Delilia: Queen of New Samona/mother of Ibula, Lakin, Gael and Hadar/ wife of King Manu/Ruala

Demanko: a demon

Demetries: a demon

Denise Froush: wife of Martin who is a wealthy ship builder in Port Friada

Denks: a soldier in the army of Wetpr

Denton: one of the spies at the Castle in Wetpr

Derek: friend of Thaos

Derlock: Huta warrior

Diana: a Venator/sister of Thor

Dieter: member of the Insidiae

Dion: Princess of Samona/wife of Yorggi who was the son of Thomas and Rewel/brother of Varden

Dixon: a Taperian soldier

Dominic Petlov: was the senior High Priest at the monastery at Malga before he was murdered

Dominic: oldest of three brothers who formed the Libertas in Ryed

Dorme: Prince of Ogg

Doros: works for High Priest Meekos

Douma: King of Ogg

Dresden: a Sergeant in the Wetprian army

Duncan: Chief of the Clan of Gesmal in Ryed/ husband of Liza

Duran: father of Nikki/Nordes Tribe

Dymas: Shettee warrior

Eachann: Shettee warrior

Edgar: father of Batina/husband of Cora/Nordes warrior

Edith: wife of Lloyd a banker in Nora

Eilig: male Ruala warrior

Elan: male Ruala warrior/son of Gunnel and Uma/

Eldridge: works with the Patronus

Elen: son of Andrus and Naomi/ brother of Rabi/ Ruala

Elexas: a female Nordes warrior

Ella: female Ruala warrior/mother of Bekka/wife of Sam

Eloise: female Ruala warrior/oldest sister of Bekka/wife of Tony

Elsa: female Ruala warrior/mother of Mia/wife of Tyron

Emeral: mother of Calen/Ruala

Emeric: a male Grand Master of the Insidiae

Emma: daughter of Luca and Lila

Emmet: workers for Gabriel

Emon: a male Grand Master of the Insidiae

Erebus: sorcerer from Ryed

Erwat: a member of the Half-Man's Tribe who helps the Clan of Gesmal

Esser: Prince/son of Segal and Cahina/nephew of King Manu of New Samona/Ruala

Esteban: a member of the Insidiae

Esther: Queen of New Norkv/wife of rebel leader Benjeman

Fabron: Prince of Ogg

Fadil: a male Grand Master of the Insidiae

Fahra: King of Zorta

Fahron: General in the Army of Lentz

Fairoot: demon/ lieutenant for Salzar

Fala: female Ruala warrior

Farnsworth: General in charge of building Fort Serpha in Wetpr

Fatima: Prince of Ryed/ son of Oren and Astrel

Fatronas: an ancient demon/one of the Old Ones

Fengu: Enrop leader who helps Gabriel and his group against Omnibus

Fennel: one of three brothers who formed the Libertas in Ryed

Ferguson: a Sergeant in the Army of Lentz

Fiona: mother of Nadia/grandmother of Michael

Fraisier: a businessman and member of the Insidiae in Nora

Frank: a villager in Telmark

Fred Stapleton: a farmer in Wetpr

Friada: King of the Kingdom of Ganz

Gabriella: sister of Marie/nurse to grandchildren of King Sudfad

Gad: male Ruala warrior

Gael: Prince/son of King Manu and Queen Delilia/Ruala

Gala: a healer from the Kingdom of Stordt

Galen: male Nordes warrior

Geoff: Prince of Lentz/son of Princess Isabella and Captain Josef

Geoff: Prince of Norkv/son of Benedict and Sasaha/grandson of Benjeman and Esther

George: an advisor for King Fahra of Zorta

George: middle son of Chief Duncan and Liza of the Clan of Gesmal in Ryed

Gita: wife of Hadi/ Ruala

Gladys: member of Nordes Tribe/ mother of Nikki

Glenda: great, great, great grandmother of Gala/ a healer from the Kingdom of Stordt

Grace: Princess of New Norkv/daughter of Benjeman and Esther

Gracie: cook for the Arthur Marcus family

Grady: worker for Gabriel

Great Ruler: God

Gregory Bancar: a wealthy landowner in the Kingdom of Wetpr and member of the Insidiae

Greta: older Ruala woman/friend of Emeral's

Greta: wife of Hugo/mother of Sasha/ sister-in-law of Sorren

Gunnel: Prince/ son of King Zachariah and Queen Noella of New Samona/husband of Uma/father of Elan/Ruala

Gus: owner of Racing Horse Tavern

Haas: a Lieutenant in the Wetprian military

Hadar: Prince/son of King Manu and Queen Delilia/Ruala

Hadi: son of Andrus and Naomi/brother of Rabi/Ruala

Hadu: female Ruala warrior

Hamon: one of the members of the Nordes Tribe who was injured in an attack at Snakes Crossing

Hamond: General of the Taperian Army who declares himself king

Hanger: one of the spies at the Castle at Wetpr

Hangered: Wetprian soldier

Hannah: physician in Nora/ Roch murdered her sister

Harold: husband of Berta/part owner of the Racing Horse Tavern

Harold: owner of the general store in Nora

Harriet Marcus: mother of Hannah and Laurabelle/wife of Arthur

Hatus: General in the Army of Lentz/on loan to Sudfad

Hecate: a powerful female demon

Hector: fighter hired by Juleta

Hector: Prince of Samona/son of Varden

Henry: and his wife Alice find Jorge in Nora

Henry: husband of Noreen/father of Jacob

Hermanas: second in command to Archetenus at Wall of Dorath

High Priest Aaron: member of the Patronus

High Priest Amos: a member of the Patronus

High Priest Barnabas: most Senior High Priest of the monastery at Leven

High Priest Caleb: member of the Patronus

High Priest Ephraim: a member of the Patronus

High Priest Gabriel: member of the Patronus/demon hunter

High Priest Gideon: a member of the Patronus

High Priest Gregory: member of the Patronus

High Priest Joseph: member of the Patronus, in charge of the Cicero Headquarters

High Priest Josiah: member of the Patronus

High Priest Meekos: priest at the monastery at Malga

High Priest Nicholas: most Senior High Priest of the monastery at Philiste and most Senior High Priest of the Patronus

High Priest Othnial: Senior High Priest of the monastery in Rubar in the Kingdom of Ryed

High Priest Paulas: member of the Patronus

High Priest Phanuel: member of the Patronus

High Priest Philetus: member of the Patronus in charge of Malga Headquarters

High Priest Pravis: priest at the monastery at Malga

High Priest Raphael: a leader of the Patronus

High Priest Rueben: member of the Patronus in charge of Nora Headquarters

High Priest Silas: a member of the Patronus

High Priest Tenebrae: priest at the monastery at Malga

High Priest Timothy: was murdered by Meekos, Pravis and Tenebrae

High Priest Tyrus: a member of the Patronus

High Priest Uriel: member of the Patronus

High Priest Vincent: assigned to the monastery at Malga before he was murdered

High Priest Zophar: priest at monastery at Malga/ trained as a healer

Hobart: a man who works for demons

Horace: father of Rachel and Zach/husband of Zelda/freedom fighter in Ryed

Hores: son of Chief Romogi and Anda, Kingdom of Marba/Huta

Horta: Prince/son of Gunnel and Uma/nephew of King Manu of New Samona/brother of Elan/Ruala

Hugo: younger brother of Sorren/father of Sasha/husband of Greta

Hunter: Prince of Samona/son of Varden

Ian Maxwell Luca: son of Koby and Bekka

Ian: husband of Mia/ brother-in-law of Calen/ Ruala

Ibula: warrior princess and healer of the Ruala Tribe/daughter of King Manu and Queen Delilia/

Iden: warrior guarding refugees/Shettee

Igor: brother of King Sharonne

Imad: a male Grand Master of the Insidiae

Ina: daughter of Mia and Ian/ Ruala

Ingr: female warrior of Nordes Tribe

Inon: one of Cisero's men/a vessel

Ipos: an ancient demon/ one of the Old Ones

Iris: mother of Vivian/wife of Joshua/Clan of Gesmal in Ryed

Irit: daughter of Hadi and Gita/ Ruala

Isabella: Princes of Lentz, sister of Mathas, Renya and Tasha, married to Captain Josef

Isadore: wife of Fahron

Isla: daughter of Prince Lakin and Princess Zada/Ruala

Isla: female warrior of Nordes Tribe

Ivan: youngest son of Chief Duncan and Liza of the Clan of Gesmal in Ryed

Jace: husband of Oda/ brother-in-law of Calen/Ruala

Jack: member of governing body of Nora

Jackson: a private in the Army of Lentz

Jackson: an escaped prisoner from Wetpr

Jacob: boy who Angelina found in the woods

Jacot: son of Prince Lakin and Princess Zada/ grandson of King Manu/Ruala

Jaden: Sergeant in the Army of Lentz

Jago: son of Elen and Batya/ Ruala

Jake: works for Talverson Transport Company in Port Friada

Jakiv: Prince/son of Segal and Cahina/nephew of King Manu of New Samona/Ruala

Jama: Enrop leader who protects Chief Sorren's family

James: Taperian soldier

Janja: Princess/daughter of Gunnel and Uma/niece of King Manu of New Samona/ sister of Elan/Ruala

Janson: Wetprian soldier

Jared: hired fighter

Jaretta: King of Stordt/husband of Queen Lillian/ father of Roch and Sudfad

Jarrod: works for Pravis/leads attack on castle in Wetpr

Jarvis: a farmer who is killed by escaped prisoners

Jasmine: young female Nordes warrior

Jasper: a large white dog that Gabriel brings home

Jasper: Prince of Lentz/son of Princess Isabella and Captain Josef

Jatu: Enrop leader who protects Fahron's family

Jeb: friend of Thaos

Jeb: one of Cisero's men

Jela: Queen of Samona/wife of Varden

Jenna: female Ruala warrior/married to Ratri's oldest brother Artis

Jeremy: cousin of Andrew the jeweler in Salar

Jerik: a male Grand Master of the Insidiae

Jess: a soldier of Wetpr

Jillian: Queen of Ogg/wife of King Douma

Jinn: an ancient demon/ one of the Old Ones

Joao: male Ruala warrior

Joey: adopted son of Elan and Cassandra

Jonas: Captain in the Taperian Army

Jorga: Princess of Ryed/daughter of Oren and Astrel/ has twin sister Andres

Jorge: a cook who is kidnapped from Endleson Hotel in Nora

Josef: Captain in the Lentz military/ married to Princess Isabella, sister of King Mathas

Joseph: male Ruala warrior/father of Ratri/husband of Clair

Joseph: nine year old Ruala boy/son of Artis and Jenna/nephew of Ratri

Joshua: father of Vivian/husband of Iris/Clan of Gesmal in Ryed

Josie: an escaped prisoner from Wetpr

Juleta: cousin to Raul and Simon/daughter and oldest child of King Mathas and Queen Rosa

Kadin: a member of Valdore Tribe

Kagen: a man who kidnaps and exploits children

Kalee: female Ruala warrior/married to Ratri's older brother Quinn

Karl: two year old Ruala boy/son of Artis and Jenna/nephew of Ratri

Karta: male Ruala warrior

Karzman: leader of Kozach Tribe/ stepfather of Michael

Kasper: Prince/son of Zeman and Oda/nephew of King Manu of New Samona/Ruala

Kata: Princess/daughter of Gunnel and Uma/niece of King Manu of New Samona/ sister of Elan/Ruala

Khryriss: an ancient demon/ one of the Old Ones

Kiana: Princess/daughter of Gunnel and Uma/niece of King Manu of New Samona/ sister of Elan/Ruala

Klass: Lieutenant in the Wetprian Army

Koby: male Ruala warrior

Koh: son of Prince Gael and Princess Mada/grandson of King Manu/Ruala

Kora: Princess/ married to Raphael son of King Zachariah and Queen Noella of New Samona/ mother of Luca/ Raphael and Kora were killed in battle when Luca was a small boy/Ruala

Korth: son of Tristt/Shettee

Kraus: hired fighter and intended vessel, works for Dieter

Kretcher: Commanding General of Fort Polta in Wetpr

Krister: Princess of Samoan/daughter of Thomas and Rewel

Kyra: young sister of Marie/ friend of Petra

Laban: Prince of Samona/son of Yorggi and Dion/grandson of Thomas and Rewel

Lael: daughter of Nina and Rhea/ Ruala

Lakin: Prince/son of King Manu and Queen Delilia/husband of Zada/Ruala

Lala: Princess/daughter of Adwell and Nada/niece of King Manu of New Samona/ sister of Misha/Ruala

Lana: female warrior of the Nordes Tribe

Lana: Princess/daughter of Segal and Cahina/niece of King Manu of New Samona/Ruala

Lani: daughter of Mia and Ian/Ruala

Lara: one of Usman's wives

Larson: a fighter hired by Juleta

Laurabelle: Hannah's sister who was murdered by Roch

Laurel: Annabelle's mother and former servant of King Roch's parents

Lazo: fighter hired by Juleta

Lea: Princess/daughter of Adwell and Nada/niece of King Manu of New Samona/ sister of Misha/Ruala

Leith: four year old Ruala boy/son of Quin and Kalee/nephew of Ratri

Leo: Prince of Samona/son of Darius and Rebek/grandson of Thomas and Rewel

Lieutenant Tarp: Lieutenant in the Wetprian Army

Lila: seventeen year old girl who Luca saves from the Hutas/sister of Christopher

Lilian: female warrior of the Nordes Tribe

Lillian: Queen of Stordt/wife of Jaretta/ mother of Roch and Sudfad

Lily: daughter of Calen and Natasha/Ruala and human

Liza: wife of Duncan the Chief of the Clan of Gesmal in Ryed

Lloyd: banker in Nora

Loftus: Commanding General of Fort Styls

Loni: daughter of King Friada and Queen Marla of the Kingdom of Ganz

Louie: works for Talverson Transport Company in Port Friada

Luca: male Ruala warrior

Lucene: male Nordes warrior/oldest son of Hugo and Greta/older brother of Sasha

Lucifer: an ancient demon/ one of the Old Ones

Luque: Prince/son of Segal and Cahina/nephew of King Manu of New Samona/Ruala

Mab: a female Grand Master of the Insidiae

Mabon: warrior guarding refugees/Shettee

Mada: Princess /wife of Prince Gael/Ruala

Madam Bular: owner of a dress shop in Port Friada

Maggie: elderly store owner in Salar

Mahon: son of King Neputa

Makalo: Prince of Norkv/husband of Grace who was the daughter of Benjeman and Esther

Malana: daughter of King Neputa

Mali: Princess of Norkv/daughter of Makalo and Grace/granddaughter of Benjeman and Esther

Maligma: an ancient demon/ one of the Old Ones

Malik: member of the Insidiae

Malus: sorcerer from Ryed

Mandrake: Taperian soldier

Manu: King of New Samona/The Chief of the Grand Council made up of Rualas and Shettees/ father of Ibula, Lakin, Gael and Hadar/husband of Delilia

Marcia: friend of Hannah's/ Roch's men murdered her family

Marcus Stephan: son of Stephan and Ingr

Margarit: daughter of King Mathas and Queen Rosa of the Kingdom of Lentz/ cousin of Raul and Simon

Margo: a young girl who was kidnapped by Sal

Margolia: girl from Nora who was sacrificed to a demon

Marie: a cook for King Sudfad and Queen Renya

Markus: a soldier in the Army of Wetpr

Marla: High Priest Meekos' housekeeper

Marla: Queen of the Kingdom of Ganz

Marsha Jarvis: a sixteen year old girl who is raped and killed by Timothy

Martha: a cook for Cerephus

Martha: hotel owner in Telmark

Martin Froush: wealthy ship builder in Port Friada/husband of Denise

Mary: Jared's young wife who was brutally murdered by Hutas

Mata: Igor's wife

Mateo: Chief Healer of the Ruala Tribe

Mathas: King of Lentz/ brother to Queen Renya

Matilda: one of Usman's wives

Matthew: son of King Mathas and Queen Rosa of the Kingdom of Lentz/ cousin of Raul and Simon

Maxwell: father of Calen/ Ruala

Maxwell: infant son of Nina and Rhea/grandson of elder Maxwell/Ruala

Melanie: female Ruala warrior/daughter of Casey and Tasha

Melina: mother of Thaos

Melinda: grandmother of Misha

Melinda: older sister of Cassandra and Joao

Mia: daughter of Maxwell and Emeral/ Ruala

Mia: female Ruala warrior/daughter of Tyron and Elsa

Mica: Princess of Norkv/daughter of Benedict and Sasaha/granddaughter of Benjeman and Esther

Micha: oldest son of Joshua and Iris/older brother of Vivian/Clan of Gesmal

Micha: son of King Sharonne/ grandfather of Sudfad and Roch

Michael: ancient king of Wetpr/father of Queen Sumona

Michael: son of Sudfad and Nadia

Milo: male Ruala warrior

Miranda: daughter of Raul and Vitomas

Miranda: emissary of The Great Ruler who takes on the disguise of a human seer

Miriam: a friend of Hannah's/works at Endleson Hotel in Nora

Misha: male Ruala warrior/lieutenant

Molach: a member of the Insidiae

Moloch: an ancient demon/one of the Old Ones

Morris: member of governing body of Nora

Muhar: Shettee warrior

Myla: wife of the owner of the Dragons Inn in Salar

Naal: warrior guarding refugees/Shettee

Nabi: male Ruala warrior

Nada: Princess/ married to Adwell son of King Zachariah and Queen Noella of New Samona/ mother of Misha/ Adwell was killed in battle leaving Nada to raise ten children/Ruala

Nadia: wife of Karzman/mother of Michael

Naomi: mother of Rabi/ Ruala

Napo: Enrop leader who protects Claudius' family

Natasha: sister of High Priest Gabriel

Nathaniel: Sorren's oldest son/ Nordes Tribe

Nebula: son of Chief Romogi and Anda/ Kingdom of Marba/Huta

Nehmota: King of Ryed

Nelpus: Shettee warrior

Neputa: leader of the Shettee Tribe when it was conquered by the Hutas

Nestor: a demon that specializes in procuring things for a price

Nica: Enrop leader who protects Sudfad's family

Nicholas: orphan boy /brother of Cerey

Nicolas: Prince of Puntd/son of King Tobias and Queen Tasha

Nieatzae: an ancient demon/ one of the Old Ones

Nikki: female warrior of Nordes Tribe

Nina: daughter of Maxwell and Emeral/Ruala

Nina: youngest daughter of Karzman and Nadia

Nita: Princess/daughter of Adwell and Nada/niece of King Manu of New Samona/ sister of Misha/has twin brother Waed/Ruala

Nobel: former prince of Ryed/son of Akasha and Norah/father of Nehmota

Noella: the first Queen of New Samona/wife of King Zachariah/mother of seven sons/Ruala

Norah: former queen of Ryed/grandmother of Nehmota

Noreen: mother of Jacob/ wife of Henry

Norris: hired fighter and intended vessel, works for Dieter

Nyla: oldest daughter of Karzman and Nadia

Oda: daughter of Maxwell and Emeral/ Ruala

Oda: Princess/ married to Zeman son of King Zachariah and Queen Noella of New Samona/Ruala

Odam: male Ruala warrior

Odell: one of the spies at the Castle at Wetpr

Omar: Prince/son of Zeman and Oda/nephew of King Manu of New Samona/Ruala

Omara: Queen of Norkv/wife of Thaddius who was son of Benjeman and Esther

Omnibus: an ancient demon/ one of the Old Ones

Omoria: former queen of Ryed/wife of Nobel/mother of Nehmota

Opago: an ancient demon/ one of the Old Ones

Orbus: a powerful demon and former lover of Hecate

Orcus: Shettee warrior/brother of King Neputa

Oren: former prince of Gandt who marries princess Astrel of Ryed

Oriah: name used by the Grand Master Banaka

Orin: male Ruala warrior/older brother of Ratri/husband of Rene

Ottillia: Princess of Lenz/daughter of Princess Isabella and Captain Josef

Otu: son of Hecate and Sampson

Padre Augustus: a member of the Patronus

Padre Bartholomew: survives the massacre at the monastery at Avaide

Padre Cornelius: a member of the Patronus

Padre Darius: a member of the Patronus

Padre Dibon: a priest at the monastery at Malga

Padre Dominick: priest at monastery at Malga

Padre Edgar: member of the Patronus

Padre Edward: a member of the Patronus

Padre Finn: Patronus priest assigned to the Cicero HQ

Padre Francis: priest at monastery at Malga

Padre Joram: member of the Patronus

Padre Lucas: a member of the Patronus

Padre Markle: a Patronus priest

Padre Nebat: alias for Dominic leader of the Libertas

Padre Octavos: runs orphanage in Salar

Padre Philip: a member of the Patronus

Padre Philip: a priest at the monastery at Malga

Padre Simpson: priest at the monastery at Malga

Padre Sorben: a member of the Patronus

Padre Sornce: Patronus priest assigned to the Cicero HQ

Padre Stephens: priest at monastery at Malga

Padre Thomas: priest at the monastery at Malga

Padre Tobias: a member of the Patronus

Padre Xavier: priest at monastery at Malga

Paj: Princess/wife of Prince Hadar/Ruala

Pallas: Shettee warrior

Pata: daughter of Chief Romogi and Trina/Huta

Paterson: a Private in the Wetprian military

Patris: six year old Nordes girl/daughter of Hugo and Greta/younger sister of Sasha

Paul: third son of Joshua and Iris/younger brother of Vivian/Clan of Gesmal

Paulas: a man who works for Cicero/a vessel

Paulas: Sergeant under Archetenus in Taperian Army

Paullo: works for High Priest Meekos

Pearl: eldest daughter of King Tobias and Queen Tasha of Puntd

Pergo: King of the Kingdom of Gandt

Peter: Sorren's second son/Nordes Tribe

Peters: member of the governing body of Nora

Petorus: an ancient demon/one of the Old Ones

Petra: peasant boy from Ort who saves Padre Bartholomew

Phifer: nine year old Nordes boy/ son of Hugo and Greta/younger brother of Sasha

Philip: Prince of Puntd/ son of King Tobias and Queen Tasha

Phillip: Court Physician to the Royal Family of Wetpr

Polgate: one of the men who kidnapped Petra

Potomas: warrior guarding refugees/Shettee

Powell: a lieutenant in the Military of Lentz/stationed at Fahron's castle

Prescott: a hired killer

Quin: male Ruala warrior/older brother of Ratri/husband of Kalee

Rabi: male Ruala warrior

Rachel: member of the freedom fighters in Ryed

Radnor: a male Grand Master of the Insidiae

Rael: Prince of old Samona/husband of Krister who was the daughter of Thomas and Rewel

Rahi: a female Grand Master of the Insidiae

Rakio: Prince/son of Adwell and Nada/nephew of King Manu of New Samona/brother of Misha/Ruala

Rako: a male Ruala warrior

Raphael: Prince/ son of King Zachariah and Queen Noella of New Samona/husband of Kora/Ruala/father of Luca/ Raphael and Kora were killed in battle when Luca was a small boy/Ruala

Ratri: male Ruala warrior

Raul: Prince/son of King Sudfad and Queen Renya of the Kingdom of Wetpr

Raum: an ancient demon/ one of the Old Ones

Rebek: Princess of Samona/wife of Darius, who was the son of Thomas and Rewel

Rebke: six year old Ruala girl/ daughter of Orin and Rene/niece of Ratri

Rene: female Ruala warrior/married to Ratri's older brother Orin

Renya: Queen of Wetpr/ wife of Sudfad

Rewel: Queen of Samona/wife of Thomas/mother of Varden

Rex: a notorious pick pocket in Port Friada

Rhea: husband of Nina/ brother-in- law of Calen/ Ruala

Riftca: male Ruala warrior

Riker: a scout in the Wetprian military

Risha: a witch who deals with potions

Roch: King of the Kingdom of Stordt/brother of King Sudfad

Rogers: one of the men who kidnapped Petra

Rolif: son of Chief Romogi and Silva/ Kingdom of Marba/Huta

Romale: member of the Insidiae

Romos: an elder of the Centras

Rosa: Queen of Lentz/wife of King Mathas

Rosalie: a dressmaker in Nora/wife of Peters

Ryan: grandson of Jeb/friend of Thaos

Sabot: member of the Insidiae

Sahil: a male Ruala warrior

Sal: a murderous pedophile/also goes by the name Tyrone

Sally: a young girl who was kidnapped by Sal

Salzar: powerful demon on Sidus

Sam: male Ruala warrior/father of Bekka/husband of Ella

Samael: a demon as powerful as Ahriman who rules the hell world Xibalba

Samara: wife of Tristt/Shettee

Samat: son of Chief Romogi and Silva/ Kingdom of Marba/Huta

Samos: Prince of Norkv/son of Thaddius

Sampson: oldest son of Chief Duncan and Liza of the Clan of Gesmal in Ryed

Sampson: Sergeant in the Taperian Army

Samuel: a high priest at the monastery at Malga who was murdered

Samuel: Prince of the original Samona/grandson of Thomas and Rewel

Samuel: second son of Raul and Vitomas

Sanuri: a holy man/emissary of The Great Ruler/warrior

Sar: an Enrop

Sar: male Ruala warrior

Sara: daughter of Usman

Sarah: baby granddaughter of Mathas and Rosa

Sarah: housekeeper for Claudius and Bella

Saran: daughter of Karzman and Nadia

Sasaha: Princess of the original Samona/granddaughter of Thomas and Rewel

Sasha: young female Nordes warrior

Sasha: female warrior of the Nordes Tribe/wife of Galen

Satan: an ancient demon/ one of the Old Ones

Satter: male Ruala warrior

Sattleman: a Sergeant in the Wetprian army

Sauer: male Ruala warrior

Saunders: a Taperian soldier

Schroeder: man who works for Insidiae leader Dieter

Segal: Prince/ son of King Zachariah and Queen Noella of New Samona/husband of Cahina/Ruala

Seguna: former princess of Ryed/daughter of Akasha and Norah/ committed suicide

Selen: house keeper for Juleta

Shanksaw: mercenary

Shara: wife of Sorren/Nordes Tribe

Sharonne: King of Stordt; great, great, grandfather of King Roch and King Sudfad

Shon: son of King Fahra and Queen Sitha

Shone: Princess/daughter of Zeman and Oda/niece of King Manu of New Samona/Ruala

Sicily Bella: daughter of Stephan and Ingr

Sila: Princess of Ogg

Silva: one of Chief Romogi's three wives/Huta

Simmons: Commanding General of Fort Nir

Simon: adopted son of King Sudfad and Queen Renya of the Kingdom of Wetpr

Sinclair: King of Lentz/father of King Mathas

Sirius: works for High Priest Meekos

Sitha: Queen of Zorta

Smoking Joe: a regular patron at the Ghost Ship Tavern

Sonja: female warrior of the Nordes Tribe

Sophie: cook and servant of King Roch

Sorren: leader of the Nordes Tribe

Soto: male Ruala warrior who leads first death squad for criminals

Sporos: priest turned demon

Stephan: Captain in Army of Lentz/son of Claudius and Bella

Stiller: a fighter hired by Juleta

Stolas: an ancient demon/one of the Old Ones

Stone: hired fighter and intended vessel, works for Dieter

Sudfad: King of the Kingdom of Wetpr and brother to King Roch of Stordt

Sudfad: little Sudfad is grandson of King Sudfad

Sumona: Queen of Wetpr/wife of Alexandras/aunt of Roch and Sudfad

Swenson: one of Shanksaw's hired men

Syrius: a Bakken hired by Juleta

Tabeth: daughter of Fahron

Tabith: son of Tristt/Shettee

Tabitha: Princess of Lentz/daughter of Princess Isabella and Captain Josef of Lentz

Tadeo: Prince/son of Adwell and Nada/nephew of King Manu of New Samona/brother of Misha/Ruala

Tafer: a warlord who drove the Hutas out of the Kingdom of Norkv after years of wars and rebellions

Tahira: a female Grand Master of the Insidiae

Tahira: Princess of Samona/granddaughter of Thomas and Rewel

Tal: son of Oda and Jace/ Ruala

Talmai: Shettee boy who Thedes and Ibula adopt

Tambor: male Ruala warrior

Tamour: General in the Army of Lentz/on loan to Sudfad

Tanner: a Lieutenant in the Wetprian army

Tanner: a Sergeant in the Army of Lentz

Tapster: a demon who works for Meekos

Tarig: a lieutenant in the Huta army

Tarin: son of King Neputa and Queen Tiara/Shettee

Taron: Prince/son of Adwell and Nada/nephew of King Manu of New Samona/brother of Misha/Ruala

Tasha: female Ruala warrior/mother of Melanie/wife of Casey

Tasha: Queen of Puntd/ married to Tobias/ sister of Renya and Mathas

Tate: a Lieutenant in the Wetprian Army

Tatterd: a Sergeant in the Wetprian military

Tavin: son of Prince Lakin and Princess Zada/Ruala

Teddy: male Nordes warrior/son of Edgar and Cora/ older brother of Batina

Tega: housekeeper for the cabins of the captains of the Taperian Army

Tegman: soldier of Wetpr

Tehtfote: a Lieutenant for Dieter

Temark: villager of Neva

Tetro: Huta warrior who was a captive in Ogg

Thadddius: Prince of the new Kingdom of Norkv/son of Benjeman

Thaddies: member of Nordes Tribe/ father of Ingr

Thanatoes: an ancient demon/ one of the Old Ones

Thaos: a hired fighter

Thatcher: Prince/son of Zeman and Oda/nephew of King Manu of New Samona/Ruala

Thatus: Taperian soldier

The Lion: emissary of The Great Ruler who takes on the appearance of a lion when he is in the world of man

Thedes: warrior guarding refugees/Shettee

Theodore: handyman for Erebus/husband of Arlene

Thomas: King of the original Kingdom of Samona/father of Varden

Thomas: second son of Joshua and Iris/older brother of Vivian/Clan of Gesmal

Thomas: the young husband of Zoya who was murdered in Taperia

Thompson: Wetprian soldier

Thor: a Venator/brother of Diana

Thronson: one of Meekos hired killers

Tiara: Queen of Shettee Tribe when it was conquered by Hutas/wife of Neputa

Timothy: son of Fahron

Tina: Mother of Cassandra, Joao and Melinda

Tito: member of Valdore Tribe

Titus Derek: son of Thaos and Nikki

Titus: a lieutenant in the Taperian Army

Tobart: a member of the Nordes Tribe

Tobias: King of Puntd.

Tomas: works for High Priest Pravis

Tome: a businessman and member of the Insidiae in Nora

Tomi: son of Usman the leader of the Valdore Tribe

Toni: young female Nordes warrior

Tony: male Ruala warrior/ married to Bekka's oldest sister Eloise

Toomback: Huta warrior

Torance: father of Thaos

Torin: oldest son of Karzman and Nadia

Trace: male Ruala warrior

Tratz: one of the men who kidnapped Petra

Travor: Taperian warrior who was injured at the Wall of Dorath

Tresdore: son of King Sharonne

Trevor: Prince/son of Zeman and Oda/nephew of King Manu of New Samona/Ruala

Tria: daughter of Oda and Jace/Ruala

Trina: one of Chief Romogi's three wives/Huta

Trina: Princess/daughter of Zeman and Oda/niece of King Manu of New Samona/Ruala

Trist: a male Ruala warrior

Tristt the Horrible: Shettee warrior

Tritor: a powerful demon of Sidus and ex-lover of Hecate

Tye: Prince of Norkv/son of Princess Grace and Prince Makalo

Tyron: male Ruala warrior/father of Mia/husband of Elsa

Tyson: Wetprian soldier

Ulger: a demon

Uma: Princess/ married to Gunnel son of King Zachariah and Queen Noella of New Samona/mother of Elan/Ruala

Umar: Prince/son of Adwell and Nada/nephew of King Manu of New Samona/brother of Misha/Ruala

Uri: son of Nina and Rhea/ Ruala

Usman: leader of the Valdore Tribe

Valdus: name used by the Grand Master Emeric

Valerie: young female Nordes warrior

Valor: Prince of the new Kingdom of Norkv/son of Benjeman and Esther

Vandrew: Petra's male tutor

Vania: Princess of Samona/daughter of Yorggi and Dion/granddaughter of Thomas and Rewel

Varden: last king of Samona/he and his family were murdered by rebels

Vardin: one of the men who kidnapped Petra

Vasart: Queen of Ryed/ wife of Nehmota

Vinca: Queen of Stordt, wife of Sharonne

Vincent: Prince of Ryed/son of Nehmota and Vasart

Vinus: Queen of the Kingdom of Gandt

Visterle: a powerful demon

Vitomas: Queen of Stordt

Vivian: a demon hunter from the Clan of Gesmal

Voltar: Prince of Samona/son of Darius and Rebek/grandson of Thomas and Rewel/later becomes King of Wetpr

Vuall: a demon

Waed: Prince/son of Adwell and Nada/nephew of King Manu of New Samona/brother of Misha/has twin sister Nita/Ruala

Wallis: member of governing body of Nora

Wilard: Captain at Fort Polta

William: son of Jared and Zoya

Willis: son of King Pergo and Queen Vinus/ Kingdom of Gandt

Xeni: a female Grand Master of the Insidiae

Yara: daughter of Nina and Rhea/Ruala

Yorggi: Prince of Samona/son of Thomas and Rewel/brother of Varden

Yori: son of Usman the leader of the Valdore Tribe

Yuri: Prince/son of Adwell and Nada/nephew of King Manu of New Samona/brother of Misha/Ruala

Zac: one of the men who kidnapped Petra

Zachariah: first King of New Samona/husband of Queen Noella/father of seven sons/Ruala

Zack: eight year old brother of Rachel

Zada: Princess/wife of Prince Lakin/Ruala

Zadok: a male Grand Master of the Insidiae

Zede: an ancient demon/ one of the Old Ones

Zehmann: an ancient demon/ one of the Old Ones

Zelda: mother of Rachel and Zack

Zeman: Prince/ son of King Zachariah and Queen Noella of New Samona/husband of Oda/Ruala

Zieman: a demon

Zorda: Taperian soldier injured in battle at the Wall of Dorath

Zortus: demon/lieutenant of Visterle

Zoya: a seer from Taperia

Glossary of Terms

Aboultis: the calling cards of demons

Abrax: the planet that orbits closest to the three suns/ uninhabited

Abyss: a vast void used to imprison demons

Acura: the whispering shadows/are in the inner circle of demons that directly serve the Old Ones

Alferto: a type of grain that is common in Opots

Amark: ancient language of The Great Ruler

Amulth: means filth in the language of demons/these monsters are made out of the waste of tortured souls from the hell dimensions

Anewa: one of seven continents in the World of Nunc

Aplewort: an herb when mixed with water purges poisons from a body

Asherane: ancient tribe that lived in the northern regions of the Kingdom of Lentz

Ashta: a common herb/when the dried leaves are boiled they give off a pleasant scent

Astras: the ancient underground city of the Centras

Astrum: the solar system that consists of three suns that form a triangle and seven planets

Beltrad: a species of lower level demons

Blood Moon Prophesy: a demonic prophesy that foretells of a time when the doors to the hell worlds will open

Blood rings: Large red rubies set in silver with markings of the Old Ones

Boca: a covered wagon pulled by horses

Box of Itifer: a gift to the world of man from The Great Ruler; this gift affects the balance of creation

Bozie: a game of skill played by the Nordes Tribe

Cava plant: a poisonous plant that grows freely near bodies of water

663

Centras: ancient race of creatures who have the responsibility of protecting the Holy Box of Itifer

Cerfic: an ancient language widely spoken among many kingdoms/a language of the masses not royalty

Chalice of Ascension: a gift from The Great Ruler, this gift contains unimaginable powers

Cicero College: in Wetpr, outside of Salar, where Raul, Simon and Hannah attended college

Clan of Gesmal: a tribe of demon hunters who live in the southern region of the Kingdom of Ryed

Crystal pillars: in the Ice Caves of Mordv/are blessed by The Great Ruler and filled with spiritual life force

Czarsta: one of seven continents in the World of Nunc

Demalogs: an inferior species of demons

Demosa: a slow acting poison from the cava plant

Diamond of Cazo: a gift from The Great Ruler, this gift can unleash powers from the center of the world

Durisks: large demonic birds/their elongated beaks contain rows of fangs

Ekel Beast: similar to a deer

Engas: a wild cat that inhabits the Vandrew Mountains

Engor: a small pack animal that lives in trees

Enrop: a large species of bird that can speak many human languages

Farduth: a Shettee necklace that symbolizes a male has completed his rite of passage to become a warrior

Filsum: the sixth planet in the Astrum Solar System/ two moons

Gafet: an ancient Shettee weapon

Gants: large apelike creatures/Watchers of the Caves of Muldun

Gate of Isula: the only opening in the great Wall of Dorath

Gefrey Games: games of sport where men fight each other and great beasts to the death

Grand Masters: the first people to call to the demons and invite them into this world

Great Ruler: God

Half-Mans: a tribe of creatures that are partially human and partially nature. They are three feet tall and walk on two legs but can change their coloring to match their environment.

Hall of Antiquities: a giant hall located in the monastery at Malga/ a sanctuary for holy items and manuscripts

Hall of Light: the Great Hall in the Ice Caves of Mordv

Hengers: giant blue eagles/ birds of war

Highland Pass: the only passage through the Rosu Mountain Range

Holy Scrolls: gifts given to each kingdom by The Great Ruler, these gifts contain powers, wisdom and immortality

Holy Vault: a secret vault under the King's study in the castle in Wetpr designed to protect holy objects

Horn of Asher: a horn used by the Patronus warrior priests to signal each other

Horn of Cass: a horn used by the Wetprian soldiers to signal each other

Horn of Cornwell: a horn used by Dieter's men to signal each other

Horn of Eel: a horn used by the Ruala warriors to communicate with each other

Horn of Esker: a horn used by the Valdore Tribe to communicate with each other

Horn of Ire: a horn carried by the Taperian soldiers to communicate with each other

Horn of Shana: a horn carried by the soldiers of Lentz to communicate with each other

Horn of Tula: a horn used by the members of the Nordes Tribe for communication

Horn of Vamont: a horn used by the Kozach Tribe for communication

Horn of Xepoltr: a horn used by the Shettee warriors to communicate

Huta: a race of humans that is driven by hatred and ideas of racial superiority who live in the Kingdom of Marba

Infineotous Text: a demonic text hidden within a plyogram/contains prophesies of the balance of power between good and evil

Insidiae: means conspirators/a highly organized secret group of humans who have sold their souls to demons

Jacar: giant leech-like creatures

Jacept Plant: a plant that a powerful poison is made from

Kafer: a small crescent shaped knife carried by the Beltrad

Keepers of the Scrolls: the Royal Family of the Kingdom of Wetpr entered into a covenant with The Great Ruler to protect his gifts until a time when they can be safely given back to the world of man

Kozach: a tribe that lives in the far north central regions of the Kingdom of Wetpr

Lamsman: an ankle bracelet worn by Venatores/stones in the bracelet signify great feats they had to accomplish to become a demon hunter

Learning Center: the first of its kind/a complex educational facility that is open to multiple peoples and guards the students and staff from terrorists

Libertas: the name of a group of freedom fighters in northern Ryed

Linges plant: a plant that grows in damp, swampy regions in Opots/the white berries are used to make the drug Melanwhop

Lynswood: an herb that reveals tracks that are concealed by black magic

Mark of Satan: a coiled red snake with green eyes and a yellow tongue

Matu potage: a food staple of the Shettee Tribe

Mayka: one of seven continents in the World of Nunc

Melanwhop: a drug made from the linges plant, causes lethargy and apathy

Mordov: the special place in hell for hypocrites

Motfer: the land of the dead

Nefandus: a secret sect within the Insidiae

Nordes: a tribe of fiercely trained warriors who live in the northern region of the Kingdom of Lentz

Nunc: the world where this story takes place/third planet from the three suns

Old Ones: the original demons that came to the World of Nunc

Opatu bread: a food staple of the Shettee Tribe

Opots: one of seven continents in the World of Nunc/the continent where this story takes place

Oran: a tobisk that is filled with a mixture of ramni oil, buruto powder and meno salts, designed to explode on impact

Orantho: the seventh planet in the Astrum Solar System/inhabited/four moons/ large planet/many hell worlds

Patronus: an elite group of men who serve as the protectors of the church

Pfison screen: a type of demonic cloaking devise/it is sensitive and has to be calibrated for the specific individuals it is intended for

Planteen: the fourth planet in the Astrum Solar System/inhabited/two moons

Plyogram: an ancient form of coding information/the information is hidden within pictures

Porto: one of seven continents in the World of Nunc

Prophesy of the Blood Moon: a demonic prophesy that predicts the doors to hell being opened.

Prophesy of Isdod: is contained in the demonic Book of Horror/this prophesy explains the significance of the thirteenth level.

Propilatry: a powerful form of demonic curse

Prostras: an ancient tribe that once inhabited the Ice Caves of Mordv

Raftifa: ancient bat-like creatures that devour human flesh

Ravens: messengers used by the dark lords

Recupero: a sect within the Insidiae that worships the demon Omnibus

Rogetts: a tribe of humans that have digressed into murderous mutant monsters

Rualas: an ancient tribe of warriors said to be half human and half bird

Salszar: one of seven continents in the World of Nunc

Salts of Envoy: a sleeping potion

Scio: a crystal ball

Scroll of Imari: a gift of The Great Ruler, a scroll that unleashes the power of the Box of Itifer

Seal of Natun: a gift from the Holy Ruler that can open doors to other worlds

Serpents of Satan: can only be called forth by dark lords and demons, large red snakes with green eyes and yellow tongues

Seven Sons Prophesy: an ancient prophesy about seven sons who stand up against the demons and dark lords

Shesone: an ancient fighting style of the Shettee Tribe

Shettee: an ancient tribe of warriors said to be half human and half lion

Sidus: the fifth planet in the Astrum Solar System/inhabited/red fog surrounds the planet

Solv: a specific prison within The Abyss

Song of the Second Son: an ancient prophesy about an evil that is passed between second son's of a family resulting in a monster that brings terror and darkness to the world of man

Sundra Templer: a gift from The Great Ruler that was stolen by dark lords/an orb with extraordinary powers that can be used in multiple ways such as transporting humans through other worlds

Tabutu: an ancient form of fighting developed by the Asherane Tribe of the Kingdom of Lentz

Talisman: an object with magical or supernatural meaning

Talmuth: giant red dragon-like creatures

Taluth: a light weight metal used to make the ancient Shettee weapons called the Gafets

Tameric: the place where Karzman claims he came from although it does not exist on any map of Opots

Tangers: large wild, grazing animals that travel in herds

Tansof: one of seven continents in the World of Nunc

Tarus demon: huge, power creatures that walk on two legs but have the head, neck and shoulders of an ox

Telgras: a hell beast that looks like it is half wolf and half panther

Teragon: death terror/a monster created as a result of diabolical acts

Terbot bear: a bear that roams in the northern regions of the Continent of Opots

Tervator: fourteen foot monster that walks like a man with long dark hair over its entire body and bull-like horns protruding from its head

Texts of Semalia: ancient texts about demonic language and rituals

The Book of Horror: a book that is worshipped by demons/contains prophesies

The Celebration of Days: an annual celebration of the Centras

The Hall of Understanding: the building in Astras where the history of the Centras is documented in drawings

The Hunters: another name for the Shettee Tribe

The Lion: a very powerful messenger of The Great Ruler assumes the form of a lion when he walks in the worlds of man

The Thirteenth Color: not seen in the world of man it is the color of horror/hell

Timbar: ghost dragons/ demons that can fly

Tinchure water: an herbal pain remedy used by the Nordes Tribe

Tincture of the Redeti Plant: Hutas dip the tips of their weapons in this insect infested liquid. The insects lay eggs inside of the victim. When the eggs are mature and hatch, two inch worm-like creatures are produced and will eat the organs of the victim causing a long and painful death

Tobisks: sphere shaped objects, metal and hollow inside that are designed to be launched from a Trebuchet

Traxsor: the second planet in the Astrum Solar System

Trebuchets: wooden machines used to catapult objects

Trimoth: a game of skill, strength and speed

Triolie: a Nordes gambling game

Tygrus: a ship that docked in Port Friada

Unholy altar: altar used to worship demons

Valdees: the tribe that lives in the underwater Kingdom of Ogg

Valdore: a tribe of merciless separatists who live in the extreme northern regions of the Kingdom of Lentz

Venator: means hunter in the old language

Venom of the Atha serpent: one of the poisons that Hutas put on their arrows

Vessel of Darkness: a human created from darkness to hold the essence of a powerful demon

Wall of Dorath: a giant wall that separates the Kingdoms of Norkv and Xepoltr from the Kingdom of Marba

Willimonns: small furry creatures that are hunted for food and sport

Xelope: the oneness of spirit with all that lives

Yellow Jay: a bird native to Opots

Yellow Mandeze: a song bird common to Opots

Zehno demon: thin, creature with long red and blue plumes on the back of its head with large eyes and round mouths

Zendoti: demons that are distinguished by the geometrically shaped tuffs of hair that protrude from their heads

Glossary of Maps

The maps are displayed in order of relevance

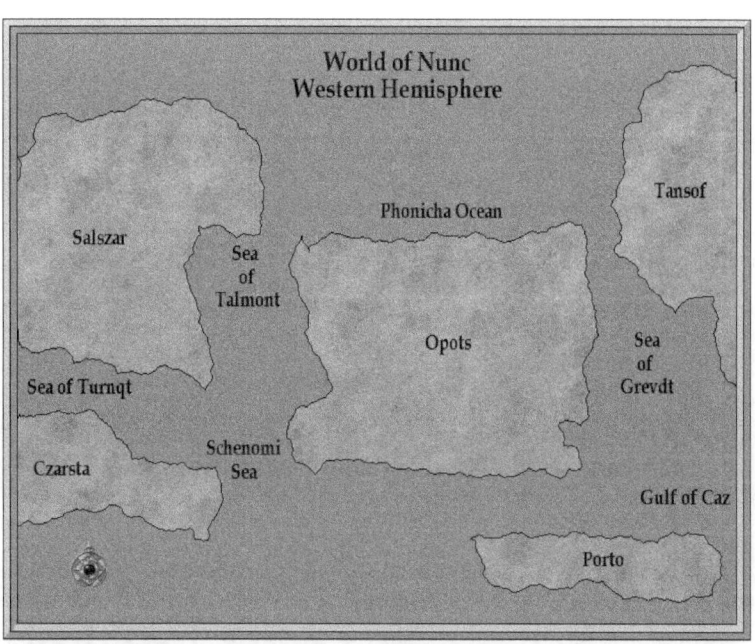

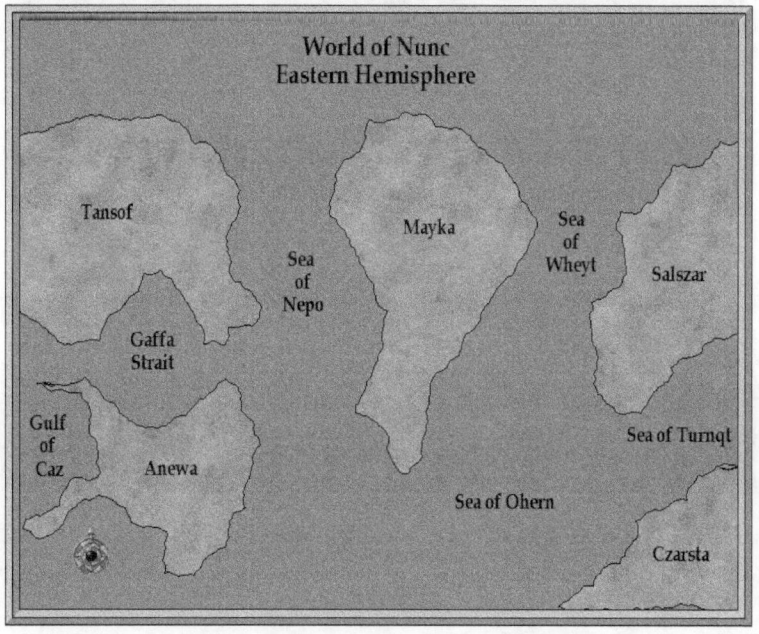

Continent of Opots
With new forts

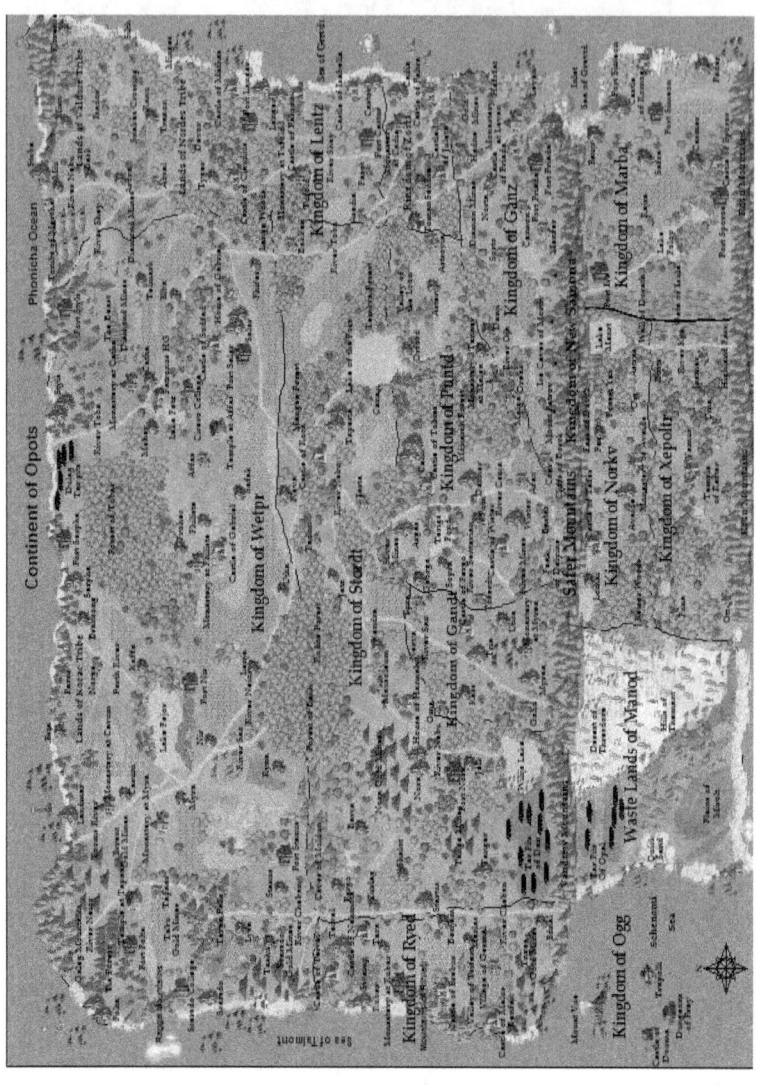

674

Western Stordt
With Fort Nora

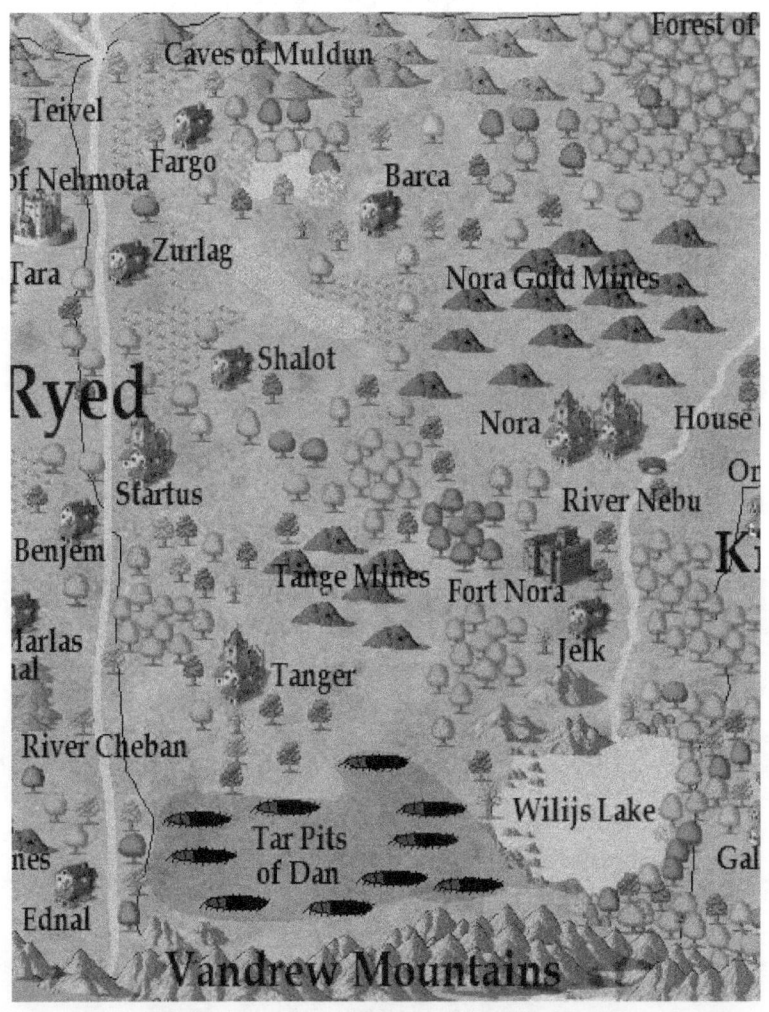

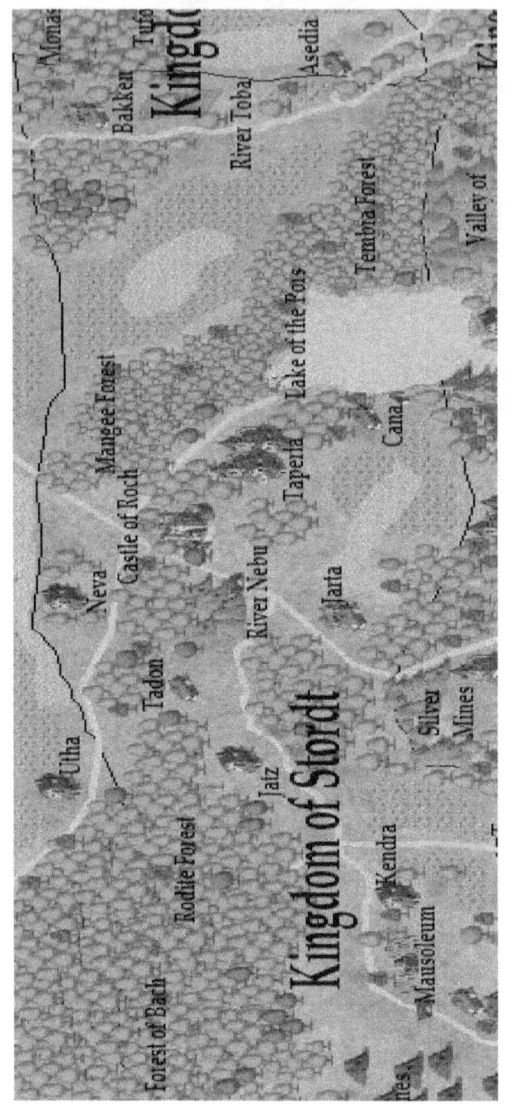

Western Wetpr
With Fort Stanus

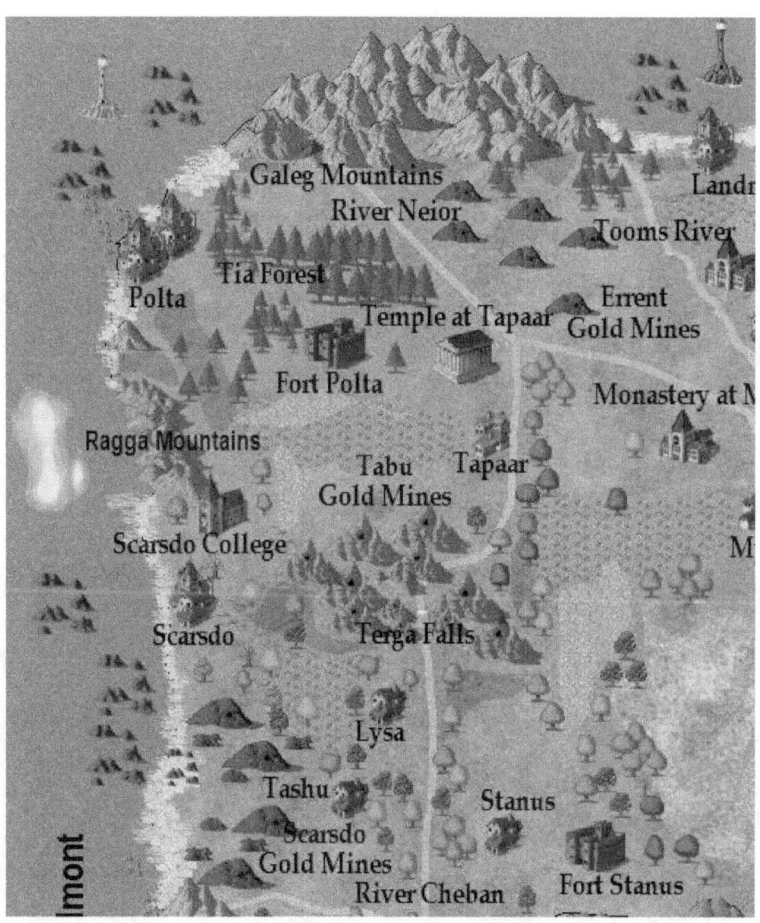

Marba

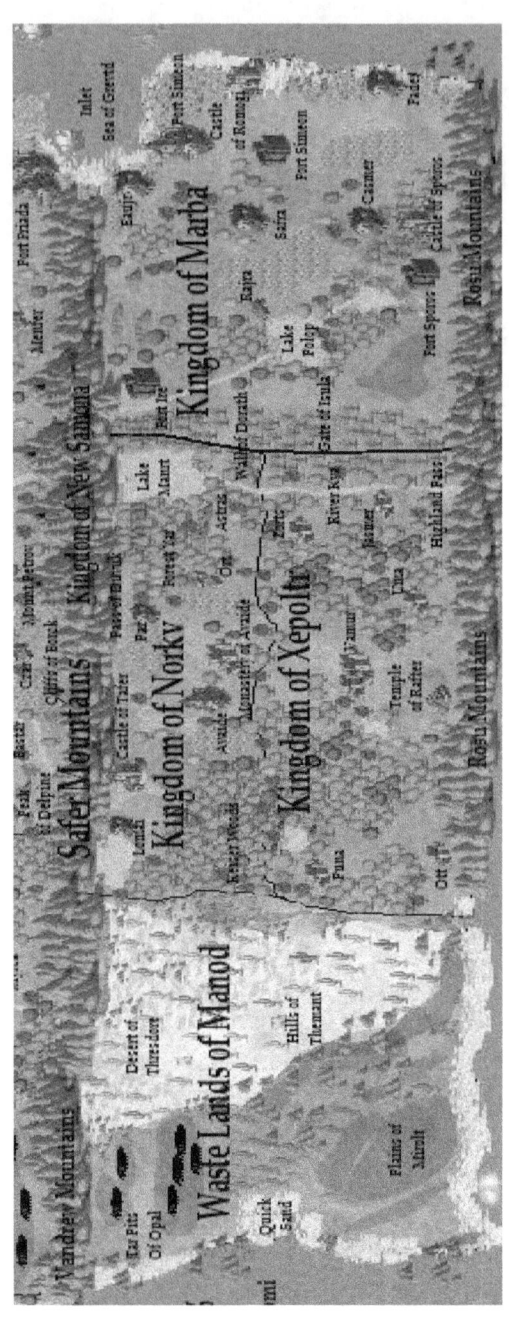

Astrum Solar System

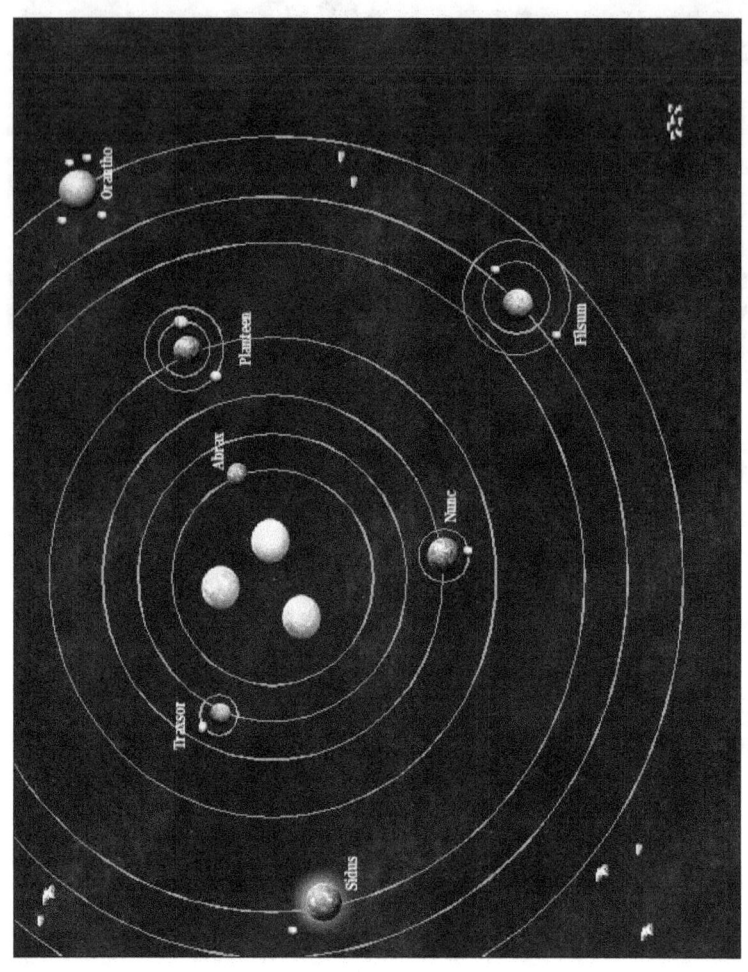